The Clue of the Stone Lantern

The Famous JUDY BOLTON Mystery Stories

By MARGARET SUTTON

In Order of Publication

A JUDY BOLTON Mystery

The Clue of the Stone Lantern

BY
Margaret Sutton

Illustrated by Pelagie Doane

APPLEWOOD BOOKS
Bedford, Massachusetts

The Clue of the Stone Lantern
was originally published in 1950.

Reprinted by permission of the estate of Margaret Sutton.
All Rights Reserved.

———

For a complete list of titles in the Judy Bolton Mysteries,
please visit judybolton.awb.com.

Thank you for purchasing an Applewood Book.
Applewood reprints America's lively classics—books from
the past that are still of interest to modern readers.
For a free copy of our current catalog, write to:

Applewood Books
P.O. Box 365
Bedford, MA 01730
www.awb.com

ISBN 978-1-4290-9041-4

MANUFACTURED IN THE U.S.A.

"Roberta's letter!" Judy whispered. "How can that be?"

The Clue of the Stone Lantern

A Judy Bolton Mystery

THE CLUE
OF THE
STONE LANTERN

BY

Margaret Sutton

Grosset & Dunlap

PUBLISHERS   NEW YORK

To

My Four Daughters
DOROTHY, PEGGY, ELEANOR
and LINDA

Contents

ix

x   Contents

CHAPTER I

The Moving Shadow

"IT WAS a good play, wasn't it?"

"Wonderful," agreed Judy, turning to her friend Lorraine, who had asked the question. "Those student nurses really know how to act."

"Tonight proved that they rate an auditorium of their own if nothing else," put in Lois Farringdon-Pett.

Laughing and chattering as they left the auditorium of Farringdon Girls' High School, borrowed for the occasion by the student nurses from Farringdon's only hospital, the three girls started walking down Grove Street.

This was the first time either Judy or Lorraine had been inside the new building since before the double wedding when Judy became Mrs. Peter Dobbs and

Lorraine became the bride of Lois's brother, Arthur Farringdon-Pett. Lois, oldest of the three, considered herself too young to marry.

"We're just out of high school, really," she reminded the other two girls.

It was true. Although so many events had crowded in that it seemed longer, actually it was not so long ago that Judy herself had stood on the stage—the same stage where she and her friends had just watched the play—and received her white-ribboned diploma.

Many of Judy's classmates were still students in out-of-town colleges. There was no college for girls in Farringdon, but there was a business school where she had taken a short course in order to be able to help Peter with his work.

Now she was the young FBI agent's secretary as well as his wife. Unlike Lois, Judy never postponed anything because of her youth. And she did love Peter. She had waited long enough to be sure of that.

To Lois, marriage was something to think of in the future.

"Right now," she declared, "I'm not ready to take on any more problems than I already have."

"Such as?"

"The hospital bazaar, for instance."

"Don't speak of it!" exclaimed Judy. "I never go to any of these benefit shows without getting roped into something. Now I'm chairman of the refreshment committee!"

"That's what you get for being Dr. Bolton's daughter," teased Lorraine. "Anyway, we got roped into more than you did. The bazaar's being held on our lawn."

Judy was not surprised to hear this. The Farringdon-Pett lawn was the size of a park, and many times in the past had been the scene of parties, bazaars, and even weddings. Judy herself had been married on the spacious lawn just behind the barberry hedge which the three girls were now passing.

The lawn sloped gently toward a grove of gnarled old trees that now cast weird shadows in the moonlight. At the foot of the slope was a crystal lake where moonbeams shimmered and danced like ghosts across the water.

"It's beautiful," breathed Judy, standing motionless for an enchanted moment.

She had to remind herself that this was not a scene on a strange planet. Why, it was even lovelier than she had imagined it when Peter first had described it to her and she had charged him with making up the story of swans on a blue lake.

There were no swans to be seen now, only the shimmering moonlight and the black, black shadows of those gnarled old trees.

The house with its turrets looked weird in the moonlight, like a fairy castle. Now more than a hundred years old, the original mansion still stood to remind people of the wealth and influence of the family for whom the city of Farringdon was named.

"It's too big," Lois said with a shiver as they turned

up the walk. "I don't like coming home to it when the lights are out."

"They aren't all out," Lorraine observed. "Someone has left the outside light on for us. Doesn't it look pretty the way it glows on the forsythia bush by the door?"

"Like gold," Judy said. "Remember the story of King Midas and the golden touch? It's in Roberta's reader. She read it aloud to me the other night and I actually cried over it. Whether it was the idea of all those beautiful roses turning to gold or because I was sorry for the king, I don't know. Roberta says there's something about a garden—"

But what Judy's little boarder had said about a garden, her friends were not to hear. Judy never finished the sentence. She stopped suddenly, clutching Lorraine's arm, and gasped, "What was that?"

"What?" asked Lorraine, more startled by Judy's sudden movement than by anything she saw.

"That shadow on the wall!"

Darting toward the forsythia bush, Judy parted the drooping branches and peered through them. She could see nothing of the moving shadow that had frightened her. She looked along the side of the house to the wide lawn beyond, but there was no further movement.

"What is it?" asked Lois, when Judy had persuaded herself that there was no one prowling about the Farringdon-Pett grounds.

"Nothing now. You didn't see anything moving behind this bush, did you?"

"Not a thing," declared the dark-haired girl.

Lorraine was equally sure that the shadow Judy had seen was only a tree shadow.

"If it moved it was probably because of the wind," she added, "or else it was a bat or an owl that flew out of the grove. We do have them, but not usually this early in the spring."

It was April and warm enough for Judy's spring suit in the daytime. She had worn a light coat over it tonight, because the evenings were still chilly. She was shivering now, but not from cold.

"Why don't you come in and let us give you something hot to drink?" Lois invited her, opening the door with her key.

A little later, seated around the coffee table in the luxurious living room of the old Farringdon-Pett mansion, it was easy to explain away the shadow Judy thought she had seen.

"The lawn is full of shadows. It always is, especially in the moonlight," declared Lois. "It was nothing else, I'm sure. You really frightened us for a moment, Judy. It's scary enough when Lorraine and I come home by ourselves without imagining the shadows are alive. Mother and Dad are away, and it looks as if Arthur isn't home yet. He drove over to the office in Roulsville to work out the details of some real-estate deal he had scheduled for tomorrow morning."

"Can you discuss it?" asked Judy, who was used to matters that could not be discussed in Peter's work.

"I guess so. There's nothing secret about it," Lois replied. "It's that old wreck of a place that's been standing empty ever since the Roulsville flood. The owner, a Mr. Heffly, has been in England, and the story is that he's held onto the place hoping to repair it and live in it again, but now he's decided to sell."

"And if you think this place is spooky," Lorraine put in, "you should see that one! Naturally, Arthur's going to tear it down and put up new houses on the land. There are four or five acres, he says, right near the center of town."

"But on the hillside, of course," Judy remarked. "Otherwise, the Roulsville flood would have saved Arthur the trouble of tearing down the old house. When the dam broke, everything in the valley went with it."

"You should know," Lorraine said, helping herself to one of the little cakes on the tea tray. "Your house went, too."

"And then you moved to Farringdon and the school burned down!" Lois added reminiscently.

"Things do seem to happen when I'm around," Judy agreed, giggling. "Peter says I attract mysteries and I'm afraid I do. Weird things have popped up for me to solve ever since I can remember. I told Peter that when we were married I would settle down and forget mysteries, but he knew better. If I don't look for them, they come to me."

"I hope you don't attract any of the more gruesome ones to the hospital bazaar," Lois said jokingly, although she was serious enough about wanting the bazaar to be a success.

"I'll try not to," Judy promised.

She was ready to admit now that she had been too hasty in agreeing to serve as chairman of the refreshment committee. It would take half a dozen waiters, at least, to serve all the people who were expected to attend the bazaar.

"And where will I find half a dozen waiters?" she wanted to know.

"What about Mrs. Beck's agency?" inquired Lois. "Mother always goes there for extra help."

"You mean I'm going to have the job of hiring professional waiters?" Judy was aghast at the suggestion. "I should think there'd be enough people interested in the hospital and its work to volunteer."

Lois and Lorraine had to laugh at Judy's sudden dismay.

"Go ahead! Round up volunteers, then," they told her. "Your brother Horace would make a good waiter. It would give him a chance to get the inside story of the bazaar."

"That's an idea," agreed Judy. "He could write it up for his paper afterward. He'd do anything for a stickful of news. That is, anything ethical," she added, remembering that her brother was nothing if not conscientious.

"So would Donald Carter. I'll ask him, if you want me to," Lois offered.

"Good!" applauded Judy. "I don't know how much Donald would do for news, but he'd do anything for you. I think I can manage everything else.

It will give me something to think about while Peter is away."

"It's a shame you couldn't go with him, Judy," declared Lorraine, who was presiding at a silver teapot that had been a wedding gift. "It doesn't seem fair for you to be tied down with a little girl to take care of when you're practically a bride still. Couldn't Roberta board with your mother?"

"She could, I suppose." Judy paused, her gray eyes clouding. "As a matter of fact, we are staying with Mother and Dad tonight. But Roberta will be just as eager as I'll be to get back to the house in Dry Brook Hollow in the morning. From the day Peter and I were married, she practically adopted us as her family. She really hasn't anyone—"

"What about her father?" Lois broke in. "He's a sea captain or something, isn't he? I'm surprised she doesn't show more affection for him. They do write to each other, don't they?"

Judy shook her head.

"Roberta doesn't want to. She didn't say anything, but I know she was disappointed when he didn't show up at Christmas as he'd promised. We haven't heard from him in months. If people still believed the world was flat, I'd say his ship must have sailed right off the edge of it."

"Maybe it did go down!" exclaimed Lois.

"I don't think so," Judy objected. "We would have been notified by the shipping company. More likely, Captain Dunn is the type of man who doesn't express himself very well in letters. He's probably been held up in some foreign port—"

"Or he may be nothing but an old meanie who doesn't care anything about his little girl," Lorraine put in.

"All the more reason why I should care about her then," Judy retorted.

Her temper matched her red hair, and she was beginning to wonder if what her friends really thought was that she was too young or too irresponsible to be left alone with Roberta while Peter traveled.

This answer silenced Lois and Lorraine for a moment. But they were laughing again and making plans for the coming bazaar when Judy decided it was time for her to leave.

Nothing more was said about the moving shadow, although Judy did stop and wonder what it could have been, when she was outside in the moonlight. Someone *must* have darted behind the forsythia bush to cause the black silhouette she had seen against the wall of the house. None of the trees could possibly have thrown such a shadow.

Judy was still trying to shake off the feeling she had that there might be someone prowling around on the Farringdon-Pett grounds when, suddenly, she heard footsteps behind her.

CHAPTER II

A Puzzling Question

STARTLED, Judy whirled around. She could see no one, for the high, curving barberry hedge that surrounded the property hid both the garden walks and the front sidewalk.

"I don't like hedges," Judy decided. "I'm glad we don't have them around our house in Dry Brook Hollow."

She couldn't help thinking, as she looked back at the old Farringdon-Pett mansion, that she wouldn't trade her remodeled farmhouse for a dozen houses with turrets. Everything was dark except for the light in the living-room window and the porch light, which had been left on so she would be able to see her way down the walk.

Judy stopped only a moment to look up at the turrets and the suddenly darkened sky. Then, still wondering uneasily whose footsteps were following along behind her, she continued her walk up Grove Street.

Beyond the curve by the barberry hedge the winding street turned and went uphill toward the lonely section known as Upper Grove Street. Just as Judy passed the spot where the old factory used to stand, the footsteps behind her quickened.

"What's the idea of walking along this dark street unescorted?" her brother's familiar voice demanded.

"Oh, it's you!" Judy laughed a little shakily as she recognized Horace and Honey. "The hedge was in the way. I couldn't tell who was coming around the bend. It isn't really dark," she added. "The moon was shining until a moment ago. Or didn't you and Honey notice it?"

Peter's pretty sister laughed and brushed her honey-colored hair away from her face in a characteristic gesture.

"Did we, Horace? Or were we too busy trying to rhyme 'April' with 'moon'?"

"It's 'June' that rhymes. What about 'June'?" Horace inquired seriously.

"I hope I didn't interrupt something important," Judy said, laughing.

"Only a poetic discourse. Horace and I decided we were hungry after the play. So we ate and danced, and now we're composing poetry, but neither of us is very good at it. This is as far as we've gone:

"Oh, give me a night in April
Under an April moon—"

"You can have your night in April," Judy laughed.
"I'll gladly give it to you, moonlight and shadows
and all. Sometime, when you feel really poetic, you
should walk around the Farringdon-Pett estate.
There's a sort of weird beauty to that lake with the
tree shadows around it. Some of them almost seem
alive."

"Were you walking down by the lake?" asked
Horace. "That was an odd thing to do at this hour of
night."

"Not walking, just looking," Judy said, and told
him about the shadow she had seen and how Lois and
Lorraine had invited her in for a cup of tea and had
tried to convince her that it had been nothing but the
shadow of an oddly shaped tree.

"Actually, they didn't convince me," Judy said,
"although, goodness knows, they tried hard enough.
We talked about Roberta, too," she added abruptly.
"They think I should leave her with Mother and Dad
and travel with Peter. Do you think she'd be happy
with anyone except me?"

"With her father, perhaps," Honey ventured.

"That's what Lois and Lorraine said. But a merchant
ship is no place for a little girl. She wouldn't want to
quit school, either. She adores her teacher."

"She adores you too, Judy," Honey said. "You're

the one she always comes to when she's in trouble."

"Which is just about all the time," Horace finished. "Mother couldn't stand it. She deserves some peace after raising you."

He was teasing her, Judy knew. But there was truth in what he said. When they had taken Honey home and returned to the Bolton house, Judy discovered that Roberta and the Dakin twins had been cutting pictures out of old magazines all evening and had left the floor littered with clippings. To make matters worse, Blackberry had tossed them about as if he were still a kitten, and Roberta's puppy had chewed some of them into shreds.

"See what I mean?" Horace pointed out.

Judy saw. The twins had not helped straighten the room, and Roberta had been too tired to do it after they left. Now they found her asleep upstairs in the exact center of Judy's bed, her golden curls streaming across both pillows and her arms outstretched. It was what Horace called the spread-eagle position.

"A sign of utter exhaustion," he explained.

"It's Mother who's probably utterly exhausted. I'm sure she went to bed with a headache," Judy said.

Horace sniffed the air like a dog on the scent of a rabbit.

"You're right, Sis," he agreed. "I smell camphor."

"That does it," declared Judy.

The next day was Saturday, but she decided not to spend it with her parents as she had planned, but to return to Dry Brook Hollow and give her mother a rest. The shopping she had been going to do could wait until the bazaar opened.

"There may be some pretty wash dresses and aprons for sale," she thought, "and I'll be helping the hospital besides."

Dr. Bolton was on the staff, and Judy felt that anything she did to help the hospital helped her father too. At breakfast she told him how she had volunteered to serve as chairman of the refreshment committee and how she hoped Horace and some of his friends would be willing to wait on the tables.

"But that's a girl's job," Horace protested.

"Nonsense!" said Judy. "Men make far better waiters than women. They can carry heavier trays."

There was no use arguing that point. Still Horace was not enthusiastic about acting as a waiter, although he did promise to put a notice in the paper, in the hope of rounding up volunteers.

The bazaar was the chief topic of conversation at breakfast. Roberta came down just in time to hear the word hospital mentioned and asked who was sick.

"Plenty of people," declared Dr. Bolton, rising from the table. "My job is to see that they get well, and I'd better be about it."

"We were talking about the hospital bazaar," Judy explained when her father had left.

"That wasn't where you were last night, was it?" Roberta questioned.

"No, we went to a play the student nurses put on

in the high school auditorium. Don't you remember?"
asked Judy. "You could have gone with us if the
Dakin twins hadn't come over to see you."

"Was it a good play?"

"Very good," declared Judy, "but a little too serious for you. Afterward, we talked about the bazaar.
That's something I know you'll enjoy. There's going
to be a candy house and a puppet show and ever so
many other attractions."

"Will they sell things?"

"Lots of things. I may buy your new school dresses
there instead of shopping here in Farringdon as we
planned. I do want to be home in case Peter gets back
from his trip."

Roberta wanted to be home, too, but she was eager
to come back to Farringdon for the bazaar. Judy
promised that she could have her weekly allowance
ahead of time, so that she would have a little extra
money to spend.

"My allowance comes from my father, doesn't it?"
Roberta asked after they had started for Dry Brook
Hollow.

"It used to," Judy said.

She didn't want to tell Roberta how long it had
been since her father had sent either her allowance or
the weekly sum he was supposed to pay for her board.

The little girl gave Judy a quizzical look, as if reading her thoughts. Then she turned her attention to
Tuffy, who was romping all over the back seat of the
car. Blackberry was curled up between Judy and

Roberta, sound asleep and purring contentedly. He had grown so used to riding back and forth between Dry Brook Hollow and Farringdon that now the car was exactly like his own favorite rocking chair.

Although Roberta continued to cast occasional puzzled glances in Judy's direction, she asked no more questions until they were turning down the road that led to the house in Dry Brook Hollow that Judy had inherited from her grandmother. With Peter's help, she had transformed it into what they both liked to call their dream house. Red Burnett, who took care of the land, was plowing a strip by the road.

"What's he going to plant there?" Roberta asked suddenly.

"Corn, I think."

"Goody! I'll husk the corn for you, Judy," Roberta offered eagerly. "I know how, and it'll be a lot of fun."

"You're a big help to me," Judy told her. "I really don't know what I would do without you."

"Then it wouldn't matter if my father didn't pay my board? I mean, ever? If his ship went down and he got drowned or something, I could keep right on living with you?"

Judy was stunned by the suddenness of this question, although she had thought of the possibility herself.

"Why, I—I guess so," she replied uncertainly. "That is, unless you have some relative—"

"But I haven't," the little girl interrupted. "Aunt

Alma wasn't my real aunt, and the grandmother I lived with right after my mother died is dead, too. There isn't anyone except my father. Look, Judy!" she cried out, as they came in sight of the house and the puppy began to bark. "There's someone at the door. It looks a little like my father's back."

The man, apparently, had just rung the bell and was now peering through the glass in the front door, obviously trying to determine if anyone was at home.

"It's a good thing we didn't stay in Farringdon today, if that should turn out to be your father," declared Judy, a little excited herself at the prospect of meeting the mysterious Captain Dunn.

"You won't let him take me away from here, will you, Judy?" Roberta pleaded.

"Take you away!" Judy exclaimed. "What an idea! What would he do with you on a merchant ship? He's probably just here on a visit. I should think you'd be glad to see him, Roberta. He'll probably have all sorts of interesting stories to tell—"

"I don't want to hear them," the little girl said stubbornly.

"But he's your father," Judy insisted, shocked at Roberta's lack of affection for him, "and if you don't love him, how can you expect him to love you and want to come and visit you?"

"He doesn't love me, or he would have come to see me before. Oh, good!" Roberta exclaimed as the man turned around. "It isn't my father after all."

Judy didn't know whether to feel relieved or sorry.

After she had stopped the car she sat behind the wheel for a moment, trying to collect her thoughts.

"Roberta should have been disappointed," she reasoned. "It isn't natural for a little girl not to want to see her own father."

Beside Judy, Blackberry stretched himself and looked at his mistress inquiringly.

"Are you getting out of the car or aren't you?" his green eyes seemed to say.

Deciding that she wasn't, he curled himself into a tight ball and went back to sleep. But the puppy bounded out ahead of Roberta, barking frantically.

"Quiet, Tuffy!" the little girl commanded. "Let's go see who he is!"

They were racing toward the house before Judy quite realized what was happening. Seeing them coming, the man whose back looked a little like Captain Dunn's picked up a suitcase standing beside him and opened it.

"Oh, Judy!" Roberta called excitedly from the porch. "Come here and look!"

CHAPTER III

A Package of Flower Seeds

"Look, Judy, he's selling flower seeds," Roberta exclaimed eagerly, as Judy came up onto the porch. "You're going to buy some, aren't you? You promised me I could have a garden this year and we haven't any seeds. April isn't too early to plant them, is it?"

"It's the best time for hardy flowers," the peddler told her.

His voice quavered a little. He was older than Judy had thought when she first saw his back. Suddenly she wanted to help him, but the first seeds he showed her were all annuals.

"Haven't you any perennials?" she asked. "I like flowers that come up year after year. We have quite a few bulbs in the ground. The crocuses are in bloom already, and there are hollyhocks for later, and chrys-anthemums and phlox."

"I can't add much to that, lady, unless you want biennials. These pinks will come up next year, but I can't guarantee them after that." He flipped through the packages as if they were a deck of cards. "Ah! There you are!" he announced. "I do have one package of painted daisies. They're genuine perennials, guaranteed to blossom."

"Lovely!" exclaimed Judy, growing enthusiastic when she saw the pictured daisies on the seed package. The centers were yellow, the petals shading from pale pink to deepest lavender.

"These are just what I want for my cutting garden," she added. "See how colorful they are, Roberta. Can't you imagine how they will look in a vase?"

To Judy's surprise, the little girl did not answer her question. She did not so much as look up from the package of flower seeds in her hand but stood in rapt silence, gazing at the picture on the package.

Looking over her shoulder, Judy could see that it was a package of alyssum seeds that had captured her attention. It was marked "Annual."

"Isn't there a perennial variety of alyssum?" Judy asked.

"No! No!" cried Roberta, suddenly finding her voice. "I want this package, Judy. This very package! Please buy it for me."

"For goodness' sake, what's so special about it?" Judy wanted to know. "We can buy alyssum anywhere, and I'd rather have the kind that will come up next year too."

"But I want this!" Roberta insisted. "It's just like my garden. My own dear garden! I had forgotten all about it until I saw this picture, but now I remember."

"May I see it?" asked Judy.

Roberta handed her the seed package a little reluctantly. On it was pictured a formal garden with flower beds in neat patterns and gravel walks between. In the very center, bordered by a circular walk, alyssum had been planted around what looked to Judy like a birdhouse on a post.

She laughed.

"If it's the birdhouse in the picture that's been holding you spellbound, we could have one like it—"

"That isn't a birdhouse!" Roberta interrupted. "It's a lantern. It has a candle in it and when you light it the whole garden looks like fairyland. There's a stone bench farther down the path. You can sit there and look at the garden and listen to the Christmas trees talking with each other. You can see the house, too."

"What house?" asked Judy. "How can you see what isn't in the picture? There's no house and no bench and no Christmas trees—"

"But there is!" Roberta cried. "It's a glass house all filled with flowers."

"I guess she means a greenhouse, lady," the old peddler remarked.

"Yes! Yes! A greenhouse!" Roberta gave the peddler a grateful look and went on excitedly. "The path

goes right past the greenhouse and under the trees. It's
just like the woods until you come to the gate and see
all the cars on the next street."

"I'm sure I don't see any cars."

"There *are* some evergreens in the background,
lady. The little girl is right," declared the peddler,
who had taken the seed package and put on his glasses
to look at the picture more closely.

"Maybe I need glasses, too." Judy laughed. "I do
see the evergreens now, and it does look as if there's
a path between them and a stone bench at the side,
but how anyone could tell there was a greenhouse or
a gate at the other end of the garden is beyond me!"

"Where was this garden, little girl?" the flower-
seed peddler asked curiously.

"I've forgotten," Roberta replied sadly, "but I know
exactly how it looked now that I've seen the picture
of this one. There was a big tree with a swing on it
somewhere, and I'm sure there was a brook."

She paused to sigh wistfully, as though remembering a favorite dream.

"Like my dream of floating on a pink cloud,"
thought Judy. Aloud, she said, "You win, Roberta!
Since you think this garden is so beautiful, we'll try
and make our garden as near like the picture as we can.
I don't know about the—the ornament." She had
almost said birdhouse. "But we certainly can have the
same flowers."

Turning to the peddler, she said, "I'll take the
alyssum seeds and the painted daisies. I would like the

pinks, too, but I'm afraid I haven't enough change. If you want to wait, I'll run back to the car where I left my pocketbook—"

"Sure, I'll wait," the old man said good-naturedly.

Presently Judy returned with Blackberry, aroused at last from his slumbers, following her.

"I'm sorry," she apologized, "but I may not be able to buy those flower seeds after all. I have only eleven cents—"

"I've got money, Judy! I've got money in my piggy bank! I'll buy them—"

"Wait a minute, Roberta!" Judy stopped her. She couldn't understand the little girl's excitement. "I was going to say I only have eleven cents in change, but I do have a twenty-dollar bill."

"I think I can change it, lady."

Saying this, the peddler began to pull bills from his various pockets. He had money stuffed away all over his person, it seemed. Judy watched in amazement as he drew forth a crumpled ten, a five, and three singles.

"Will this do?" he asked. "I reckon you'll want to buy about two dollars' worth of seed."

"Perhaps more. We want to duplicate the other flowers in the picture on the alyssum-seed package if we can," Judy told him. "I already have some, but the perennials will need transplanting. Luckily, we have similar shrubs, and the potted bulbs are already in bud, but the tall flowers will have to be grown from seed. Let's see, we'll need marigolds and balsam and snapdragons . . ."

One by one, the obliging old man helped Judy pick them out until she had them all.

"Thank you very much, lady. And you, too, little miss," he said as he turned to go. "You're going to have a beautiful garden."

Just then the telephone rang and Judy rushed into the house to answer it. To her delight, it was Peter. He couldn't reveal his whereabouts but told her he would be home that evening.

"In time for dinner?" she questioned.

"If you make it late. Say, seven-thirty."

"Seven-thirty it will be."

Judy liked late dinners with no rush, no pressing engagements to be kept afterward. She liked sitting quietly around the table by candlelight. There was always so much to talk about, so much to plan.

"Our garden, for instance," she thought, already anticipating the talk around the table.

"Roberta!" she called. "Aren't you coming in?"

There was no answer.

Going out on the porch once more, Judy found her little boarder still standing like a statue, the flower seeds they had bought in her hand. The package of sweet alyssum was on top.

"For goodness' sake!" exclaimed Judy. "Are you still dreaming over that garden? You didn't even ask me who called on the telephone."

"Was it my father?" Roberta's voice had a faraway sound to it. "If it was, I do want to see him. I want to show him my garden after it's all planted so it looks exactly like the garden in this picture. It will make him remember how I used to run down the path to meet him and throw my arms around his neck and kiss him. I did love him then, Judy, really I did."

"Of course you did. You still do," declared Judy. "I was sure you didn't mean what you said. But that wasn't your father on the telephone, Roberta. It was Peter. He's coming home this evening."

The little girl sighed. "I wish my father *would* come."

"Perhaps he doesn't know that, Roberta. Why don't you write to him in care of the shipping company? They'll forward your letter, and when your father realizes how much you want to see him I'm sure he will come home as soon as he can."

"He didn't come for Christmas."

"Did you honestly want him to, Roberta?" Judy questioned. "You've been acting as if you didn't care anything about him, and you never write."

Roberta hung her head, looking ashamed, until Tuffy jumped up and licked her face. That made her laugh.

"My father doesn't even know I've got Tuffy. Why, we're almost strangers and I guess it is my fault, Judy. I'm going to write him a long letter right away."

Roberta was busy with her letter when it was time for her to set the table that evening. Judy glanced at the golden head bent over the writing desk and decided not to call her away from her letter, but to set the table herself.

"I'll miss Roberta when her father does come for her," she thought.

Judy had known she would not have her little boarder forever, but, somehow, the child's sudden yearning for her father made Judy feel that perhaps she should have done something to bring them together before this. Captain Dunn's first letters had been brief, both to her and to Roberta. Finally, with Judy's assurance that Roberta was happy in her new boarding place, both letters and checks had stopped coming altogether.

"What has happened?" Judy wondered.

She was still standing in a wondering attitude with the silver in her hands when Peter suddenly startled her out of her thoughts by kissing her on the back of her neck.

"Peter!" she exclaimed, whirling around to return the kiss. "It's good to have you home," she murmured into his coat. "You've only been gone a week, but it seemed like forever. This house is so lonesome!"

"With you in it? Impossible," declared Peter. "What's the matter with old Blackberry? Isn't he good company any more? And where's our little boarder and her demon pup? Isn't she supposed to be setting the table?"

"She's busy," Judy replied. "She's writing a letter to her father."

"It's about time! I don't believe she's written him so much as a card since Christmas." Peter sniffed the air. "What's cooking? It smells like pot roast."

"It is pot roast," Judy said, smiling. "And for dessert there's something else you like. Apple pie with big pieces of cheese to go with it. We won't have to rush through dinner, will we? I'd like to light the candles and just sit around and talk afterward, or maybe listen to some music."

"I'll see what's on. You cut out the week's programs last Sunday, didn't you?"

"Roberta did. They're right in the top drawer of the telephone table where we always put them."

Peter walked over to the table and opened the drawer, then whistled suddenly in surprise. "What's this on top?" he asked, picking up one of the bills Judy had received from the flower-seed peddler.

"Where did you get this?" Peter demanded urgently, studying the ten-dollar bill. "Every FBI agent in the country is looking for it!"

CHAPTER IV

The Telltale Bill

JUDY WAS STRUCK SPEECHLESS for a moment by Peter's unexpected question.

"I—why, I got the money from a flower-seed peddler," she faltered. "He simply changed the twenty dollars you left me for the housekeeping money, so I could pay for the seeds we bought for Roberta's garden."

"Do you remember what this peddler looked like?"

"I do, Peter," Judy declared. "I'd know him anywhere. He was a—well, a sort of gentle old man with a pleasant way of speaking. I judged him to be at least sixty. His hair and moustache were white, but he didn't wear glasses except for reading."

"About how tall was he?"

Judy hesitated only a moment.

28

"Five feet eight, I would say. He carried himself very erect for a man of his age and seemed much more refined than the ordinary house-to-house peddler. In fact, I rather liked him."

Peter's blue eyes narrowed.

"Likable, was he?"

"Oh, yes," Judy agreed enthusiastically. "He was ever so helpful when it came to planning the garden. What I can't understand is what a nice old man like that would be doing with money that the FBI is looking for. Is it counterfeit, Peter?"

"Something like that," he replied, not answering her question directly.

"Oh, Peter! It's one of those horribly secret things, isn't it?" she cried. "I don't like to have you working on cases like that. They're so dangerous!"

"Not while nobody knows I'm working on them."

"I only hope that poor old peddler isn't involved," sighed Judy. "He had such a kind, honest face."

"They all do," declared Peter. "The prisons are full of refined old gentlemen with kind, honest faces. They get by on their appearance—"

"But, darling," Judy teased him, "you have a kind, honest face. So that doesn't prove a thing."

"Thanks!" Peter's kind, honest face broke into a grin. "I'm sorry if I was abrupt, Angel. But it was such a surprise to find that ten-dollar bill right here on our own telephone table. I'll have to call the field office and report it right away."

Saying this, he disappeared into his den.

"Oh dear!" sighed Judy. "There go my plans for a quiet dinner. Everything probably will get cold while he telephones."

Peter was making his call from the extension in his den, where he kept all his private papers. His sanctum sanctorum, Judy called it, whenever she found herself excluded which wasn't often. As his secretary, she usually worked with him.

"We have solved practically all our mysteries together," she thought, a little piqued because she had no share in this one.

Just as she had predicted, it took Peter a long time to complete his telephone call. Meanwhile, Roberta, her letter finished, came into the kitchen and said, "I'm hungry. Where's Peter? Oh, thank you for setting the table, Judy."

The large country kitchen with its fireplace and old beams had a dining section right by the front window. It was the most cheerful room in the world when there was a fire flickering in the grate and lighted candles on the table.

"I thought we'd be ready before you finished your letter," Judy explained, "but Peter had to make a phone call, so we must wait a little longer."

"While we're waiting, would you like to read my letter?" Roberta asked.

"If you want me to."

Judy took it with the respect she always had for personal mail and sat down in her grandmother's rocker by the fireplace to read it. The letter was so

fat that it would need an extra postage stamp. She
could see that right away.

Tuffy already was under the table, ready for the
tidbits he knew Roberta would let fall in his direction
when they finally sat down to supper. But Blackberry, seeing that his mistress had made herself comfortable by the fire, leaped into her lap.

While she read, he occasionally stretched forth a
paw to rustle the pages of the letter.

In it Roberta had told her father all about her life
at the farm in Dry Brook Hollow. She had told him
about Tuffy and how wonderful it was to have a little dog all her own to love and take care of.

I take care of the chickens, too, she had added.
They follow me whenever I go out into the yard.

There was a whole page listing the different things
Roberta did to make herself useful, and another one
telling her father about the school she attended in
Roulsville and how much she liked her teacher and
her best friend Muriel Blade.

Finally she had told her father how much she
wanted to see him and how sorry she was that she
had not written before.

I haven't seen you for so long, the letter confessed,
*that I began to feel as if I'd always lived with Judy
and Peter. Then something made me remember the
garden and the lantern. You will see what it was when
you come to visit me here in Dry Brook Hollow. The
house is hidden behind trees, but I think you can find*

it, because the name Dobbs is on the mailbox where our little road turns off the main road from Farringdon to Roulsville.

Roberta had given her father explicit directions. Not only had she told him how to reach the house from the highway, but she also had mentioned the fact that the nearest railway station was Roulsville and that there was an airport in Farringdon, in case he wanted to fly.

"I didn't tell him anything about the garden we're going to have," she explained, "because I want to surprise him when he comes. He will come, won't he, Judy?"

"I hope he will," she replied. "This is a warm enough invitation. He will certainly know his little girl wants to see him."

At Roberta's request, Judy corrected a few errors in spelling. There weren't many. It was such a tender, sweet letter in places that Judy's eyes were a little wet when she had finished reading it.

Roberta read it over once herself and then added:

P. S. I love you, Daddy. I always loved you, but it is hard to remember what you are like when you stay away so long. Please send me a picture of yourself to keep beside the picture I have of Mother.

She signed the letter *Bobby*.

"That's what he used to call me," she explained.

"Nobody ever called me Roberta until I went to live with my grandmother. She was strict and made everybody, even my father, call me by my full name."

"Was she your father's mother?" asked Judy.

Roberta thought a minute.

"No, my mother's," she replied. "Her name was Mrs. Ridley. I never liked the way she said 'Roberta!' with her mouth in a straight line."

Judy could imagine what a stern old woman Roberta's grandmother Ridley must have been.

"Would you like it if we called you Bobby?" she asked.

Roberta laughed and shook her head.

"I guess not. It sounds too much like a boy's name. But I did like it the way my father said it when he used to come to the door and call, 'Bobby! Bobby!' The garden was so big that sometimes he had to call two or three times before I heard him. Then it would sound as if the big trees were calling, 'Bobby! Bobby!' It makes me homesick just to think of it," Roberta finished.

"You mustn't be homesick here. This is your home," declared Judy. "Maybe you're just hungry. I'll give you your dinner now. We may have to eat in a hurry when Peter comes to table. He probably will have plans."

"You had plans," Roberta said. "We were going to take our time and listen to some music. There's a play that goes on the air at eight-thirty—"

"How would you like to listen to that play with

your little friend Muriel Blade?" asked Peter, coming in just as Judy placed the pot roast on the table. "I called her mother and she says you may stay there for an hour or two while Judy and I go on rather an important errand in the car."

Judy's eyes told Peter she understood. But it was not until after they had finished their meal and driven Roberta over to Muriel's that Judy asked questions. Then she said, "We're going after that flower-seed peddler, aren't we?"

"You bet we are!" declared Peter. "Apparently he canvassed the road all the way to Roulsville. I just talked with Mr. Blade and he says he bought some seeds of him and that Mrs. Blade gave him a cup of coffee. Our story will be that he shortchanged you, Judy. Do you think you can stick to it?"

"I'll try," she promised, "but I won't like it. Wouldn't it be better if we said we were rounding up volunteers for the hospital bazaar? I am chairman of the refreshment committee, and we do need waiters and people for the booths and for entertainment. Afterward, I could say, 'By the way, was there a flower-seed peddler here this afternoon?'"

Judy's voice was so comical as she imitated herself making the inquiry that Peter had to laugh. But he agreed to the plan and admitted that it was a better idea than his own.

"What do we do?" asked Judy. "Stop at every house?"

"Let's skip a few to save time," Peter suggested. "Then, if we find we've missed him, we'll work back."

They were driving past some of the houses Peter wanted to skip as they talked. A sign just below the broken pieces of the old dam welcomed them to Roulsville. Here the houses were all new except those that stood on the hillside out of reach of the flood that once had swept the town.

At the first few houses, all of which had little gardens in back, they found that the peddler had accepted nothing but change for the seeds he had sold.

"Selling seeds from door to door wouldn't be a very good way to get rid of 'hot' money, if that's what you think he was doing," declared Judy. "Most people wouldn't give a peddler large bills to change."

"You're right," Peter agreed. "He may be entirely innocent, but we have to trail him anyway to find out where he got that telltale ten-dollar bill. I was instructed to bring you along to make the identification in case we do run across him."

"And I thought you brought me just for company!"

Judy was not taking Peter's case very seriously. How could she when she knew nothing about it? But she was enjoying the ride. They did not often go out driving alone in the evening. Usually Roberta was with them. Ever since their wedding day, when she had arrived so unexpectedly to take the place of

Judy's chosen flower girl, who had come down with chicken pox, Roberta had been almost like a little sister to Judy.

And yet, although Judy would not admit it even to herself, it was more romantic when she and Peter were just by themselves.

There was almost a full moon again tonight, the same as there had been the evening before when Lois and Lorraine had tried to convince Judy that what she had seen was only a tree shadow. The moon was just rising over the ridge of the wooded hill on the upper side of the road.

Suddenly Judy pointed.

"See that old house all by itself with the trees around it?"

"You mean the old Heffly house?" Peter questioned.

"Yes, that's the one. Lois and Lorraine tell me that Mr. Heffly has decided to sell it at last. Arthur intends to buy it and tear it down and put up new model houses on the land."

"There's a light behind the shutters in that upstairs window," Peter observed suddenly. "That old house would be an ideal place for a homeless flower-seed peddler to spend the night. Shall we stop and investigate?"

"Yes, let's!"

Judy was enthusiastic until they stood on the creaking porch. To her surprise, there were curtains at the lower windows.

"Somebody's been living in it!" she exclaimed, surprised that anybody would live in such a dilapidated old house without making repairs.

Peter banged the knocker. Presently they heard footsteps. The door was opened by a gaunt young man almost too tall for the doorframe.

"Well? What is it?" he demanded, and his voice was anything but cordial.

"We just wanted to make an inquiry—" Peter began.

"Inquire somewhere else then," snapped the man, and shut the door almost in their faces.

Startled, Judy would have backed right off the porch if Peter hadn't caught her. Together they walked back down the ancient board walk and descended the rickety wooden steps that led to the street.

"A pleasant character, wasn't he?" Judy remarked when they were safely on their way again. "I'm glad you're tall, Peter, but not that tall. Why, he was practically a scarecrow. And that creaky old house! It gives me the shivers just to look back at it. Lorraine said it was spookier than the Farringdon-Pett mansion, and now I believe her."

"Shall we stop at that cozy little white cottage on the next corner for contrast?" asked Peter.

Judy agreed, but they had no more than turned in at the walk when a voice from inside called out, "Here they come now!" and the door was flung open.

The girl who rushed forward to greet them was as

plump as the "scarecrow" in the old Heffly house had been thin. But it was her hair that fascinated Judy. It was obvious that nature had not given her the mass of golden curls that adorned her head.

"Come in! Come in!" she invited, waving her hand. "The party's just beginning."

"Sophie!" a voice screamed behind her. "They're not the right people. They'll think you're crazy going to the door in that wig."

"We think she's perfect," declared Judy, who could see at once that the young people were having a masquerade party. "We're rounding up volunteers for the hospital bazaar. If you'll volunteer to be one of the attractions, I'll see if that tall, thin man in the house across the street will volunteer, too."

"You mean—the old Heffly house?"

"Yes, the one on the hill. There was a tall, thin man who answered the door—"

"But there couldn't have been," the girl called Sophie interrupted, her eyes wide and frightened. "Nobody lives there. That house is empty!"

CHAPTER V

A Weird Encounter

"You mean—" Judy glanced at Peter. "But that's ridiculous," she said. "We saw him with our own eyes. He was tall, practically a living scarecrow. But he was certainly no ghost."

"There is a rumor going around that the old Heffly house is haunted," Sophie's friend reminded her.

She had been laughing when she first came to the door, but now she was surprisingly serious. Three or four other young people had gathered in a group behind her. Some of them were in costume. One girl, looking amazingly like an animated rag doll, flopped forward and pointed a stocking-covered arm.

"They're right!" she cried. "There's a light up there."

"There are curtains at the lower windows, too. Ghosts don't hang curtains," Judy said.

At that, the whole idea began to seem comical. Sophie started to laugh, and the others soon joined in.

"You should know," a tall youth, unrecognizable in a clown costume, declared. "You're Judy Bolton, aren't you? The famous Judy Bolton," he explained, bowing to the others. "She's an authority on ghosts. You all know her, by reputation at least. Her brother was the hero of the Roulsville flood, but she put him up to it. And she's dehaunted more houses than you could shake a stick at, including her own house in Farringdon."

"Do you still live there?" inquired another boy, who remembered Judy from grammar school.

Introducing Peter to those who did not already know him, Judy explained that they were married and now lived in her grandmother's house in Dry Brook Hollow.

"Why, we're practically neighbors!" exclaimed Sophie, whose last name turned out to be Howell.

She was a jolly person, as cordial as the "scarecrow" in the old Heffly house had been forbidding. Judy was soon telling her all about the coming bazaar.

"We really do need you. Please come in costume, just as you are now, and help us entertain," she urged. "You and your friends would make a top-notch circus, and you'd be doing a good turn as well. The whole county needs a new, modern hospital annex."

"We'll come," the fat girl promised. "We'll do a

few acts we've been rehearsing, too, if you like. But are you serious about asking that—that Heffly ghost—"

"I'd certainly like to," replied Judy. "That is, if he doesn't vanish before my eyes. He must be seven feet tall. He'd make an excellent giant, especially if you appeared beside him. You're about four feet eleven—"

"A good guess!" Sophie giggled and swished her wide skirt. "This isn't all me," she confessed. "My friends tell me I'm just pleasingly plump, but with these pillows and this curly wig, I think I'll do for your circus fat lady."

"You'll come then, pillows and all? I want the rag doll and the clown too. In fact, I want all of you. By the way," Judy added, trying to make her voice sound casual, "was there a flower-seed peddler here this afternoon? An old man—"

"What's he got to do with it?" the rag doll wanted to know.

"Judy Bolton, if you're going to ask that poor old man to appear in your freak show—"

This was one of the girls Judy had known when she went to school in Roulsville before the flood.

"I just won't be in it if you do," Sophie chimed in with a childish pout.

"I had no intention of asking him to appear," Judy reassured her. "I was just wondering if he stopped here, too. You've just moved in, haven't you?"

Sophie admitted it. The party, she confessed, was a sort of housewarming. Like Judy and Peter, she and

Jack Howell, otherwise known as the clown, were newlyweds.

"In that case," said Judy, "you'll probably be gardening for the first time and could—well, use a few tips."

She glanced helplessly at Peter, but he was talking with one of his old school friends and did not come to her rescue.

"We're not experienced gardeners, by any means," she went on, floundering for words, "but we do have plans. You must visit us and see our garden. We bought quite a lot of seeds. I mean, from the peddler."

"We bought some asters and marigolds," Sophie told her at last. "I wasn't going to plant any garden this year, but I felt so sorry for the peddler that I just had to. He said he'd been peddling his seeds all day but that he intended to make only a few more stops before he took the train. . . ."

Again Judy glanced at Peter. This time he nodded slightly.

"This is the information we want," his eyes said wordlessly.

Their next stop, Judy knew, would be the railroad station. Sophie had saved them the trouble of canvassing all the houses.

At the station, fifteen minutes later, Judy and Peter were relieved to find their old friend Jed Baker, who was just about to close the ticket window. No more trains were due until the midnight flyer would come whizzing through with only a warning toot for Roulsville.

"Well, if it ain't Judy and Peter!" the old ticket agent exclaimed warmly. "How's your grandfather these days, Peter? We've missed him at the last couple of get-togethers down at Sam Tucker's farm. The old crowd's thinning out now that your grandparents are gone, Judy." He shook his head sorrowfully and added, "Too bad you missed your train."

"We didn't miss it," Peter replied. "We were just a mite curious about who got on it. How about giving us a little information for old times' sake?"

"Sure. Be glad to." He paused, glancing at Judy. "Thought it was your brother, the newspaper fellow, who did the checking up on people who take the train. Not much use nowadays, since so many go places in autymobiles and airplanes. Next thing, 'twill be rocket ships."

"We're planning to fly to the moon ourselves when that day comes." Judy's gray eyes twinkled. "But right now," she added, "we're interested in a flowerseed peddler who traveled the old-fashioned way."

Jed Baker chuckled appreciatively.

"By foot, you mean? Well, to tell you the truth, he did take the train, but only to the next town."

"Farringdon?" Peter questioned.

"Nope." The ticket agent squinted one eye at Peter. "It was an earlier train going in the other direction. He bought a ticket to Emporium and said something about going to church tomorrow. Now, mind, I wouldn't give this information to everyone. Where a man goes is his own business, I always say, but you two kids are different. You're like your grandfather, Peter, always up to something."

Peter grinned. "That's right, Uncle Jed." The whole town called the old ticket seller Uncle. "Just nosy, that's me!"

Laughing, he and Judy left the station. It was seldom necessary for Peter, who was so well remembered in Roulsville as a snub-nosed little boy trailing around after his grandfather to pick up odd bits of information, to reveal the fact that he was now working for the big uncle, otherwise known as Uncle Sam.

"We'll go to church in Emporium tomorrow," he declared enthusiastically when they were in the car again. "With the same luck we've had tonight, we're sure to locate our missing flower-seed peddler."

Somehow, Judy could not share Peter's enthusiasm for trailing an innocent-appearing old man who had done nothing at all except change her twenty dollars with a telltale bill he probably had received from another flower-seed customer.

"Is it so important that we have to follow him to church?" she questioned. "Probably he'll be just as surprised to hear there's anything wrong with that ten-dollar bill as I was. I shouldn't ask, but was it part of the loot from a train robbery, a bank holdup, or what?"

"That's right," replied Peter, grinning in the boyish way he had.

"What's right?" asked Judy curiously. "I made a couple of guesses."

"You're right. You shouldn't ask."

Judy made a face at him and was silent. Luckily there was no opportunity for her to ask any more questions, as they had arrived at the Blade farm. Roberta was bundled, half asleep, into the back seat of the car and taken home to be put to bed. Judy had to undress her as she was too sleepy to do it herself.

"Poor baby!" she said to Peter when Roberta was all tucked in. "We shouldn't have dashed out the way we did tonight and parked her with a neighbor, to go chasing—well, adventure."

"It was more than that, Judy."

Even though he would tell her nothing about it, he couldn't keep her from wondering.

"That telltale ten-dollar bill must be part of the loot from a robbery," she decided, "or he would have told me it wasn't. Maybe the bandits are still at large."

Judy went to sleep with this comforting thought. She was peacefully dreaming of a train robbery, probably suggested to her subconscious mind by the distant whistle of the midnight flyer as it whizzed through Roulsville, when another sound that she did not immediately recognize startled her awake.

CHAPTER VI

A Midnight Mystery

"WHAT WAS THAT?" Judy whispered across to Peter, who also had been awakened by the strange sound and was now moving restlessly in the dark.

"It could be a door banging somewhere," he replied. "There's a strong wind blowing outside. Hear it!"

"That isn't all I hear," declared Judy.

The banging continued. *Bang!* Then a little silence while the wind whistled through the trees. And *bang* again. It reminded Judy of the noises they used to hear in the Grove Street house when everyone believed it to be haunted.

Now they were saying the same thing about the Heffly house! Judy had to laugh to herself as she remembered Sophie and her friends and how alarmed they had been. Even the Scarecrow, as she had called him, seemed funny to Judy as she thought back over the events of the evening.

"You don't suppose Sophie's ghost from the old Heffly house followed us home, do you, Peter?" she asked.

"Whatever it is," Peter replied, "nobody could sleep through it. I'll go down and investigate."

Judy was curious, too. Pulling on her quilted satin housecoat, she was about to follow Peter downstairs where he already had turned on the lights, when something dark and furry brushed past her and almost made her trip.

"Blackberry!" she exclaimed. "Peter, I thought you said you put him out. He nearly made me fall head-long down the stairs."

"Was it Blackberry or that sweeping, rose-colored thing you're wearing?" Peter asked impishly as she came downstairs.

"This is a housecoat," Judy replied with dignity. "It's supposed to make me look glamorous when I have to get up in the middle of the night to put out cats and do other things you forgot—"

"But I didn't forget," Peter interrupted. His voice told Judy that this was no joking matter. "I did put Blackberry out. I locked the doors, too, just as I told you I would when you went upstairs to bed. The windows down here were all closed and locked, too."

"Then how did Blackberry get back in?"

Puzzled, Judy picked up the cat and began talking to him.

"You'd tell us if you could, wouldn't you, Blackberry? You always were a mysterious animal. From the very day Peter gave you to me you've been involved in mysteries almost as much as we have. If you could talk, I know you'd tell us—"

Another bang interrupted her.

"It's probably a loose shutter somewhere. I'll have to look around for it," declared Peter. "It may have broken a window. That would explain Blackberry's mysterious presence in the house when he should be outside catching himself a midnight snack."

"Speaking of midnight snacks, how would you like a piece of that apple pie in the icebox? I'm a little hungry myself," Judy confessed. "I always am when wc have to rush through dinner. I believe I'll cut a couple of pieces. Will you have milk with your pie, or a piece of cheese?"

"Both."

Peter had hardly spoken when a still louder bang sounded in their ears. There was no mistaking it now. The noise came from the kitchen.

In the doorway, Judy stopped short. Peter was just behind her. Now they were both staring in disbelief at the wide-open kitchen door, which was swinging back and forth on its hinges and banging against the outside of the house. The wind had risen and, with every fresh gust, the door would bang again.

"That explains it," Peter said at last. "Now we know how Blackberry got in."

"It doesn't explain very much to me. Who unlocked the door?" Judy wanted to know. "Blackberry couldn't have done that all by himself."

"No," Peter agreed. "He's a smart cat all right, but not that smart. I had the night catch on. Nobody could have opened the door from the outside without first breaking the lock."

"Then it stands to reason that the door must have been opened from the inside," Judy said. "But by whom? Our Heffly ghost?" she suggested, giggling. "I can't think of anyone else who could get in through a locked door."

"Someone else might have gotten in through one of the upstairs windows—"

Judy's first thought was of Roberta. Her window was open! But when she raced upstairs to make sure the little girl was safe, she found her sleeping so peacefully that she had to stop and say a little prayer of thanks.

Somehow, Judy always felt reverent when in the room with a sleeping child. Roberta looked so sweet and helpless, curled up, kitten fashion, under the covers that Judy had to bend over and kiss her, ever so lightly, in her sleep.

"I shouldn't have done that," she told herself as Roberta stirred slightly and threw out one hand. Judy was surprised to find it clutching the precious package of alyssum seed.

"Roberta is so eager to plant her garden that she took one of the seed packages to bed with her," Judy told Peter when she was downstairs again. "There's a picture on it that actually has made her homesick."

This was a little difficult for Peter to believe.

"But it's true," Judy insisted. "She said it was just like her own dear garden, but she couldn't remember where the garden was. I thought at first it was one of those imaginary places she makes up sometimes. But the more I think about it the more certain I am that it was real. Wait a minute and I'll show you!"

Judy ran upstairs again and, without waking Roberta, carefully removed the seed package from her hand. The hand seemed a little cold, so she tucked it under the covers and then hurried downstairs to show Peter the picture.

"You see that—that object in the middle of the garden," she said, indicating it. "What would you say it was?"

He studied the picture on the seed package a moment before he replied, "Why, it's a Chinese stone lantern! I saw one in a museum once. They have them to illuminate Chinese gardens. They put a candle inside—"

"I knew it!" cried Judy. "That proves what I was trying to tell you. Roberta wouldn't have known it was a lantern if she hadn't remembered one like it in some other garden. It looked to me exactly like a birdhouse. But when I called it that she spoke up and said, 'That isn't a birdhouse. It's a lantern. It has a candle in

it and when you light it the whole garden looks like
fairyland!'

"She described other things," Judy continued. "A
gate, for instance, and a greenhouse. There's no greenhouse in this picture. It's obvious that she remembers
some garden—"

"Her grandmother's, perhaps. She lived with her
grandmother Ridley for a while."

"Yes, Peter. But she's dead. So is Roberta's mother.
So, even if the garden was a real one, it isn't going to
do Roberta any good to keep on longing for it. I
promised her I'd make ours as near like it as I can."

"I don't think I can provide the stone lantern,"
Peter said skeptically. "They must cost a mint of
money. Probably whoever owned this garden in the
picture did some traveling and brought this lantern
back from China himself. You could set up your
mystic ball in our garden as an ornament, though."

"Lovely!" exclaimed Judy. "It will be even better
than a stone lantern because it will remind us of another mystery we solved."

"Another? Why be reminded of them? Haven't
you enough to puzzle over for one night?" asked
Peter.

Judy laughed. She still was not too sure that Peter
himself had not left the door unlocked. If he had, the
wind could have blown it open. But he insisted that
he had locked the door.

"Well, anyway, let's forget it and have our pie,"
she suggested, unconvinced. "If you think the Heffly

ghost is still here, I'll pull up a chair for him and invite him to join us around the table. From past experience, I've learned that it's always best to be cordial when you're entertaining invisible guests."

Judy was still laughing, but her face sobered when Peter said, "I'm afraid our guest was not as invisible as you think. I may as well tell you, Judy, that this may be a serious matter. As yet I have no proof of what happened. But it's just occurred to me that someone, possibly the flower-seed peddler himself, may have entered the house in the hope of getting back that telltale ten-dollar bill before it was spotted."

"You mean you think he was involved in the—the robbery or whatever it was, and gave me the bill by mistake? Well, I don't," declared Judy. "Call it woman's intuition if you like, but I don't believe it."

Peter pushed aside his empty plate and rose from the table.

"Facts speak for themselves," he said gravely. "I suggest that you look in your pocketbook to see if anything has been disturbed, while I search the den. If the bill is missing I think we can be pretty sure the peddler is guilty."

"Of what?" Judy asked the night as she turned toward the shadowy living room where she had left her pocketbook.

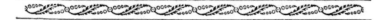

CHAPTER VII

The Finger of Suspicion

THE HOUSE was so far back from the main road, so entirely by itself, that Judy very much doubted that anyone had been near it. But, to please Peter, she carefully checked the contents of her pocketbook before going upstairs to bed.

"Everything is just as I left it," she reported to Peter when he came into their room a little later. "And all the money is in the drawer except the ten-dollar bill you seem to think is attracting all this trouble. You took that yourself for safekeeping."

"I know I did. I put it with my papers in the den downstairs, and it's still there. Nothing has been disturbed. It is strange," Peter went on. "I was so sure I'd hit on the right answer."

"I'm glad you didn't if it meant blaming that poor old peddler," declared Judy. "Now that I think of it,

I'm sure he couldn't have known there was anything queer about that bill, because he had it wadded up and stuffed in his pockets with all the rest of his money."

"You're probably right," agreed Peter. "But, as I said before, we have to trail him anyway and find out where he got it. Let's grab a little sleep before daylight. Tomorrow may be a busy day."

"Today, you mean."

It was long after midnight. Judy was so tired from her adventures that she had no difficulty at all in going back to sleep.

It was waking up the following morning that was really difficult. Roberta must have been calling her for some time, but the first thing that Judy heard was ". . . breakfast, Judy?"

"Wh-what about breakfast?" she asked, still half asleep.

"I said, aren't you coming down to breakfast?" the little girl repeated, coming into the bedroom. "Peter fried some eggs and made the coffee. He's going to take me to Sunday school, and then I can play with Muriel again. Are you going to church?"

"We're probably going to two or three churches," declared Judy, "but not in Roulsville. Peter is planning to drive on to Emporium."

"I know," Roberta said above the noise of the water Judy was running for a quick shower. "Peter told me. He didn't say so, but I think you're going to follow that flower-seed peddler. Do you think he can help you find my garden?"

"We do intend to ask him about it," Judy replied truthfully.

"Do you think he came on purpose to show the picture to me?" Roberta persisted.

"He didn't show you anything," Judy reminded her. "You found the picture on the seed package yourself and showed it to him. Peter thought it might be your grandmother's garden."

"You mean my grandmother Ridley? She didn't have any garden. She lived in two little rooms on the top floor of a house in Albany. I didn't like it there," Roberta declared emphatically. "Whatever I did, she was always watching me. She'd sit humped over like an old witch and watch me out of the corner of her eye. Once I tried to run away—"

"You shouldn't have done that!" exclaimed Judy. "Lots of times old people don't understand children. It's been so long since they were children themselves that they've forgotten how it feels, I guess. But they mean to do what is right."

"She did bake cookies," Roberta conceded.

"It's like the old rhyme," declared Judy:

> " 'There's so much good in the worst of us,
> And so much bad in the best of us,
> That it scarcely behooves the most of us
> To talk about the rest of us.' "

"What does *behooves* mean?" asked Roberta.

"Something that it's right to do, I guess."

"Then it behooves you to hurry. Peter said so. I

don't want to be late for Sunday school and miss the singing."

"It sounds to me as if you've already had your Sunday school lesson," said Peter, appearing at the door unexpectedly. "Come on down, Judy! You can brush your titian locks another time."

"I'll tie a kerchief over them and let them go. There!" Judy announced, pulling on her coat. "I'm all ready to swallow my coffee and dash off."

Judy did full justice to her breakfast. But she ate in record time.

It was only a short drive to the church in Roulsville where they deposited Roberta in plenty of time. From there they took the short route through the woods and past the state park where Judy remembered being left behind once on a school picnic.

From the picnic grounds on, the scenery changed. Emporium was a manufacturing town with factories in the valley, while most of the houses dotted the surrounding hills.

"I'm sure I don't know where you'd look for a church in a town like this!" exclaimed Judy. "All I've seen so far are factories and little ramshackle houses. Oh, there's one now with a big sign over it, 'Emporium Mission.' "

Peter stopped the car to listen.

"It sounds like a revival meeting going on inside," he commented after a moment. "Shall we go in?"

"Yes, let's," agreed Judy.

They stayed for a few minutes singing hymns and

hearing what the preacher called Testimonials. None of the men who had come to the service looked at all like the flower-seed peddler.

"I enjoyed the singing," declared Judy when they were out in the sunshine again. "Some of those people really raised their voices, didn't they? Did you hear that young man down in front? I was half tempted to ask him if he'd sing at our hospital bazaar."

"When is the bazaar?" asked Peter. "I don't believe you told me."

"It's the week after next. Thursday, Friday, and Saturday, but Saturday is the big day. I have a lot to do before then. I still don't have enough waiters. Singing waiters would be nice, wouldn't they? Here comes that young man now. I believe I will ask him."

The singer gladly consented. When they had talked a little while, Peter asked him if he had seen the flower-seed peddler.

"Oh, sure!" he replied. "Everybody around here knows him. He sells seeds every spring, but don't ask me where he goes to church. I haven't the faintest idea. But if you can wait until noon you'll be apt to find him in one of those coffee shops down by the railroad station. He generally eats around there."

Judy and Peter thanked the man who had consented to be a singing waiter, and, after they had stopped briefly in another church not far away, they decided to continue their search for the peddler in the various restaurants.

"We'll have soup in the first one, a sandwich in the

second, and dessert in a third," Peter said with a chuckle.

"But suppose there are more than three—"

"We'll just keep on eating," declared Peter. "Both of us could use a few extra pounds."

In the first restaurant they saw no one in the least resembling the peddler whom they were seeking. The same was true of the second place, where they had nothing but coffee, as the sandwich filling did not look inviting. But in the third restaurant, a dingy place near the railroad station, Judy recognized a familiar back.

"Peter!" she whispered excitedly. "There he is on that stool by the counter. I'm almost sure."

In order to make quite sure, Judy walked around to the other side of the counter where she had a view of the man's face. It was the flower-seed peddler all right. He was eating a huge portion of lamb stew and did not once look up from his plate.

Glad that she had not been seen, Judy walked over to the secluded corner where Peter was standing and whispered, "He's your man! I'll vanish while you talk with him. It will be better that way, won't it?"

"Much better," agreed Peter. "In fact, I was going to suggest it. I'll have to identify myself as an FBI agent," he added in a lower voice. "For your own safety, it will be just as well if we appear to be strangers."

For some reason this seemed funny to Judy, but

the seriousness in Peter's blue eyes kept her from laughing.

"Don't be such a worrybird! I'm safe enough," she began.

"Are you?" asked Peter. "After all, if he is involved in this crime, you must not forget for a single minute that he knows where you live."

What did Peter mean? Was he thinking of the kitchen door that had opened so mysteriously at midnight? Or did he suspect that the peddler had had some secret motive when he came to the door selling flower seeds?

"See if you can find out if he knew anything about that garden on the seed package, won't you?" she begged. "I didn't think he did, from the way he spoke. But Roberta is so interested."

"I'll get as much information as I can," Peter promised. "Where will I find you? In the car?"

Judy nodded and walked outside where there was a newsstand. The Sunday paper made the wait seem shorter, but, even at that, Peter spent a lot of time in the restaurant.

When he did come out, the flower-seed peddler was with him. They chatted for a while like old friends, ignoring Judy. It was not until after the old man was out of sight down the street that Peter finally walked over to the car.

"Hello, Angel!" he greeted Judy. "Where have you been all my life?"

"Waiting for you," she replied sweetly as he slid behind the steering wheel.

"Well, he didn't know anything about Roberta's garden, but I got the information I wanted," he announced, starting the car. "The peddler cleared himself. You were right about him being innocent. Believe it or not, the finger of suspicion now points to a certain young architect named Arthur Farringdon-Pett!"

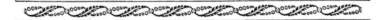

CHAPTER VIII

Serious Business

"No!" JUDY EXCLAIMED in disbelief. "Arthur couldn't have had anything to do with any crime, whatever it is. He will have some perfectly good explanation."

"No doubt he will," agreed Peter. "But the peddler's explanation satisfied me, at least for the moment. His name, by the way, is Abner Higgins."

"The Farringdon-Petts have a gardener named Higgins, don't they?" asked Judy.

"They do," Peter declared. "He is this man's brother. He's taken care of the Farringdon-Pett grounds for years, and Abner has supplied him with seeds and helped out around the place when there was any planting to be done. He also sells seeds to the people in and around Emporium."

"Then what was he doing selling seeds in Dry Brook Hollow?" Judy asked.

Now it was her turn to be suspicious of the flower-seed peddler.

"He says Arthur suggested it when he rode over with him yesterday morning," Peter explained. "He had a couple of regular seed customers along the main road, and our place wasn't much out of his way."

"I suppose he was peering through the door just to see if we were home. But I don't like it," Judy said. "I thought he was honest, but it seems to me he cleared himself and placed the blame on Arthur altogether too quickly."

"He didn't place the blame on anyone," declared Peter. "He merely told me where he got the bill. Arthur gave it to him in payment for some grass seed and fertilizer he bought. Where Arthur got it is the question we have to answer next. For all we know, there may be half a dozen people innocently involved."

"Does that mean I spend the day waiting in the car while you talk with them?"

Peter grinned in that impish way of his.

"Perhaps. We'll see what Arthur has to say for himself first."

"You didn't tell the peddler you and Arthur were friends, did you?"

"No, I didn't tell him anything," Peter replied. "I was getting information, not giving it out. Well, Angel, it looks as if our next stop is the Farringdon-Pett mansion."

"No, it's Muriel's house," Judy objected. "We can't leave Roberta there all day."

"How about taking her along with us and leaving her with your mother?"

Judy thought that was an excellent idea. But when they reached the Blade farm Mrs. Blade told her that Muriel and Roberta had decided that it was a good day for gardening.

"I gave them their lunch and they went over to your place," Mrs. Blade explained. "Roberta said she knew just where you wanted the seeds. She was so eager to get them planted that I let Muriel go along to help her spade up the ground."

"But they're all by themselves," Judy protested.

Mrs. Blade smiled the experienced smile of an older woman.

"They're ten years old, aren't they? Like as not, your mother left you by yourself plenty of times when you were that age. Don't you worry! No harm will come to them. What I always say is, when youngsters want to work, let them."

"I guess you're right at that," Judy agreed with a laugh.

Still a little uneasy about leaving the two little girls by themselves, Judy and Peter bade her good-bye and drove on toward Farringdon.

As they passed their own house they could just see Muriel and Roberta, their sweaters two bright spots of color through the trees. They were both as busy as beavers, running back and forth with rakes and pails. It didn't look to Judy as if they were either spading the ground or planting flower seeds. What were they doing?

"They'll be all right," Peter reassured her as they drove past.

Did Judy imagine it, or was he a little anxious, too?

"They're probably better off there than they would be with us," he commented after another few minutes of driving. "I feel certain that Arthur came by that telltale bill as innocently as the flower-seed peddler claims he did, but if we do run into the real criminals, there's no telling what they'd do to throw us off the trail."

"If it's that dangerous, I should think the police would handle it. They often work with you—"

"But not on assignments as delicate as this," Peter interrupted.

"You're certainly leaving me in the dark about it," Judy said, "but that's all right. I like mysteries, and even if I don't know why you're following this trail, you're letting me help. I guess I should be grateful for that."

Judy was silent as they drove over the next hill and down into Farringdon, which, like Roulsville, was situated in a valley. All the towns in this section of Pennsylvania were nestled among wooded hills. "The hills of home," Judy called them. She knew she would always want to come back to them even if she did, someday, realize her dream of traveling with Peter to other parts of the country.

"But there's no use dreaming about it now," she told herself firmly.

Even if she didn't have Roberta and the house, to say nothing of the garden, there still would be Peter's job. As resident agent, it was necessary for him to investigate any crimes in his own locality that came under the jurisdiction of the FBI.

It seemed impossible that quiet, dignified Arthur Farringdon-Pett could have become involved in a crime, however innocently. Suddenly Judy became apprehensive.

"This won't mean that Arthur will be arrested or held for questioning or anything, will it?" she asked.

"Not if he can tell me where he got that bill," Peter replied, halting the car in front of the Farringdon-Pett mansion, "and knowing Arthur, I'm sure he can."

It was Judy who rang the bell. The door was opened, as usual, by the quiet little colored maid Hetty, who had worked for the Farringdon-Petts for years. She was always in uniform. Judy had been greatly impressed by her polite way of speaking, as well as by her uniform, when she first met her. In those days, maids were something rare indeed in the young redhead's life.

"Come right in, Miss Judy," Hetty invited her now. "Miss Lois and Miss Lorraine—" She broke off with a low laugh. "I always will forget you girls are married now. It seems only yesterday you were calling for Miss Lois and looking scared to death because you didn't know the way to school."

"Or the way home," Peter put in, stepping into the light and causing the maid to give a little start.

He had been standing in the shadow of an evergreen tree and she had not seen him until this minute.

"Excuse me!" she apologized, inviting them both inside.

"Who is it, Hetty?" Lorraine called from somewhere upstairs.

"It's Judy and Peter," they called back. "Is Arthur home?"

"Arthur!" shrilled Lorraine. "Come on down! Judy and Peter are here."

"How do you ever find each other in such a big house?" Judy wanted to know, when they were all together in the spacious living room.

"We throw pebbles like Hansel and Gretel," Lois replied with a laugh. "They always lead us to food. Are you hungry, I hope? We're having a late dinner, and we'd love to have you stay."

"Thanks," Peter said, "but we've had ours. Three of them, in fact."

He grinned at Judy, and she breathed a sigh of relief. This wasn't going to be the ordeal she had anticipated.

"Three dinners!" exclaimed Lorraine. "How did that happen? Were you going on a diet in reverse?"

"Something like that." It was Peter who answered. "We were trailing a peddler who turned out, surprisingly enough, to be the brother of your gardener."

"I bought some flower seeds of him," Judy added.

"I presumed you would. I sent him to you." Arthur was beginning to sense something was wrong. "Don't tell me he shortchanged you! I'm sure, if he did, it was unintentional. Old Abner is as honest as the day is long."

"No," Judy said, "he didn't shortchange me."

"Suppose I tell Arthur something about it?" Peter suggested. "Confidential stuff, you know. Where can we talk?"

Arthur motioned him toward the library. Judy noticed that Peter was careful to close the door as they went inside.

"Oh, so it was Arthur he wanted to see?" Lorraine tilted her head in mock dignity. "Never mind, Lois! Let them have their confidential stuff. Are you in on it, too, Judy?"

"No," she replied, "but I'd like to be. You know how I feel about anything mysterious. Usually Peter tells me a few things. But this time it's different. I just tag along and do what I can. The hardest part is not being able to ask questions."

"What would you ask, Judy?"

"That's just it," she replied. "I don't know."

There was a little silence broken only by the sound of voices indistinguishable in the adjoining library.

"Peter seems to know what to ask," Lois commented. "This isn't anything serious, is it, Judy?"

"I'm afraid so," she admitted. "But don't worry. I'm sure Arthur is just as good at answering questions as Peter is at asking them. Here they come now!"

CHAPTER IX

A Shocking Revelation

THE DOOR to the adjoining library where Arthur and Peter had gone for their conference opened slowly, creaking a little on its hinges.

"I can't understand it," Peter was saying as they came out. "No bank in the country would let that many ten-dollar bills go through without checking the serial number against our list of wanted bills. It doesn't seem possible—"

"It's the truth," Arthur insisted. "I drew the whole ten thousand out of the First National Bank on Friday afternoon and put it in my safe at home."

"Ten thousand!" exclaimed Lois with an apprehensive glance toward Lorraine. "I had no idea Arthur had that much money in the house, did you?"

"Goodness, no!" the blonde girl replied. "I wouldn't have slept a wink."

"Judy, I want you to hear this," Peter said gravely. "Arthur declares he paid the seed peddler with one of the ten-dollar bills he got from the bank to close the real-estate deal with Mr. Heffly."

"Is he the Scarecrow, who came to the door of the house?" asked Judy. "The giant seven feet tall? I might have known he'd figure in this somewhere."

"You say a—a man came to the door of the Heffly house?" Arthur's voice was puzzled. "Surely I would have been told if the house was rented. Why, it isn't fit to live in. As you probably know, I had planned to have it torn down. All I wanted was the land."

"It looks as if you're getting tenants, too," Peter told him. "The tall, thin gentleman Judy referred to as a scarecrow was certainly there last night. He may come with the house. I'd look into it if I were you."

"From what you've been telling me, there are a lot of things that need looking into," declared Arthur. "I doubt if the mysterious figure you saw can be Mr. Heffly himself. His lawyers spoke of him as a typical English gentleman, with no mention of anything unusual about his appearance."

"Is he tall?" asked Judy.

"I've never heard that he was. As a matter of fact," Arthur admitted, "I haven't had the pleasure of meeting him. I was dealing with his lawyers until Friday when he telephoned and said he'd be in town Saturday afternoon for the title closing and wanted the whole ten thousand in cash."

"Isn't that much money an invitation to burglars?" Lois ventured. "I mean, wouldn't it be, if anyone knew you had it in your safe?"

"Mr. Heffly knew," Judy remarked.

"Of course." Arthur's voice was impatient. "He asked me to have the money ready and stipulated that it should be in small bills, preferably tens."

"Why was that?" Peter questioned.

It seemed a little strange to Judy, too.

Arthur shrugged. "It sounded rather eccentric, but Mr. Heffly said he needed immediate cash to meet legal fees and other expenses in connection with another house he's buying. It was obvious that a certified check wouldn't do, as the banks would be closed. You see," Arthur pointed out, "he bought the new house on a ninety-day closing in order to give him time to sell the house in Roulsville."

"Where is this new house?"

"He didn't tell me," Arthur admitted. "But, wherever it is, the ninety days were up yesterday, which made it necessary to have both closings on the same day. Mr. Heffly's lawyers were to have been with him, and he was to have given me other satisfactory proof of his identity, but as it turned out, both closings were postponed indefinitely because of a delay in the title search."

"It sounds good," declared Peter. "I can see why

you fell for it. But it could have been just a scheme to get hold of your ten thousand."

"I don't see how. I wouldn't have turned it over to Mr. Heffly until I had the deed to the property and everything was in order."

"But you would have carried the money around with you?"

Arthur shook his head.

"You're wrong there, Peter. I wouldn't have taken it from my safe. Mr. Heffly wanted me to bring it to the real-estate office in Roulsville, but I refused. You know yourself that the office is situated in rather a lonely spot. I didn't think the money would be safe there, so it was agreed that the title closing would take place right here in the library of my own home."

Judy was listening carefully to all this. The legal terms Peter and Arthur were using were perfectly understandable to her as she had heard them almost daily when she was working with Peter in his little law office in Roulsville. Most of their clients had been either buying or selling real estate.

What she couldn't understand was how Arthur happened to have taken ten dollars from the money he had set aside to pay Mr. Heffly.

"That was after I learned of the postponement," Arthur explained when she asked him, "when Mr. Heffly called me again late Saturday morning. It just happened that I was in need of cash. So I decided to withhold part of the ten thousand and put the rest back in my account as soon as the bank opened on Monday morning."

"How much did you withhold?" asked Peter.

"Only fifty dollars. After all, it was my own money," Arthur was beginning when Peter interrupted to ask him if he had spent any of it except the ten-dollar bill he gave the flower-seed peddler.

"Not yet," Arthur replied. "I still have it in my wallet."

"And the rest of the ten thousand is in your safe?"

"I certainly hope so!" declared Arthur. "It was there yesterday. But maybe I'd better check to make sure."

Saying this, he hurriedly left the room. Judy glanced at Peter, whose face told her nothing. Lorraine paled, and Lois gave a little gasp. The same thought hit them all at the same time. But it was Judy who exclaimed, "I hope the money hasn't been stolen!"

"This is terrible!" cried Lorraine. "You might know something like this would happen if Arthur bought the Heffly house."

"He hasn't bought it yet," Lois reminded her. "And even if he had, you and Arthur weren't going to live in it, you know."

"I should think not!" Lorraine agreed. "I wouldn't live there for anything. I wouldn't even stay there overnight."

"Why not?" asked Judy. "You're not afraid of

those rumors about it's being haunted, are you? Any
house can get a reputation like that. Look at our
house on Grove Street! I've forgotten how many
families were frightened away by what they thought
were ghosts. But they were explained. Such things
always are. Why, only last night our kitchen door
opened all by itself just at midnight—"

"In the Grove Street house?" Lois spoke as if she
still believed there might be a ghost or two lurking
about the place.

"No, in our house in Dry Brook Hollow," Judy
replied. "Peter declares he locked the door, but,
somehow, it opened by itself and let Blackberry in.
We were a little unnerved by it last night, but we'd
practically forgotten it by morning. As for that 'scarecrow' who came to the door of the Heffly house, anyone can be tall. I even thought of asking him to be
our circus giant."

"What do you mean?" asked Lois.

"I didn't tell you, did I? We're going to have a
circus at the bazaar. I already have the fat girl and a
clown—"

Judy stopped, feeling suddenly that this wasn't
exactly the right time to be planning a bazaar on the
Farringdon-Pett lawn. If Arthur really was in serious
trouble, all their plans might have to be changed.

She answered a few more questions, trying to
change the subject, and then Lorraine said, "I hope
you don't ask that—that giant or whatever he was,

Judy. It isn't that—that I believe any of those rumors, but it's just a feeling I've always had about the Heffly house. Like the feeling I have now that Arthur won't find the rest of that ten thousand—"

A relieved shout from Arthur himself interrupted her.

"It's here all right, exactly as I left it!"

"There, you see, Lorraine, we had nothing to worry about," declared Lois. "Come in to dinner and forget it. Are you sure you and Peter won't join us, Judy?"

"Quite sure, thank you," she replied. "We'll be going soon, won't we, Peter? We really must get back because we left Muriel and Roberta all by themselves. They were busy spading the garden. Probably it's ready for the flower seeds I bought by now."

Lorraine laughed.

"I see. And, naturally, you want to plant them yourself?"

"Not necessarily," said Judy. "Roberta probably will want to. She loves flowers. But I should be there in case there's some question as to where they should be planted."

"Or in case your invisible guest opens the door again and frightens your little boarder."

Lois had meant this to be funny. But, somehow, her remark failed to amuse Judy. Always, in the back of her mind, there was the fear that something might happen to Roberta when she was away from the little girl.

At Peter's suggestion, Lois and Lorraine went into the dining room. He detained Arthur to ask if he might see the bills he claimed were still in his safe.

"Sure, you can." Arthur's voice was puzzled. "I have no objection to showing them to you if you don't want to take my word for it that they're there."

"I believe you, all right." Peter paused, cleared his throat, and then said, "I hate like the very dickens to do this, old man, but it's Uncle Sam's orders."

"I see."

Without another word, Arthur led the way into the library, opened his safe, and took from it nine packs of ten-dollar bills. The tenth pack had been opened, but he returned the four tens he had in his wallet before placing it on the desk with the others. Only the telltale ten-dollar bill he had given the flower-seed peddler was now missing from the pack.

"There must be a thousand dollars in each pile!" exclaimed Judy. "Wow! What couldn't that buy?"

"A clear conscience, for one thing," Peter said grimly as he began checking the bills against the list furnished him by the FBI.

Even with Judy helping, it took a long time.

"What was that ten, anyway?" Arthur asked finally. "A counterfeit bill?"

Peter shook his head, still checking the serial numbers as Judy picked up one stack of bills after another and read them off.

"That's Treasury Department stuff. This comes under our jurisdiction, and I may as well tell you that, so far, every serial number is identical with those on the bills we've been looking for." Peter's face was grave and his voice a little husky as he added, "Sorry, Arthur, but I can't tell you anything more until I've reported this and received further instructions."

"But Peter, you can't report Arthur—" Judy started to protest.

"I'm afraid he can," Arthur interrupted quietly. "I haven't the faintest idea how I became involved in this mess, whatever it is, but Peter's duty is clear. The telephone is right there on the desk if you want to use it."

"No!" cried Judy as Peter lifted the phone. "Wait just a minute! There must be some explanation. Maybe these bills were substituted, somehow, for the bills Arthur received from the bank. You say you got them Friday?"

"That's right," Arthur said.

"Friday— Oh!" Judy gasped. "Listen to me, Peter, please!" she begged. "I think I know what happened!"

CHAPTER X

Judy's Idea

"Sorry, operator! I'll make that call later," Peter said and put back the phone.

"We'd better listen," he continued, turning to Arthur, whose face was now noticeably pale. "Maybe Judy really has something. I haven't told her one single thing about this case. Strict orders, because of its delicate nature. But I know, from past experience, that my young wife has an uncanny habit of delving into things she doesn't understand and coming up with the right answers."

"I do? Oh, Peter!"

A look passed between them that Judy would never forget. Of all the praise in the world, Peter's was the sweetest.

"Let's hear your idea," Arthur said. "I'm like the well-known drowning man. I'm willing to grasp any straw that happens to float by."

Judy laughed and they all felt better.

The tension of the last hour, when Judy had been reading off serial numbers as rapidly as she could, waiting only for Peter to say "check" before going on to the next one, had been almost unbearable.

They hadn't finished. It would have taken them all afternoon to check each separate bill. But they had checked enough from each pile for Peter to be fairly certain they were all on his list.

But why?

This question still bothered Judy although she now felt sure she could clear up the mystery of how the wanted bills happened to be in Arthur's safe.

"The way I figure it, it must have happened Friday night," she began. "I don't know the exact hour, but it must have been around ten-thirty. That was when the play was over."

"What play?" asked Arthur. "You mean that one put on by the student nurses in the high school auditorium? What could that have to do with it?"

"Nothing," Judy said. "That is, not directly. Indirectly, it could, because the crook probably counted on Lois and Lorraine going to see it. That took them conveniently out of the house. You were in Roulsville Friday evening, and your parents were out of town."

"They still are, thanks be! I wouldn't want them to walk in on a mess like this," declared Arthur. "But go on, I'm just as eager to hear what you think happened as you are to tell it."

"What I wanted to make clear was the fact that nobody was here Friday evening except the servants, and they stay in their own part of the house. Is that right?" asked Judy.

"Why, yes," Arthur admitted. "I believe it is."

"I'm beginning to get the idea, too," declared Peter. "I was right about you delving into things you don't understand."

"I do understand that there has been a crime committed. A crime so serious that it's the business of Uncle Sam to see that the criminals don't get away with it," Judy added. "But I also know that Arthur couldn't possibly have committed it, because—well, just because he's Arthur."

"Thanks," Arthur said.

"Don't thank me until I've finished. Now comes the idea," Judy continued. "I think the real criminal broke into the house Friday night and switched the money around on purpose to throw suspicion on you, Arthur. It looks almost as if it had been planned that way. Were you called to Roulsville?"

"Why, yes. Mr. Heffly—"

"I thought so!" exclaimed Judy. "You see, it was a trick to get you out of their way. Your Mr. Heffly knew the money was in your safe. My theory is that he either switched the money himself or hired a professional burglar to do it. They have sensitive fingers or something, don't they, Peter?"

"Some burglars do," he replied. "They've been known to sandpaper the ends of their fingers in order to make them so sensitive that they can feel the tumblers of the lock fall into place—"

"That could be how they opened the safe without Arthur knowing it, couldn't it?"

Judy was too excited by her idea to allow Peter to finish his explanation.

"It could be," he admitted, "but this is all theory. It would sound pretty corny if I told my superiors that Arthur couldn't have committed this crime just because he's Arthur and that someone might have broken into his house and substituted the wanted bills, which, by the way, were all tens, for the bills he received from the bank. I see your point. But the FBI works with facts."

"I have the facts, too," Judy declared. "Lois and Lorraine will tell you! Just as we came up the path to the house on our way home from the play, I saw what I thought was someone darting behind the forsythia bush just under the library window. Was the window locked?"

Her question was directed to Arthur. When he assured her that it had been, Peter pointed out that professional burglars had tools for opening locked windows, too.

"And locked doors?" asked Judy, thinking of the still unsolved mystery of the door that had opened by itself in their own house.

"Not ours," said Peter. "Not without removing the

lock. But let's hear about this prowler. Did Lois and Lorraine see him, too?"

"No," Judy admitted. "None of us actually saw him. We only saw his shadow against the wall. It was bright moonlight, and the trees do make shadows. I didn't figure out until afterward that no tree could possibly have thrown the shadow that we saw."

"You're sure of that?"

"Positive," Judy said. "I would have told you about it before this, but after I'd looked around a little and found nothing I let Lois and Lorraine talk me into coming inside. We had tea and cakes, and then we got to planning the bazaar and I didn't think anything more about what I'd seen until now."

"It's worth considering," Peter said thoughtfully. "Think you'll have time to type it for me this evening? Better make a couple of carbon copies. But stick to facts, not theories, Angel."

"I'll simply state that on Friday evening, about ten-thirty, I saw the shadow of an unidentified person dart behind the forsythia bush under the library window and that his shadow led me to believe he had jumped from the windowsill. Shall I add that I helped you check the serial numbers on these bills Arthur was supposed to have received from the bank?"

"That won't be necessary. If the bills were switched, it will be easy enough to prove Arthur's innocence," Peter declared. "The bank undoubtedly kept a record of the bills they gave him, as they would be likely to do in the case of such a large sum of money as this."

"Then if you do have to report this," Judy indicated the stack of telltale bills, "you will report what I saw, too, and let the FBI look for the prowler, won't you? I'm sure he must be the criminal."

A relieved look crossed Arthur's face.

"I'm glad you don't think I am. I'm still in the dark about what I'm supposed to have done. It must be something pretty bad."

"It is."

Peter's two words were followed by a dead silence, broken only when he pulled the phone an inch or two nearer him and said, "Sorry, Arthur, but I'll still have to use this."

CHAPTER XI

A Suggested Trap

PETER'S REPORT to the field office was brief. He gave the address of the Farringdon-Pett mansion on Grove Street, and then Judy heard something about the "Doe case" and "no arrests as yet."

Arthur's face was chalk white.

"What does Peter mean, 'as yet'?" Judy asked herself. "And what is the 'Doe case'?"

"These bills are our first real break," Peter was saying over the telephone. "It looks like a switch. What are your instructions?"

Whatever they were, it did not take Peter long to start acting upon them. As soon as his call was finished, he turned to Arthur and said gravely, "You'll be questioned, of course. So will the bank officials. But if we can prove the existence of Judy's prowler, and if the bank can prove these were not the bills they issued to you, you will be in the clear. You'll just about have time to have your dinner before the squad car gets here. I'll have to send for it to pick up those wanted bills."

Judy stared at Peter.

"Did I hear you right?" she demanded. "Did you say you were sending for a squad car? But that's the police! Peter, you can't—"

"Look, Angel," he interrupted, "just trust me to do the right thing, won't you? Arthur understands."

"Well, I don't," declared Judy, her temper flaring up. "First you say you can't work with the police because this is too secret, and then you call the squad car to pick up the ten thousand dollars just as if Arthur had stolen it or something. If I could talk with Horace—"

"Not a word to your brother!"

Peter was firm about this.

"But won't the police tell him? He goes to them for news reports."

"The police don't give out news reports where a life may be at stake," Peter said soberly.

"Oh!" said Judy, instantly ashamed. "I'm sorry, Peter. Isn't there anything I can do to help?"

"There will be," Peter promised. "Thanks to you, Judy, it's now obvious to me that these criminals are trying to get rid of the hot money by putting it in the place of the genuine article whenever the opportunity can be arranged. One ten did turn up in a busy restau-

rant along the Roosevelt Highway, but it wasn't discovered until long after the customer, whoever he
was, had driven away."

"Is that what started you on the trail of this—this
'hot' money?"

Judy had to smile at Arthur's reluctance to use the
word adopted by gangland to describe money wanted
by police or Federal authorities.

"Let's say we redoubled our efforts."

Peter's reply was cut short by the appearance of
Hetty with coffee and roast beef sandwiches on a
tray. Since Arthur had not come in to dinner with
Lois and Lorraine, she had decided to see to it that
Master Arthur, as she still called him, did not go
hungry.

"Hetty," Judy asked as the maid turned to leave,
"were you here Friday night? Did you see or hear
anything unusual?"

"I thought I did," Hetty admitted. "I went to bed
early with a headache, but something woke me up
just before you girls came in. I couldn't tell you what
it was."

"Could it have been a—a burglar?"

Hetty shivered.

"I hope not, Miss Judy. That was what came into
my head when I heard it, but then I told myself it
was only Mr. Higgins helping himself to a book from
the library. He does like to read, especially those
garden books. They help him with his work. But he's
honest. Has anything been taken?"

"Nothing that wasn't put back," Judy replied, pretending to make light of the whole thing.

The maid was obliged to repeat her story to the FBI agents and the chief of police when they arrived a few moments later. It made what Judy had to say sound more believable.

"You see, Chief Kelly, there *was* somebody in the library," she pointed out. "I knew Arthur couldn't be guilty of this—whatever it is. But now that you're here, everything is sure to turn out all right."

"*I* was sure of that when I heard *you* were here," returned the chief, his eyes twinkling.

With him was David Trent, Peter's immediate superior, and another FBI agent who was a stranger to Judy. He was introduced to her, but afterward she couldn't, for the life of her, remember his name. There was too much else on her mind.

"I wish I could help trap these criminals," she said thoughtfully, "but how?"

"That's our worry," declared the young stranger. "This isn't the sort of thing for a girl to be messing around with, especially if ten thousand dollars have been switched. We expected these bills to turn up singly, not a quarter of them at once."

He had, unwittingly, given Judy a clue.

"If ten thousand dollars is a quarter, there must be another thirty thousand, or nearly that, still to be switched. Do you think they might try it again? I mean," Judy explained, "if we sort of created the opportunity by setting a trap—"

"There's an idea!" Chief Kelly agreed.

Judy's ideas had helped him trap wanted criminals before. But David Trent was skeptical.

"How do you propose to bait this trap?" he asked.

"With money," Judy replied. "We could let it be known that a large sum was being taken in at the bazaar. Or wouldn't criminals come to a hospital bazaar?"

"These criminals would, if they thought there was anything in it for them," Mr. Trent declared. "They're so cold-blooded they wouldn't mind helping themselves to every cent the hospital makes."

"It is a good idea, Judy, but suppose you leave it to us," Peter suggested. "I'll be going back to the field office with Mr. Trent when we've finished what has to be done here. We'll use his car."

"Then I'll take ours," said Judy. "The afternoon is almost gone, and those two little girls have been by themselves all this time. I'm really worried."

"You have good reason to be," declared Chief Kelly, who remembered Roberta well, having once fed her cake and cookies as she sat on top of his desk at police headquarters.

"Is this the way you usually treat little runaway girls?" Judy had asked, when she and Peter had found Roberta there.

It was then that Chief Kelly had explained the Rainbow Riddle, one of the strangest mysteries Judy had ever solved. The thought came to her now that it might have been her last, had it not been for the courage and devotion of her unpredictable little boarder.

"Don't let anything happen to my sweetheart," the chief cautioned Judy now as she turned to leave.

Lois and Lorraine appeared from somewhere to bid Judy and Peter good-bye. It was obvious that they blamed neither herself nor Peter for the trouble that was crowding the house with police and G-men. More of them arrived just as Judy drove off.

It was good to be alone in the car with only her thoughts for company, even though they were a little frightening. Were her suspicions correct? If so, how safe was she or Roberta or anyone until the wanted criminals were behind bars? A shiver passed through Judy as she thought of the life Peter had said might be at stake.

It was a picturesque drive over the hills and down into Dry Brook Hollow. But today Judy did not notice the scenery. She drove as fast as she dared. The road was winding and dangerous in places, and she was not an experienced driver. When she finally reached home, it was after six o'clock. There was no one but Blackberry on the porch to meet her.

"Where is everyone?" she asked the cat, reaching down to stroke his glossy head.

His black fur always shone as if it had just been brushed, and the few white spots on him were so very white. It was no wonder Judy had exclaimed, "Why, he looks just like a blackberry dipped in sugar!" when

Peter had first placed the chubby kitten in her arms.

Now he was a lean black cat, but the name still fitted him. His answer to Judy's question was a plaintive yowl which said, as clearly as words, that he was hungry. He stood at the door, waiting for Judy to go into the house.

"Be patient," she scolded him. "You'll get your dinner. First I want to put the car away and see what Roberta and Muriel have done with the garden."

The plot Judy had chosen was at the far side of the house where there would be a full view of the garden from the window seat in the bay window of the living room.

After she had carefully closed and locked the garage door, Judy walked around there. She stopped short in amazement at what she saw.

Although there was still no sign of the two little girls who had done it, the earth in several flower beds was nicely turned over and the bulbs transplanted in neat rows. But most surprising of all, there were paths marked out between the beds exactly as there had been in the pictured garden on the package of alyssum seed.

"It's unbelievable!" Judy whispered.

Yes, there was the circular bed in the center of which she intended to place her silver ball instead of the stone lantern Roberta was so sure she remembered. The garden would end at the fence instead of a busy street. And, of course, there was no greenhouse. But the evergreen trees were there, and now there was a path under them that was edged with pretty little stones and led straight to the pasture gate.

"The children certainly have been busy," thought Judy. "Now I know what they were doing. They were carrying pebbles from the brook to mark out all these paths between the flower beds."

But where were they?

Suddenly remembering Chief Kelly's "Don't let anything happen to my sweetheart," Judy rushed into the house and began to call.

CHAPTER XII

Roberta's Surprise

"ROBERTA! Roberta! Where are you?"

Judy tried to keep the anxiety she felt out of her voice. Chief Kelly's warning had made her apprehensive, although she had no reason for her fears.

Roberta could have gone back to Muriel's house, of course.

"I'll call Mrs. Blade," Judy decided.

But before she reached the telephone, she stopped short and stared at the table. It was all set with crisp salads of lettuce leaf, pineapple circles, and cottage cheese topped with cherries, at each of the places.

The big lace tablecloth hung a little unevenly. Suddenly something moved underneath it.

"Keep still, Tuffy!" a voice whispered.

91

But, in spite of efforts to pull him back, the puppy struggled out and greeted Judy with leaps and tail wags.

Blackberry, looking on disdainfully, was obviously thinking, "That's *my* mistress. What are *you* so excited about?"

But now Judy knew where Tuffy's mistress was!

"Roberta! You little imp," she exclaimed. "I do believe you're hiding under the table. Is Muriel with you? Come out of there and help enjoy the dinner you prepared. And I had visions of lost keys and two little sunburned girls locked out of the house or lost or—but why tell you about it?" she broke off quickly. "This is such a nice surprise!"

"Golly, we're glad you came!"

Muriel crawled out first, and then Roberta. They were both talking at once, telling how their feet went to sleep waiting. Then they asked in the same breath, "Did you see the garden?"

"I did," declared Judy. "It's a work of art. Those paths with all the little colored stones at the edge are really beautiful. And the beds are so smooth and nice with the bulbs in neat rows just the way I wanted them. Don't tell me the seeds are in, too?"

"Only the alyssum. I thought maybe you'd want to plant the rest. Besides," Roberta confessed, "I was getting tired of bending over."

"So you did some more work to rest yourself? What a girl!" exclaimed Judy. "You're both hungry, aren't you? So are Blackberry and Tuffy. But they can wait for us. Is the main dish soup?"

"It will be if you can find the can opener." Then Roberta had to laugh when she found it herself right on the wall by the kitchen sink. "I'd forgotten you had a new one," she explained.

"Yes, Peter bought it. He likes gadgets in the kitchen to make the housework easy for me. Really, it's the radio that makes it easy," Judy added. "I like working to music."

"So do I," agreed Roberta, tuning in on Judy's favorite Sunday night program. "We'll have the nice, quiet supper we missed last night."

"Quiet? With the radio?" Muriel laughed. "That isn't the way my mother feels about it."

"There are different kinds of quiet, I guess."

Judy was thinking of the sudden quiet that had followed Peter's discovery of the telltale ten-dollar bill she had received from the flower-seed peddler. Was it only last night? So much had happened since then that it seemed impossible.

"If ever I needed a quiet evening meal, it's right now," declared Judy, struggling with the can opener that was supposed to make her housework easier.

"You do it like this," Muriel explained.

She clamped the thing down and, with one turn, the can was open. When she had emptied its contents into a pan and put the soup on to heat, she turned and said, "We could have had sandwiches, too, but Roberta thought you wouldn't want us to cut into the cold meat. The knife is so sharp."

"Roberta was right," declared Judy. "I'll slice it if you still want sandwiches."

"We do," chorused the two little girls.

Blackberry and Tuffy were equally interested in the slicing process and took turns gobbling up the scraps.

When everything was ready, Roberta looked at the table and noticed that there were only three bowls of hot soup.

"Isn't Peter going to have any soup?" she asked Judy. "He's home, isn't he? I thought he was still outside looking at the garden."

"No, he hasn't seen it. He probably will be as surprised as I was. I drove home by myself," Judy explained, "because Peter had to go back to the field office with Mr. Trent."

"On Sunday?"

"Yes, it was important."

"Golly! It must have been. I wish the Junior FBI hadn't broken up," Roberta added, when they were sitting around the table with the candles lighted and soft music playing. "Maybe we could help him. We did before. Afterward, everybody except Muriel and me lost interest because there weren't any more mysteries to solve."

"There are always mysteries," declared Judy, her gray eyes dreamy. "Maybe not big ones, but nice little ones. Seeds, for instance, with what will someday be beautiful flowers tucked inside, ready for the sun and rain to make them grow. Couldn't your club work on mysteries like that instead of trying to help the FBI solve the more dangerous ones? Look what you and Muriel have done this afternoon! And the rest of the seeds are still to be planted."

"Maybe we could reorganize the club to help us!" Muriel suggested. "I'd like that. Roberta says we have to carry a lot more pebbles up from the brook if we want this garden to look as pretty as the one she re-members. It's funny how the picture on the flower-seed package made her think of it, isn't it? Where do you suppose her garden was?"

"I haven't the faintest idea," Judy replied.

For the rest of the evening the conversation cen-tered around the garden. And when Mr. and Mrs. Blade drove over in the car to take Muriel back home, they had to go out and see it, too.

It was so dark by then that Judy took the barn lantern along and placed it in the center bed so they could see how the two little girls had marked out the garden paths.

"See how it lights up the whole garden!" exclaimed Roberta, now greatly excited. "Imagine how beauti-ful it will be when all the flowers are in blossom. Oh, Judy! I wish we could have a lantern with a candle—"

"Do you mean a stone lantern?" asked Judy.

"Yes, it was stone! I remember now!" cried Ro-berta. "But how did you know, Judy? You said you hadn't the faintest idea where my garden was, but you've found out something about it, haven't you?"

Her voice was so eager that Judy could hardly bear to disappoint her.

"No, dear," she replied. "I'm afraid not. I showed the picture on the seed package to Peter and he recognized the stone lantern as a Chinese garden lantern. He saw one like it in a museum once."

"I hope it wasn't ours," Roberta said. "It did look so pretty in the garden. It made all the little stones around the edges of the flower beds shine like silver. They were so even, Judy. The stones, I mean. Not like these. We picked out the very smoothest pebbles we could find, but still they don't shine the way the stones in my garden did. Maybe it was on account of the lantern. Couldn't we have one? Please!"

"I don't know where we'd get one," Judy said doubtfully. "Maybe, if I wrote to the seed company, they could tell us where the lantern in the picture came from. Do you still have the seed package, Roberta?"

The little girl had it in her pocket and handed it to Judy eagerly. She turned the package over and made out the words: Bell Seed Company, Chicago, Illinois.

"I'll write them and see what they can tell us about it," Judy decided.

"What is a stone lantern?" asked Mrs. Blade. "I don't believe I ever heard of such a thing."

Judy explained how the Chinese used to use them to illuminate their gardens.

"But the ones in this country are imported," she

added, "and Peter says they're awfully expensive."

"We can't have one, then, can we?" Roberta sighed.

"I'm afraid not, Roberta," Judy replied honestly. "But we can have something pretty in the center of the garden. How would you like a big silver ball?"

"Could you see it when the flowers grew up all around it?" the little girl questioned doubtfully.

"Oh, yes, you could see it easily. It won't be on the ground. It will be on a stone pedestal, like the stone lantern you remember," Judy explained. "It will shine, too. You see, Roberta, I already have such a ball. It used to belong to a fortuneteller. She had some sort of liquid inside, but I planned to have the inside silvered with the kind of silver they put on the backs of mirrors. Then it will reflect the whole garden, only smaller. It will be every bit as pretty as a stone lantern when it's set up in the center of this garden. You'll see! We'll set it up tomorrow."

Roberta agreed that it would look lovely. The others were enthusiastic. Her plans for the garden nearly put the fact that she had to type a statement for Peter out of Judy's mind.

It was so late when she thought of it that she decided to do the typing in her own room with the door closed so that she would not disturb Roberta, who was already in bed.

The typewriter keys banged away until midnight as Judy did the statement over two or three times before she was satisfied with it. Then, late as it was, she wrote a short note to the Bell Seed Company, asking for information about the garden pictured on the seed package.

When it was finished, she gathered up Blackberry from the rug at her feet and crept downstairs to put him out and make sure the doors were locked. Peter had his key. But Judy intended to make quite certain that no one else entered the house during the night.

Soon after that, in spite of a vague uneasiness about Peter, Judy was in bed and sound asleep.

CHAPTER XIII

Peter's Secret

"I TYPED THAT STATEMENT you wanted and was going to give it to you last night," Judy told Peter the following morning, "but I didn't hear a sound when you came in."

"That's obvious," said Peter with a glance toward the back kitchen door.

They had just come downstairs to the kitchen together and now stared incredulously. The back door was wide open.

"Didn't you open it last night?" Judy asked Peter suspiciously. "Blackberry was in again, too. Didn't you open the door to let him in?"

Peter shook his head slowly, watching Judy's face.

"Then who did?" she cried. "I put him out and locked the door just before I went to bed. I not only locked it, but bolted it from the inside. Peter, are you sure you didn't—"

"I didn't touch it," he declared. "I saw it was locked and bolted, so I didn't go near it, but I did try the front doors to make sure they were locked."

"It's unbelievable," Judy said. "Nobody but a ghost could get inside to open it. And what's this?"

She picked up the barn lantern which was standing lighted on the floor, and blew it out.

"But Peter, I blew it out before," she protested. "This is the lantern I took with me when I went out to show Mr. and Mrs. Blade what the children had done with the garden. But I blew it out. I—I'm almost positive I did."

"That is odd." Peter frowned. "I didn't light it. I was so tired I went directly upstairs to bed. Mr. Trent brought me as far as the mailbox, and I practically stumbled the rest of the way home. The numbers on those bills were still going around in my head when I went to sleep."

"Poor Peter!" sympathized Judy, beginning to prepare breakfast. "I was dreaming of them myself."

She lifted the bacon from the frying pan and broke three eggs into the hot fat. Then she asked, "What time was it when you got in, Peter?"

"Three o'clock in the morning," he replied. "Just like the old song."

"Seriously," she questioned, "was it that late?"

"All of that. I was too weary to look at the clock when I got in, but it was half past two when we drove past the courthouse in Farringdon."

"Then our ghost didn't time himself right," declared Judy. "He appeared at midnight the night before last. He didn't seem to need a light for his ghostly wanderings the other time, either."

"You can joke all you want to," said Peter, "but this is something that's going to be investigated as soon as I have time for it."

"I have time. That is, I would have," Judy added, "if I hadn't promised to give so much of it to the hospital bazaar. Do you think it still can be held on the Farringdon-Pett lawn, Peter? This business of the money won't make any difference, will it?"

"We hope not. Arthur probably will be cleared of all suspicion this morning when we talk with the bank officials. We can't return his ten thousand dollars, though, until we catch whoever broke into his house and made the switch."

Judy glanced toward the door that had opened so mysteriously and shivered as she asked, "Peter, do you think the—the same burglar broke into our house?"

"You'll feel a lot safer," he declared, "if you keep on pretending it was a ghost."

"Whatever it was, I don't like it." Judy looked at Peter wistfully over the rim of her coffee cup and then put the cup down with a sigh. "If only I knew more about this 'Doe case,' as you call it, so I could be sure it wasn't someone trying to find out things or keep you from investigating—or burn the house down," she added, with a glance at the lantern.

"Look, Angel," he interrupted, "nobody except

Chief Kelly and our own personnel have any idea I'm working on this case. Besides, I have all the papers pertaining to it right here in my portfolio."

"Nothing was taken the other time," Judy said thoughtfully.

"We'll look around, of course," Peter said, "but I don't think we'll find anything missing today, either. I can see from where I'm sitting that the china and silverware are safe. You're wearing your rings, and we simply don't have anything else valuable enough to tempt a burglar. That's one of the blessings of poverty!"

"We aren't exactly poor, Peter. Just look at that breakfast!"

"I'd rather eat it than look at it," he returned, finishing his bacon and eggs and topping it off with a huge baked apple.

There was another apple, equally large, at Roberta's place. But, although the little girl had been called, she was not expected for another half hour. Dressing was a slow process with her unless Judy helped, and this morning she had to get Peter off first.

"What I mean," he explained, helping himself to more cream for his apple, "is that, while we certainly do have our share of the good things of life, we're not exactly wealthy. We couldn't raise forty thousand dollars at a moment's notice, not even if we sold the farm. I'm thinking of the—the Does, I guess. They managed to raise it."

"Can you tell me about them?" Judy asked eagerly.

"A little," he replied. "I talked it over with Mr. Trent and two or three others at the field office, and we've decided we'll need your help at the bazaar in order to set the trap you suggested. That means, of course, that I can let you in on some of this now."

"I think I've figured out part of it anyway," confessed Judy. "When you were in school you sent me a list of the crimes that come under the jurisdiction of the FBI. Well, I kept the list, and last night after I'd finished typing that statement I gave you this morning, I got to thinking about it and went through the list. It's an alphabetical list, you know, and I got as far as the F's—Federal Kidnaping Act.

" 'That's it!' I told myself. You see, I remembered what you said about a life being at stake and simply put two and two together. But, even before that, I had a pretty fair idea of why you had to check those bills so carefully and afterward give them into police custody. They were ransom bills, weren't they?" Judy's voice was low. "Peter, is the—the victim still alive?"

"To tell you the truth, we don't know," Peter replied slowly. "Mr. and Mrs. Doe—that's not their real name, of course; we refer to them by the name of Doe for security reasons—have begun to give up all hope of ever seeing their baby again, but our men feel differently." He paused. "Now you know," he finished abruptly, "but we still can't discuss it. Walls have ears, they say."

"Yes, and doors open by themselves, so we never know who may be listening. I won't talk," Judy promised, "but oh, those poor people! It makes a person's blood boil, doesn't it, to think that there are fiends capable of committing crimes like that? You knew Arthur couldn't—"

"Of course," he broke in. "What I'm still not sure of is whether some friend of his, or possibly some business associate, hasn't involved him in this thing without his being aware of it."

"What about Mr. Heffly?"

"We're working on that angle. As soon as we're through at the bank, we intend to have a talk with his lawyers."

Peter glanced out the window and saw a car turning in from the main road.

"That's David Trent coming to pick me up now!" he exclaimed. "I may be home late, but don't worry!"

He kissed her and was off.

"Don't worry!" Judy echoed when he had gone. "As if I didn't always!"

CHAPTER XIV

The Trap Is Set

IT WAS the Saturday before the bazaar was to open when Peter finally came in and announced that the trap to catch the criminals involved in the Doe case was being set. To prove it, he handed Judy the morning paper.

The first thing that met her eyes was a full-page ad announcing, in inch-high type, that there would be a number of valuable door prizes given away at the bazaar to members of the ten-dollar club.

"What's the ten-dollar club?" Judy asked in bewilderment. "I've been working on the bazaar all week and this is the first time I've heard anything about it."

"You will soon hear more. Much more," prophesied Peter mysteriously.

Judy was all interest. Time had flown by with little opportunity for Peter to tell her how his investigation was coming along. She did know that the serial numbers of the bills the bank paid to Arthur had proved to be entirely different, and had confirmed her own suspicions. The FBI now believed that on the night she had seen the sudden shadow thrown against the wall of the old Farringdon-Pett mansion, someone actually had opened Arthur's safe and stolen the ten thousand dollars he had received from the bank, leaving the telltale ransom money in its place.

Now, as Judy read on, it was obvious to her what Peter meant by saying the trap was being set. She only hoped enough people would take advantage of the admission price of ten dollars to pile up a substantial stack of ten-dollar bills.

The prizes offered were certainly an inducement. The winners were to have such prizes as a new car, the latest model television set, or a completely modernized kitchen. But the club members got their ten dollars' worth in merchandise, food, and entertainment even if they didn't win one of the prizes that had, almost miraculously, been donated at the last minute.

"What do you think of it?" asked Peter when Judy had almost finished reading the item in the paper.

She nodded approvingly.

"I think whoever donated these prizes is more than generous."

Peter smiled cryptically but said nothing.

"Horace wrote the ad, didn't he?" Judy asked. "How much did you tell him?"

"Not much," replied Peter. "I only mentioned the fact that we're trying to locate some hot ten-dollar bills and that we're making every effort to see that a lot of tens will be taken in at the bazaar, to give us something to work on. The receipts will be kept on the premises until the bazaar ends, instead of being banked each day. Posters are being printed, and the news of the bazaar is being broadcast over our local radio station. The crooks can't miss it."

"What about Mr. Heffly's lawyers?" asked Judy. "Have you thought of the possibility that the criminals you're after might be in their office?"

"We've eliminated that possibility. We investigated the firm, of course, but the lawyers are both perfectly reputable men. They did have a clerk in their office at one time who was convicted of a felony, but the man was arrested and sent to prison a good while before Arthur's ten thousand was stolen."

Peter broke off quickly as Roberta rushed in, her hands grubby and her face smudged.

"I have the most wonderful news," she announced excitedly. "The bulbs we transplanted from the flowerpots are all in blossom, and I *think* the alyssum is beginning to come up. You can see teeny little green shoots all around that silver ball we set up in the garden."

Judy and Peter had to see it themselves before they would believe it. The hyacinths and jonquils seemed to have blossomed overnight. The effect was even more beautiful than Judy had imagined it would be, as the pink, white, and blue of the hyacinths blended with the yellow of the jonquils and was reflected in the silver ball. Tiny little green spikes were just beginning to poke up through the earth close to the base of it.

"Is it alyssum?"

Judy assured Roberta that it was.

"The other seeds we planted will begin to come up soon, won't they? It's going to be so lovely when my father comes home."

Roberta stopped abruptly and turned to Peter, who had picked up one of the little stones she had placed around the flower beds.

"He will come, won't he?" she asked anxiously.

"We'll know when he answers your letter." Peter was examining the stone he had picked up and wasn't paying much attention.

"Don't you think he's had time to answer it?" Roberta persisted.

"That depends on where he is," replied Peter. "The letter goes to the shipping company first, and they forward it to him. You see, they know where his ship is."

"I wish I knew!"

All the pleasure she had found in the garden faded, suddenly, from Roberta's face. And when Judy turned to go back into the house with Peter, she noticed a big tear on its way down the little girl's cheek.

"Roberta is unhappy. I knew it!" she declared.

"We'll have to get in touch with that shipping company ourselves," Peter decided. "If they can't locate Roberta's father, Navy Intelligence can. It isn't right for the poor kid to be eating her heart out that way, making plans for something that may never happen—"

"You don't really think her father's ship is los:, do you?" Judy interrupted.

"To tell you the truth," Peter replied, "I don't know what to think. But leave it to me. If Roberta's father is still in the land of the living, he'll be here to see that garden before the alyssum blossoms."

It was a promise, and Peter did not regard promises lightly. Satisfied that it would be kept, Judy returned to the notice in the paper, which she had not quite finished reading when Roberta came in from the garden.

"What's this about the bazaar being held on the courthouse square, with refreshments served in the basement of St. Mark's church?" she asked. "Did you think it might look suspicious if it was held on the Farringdon-Pett lawn the way we originally planned?"

"I certainly did." Peter was positive about it. "So did Arthur. Lois and Lorraine will be a little disappointed, of course. But it will make things easier all around."

"Especially for me," Judy added. "In case of rain we'll still have a place to serve the refreshments and set up the booths. The Farringdon-Petts wouldn't have wanted them in the house so we had planned on a tent. It would have made my side show more effective, of course."

"You can still set up your tent on the courthouse square."

"I don't think I'll bother now," Judy said. "I'm afraid my side show won't be very effective anyway without the giant. I've stopped at the Heffly house two or three times, but there's nobody there now. Anyway, nobody answers the door. I can't understand it. Sophie will be sure he was a ghost now."

"The ghost of the old Heffly house?" Peter questioned, laughing.

"If there is one, we've met him," affirmed Judy. "And it is odd about the curtains. They are still at the windows, but, outside of that, the Heffly house is as empty as ever."

"Arthur will be glad to hear it," said Peter. "When, and if, he takes title to the house, he won't want to annex a lot of strange tenants who will have to be evicted before he can tear down the house."

"Strange is right!" agreed Judy. "The more I think about it, the stranger it seems that someone should have been there that night we called. Did you tell Mr. Heffly's lawyers about it? What did they say?"

"They weren't greatly impressed. So many rumors have been floating around that the house has quite a reputation. I suppose tramps do stay there overnight."

"I suppose so," Judy was reluctant to accept the ordinary explanation Peter had suggested. "What else did the lawyers say? You were going to tell me when Roberta rushed in all excited about the garden."

"That's the strangest development yet," declared Peter. "Mr. Heffly's lawyers tell me that he has been in England for months and had authorized them, before he left, to sell the property."

"But if he's in England, how could he call Arthur and make an appointment to meet him the following morning?" asked Judy.

"That's the point. He couldn't have made that particular telephone call. What we think now is that a third party got wind of the real-estate deal somehow and posed as Mr. Heffly in order to persuade Arthur to bring all those ten-dollar bills home from the bank. Probably there never was any intention of completing the deal."

"And this third party—"

"Is probably the criminal we're after," Peter finished, "but, so far, we haven't a clue. He was careful not to leave his fingerprints on anything when he opened Arthur's safe. We've been over the place with a fine-tooth comb, but there's nothing of any importance to be found. If he doesn't try to switch the rest of the ransom money, we'll be just as far from solving the case as we were in the beginning."

"So the whole case hangs on whether or not he falls into the trap we're going to set at the bazaar?"

"That's about it," agreed Peter, "so let's hope for a big crowd and fair weather."

CHAPTER XV

At the Bazaar

IN SPITE of their fervent hopes, the opening day of the bazaar dawned gray and cold.

"Wouldn't you have known it!" exclaimed Judy, looking out the window. "We'll never get a crowd in such weather as this, and we'll have to set up all the booths in the basement of the church."

Discouraged, she sank into a chair beside the breakfast table and continued, halfheartedly, eating her grapefruit.

"It will be good for the flowers," Roberta remarked, pushing her plate aside and running to the window to look out at the garden. She could only see a corner of it from this side of the house, but it seemed to satisfy her as her face broke into a smile.

"You're a regular Pollyanna this morning, aren't

you?" asked Judy. "But why shouldn't you think of your garden first? You've worked on it every bit as hard as I've worked on the bazaar, if not harder. I hope you won't mind tearing yourself away this afternoon when Muriel and Louise and all the other children in your class attend the bazaar. School is going to be dismissed early, and you're going to be taken over in the bus. It's all been arranged."

"Where will you be?" asked Roberta.

"Serving refreshments on the courthouse lawn—I hope," Judy added, still dubious about the weather.

Not until noon did the sky begin to clear. Then the sun seemed to catch the cheerfulness of the various committees who had been hard at work setting up their booths and tables outside in spite of the earlier threat of bad weather.

Judy had arrived in Farringdon shortly after ten o'clock. She had picked up her mother, without whose help she would have been lost, and Peter's sister Honey.

They had hardly put away their wraps when the food began to arrive. There were salads, pickles, olives, cakes, and a multitude of sandwiches as well as chopped meat and frankfurters to be cooked on an outside grill and served between sliced rolls.

The big urn in the church basement was made ready for coffee. Another one was filled with hot water to be poured over individual tea bags, and later there would be cold milk and plenty of ice cream.

"Thank goodness, it's warm enough outside now

so people won't get the shivers eating it," Judy remarked when the ice cream wagon arrived.

"You and your shivers!" teased Honey. "Ghosts don't bother you, but ice cream does. Believe me, I'd have the shivers for real if the door in our apartment ever flew open by itself—and when I'd locked it, too!"

"Did yours, Judy?"

An eager group of girls was standing around questioning her. She was almost sorry she had told Honey anything about it. Suppose the opening door should prove to have something to do with Peter's case!

"Judy, come here and help me get this table ready for the cigar boxes," Lois called at that moment.

"Cigar boxes!" exclaimed Judy, glad to escape from so many questions. "What in the world are they for?"

"To hold the money. You've heard about the ten-dollar club, of course. Everybody is talking about it. I wonder how many will join."

Lois had not long to wonder, as the people soon began to arrive. The first group were unanimous in their desire to contribute to the fund being raised for the hospital. The ten-dollar bills they placed in the cigar box on the table soon made a substantial pile.

More and more people arrived. Farringdon was a wealthy town, and many of its citizens joined the ten-dollar club without question. In exchange for the admission price, each club member was given a number that later would be placed in a hat. Then on Saturday

the most exciting event of the bazaar would take place
—the drawing of the prize-winning numbers.

"Would I love to win the television set!" exclaimed
Sophie, the "fat lady," who had arrived in her circus
costume.

She and her friends, also in their circus costumes,
were to take charge of the toy booth to attract the
children. Later in the day they would entertain them
by parading, circus style, and then putting on their
show. But now it was time for the formal opening of
the bazaar.

Suddenly the leader of the high school band raised
his stick, and the music began. The crowd swelled as
voices were raised to sing the National Anthem.

Afterward, there were speeches by doctors, nurses,
and trustees of the hospital. Judy could not help feeling proud of her father as he mounted the base of the
statue that was being used as a speaker's platform.

Briefly he stated the object of the bazaar, which
was to raise enough money to make possible a new
annex to the hospital and a convalescent home for
those who no longer needed to stay in bed but who
still required nursing care. A few case histories from
the now overcrowded wards made the appeal irre-
sistible.

"Dad made the best speech of all," Judy declared
when the opening ceremonies were over.

The whole crowd now moved in the direction of
the booths, which were beautifully decorated. Every-

thing from flowers to kitchenware was on sale. But it was the display of handmade dresses for little girls that attracted Judy.

"I'll pick out two for Roberta now," she decided. "The pretty ones will be all gone if I wait."

Judy was right. By the time Roberta and her crowd arrived in the school bus, the dainty handmade dresses on the rack were pretty well picked over.

"Thank you for saving those dresses for me. But Judy, Muriel wants one. May she have it?" Roberta pleaded. "Her mother will pay for it. She belongs to the ten-dollar club, so it will come out of her admission. Do we belong?"

"We certainly do. So go ahead and buy whatever pleases you," replied Judy. "People are beginning to get hungry, so I can't go around to the different booths with you, but you'll find me wherever there's food. I have to see that it keeps coming."

It was no easy task. But Judy had willing helpers.

"Almost too willing," she thought as she watched the young men who were working at the grill.

They looked quite impressive in their white aprons and tall chef's hats. They also acted as waiters. Judy supposed they were college students, but she had been so glad to have them volunteer that she had not bothered to ask them who they were.

One, who said his name was Dave Everett, seemed especially helpful. Whenever anyone complained of the food or the service, he was right there to straighten things out. Peter's grandmother, in her wheelchair, was being served like an empress.

"Here, boy!" called an irritable old woman who seemed perfectly capable of waiting on herself. "More tea over here, if you please. Mine's cold. And, if you don't mind, I'd like another of those grilled cheese sandwiches. But see that it's hot when you bring it."

"It will be, madam," Dave replied serenely.

Judy nudged Honey, who was busy at the flower booth.

"Why, he's even bowing to her! Who does she think she is, anyway?"

"I heard someone call her Mrs. Madders-Madders," Lorraine volunteered. "We made the corsage she's wearing."

"It's a beauty, fit for a queen," approved Judy, "too nice for Mrs.—what's her name?—Madder and Madder? Well," she added, as Honey giggled, "I mustn't be catty. After all, we're piling up the money. All the elite of Farringdon are here."

She walked over to the table at the entrance to see how Lois was doing. The pile of ten-dollar bills in the cigar box at her elbow had grown several inches higher. Judy said she was thrilled.

"I don't see anything thrilling about it," Lois complained. "I'm missing all the fun."

"You don't have to sit here all day, you know," Judy told her, remembering certain instructions Peter had given her. "If anyone offers to take charge of the money while you shop around a little, Lois, let him."

"You mean—Judy, you don't really mean I'm to trust any stranger who comes along and wants to mind this money?"

Lois was plainly puzzled.

"Exactly. He will be watched." As Lois hesitated, she added, "It's all right, Lois, take my word for it."

Judy glanced toward the courthouse window which was just back of Lois's table. She could not see Peter through the half-drawn blinds, but he had assured her that he would be there for the entire three days of the bazaar. He wouldn't be having much fun either, unless, as Judy suspected, he enjoyed working more than he did simply having a good time.

As soon as word was passed around that volunteers were wanted to relieve Lois at the admission table, she was besieged with offers. Most of them came from the young men at the grill.

It was Dave, the polite one, who approached Lois on the third and busiest day of the bazaar. Judy was watching him as she had watched all the others, although she had just about decided that the trap she and Peter had set wasn't going to catch anyone after all. No attempt had been made to steal the bazaar money during the two previous nights, and surely, no one would be rash enough to try to steal it from Lois's table, in plain sight of everyone!

"Aren't you hungry, Miss Farringdon-Pett?" Dave asked solicitously. "There are some hamburgers and cheese sandwiches on the grill now. I'll bring them over—unless you want to trust me with this loot."

"Of course I'll trust you." Lois smiled her sweetest smile. Dave had made himself generally liked. "I've been hoping someone would relieve me again today," she added as she left the table and crossed the lawn to the grill.

It was only a few minutes later that a terrific crash sounded, as someone tripped against the toy counter and upset the whole booth. Much to her dismay, Mrs. Madders-Madders unexpectedly found herself sitting on the lawn with a large pink Teddy bear in her lap.

Toys flew in every direction. The clown scrambled to his feet and rubbed his head where it had been hit by a huge rubber ball. Sophie, on hands and knees retrieving the scattered articles, made an equally amusing picture. The shows they had put on previously to amuse the children were nothing compared to this. Everybody shrieked with laughter.

"Did you plan this part of the circus, too, Judy?" Roberta asked, when the laughter had subsided.

"Did I—"

Judy stopped short. No, she hadn't planned it. But someone had!

She glanced toward the table at the entrance to the bazaar and saw Dave Everett in his tall chef's hat still sitting there.

But, in the moment when the crash at the toy booth had caused everyone to look in the other direction, what had happened?

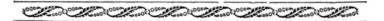

CHAPTER XVI

A Figure in White

WHEN JUDY found Peter in the Register and Recorder's room of the courthouse and told her suspicions to him, he merely smiled and drew her over to the window. It overlooked the lawn, so that anyone standing there could see practically everything that went on beneath it.

"You certainly had a good view!" exclaimed Judy after she had watched the bazaar a moment from this new angle. "But what did you see?"

"Precisely what I wanted to see," Peter replied. "Before this man who calls himself Dave Everett tries to leave the bazaar, two of us will step up and quietly place him under arrest."

"Quietly?" asked Judy. "If that crash at the toy counter is any sample—"

"It will be quiet," he assured her. "When we tell

120

him we have witnesses who saw him remove the bills from the cigar boxes and substitute others from his own pockets, he will know better than to resist."

"You did see him then? How did he do it so quickly?"

"He had already counted the bazaar money on the table quite openly. It's a considerable sum by now, because, as you know, we purposely haven't banked the first two days' receipts. Then he counted out the same amount of his own money under the table. The switch took only a moment."

"But you said the 'hot' money is all in tens," Judy pointed out. "That would make quite a bundle of bills. I didn't see him carrying a package in his hand when he came over to relieve Lois."

"He had the money in flat stacks with rubber bands around them, in the big, deep pockets of his white chef's apron. I suppose he knew how much was in each stack, because he didn't have to take much time to count out the right amount."

"I wish I'd had sense enough to watch," lamented Judy.

"It doesn't take sense. It takes training."

Peter was referring to the training he had received at the FBI Academy.

"That was an old trick," he continued, "but it points to another possibility. Dave Everett undoubtedly has a confederate. Who else would have tripped Mrs. Madders-Madders and knocked over the toy booth at such an opportune moment?"

"You're right," agreed Judy. "Then there are two

to catch, and this is the last day of the bazaar. Oh, my goodness!" she exclaimed. "While we've been talking in here, we've missed the awarding of the prizes. Come on, Peter, let's hurry out there before they finish calling the numbers."

They were in time to see the last prize awarded—to Jack and Sophie Howell. It was the television set.

"We accept this as a consolation prize to heal our wounded vanity," Jack was explaining to the crowd that gathered around to congratulate him and his wife on their good fortune.

"No more circuses for me," put in Sophie. "I've had enough. From now on I'll just sit back and watch television shows."

"Who stumbled into the toy booth? Did you happen to notice?" Peter asked at the first opportunity.

"It was that clumsy lummox over there," the fat girl declared, pointing to an awkward boy from Roberta's class in the Roulsville school. He was overage and oversize for his grade, but certainly he was innocent of any criminal intentions. And when Peter spoke to him, he said one of the men at the grill had dared him to trip up Mrs. Madders-Madders by the toy booth the next time the man relieved Miss Farringdon-Pett at the ticket table. He said the man had told him he wanted to be able to see the fun.

"It was the good-looking one," he added.

Dave Everett lost a little of his good looks when Peter stepped up to him a moment later, said something to him in a low voice, and then, with Mr. Trent holding him firmly by the other arm, escorted him off the grounds. He was wearing what Horace later described in his news report of the arrest as a frozen stare.

"You and Mr. Trent certainly did a quiet job of arresting him, Peter," Judy commented that evening, after the bazaar was all over and they were home again. "Was Dave Everett actually the—the kidnaper?"

Judy hesitated to use the word even though Roberta was upstairs fast asleep. It had such a grim sound that she would surely be frightened if she heard it.

Peter shook his head.

"No, Judy. I should have known it wouldn't be that easy. Apparently he was hired to switch the money at the bazaar. He says he doesn't know the name of the man who hired him, but he gave us a description."

"Was the man tall?"

Peter laughed at her question. He could just about read her thoughts.

"He was no giant, if you're thinking of that man who came to the door of the Heffly house. No, according to Dave's description, he was of medium height, with medium-brown hair. In fact, there seems to be nothing at all unusual about his appearance. The only thing Dave remembered particularly was that the man seemed to have a slight hesitation in his speech. Dave was to have met him on that lonely road out of Roulsville just where the pavement ends. You remember it. Out where Dr. Burlingame used to live. I believe the house is vacant now."

"And probably just as haunted as ever! I know. We got stuck in the mud and had to take shelter there once."

Judy was recalling another mystery she and Peter had solved and one of the few cases he had lost when they were working in the little law office he had established in Roulsville before their marriage.

"One of our men, Robert Reed, is keeping the appointment," Peter continued. "Luckily, he looks a little like Dave."

"That's right. He does. I noticed the resemblance."

"It may not work. The appointment is at midnight." Peter looked at his watch and decided he'd better hurry. "I'm going to be parked in the vicinity of the Burlingame house myself, in case there's trouble. And this," he finished decisively, "is one little adventure you stay out of, darling."

"Oh, it is!" Judy tossed her head disdainfully.

She had plans of her own, but she wasn't telling Peter. He would object, she knew, if she divulged the fact that she was planning to sit up tonight and watch for whoever it was who had been opening the back door.

Peter had his own ideas about it, she knew. But, for some reason, he wouldn't discuss them with her.

"You'll feel a lot safer," he had told her, "if you keep on pretending it was a ghost."

That was pure nonsense, and he knew it. But to-night he would be out, and there would be nothing on earth to keep her from sitting up and watching for the mysterious intruder. She even felt a little brave when, a few minutes before midnight, she pulled a high, wingbacked chair into a spot where she could keep her eyes on the back door.

"I won't fall asleep," she thought. "I'm so wide awake now I don't feel as if I could ever fall asleep again. And certainly not with a—well, a ghost, if Peter must have it that way—creeping into the house. Funny—he creeps in without opening the door but has to open it to get out. A strange sort of ghost . . ."

Judy started up quickly as the back door banged shut. She had fallen asleep after all. How could she have slept through the intruder's entry? That was what she had most wanted to see.

"I may still catch him, though," she thought, grabbing her coat and throwing it over her shoulders.

Outside, the mystic spell of night was over everything. The stars glittered and winked, and the moon, now only a thin crescent, rode like a silver boat through the clouds.

Below there was nothing unusual, only the trees down by Dry Brook swaying a little in the wind and whispering, as they always did, and the babbling of the brook. It was swollen from a recent storm and made a little rushing noise where it flowed under the bridge that Judy could see dimly through the darkness.

There was no one crossing the bridge. No one at all.

Then, suddenly, as Judy turned to look out in the other direction toward the garden, she saw a light. It was moving, as if by itself, along the paths.

"Good heavens!" she gasped, creeping toward it. "I do believe it's the barn lantern."

The figure in white that she could now dimly see carrying the lantern moved along as noiselessly as a ghost. For a moment Judy was filled with sheer terror. Then, as the figure turned, she recognized Roberta in her white-ruffled nightgown and bunny-fur slippers. She was holding the lantern high, stopping every few moments, and then moving on. Her eyes were wide open, but Judy could tell she was still asleep by the dreamy way the child looked at her, not seeing her at all.

"I mustn't call," she thought.

Someone, sometime, had told her it was a dangerous thing to waken people who were walking in their sleep. Judy didn't remember exactly why it was supposed to be dangerous. But, whatever it was, she was not anxious to bring it about.

So, instead of speaking to the little sleepwalker, she simply walked along the garden path beside her and quietly took her hand. It was so cold it sent the shivers through her.

"She'll be sick," she thought, forgetting the other times Roberta must have walked in her sleep with no ill effects.

It was not until the little girl stopped to put down the lantern that Judy remembered it. Roberta had left the lantern without blowing it out, just as she had left it before. Judy was amazed that she had been able to light it in her sleep.

"She must have unlocked the door while she was sleeping, too," thought Judy. It was not hard to unlock from the inside. "And she would have gone back to bed by herself if I hadn't seen her."

Roberta was already on her way upstairs. Judy stayed just behind her and watched her take off her slippers mechanically and climb into bed. Then Judy made sure the child was warmly covered. Tuffy, in his box at the foot of Roberta's bed, had dozed through the whole adventure. But Blackberry, who was always on hand when anything mysterious was happening, had followed Judy upstairs and was now arching his back and purring around her ankles.

"So that's how you got in. You followed Roberta. Faithless cat! Don't you know you're not supposed to follow anyone but me?"

Judy had picked up Blackberry and was scolding him gently as she carried him back downstairs to put him out. It was all clear to her now. Or so she thought. But she had hardly closed the back door when, suddenly and without warning, a piercing scream echoed through the silent house.

CHAPTER XVII

A Haunting Memory

JUDY TOOK THE STAIRS two at a time in a mad dash for Roberta's room. The screams were coming from there and, for one panic-stricken moment, she had visions of the little girl being carried off bodily.

"Thank Heaven!" she breathed, pausing just inside the bedroom door to catch her breath.

Roberta was still safely in bed. But she had thrown aside the covers and was sitting bolt upright, her eyes wide with terror.

"Where am I?" she demanded, looking at Judy as if she had never seen her before.

"Why, you're right there in bed. I can't think of a safer place," replied Judy, sitting down beside her and taking her hand to quiet her screams.

For several moments she sat there, not saying any-

thing, just holding Roberta's hand. Had she frightened her by talking to Blackberry? She didn't think
so, as she had only whispered her scolding playfully,
as she often did, into the cat's soft fur.

Finally, when Roberta had stopped sobbing, Judy
asked gently, "Where did you think you were, darling? Was it such a terrible place?"

"N-no," Roberta replied falteringly. "It was—it
was—"

But here she gulped a couple of times and broke
into fresh sobs. Again Judy had to wait until she had
controlled them.

"What could have frightened her so?" Judy asked
herself.

There was nothing in the room to frighten anyone.
Tuffy was still curled up in his box. He had cocked
a listening ear, but he hadn't barked, and he certainly
would have if any real danger had threatened his
little mistress.

Or would he? As a watchdog, Judy did not think
much of the shaggy little terrier Roberta had adopted.

She was still sobbing and Judy was still sitting on
the edge of her bed trying to quiet her, when she
heard Peter come in. He must have seen the light in
Roberta's room, because he immediately called:

"Everything all right up there, Judy?"

"I guess so," she called back. "Roberta must have
had a bad dream—"

"I was lost," the little girl said. She had stopped
sobbing and now spoke in a bewildered voice. "I was

so-oo frightened. I went through the gate, and people walked by going both ways, but nobody paid any attention to me or knew I was lost. Somehow, I had to get back—"

"Where?" asked Judy quietly, putting her arm around Roberta.

"Back to my garden," she answered, choking back another sob.

"Darling, you've been dreaming—" Judy began, not thinking it wise to tell the little girl she also had been walking in her sleep.

"But it was a real garden!" Roberta cried. "The one I told you about with the stone lantern in the middle like the one on the seed package, and the walks all around, and flowers. I do have to get back there, Judy."

"Not tonight. Try and forget it and go back to sleep," Judy advised. "Tomorrow you'll have your garden to work in, and maybe you'll forget this dream."

"But what I dreamed wasn't just a dream," Roberta insisted. "I used to play there, wheeling my doll carriage in and out among the flowers, but I never picked any. My mother said I mustn't—"

"Your mother?" Judy looked puzzled. "Roberta! Do you remember her, too?"

"I didn't think I did," replied Roberta. "But I wouldn't have said that if I didn't remember her a little bit, would I?"

"You have her picture right there on your bureau," Judy reminded her.

"I know I do," Roberta agreed, "but when I look at her picture, I don't seem to remember her at all."

Judy thought about all this for a moment. It was strange how Roberta suddenly was remembering so many things she had, apparently, forgotten. And all because of the picture on a package of flower seeds!

Peter had come in quietly while they were talking. He had been standing in the doorway, but now he came closer.

"What else happened in your dream, Roberta?" he asked.

The little girl said slowly, "I remember going through the gate at the end of the garden. You know, Judy, the one that doesn't show in the picture. The gate was always closed before, but this time it was open so I went through—"

"All by yourself, Roberta?"

"Yes." She hesitated, trying hard to remember. Then she said, "I was lost for a long time before my father found me. He told me my mother had died, and after that he would never let me talk about the garden."

"Perhaps it made him sad to think of it," Judy said thoughtfully.

"I can see why it would," declared Peter.

"I can, too, a little," Roberta admitted, "but he didn't need to be so cross about it. Once I asked him for a picture of the garden so I wouldn't forget, and he said in a very cross voice, 'Which do you want to remember, the garden or your mother?' That was the time he gave me my mother's picture."

"She was very lovely," Judy said, looking at the wistful, heart-shaped face pictured in the frame on Roberta's bureau.

"But you say this doesn't look like her?" Peter questioned, studying the picture more closely.

"Oh, I guess it does. My father says it does. And my grandmother used to hold it and rock back and forth and moan."

Judy's eyes met Peter's. How much of all this was a memory and how much a dream?

From the first, there had been a good deal about Roberta's background that had not been clear to them. The little girl had been vague about it herself. She had not really wanted to remember until now.

This was understandable. Her life with Mrs. Griggs, Judy knew, had been almost unbearable. It had turned out that the Griggses were involved in a series of crimes about which Roberta's father knew nothing. The letter Judy had written informing him of this had been answered promptly. In it she had also offered her home as the little girl's new boarding place.

"This solves my problem," Captain Dunn had written. "I will now entrust Roberta to you."

There had been other letters, including the one in which he had promised to come for a visit at Christmas. That letter had been his last. How tragic, Judy thought now, if his ship actually had gone down. As far as she knew, it would leave Roberta without a single living relative.

"And how did your dream end, Lamb Pie?" Peter

was questioning the little girl gently. "You say your father found you when you wandered out of the garden and got lost?"

"Oh, yes," Roberta replied, "but he didn't bring me back to the garden. He brought me to my grandmother Ridley's house. I never saw the garden after that. Not one single time! If you could just take me there—"

"I don't see how we could do that, Roberta, when we don't know where the garden is."

"You and Judy are good at finding things. Couldn't you find it for me?"

"We can try," Peter promised. "We've found all sorts of lost things. But a lost garden is something a little out of our line."

"Won't our garden do?" asked Judy, hoping to divert Roberta's mind from this other garden that seemed to be haunting her dreams. "When the seeds come up, and all the many-colored flowers are growing straight and tall and casting their reflections in the silver ball—"

"You make it sound like a poem," Roberta murmured.

But Judy went on as if she had not heard the interruption.

"There won't be a lovelier garden anywhere, Roberta. Even your dream garden with the stone lantern won't be as lovely as ours when the sun is shining. You will try to like it just as well, won't you, darling?"

Judy glanced at Roberta when she did not answer. She had cuddled down under the covers again and turned her face in the other direction.

"She's asleep," Peter whispered. "If we go out quietly, we won't wake her. I want to hear what happened just before I came in."

"And I want to tell you," Judy whispered back. "That is, if I didn't dream it myself. It was all so strange!"

CHAPTER XVIII

Tragic News

"You have something to tell me, too," Judy reminded Peter. "Knowing what I do about your case, you can imagine what I thought when I heard Roberta scream."

"I sure can," agreed Peter.

Judy had just finished telling him about the vigil she had kept and how, after the door had opened and closed again, she had looked out and had seen Roberta walking in her sleep, the lighted lantern in her hand.

"It must have happened the same way the other nights," Judy continued. "Roberta has that garden on her mind so much that she can't forget it even in her sleep."

"I suspected as much, when—" Peter started.

"Peter!" Judy interrupted, glaring at him. "You

said you thought somebody was after that ten-dollar bill! If you suspected Roberta was sleepwalking, why didn't you tell me? How was I supposed to take care of her if I didn't know—"

"Just a minute, Angel," he stopped her. "Don't flare up so quickly. What I started to say was that when nothing was ever taken, I suspected someone was sleepwalking. But, to tell you the truth, I thought the sleepwalker was you."

"And I half suspected *you* had left the door unlocked and the wind blew it open! That was why I waited up tonight when you were out—so I could catch you absent-mindedly unlocking it!"

They both laughed at that. But Judy was serious a moment later when she reminded him again that he had something to tell her.

"Was there any trouble?" she asked anxiously. "Did the—the kidnaper keep that midnight appointment?"

"No, he didn't," replied Peter. "Nothing happened. I'm afraid he knows now that we're on the lookout for him. That will make him more cautious than ever."

"What became of Dave Everett? He won't give you any more trouble, will he?"

"No. He's safe in jail where he belongs," declared Peter. "His name, by the way, is Butch Davis, and he's wanted for a series of petty crimes. Nothing big. He swears he knew nothing about Arthur's money, and I'm inclined to believe him. We may get something more out of him, but I doubt it. Meanwhile, we'll keep on looking for the criminal who hired him, and the balance of the ransom money—and, of course, we still hope to recover Arthur's ten thousand."

They had been talking in the kitchen where Peter, as usual, had helped himself to a late snack from the refrigerator.

"Well, we solved one mystery, anyway," Judy said with a yawn as she turned to go back upstairs. "The mystery of the opening door. As far as I'm concerned, that's enough for one night. I'm dead tired. If there should be an earthquake or anything like that, just let me sleep, will you? Are you coming up?"

"In a minute," Peter said. "I have a report to make out while it's fresh in my mind."

He disappeared into his den, and Judy went upstairs, but not to sleep. The events of the past two weeks kept turning themselves over in her head until nearly morning.

Church bells were ringing when she awoke. Today, she resolved, she'd spend a quiet Sunday and not even think of the mysteries that had robbed her of so much time and sleep.

But Roberta had other plans. Right after breakfast she appeared in the new dress Judy had bought her at the bazaar and asked, "Are we going for a ride? I still have the empty seed package. Maybe that will help you find it."

"Find what?" asked Judy.

She had been busy clearing the table and had not paid much attention.

"My garden," Roberta said. "Remember? You and Peter promised last night that you'd help me find it."

"But not this morning," Judy objected. "To tell you the truth, Roberta, I'm too tired to even think about it. Why don't you just run along to Sunday school and let it wait until tomorrow?"

Roberta sighed deeply.

"But it's waited so long, Judy. And tomorrow there's school."

"Today there's Sunday school, and you'll be late if you don't hurry."

Without another word, Roberta put on her new spring coat and yellow straw hat with the flowers on it and hurried off.

"Good-bye, Roberta!" Judy called after her.

But the little girl was already halfway to the bridge.

"I think I hurt her feelings," Judy confessed to Peter, who had come in the room at that moment.

"What was wrong?" he asked. "She did run off a little faster than usual. I saw her from the window."

"She had plans," Judy said, "and now I have plans, too. The bazaar's over, thank goodness! You've no new clues to track down in connection with your case, and our ghost is explained. So I guess the next thing on the program is Roberta's garden. She wanted us to start looking for it this morning, but I suggested Sunday school instead."

"So that was it? Any ideas?"

"Nothing immediate," Judy replied. "I wrote to the Bell Seed Company two weeks ago, but they never answered. Anyway, Roberta's father will know, won't he?"

"First we have to find him," Peter reminded her. "Apparently, the shipping company whose post-office box number he gave us is out of business. When they didn't answer my letter, I tried to locate them and was told there was no such company listed. The next thing to do was contact Navy Intelligence. I expect to hear from them any day now. Today I have to give David Trent that report I told you about. I think I hear his car now."

"Maybe," Judy said rather wistfully, "if you get back soon enough, we might drive somewhere together this afternoon and look at gardens along the way."

"It's a date then. I'll be back by two o'clock. Don't bother with Sunday dinner. We'll eat out somewhere."

He kissed her and was off before she could ask any more questions.

An hour later, when she was upstairs getting ready to go out with him as soon as he returned, she happened to glance out the window. A cream-colored car was just turning in from the main road.

"But Peter left in Mr. Trent's green car. It must be Horace," Judy thought.

Her brother had a cream-colored roadster. But she soon realized that the car was not his. It was a different make altogether.

"I wonder who it can be," she said to herself,

quickly zipping up the skirt of her suit and arriving at the front door just as the bell rang.

"How do you do," a prim voice greeted her. "You're not—I was told a Mrs. Dobbs lived here, but you're too young—"

"I am Mrs. Dobbs," Judy said with dignity.

"You don't mean it!" the strange woman exclaimed. "Why, you're hardly more than a child yourself. Can it be that my sister's little girl is boarding with you? We've come to take her—"

"To take Roberta?" Judy questioned in surprise.

"Maybe we'd better introduce ourselves," the man said quickly. "I'm Clyde Rees, and this is my wife Lillian. We've brought sad news, I'm afraid. May we come in?"

"Yes, do!"

Judy showed them into the living room and said, "Roberta will be home soon. She just went to Sunday school—"

"In that case we'll state our errand quickly. The poor child has lost her father. We received word only this morning. His ship went down last November—"

"No!" gasped Judy. It was the news she had feared they were bringing. But how would she tell Roberta? "This is terrible," she exclaimed. "We haven't heard from him in so long that I was beginning to be afraid something like this had happened."

"And that you would be stuck with her? Is that it? Well, you don't need to worry, Mrs. Dobbs. That's what we're here for, to take her off your hands. It isn't fair for a young girl like yourself to be tied down with someone else's child."

Judy wanted to say that she didn't feel tied down, that she loved taking care of Roberta, and that she and Peter had thought of adopting her if anything happened to her father. But Mrs. Rees didn't give her the chance. She talked on and on, with only an occasional interruption from her husband and none at all from Judy.

The gist of her talk was that she was a woman who always did her duty. She had raised three children of her own, but they were grown up and gone now, there would be plenty of room for Roberta, and she would be willing to take her that very afternoon.

"I do hope she's a quiet child," she finished. "My nerves couldn't stand a noisy youngster."

"I expected a little peace myself—"

"But, Clyde," his wife interrupted before the man could finish his sentence, "you know it's our duty. Nobody is ever going to say that Lillian Rees didn't do her duty by her sister's daughter."

This sharp-featured woman didn't look to Judy as if she possibly could be the sister of the lovely young girl in the frame upstairs. Would Roberta be happy with her? And what about her garden?

Then, suddenly, Judy had an idea. Roberta's aunt and uncle might be helpful after all. Certainly they would know where her lost garden was—if there really had been a garden. Judy was about to get the seed package and show them the picture on it when the back kitchen door slammed shut with a bang.

"That must be Roberta now!" she exclaimed. "I think I'll let her decide about this. After all, it's her happiness that we must consider first. Roberta!" Judy called. "Come in the living room a minute. You have some unexpected company!"

CHAPTER XIX

After Them!

WHEN ROBERTA did not answer her call, Judy arose from the sofa where she had been sitting beside Mrs. Rees and went out in the kitchen to see what was the matter.

"Roberta, where are you?" she called again.

Still there was no answer. The kitchen was quite deserted except for Blackberry, who was sitting squarely in the doorway regarding the pair in the other room as if he had no liking for them.

Again the thought came to Judy, "Blackberry couldn't open a door."

Someone had opened it, certainly. And someone had closed it with a bang. It was not locked this time, so there was nothing puzzling about that. Roberta could have come in and gone out again, although it

143

did seem strange that she would have done such a thing without calling out her usual cheerful greeting to Judy.

Opening the door herself, Judy looked down the road, which could be seen plainly from this side of the house. There was no one in sight.

"And I thought I'd solved this mystery," she said to herself as she turned to look in the other direction —toward the garden.

It, too, was deserted. A solitary bird was sitting in the top branch of the big cedar tree, singing. But there was no other sound.

"Roberta! Roberta!" Judy called, thinking as she did so of all the other times she had called the little girl. What was this fear she had of something happening to her? She had never felt that way about anyone else. Judy was not the type of person who worried needlessly.

There was nothing to worry about now, she told herself firmly. Roberta, undoubtedly, had come in the door and put something down—the pocketbook she had carried with her to Sunday school, perhaps—and then run out to play somewhere away from the house. Probably this very minute she and Muriel were whispering and giggling over some of the many things that always seemed to amuse them whenever they were together.

"Muriel will miss Roberta if we let her go," thought Judy.

Muriel would have Louise, of course, but whom

would Roberta have for a friend? She'd need one, too, if she lived with her aunt and uncle, as it certainly didn't look as though she'd get much affection from them.

These and many other thoughts went through Judy's mind before she returned to the house to look for the pocketbook Roberta might possibly have left inside the door.

No, it wasn't there. Roberta hadn't come in to put her pocketbook down. That was evident.

Why had she come in, then?

To take Tuffy out, perhaps. The hook where the puppy's leash usually hung was empty, and the little black-and-tan terrier was nowhere about.

Satisfied that she had the right answer to her question, Judy returned to the living room.

"You'll have to wait a little longer, I'm afraid," she told Mr. and Mrs. Rees, who seemed to have grown impatient in her absence. "If that was Roberta who came in, she's gone out again now. The puppy's leash is gone, too. I think she just took him for a walk."

"Don't tell me there's a dog too!" Mrs. Rees exclaimed. It was evident from her expression that she did not approve of pets for children.

In her next breath she said so, voicing her disapproval in no uncertain terms. But Judy made it clear that where Roberta went, Tuffy went, too. The little girl and her puppy were inseparable.

"I suppose I'll have to take them both, then. But I honestly don't know how I'll manage with an impolite child and a bothersome dog under my feet all day," Mrs. Rees complained.

"How can you say Roberta is impolite when you've never met her?" Judy wanted to know. "Why, she doesn't even know she has an aunt. She told me she had no relatives except her father."

"She said that?" the man spoke sharply. "Are you sure?"

Judy nodded.

"Then she's not only impolite, but she tells fibs!" Mrs. Rees put in triumphantly.

Judy rebelled at that. She had come to a decision. Roberta was not to go with this pair, no matter who they were, if Judy could possibly help it. As she had told them from the beginning, the little girl's happiness came first.

"You are mistaken, both of you," she said decisively. "Roberta is not impolite, and she doesn't tell fibs. In fact, she's so sweet and polite and helpful that I don't see how my husband and I could possibly get along without her. You see, we didn't take her out of pity. We—we took her because we loved her."

Judy had faltered on that last sentence. The thought of turning over her little charge to the unpleasant pair who called themselves her aunt and uncle had been too much.

"If you love her so much," Mrs. Rees returned with biting sarcasm, "no doubt you will be willing to keep her without pay. There won't be any more board money coming from her father now that he's dead."

"There hasn't been any for the past five months," Judy replied, "but we haven't complained. Naturally, we wouldn't expect you to pay—"

"You'd be disappointed if you did," Mr. Rees snapped. "Come on, Lillian, we can't waste any more time here."

"Wait a minute!" cried Judy. They seemed, suddenly, in too much of a hurry, and she had found out so little about them.

"What is there to wait for?" Mr. Rees asked bluntly.

"For Roberta, of course. Don't you want to see her?" Judy questioned in surprise.

The man shrugged.

"She's not here."

"But surely you want to wait and see her, Mrs. Rees," Judy insisted. "She won't be gone long unless she's taken her puppy over to Muriel's house. Muriel Blade is a little neighbor of ours, and she and Roberta are very good friends. She often goes there to play."

"Why don't you call up and see if that's where she is?" Mrs. Rees asked impatiently. "We can't wait here all day."

"I will call."

For her own peace of mind, Judy felt the call was necessary. But Mrs. Blade, who answered the telephone, said she knew nothing of Roberta's whereabouts. Muriel hadn't seen her at Sunday school simply because she hadn't gone there herself. She had a cold.

"Louise might have seen her, though," Muriel's mother added. "Or she may be playing on the way home."

"I think she did come home," Judy said, "but I'm not sure. Probably she took the puppy for a walk. I thought they might have walked over to your house. Thank you, anyway, Mrs. Blade. I hope Muriel's cold is nothing serious."

When she had hung up, the couple rose.

"We really must go," Mrs. Rees said. "It's too bad Roberta had to run off without coming in to see us. I can assure you, if she had been living with us, we would have taught her better manners."

"Oh, would you?" said Judy hotly. But she curbed her temper a moment later when she realized that they were actually leaving without telling her where they lived.

"If you'll give me your address, we'll get in touch with you," she said. "We'd like to keep Roberta, but of course you'll want to see her. After all, Mrs. Rees, if you're her mother's own sister—"

"*Tell her half sister.*"

The whisper from Mr. Rees was almost inaudible, but Judy caught it. She had had an uneasy feeling about the pair all along. Now her suspicions were thoroughly aroused.

"We were half sisters," Mrs. Rees explained quickly. "I was grown up and gone before my father married again, so, you see, the little girl's mother

and I were not very close. It was only that I wanted
to do my duty by Roberta."

"I see," Judy said. "Well, if you'll give me your
address—"

"I only wanted to do my duty by her," Mrs. Rees
repeated, "but, of course, if you want to keep her—"
She shrugged and turned to go. Judy asked several
more questions which Mrs. Rees successfully evaded
before she and her husband drove off in the cream-
colored car. On impulse, Judy decided to follow
them.

"I'll wait till they've crossed the bridge," she told
herself, "and then follow them in our car. It will be
interesting to see just where they go."

It took Judy but a moment to back the car out,
turn around, and pick up speed. The car shot forward
as if it, too, realized the need for haste. It frightened
Judy a little. Peter had often said, jokingly, that the
car knew where to go when he was in doubt. Now
Judy was at the wheel, hardly knowing why, and
driving faster than she had ever driven before in her
life.

"Why am I doing this? It's just a hunch." Her
thoughts raced along with the speeding car. There
was something very peculiar about the way that pair
had arrived so unexpectedly, demanded Roberta, and
then, suddenly, lost interest in the whole thing.

Judy passed the broken dam with hardly a glance
toward the valley. But at the railroad crossing she

was forced to slow down. A whole line of cars was waiting for a big freight train to pass. Surely the cream-colored car was among them!

"It's not there!"

Keenly disappointed, Judy turned back. But she had driven only as far as the Heffly house when, through the neglected shrubbery that surrounded the place, she caught a glimpse of a cream-colored car in the driveway.

"I knew it!" she exclaimed. "Something suspicious is going on in there, and this time I intend to find out what it is."

CHAPTER XX

In the Old Heffly House

IT WOULD NOT BE SAFE to park her car too near the cream-colored automobile she had been following, Judy decided. So she drove over to Joe's parking lot and left it there.

"I may overhear something," she thought as she hurried back to the old Heffly house.

Instead of risking a fall on the rickety front steps, she climbed a steep bank overgrown with honeysuckle and approached the house from the back. The yard, though neglected, was still picturesque with unusual shrubs and evergreens. Judy took advantage of their shelter and cautiously crept around until she reached the back porch. A door opened, and voices came to her distinctly.

"You should have waited and brought her along,"

a man's voice was saying. "That—was your chance."

"How could I?" This was the sharp voice of Mrs. Rees. "She wasn't there, and there was no telling when she'd get back. It's a pity you couldn't have left well enough alone!"

"You're sure the girl doesn't—suspect?"

"Why should she?"

Judy had edged closer in order to listen, and could now see Mrs. Rees standing on the back porch with her husband and another man, whose voice she heard again, as he said, "We'll have to be careful. We can't take a chance on the kid remembering things—later."

The voices faded as the three of them started walking down to the driveway to where they had left the cream-colored car. Suddenly Judy realized they had not locked the back door of the house.

"Now is my chance," she thought.

Quick as a flash, she darted inside and stood concealed behind the door until her heart stopped pounding.

"What don't they want Roberta to remember?" Judy was thinking.

There was a garden that Roberta's father hadn't wanted her to remember either, according to the little girl's own story. But why? What secret did the garden hold? And why would this mysterious couple now leaving the Heffly house pose as Roberta's aunt and uncle unless the news they brought was as fictitious as they were?

The answers to the questions Judy was asking herself presented alarming possibilities. She was anxious to talk over her ideas with Peter, especially the last one. It immediately gave rise to another question.

What of Roberta's father and his long silence? If his ship had not gone down, why would anyone want to pretend that it had?

Navy Intelligence might throw some light on the mystery as soon as Peter heard from them.

It was hard to see just where the Heffly house fitted into the jumbled pieces of the puzzle Judy was trying to put together in her mind. But fit it must. Of that she felt certain. And she intended to find out how, if she could, before she left the place.

It seemed reasonably safe to come out from her hiding place now. One look at the kitchen in which she found herself convinced Judy that nobody was living in the house. There was no place to cook, for one thing, and no dishes on the dusty cupboard shelves.

As she looked around, Judy could see that once the kitchen had been beautifully decorated and expensively tiled. But now the tiles were loose and broken. Half of them lay on the floor mixed with bits of fallen plaster. The sink and stove had been removed, and great brown stains overhead proclaimed the fact that the roof was open to wind and rain. The once gay border of red and blue windmills could scarcely be seen through the dust.

"What a shame to let a house fall to pieces like this!" Judy thought. "And after the flood, there were so many who would have gladly taken shelter here."

It had not been the flood, but sheer neglect, that had destroyed the Heffly house. No wonder Arthur had said it wasn't fit to live in! Obviously, no one had been living in it. And yet . . .

As she picked her way around the fallen tiles and began her exploration of the rest of the house, Judy couldn't help wondering about the tall figure who had come to the door that evening—the figure that Sophie Howell had called "that Heffly ghost!" Judy preferred to think of him as the Scarecrow until she learned his real name. She did hope to explain him, although his presence in the house was no more puzzling than the presence of the couple she had just been following.

"I'll look through the rooms quickly and then hurry home and tell Peter about this," she decided.

It was almost two o'clock by her wrist watch. He would be home soon, and surely Roberta would be back from her walk with Tuffy. Probably it was just as well she had missed seeing the pair who claimed to be her aunt and uncle and who had brought such tragic news. Had she ever seen them before? And, if so, could she have recognized them and stayed away on purpose? Judy didn't think so. Roberta would have wanted to ask them about her garden.

"It's going to be fun looking for it—though I don't think Peter really believes it ever existed," thought Judy.

Exploring the old Heffly house would be fun too,

if Roberta or Peter or both of them could be sharing her adventure. Alone, it seemed a little too spooky with its creaking boards and rattling shutters.

All the rooms had a not-lived-in aspect in spite of the curtains hanging crookedly at most of the windows. There was no furniture except an ancient round oak dining table and a few broken chairs in the once magnificent dining room.

The living-room door was closed, but, after a few tugs, Judy managed to open it. Cobwebs were everywhere. A busy brown spider in the act of spinning a new one missed Judy by inches as he dropped from the paneled ceiling.

"What a splendid living room this must have been!" thought Judy as she gazed around.

Little of the old splendor remained, although there was a huge brick fireplace with carved mantel still unhurt and a magnificent circular stairway leading upward.

"It looks safe."

Judy grasped a rail and shook it to test its safety. Just then she heard what sounded like a footfall upstairs and stopped to listen. Had she imagined it? The couple who had claimed to be Roberta's aunt and uncle certainly had gone by now. Their companion? But a third person had been walking with them when they had started down the driveway. Who had remained behind if not . . . the Scarecrow?

"There's only one way to find out," thought Judy, mounting the stairs.

She knew there must be some logical explanation for the sound she had heard. Perhaps it was a broken branch thumping against the house that had given the effect of the sound of footsteps.

The first two rooms Judy looked into confirmed her belief that there was no one walking about the upstairs rooms. They were bare of furniture and showed the effects of the weather even more than did the rooms on the lower floor. Plaster had fallen from both the ceilings and crunched under Judy's feet as she walked across to a third door.

She had a vague feeling of uneasiness, as if someone were watching her, but quickly shook it off. People always felt that way, she reasoned, when they were exploring empty houses.

It did look a little as if someone had cleared away the plaster in front of the closed door, though. Was that a footprint in the dust?

She turned the knob cautiously and gave the door a gentle push, expecting that it would stick a little as the living-room door had done. To her surprise, it opened so easily that she almost fell into the room.

Looking around the room in the dim half-light from the hall, Judy could hardly believe her eyes. Shutters across the one window kept out the daylight except for the few sunbeams that managed to find their way in through the crescent-shaped holes cut in the center of each shutter. Nevertheless, Judy was able to make out the heavy draperies that hung at each side of the window. She could see that there was

a cot bed, neatly made, in one corner of the room;
also an easy chair and a desk upon which stood what
seemed to be a kerosene lamp. She could feel a rug
under her feet, and on one side she saw that a number of books filled the built-in bookshelves that lined
the wall.

A short toot interrupted her survey and made her
start nervously.

"Good heavens!" Judy exclaimed. "It must be the
cream-colored car. I thought they'd gone."

Panic seized her. Suddenly she felt that everything
she had done for the past half hour had been watched,
if not by the pair who had visited her, then by their
mysterious companion.

"I'd better get out of here, but fast!" she told herself, turning toward the door which she had left open
behind her. Then a scream rose in her throat as she
saw the door slowly closing—closing on a tall, shadowy figure standing out in the hall.

Judy made a leap for the doorknob, but before she
could reach it she heard an ominous click and knew
that the door was locked.

"Let me out!" she cried, rattling the knob desperately. But there was no answer. There was only the
same sound of footsteps that she had heard before, but
now they were going down the stairs very rapidly,
out across the porch, and down the driveway.

"Why, it was the Scarecrow!" she gasped. "He's
made me a prisoner!"

She let go with another ear-splitting shriek, but it

was no use. No one paid the slightest attention to her. And when, only a minute or two later, she heard the sound of a starting motor, she knew very well what was happening.

"They're getting away—all four of them," she thought.

Judy's heart sank lower and lower as the sound of the motor diminished in the distance and she was left alone locked in the dark little room.

CHAPTER XXI

A Scrap of Paper

At first it was hard for Judy to believe that the tall man she and Peter had called the Heffly Scarecrow had deliberately trapped her in the room he must have been occupying in the deserted house. Although she knew it was useless, she continued to rattle the locked door and bang against the panel.

Failing to budge the door, Judy ran to the window, which seemed to be nailed shut. Undaunted, Judy pulled off her shoe and shattered the glass.

"I'll get out of here yet," she told herself fiercely as she struggled to open the shutters. But for some reason, although she found the catch which held the shutters together, they would not open. Finally her groping fingertips recognized the outline of nailheads, and Judy realized with a sinking heart that the shutters, too, like the window, were nailed tight.

Exhausted from her efforts to escape, Judy leaned her head against the window frame, trying to think. In spite of all of her past experiences, she would never understand the ways of criminals. Their minds worked so differently from hers. They were not motivated by feelings of sympathy, loyalty, and love as she was.

Perhaps, she reasoned, it was just as difficult for them to understand her. Mrs. Rees had given her such a strange look when she had said she loved Roberta, as if such a thing couldn't possibly be true. That was something she'd have to tell Peter.

"When he finds me," she concluded with a sigh.

First he'd have to find the car. She wished now that she had not left it in Joe's parking lot. If she had parked it nearer the Heffly house it would be a clue, at least, to where she was. Joe didn't worry much about who parked in the lot next to his diner. The car might not be noticed for several days.

Judy gulped when the realization of this fact struck her.

"There must be *some* way out of here," she thought, firmly quelling the panic that suddenly threatened to engulf her once more. "The first thing to do is make some kind of a light. This darkness is awful."

Remembering that she had glimpsed an old-fashioned kerosene lamp in the few moments before the mysterious stranger had trapped her, Judy groped her way to the desk where it had stood. She sighed with relief when her fingers closed around the base of the lamp.

"It isn't going to do me a bit of good, though," she thought in dismay, "unless there are some matches here too."

She brushed her fingers across the top of the desk and located what felt like a metal letter opener and a box of paper clips, but no matches.

"They must be in the desk drawer," Judy assured herself, and hoped there was a drawer. After a little more fumbling, she found it and managed to open the drawer. At first it seemed to be empty, but in the far corner she felt what apparently was a slip of paper, and then her fingers closed triumphantly on a package of matches.

"Now we're getting somewhere," Judy thought, "*if* there is some oil in the lamp."

She struck a match and then held her breath until she saw that the wick was going to hold the flame. When the lamp was burning steadily, Judy straightened up and looked about her again.

In the mellow, flickering light of the lamp she could see that the door was made of solid oak. Nevertheless, she tried it again. It resisted all her efforts. After she had banged away at it for half an hour, there wasn't so much as a crack in the panels.

The hinges were just as solid. With the proper tools, it might be possible to remove them. But Judy had nothing to work with.

She tried calling again. She called until her throat

was hoarse and dry. But not one of the people in the cars going by on the road heard her lusty screams at all. Or if they did, they passed them off as a joke.

"It's no use," Judy finally decided. "If I expect to get out of here today, I'll have to get those shutters open somehow."

She knew now how she had been trapped in the first place. The Scarecrow must have heard her creeping up the stairs. He evidently had waited, knowing she would investigate the little study eventually, and then neatly locked the door on her when she entered the room.

Judy went back to the desk, hoping to find something she could use as a tool with which to attack the shutters. The scrap of paper she had felt in the corner of the drawer caught her eye, and she picked it up. A piece torn from a letter, Judy decided, and stared at it a moment before she recognized the familiar round handwriting.

"Roberta's letter!" she whispered. "How can that be?"

On the slip of paper were the words:

Then something made me remember the garden and the lantern. You will see what it was when you come to visit me here in Dry Brook Hollow.

The word "lantern" had been circled in pencil.

"This is terrible," thought Judy, putting the scrap of paper in her pocket. "He can't be dead when he's hiding here. Or did someone else receive this letter? And why is 'lantern' circled? I'll have to ask——"

Then Judy thought of something.

The letter, originally, had been sent to a shipping company that didn't exist. Peter had found out that much. And he had been on the verge of finding out more. How had the letter reached these people? Was it the reason for the sudden appearance of the fictitious aunt and uncle? Were they the "shipping company"? If so, what was their purpose?

These questions, all of them unanswered, were beginning to spin around in Judy's mind until they made her dizzy. Or was it because the room was so stuffy and she was so hungry and thirsty?

"The whole day will be gone!" she mourned, "and here I am letting those criminals escape and no way to stop them. What if they should go back to the house and find Roberta there alone!"

This disquieting thought spurred Judy on to fresh efforts. She picked up the metal letter opener and considered it appraisingly. It was too thick to use on the nails in the shutters, but it might have other possibilities.

"If I should heat it in the flame of the oil lamp until the blade was red-hot," she thought, "I might be able to burn away the wood around the fasteners and get the shutters open that way."

Judy set to work quickly. She turned up the wick of the oil lamp and held the metal opener in the flame. Metal being a quick conductor of heat, Judy soon had to double over her handkerchief and wrap it around the handle of the opener in order to hold it.

After a while the blade glowed red, and she ran to the window with it before it had a chance to cool. She scraped the wood around one of the shutter fasteners with the red-hot opener, and had the satisfaction of seeing the surface of the dry old wood begin to char slightly.

She thrust the metal blade into the lamp's flame once again, and again applied it red-hot to the ancient wood. Steadily she worked, on into the late afternoon, and still the wood had not burned through sufficiently to release the catch of the shutters.

Finally Judy, her throat parched, and her nose and eyes stinging, was forced to throw herself down on the cot and rest her tired arms and aching back.

"But I won't give up," she told herself fiercely. "I'll get out of here if I have to burn the house down."

She must have dozed for a while after that, for when she roused there was no longer any light coming through the two half moons cut in the shutters.

"Oh!" Judy gasped, starting up. "I must have dropped off to sleep. Goodness knows how much time I've lost."

She set to work again quickly, and after another two hours of heating, scraping, and heating again, at last the ancient fasteners gave way, and Judy threw open the shutters triumphantly.

"Thank heavens for some fresh air," she exclaimed, taking deep, grateful breaths of the cool night air that now flooded the little room. Then she leaned out the window to estimate the drop to the ground below.

One would need wings to escape that way, she realized immediately. To jump would be suicide, as the cement driveway with its high retaining wall was directly under the window.

Judy could see the headlights of the cars on the main road, and the smaller, half-hidden lights of distant houses. She let out an experimental, but effective, shriek, then waited a few moments to see what results it would produce. No cars stopped, no windows were flung up, no curious heads were poked out; the peaceful countryside slept on.

"H-mm," thought Judy. "Well, I guess it's out the window for me."

She went over to the neat cot and stripped the sheets from it. Tying them together, she twisted them into a crude rope. Then she tied one end to the sturdy frame of the cot and threw the other end of the improvised rope out the window. It almost reached the ground.

Next she tested the strength of the sheets and decided they would hold. Then Judy blew out the lamp and climbed up on the window sill. Twisting one foot around the sheet-rope until she had it doubled around one leg to act as a brake, she took a firm grip with her hands and let herself down from the sill. Although the distance to the ground was not more than fifteen feet, it seemed a long time to Judy before her toes touched cement and she let go of the rope.

For a moment she stood in the dark driveway, listening. She heard nothing but the usual cheerful country sounds in the night. Then Judy set off briskly down the driveway and out to the main road. On the highway she walked on the side facing approaching cars so that she would not be run down before she reached Joe's parking lot.

Once there, Judy quickly located her car and started the engine. She backed the car out of the parking lot a little gingerly, as she had not done much night driving. But when she had successfully negotiated the turn onto the highway, Judy drove at a steady pace. Now that she was nearly home, it seemed as if she could not get there quickly enough.

On the way, she tried desperately hard to remember all the things she wanted Peter to know. The thought had come to her again and again during her imprisonment that there was something in particular that she must tell him. But now, somehow, everything escaped her.

The lights of the house in Dry Brook Hollow had never seemed so dear to Judy as they did when she finally turned into their own driveway. Suddenly the front door was flung open and a haggard-faced Peter dashed out. He had recognized the sound of his own car's motor and was alongside the front window almost before Judy had time to put on the brake and climb out.

"Judy! Oh, Judy," he said hoarsely and took her in his arms.

"I'm all right, Peter," she said, "and I'm so glad to be home," she added, sobbing happily into his coat.

CHAPTER XXII

A Night of Suspense

"Peter, I have so much to tell you," Judy said at last, when Peter had led her inside the house and seated her in the rocker before the kitchen fireplace. "I hardly know where to begin. Besides, I'm starved, and I'm dying for a long drink of water."

"Sit right there, Angel, and I'll bring you everything in the refrigerator," Peter promised. "I don't ever want to let you out of my sight again," he added.

"Were you terribly worried, Peter?" Judy asked.

He tilted her face toward his and gave her such an adoring look that she needed no further answer.

"I suppose Roberta's sleeping so soundly she didn't hear me drive in, or she'd be down here," Judy was continuing when Peter interrupted her:

"You mean you didn't leave Roberta and Tuffy with someone?" he asked anxiously. "When she didn't come home, I took it for granted you'd made some arrangement—"

"But I didn't!" cried Judy, white-faced. "I thought I'd be right back. You were coming home soon, and Roberta was out somewhere with the puppy. Anyway, I thought it was Roberta who came in and took down his leash. Peter, I haven't seen her since she left for Sunday school."

"I'm afraid I don't get it," said Peter.

"I don't either. Oh, Peter!" she exclaimed. "If anything has happened to Roberta, I'll never forgive myself for following that couple without making sure she was safe before I left. They talked so strangely about her that I was worried for a while, but I thought of course she had come home and found you here—"

"Wait a minute, Angel," Peter interrupted. "What couple? This is the first I've heard about any couple you were following."

"I'd better start at the beginning and tell you about them, then," she declared.

"First let me call your mother and father and let them know you're home safely," Peter said. "When you didn't come and didn't come, I telephoned to see if you were over there, and I promised to let them know the moment you showed up."

When Peter had reassured Judy's parents, he came back to her and said:

"Now let's have it, Angel. Give me the important facts first. You can fill in the details later, but we've got to get a line on Roberta, and fast."

"They called themselves Mr. and Mrs. Rees," Judy
began. "I should have known they were up to something when they first came to the house and wanted
to take Roberta. They said they were her aunt and
uncle and they were bringing news of her father's
death."

She stopped abruptly.

"But why are you looking at me with that strange
expression on your face, Peter? Were you told about
it, too, or did you only suspect that he was dead?"

"Roberta's father didn't die," Peter said evenly.
"He never existed. Navy Intelligence sent a reply
to my inquiry by Special Delivery. There's no such
captain as Robert Dunn and no such ship as the *Merchant Queen*, which was the name he gave us. Obviously, the whole story was manufactured to cover
his real identity."

"But why?" asked Judy. "I can't understand any
of this. The shipping company didn't exist. The aunt
and uncle were fictitious, and now you say even her
father is a made-up character. Goodness!" she exclaimed with a giggle that was almost hysterical.
"Isn't *anybody* real?"

Peter looked at Judy's tired face and decided that
she had been through enough for the present.

"You are real," he said, placing a huge sugar bun
and a glass of milk before her, and bringing more food
from the refrigerator, "but you won't be much longer
if you don't eat something."

"Peter, I saw the Heffly Scarecrow," Judy broke

in, her mouth full of bun. "He was the one who locked me in. I'm sure of it. And I heard his footsteps on the driveway. He must have driven off with those other three."

"Three?" questioned Peter, who had now joined Judy at the table. "Who was there beside the couple who called themselves Mr. and Mrs. Rees and this other character we call the Scarecrow?"

"There was a—well, an ordinary-looking man. He seemed to be the one who was directing the Rees couple, and, from the conversation I overheard, he was afraid I might suspect something. I'm sure I don't know what. I don't think I caught everything he said," Judy confessed, "because he'd sort of stop and grope for a word every once in a while. But I did hear him say something about the possibility that Roberta might remember things later."

"That's odd," Peter said, frowning. "Can you tell me what this man looked like?"

Judy waved what was left of her bun in a helpless gesture. "You'd never pick him out of a crowd, Peter, for any one distinguishing characteristic. He had what I used to call man-color hair when I was a little girl. You know, not brown but not exactly gray either. He wore a gray suit and a tweedy-looking topcoat. He—well, he's just one of those people you'd call medium," she finished vaguely.

"You would!"

Judy was surprised at Peter's sudden excitement.

And when he jumped up from the table and rushed into his den and began making one phone call after another, she was even more baffled. She realized, of course, that the first thing to do was to send out an alarm for the four who had escaped, just in case they had found Roberta and had taken her with them. But why would they take her? The couple who had called themselves Mr. and Mrs. Rees hadn't seemed to want her when they had left after talking to Judy.

"I think you're wrong, if you're thinking that this is another kidnaping case," she told Peter, following him into his den. "I thought it might be, myself, at first, but Roberta isn't a millionaire's child like the little Doe baby. She's only boarding with us. They wouldn't hold her for ransom. It looks to me as if she simply wandered off somewhere by herself and got lost."

"It looked as if the Doe baby wandered off somewhere, too—until the parents got the ransom note," Peter replied grimly. "And if you'll remember Dave's description of the man who hired him to switch the ransom money," he added, "he said it was a man who *hesitated when he spoke*."

Still Judy could not believe any such dreadful thing had happened to Roberta. Too many incidents pointed to the fact that she had left the house of her own accord.

"There's the fact that she took Tuffy, for one thing," Judy began enumerating them. "Secondly, they couldn't have picked up Roberta after they left the Heffly house, because they drove away in the opposite direction."

"They could have turned back—"

But Judy didn't think so.

"Why would they risk taking Roberta with them when it was perfectly obvious that I would get out of there sooner or later and be able to identify them?"

"I don't know why," Peter said honestly. "It's simply that if this is the gang we're after, we know what they're capable of—and Roberta is missing."

Judy shook her head. "My guess is that they locked me in that house simply to give themselves time to get away before the police caught up with them. They were in hiding for some reason. Anyway, the Scarecrow was. And they all were quarreling and saying I might suspect them of something. Of lying to me, maybe."

"Usually people lie when they are afraid," Peter said thoughtfully. "But whatever they were afraid of, they aren't apt to go far in that cream-colored car. I had your description of them put on the teletype. It's being flashed to police and FBI agents all over the country, with an added warning to be on the lookout for a little girl in a new pink dress. You said Roberta was wearing the dress you bought her at the bazaar, and the light tan coat and yellow straw hat, didn't you?"

"Yes, and she was carrying her pocketbook. It was a little red one," Judy said. "When she left for Sunday school, she had the quarter in it that I gave her for the collection."

"Was that all? The police will be here soon with a missing-persons report to fill out, and one of the questions is about money. They figure it will take a person quite a long way by bus or train . . ."

But Judy had raced upstairs while Peter was still talking. She was back in a minute, a little out of breath, but with the information he wanted.

"Peter, she did have money! She took all the money in her piggy bank, and she took something else, too. That flower-seed package with the picture of the stone lantern on it. I don't know where she went. But I'll bet I know why. She went in search of her garden!"

"I hope you're right," Peter said gravely. "It isn't like her to run off without telling us, though."

"That was my fault!" cried Judy. "She wanted me to go with her to look for the garden, but when I suggested Sunday school instead, and then, when she came back and heard that woman talking and me not saying a word . . . Oh, Peter!" cried Judy. "I can just imagine how she felt if she heard that terrible news about her father. And then that awful Mrs. Rees went on and on saying how it wasn't fair for a young girl like me to be saddled with a child. She was the kind who doesn't give anyone else a chance to put in a word. It wasn't until after the door banged and Roberta went out with Tuffy that I told the woman we loved Roberta and that the board money didn't matter. Mrs. Rees gave me such a look—as if she'd never heard the word love. But it's true, Peter! We do love Roberta, and now she's somewhere, goodness knows where, eating her heart out because she thinks she's an orphan and nobody wants her. I'd go out in search of her this very minute if I had the faintest idea where to look."

"The police will have an idea. They always do. Here they are now!" Peter exclaimed as a loud rap sounded on the front door.

It was Chief Kelly himself and Ralph Flynn, one of his most trusted inspectors. They listened sympathetically to all Judy and Peter had to say.

"We can't overlook the possibility you mentioned on the phone, Peter," Chief Kelly said, "but my guess is that your little bird hasn't flown very far from the nest. We found one missing person fast asleep in her own bed. Her parents had looked everywhere else and, in the meantime, the little miss had changed her mind about running away and had crept back into the house without being heard by anyone."

"But Roberta isn't in bed, Chief Kelly," Judy protested. "I went up to her room to look in her piggy bank just before you came."

"Have you looked in the barn?" Inspector Flynn inquired. "Hay makes a nice soft bed."

A party was soon organized to search the entire farm. The lantern Roberta had carried on her sleepwalking expedition flitted once more through the garden, but this time it was in the hand of Chief Kelly, who had to admit at last that any further search must wait until morning.

The night of anxiety and suspense was almost over when Judy happened to put her hand in her pocket. Her fingers closed on a scrap of paper.

"Peter!" she exclaimed, hurrying into the den where he was sitting at his desk surrounded by papers. "This is what I had in the back of my mind to tell you about! It's a piece torn from Roberta's letter. I found it in the drawer of the desk up there in that study room where I was made a prisoner. I had forgotten it until this very minute when I discovered it in my pocket, but I saved it on purpose to show you."

"It doesn't add up," Peter muttered in exasperation when he had looked at the scrap of paper. "If they have got her, why would they care about some lantern that she thinks she remembers from the *past?* It just doesn't add up—or does it? Good grief!" he exclaimed, jumping up from his desk, "The whole thing adds up! Judy, how would you like to take a little trip to Chicago with me? We'll fly, of course, to save time."

"Without Roberta?" she questioned in amazement. "If you think I would fly all the way to Chicago before we find her, you don't know me, Peter. What I can't understand is why you would even suggest it."

"Well, you've never been there for one thing," he said teasingly, and added, "besides, I'm beginning to think now that you're right in believing Roberta went looking for her garden."

"I would love the trip," Judy admitted rather wistfully, "but we have to find Roberta first."

"We certainly do have to find her, and fast," Peter agreed. "Meanwhile, I'm going to make reservations on the plane that leaves Farringdon airport at two o'clock this afternoon."

CHAPTER XXIII

In the Morning

JUDY WAS PUZZLED. Peter refused to say anything more about the proposed trip, but he seemed so confident now that Judy felt sure he had made some discovery. But what?

He wanted her to get a little rest, and she did sleep some. But morning found her at the telephone making all the calls she had hesitated to make the night before for fear of getting people out of bed.

First she called Horace, who had not been asleep, he claimed. He couldn't understand why his cream-colored roadster had been stopped three times by police during the night, and Judy wouldn't tell him. She did tell him about Roberta, though. His theory was that she had simply wandered off in the woods and lost her way.

"Or maybe she passed the old Heffly house and was scared off," he added, trying to make a joke of it to cheer Judy, who had let some of the anxiety she felt creep into her voice.

Her next call was to Mrs. Blade.

"Roberta's been gone all night," she told her neighbor. "The police and everybody have been searching, but I thought maybe you might have some idea—"

"Let me talk to her! Let me talk to her!" Judy heard the hoarse voice of Muriel repeatedly insisting. Obviously, her cold was no better, but she was determined to talk, and finally her mother consented.

"Did you look in the hut?" Muriel questioned. "There's a bed there, sort of. It's fir branches spread over some dry leaves, but it isn't bad. If Roberta ran away on purpose, that's where she'd go."

It was a hut the children had built themselves when their club, the Junior FBI, was in full swing. It was supposed to be secret, Muriel explained. The club members had promised each other that they wouldn't tell anybody about it.

"But sometimes," Muriel said in a lower voice, "it's right to break a promise, so I'm telling you."

Judy thanked her and after having been given specific directions, she set out for the hut. Someone had to be at the house to receive messages, so she went without Peter. She was not entirely alone, though, as Blackberry marched ahead of her waving his tail like a signal flag and looking back every few minutes to make sure she was coming.

The woods were beautiful at this time of year. The first spring flowers were beginning to peep from hidden places beside the path Judy was following, and the birds were having a regular morning concert in the branches over her head. She couldn't help feeling hopeful. Hope was in the air.

Twice something darted across the path in front of her, and Blackberry raced off in pursuit. He had just succeeded in scaring a mother partridge off her nest in the brush when Judy's ear caught another sound not at all like the squawking and wing-flapping of the frightened partridge. It was the persistent barking of an excited puppy.

Never, in all her life, had Judy been so glad to hear a puppy bark. She couldn't help remembering a little ruefully a time when she had not wanted Tuffy because she had been afraid the puppy and Blackberry would not get along. But now they were the best of friends.

Barking and wagging his stub of a tail, Tuffy came bounding out of the brush while Blackberry turned to walk more sedately a little way behind him. But when Judy patted him, the puppy began to whine.

"What's the matter, Tuffy? Where's your mistress?" Judy questioned. "Are you worried about her? Well, so am I. Come along and show me where she is."

It was Blackberry who finally led the way to the hut. Judy was amazed. It was nothing but four poles placed crosswise on the lower branches of four trees that were growing close together, making a perfect square. A large piece of canvas had been thrown over the poles and secured at the sides by little piles of stones that were heaped upon the corners. But, at least, it was dry inside.

Peeping in, Judy could see that one of the stone piles had been used as a little fireplace. There was no other furniture except the bed of fir branches Muriel had described. There lay Roberta, peacefully sleeping, her tear-stained face pressed hard against what once had been her new straw hat. The sight of the little girl made Judy's heart sing with the chorus of birds in the trees above.

"Roberta! Roberta!" she whispered softly. "Oh, darling! What made you do it? Could you really believe we didn't love you?"

Roberta's eyes flew open. She sat up, straight as a rod.

"Judy!" she exclaimed. "You shouldn't have come here. This hut is secret. Nobody is supposed to come here but Muriel and me. I didn't want anybody to find me."

"But what were you going to do?" asked Judy. "Live in the woods like a rabbit? I'm afraid that sort of life wouldn't suit a little girl very well. You'd be cold and hungry, and there'd be no one to kiss you good night when you went to bed. There's school, too—"

"I know," Roberta interrupted. "I didn't mean to skip school. It was just that I have to find my garden.

Won't you and Peter please help me find it, Judy?"

"Of course we will, if that will make you happy. We want your happiness more than anything, Roberta."

Judy held her close for a moment. It was so good to know she was safe. But soon she jumped up, saying cheerfully, "Well, if we're going to find your garden we'd better start looking for it. Peter said something about an airplane trip to Chicago. We can look for your garden on the trip."

"Oh, Judy! I'm sure we can find it! And I'm awfully sorry if I worried you. I just didn't want you to be stuck with me, and I didn't want to go with that horrible woman who came to take me off your hands—"

Roberta stopped abruptly and burst into painful sobs.

"So you did hear that ridiculous woman talking!" Judy exclaimed, hugging her close. "Why, Roberta, don't you know how glad we are to take care of you? Every young thing requires care, you know. Even kittens and puppies—"

"Their mothers take care of them," Roberta said wistfully. "It's different then."

"That's the best of all," Judy agreed. "But often people have to accept a little less than the very best. We can't take the place of your mother and daddy, but don't you ever again think we don't want you."

"I didn't think that until I heard that woman—"

"Forget everything she said," Judy advised, taking

Roberta's hand and urging her to hurry. "We must let Peter know you're all right," she explained as they hurried along with the puppy frisking about behind them and Blackberry marching proudly ahead.

"Look at him!" exclaimed Judy when they were nearly home. "You'd think he was leading a procession the way he walks."

Peter saw them coming down the hill and rushed out to meet them.

"You're a miracle, Judy!" he exclaimed. "You and that enchanted cat of yours. I knew you'd find Roberta when you set off this morning with such confidence. Running away seems to be a habit with you, Lamb Pie," he added, trying to be severe and failing utterly.

"Oh, Peter!" Roberta cried, hugging him. "You are good. You and Judy are both good. And I'll be happy with you even if I never find my garden. Judy said you were going for an airplane ride. May I go, too?"

"I think it can be arranged."

"What about school?" asked Judy. "I thought, if we hurried, Roberta could still catch the school bus. She's kept her dress fairly clean."

"Clean enough to wear on our trip?" he inquired. "Or don't you think perhaps she should have a bath and put on her very prettiest dress, the one with the brown butterflies and the yellow ribbon? I think a little girl's first airplane trip is important enough to excuse her from school. How about it, Judy?"

"To tell you the truth, Peter," she replied, "I don't

know what to think. Things are happening too fast for me."

"If it hadn't been for some pretty quick thinking on your part," Peter returned mysteriously, "I'm afraid they wouldn't be happening at all."

"You realize, of course, Mr. Dobbs," Judy remarked sweetly, as Peter held open the front door for her, "that that tells me absolutely *nothing*."

Peter, chuckling, went to the table and picked up a letter. "The mailman came while you were out looking for Roberta," he said, handing the letter to Judy.

Noting that the postmark said Chicago, Judy tore open the envelope eagerly.

"At last!" she exclaimed. "It's the reply to my letter to the Bell Seed Company." She scanned the letter rapidly. "They say the picture on the seed package was copied from a photograph of the garden of a Mr. and Mrs. James Floyd, of Chicago, Illinois."

"Oh, goody!" Roberta cried, jumping up and down. "Then we can watch for it while we're flying in the air."

"We can go see it while we're in Chicago, can't we, Peter?" Judy said appealingly.

For answer, he bent over unexpectedly and kissed her. As Judy looked up at him in surprise, Peter said solemnly, "Angel, I love you!"

CHAPTER XXIV

The Plan Unfolds

By AFTERNOON Judy had stopped trying to figure out Peter's plans. She just let them unfold the way the first flowers were unfolding in the beds she and Roberta had patterned after the lost garden.

It did seem strange, almost as if they were going to search for something out of a dream. Was it a real garden after all? If so, what secret did it hold?

"Shall we say good-bye to our own garden?" she asked Roberta when they were ready to start for the airport. "Some of the early flowers may be gone before we get back. Peter hasn't said how long we're going to stay in Chicago, and the crocuses are already fading."

"It seems sad, doesn't it?" asked Roberta. "The garden is so lovely, and we did try so hard to make it

like the one with the stone lantern. The silver ball is
nice. It reflects the colors of the flowers just the way
you said it would. It's every bit as pretty as my garden
in the daytime. But Judy, if you could have seen it at
night! It was magic! The light from the stone lantern
turned all the stones around the flower beds into shining jewels just as if some fairy had touched them with
her wand."

"It must have been quite a garden," agreed Peter,
coming up behind them. "But if you want to find it,
you'd better hurry."

"Can't Tuffy come too?" Roberta begged. "Please,
Peter!"

"Okay," Peter assented good-naturedly, "but you'll
probably have to keep him in the dog carrier on the
plane. Judy hadn't better decide to take Blackberry,
though. He'll have to stay here and mind the house."

"I hope he doesn't let the chickens get into the garden and spoil it, Judy. We did have such fun planting
it."

Roberta spoke a little wistfully as if she felt that she
really should have been satisfied, but Judy understood.

It was at the airport that Judy began to suspect
something really big was about to happen. Her family
and friends were there, of course, but she had not expected that the whole police force would turn out to
see her off. Chief Kelly looked especially pleased with
himself.

"Well, you found the little runaway bird not far

from the nest, just like I said. Good work, Judy!" He turned to Peter and said more gravely, "It's all arranged. We have the four prisoners down at the county jail. It won't take but a minute for your wife to identify them. I'll run you both over there myself. The plane will wait for you."

"What about Roberta?" asked Judy.

"Oh, I like jails," Roberta put in quickly.

The little girl was thinking of the police station where she had been treated royally with cake and cookies when she first came to live with Judy and Peter.

The prisoners, it turned out, were the four in the cream-colored car. Chief Kelly had reason to be proud of his part in rounding them up even if it had been not a little embarrassing to Horace.

"We found them in another deserted house," the chief told Judy when, after a fast trip with the siren screaming, they had arrived at the county jail. "So far we haven't been able to get any sort of confession out of them. But with you to identify them, we may not need it. As soon as you've had a look at them, we'd better let Little Sunshine here step inside and see if she's ever seen any of them before."

Judy quickly identified the four behind the bars. They were the pair who had claimed to be Roberta's aunt and uncle, the tall man who had made her a prisoner, and the other man who, for some reason, had not made much impression on her until now.

The rest faced her without flinching as she pointed them out, one by one, but the guard had to jerk this

man's hand away from his face forcibly. Judy
couldn't understand his agitation until she saw that
Chief Kelly had come in with Roberta, who was staring, open-mouthed, at the prisoners. Suddenly she
screamed:

"Daddy! Daddy! Those other two people lied to
Judy. They told her your ship had gone down and
you were dead!"

"I'm not your—father," the man growled.

There was nothing at all ordinary about him now.
His face was contorted with shame and anger. To
Judy it was pitiful and, at the same time, disgusting.
It was hard to believe Roberta had ever thought such
a character was actually her father. No wonder she
had shown so little affection for him!

Roberta stared at him a minute and then said in
that matter-of-fact way of hers, "No, I guess you're
not my father. You did make me think you were, but
my father was good. He didn't tell lies."

"That does it!" Chief Kelly said. "Well, you'd best
get back to the plane now. You'll have a police escort.
Good luck to you, Cookie. The best of luck!"

He grasped Roberta's hand warmly. Then, im-
pulsively, he picked her up in his arms and gave her a
hearty kiss.

"Imagine them trying to pretend you were ten
years old!" he exclaimed. "I don't believe you're a
day over eight."

"What made him say that?" asked Roberta as they
sped back to the airport.

"Don't ask me," replied Judy, who was thinking

furiously. "I've given up trying to answer questions. All I know is that we're on our way to look for your garden, and it wouldn't surprise me at all if we found it!"

There were more good-byes at the airport. Judy's mother and father, Peter's grandparents, his sister Honey, Lois, Lorraine, and Arthur—everybody was there.

Last, but by no means least, was Horace. He rushed out to the plane and took a few pictures of Roberta with her puppy before Peter could stop him.

"Hold those pictures if you want the real story that goes with them," he ordered. "I'll telephone you from Chicago."

Horace started to protest that he already had a wonderful human-interest story of the all-night search for Roberta and how she had been found asleep in the fir branches. But Peter told him to save it.

"It may be real front-page stuff," he promised, "if you're willing to wait."

The trip was everything Judy had imagined it would be—and more. Peter had seen to it that they had good seats where the wings of the plane could not get in the way of their vision. When they were finally in flight they could see everything for miles and miles.

"How funny the towns look, like little block villages!" exclaimed Roberta, gazing downward. She had opened the dog carrier and was holding Tuffy so that he could see, too.

"The fields would make a nice pattern for one of my grandmother's patchwork quilts," Judy commented after another few minutes of watching. "See, Roberta! Some are brown and some are green, and there's one that's a sort of misty yellow."

"But they're so far away!" lamented Roberta. "I don't believe I'd know my garden even if we flew right over it."

"We're flying to Chicago," Judy reminded her, "and I think Peter intends to look for your garden after we get there. He's acting awfully mysterious. Maybe he knows where it is already."

Peter shook his head.

"I won't be sure until I see it," he replied even more mysteriously.

Judy did not persist in her questioning, as the cloud formations around the plane were so unusual that she didn't want to miss them.

"Look! Down there and over there!" cried Roberta, bouncing up and down on the seat in her excitement. "I never thought clouds would look the same from the top as they do from the bottom. I used to play there were fairies riding on them only we couldn't see them because we were underneath."

"You're really going to believe in fairies before this trip is over," prophesied Peter.

He was smiling to himself as if his thoughts were very pleasant ones.

"I believe in them already," declared Judy. "I've always wished I could fly in a big airliner, and now I'm actually doing it. But Peter, Chicago is a big city, and the seed company didn't give us the local address of those people whose garden we're going to see.

How are we going to find it if they're not in the directory?"

"We'll find it," he replied. "One of our agents from the Chicago office is meeting us at the airport and driving us out into the suburbs. This is a business trip, Angel. You'll probably be taking a lot more like it."

What did Peter mean?

"But where are we going?" she asked impatiently. "So far you've told me nothing. 'The suburbs' could be anywhere within fifty miles of Chicago. Aren't we going to any one specific house?"

"We are, eventually. I wouldn't wonder if it's an English-type house with a stone chimney like ours and lots of peaks and gables. And that's absolutely all I can tell you at this point, Angel."

Judy eyed him intently. "Well, if it's that definite, I'm just going to relax and enjoy the trip without asking any more questions," she declared at last, leaning back in the comfortable seat and closing her eyes.

Both she and Roberta slept part of the way. Peter confessed later that he dozed off once or twice, too. But all three of them were wide awake when the plane roared into Chicago.

They were met by a young man who introduced himself as Phil Spear.

"Why not let the little lady sit up in front with me," he suggested as he escorted them to his own car. "We'll have to get acquainted. What's that you have in the basket? Not a lion, I hope."

"It's Tuffy," Roberta replied. "Peter said I could

bring him along because he wants to see my garden too."

"Oh, so you know you're going to see the Floyd garden!" Phil Spear exclaimed. He turned to Peter. "I understood we were to proceed cautiously. Good news is sometimes just as hard to break as bad news, and—"

"Don't worry," Peter said. "We'll break it gently. When you see a light in the stone lantern you'll know what to do."

"Peter!" Judy gasped, almost stuttering in her excitement. "If what I've been thinking you were thinking is really true—"

"Wait," Peter said quietly. "Just let's wait and see."

CHAPTER XXV

The Lost Garden

PETER'S PLAN, Judy soon discovered, had been carefully worked out over the telephone. Although he had not introduced himself as an FBI agent, Phil Spear must be the G-man from the Chicago office Peter had said would meet them.

"From here on you'll have to keep your eyes open, little lady," the young man advised Roberta. "Does anything look familiar?"

They were driving along a street lined with stores and shops. At the very end of it, as they looked back, they could still see the blue of Lake Michigan. The first part of their drive had been along the lake shore.

Roberta looked puzzled.

"Should it? There aren't any gardens along here."

"He means," Peter pointed out, "does it look at all like the street where you said all the people walked by without paying any attention to you that day you were lost?"

"In my dream, you mean?"

"It was no dream, Roberta. Think! We're trying to take you back along the same route you must have followed when you first wandered out of the garden and that man you thought was your father found you and told you your mother was dead."

"And took me to my grandmother's in Albany? Or wasn't she my grandmother, either? I never liked her very much so I hope she wasn't," Roberta added mat-ter-of-factly.

"She couldn't have been, could she?" asked Judy, who still could not believe the surprise that was in store for Roberta.

Peter shook his head.

"None of them were real relatives," he said gravely.

There was a little silence after that. It was a silence filled with suspense as Roberta watched eagerly from the car windows.

"If you recognize anything," the Chicago agent re-minded her, "just let us know."

They drove for another block.

"Anything familiar?"

"That movie!" Roberta exclaimed, almost falling out of the car in her excitement. "That was where all the people walked by!"

Phil Spear smiled his satisfaction.

"I thought so. In that case we'll park here and walk the rest of the way. It's about time that puppy had a walk anyway," he added, stopping the car. Tuffy bounded out eagerly when Roberta opened the door.

"Wait, Tuffy! Wait for us!" Roberta cried, running after him and fastening his leash to the little red harness he wore.

She stopped, her eyes bright with excitement.

"Hurry, everybody!" she called. "Pretty soon we'll come to the fence!"

"Is there a fence around the garden?" asked Judy.

"You'll see," Peter began. But Roberta was running again, the puppy leaping and barking at her side.

Judy hurried to overtake her. The little girl had reached the fence. Nothing could be seen beyond it but flowering shrubs and the upper branches of the evergreens that hid the garden she was so eager to see. Roberta ran on until she reached a high wrought-iron gate.

"It's locked!"

She rattled the chain on the gate she had discovered and then peered through it wistfully. Tears were streaming down her cheeks when Judy overtook her.

"Is it your garden?" Judy asked eagerly. "If it is, you have nothing to cry about. We'll get in, somehow, won't we, Peter?"

"Sure, we will," he replied. "You don't think we'd let a little thing like a gate stop us, do you?"

Roberta sighed deeply and dabbed at her eyes.

"In my dream it stopped me. I always woke up when I came to the gate."

"Watch this!" cried Phil Spear, vaulting over the

fence. "Now Peter can boost you and Tuffy up, and we'll be inside the garden."

"What about us?" asked Judy. "Aren't we going to see the garden, too?"

"Eventually," said Peter, lifting first the little girl and then the puppy to the top of the fence.

Phil Spear smiled as he put Roberta down, cautioning her not to run along the path between the evergreens, but to wait for him and to walk slowly.

"We mustn't be seen until the people in the house have been prepared for our coming—"

"I know," Roberta interrupted. "We must wait for the light in the stone lantern. Peter said so. We'll sit on the stone bench, if it's still there, and I'll read to you from this book of fairy tales I brought along. Tuffy likes to listen, too."

It all seemed to be part of the prearranged plan. They separated, and Judy and Peter walked around the block to the front of the house.

"Do Mr. and Mrs. Floyd expect us?" Judy asked in confusion. "If not, what will we tell them? It's going to sound awfully strange just to say we've come because Roberta wants to see their garden—"

"We won't say anything about Roberta at first," Peter declared as they rounded the corner. "See, it is an English-type house with little gables and a stone chimney, just as I told you. And I think you've guessed what I couldn't tell you until Roberta recognized the garden: Mr. and Mrs. Floyd are the 'Mr. and Mrs. Doe' whose baby was kidnaped."

"I did guess it," Judy confessed. "But, Peter, I still can't understand it. I thought the child who was kidnaped was just a little baby."

"She was," Peter replied. "She was only three years old at the time. It happened five years ago."

"Five years!" Judy exclaimed. "That's why I've been so baffled by all this, Peter. I thought it happened just recently."

She stopped. She couldn't tell what to think. It was all so unbelievable.

"The house looks so gay," she continued, still trying to make herself believe it. "Aren't those Oriental cherry trees in blossom? They're beautiful! And just look at the azaleas! Why, the whole place is just one big garden. It doesn't seem as if a tragedy could have happened here."

"We're pretty sure now that it isn't the tragedy Mr. and Mrs. Floyd believe it to be," replied Peter. "The first thing we have to tell them, though, is that four new suspects have been rounded up. This is going to be very official to begin with. We don't want to excite Mrs. Floyd."

"I can understand that," said Judy as Peter rang the bell, "if you think—"

She broke off abruptly as the door was flung open by a sturdy little fellow about five years old.

He stared at them with round eyes for a moment and then called at the top of his voice, "Mother! A man and a lady are here to see you. Can they stay to the party? It's an awfully big cake for just us."

The mother came hurrying to the door, her dark

hair a little disheveled and her face flushed. Judy forgot herself momentarily and frankly stared. There was something about her eyes . . .

Meantime, Peter was introducing Judy and himself very officially, showing his credentials. Mrs. Floyd immediately invited them in. Then she turned to the little boy.

"Ronnie, run upstairs and help little sister get ready. Mother doesn't want to be disturbed for a few minutes. This lady and gentleman may have something important to tell me."

"Can't they stay to the party?"

"We'll see. Now run along." She turned to Peter apologetically. "This is always an exciting day for the children," she explained. "You see, it's Barbara Sue's birthday. She would be just eight years old. You may think it odd, and perhaps it is, but we always have a little celebration with cake and ice cream just as if— well, just as if she were still with us. This year is the last time we'll do it, though, as both my husband and I have decided it will be easier if we stop entertaining false hopes. After all, we do have the other children to think of, and it's been five years— It will be better to try to forget."

"I know how you feel, Mrs. Floyd," replied Peter kindly, "but since I'm new on this case and my wife knows even less about it than I do, I may have to ask you to review some of the facts. You see, we've just recovered some of the ransom money and arrested four new suspects."

"I'm glad to hear that. They shouldn't be at large

to harm other children. But what about our little Barbara Sue? Is there no trace of her?"

There was a pause. It wasn't a question that could be answered immediately. Good news as well as bad, the Chicago agent had said, had to be broken gently. Judy could see that Peter was waiting for her to make the next move.

"Suppose we talk about it in the garden," she suggested.

If Mrs. Floyd thought this an odd request, she said nothing but merely smiled a little wearily as she led Judy and Peter through the house and opened a door that took them directly outside. The garden was just beyond an open patio where the party table was already set. Judy walked past it and stood speechless for a moment, gazing at the scene before her. Except for the taller flowers that would grow up and blossom during the summer, the garden was exactly like the picture on the package of alyssum seed.

"That is a stone lantern in the center, isn't it?" cried Judy, unable to curb her excitement. "And all those shiny stones along the edges of the flower beds. What are they?"

"Imported tiles. They do give a pretty effect, don't they?"

Mrs. Floyd was evidently pleased with her garden. She stood admiring it, little dreaming what was going through Judy's mind as she fully realized that the search for Roberta's lost garden was at an end.

CHAPTER XXVI

By Lantern Light

"WE HAVE A GARDEN almost like this," Judy said finally, when she could recover her voice. "We patterned it after a picture on a package of alyssum seed. Is that alyssum planted around the base of the lantern?"

"It is," replied Mrs. Floyd. "We always plant it there. I'm surprised you recognized it, though. It won't be blooming for another month."

"It was already in bloom on the seed package," Judy said.

"On the seed package?"

Mrs. Floyd was plainly puzzled.

"Wasn't your garden ever photographed?" asked Peter.

"Why, yes," she replied slowly, "Mr. Floyd won

several prizes before—before our tragedy. The photographs could have been copied without our permission, I suppose. We did try to avoid publicity."

"It's a good thing you didn't avoid it altogether," declared Peter. "You see, Mrs. Floyd, we don't want to raise false hopes, but we've had a little boarder at our house, and if she should turn out to be only eight years old instead of ten, as we thought—"

"But, Peter," Judy protested quickly, "we had her birth certificate. It was sent to us from the school in Albany along with her record card. According to her birth certificate, she is ten, and her name is Roberta Dunn. Could the certificate have been as fictitious as everything else?"

"No," Peter said, "It was genuine, but it wasn't hers. I told you there was never any Captain Dunn, but our investigation did reveal that a certain Robert Dunn was paroled recently from a western prison.

"I think," he continued, turning to Mrs. Floyd, whose dark eyes were now watching him tensely, "I'd better outline for you some of the facts as we now interpret them. This man's police record shows that he was once a presumably respectable citizen living with his wife and little girl, Roberta. He was a reckless driver, though, and due to his carelessness both his wife and child were killed in an accident."

"Oh!" exclaimed Judy. "How tragic. What happened after that?"

"Well, a man can either get over a thing or he can't. Evidently, Robert Dunn couldn't. He became bitter

—and greedy. The way we figure it, he found little Barbara Sue Floyd wandering alone on the street and recognized her. He took her with him, left Chicago, and brought her to his mother-in-law in Albany. He had no scruples whatever about substituting his own daughter's name for Barbara Sue's, and forcing his mother-in-law to pass the child off as her own granddaughter.

"In the meantime, his demands for ransom had been met, and Robert Dunn had forty thousand dollars that he didn't dare spend. He began to build up a fictitious background for the little girl, and Barbara Sue, who knew herself as Bobby, was taught that her real name was Roberta. He must even have taught her to call him Daddy."

"But she called all men Daddy!" Mrs. Floyd broke out, greatly excited. "We thought it was cute, but now I see it may have led her to trust this criminal."

"Apparently she thought, from the very first, that he really was her father," put in Judy. "Remember, Peter, she said herself that after she wandered off, her daddy found her and brought her to her grandmother's house because by that time her mother was dead."

"Is that what they told her? The poor baby!" gasped Mrs. Floyd.

"They even sent her a picture of the real Roberta's mother. I can understand now why the old woman moaned over the picture," Judy said.

"Then," Peter resumed, "after the grandmother

died, Dunn sent the child to live with an unsavory
pair named Griggs, who later were arrested on another charge. When Roberta landed with us, Robert
Dunn, for the first time, began to feel safe. He knew
from our letters that we were glad to have her and
that she was happy with us. He was reasonably sure
that Roberta—or Barbara Sue—remembered nothing
from the past and eventually would forget him altogether. Nearly five years had passed, and he had just
about decided it would be safe to start spending the
ransom money, when he was arrested for a relatively
minor crime and sent to prison. Recently he was paroled, but now he didn't dare spend the 'hot' money
because he had a criminal record. So he conceived the
idea of having a confederate steal good money in
large sums and leave the ransom bills in its place
whenever the opportunity could be made. The Scarecrow, Judy ^learned, was a professional burglar whom he had
met in prison.

"It was a risky business at best," Peter continued,
"but when he received Roberta's letter saying she
remembered the garden and the lantern, he must have
become panicky—"

"And sent the 'aunt and uncle' to take Roberta
away if they found she really did remember too
much!" Judy finished eagerly.

"But where is my baby now?" Mrs. Floyd asked,
and for the first time, there was hope in her voice.

At a nod from Peter, Judy took Mrs. Floyd gently
by the arm, intending to lead her down the garden

path. But just then Ronnie rushed outside, pulling his baby sister by the hand.

"Haven't they gone yet?" he demanded. "Joanie and I are hungry. When do we get the cake?"

"Patience," said his mother, who was now trembling noticeably. "We may invite them to stay for the party, but first they would like to take a walk in the garden."

Peter whispered something to the little boy, and his eyes grew round.

"Gee, Mother! We'll wait. We'll sit right here on the steps and not move till you tell us you're ready."

She smiled, and suddenly her eyes filled with tears. But she quickly composed herself and was smiling again as Judy walked over to the stone lantern.

"I'd like to light it if I may, Mrs. Floyd," she said, her own voice a little shaky.

"It is growing dark," Peter admitted.

Judy could feel the spell of the oncoming darkness. The sun had just set behind the evergreens that Roberta had called her Christmas trees. The rosy glow in the sky was still fading when Judy struck the match Peter handed her, and held it to the wick of the candle inside the lantern. Like magic the garden was aglow again.

"You see how it lights up the flower beds—"

"I do see," Judy returned softly. "Mrs. Floyd, you're going to bless this stone lantern. It was the only real clue we had."

"If the criminals hadn't circled the word 'lantern' in

Roberta's letter, that Judy found," Peter said, "we would not have realized it was something in the *past* and not in the future that they were afraid she'd remember."

"And if Roberta hadn't recognized the lantern on the seed package," Judy added, "we wouldn't have known the lost garden she was always talking about was anything more than a dream."

"It will be a dream come true for me," declared the excited mother, "if you have actually found her. How soon may I see this child you call Roberta?"

"Very soon," Peter promised. "I believe I hear her coming now."

There was a sudden sound of laughter and running footsteps on the walk under the Christmas trees. A happy voice exclaimed, "It is lighted! Now I can see it, too. Come on, Tuffy! Please, Mr. Spear, let's hurry. Now I *must* be dreaming. That lady with Judy and Peter looks the way my mother did in my dream. But who are the children on the steps, and whose party is it?"

"It's your party!" called Judy. "Surprise! Surprise! The children are your own brother and sister, and this—"

"It *is* my mother!" shrieked Roberta, running headlong into the arms that were outstretched to receive her.

They clung to each other for a moment, mingling tears with laughter. Then, with both hands, Mrs. Floyd held her little daughter away from her.

"I must look at you, dear," she said brokenly. "You've grown so tall, and your hair is so much lighter than it used to be. But your eyes are the same."

"They're like your own, Mrs. Floyd," Judy put in. "I noticed it the moment I saw you. I always called them chocolate brown."

"That's what her daddy used to call them. Oh, I can see how good you've been to her."

"We only made one mistake," confessed Peter with an understanding look in Judy's direction. "We loved her so much that it's going to be awfully hard to give her up."

"Bless you both!" exclaimed Mrs. Floyd. "My prayers have been answered. All I asked was that she might be kept from the evil influence of the criminal who tortured us with demands for ransom and then sent not one word of assurance that she was safe or—or even alive."

"Did *you* think *I* was dead, too, Mother?"

It was Barbara Sue Floyd who was asking the question. Judy was still trying to get used to the idea of calling her Barbara Sue instead of Roberta when the two younger children claimed her attention. They were excited, particularly when they discovered that the puppy had come to live with them, too. But they were not as surprised as Judy had supposed they would be. Ronnie had the same matter-of-fact way of speaking as his older sister.

"We knew you'd come home sometime," he stated. "Now can we have the cake?"

It was a wonderful party. Mrs. Floyd had rushed to the phone to tell her husband the marvelous news, but had been informed that he had already left his office and was not expected back that day. It was decided not to wait but to begin the celebration at once. Extra places were set and extra favors brought out. There were party hats and noisemakers for everybody, as well as ice cream and a big birthday cake with eight candles on it.

"Blow!" little Joanie directed when the cake was brought to the table.

"Wait!" cried Ronnie. "First we must sing." He opened his mouth wide and sang lustily:

> *"Happy birthday to you,*
> *Happy birthday to you,*
> *Happy birthday, dear Barbara,*
> *Happy birthday to you."*

Tuffy barked shrilly as the others joined in, some of them singing "Barbara," while Judy, by mistake, still called the little girl Roberta. Changing names wasn't easy. Neither was changing ages. Barbara Sue found it hard to believe that this was only her eighth birthday when, as Roberta, everybody had thought she was ten and small for her age. Her mother was surprised to hear that she was already in the fourth grade.

"I'm afraid I pushed her ahead a little," Judy confessed. "You see, when we received her birth certificate and her school record card, we—we thought she must be a little slow."

"Slow? With that memory?"

Phil Spear considered this a great joke.

He excused himself early, saying he had a report to make, but the others talked around the table until the garden had grown quite dark except where the light from the stone lantern shed its magic glow over the flower beds. There was so much to tell, so much lost time to be made up. Her family had missed five of the most precious years of their little girl's life. This thought sobered Mrs. Floyd even in the midst of all the gaiety.

When it was finally time to blow out the candle inside the lantern and go indoors, Judy managed to steal a moment alone with Barbara Sue.

"Is your lost garden everything you dreamed it would be?" she asked softly.

She wanted to be quite sure she was leaving the little girl she had known as Roberta completely happy with her newly discovered family.

Her face, as she turned to answer Judy's question, was radiant.

"It's more," she said, "much more. I didn't dream I'd have a brother and sister. I only wish my father—"

As if in answer to her wish, a shadow fell across the garden just as Judy was about to blow out the light. The face of his little girl appearing so suddenly before him took Mr. Floyd completely by surprise. Judy, seeing his white face, called out in swift alarm.

"Oh, Peter—quick! He's going to faint!"

If Peter had not instantly rushed to his aid, the shock

might have been too much for Mr. Floyd. After seating him quickly, Peter explained everything in a quiet voice, while Roberta's chocolate-brown eyes never once left her father's face.

"Daddy!" she burst out at last. "I should have known that man wasn't my real daddy. Now I remember your face as well as if I had walked out of the garden only yesterday."

"I recognized your face, too," the distraught father confessed, "even though you were only a baby when —when someone carelessly forgot to close the garden gate—"

"And I walked out. I do remember that. I remember running to meet you, too, and how you used to toss me up in the air and kiss me . . ."

It was amazing how much she did remember, Judy thought. The story would be in all the papers, of course. Peter already had telephoned Horace as he had promised, and photographers had arrived to take pictures of the reunited family. Again it was explained how the lost child had called Robert Dunn "Daddy" and how the idea of holding her for ransom had come to him, together with the notion of teaching Barbara Sue that her name was Roberta Dunn.

While Judy and Peter were still at the Floyds', David Trent called Peter long distance to report that a full confession had been obtained from the prisoners in Farringdon. Confronted by the fact that Roberta had been identified positively as Barbara Sue Floyd, Robert Dunn had admitted the whole crime. It was pure coincidence, he explained, that his first attempt to substitute ransom money for legitimate bills had taken place in Farringdon, so near where Roberta lived. During his sojourn in prison, another man, a former clerk in the offices of Mr. Heffly's lawyers, had told him how Mr. Heffly's affairs were being handled.

Seeing the possibilities of a successful swindle, Robert Dunn had come to Farringdon upon his release, and managed to ferret out the details of the real-estate deal with Arthur. He was careful, however, to keep under cover, as he was well aware of the danger of Roberta seeing him. The Scarecrow was to do all the actual work.

"Roberta's been boarding with us for nearly a year," Peter said, after he had repeated Mr. Trent's report to the others. "We hadn't the slightest notion, when we first agreed to the arrangement, that Captain Dunn as well as his shipping company were entirely fictitious. In fact, nothing more than a post-office box number, with the pair who posed as the aunt and uncle to answer any mail. When Dunn learned that Barbara Sue remembered more than he had thought she did, he was not at all eager for the surprise she promised in her letter, and sent the Rees couple on from Chicago to investigate."

"You might remind Robert Dunn when you see him in prison," Judy said, giggling, "that the last place in the world to board a kidnaped child is with an FBI man and his wife."

"For that matter, Angel," Peter pointed out with a smile, "you cracked the case before we did even though you didn't know it." He turned to Mr. and Mrs. Floyd. "You see," he explained, "Judy believed in the dream of the lost garden enough to write to the seed company. And just when I needed something to clinch my suspicions, along came their letter telling us that it was your garden that Roberta—Barbara Sue —had recognized on the seed package."

Judy sighed. "We couldn't have asked for a happier solution, could we, Peter? The Floyds have their lost baby, Roberta has found her garden, Arthur will get his ten thousand dollars back—"

"And you and I soon will take that wonderful vacation we've been talking about so long," Peter finished.

It would be wonderful, too. And exciting! More exciting than either of them guessed.

"You thought everything would work out like this when you planned the airplane trip, didn't you, Peter?" Judy said. "But you wouldn't tell me until you were sure you had the right answer and that I— I would be glad to give Roberta back to her own people. I am glad, of course."

Judy's voice did not betray her. But she had to turn her face toward the darkened garden so that Peter would not see the tears in her eyes.

Judy's vacation proves to be a "busman's holiday" right from the start. Mystery dogs her footsteps from the moment she receives the strange message on the deserted pier until she uncovers Fog Island's last terrifying secret. You won't want to miss THE SPIRIT OF FOG ISLAND.

Printed in the United States
119501LV00005B/1-78/P

FREDERICK LEONG
3406 TULANE DRIVE, APT. 14
HYATTSVILLE, MARYLAND_ 20783

November, 1981

D1320348

USING TESTS
IN COUNSELING

Leo Goldman

*The City University
of New York*

USING TESTS

IN COUNSELING

New York

APPLETON-CENTURY-CROFTS
EDUCATIONAL DIVISION
MEREDITH CORPORATION

ACKNOWLEDGMENTS

AMERICAN COUNCIL ON EDUCATION, quotation from *Educational measurement*, E. F. Linquist (Ed.) , 1951.

AMERICAN JOURNAL OF ORTHOPSYCHIATRY, quotation from *Motivational factors in aptitude testing*, R. Sears, 1943, 13.

AMERICAN PSYCHOLOGICAL ASSOCIATION, quotations from: *Ethical standards of psychologists*, 1953; Wanted—a good cookbook, P. E. Meehl, *Amer. Psychologist*, 1956, 11; Some correlates of test anxiety, S. B. Sarason & G. Mandler, *J. abnorm. soc. Psychol.*, 1952, 47; Increase in spatial visualization test scores during engineering study, M. F. Blade & W. S. Watson, *Psychol. Monogr.*, 1955, 69, No. 12 (Whole No. 397) ; Differentiation of individuals in terms of their predictability, E. E. Ghiselli, *J. appl. Psychol.*, 1956, 40; Long-term validity of the Strong Interest Test in two subcultures, C. McArthur, *J. appl. Psychol.*, 1954, 38; An investigation of client reactions to vocational counseling, J. Seeman, *J. consult. Psychol.*, 1949, 13; Personality inventory data related to ACE subscores, C. L. Pemberton, *J. consult. Psychol.*, 1951, 15; The intra-individual relationship between interest and ability, S. M. Wesley, D. Q. Corey, & B. M. Stewart, *J. appl. Psychol.*, 1950, 34.

EDUCATIONAL AND PSYCHOLOGICAL MEASUREMENT and the authors, quotations from: Present progress and needed improvements in school evaluation programs, W. N. Durost, 1954, 14; A study of client self-selection of tests in vocational counseling, J. Seeman, 1948, 8; A study of faking on the Kuder Preference Record, O. H. Cross, 1950, 10; The Tab Item: a technique for the measurement of proficiency in diagnostic problem solving tasks, R. Glaser, D. E. Damrin, & F. M. Gardner, 1954, 14; Effect of coaching on an aptitude test, J. W. French & R. E. Dear, 1959, 19; Problems of differential prediction, A. G. Wesman & G. K. Bennett, 1951, 11.

EDUCATIONAL TESTING SERVICE and the authors, quotations from: New light on test strategy from decision theory, L J. Cronbach, *Proceedings 1954 invitational conference on testing problems*, 1955; The logic of and assumptions underlying differential testing, J. W. French, and Clinical versus actuarial prediction, L. G. Humphreys, *Proceedings 1955 invitational conference on testing problems*, 1956; What kinds of tests for college admission and scholarship programs? R. L. Ebel, and The nature of the problem of improving scholarship and college entrance examinations, E. F. Lindquist, *Proceedings 1958 invitational conference on testing problems*, 1959.

HARPER & BROTHERS, quotation from *Guidance policy and practice* (2nd ed.) , R. H. Mathewson, 1955.

JOURNAL OF COUNSELING PSYCHOLOGY and the authors, quotations from: The effects of client and counselor personality characteristics on client learning in counseling, A. H. Tuma & J. W. Gustad, and When shall we use our heads instead of the formula? P. E. Meehl, 1957, 4.

iv

UNIVERSITY OF MINNESOTA PRESS, quotations from *Clinical vs. statistical prediction,* P. E. Meehl, copyright 1954 by the University of Minnesota.

NEWSWEEK, quotation from Testing: can everyone be pigeonholed? July 20, 1959.

OHIO STATE UNIVERSITY PRESS, quotation from Appraisal of special tests and procedures used with self-scoring instructional testing devices, D. G. Severin, *Abstracts of Dissertations,* 1955, No. 66, p. 330.

PERSONNEL AND GUIDANCE JOURNAL, quotations from: Guidance: manpower utilization or human development? D. E. Super, 1954, 33; A method for counseling engineering students, P. J. Stinson, 1958, 37; Educational and vocational counseling from the actuarial point of view, P. Horst, 1956, 35; The evaluation interview in vocational counseling, J. W. Gustad, and The preliminary appraisal in vocational counseling, D. E. Super, 1957, 36.

STATE TESTING AND GUIDANCE PROGRAM, THE UNIVERSITY OF TENNESSEE, quotation from The place of standardized testing in a guidance program, *Tennessee state testing and guidance program annual report, 1956-1957.*

TO MY PARENTS

Preface

My AWARENESS of the need for a book on this subject has been developing for a number of years. It has grown primarily out of experiences teaching graduate courses in testing and counseling and supervising students in the laboratory and in field-work placements in schools and agencies. Even though they were well-trained in guidance and counseling, or in counseling psychology, few students were ready to use tests skillfully as tools in the counseling process. In this important area, there seems to be a serious gap between the training program and the fully competent practitioner.

The introductory course in measurement can draw upon several excellent textbooks dealing with basic principles of tests and measurement and introducing the student to various types of tests. In addition, this basic work can be enriched with a variety of materials about tests, including the invaluable *Mental Measurements Yearbooks,* various series of bulletins from test publishers, and specimen sets of tests. However, in teaching a second measurement course for counselors, first at the University of Buffalo and more recently at Brooklyn College, I began to realize that additional areas of competency are necessary for the professional use of tests, and these are not adequately covered in our courses or in textbooks.

Perhaps the most important one is competency in *interpretation* of test results—the process of drawing information and hypotheses from a set of test scores. As I spent many hours discussing cases and interpretive problems with students, I became more and more aware of the considerable body of relevant materials and ideas, some published and others not, which had not been brought together and organized for the graduate student and the practitioner. Some of this consists of theoretical treatment and some of research reports, but a great deal is the accumulated experience of those who have counseled with adolescents and adults, especially in educational and vocational areas.

Another skill that is inadequately taught in measurement courses is that needed in *selecting* tests. True, this ability draws upon an understanding of basic principles of counseling and a fund of information about particular tests and their validities. However, these are not enough; here, too, there is a specialized body of theory, research, and practical skills that the counselor-in-training should acquire.

Observation of graduate students in their courses and on the job has indicated also that they have been insufficiently prepared to *communicate* test interpretations effectively to counselees, their parents, and other professional workers such as teachers and school administrators.

Other neglected topics were suggested by questions raised in classes, in the field, and at conferences. Some people have asked about the effects of excessive *anxiety* on test scores. Many did not know how to reconcile two apparently *contradictory scores* on ability tests or on interest and personality inventories. In high schools, teachers and administrators questioned the value of various kinds of *coaching* programs for college entrance examinations. Even with a matter as straightforward and concrete as the *scoring* of answer sheets, there appear to be unsatisfactory practices and a lack of awareness of desirable techniques.

In organizing these ideas and materials, I have committed myself to the point of view that competence on the part of the counselor requires his continuing efforts to understand and build upon current theories and research findings. Wherever possible, I have tried to interweave theory, research, and practice and to base discussions of techniques on a prior examination of pertinent research and theory. Although this book is intended primarily for the counselor-as-practitioner in schools and agencies, the counselor-as-research-worker should find many suggestions for hypotheses and for the design of studies.

A sabbatical leave from the University of Buffalo made possible a review of the literature and an attempt to organize the large amount of information that had accumulated over the years. The illustrative case materials were readily available, since I had been using them in teaching for some time, and my discussion of them has benefited from the thinking of many students. Other materials have been developed as lectures, particularly in the advanced measurement course given at Buffalo to majors in Guidance and Student Personnel and in Counseling Psychology. During the past two years much of the content of this book has been tried out in a similar course at Brooklyn College and in guidance institutes at the municipal colleges in New York City, at Rutgers University, and at the University of Buffalo.

Thus many graduate students have contributed to this volume. They helped to define their areas of need, they brought in reports of practices —good and bad—from their schools and agencies, and they brought a wealth of ideas.

It is not possible to name all the people who have in one way or another made contributions. One to whom I have long been indebted is Dr. Donald E. Super. For me, as for many graduate students at Teachers College, Columbia University, he provided not only an introduction to measurement but, much more broadly, an initiation into the manifold roles of the counseling psychologist. Perhaps, most important is his embodiment of the balanced and truly liberal approach of the scholar who can be both scientist and artist in a service profession. Dr. Super encouraged the undertaking of this volume and reviewed the entire manuscript, making a number of valuable suggestions.

Dr. Benjamin Rosner, a colleague first at the University of Buffalo and now at Brooklyn College, also reviewed the entire manuscript, with particular attention to statistical aspects. Portions of the manuscript were read by Dr. Michael A. Guerriero of The City College of New York and by Dr. Harry Beilin of Brooklyn College.

A counselor's skills in the use of tests are to a large extent developed on the job. One is fortunate to be on the staff of an agency or institution where competent and thoughtful colleagues share ideas and experiences. I have learned about testing from many colleagues at the Laboratory of Psychological Studies, Stevens Institute of Technology; at the New York Regional Office of the Veterans Administration; and at the Vocational Counseling Center of the University of Buffalo. I have also had the good fortune to teach graduate students who were on the staffs of a variety of institutions. In this way, it has been possible to learn about applications of tests in a number of elementary and secondary schools, colleges, state employment offices, rehabilitation agencies, vocational guidance centers, and in business and industry. It is a pleasure to acknowledge my indebtedness to all of them.

Thanks are due those authors, editors, and publishers who have given permission to quote at length and to reproduce tables, figures, and profile forms. They are mentioned specifically elsewhere.

Not least of all, my wife and two young daughters have helped more than I can say. They ungrudgingly did without vacation trips and spent many fine summer days at home so that the work could be completed.

East Rockaway, New York **L. G.**

Contents

Figures

Tables

USING TESTS
IN COUNSELING

CHAPTER 1

Introduction

THE PRODUCTION and consumption of educational and psychological tests have reached a level that is surely beyond the wildest dreams of those who developed the first standardized tests a half century ago. In a special report on testing in its issue of July 20, 1959, *Newsweek* reported that 122 million test booklets and answer sheets had been sold to schools alone during the previous year and that this represented an increase of 50 per cent over the sales figures for 1954. Equally impressive figures were reported for the use of tests in business, industry, and government.

Not only are more tests being used, but, at least in schools, they are being used increasingly for purposes of evaluation and guidance of individuals and less for administrative purposes (Traxler, 1959).

For a long time, the primary concern of those interested in tests has been the improvement of the tests themselves and the understanding of what tests can tell about a person. These goals have been approached by development of new tests and by research regarding the reliability and validity of existing tests. Textbooks on tests and measurement have for the most part emphasized the *facts about tests*.

Increasingly of late, however, there is a concern with the test *user* and with the operations involved in *using* tests with individuals and groups. Those who have observed the situation at close range are often appalled at the amount of misuse of tests which they see. Gross errors are made in all phases of testing operations—in the selection of tests, in their administration and scoring, in the selection of norm groups, and in the interpretation and reporting of the scores. For most of these phases it is difficult to obtain specific evidence of malpractice, but some estimate of the magnitude of the problem is conveyed by Durost's report of the prevalence of errors in the scoring process, which is perhaps the simplest of all the operations in a testing program:

. . . in handling hundreds of thousands of teacher-scored tests, I have found that from ¼ to ⅓ of them have to be completely rescored or re-interpreted to provide even enough accuracy for mass statistical treatment. As the operator of an IBM Test Scoring service, I am now finding that anywhere from 10 to 50 per cent of the answer sheets coming to me have to be re-marked and cleaned up before accurate scoring is possible. (Durost, 1954: p. 252).

It has been the author's observation that even relatively well-trained counselors are often quite at a loss in applying tests to problems of vocational planning, of educational appraisal, and other areas in which tests are used. Over and over one encounters questions like: "What is a good social studies test at the high school level?" asked by those who should be expected to know where to seek information of this sort and who should know also that one must first ask other questions, such as "What kinds of goals do we have in our social studies courses?" and "For what purposes is this test intended?" Similarly one observes frequent misinterpretations of test results: sometimes the interpreter implies a degree of precision that doesn't exist (such as "his IQ *is* 119"); sometimes he compares scores which are not comparable because of differences in norm groups; sometimes he implies a prediction for which there is absolutely no basis in either "statistical" or "clinical" validation. Finally, there is an alarming amount of misuse and disuse of test results. The former is illustrated by the practice of sending home to parents a copy of their child's test profile with the assumption that they are qualified to interpret it. The latter is seen in the "filing and forgetting" of test results in schools which lack the guidance staff to do anything with the scores after they have been obtained.

From the vantage point of this observer, the impression has been that many, if not most, of the tests currently in use are either wasted or, even worse, used in such a way as to misinform and mislead. Perhaps this is one of the reasons that tests stand in disrepute among so many teachers, parents, businessmen, and others. It is becoming clear that we need to be much more concerned than we have been in the past with the *use* of tests and with the *users*. In the *Newsweek* report cited earlier, Dr. Harold Seashore, vice-president of the Psychological Corporation, is quoted as saying: " 'The biggest problem today is not the tests themselves. . . . It is getting a supply of competent professionals to interpret and make proper use of the tests. For every $500 a school spends on the tests themselves, it should spend $15,000 on salaries for personnel to supervise and interpret the tests.' " *(Newsweek,* July 20, 1959: p. 93) .

What factors are responsible for the unhappy situation which prevails? First, and most obvious, is the inadequate training of large numbers of test users, including even many who carry such titles as "counselor" and "personnel manager." Second, perhaps not so obvious, is the underdevelopment of that area of counseling psychology which has to do with the *use* of tests as contrasted with their development and standardization. It is the aim of the present work to focus on the second of these factors, to bring together available knowledge of the use of tests, and to point out some of the major gaps in the current state of knowledge in this area. The remainder of this chapter deals briefly with each of these two factors and in doing so provides an overview of the structure and contents of the chapters which follow.

QUALIFICATIONS OF TEST USERS

Large numbers of teachers, counselors, advisers, and personnel people in schools, colleges, businesses, and government and other agencies have few qualifications for using tests other than a background in the school, business, or agency in which they work, and perhaps some interest in studying and helping people. They are all too often encouraged in their gropings by salesmen of "self-administering" and "self-interpreting" tests. They are all too seldom supervised by a person who knows any more than they do about tests and their use. If the test user is on the staff of a school or a business firm, he has fairly easy access to most tests of almost all publishers. Although some publishers have established minimum qualification for test purchasers, these are generally quite liberal for those who order on a school or company letterhead. Presumably what they do intramurally is "their own business," but it is obvious that these intra-institutional testing programs affect large numbers of people; indeed, we are rapidly approaching the time when every American school child is on the receiving end of one or more standardized tests.

It cannot be assumed that state and local certification requirements provide assurance of the competency of test users in schools, for two reasons: First, certification for guidance workers, even in those states in which it exists, often calls for only a bare minimum of relevant professional education. Second, testing activities in many schools, particularly at the elementary level, are under the direction, not of counselors or psychologists, but often of teachers and administrators whose certification usually calls for no training at all in such relevant areas as statistics, measurement, and counseling.

In colleges, business firms, and government and community agencies, there is usually not even the small protection afforded by certification procedures. Some business establishments have turned over their testing operations to high-pressure "consultants" of no professional standing, who do not hesitate to give interpretations and to make recommendations which go far beyond what they or their tests can properly do. Since a sense of professional ethics does not stand in their way, they can make promises which are far more appealing than the more conservative statements of competent psychologists. The uncritical acceptance of test interpretations was demonstrated vividly by Stagner (1958). He showed that half of a group of personnel managers were ready to accept as accurate descriptions of themselves a set of uniform generalizations, extracted from dream books and astrology charts, but presented to them as individualized interpretations of a personality inventory which they had filled out. For the sake of balance, it should be added that the use of tests is, in some companies and in many agencies and colleges, under the direction of well-qualified psychologists, counselors, personnel workers, and others. It should also be noted that a similar uncritical attitude was found in an earlier study with college students (Forer, 1949).

For the protection of the community, it seems time to set considerably higher standards for test users and to establish controls, whether voluntarily by test publishers or by certification or licensing, to eliminate at least the blatant malpractice. As a minimum, the public is entitled to assurance that all testing activities are carried on under the direct and responsible supervision of individuals who have had training in accredited programs, whether in counseling psychology, educational guidance, or tests and measurement. Ideally, the training should be at the doctoral level, but it is certainly not too soon to insist on the master's degree in one of these fields as the minimal level. To the objection that these qualifications are unnecessary, one need only point to the vast amount of misuse of tests and to the rapidly increasing body of knowledge about tests and about their uses; the misuse must surely be at least partly attributable to ignorance of this body of knowledge. To the objection that the proposal is not feasible, there are at least two answers: First, it has been done in other similar fields, as witness the rapid raising of standards in recent years for some kinds of applied psychological specialists, including counseling psychologists in the Veterans Administration, rehabilitation counselors in state agencies, and, in some parts of the country, the school psychologist. The funds being expended under the National Defense Education Act for training of secondary school counselors are further evidence of the readiness to raise standards.

Second, if it is truly not possible for test users to attain the minimal level of training here proposed, then there is the question of whether they are likely to do more harm than good with tests and whether, therefore, their schools, companies, or agencies would be better off to use no tests at all than to run the risks attendant on unprofessional use. It is difficult to justify a position in this matter any different from the one we would expect if it were suggested that a school institute a program of chest X-rays for all students, administered and the pictures interpreted by the biology teacher or school nurse, because a properly qualified physician was beyond the means of the organization. True, our testing devices do not have nearly the precision of X-ray pictures, but this is even more reason to insist that educational and psychological tests be used only by those who are aware of all the limitations. If it be argued that the tests used in counseling are so crude that it makes little difference whether one has much training or not, this should be followed to its logical conclusion: that such instruments have no place in a program of assessment and counseling. However, the fact is that, limited as it is, there awaits the serious scholar of tests and measurement a large body of research, theory, and techniques, all of which contribute toward making tests a useful tool in the hands of competent practitioners.

The Reader

It is assumed that the reader has attained or is in process of completing the minimal level of professional education defined above and that he has at least the following specific background:

1. A foundation in relevant areas of psychology and sociology, with particular emphasis on courses usually designated as "developmental psychology," "personality," and "individual differences."
2. A framework for the use of tests in his particular setting. This will normally come from such courses as "principles of guidance" and "introduction to counseling psychology."
3. A background in elementary statistics, which provides both a reading knowledge of statistical concepts and terms and some skill in computation.
4. Understanding of the basic principles of tests and measurement. Whether it was obtained in a previous course or in the same course in which the present material is used, the reader is assumed to have fairly substantial understanding of such concepts as reliability and validity, to be familiar with the types of tests used in counseling, and to have had some first-hand experience (even if only of an observational nature) with a sampling of the more widely used tests of aptitude, interest, personality, and intelligence.

It might be added somewhat parenthetically that graduates of some reputable graduate training programs in guidance and in counseling psychology have not had adequate course and laboratory work in what is here called the *use* of tests in counseling. As is detailed in the following section, the emphasis in most graduate programs has been on the tests themselves and their characteristics. Few programs have provided courses which deal with the *utilization* of tests in the counseling process.

THE LITERATURE ON USING TESTS IN COUNSELING

A distinction is made here between those articles and books which focus on the tests themselves, their validities, norms, and other characteristics and those which report research, theory, and techniques related to the use of tests in the counseling process. The latter group deal with such aspects as selecting tests for particular purposes, administering and scoring them, interpreting their results, and reporting the interpretations to counselees, teachers, and others.

In the first area—that concerning the tests themselves—the body of literature is now quite large, having been built up over the years since the first extensive use of paper-and-pencil tests during World War I. During the period beginning with the second World War, research and theory have expanded considerably, and a number of new and improved tests have been introduced. During this same period, professional associations have sponsored and distributed criteria for tests and for test manuals (American Educational Research Association, *et al*, 1955; American Psychological Association, *et al*, 1954). As a result of these and other developments, today's typical test manual is a far cry from the two- or four-page manuals which were common a decade ago. Now manuals are often small books packed with technical information, reflecting the extensive test development procedures, large-scale normative studies, and other research which are demanded by the new standards.

In addition to the literature on the tests themselves, there have been in the past decade at least the beginnings of long-range and large-scale studies of measured characteristics as they relate to educational, vocational, and personal development (see, for example, Flanagan and Dailey, 1959; Super, 1957a; Thorndike and Hagen, 1959). These studies, like those involved in test development, require the organized efforts of numbers of workers and, often, financial support of foundations and the Federal Government. Although there are still important contributions being made by individual research workers operating on small budgets, it seems clear that the large-scale studies are necessary if we are to have the data which will some day make it possible to remove much of the guesswork from testing.

The foregoing paragraphs have dealt with the first of the two subdivisions of the professional literature—that which concerns itself with the tests themselves, with the human characteristics which they represent, and with the later behaviors which they predict. When we shift our focus to those articles, monographs, and books which deal with the *uses* of tests in the counseling process, we find far less material, whether in the way of theory, research reports, or descriptions of techniques and programs. Most textbooks on tests and measurement in guidance and counseling devote far more space to the tests than to their uses. Yet, as will be seen in the chapters that follow, there is no shortage of important and perplexing topics in this area.

In seeking an explanation of this state of affairs, one is led to place a great deal of weight on the changing emphases in counseling and in counseling psychology. The 1940's and 1950's saw an increasing emphasis on what might be called the therapeutic aspects of the counseling process—those aspects which have to do with helping clients to achieve insight, to accept themselves, and to deal with their *feelings* regarding their plans and decisions. It was more fashionable to talk about the "helping" process than about the appraisal process, whether at professional conferences or in graduate seminars. Similarly, occupational and educational information was played down as being of little importance as compared with the client's *feelings* about an occupation or an educational program. In general, there was a devaluation of educational and vocational counseling and a corresponding increase in the value assigned to personal and emotional counseling.

In retrospect, these developments seem to have been a necessary and desirable antidote to the earlier neglect of emotional aspects of guidance and counseling. However, after a while it became apparent that there could be too much of the antidote, beneficial as it might be in small doses. We now recognize the values both of facts and of feelings and are moving toward a better balance, indeed a synthesis, between the two. During the past few years there has been something of a renascence of educational and vocational counseling, and of cognitively oriented guidance in general, as contrasted with the earlier preoccupation with pathology and with emotions. There seems to be some movement of counseling back toward its earlier role of helping people to make plans and decisions about very concrete aspects of their lives. Associated with this development is the growth of *counseling psychology* as a full-fledged specialty of professional psychology, with increasing stress on the doctorate as the standard requirement for independent functioning. Along with this trend have come an expanded literature, including a number of new books on old subjects, but now at a higher theoretical level. There have also been a number of substantial research studies and finally a journal devoted to psychological aspects of the new specialty, the *Journal of Counseling Psychology*.

It is interesting to note that books on tests and measurement in counseling and in counseling psychology have emphasized the tests themselves, with stress on evidences of validity. The comparable literature of testing as applied to clinical psychology has dealt much more with the use and interpretation of tests and much less with their validities. Clinical psychologists have available to them a number of books which deal primarily with interpretation of such tests as the *Rorschach* and the *Thematic Apperception Test* (and which sometimes neglect the topic of validity). It is hoped that the newer interest in the counseling field in test interpretation (and test utilization in general), when synthesized with the earlier interest in validity, will result in a higher level of usefulness of tests.

It is likely that a book on this subject published ten years hence will reflect a far superior level and organization of testing theory, research, and practice, all of which will make possible considerably more effective use of tests in counseling. Indeed, the more theoretically inclined may feel that such a book should await those further developments, rather than reflect the patchwork quilt which is today's knowledge in this area. Unfortunately, or otherwise, the practitioner does not wait for more adequate theory and research. He uses tests in his counseling practice as best he can, keeping up with the literature to an extent commensurate with his training, his professional conscience, and the prevailing attitudes of his work-setting. Any attempt to organize for him the current knowledge in our field, however limited it may be, will provide the practicing counselor with some basis for evaluating and improving his work in the utilization of tests in counseling.

LIMITS OF THE PRESENT WORK

We shall deal here with that cluster of tests sometimes called "guidance tests." These are for the most part those paper-and-pencil, group-administered tests and inventories that are used by guidance counselors in schools and by counselors and counseling psychologists in colleges, the Veterans Administration, and in a variety of agencies. The applications to be highlighted are those which have to do with educational and vocational planning, including the appraisal of maladjustment in these areas of living. Even more specifically, we are concerned with tests as they are utilized by counselors and counseling psychologists in connection with *individual counseling* in these various settings.

Because the direct experience of the writer has been for the most part with adolescents and young adults, most of the illustrative cases and the types of tests discussed are appropriate to those age groups and to the educational-vocational counseling setting. It is hoped, however, that the principles discussed will have some applications for counselors who work with younger or older groups than these.

The particular tests used in the cases also reflect the experiences, preferences, and limitations of the author. Thus, the *Strong Vocational Interest Blank* receives considerable attention, in part because it is one of our most valuable instruments, but also because of personal experience with it in settings where it was especially useful. On the other hand, little mention is made of the *Minnesota Multiphasic Personality Inventory* and of a number of other useful instruments, including the individually administered tests of intelligence. In some settings, the *MMPI* is a standard tool; this seems especially so among college counseling centers. In some agencies, the *Wechsler* tests of intelligence are used fairly routinely in counseling regarding educational, vocational, and personal matters. One can, however, best instruct others in the use of tools and techniques with which he has had personal experience in a counseling setting.

It does not necessarily follow that the reader will develop understandings and skills only in the use of the particular tests given here for illustrative purposes. On the contrary, it has been the author's intention to stress *principles* rather than specific techniques and to describe methods, as far as possible, in a framework of theory. The reader can then generalize some of these techniques and methods to other tests by studying those tests and their respective literature and by trying them in his own counseling practice. For a few tests, there is such an extensive literature that entire volumes have been devoted to them; in the counseling area, this is true of the *Strong* and the *MMPI*. An annotated list of such references may be found at the end of Chapter 4.

Similarly, it is hoped that some of the methods discussed here will be found usable in appraisals other than those of an educational and vocational nature. For example, to the extent that specific tests are found to be valid for predicting marital adjustment, successful outcomes of counseling, or likelihood of engaging in delinquent behavior, many of the same principles and practices of test selection, administration, and interpretation which apply to educational and vocational prediction may be applied to those kinds of counseling. Ideally, it would be desirable to have a separate treatment of the use of tests in each of these content areas, but until this is available, the thoughtful reader can extemporize by making use of available resources.

Also excluded here is a systematic treatment of nontest methods of studying and appraising individuals. There are presently in print a number of books which focus on the use of interviews, sociometrics, autobiographies, rating scales, and other techniques in the appraisal process. As will be noted in later chapters, the nontest devices are used together with tests in the "clinical" process of test interpretation, and even sometimes in "statistical" interpretations.

WHAT IS TO FOLLOW

We shall follow a chronological sequence, dealing with each of the aspects of test usage in the order in which they normally occur in the counseling process. Thus, Chapter 2 deals with *purposes* of tests, stressing the counseling uses, but including some noncounseling uses, in part for the sake of broader perspective, but also because a single test score may serve several different purposes—counseling, curriculum evaluation, or research. Chapter 2 also makes an attempt to provide a broad *framework* for the use of our tests, in terms of the society as a whole, as well as the particular institutions.

Chapters 3 and 4 are concerned with the *selection* of tests for particular individuals or groups, the first dealing with *process* aspects, primarily with the question of client participation in the process of selection, and the second emphasizing the principles, methods, and materials used in choosing a particular test for a particular purpose.

In Chapter 5 several topics having to do with the process of test administration are brought together. However, little attention is given to mechanical aspects of the process—directions, time limits, and so on. Instead, the emphasis is on the *psychology of test-taking* in terms of the client's feelings as he takes a test, the relevant attitudes that he brings to tests, and the processes by which he arrives at his answer to a test item.

Chapter 6 deals with the scoring of tests, including both machine and hand methods. There is detailed consideration of what should be recorded on an answer sheet to make it optimally useful to the test interpreter.

Continuing the chronological process, Chapters 7 to 13 focus on several aspects of the process of *interpretation* of test scores. First, in Chapter 7, there is a *theoretical framework* for interpretation, followed by discussion of statistical and clinical methods of interpretation in Chapters 8, 9, and 10. Chapter 11 consists of *case reports* which serve to illustrate the principles and the general methods of interpretation. Chapter 12 contains a detailed discussion of two related problems in test interpretation—first the question of deciding when two scores are actually different from each other and second, the problem of explaining and reconciling apparent *contradictions* between two or more test scores. Completing the treatment of the interpretive process, Chapter 13 includes a miscellany of topics which, for one or another reason, seem to warrant separate consideration.

The chronology ends in Chapters 14 to 16 with that phase of test use which has to do with *reporting* results to clients and to others who have some legitimate use for them. These last chapters move from theory and research foundations to principles and finally to specific methods and materials for communicating results of tests to our relevant audiences.

CHAPTER 2

Purposes of Testing

THE SPECIFIC PURPOSES for which tests are used in counseling need first to be considered within the broader framework in which counseling occurs, beginning with the culture as a whole and then narrowing down to the particular institutions in which counseling activities are carried on. Both the culture and the particular institution play important parts in setting the goals and the limits of the counselor's work. Then, to add further to the framework, there is a summary of some of the noncounseling uses of tests, followed next by the counseling uses themselves. The chapter ends with a discussion of some ethical considerations in the use of tests.

THE CULTURAL FRAMEWORK

As Super (1954) has pointed out, certain characteristics of North American culture have influenced vocational counseling to develop with an orientation quite different from that in a number of European and Asian nations. The democratic traditions and values of the United States and Canada have resulted in a conception of vocational counseling, for example, as "human development," to use Super's phrase. In France, India, and various other countries, by contrast, it is "manpower utilization" which has tended until recently to be the ultimate purpose of vocational counseling services. Here, then, guidance tests are used primarily to help the individual develop his potentialities to the fullest and to his own satisfaction. In the other countries, both the ". . . underdeveloped but dynamic countries and in more industrialized countries with disturbed economies, guidance tends to be viewed, as (a) a vocational problem and activity, and (b) a means primarily for obtaining the needed supply and distribution of trained manpower. . . ." (Super, 1954: p. 14).

The North American cultural framework thus provides the counselor as test user with his ultimate criterion in the use of tests, that is, how will this help my client? This orientation, however, may be modified and even negated by the influence of the particular institution employing the counselor, as we shall see later.

To Choose or to Change

A related philosophical conflict, this time within psychology, has been discussed by several writers, most recently by Cronbach in his Presidential Address to the American Psychological Association (1957). Cronbach contrasts the "correlational" stream of psychology with the "experimental" and points out that test development and interpretation have been largely in the former tradition. That is, there has been an interest primarily in appraising the individual for the purpose of finding his place among other individuals in school, on the job, and elsewhere. The emphasis has been on estimating in which of several possible placements the individual is most likely to be successful and/or satisfied. The counselor says to the client, although not necessarily in so many words, "If you try for a drafting course in a vocational high school you should have an easy time of it; if you aim at a two-year technical institute program, you will have your hands full but should do average work; and if you attempt a four-year engineering program, your chances are quite poor."

With the "experimental" approach, on the other hand, the concern is less with individual differences and more with the effects of different "treatments" (courses of study, jobs, psychotherapy) on people in general. The implication here is that the environment (jobs, school courses) is modified in such ways as to make it likely that people will learn and function more effectively than they would otherwise. This approach is in the tradition of the experimental psychologist in the laboratory, who has little interest in individual differences among his animal or human subjects (as Cronbach says, he considers such differences an annoyance). Instead, the experimenter attempts to manipulate his equipment, the arrangement of trials and types of stimuli, so as to discover which conditions lead to optimal learning and functioning by the subjects *as a group*.

As Cronbach points out, each of the approaches has a blind spot. The correlational approach, although it is sensitive to differences among people, has a kind of sterility, in that "By reducing failures, they remove a challenge which might otherwise force the institution to change" (Cronbach, 1957: p. 679). The experimental approach, on the other hand, which encourages man to shape his environment, has as its blind spot a considerable degree of insensitivity to differences among people. As a result, all are treated alike, and the "treatment" which is considered most effective is that which yields the highest *average* performance level.

Applied to measurement in guidance, the experimental approach in its pure form would use tests to determine the conditions under which abilities, interests, and personality characteristics develop and would recommend those conditions which lead to the most desired changes in groups of people. Test scores would be seen as *results* of the particular environmental conditions. The correlational approach, by contrast, *begins* with test scores and seeks to locate those existing environments in which a person with a particular constellation of abilities, interests, and other characteristics, is most likely to do well. Here the person's characteristics are *causes* rather than results.

Ideally, the user of tests in counseling should be able to benefit from a careful synthesis of selected elements from both approaches. A school or college counselor, for example, may feed back to those responsible for curriculum development selected information regarding the distribution of abilities and other characteristics of the student body. Not only can he describe them, but he has also learned (if he has listened) something about the effects of the environment: which courses have produced beneficial effects, and which have not, which particular teaching approaches stimulate students and which interfere with learning. But now we must add an element from the correlational approach: It should be even more valuable to teachers and curriculum evaluators to know something about the experiences of *different kinds* of students. How many do we have, for example, who function best with concrete facts and materials rather than with abstract ideas? Having answered this descriptive question, the test user can contribute even further if he can offer some insights as to the curricular content and methods which lead to desired goals for one kind of student and which serve better for the other. In fact, Cronbach suggests that we need a new kind of test, one which will not only reflect differences among people but also will suggest new kinds of environmental change which could lead to a higher order of functioning for the individuals.

The counselor can in this way make additional contributions to his clients, not so much in the old sense of *manipulating* their environments, but rather with the intent of feeding back to those responsible for planning the curriculum or the job what he has learned about the effects of existing and proposed conditions on people as he knows them. None of this implies that it is desirable for counselors to eliminate or even to reduce their more traditional practice of helping individuals to learn what their chances are likely to be in one existing school program as compared with another, in one occupation as compared with another, in one social or community activity as compared with another.

Another kind of synthesis of elements from the two approaches is expressed in a test interpretation such as this:

The way you are now, with a reading handicap and a lack of verbal fluency, your chances are poor in colleges *A, B,* or *C,* but you should be able to do fairly well in colleges *X, Y,* or *Z.* However, from your measured intelligence and from various other things we know about you, the chances are good that remedial work in reading and in English, of the kind offered in such-and-such courses, would raise your level of functioning in those areas. If that happens, then our estimate of your chances of succeeding in colleges *A, B,* or *C* would go up proportionately. You must decide whether to enter that environment in which you have the greatest likelihood of success *as you are* (but which you don't prefer), or whether to try to *change* yourself and thereby to be better equipped to function in the environment which you do prefer.

As Buckton and Doppelt have pointed out in referring to remedial work of this kind: "This actually means that the counselors are trying to upset predictions implied by the test scores" (1950: p. 358).

THE INSTITUTIONAL FRAMEWORK

All counselors, except those in private practice, work within the framework of a particular institution, be it a school, college, government or community agency, or business organization. The characteristics of the setting inevitably affect the way in which counseling in general and testing in particular are carried on. These effects may be in terms of *demands* upon the counselor for certain kinds of contributions, such as emphasis on measures of academic aptitude for purposes of sectioning in a high school. The effects may be *proscriptions* upon certain kinds of testing, such as personality testing because "it's too personal." Finally, the effects may be *limits,* such as those which make it difficult to use as many tests as one would like to, because of the cost or the limits of a heavy case load, which makes it impossible to do extensive test interpretation except for a small number of cases.

To the influences exerted by the institution proper should be added those emanating from the *community* of which it is a part.[1] This kind of influence seems to be most prevalent in schools below the college level; parents and taxpayers have certain expectations, ill-defined as they may be, which affect the work of counselors in the area of testing. They may, for example, put pressure on the school to emphasize college application and placement and thereby to emphasize academic aptitude and achievement tests.

The values, needs, and perceptions of the institution and its community (including the students or whoever are the test-takers) inevitably affect the testing activities of the counselor. In many high schools, counseling is perceived as educational-vocational in nature, and neither students nor teachers see the counselor as one to whom personal matters are brought (Grant, 1954). It might be expected, as a result, that aptitude and achievement tests, and perhaps interest inventories, are emphasized

---

[1] A dramatic example was the decision by a Texas school board to burn answer sheets of 5,000 ninth graders on six sociopsychometric instruments (Nettler, 1959). Local newspapers reported that some parents objected vigorously to such inventory items as "I enjoy soaking in the bathtub" and "Sometimes I tell dirty jokes when I would rather not."

in such a setting, but not personality inventories. (One might wonder which is cause and which effect: Do the kinds of services offered in the guidance program cause the reported student perception, or did student expectations and preferences cause the program to be structured in that way?) In some colleges and universities, on the other hand, the counseling center is perceived as a place to which one refers disturbed and mal-adapted students; with such referrals, relative emphasis on personality measures is not surprising. Finally, referrals to specialized vocational counseling centers are frequently made by school counselors and by others in such a way that the client expects to be appraised and advised. In these cases, counselors find it difficult to avoid a prescriptive and diagnostic kind of testing approach and to involve their clients in a more active and more personal counseling relationship.

The limits may be explicit, as in the Veterans Administration counseling program in regional offices and contract centers, where there has been a list of "approved" tests, other tests requiring special permission of higher headquarters. More often the limits are less obvious and direct (though sometimes even more controlling) as in the college counseling program where a single battery of freshman tests is expected to provide most of the test data needed for selection of students, for sectioning, for referral to remedial courses, and for guidance. Such a setting encourages "saturation" rather than "precision" testing (Super, 1950) ; that is, the battery may include everything that might be wanted for one or another student, with the result that each student takes some tests that for him are not functional. In fact, it seems to be generally true in schools and colleges that most of the tests used in counseling are those which have been given to entire groups (such as applicants for admission to a college or the entire ninth grade of a junior high school) . Such mass testing programs are encouraged by administrators for their advantages of economy of time and money; there is less concern about the motivational problems and the resulting doubtful reliability of the test scores obtained. (There will be further discussion of problems related to group testing programs in Chapter 3.)

Such, then, are some of the institutional influences on testing activities in counseling programs. All too rarely, apparently, do counselors in institutions have opportunities to plan their programs in the manner described by Dingilian (1956) , so that testing is carried on in the framework of a carefully conceived rationale. Instead, testing, whether done programmatically or on an individual client basis, seems more often than not to be the result of a haphazard series of occurrences and subject to change in an equally casual manner. This is especially true in schools, where often there are no persons responsible for the planning of testing activities who have the necessary qualifications in terms of training and experience.

THE COUNSELOR'S PERSONAL ORIENTATION

In addition to the influences previously mentioned, there are others resulting from the counselor's personal approach to his work with clients. The "client-centered" counselor, for example, may not use tests at all, or perhaps only at a client's specific request, while a "trait-and-factor centered" counselor is likely to measure rather routinely early in the counseling process.

The counselor's "degree of leadingness" (Robinson, 1950), affects not only the extent to which he will use tests at all, but also his manner of selecting tests and the way in which test results are later interpreted and then reported to the client. Each of these aspects of test usage—selection, interpretation, and reporting—will be reviewed in considerable detail in later chapters. For now it should suffice to say that the counselor's degree of directiveness is one determinant of the manner in which he selects tests and uses the test results. Less directive counselors are more likely to share the planning of tests with clients and, in the interpretation process, to stay close to the scores themselves, or perhaps to go one step further and state only the probabilities of whatever it is the test is being used to predict. More directive counselors can be expected to assume greater responsibility for choosing the tests to be used and later to go beyond mere reporting of scores and to suggest alternative courses of action and even to recommend a particular one.

Counselors also differ in the confidence which they place in tests; this is somewhat independent, it would seem, of the directiveness variable mentioned previously. Directive counselors often, though not always, use tests as a basis for their recommendations or suggestions; they may, however, be equally directive without tests, basing their suggestions or advice on data collected in the interview, from school records, and from other nontest sources.

USES OF TESTS

Having considered some of the cultural, institutional, and other personal determinants of the uses to which tests are put, we now move on to a closer look at these uses. Although our focus is to be on tests in counseling, it will be wise first to summarize some of the noncounseling uses, if only to sharpen the focus later. Often the same tests may serve both kinds of purposes. As Weitz *et al* (1955) have pointed out, institutions often overlook multiple uses of a single test, thereby incurring unnecessary duplication of test activities. It is particularly important, as educational guidance programs broaden their bases and provide consultant assistance to teachers and others, to be aware of these extracounseling values of tests.

The Principle of Validity

Since this applies to almost all uses of tests (a few exceptions will be noted among the counseling applications), a word should be said about the principle of *validity* and about the related topic of *decision theory*.

In most of the uses of tests, *information* is collected for the purpose of improving the nature of decisions, plans, and adjustments. This is as true of the decision regarding a pupil's grade placement as it is of the decision regarding an adolescent's vocational plans. There is always an assumption, whether stated or not, that the test results provide information which is *valid* for the action in question. In connection with grade placement, for example, it is assumed that a pupil's scores on achievement tests tell something about how well he will do in one grade as compared with another. Specifically, we might judge that a fifth grade pupil with grade equivalent scores in reading and mathematics at the 7.8 level, using local norms, would, in terms of academic work, be more appropriately placed in the sixth grade, or even in the seventh grade.[2] In the case of vocational decisions, it is assumed that measured aptitudes in some way are related to success and/or satisfaction in an occupation. As an example, one might conclude that because a youngster has higher verbal than nonverbal scores, he would be more successful in a verbal than a nonverbal kind of occupation.

The fact of the matter is that validity is very meagerly established, when at all, for most of the situations in which tests are used in guidance work. We are, for the most part, assuming certain validities on the basis of "common sense," "clinical judgment," and sometimes sheer speculation. Sometimes we seek to avoid the assumption of validity by declaring that we are simply *describing* the individual to himself and then permitting him to draw his own conclusions as to the educational, occupational, and other implications of his appraisal portrait. There is implied here an even more questionable assumption, namely, that the client knows something about the validity of these tests that the counselor does not. Here is the *reductio ad absurdum* of a completely client-chosen battery of tests. Knowledge of validities is the counselor's province; what the client *can* participate in are decisions as to *what* is to be predicted, or what decision theory refers to as the decision and its "outcomes" (Bross, 1953; Cronbach and Gleser, 1957). That is, the client may have ideas as to which decisions—courses of action such as school courses and jobs—he is interested in considering. He certainly must have preferences regarding outcomes or goals, such as salary, grades, amount of leisure time, prestige or parental approval. But it is the responsibility of the counselor to decide which tests can furnish

---

[2] This assumes that the 7.8 grade equivalent is not just an extrapolation but actually represents a level of functioning comparable to that of an average pupil in the eighth month of the seventh grade.

the *information* related to the various *decisions* or plans that might be made by the client. Furthermore, information theory and decision theory tell us that the information obtained from tests must add something to existing information about the individual. It is therefore the counselor's responsibility to judge whether the necessary information can be obtained just as well from existing records or other sources as from new tests.

It will be well to keep in mind, during the remainder of this chapter, the implications of information theory and decision theory. In all but the last few uses of tests described, assumptions are always made regarding the validities of tests for the particular decisions, whether these have to do with selecting the freshman class of a college, adjusting school curricula to the needs of students, or helping an adolescent make an individual career plan. In all the uses, it is assumed that the counselor has judged that already existing sources of information are inadequate and that tests have something to add.

Noncounseling Uses of Tests

In discussing uses of tests other than those directly related to counseling, we are dealing mostly with admission and placement procedures in schools and colleges and, to a lesser extent, in business organizations. In the other kinds of settings in which counselors work, such as the Veterans Administration, YMCA counseling centers, and rehabilitation counseling agencies, there are few uses of tests other than those concerned with the counseling process itself or with a research project for which test data are being collected.

It is also necessary to point out that we are using *counseling* in a fairly narrow sense, limiting the term to those activities of counselors which center on a particular individual and especially those which involve face-to-face contacts. Others prefer to define counseling more broadly, sometimes going so far as to include almost everything that counselors do. In that case, many of the "noncounseling" uses which follow would be classified as "counseling."

In actual practice there need not be, and frequently is not, a complete and rigid separation of the counseling from the noncounseling uses of tests. This is especially true in schools; while studying the test results of a single child, the counselor may develop hypotheses about the *child's* needs to change goals, a *teacher's* need to change rewards, and the *school's* need to add a new course of study. Similarly, in higher education, college admissions committees sometimes try to decide whether a low-scoring applicant should be rejected as unlikely to succeed, or whether he should be accepted as one potentially able to succeed provided he seeks counseling help and makes judicious selection of courses. Despite the fact that this kind of intermeshing of test implications is frequent, there is still value in separating the two categories to gain a sharper focus on each. There is also the matter of establishing the locus of primary responsibility for a particular application of tests. In the case of what we are labeling the counseling uses of tests, the primary responsibility is with the counselor. With noncounseling uses, responsibility is more likely to belong to classroom teachers, curriculum co-ordinators, and administrators.

A thorough treatment of the purposes for which tests are used in education is to be found in *Educational Measurements* (Lindquist, 1951) ; this has been a major resource for the discussion which follows.

The noncounseling uses of tests seem to fall into the following categories, with regard to both educational and business organizations:

1. Selection of candidates *for* the institution.
2. Placement of individuals *within* the institution.
3. Adaptation of institutional practices to meet the needs and characteristics of particular *individuals*.
4. Development and revision of institutional practices to meet the needs and characteristics of students or employees *in general*.

Selection of Candidates for the Institution

Few public schools select students through examinations; the exceptions, which for the most part are located in large cities, are high schools specializing in technical or vocational subjects, music or art. Tests are occasionally used to select pupils for special schools for retarded children or for emotionally disturbed children. On the other hand, the use of tests for selecting college students is quite widespread. In addition to the College Entrance Examination Board and other national and regional testing programs, many colleges use their own batteries, made up sometimes of commercially published tests and sometimes of their own tests. The most frequently used tests include general academic aptitude, reading comprehension, academic achievement, and, to a much lesser extent, tests aimed at tapping noncognitive variables such as motivation, personality adjustment, and study habits (Chauncey and Frederiksen, in Lindquist, 1951; Dragositz and McCambridge, 1952).

Beyond the selection of entering freshmen, some colleges and universities also use tests for admission to upper-class programs and to graduate and professional schools. One additional special use of tests is in connection with the award of scholarships, loans, and other forms of financial aid.

In business, there has been a wide variety of measurement techniques used for selecting employees, ranging from ten-minute intelligence or clerical tests to all-day programs which sometimes include projective tests, leaderless group discussions, and other appraisal devices for higher level positions.

Placement of Individuals Within Institutions

Elementary and secondary schools sometimes use test data (along with other data as well) to place students in multitrack programs. Here the variables of greatest concern usually are the individual's past achievement and his level of capability; accordingly, achievement and general mental ability tests are used to place the student with a group of similar learning speed and level. In elementary schools, teachers sometimes group pupils within a single class (most often for reading) in an attempt further to restrict the range of abilities.

Occasionally a secondary school is known to use tests as selection devices for particular curricula, such as business or vocational programs. Often, however, these are crude (and unvalidated) methods to send to these curricula students who are not acceptable for college preparatory work. Some schools also use test data for selecting students for particular courses, such as algebra and foreign language; here, too, local validation studies seem to be rare.

This kind of test application seems less prevalent in colleges; instead the general practice appears to be to admit a student to the institution or to one of its subdivisions and then to permit him to try any elective course for which he has the prerequisites. The large percentage of failures in certain courses reported by a number of colleges would indicate that testing programs might be worth a trial.

Business and industry have probably made somewhat greater use of tests for differential placement than have educational institutions. In part, this is probably because business firms rarely adopt the policy, common to schools, of permitting people to try themselves at activities in which failure is likely or even certain. With the present crowding of junior and senior high schools and the anticipated bulge in college enrollments, schools too may decide that they cannot afford the luxury of courses in which as many as half the students fail. In industry, interestingly, there have been instances in which labor unions have opposed the use of tests for differential placement and for promotion. These unions have preferred to let seniority be the deciding factor. In effect, they have somewhat the same attitude as exists in schools, that is, that each person should be permitted to try himself in any endeavor. The motives of unions in these cases, however, are not quite the same as those of educators, involving as they do a desire to exercise some control over placement and promotion.

Adaptation of Institutional Practices to Meet the Needs and Characteristics of Particular Individuals

In this category are such adaptations as the provision of special reading materials for deficient readers and individual help for slow-learners. Also included are the practices of giving encouragement and opportunities for success experiences to students who lack self-confidence, and increasing a student's motivation for a particular subject by relating it to some of his known interests.

Sometimes the adaptation includes referral to special services within the institution, such as counseling and remedial work in reading or other areas. Some schools arrange work-study programs for students whose interests, abilities, and financial needs make this appropriate.

In its broadest sense, this category includes every use of test data to help teachers and others to know a student and his particular characteristics. If the information results in increased understanding of the student, it may then be possible to make better use of the institution's resources for more effective learning and development. As Cronbach (1955) has noted, however, it cannot be assumed that the resulting individualized treatment is any more effective than what would otherwise have been the case. It must be demonstrated in some way that the course of action recommended on the basis of certain test scores is valid, that is, that it will improve the chances of success, however this is defined. Like any other prediction, this one too must be validated.

This kind of adaptation is less often heard of in industry, but even there jobs are sometimes modified so they may be performed by handicapped workers. Also, as in schools, supervisors may be able to increase the effectiveness of workers through increased knowledge of their personal problems, their strengths and weaknesses.

Development of Institutional Practices to Meet the Needs of Students or Employees as a Group

As applied to schools and colleges, this category has to do primarily with the organization of curriculum and extracurriculum. In its most general form, this is a matter of building school programs around established knowledge in the areas of psychology and sociology. Included are facts about developmental sequences of abilities and interests, about emotional needs of children and youth, and about the characteristics of small groups. Tests, with their norms and other standardization data, have provided us with something of a foundation on which to base curriculum-planning.

Applied more specifically to a particular school or school system, tests can provide information not only about the achievements of students but also about their capabilities (Seashore, 1951). The achievement data tell us what students know when they begin, whereas tests of mental ability provide a further basis for judging what they are capable of becoming. As Seashore indicates, a school's program and plant can be more adequately planned if information regarding the occupational aptitudes of the student body is available. For example, a survey of aptitudes provides at least one basis for judging the relative proportion of vocational subjects, business subjects, and so on, in a school's program.

Achievement tests used after a year or a term, or some other period of instruction, provide some basis for evaluating instructional activities. The evaluation in turn is useful to supervisors in helping teachers to do a better job and to administrators in making their judgments about text materials, teaching methods, and retention and promotion of teachers, as well as in interpreting the school to the community.

Tyler describes another contribution of testing in terms of stimulating the faculty to formulate objectives of instruction and to express them clearly, in behavioral terms. Concerned primarily with achievement testing, he points out that "It is not possible to construct a valid achievement test, or to use one properly, without clarifying the objectives which the test is supposed to measure" (Tyler, in Lindquist, 1951: p. 49). It does not appear, however, that many schools approach either achievement-measurement or curriculum-planning in a very organized manner. A broader conception of the functions of guidance programs might result in greater contributions of tests to curriculum, mainly by demanding answers to questions about goals and purposes.

This kind of use of tests does not seem to be widespread in industry. Nonetheless, some applications are obvious; a plant or office cannot maintain maximum productivity unless the machines, processes, and methods are optimally adapted to the abilities, proficiency, and other characteristics of workers. Some companies employ psychologists, engineers, or personnel specialists for the purpose of evaluating the adequacy of their equipment and procedures in relation to the characteristics of workers.

Counseling Uses of Tests

These may for convenience be arranged in two broad clusters: first, those uses which are intended to provide information, and, second, those which are intended to serve other purposes.

For Informational Purposes

These uses are intended to add information not previously available or perhaps to check available information for reliability by repeating the test or using a different test of the same function. In its most rigorous form, the theoretical model for this use of tests, called "decision theory," requires that ". . . the value of test information should be judged by how much it improves decisions over the best possible decisions made without the test, whereas the conventional validity coefficient reports how much better test decisions are than *chance* decisions" (Cronbach, 1955: pp. 31-32). Although in practice this degree of rigor is not approached, the theoretical formulation has important implications for test users. For example, Cronbach points out that, if one is interested in predicting school grades, a scholastic aptitude test adds little to what is already contributed by previous grades. A good achievement test with high validity, he goes on, adds much less to a teacher's knowledge of a pupil than does a less valid personality inventory. He concludes that it may be wiser to use imperfect tests of important objectives that are hard to measure, such as creativity or attitudes, than to use highly valid tests that merely supplement nontest data.[3]

Cronbach discusses the implications of decision theory for testing *programs:* Rather than administer an entire battery to all students or employees, it is recommended that just a short test be given to all. For some people, this provides enough information to make whatever decision it is that needs to be made (acceptance, hiring, or assignment to sections). For the remainder, there is a continuing process of narrowing-down, each person dropping out at the point that a decision can be made, and the entire testing procedure being terminated at such time that the added value of further testing is less than its cost. (This interesting idea of sequential testing is considered at greater length in the section in Chapter 3 on "When Is Testing Done?").

Adapting schemes developed by Super (1957b) and Bordin (1955) the information to be sought may be arranged in three categories: precounseling diagnostic information, information for the counseling process itself, and information for postcounseling.

Precounseling diagnostic information is intended to help the counselor (with or without the client's collaboration) to decide whether the client's needs are within the purview of his services. This intake process may actually be a separate preliminary step in counseling or may be merged with the other elements of counseling. Counselors who work in a nonmechanical fashion see intake and diagnosis (as here defined) as a continuous process extending throughout the duration of the counseling relationship. There is an attitude of flexibility in this kind of counseling, with regard both to the analysis of the problem situation and to the decision as to whether this client should continue with his counselor. For example, it is entirely possible that the counselor's first judgment is that a particular client is well enough integrated to proceed with counseling. Later, however, a personality inventory used in relation to a particular occupational goal may indicate a degree of disturbance to warrant introducing the topic of referral. Or it may be the client himself, who, after gaining increased confidence in the counselor, feels ready to introduce the topic himself.

Included in this category are questions about the *locus* of the problem, whether in such areas as Personality, Educational, Vocational, Financial, or Health Problems. Some counselors specialize in one or another of these

[3] As will be seen in Chapter 4, there are instances in which a counselor may justifiably use tests of functions which have been previously tested. There must be a rationale, however, perhaps in terms of questioning the reliability of the previous measure for some good reason, or perhaps because there is reason to hypothesize that the client has changed significantly in the attribute to be retested since the earlier testing.

areas, and others function as general practitioners. The latter may not need to be so concerned with differential diagnosis; specialists must decide early, however, whether to work with a particular individual or to try to refer him elsewhere.

A related question refers to the *severity* of the client's disturbance: Is he well enough in control and well enough oriented to reality to be able to use the services of a counselor as contrasted with those of a psychotherapist? Despite the rejection by some counselors of any distinction in theory between counseling and psychotherapy, the fact remains that some practitioners do short-term counseling of a relatively cognitive nature, whereas others do long-term, relatively affective work with more disturbed persons.

Information of these kinds normally is obtained from interviews and questionnaires rather than from tests, although personality inventories may be used in diagnosing severity of disturbance, and problem checklists, in identifying the locus of the problem. Having decided that this client can be served, the counselor moves on to seek information in the next categories.

Information for the Counseling Process Itself. The counselor ordinarily is able to offer a larger number of particular services than will be utilized with any one client. Somewhere along the line, decisions are made as to *which methods, approaches, tools, and techniques* are to be used. The use of some classification system, even though imperfect, is helpful to counselors at this point. Perhaps the most well-developed system was originated by Bordin (1946) and modified and tested in research by Pepinsky (1948). It includes the categories: Dependence, Lack of Information, Self-Conflict, Choice-Anxiety, and Lack of Assurance. This kind of diagnosis is usually based on nontest information derived from such sources as interviews and questionnaires, although here also personality inventories, and sometimes other kinds of tests, are found useful.

Bordin also refers to a use of tests to *aid the client in developing more realistic expectations about counseling.* He applies this particularly to those cases in which (1) clients are overdependent on tests to solve their problems and (2) clients seek escape from threatening feelings by focusing on tests. The economical counselor tries to clarify these needs without tests but, failing this, may find it effective to give his client actual experience in learning the inadequacies of tests for his particular needs. In a way, this is a *negative information* use of tests, since the counselor intends the client to realize that the particular information he seeks will *not* provide the help needed.

Here, too, the skillful counselor is on the alert for changes in what he or the client sees as the needs and the problem. He regards each such definition of the problem and each resulting plan for counseling as hypotheses which may be modified, or rejected entirely, as they are tested by succeeding events. It is quite common, for example, for a client to present a relatively simple need for information about his ability to achieve a particular educational goal and then to express anxiety or conflict about this goal, after he has found that the test information itself (whether favorable or unfavorable) has been of no real help. At this point counselor and client may re-examine their definitions of the problem and then redefine the goals and methods of counseling.

In other cases, interest test data, originally sought as simple confirmation by the client of a tentative vocational choice, may reveal an underlying conflict between two quite different ways of life and sets of values. At this point, the sensitive and flexible counselor may try to restructure counseling in terms of the conflict and its attempted resolution. Further tests may then be planned to aid in determining this new goal.

Information Relating to the Client's Postcounseling Decisions. Here we come to the major use of tests in counseling. An almost universal characteristic of counseling as here conceived is that it deals with decisions and plans. This is not to imply that all clients are involved exclusively in a rational, cognitive process. On the contrary, counseling differs from processes such as appraisal, information-giving, and advisement in that one deals not only with facts but also with an individual's *feelings about* them. The purpose of counseling, however, is usually to give help in making decisions and plans for the future and in choosing among alternative courses of action in the world of reality. In this category tests contribute to the planning and choosing process by giving the client additional information (including clarification and confirmation of previous information) about himself *in relation to* the facts about an occupation or an educational program.

Bross (1953) has described, in the framework of *decision theory,* the increased difficulty of making decisions in today's world. Not only are the alternatives many in number, but there are conflicting values facing the individual (need for security vs. an opportunity to grow; gaining prestige vs. doing interesting work). Many people can use help with both elements of this process, first, in deciding on particular goals (outcomes) and, second, in considering the relevant alternative choices (decisions) and weighing them in relation to their own characteristics to determine in which they have the best chances of reaching their goals. Rarely is such a decision unequivocal; more often compromises must be made among conflicting goals (outcomes) and among inconsistent pieces of information.

Before listing the several uses included under this heading of Postcounseling Decisions, it will be helpful to discuss briefly three dimensions, or variables, of the information-getting process: the degree of affect, the degree of superficiality, and the degree of realism with which information is sought.

The *degree of affect* attached to the process of information-getting varies. It may be very little, as in the case of the high school senior who simply doesn't know whether a chemistry major or a chemical engineering major in college is more appropriate to his abilities and interests. There may be, at the other extreme, a great deal of feeling, as in the case of the student who wants very badly to attend College X but may not be acceptable and would then have to settle for a much less desirable college. In this case, whatever comparative predictions are made from academic aptitude tests will be received with strong feelings. Even the *taking* of the test will be different for these two students; for one it is a relatively unthreatening and perhaps even interesting experience; for the other it will be fraught with anxiety. Likewise, client reactions toward the counselor's later interpretations of test scores may be expected to differ in terms of amount of resistance, and the use of such defense mechanisms as rationalization and projection.

The counselor's handling of feelings related to information needs is considered further in Chapter 3 in connection with selecting tests, in Chapter 5 in connection with the effects of emotions on test-taking itself, and in Chapters 14 to 16 in connection with reporting test interpretations.

The second variable is the *degree of superficiality* of the client's stated need for information. In other words, to what extent is the presenting problem the true source of the client's need for counseling? Two clients may present identical questions, such as, "What are my chances of being a toolmaker?" For one this may represent a need for confirmation or reassurance regarding an essentially realistic goal. For the other, the quest for information may be a defense against dealing with the individual's fear of being "stuck in a factory job for the rest of my life." In terms of mechanical and other relevant aptitudes, a semiskilled job may indeed be more appropriate for the second person, but for him such a job could be unacceptable because of its implications in terms of status, limited wages, or lack of responsibility. The counselor may be able, before or after testing, to help him to look at the more basic problem, which may or may not require information from tests.

As both Bordin (1955) and Super (1955b) have pointed out, it is sometimes necessary, and even desirable, to begin to work with the client at the more superficial level. In some instances, the counselor's attitude of acceptance, as well as information from tests, help the client to reduce his defenses and deal with underlying matters. In other cases, of which Super discusses one in detail, counseling at a surface level which deals with cognitive, factual matters, may help the individual to make a concrete decision, no matter how small. The results may eventually lead to improvement of the "underlying problem," perhaps through greater confidence to face it or perhaps as a chain reaction, in which success in one aspect of life, such as the job, leads to changes in behavior. These changes in turn may permit success in other areas.

A third dimension, related to the others but having some independence, is the *degree of realism* of the alternatives being considered and of the request for information. Here we are concerned with the extent to which the client is seeking information which is *pertinent* to or necessary for the decision he must make. If, for instance, the decision is whether to go to college and the counselee has a barely passing high school average and low scores on intelligence tests in school, it is not realistic for him blandly to ask for a test to predict his college success, since the additional information is not *necessary*. (Whether the counselor accedes to the request is another question and is considered elsewhere) . In some cases the *decision* or alternative being considered may be realistic enough, but the information requested is not pertinent. Consider the counselee who requests a personality test to help him decide between becoming an auto mechanic or an electrician. There may be tests which could be of assistance with such a decision, but they are not likely to be in the area of personality.

Having considered these three dimensions of the client's needs for information in relation to decisions and plans, we may now go on to spell out four subdivisions of this kind of need.

1. *Suggestion or identification of possible courses of action.* Here the assumption is made that the client really means what so many clients say, but sometimes without conviction: "I don't know *what* to do." It may be a matter of deciding on an appropriate course of study in high school, or planning education after high school, or choosing an occupation. It might also be a search for an explanation of a student's failure in school or an employee's dissatisfaction with a job. As implied above, the client's statement may be high in superficiality and not therefore to be taken at face value; he may actually have one or more alternative explanations or courses of action in mind but be unable or unwilling to say this at the outset of counseling. If one considers the variety of experiences that an adolescent or adult has had, whether in school subjects, extracurricular activities, part-time jobs, or whatever, it is obvious that very few people can genuinely have no ideas at all about what they want to do or can do. More often than not it turns out that they do indeed have some ideas, at least as to what they *don't* want to do, or don't do very well.

2. *Evaluation of two or more alternatives.* Here the client brings a somewhat more crystallized problem. He seeks help in comparing his suitability for two different occupations, or in analyzing the relative advantages of living in the dormitory versus commuting from home, or in considering the merits of continuing to go steady versus being unattached.

In degree of affect, this evaluation of alternatives may be at one extreme a fairly objective process, whereas at the other extreme it may represent an emotion-laden conflict.

The degree of realism may vary sharply too. One client may seriously ask whether law or medicine is his better choice, when in reality they are both clearly out of his reach in terms of academic aptitudes and achievements. The counselor plans his strategy in such situations in a manner calculated to aid the client eventually to deal with reality more adequately. In one case he will face the client directly with the incongruity of both alternatives, and in another he will go along with the request for information and hope that later the counseling can move to a more realistic level.

3. *Testing the suitability of a tentative choice, plan, or decision.* The individual presents his problem as, "I think I want to be a ———, but I'm not sure and I wonder what you think about it." The experienced counselor realizes that such a statement may represent a wide variety of actual needs, ranging from those of a low-affect, nonsuperficial, highly realistic person who simply needs a piece of information, to the other extreme—a person who may be quite upset, who may have underlying problems, and be unrealistic, and who may therefore need a good deal of help, which may or may not include information at appropriate points.

Applying Bordin's (1955) classification of counseling needs, we may have any one or a combination of them here: Dependence, Lack of Information, Self-Conflict, Choice-Anxiety, and Lack of Assurance. If it is really and simply a lack of information, the need can be met quickly and easily. Often, however, there is at least some anxiety regarding the decision itself, or the decision-making process. Quite frequently, especially with adolescents who come voluntarily for counseling, lack of confidence in their ability to make decisions leads to an attempt to become dependent on the counselor. This is not to suggest that, wherever there is anxiety or dependency or lack of assurance, there is not a legitimate and realistic need for information. Rather it is to caution that simple and automatic provision of the information requested, without sensitivity to the possibilities of associated feelings and veiled problems, is likely to fall short of meeting the needs of many clients. As with other uses of tests in counseling, there is no standard way of handling these matters; sometimes the request for information is taken at face value and tests are planned. Most counselors would at least test the validity of the stated need for information by encouraging the client to "tell me more." Then, if it becomes clear that the requested information is genuinely needed, or if information is not really the need but the client seems unable to deal directly with what the counselor judges to be the "real" problem, tests may be in order. As Bordin points out, in the latter situation it is a matter of helping the client to develop more realistic expectations of the value of counseling. Expressed a little differently, the counselor here helps the individual to reach the point of readiness to share his more covert feelings and thoughts.

4. *Self-concept development and clarification.* The three uses previously described have in common a client-motivated and expressed need for information of some sort. They are limited primarily to those instances in agencies and schools in which an individual comes (or is sent) seeking

help with a particular problem. Now, however, we must add an informational use of tests which seems to be increasing in importance, especially in school and college guidance programs, but also elsewhere. Many schools apply batteries of tests on a programmatic basis, giving the same battery of achievement, aptitude, and other tests, to entire classes. In colleges this is most often at the beginning of the freshman year, but sometimes earlier, either prior to admission or as part of an orientation program. Then, in at least some of these programs, each student has an interview with a counselor or advisor, the purposes of which include a report of the test results. Sometimes this report leads to one of the other uses of counseling, such as testing the suitability of a decision or developing new interests (see below). In many cases, however, no particular focus develops, but the test information may nonetheless have performed a major function, that of contributing to and clarifying the individual's self-concept. Mathewson (1955) has described in detail this kind of *developmental* approach to guidance services, as contrasted with the *problem-oriented* approach that has received so much more attention both in the literature and in practice. Yet, as Mathewson points out, it is the more positive, developmental and preventative approach which in the long run seems likely to be of help to the largest number of people. Part of growing up is knowing oneself, and here tests have something to offer everyone.

There are pitfalls here too: Real self-concept work means skillful counseling that sometimes requires more than the perfunctory ten or fifteen minutes allowed for the "routine" interview. To be really meaningful to the client, there must be some depth and some emotional involvement. There must also be some opportunity to relate the test information to other aspects of the individual's experience, whether to his school work, his leisure-time activities, or his family's values and those of his neighborhood. Without these elements, self-concept development through information about himself is likely to be superficial and lacking in real impact on the individual.

As suggested earlier, this use of tests also occurs in problem-oriented counseling. A set of test data may add no *new* information but can contribute to the organization of the client's concept of himself in relation to whatever decisions are in focus. Thus an interest inventory of the *Kuder* type may tell the client little or nothing that he doesn't already know, but it sometimes provides a more sharply defined picture of his interests than he had before. The feeling of satisfaction which the individual gains from recognizing his perceptions in a new and clearer form can be a very worthwhile outcome of counseling.

For Noninformational Purposes

There are at least three uses of tests in counseling that do *not* seem to have the element of providing information. They are stimulation of interest in areas not previously considered, laying a groundwork for later counseling, and providing a learning experience in decision-making.

Stimulation of Interest in Areas Not Previously Considered. Some years ago Kitson (1942) described the use of short trade projects (mechanical or electrical), in part as a way of testing claimed interest in these areas, but also as a way of stimulating interest. Testing and stimulating interest, of course, have been among the major stated purposes of junior high schools in general, particularly of their "exploratory" courses, and, to a lesser extent, of senior high schools and colleges, especially in some of the courses labelled "introduction to" or "appreciation of." More recently, there has been a good deal of this kind of activity in prevocational try-outs with handicapped counselees.

Tests can make a contribution toward stimulation of interests in educational and vocational areas. In fact, many schools use interest inventories somewhere around the eighth or ninth grades, not so much for purposes of predicting or selecting, as of stimulating further thinking about the world of work in general and about specific areas of activity as well. For many youngsters it is unlikely that anything very new in the way of interests is learned from these inventories and from tests in general. There are cases, however, in which a youngster learns, from test interpretations, about potentialities for schooling or for occupations, indeed for a whole way of life, of which he had little awareness. Such occurrences, although rare in many agencies and schools, are observed especially among underprivileged groups, those who, living at a low socioeconomic occupational level, have had limited opportunity to think about themselves in relation to higher level activities.

It is becoming increasingly important to locate such high-potential youngsters and to stimulate their upward movement, not only for the sake of their own happiness and fullness of development, but also because of the needs of our economy. The current manpower situation is such, according to recent estimates (Wolfle, 1958) that our needs for skilled, technical, and professional workers can be met only by increased upward mobility of those in underprivileged groups who lack not only the money but also the conscious interests and the motivation to seek out advanced education and training. It is here that guidance workers, with tests, as well as with other techniques, can contribute to the stimulation of interests and to the development of changed self-concepts (Beilin, 1956).

Laying Groundwork for Later Counseling. Some high school and college counselors spend a considerable amount of time in "routine" interviews with students; included frequently in such interviews are reports of results of tests taken at the time of admission or at other group-testing occasions. Self-concept development was the focal point of the fourth informational need discussed above. Now we consider another use of the same kind of interview, namely, to communicate to the student the counselor's interest in him and his availability to discuss abilities, in. terests, and other characteristics, in relation to school adjustment and planning for the future. The student may become immediately involved in one of the other uses of tests, or he may do this at a later date, when something happens either internally or externally which leads him to feel the need of counseling.

Learning Experiences in Decision-Making. This use of tests deserves considerably more emphasis and recognition than is reflected in the literature. Dependent clients tend to shirk responsibility for planning their counseling procedures, including decisions as to whether to take tests, and if so, what kinds and for what purposes. It is all too tempting for the counselor to give in to these client attitudes and take the easy way (easy for *some* counselors) of assuming all responsibility. This is especially tempting since it places the counselor in the position of the esteemed and respected authority figure. The counselor who resists these temptations can look forward to only the occasional reward of a client's having the experience of making a good decision, or of making a poor decision and realizing that the skies don't fall in as a result. A good deal more will be said about this in the discussion of test selection methods in Chapter 3.

Research. Although research is not, strictly speaking, a counseling function, it can be a responsibility of counselors and can be intimately related to their service functions. As Pepinsky and Pepinsky (1954) have made clear, the counselor-as-researcher performs operations and has a set of attitudes quite similar to those of the counselor-as-helper. In both instances, he tries to organize data into hypotheses which are then tested against further data. Perhaps the richest source of hypotheses for research is the day-to-day experience of counselors.

An illustration of interaction between practice and research is the study of Blade and Watson (1955). They had the impression that at Cooper Union (a college specializing in engineering and artistic fields) there was not a very high correlation between scores on spatial visualization tests and grades in related engineering courses. They speculated that increases in scores of some individuals on tests might be a cause of the low correlation. A carefully planned series of studies over a period of four years showed that a number of students had marked increases in scores in the first year, apparently as a result of course experiences which developed latent abilities. This was particularly true among those students who had had limited experience with hobbies and courses of a related nature. These results led to the conclusion that spatial visualization would be better measured after a year of engineering study. A stimulating contribution to the literature thus resulted from the sensitivity of practitioners to inadequacies of tests which, in this illustration, were being used for admission purposes.

Closing Comment

The organization of concepts and activities into categories is sometimes so intellectually satisfying an activity that we are deluded into seeing the resulting orderly list as an end in itself. Actually, organization of experience has real value (outside of its aesthetic gratification) when it contributes to improved theorizing, when it leads to hypotheses for research, and when it provides insights and helpful guides for the practitioner. It is for this purpose that the preceding pages have been included.

It must be obvious that the lines of demarcation among the categories in this chapter are elastic. Counselor and client shift back and forth as counseling proceeds and as new data lead to new hypotheses, to increased readiness, and to changed relationships. Thus it is clear that skillful work with tests is no more mechanical than any other part of the total counseling process.

One final word: Not only do the purposes of tests change during the course of counseling, but at any one time there may be more than one purpose being served. As if this were not complicated enough, counselor and client may at one and the same time have different perceptions of the role of a test. Careful and repeated explicit structuring of what is going on may reassure the counselor but doesn't necessarily communicate to the client what is intended. Clients may persist in meeting their needs by perceiving interest inventories as measures of abilities and academic aptitude tests as conclusive evidence of being or not being "college material."

ETHICAL CONSIDERATIONS IN THE USE OF TESTS

The basic principles of ethical practice in the use of tests are essentially the same as those for counseling in general, and in fact for all helping professions, including social work, medicine, and others. Fundamentally, the ethical practitioner is guided by two principles: The first is that he provide services which are as competent as possible, within the limits of his own and his profession's development. The second principle is that the welfare of his client, the institution, the community, and society in general are the criteria for judging whether one or another course of action is taken.

The professional counselor should be familiar with some of the more extended statements of ethical practices in relation to psychology (American Psychological Association, 1953; American Psychological Association, 1958) and to counseling (Wrenn, 1952). For present purposes, it has seemed desirable to highlight two areas of ethical consideration which are especially relevant to the use of tests by counselors. The first includes situations in which conflicting demands are made upon the counselor, or in which a demand made by a person other than his counselee seems to conflict with ethical responsibilities to the counselee. The second area has to do with the competencies of those using tests.

Conflicting Demands and Obligations

Conflicts of this kind are found in situations in which counselors deal with persons other than their individual clients, as, for example, with the client's parents, with teachers, principals, supervisors, or with employers or prospective employers. For the private practitioner who works with adults, this is not a frequent problem, since his obligations and responsibilities can usually be seen as being restricted to his clients, who have come voluntarily seeking help and who see the counselor over a limited period of time. In marked contrast is the position of the counselor in a school, college, business firm, and other such institutional settings, who has responsibilities to his employer, to colleagues, and to parents, and who in fact may himself have other relationships with his clients, such as those of a teacher or a source of references for colleges or employers.

With particular reference to testing, here are some illustrations of specific conflicts which involve ethical considerations; although drawn from real life, these incidents are composites rather than specific examples from one particular school or agency:

A high school senior is interested in mechanical occupations, but his parents insist he apply to an engineering college. The vocational counselor in a community agency is urged by the parents to administer an engineering aptitude test to the boy, or even worse, to interpret test results to indicate that engineering is an appropriate choice.

An elementary school child has low scores on intelligence tests; normally the results of such tests are reported to classroom teachers. In this case, however, the counselor judges that the results are an underestimate of the pupil's capabilities. He also knows that this youngster's teacher is likely to reach an unwarranted conclusion about the child's learning potentiality. Should test scores be withheld from this teacher?

A high school counselor receives a phone call from a vocational counseling agency in the city, to which a present student in the school has applied for service. The agency would like to have a list of all test scores in the school's possession. Should such requests be routinely concurred with or routinely rejected, or is there some other course of action which would be better?

Phone calls are received quite frequently at one school from prospective employers of their graduates. The employers want to know, among other things, how the graduates did on intelligence and aptitude tests. The counselor has always given such information freely but now wonders whether this is proper.

A failing college freshman has sought help from the college's counseling bureau; personality tests and interviews reveal serious emotional problems which the student asks be held in strict confidence. The Dean, who is considering dropping the student from college, asks the counselor for a complete report. Should the confidential information be withheld?

Such illustrations could be multiplied in almost any counseling office. In all of them the counselor faces a conflict of obligations between those due his client and those due others in the school or agency or community. He is, after all, a member of an institutional staff, and as such, is expected to be of help to teachers, administrators, and others. Also, to maintain good community relations, he would like to be helpful to employers. Finally, as a practitioner in the field of counseling, he feels a responsibility to share information with professional workers in other agencies and institutions.

In many of these problem situations there is no clear-cut and obvious right answer. One cannot always assume, for example, that the counselor's first responsibility is to the individual client; it might in some cases be to the institution and its programs. Perhaps the one universal dictum is that there should be a clear statement of the counselor's roles and relationships. This position is taken in the *Ethical Standards of Psychologists* (American Psychological Association, 1953: p. 56) on the handling of confidential materials: "In clinical and consulting situations where possible division of loyalties exists, as between the client and the employer of the psychologist, agreement concerning handling of confidential materials must be worked out and the nature of the agreement made known to all concerned."

In schools, colleges, and in business, it would be desirable that such an agreement, regarding confidentiality as well as other ethical problems, be prepared with the collaboration of as as many as possible of the parties concerned (teachers, administrators, supervisors) in order that the needs and points of view of all are understood. In one school, as a result of such a process, it might be decided that the counselor shall reveal only those items of information which he deems appropriate. In a second institution, there might be a policy that written permission of the client or his parents must be obtained before test scores are given to anyone outside the school. Whatever the policy, it must be communicated to all concerned, including new staff members, counselors as well as others, so that all are acquainted with the "ground-rules." It may be necessary, as pointed out in the principle of the *Ethical Standards* (p. 56), to inform counselees of certain aspects of the policy: "When the psychologist's position is such that some departure is required from the normal expectation that clinical or consulting relationships are confidential, it is expected that the psychologist will make clear to the client the nature of his role before the client enters the relationship."

Finally it cannot always be expected that all parties will be equally satisfied with the policy statement as it is worked out. The counselor may be so dissatisfied that he decides he cannot work within those limits and must leave the job. On the other hand, he may feel that it is the best compromise possible at that time and that he can hope to improve it later, through a continuing process of evaluation and development. It is important to remind ourselves that ethical standards are not the same for all time in any situation, even the best; they sometimes change as a result of changing definitions and theories of counseling, and changing conceptions of the nature of man himself.

Competencies

The second general kind of ethical situation involves competencies, particularly those of the counselor but also those of others involved in using tests. As with the question of conflicting responsibilities, there are no obvious answers or hard-and-fast rules. Often the counselor must decide for himself whether he is qualified to give a particular service. Unfortunately, the less training he has, the less likely he is to know his limits. The untrained counselor, for example, may be quite gullible about the "self-administering" and "self-interpreting" virtues of a particular test. A convincing test manual and a persuasive publisher's representative are more likely to lead the poorly trained than the well-trained into unethical practices. The paradox here is that those least qualified to do a good job with tests are, because of lack of training, least likely to be aware of their shortcomings and therefore more likely to practice beyond the bounds of their skills.

In Chapter 1, the position was taken that all testing activities should be under the immediate and active supervision of persons with at least a master's degree in guidance and counseling, counseling psychology, or other similar fields. It is sometimes implied, if not directly stated, that there are *types of tests* or *elements* within the total testing process which require less competency than others.

For example, some publishers discriminate among different types of test by restricting the distribution of some tests (notably those of personality) more than others (achievement tests usually being the least restricted). Such a practice may imply that a higher order of knowledge and skill is needed with one type of test than another. Although there may indeed be something of a hierarchy along these lines, careful consideration indicates that a substantial amount of training is necessary for proper use of any and all standardized tests. Achievement and intelligence tests can just as readily be selected inappropriately, administered improperly, scored incorrectly, and even interpreted poorly, as can interest and personality inventories. The proper professional use of *all* tests requires deep understanding of concepts of validity and reliability, of norms, of individual differences, and of sociological and psychological factors which affect test performance.

Over and above these fundamental understandings, each kind of test requires special competencies. For example, academic achievement tests require knowledge of subject matter, which teachers are indeed likely to have. Personality tests require knowledge of the psychology of personality, which teachers are *less* likely to possess. To the extent that these additional competencies are necessary, there is some rationale for the practice of requiring different qualifications for purchasers of each type of test. Carried a step further, however, this rationale might lead to the conclusion that achievement tests should be sold only to those with knowledge of the relevant subject matter. That this is not done suggests that there is indeed an assumption of a hierarchy in which some kinds of tests require simply *more* competency than others. The point of view taken here is rather that, first, there are basic competencies required for interpretation of *all* types of tests, and, second, that different additional competencies may be required for some types of tests.

As to the particular *element* of the testing process, it does indeed seem possible for classroom teachers and others to perform the more routine operations of administration and scoring. Experience indicates, however, that even these operations are fraught with the possibility of errors if not carefully supervised and if the administrator is not carefully trained. Certainly the more complex operations of selection, interpretation, and the reporting of almost any test score require, as well-trained practitioners know, all the skills one can muster. Proper interpretation of a "simple" IQ may involve understanding of the factorial composition of the particular test used, the range of difficulty of the items, the possible influence of reading handicaps, the effects of anxiety and motivation, and a whole host of factors both in the individual and in the instrument which might affect a single score.

It seems clear that *all* types of tests and *all* elements of the testing process must be under the responsible supervision of those with the minimum training which has been defined earlier. It should be regarded as an unethical practice to release tests and test results, without supervision, to classroom teachers, school principals, untrained "counselors," personnel clerks, and others who are not professionally competent test users. When such people, and their colleagues, later denounce tests as "useless" or "misleading" or "confusing," they often are criticizing tests for faults which lie in the users.

CHAPTER 3

Test Selection as an Aspect of the Counseling Process

THE PLANNING, selection, administration, and scoring of tests are sometimes perceived by counselors as quite separate from those portions of the counseling process which precede and follow testing. It is as if testing were an interruption of the counseling process—taking time out to collect data mechanically and "objectively" before returning to the more affect-laden relationship between counselor and client. It is clear, however, that for many clients, if not all, testing is *not* objective. The experience of testing is permeated with those emotions which the counselee has in relation to the *purposes* of testing, as he perceives them. If, for instance, the question is "Can I succeed in College X?" the test itself is likely to be imbued with the threatening qualities of the student's fear of failure. In similar fashion, the client who is under parental pressure to make a decision different from his own preference, may project his anxiety into the whole testing situation.

It is not surprising, then, that an anxious and insecure client reacts to the test itself, and even to the counselor's suggestion of a test, with such irrational behavior as resistance, rationalization, and withdrawal. Even when the counselee expresses objective attitudes similar to those of the counselor, we cannot assume that these attitudes represent his real feelings. In fact, sometimes the client who approaches tests with no directly expressed anxiety may be suspected of not really letting himself become involved. It is as if the threat is so great that it is denied completely. After all, if one seeks counseling help in planning a career, or choosing a school or college, or making a better adjustment to school or the job, it is "normal" to feel at least a little apprehensive about what the tests will indicate as to one's abilities, interests, and personality.

This whole situation—the gap between testing and the rest of the counseling—is subject to greater control by the counselor in those instances where he does his own testing as part of his counseling relationship with each individual. This is probably not the case for most counseling users of tests. In schools, most of the tests used are given prior to the establishment of a counseling relationship and usually are given by someone other than the counselor—most often by teachers in the classroom. In larger counseling centers, both in colleges and agencies, it is often the practice to have all testing done by a psychometrist. Here there is usually an interruption, for a period of days or weeks, in the relationship between the counselor and client. The merits and demerits of these various organizational arrangements will be discussed more fully later in this chapter; now we need only recognize the implications for test selection. Briefly stated, these are that testing and its subdivisions, including test selection, is an integral part of the counseling process. In the process of selecting tests, attention should be paid to the same basic principles which apply to all counseling activities. Tyler (1953) has conveniently summarized these as *understanding* the client, *accepting* him and his perceptions, and *communicating* to him both our understanding and acceptance.

Test selection, however, involves more than the application of general principles. In addition to what we will call the *process,* or *how* aspect of test selection, which was emphasized above, there is the *content* aspect, the *what* of testing (Goldman, 1954). It is here that we are concerned with using those tests which are most likely to answer the questions, to provide the information, or to do whatever is the goal of testing. Our goals, then, are twofold: first, to select those tests which are most likely to serve the particular purposes of testing (content), and, second, to select and plan tests in such a way as to make the greatest contribution to the growth and development of our client (process). Although the "how" and "what" are as inseparable in operation as are an electric wire and the current which flows through it, it will be helpful to study them separately, just as a wire and current may be studied independently.

In the case of test selection, content and process each have some degree of uniqueness in terms of methods and resources used, training and competencies needed, and special problems. The present chapter deals primarily with process aspects, with particular emphasis on the role of the client in the selection and planning of tests, and includes also some discussion of *program testing* in schools, where entire classes may be tested at once. In Chapter 4 we shall discuss the content phase, that which has to do primarily with the question of which specific test is selected for the particular purpose at hand.

CLIENT PARTICIPATION IN TEST SELECTION

Awareness of the process aspect of total test selection seems to be a contribution in the first instance of Carl Rogers (1942) and then of others stimulated by his ideas. For some counselors, their perceptions of "client-centered" theory led to virtual abandonment of tests as part of counseling. (In all likelihood, many of these counselors also changed the foci of their counseling work from educational-vocational to personal and social areas.) For counseling in general, client-centered theory has stimulated interest in the process of test selection and especially in what has been referred to as "client participation" in the process. Although a number of years ago Bordin and Bixler (1946) analyzed the psychology of test selection and suggested needed lines of research, the actual published reports of empirical research in this area have been few in number (Seeman, 1948, 1949; Gustad and Tuma, 1957; Strange, 1953; Tuma and Gustad, 1957; Forgy and Black, 1954) and quite inconclusive.

The pages that follow will offer first a theoretical analysis of the process of test selection, with emphasis on the issue of client participation, and then will review the published research which bears on this topic. Following this will be some discussion of the implications of the current state of knowledge and theory.

Arguments in Favor of Client-Participation

Bordin (1955) has presented the case for client participation in selecting tests:

1. Clients may not return for further interviews if tests are planned without their active participation. This happens sometimes because ". . . the counselor has failed to establish specific relationships between the tests assigned and the client's particular problems." At other times it is because of ". . . the client's unpreparedness for reality testing." In the latter case, "Clients in conflict may not be emotionally ready to subject themselves to a realistic scrutiny" (pp. 267-268) .

2. Clients who feel convinced of the purpose of testing can gain insights from self-observation during testing. With understanding of what a particular test is getting at, the counselee can better learn about his abilities and interests from his experiences while taking the tests.

3. Motivation to do his best on tests is strongest when the individual sees the relationship between them and his goals. Although not stated explicitly by Bordin, this seems to imply not only doing *well* on ability tests, but also being accurate and truthful in replying to items on interest and personality inventories.

We can add to these the following advantages for later interviews when test interpretations will be reported to the client:

4. To the extent that the client has participated in the decisions to use tests, he will be more ready to accept later interpretations with a minimum of defensiveness. He should be less likely under these conditions to rationalize the results because they disagree with his needs. He should, in short, be more objective in his perception of the results of testing.

5. Where dependence is a problem, complete counselor responsibility

for test planning does nothing to deal with the problem of dependency except perhaps to reinforce it. In effect, the counselor encourages the client to be dependent on him, as he is on other people. To the extent that a client can accept some responsibility for the test planning process, to that extent he has an opportunity to free himself from dependence on others, particularly adults.

6. Where indecisiveness is a problem, with the client fearing to make a decision either because of lack of confidence in his judgment or because of lack of successful experience in decision-making, he needs the experience of making decisions. Otherwise, his indecisiveness is reinforced or, at best, not improved.

7. Bordin and Bixler (1946) have suggested that the client's reactions to suggestions and descriptions of various tests may provide a wealth of diagnostic data. Frequently, counselor sensitivity to overt feelings about, say scholastic aptitude, will lead to a more open and helpful examination of that area.

8. Finally, a better job of test selection is done in terms of the tests selected. By giving his clients ample opportunity to express their opinions about tests, the counselor can test his own hypotheses about what information is needed. We sometimes learn from our clients that they already have adequate data about an ability, interest, or personality area, and if we can help them to use this information, further testing in that particular area may not be needed.

Arguments Against Client Participation

The main arguments against client participation seem to be that:

1. All this is much ado about nothing; it makes little difference what process is used so long as the most appropriate tests are administered and skillfully interpreted.

2. Because decisions as to the use of tests require knowledge and competencies which few clients have in this area, they must be made by the counselor.

3. The client is much too emotionally involved with his problems to make objective decisions as to the testing part of planning.

4. Dependency and indecisiveness are not problems with which the counselor legitimately should deal; they more properly are the goals of psychotherapy.

Hypotheses and Research on Client Participation

For further discussion here and for the assistance of those interested in planning research in this area, the issues are now stated as hypotheses. Some are ready for research testing as they stand, but others will need further breakdown, refinement, and translation into operational terms:

Client participation in the selection of tests:

1. does not lead to unsuitable test selection resulting from the client's *lack of competency.*
2. does not lead to unsuitable test selection resulting from the client's *lack of objectivity.*
3. results in a *higher rate of return* for further interviews after the one in which testing is planned.
4. results in the client *learning more about himself* during test administration itself.
5. increases *motivation* to do well on ability tests and to respond accurately and truthfully to interest and personality inventories.
6. leads to greater *acceptance* by the client and less defensiveness during later discussions of the test results.
7. decreases *dependency* in those for whom this is a problem.
8. decreases *indecisiveness* in those for whom this is a problem.
9. results in the client *learning more about himself* as a result of the total process of counseling.
10. furnishes additional *diagnostic data* to the counselor.
11. improves the *quality of test selection,* because the client helps the counselor to understand what the client already knows, is interested in knowing, and needs to know.

The research reports in the professional literature to date pertain to only a few of these hypotheses; even in these instances, findings are sometimes contradictory and generally inconclusive. The first study, by Seeman (1948) used 50 interviews (12 of them recorded) with college students who were self-referred for vocational counseling. The two counselors used a client self-selection method, described thus: "Client was given the responsibility for choosing the tests. Counselor limited his function to describing the values and limitations of each test in a neutral, non-persuasive manner" (p. 333). Appropriate checks were made using a control sample of 120 students counseled by four different counselors, to insure that the 50 students were representative of all counselees at that Bureau and that the two counselors did indeed use a client self-selection approach. The experimental subjects selected a mean number of 5.71 tests out of the more than 25 available, whereas the controls took a mean number of 4.70 tests each. This difference was not found to be significant, but the variety of tests taken was significantly greater for the experimental group, suggesting that these subjects were more discriminating as to individual needs than were the counselors of the control subjects, who may have had more of a stereotyped pattern for selecting tests. Seeman also reports that, of the tests judged to be suitable for making either actuarial or clinical predictions of the client's stated objectives, clients actually selected such tests in 93.2 per cent of the possible cases. In one further check, it was found that "technical" students selected a spatial relations test in significantly more cases than did "social science" students, which is in keeping with the hypothesis that students make appropriate choices of tests. These findings offer some basis for accepting Hypotheses 1 and 2 above, although without any indication of the particular roles of competency and objectivity.

Seeman's well-designed study also has some implications for the seventh and eighth hypotheses, even though it doesn't actually test them. The recorded interviews were divided into two groups, four in which the client was judged indecisive in selecting tests and eight in which he was not. Then a count was made for each of the twelve interviews, of the total number of client responses indicating indecisiveness. A clearcut differentiation was made, leading to the conclusion that indecisiveness in test selection is a reflection of a general insecurity. Seeman suggests then that ". . . the phenomenon of ambivalence and conflict in making test choices offers the same challenge and potential for therapy as a problem in any other area of personal adjustment, and may well be considered an integral part of the process of counseling" (pp. 344-345).

Another article by Seeman (1949) reports additional data regarding these same subjects, but this time obtained from the clients themselves by means of questionnaires. Subjects were asked to give reactions to the first interview, and later to make judgments about the value of each test as it was completed. These data are necessarily less dependable than those reported previously by Seeman, based as they are on expressed perceptions and opinions of clients. They do, nevertheless, bear on several of the hypotheses; in general, they offer little support for the client-participation point of view. More of the clients of the experimental (client-selection) than of the control counselors found the first interview different from their expectations, but there were no differences between groups in the extent to which they felt *positively* about the interview. Apropos of Hypothesis 4, experimental clients apparently reported no more learning about themselves during test administration than did the control group, nor, apparently, did they rate the tests as any more valuable. The experimental group recognized that their counselors were using a co-operative method of test selection, but they had even fewer positive reactions about this process than did their control peers.

Finally, Hypotheses 6 and 7 received mixed support from responses to the question about clients' expectations of the next interview. The clients of only *one* of the experimental counselors differed from the general trend of expecting information and suggestions, and only this counselor had any number of clients who saw themselves as definite participants in the interview. Seeman concludes ". . . even within the framework of apparently similar methods counselors may differ in the degree or level to which they facilitate active responses or participation by the client" (p. 104). We shall reserve discussion of this important idea for the later review of a study by Forgy and Black (1954).

Strange (1953) reports an application to group use of Seeman's methods and concludes that it is both feasible and desirable to have students in classes select their own tests. His conclusion rests primarily on impressions, however, and he quite accurately characterizes his study as "exploratory and uncontrolled." Unfortunately, this report offers no usable data for testing any of our hypotheses.

Tuma and Gustad report (1957; Gustad and Tuma, 1957) data which bear directly on Hypothesis 9, although flaws in their experimental design prevent any real test of that hypothesis. (This same study will be cited in a later chapter as it applies to interpretation of test results to the client.) These authors set out to examine two hypotheses:

1. When the same test selection and interpretation methods are used by different counselors, significant differences will result in the amount of learning about self shown by essentially comparable groups of counselees;

2. There are systematic relationships between the amount of learning about self by clients in a counseling situation and the amount of client-counselor similarity on selected personality traits (Tuma and Gustad, 1957, p. 137).

In testing the first hypothesis, the *Strong Vocational Interest Blank* was the only one of the tests used, apparently because it was the only one given during the counseling process itself to enough subjects to allow its use in this analysis. The clients of three counselors were assigned at random to three methods of test selection (ranging from complete client selection to counselor selection). The dependent variable (learning about self) was the amount of change in discrepancy from precounseling to post-counseling between measured interests and client self-ratings of interests. For the *Strong VIB* data, the Gustad and Tuma article reports that no significant relations were found between method of test selection and the self-learning variable. This would seem to be at least in part a rejection of our Hypothesis 9. However, further light is cast by the Tuma and Gustad article, which is devoted primarily to that portion of their study which deals with their second hypothesis. There was found to be little relationship between client-counselor personality similarity on the one hand and client self-learning on the other. In seeking explanations of this finding, the authors suggest factors which may explain not only this result but also the ones previously cited. It seems that the three counselors "may be generally classified as belonging to the Minnesota school" (p. 140). Furthermore, all the counselors "were well above the average on their scores on dominance, social presence, and social participation. Since the significant correlations were negative, this means that the closer the client and his counselor were on these measures, the better was the client's criterion performance. Considering the values of the counselors' scores on the three measures, this also means that clients who were somewhat more dominant than average and who had higher than average scores on social participation and social presence did better. Whether they would have done better with other counselors whose scores were lower remains in doubt, but it is an intriguing suggestion for further research" (p. 140).

The Tuma and Gustad findings, then, may well reflect, as they themselves point out, the narrow range of counselor personality and school of thought. Another likely source of error in this study is the absence of any evidence that the counselors actually used the test selection methods assigned to them. Knowing what we do about these counselors, it is likely that they were more at home and perhaps more successful with the counselor-selection approach. Further discussion of methodological concerns in this area of research are included in the review of the Forgy and Black article which follows.

The study of Forgy and Black (1954), although not limited to the test selection process, offers additional insights into the problems of research design in this area. They followed up clients three years after a follow-up study of the same clients' satisfaction with counseling. The first study (by other researchers) had led to the conclusion that clients were more satisfied with a "client-centered" or "self-adjustive" counseling approach (one characteristic of which was greater client participation in test selection) than with a "highly structured" approach. The Forgy and Black study, on the contrary, found no difference in satisfaction between the two groups of clients, nor among clients of three different counselors. When both counselors and method were examined together, however, differences were found. The clients of one counselor tended to be more satisfied when he used the "client-centered" method, a second counselor had more satisfied clients with the "counselor-centered" method, while the third had about equal satisfaction with both methods. The implications for research call for identification of the counselor-method *interaction* if comparisons are to be made of either counselors or methods.

For the practitioner, the first implication of this research is that each counselor must find the method by which he is most effective. Furthermore, he cannot rely upon his own judgment here, since Forgy and Black also found that there were differences among the three counselors as to which approach was more effective, despite the fact that all three apparently believed that the "client-centered" approach was superior. *Caveat Vendor!*

Implications of the Research

It is clear that we cannot rely upon the research evidence to date as a guide for the process of selecting tests in counseling. The research, however, is helpful in pointing up the importance of the counselor as a variable. It seems likely that there is not, and never will be, any "best method of test selection." It is more likely that further research will evaluate various methods of test selection *in relation to* relevant characteristics of counselors and clients. In turn such studies may lead to the development of instruments that will characterize each counselor, thus providing him with a basis for identifying the methods which are for him likely to be most effective in general, and for particular cases.

METHODS OF TEST SELECTION

Noting the limited contributions of research in the area of test selection, we must draw more heavily on theory, on logic, and on the accumulated experience of counselors. The major concern in our discussion of test selection (process) has been the matter of client participation. It is the author's point of view that the weight of theory, logic, and experience is in favor of a method which encourages at least some client participation in test selection. Not to engage the client in this process is likely to *increase* the probability of (1) encouraging dependence, (2) developing resistance not only to testing but to reports of the results, and (3) using inappropriate tests. Similarly, we *decrease* the probability of (1) client growth in decisiveness and independence, (2) client learning about himself through test-taking itself, as well as through the entire counseling process, and (3) counselor learning about his client through discussion of possible testing.

A hasty qualification: for some *counselors,* such a method may not be personally compatible, in some *situations* such a method is difficult and even impossible, and for some *clients* it may not make much difference which method is used. Each of these three variables will be explored before the discussion of the methods themselves.

The Counselor

As suggested by Seeman (1948), Tuma and Gustad (1957), and Forgy and Black (1954), the counselor and his personality seem to be major factors in determining the effectiveness of a particular approach to test selection. The critical element here seems to be the counselor's genuine *belief* in the client's ability to make valid judgments about taking tests. The counselor who feels this way is sincere in encouraging and even requiring client participation. Otherwise, he may be giving merely lip-service to a "right way" to select tests; as a result, the client may sense coldness on the part of the counselor, or he may soon learn that the counselor really doesn't mean it. Consider the following counseling interchange, in which a high school junior tests the limits of the counselor's structuring of test selection as a co-operative process and receives confirmation that it is the client's ultimate responsibility to make the decision. The counselor was a student in a summer session practicum in counseling held at an urban university; the client we will call Edward Schaeffer.

Co 1: Hmm . . . You could look forward to that sort of thing when you get ready for college. Probably that would be on the college level rather than the high school level.

Cl 1: I want to get me ahold of some addresses that I could write to and find out what . . . well, I would appreciate it.

Co 2: All right.

Cl 2: Well that will be fine then . . . if I could get some of those . . .

Co 3: You mentioned that you would be interested in aptitude tests sometime during the summer. Are you still interested in that sort of thing?

Cl 3: Well, would the aptitude tests . . . What will they be about, I.Q.'s?

Co 4: We could get an I.Q. test . . . or aptitudes in mechanics . . . there's quite a number of general tests in that field. Then there are preference tests to help you understand what type of thing you would be most interested in doing.

Cl 4: Well, what would those tests . . . ah . . . what's the benefit of them?

Co 5: They would help you to see your own interests and abilities a little more clearly; it would give you something to think about as to what you would best be fitted to do . . . or what you would like to do . . . (pause) . . . A test never gives you a conclusive statement as to just what you ought to do, or necessarily what you would succeed in, but it would help you to see your own abilities a little more clearly . . . and your own interests a little more clearly. That would serve as a help in trying to make decisions as to what you want to do.

Cl 5: Hmmmm. . . .

Co 6: It's entirely a matter of your choosing. If you prefer not to take them, you don't have to. If you want to, why, we have them available here and I can get someone to give them to you. Then we can talk over the results.

Cl 6: Would that be in a big class?

Co 7: Probably not. Probably just you, or maybe one other person or whoever wanted to take them at the time.

Cl 7: They just benefit to see what I know . . .

Co 8: Just you, they wouldn't be used for anyone else . . . or for any other purpose but to help you. All of what we do in here is just a matter of helping you. And anything we talk about, or any of the scores, from the tests we give, will be kept entirely confidential. So, it just is a matter of helping you . . . Whatever you want to talk about, we will talk about . . . Whatever seems to be a point of interest to you, why, we'll try to work with it.

Cl 8: Well, . . . if they're just to prove what I want to get into . . . You say they are just a . . . I already know what I want to get into, and . . . . .

Co 9: All right.

Cl 9: . . . I mean . . . I wouldn't mind taking them, but if it's just to show what I would be best in . . .

Co 10: You feel you are pretty well fixed up.

Cl 10: I know what I . . . (pause) . . . there's no way you can get high school credit at all around here, is there?

Co 11: On the campus here?

The significance of Edward's rejection of tests is not clear at this early point in the first interview, whether they are, as he says, unnecessary, or whether he is being defensive. Later interviews led the counselor to conclude that this boy was unaware of his shortcomings and assumed that drive alone would carry him to his goals. (It might be argued that in such a case the counselor should try to get the client to be more realistic. Edward's counselor would probably reply that a permissive relationship will help the boy eventually to face reality more adequately) .

Contrasted with this counselor's attitudes are those expressed in the following excerpt from the first interview with Paul Engel, a high school sophomore:

Co 1: Now, we have a number of aptitude tests that you could take here and see your ability. We have quite a few in engineering. Would you like to come in, probably some morning; I think it may take more than just one hour, and take a series of these?

Cl 1: Sure.

Co 2: Well, we'll ... by all means give you a mechanical aptitude test there, . . . I don't think we'll need another one. Maybe we'll put down a personality . . . I won't give you these; there'll be another group of fellows, probably in this room. . . .

Cl 2: Uh, what does this personality test involve?

Co 3: Well, your ability to get along with other people, how you think of them, your attitudes toward work, family, things like that. The records are all confidential,—they don't go out of this office. Unless, if you'd like, the results of this conference or others, we can send a report to your counselor over at [high school] if you'd like.

Cl 3: I see.

Co 4: But I mean, unless you request it we won't do it. (pause) Is that clear then. . . .

Cl 4: Yeh.

Co 5: I mean this is voluntary on your part. You wanted it and we're going through with it, but we're not putting it on your record at school, or anything else,—or doing anything you wouldn't want.

Cl 5: Okay. That's okay then.

Co 6: Um hm. I think then, you seem pretty set in there, but an interest inventory might be a very nice test.

Cl 6: I'm not really sure though, if I really want to take air conditioning—, I might change my mind later on.

Co 7: Well, I don't think this would change very much in the field of engineering, and I think your interests would probably be up there. This is the one where they give you a list of three or so different jobs or things to do, and you have to punch the one you'd like to do least. So, it's a very easy thing to take. You can actually score it yourself. Well, how is your mathematics, generally?

Cl 7: Well, it isn't—it's pretty easy; to high school, anyway.

Co 8: Maybe we ought to put down a mathematics there.

Cl 8: Is this general mathematics or algebra?

Co 9: Well, we'd pick one that would fit your level. Seeing you haven't had algebra, we . . . wouldn't . . .

Cl 9: Well I had a little. . . .

Co 10: You had a little bit?

Cl 10: And I've . . . I've got a book home and, but I haven't studied it very much.

Co 11: Then I think we'll give you one with a little algebra in it, to see how well you will do on it and how you probably will react.

Cl 11: I don't know what I'll do on the algebra, though, I might uh, fail that.

Co 12: Well, we have quite a list of tests. I'll pick out one that tries to fit your ability pretty well. Don't worry about the results. All we're trying to do is find out more about you, so we can help you there, and I'll arrange another conference, probably about Friday of this week at the same time, if that's all right with you.

In addition to being quite inept at interviewing, this counselor discourages client participation in test planning. His personality doesn't permit him to plan co-operatively with clients. Edward Schaeffer's counselor, on the other hand, would find it quite difficult to relate to his clients in a more authoritative manner; he would feel uncomfortable taking that kind of responsibility for another's decisions.

In addition to the kind of relationship which each counselor finds most *congenial*, there is also the matter of his *willingness to struggle* with attempts to be dependent, uninvolved, and "test-obsessed" (Hanna, 1950). Even for a counselor who emphasizes client participation, it is hard work to deal with clients who resist playing a positive and constructive role. In this situation, many find the counselor-selection approach an easy way out, and some succumb to it under pressure from the situation or from clients.

Finally, Bordin (1955) has cautioned that the counselor's *knowledge of the tests and feeling of comfort with them* are necessary for skillful work in a co-operative test selection process. Inadequate knowledge of tests may lead to hasty choice (in response to the counselor's anxiety) and therefore inadequate opportunity for the client really to participate.

The Situation

In schools and agencies where the counselor's role is generally that of an adviser or an authority figure who makes decisions about institutional actions, it is difficult for a counselor to engage clients in a co-operating relationship. Even those counselors who generally are committed to, and suitable for, a client-selection approach, find themselves drawn into the more authoritarian pattern. In part this results from the general *tone* of the institution, but there are other more specific contributing factors, such as the way *referrals* are made ("You go down there and they'll give you a test to find out what you're suited for"). Another specific factor is the existence of a separate psychometrist or examiner and the expectation that clients are turned over to that person after the first interview for "testing." This expectation, it should be noted, is shared by receptionists and secretaries as well as by counselors and psychometrists.

As with other professional disagreements, the counselor in an incompatible situation resolves the conflict by one or a combination of the following methods: trying to persuade others of the wisdom of his point of view, changing his own attitudes, suppressing his feelings and conforming to local expectations, or leaving the situation for a more congenial one. The individual's decision usually involves a variety of internal factors, such as his frustration-tolerance level, his compulsiveness, his ability to compromise, and his need of a job.

The Client

Clients in general, especially children and adolescents, in schools or school-referred agencies, usually perceive counselors as authority figures endowed with both power and wisdom, or at least with the first of these qualities (Sonne and Goldman, 1957). In addition, they frequently seem to expect a cognitive service (Grant, 1954), with tests being particularly important. These general tendencies of clients to be *dependent* and *test-oriented* probably confront most counselors in most situations. To practice a client-participating approach requires that the counselor seek to counteract these tendencies; all who have struggled in this arena can attest to the strength of their opponents.

Beyond the general tendency are the *individual differences*. Some individuals, even some adolescents, approach counseling with maturity and independence and with readiness to seek and use information positively and constructively. With such clients test selection may proceed quickly and smoothly, and it may not matter very much which approach the counselor uses. At the other extreme are the quite immature, dependent, and poorly integrated persons. Despite their great need for personal growth, these clients frequently are unable to use the counselor's efforts to help them face reality and themselves. With them, also, perhaps, it may not matter so much which approach is used, since they probably can't use the help the counselor can provide. With such clients specific planning is often not feasible, and the counselor tries instead to make a good referral or to utilize the environment to help effect deep-level changes.

It would seem, then, that client participation in test selection is most likely to be really effective with those between the extremes—the ones who can benefit from the growth experiences.

PRINCIPLES OF THE TEST SELECTION PROCESS

The methods suggested in these pages are based on the assumptions heretofore made, namely, that client participation in test selection is generally desirable.

Structuring

It is necessary to communicate to clients the procedures and "ground rules" under which we propose to operate. The particular manner in

which this is done, and the timing, are an individual matter; each counselor must find one that for him is comfortable, genuine, and effective.
The following excerpt from the case of Richard Wilson, a recent high
school graduate, illustrates one counselor's approach. The typescript begins at about the mid-point of the interview; for a half hour or so, counselor and client have been exploring the needs and problems. Further
details are given in Chapter 11.

Co 1: Well, uh, let's see where we stand now, uh, we've talked a little bit about
some of the fields that you've given thought to—mostly it's merchandising,
secondarily engineering and teaching, uh, and you would like some ideas
as to your capability of handling these different fields, your capability of
succeeding in a college course.

Cl 1: Yes.

Co 2: Well, uh, maybe we can talk for a little while now about some of the
tests that we have, uh, and see whether we can plan some tests that would
help to answer some of the questions you have 'cause you see there is no
one kind of test that everybody takes. Instead, we have oh, uh, maybe a
hundred different tests and there are different types; there are college
aptitude tests and there are interest tests, and personality tests and there
are achievement tests that tell how much you know, how much you remember in different subjects, and uh, there are mechanical aptitude tests
and engineering aptitude and clerical aptitude and art aptitude and
music aptitude, uh, so nobody could take all the kinds of tests there are,
uh, and what we try to do is together to pick out those particular tests
which, will help you to answer the kinds of questions you have, and, you
look a little puzzled—as if . . .

Cl 2: No, I understand what you mean as far as, uh, you want to, um, see just
what test, through these interviews, just what test I'll be able to take, or
should take—

Co 3: Yeh. . . .

Cl 3: Which is best for me to take. . . .

Co 4: Uh-huh.

Cl 4: I understand what you mean in that. . . .

Co 5: This is something that I think we can best do together, uh, by talking
over each kind of test so that together we can decide, uh, whether that
particular kind of test will tell you anything new about yourself and
whether it will give you information that might be helpful to you, um
. . . and we can begin this, uh, by my telling you about some of the
kinds of tests there are in relation to some of the, uh, questions you've
already raised about yourself, uh, now also, of course, the more tests you
take, the more time you'll be spending here, and, uh, the more it will cost
and this is maybe another reason why, uh, we have to do this together,
uh. . . .

Verbal structuring is only one of the ways we communicate our procedures. Perhaps more important, in convincing the client, is communication through *actions*. Earlier in the interview with Edward Schaeffer we
saw an example of testing of limits by the client; the counselor could have

negated his verbal structure by trying, subtly or obviously, to persuade Edward that he should take some tests.

The structuring illustration given above is appropriate in those agency and school settings where testing is done in a concentrated fashion. Super (1950) has recommended a somewhat different approach, with tests given in a more flexible and scattered way, frequently one at a time as needed. The structuring of test selection would then begin with a general statement of the role of tests, but would not be followed by any attempt to actually plan a battery of tests at the time. Instead, in the first interview or whenever appropriate, client or counselor would initiate the topic of testing, most likely in connection with a particular need for information which developed from the interview. This approach to test selection has much to commend it; testing goes directly along with the total counseling process. Unfortunately, in many counseling offices in schools and agencies there is a tradition, in some instances a required procedure, which would make such a flexible approach to testing impossible. Super's recommendation will be referred to later in this chapter, as one approach to the timing of tests.

Client Doesn't Select Particular Tests

Bordin has warned ". . . the counselor should not burden the client with the responsibility for deciding which specific test is the best measure of a given psychological characteristic. This is a technical question which the counselor must be prepared to answer" (1955: p. 269) . As a matter of fact, what the client is usually concerned about is a particular *decision,* and he needs (or *feels* he needs, or perhaps the counselor feels he needs) certain *information* which is valid for, or predictive of, the one or more alternative courses of action. If, for instance, he is thinking of drafting as an occupation, he may have some interest in the fact that measured spatial relations ability is one of the correlates of success in drafting, but he is much more interested in the test's *implications for him.*

If we could predict behavior and describe people better than we presently do from our tests, we might not feel so strongly the need to share with clients the decision concerning which *characteristics* to measure. Client decision-making seems sometimes to be the end result of a strange sequence of reasoning: Since the counselor doesn't know which tests have any likelihood of helping with a particular problem, the client's choice is as good as any!

An approach that seems to us to have considerable merit is to ask counselees to participate in specifying alternative *courses of action* and *questions* about these alternatives. Some of these questions have nothing to do with tests, as for example, "What salaries are usual in pharmacy?" or "Which colleges offer courses in hotel management?" For those questions which may be answerable by tests, as "What are my chances of doing well in retailing?" the counselor indicates which tests can provide answers and the nature of the answers. The client can participate in deciding, first, whether this is a question he wishes answered. Second, he can participate in thinking about whether a particular kind of predictive information is already available, from tests or otherwise, and, if not, whether he then wants to try those tests which would be appropriate.

Unfortunately, with validity data as sparse as they are, we sometimes ask clients to decide which characteristics (and therefore which kinds of tests) are appropriate for a given area, when we ourselves don't really know. We say, "Verbal reasoning ability is important for success in college, but we don't know exactly the minimum amount needed, nor can we tell you how much of a lack of it can be compensated for by effort and time spent in studies. If your score is very high, that's a positive sign, if it's very low, that's a warning signal, but between the extremes your guess may be as good as mine."

We do now have, in a small number of instances, more specific expectancy and other validity data regarding education and occupation (more of this in Chapters 7 and 8); in those instances, we can be more definite: "From your score on this verbal reasoning test we can estimate your chances of attaining a *B* average or better at State U. Combining this score with a reading test score and your high school average, we can estimate your college grade more narrowly."

In most cases at present we must do with the more vague approach, consoling ourselves with the hope that a skillful counselor's estimate, based on the best test and other data available, is in the long run better than the client's own best guesses.[1] It may be further consolation to remind ourselves that the kinds of tests we use in counseling are still better validated than the projective devices on which our clinical colleagues often rely with a good deal less skepticism.

In spite of these difficulties there is a tendency of some counselors to overwhelm a client with a very technical presentation of tests and measurements, as in this brief excerpt from the case of Bette Morgan (Callis, Polmantier, and Roeber, 1955: p. 15) :

Co 40: Mm-huh. (*very long pause*) Well, here's what I have in mind at the moment as far as that test battery is concerned. Vocational interest will be one of the big factors in determining what kind of work, or what areas you would be most satisfied in working in (*pause*). We'll get at that through two different tests, approaching it from different frames of reference. I think for your own information we might have a recheck on intelligence (*pause*) —using a different test that should come out with essen-

----

[1] Even this generalization is sometimes questionable. A study by Young (1954) showed that under certain conditions college students predicted their grades as accurately as their counselors did.

tially the same answer except that it is specifically designed for adults, whereas the one that you took starts with, oh, maybe three-year-olds and goes up to adults, too. (*pause*) You will come out with a different I.Q., because there's a greater spread, a different interpretation for I.Q.'s on the Stanford-Binet for adults than there is for the Wechsler-Bellevue. We can actually equate those, and see what they would come out to be, for instance that 127 on the Binet, oh, might run (*pause*) maybe 120 to 125 somewhere in there on the Wechsler. You don't get quite as wide a spread of scores on the Wechsler as you do on the Binet, and that doesn't mean any difference in ability. . . .

Such lectures may satisfy a need of the counselor but are unlikely to communicate anything especially meaningful to the client. In fact, they may serve to increase the client's anxiety about (1) the threat of tests, and (2) the counselor's understanding of his problems.

In summary, whether or not we ask our client to share in the consideration of the decisions to be made, and in the exploration of his present characteristics as they may be relevant to those decisions, it seems clear that the choice of specific tests of those characteristics is the responsibility of the counselor.

Flexibility

Counselees, fortunately or otherwise, rarely pursue a consistent, rational and well-organized sequence of ideas and feelings during test-planning (or any other) interviews. To derive the full possibilities of such interviews, it is necessary to sense the client's reactions and to move *with* (or at least to move with recognition *of*) these reactions. We return to Richard Wilson's first interview for illustration of this kind of flexibility. Since *Cl.* 5 where we left them, Richard and the counselor have discussed the amount of time Richard has available for counseling and have established that there is no serious problem in that regard.

Co 11: Um, hm, . . . Well, um, let me, let me go down the list then, and uh, tell you about some of the kinds of tests and, uh, uh, then let's decide together about what tests to include, um, now I think the most obvious one, from all the things you have said, uh, is a test that would tell us, give us some idea as to your general thinking ability as compared with college freshmen in general learning ability, and we call these college aptitude tests, and we, um, have, um, two main ones that we use . . . one of them, uh, is a speed test and the other is not a speed test, that is, you take all the time you want, um, . . . now, you, both of them will give us some answer to the question of, uh, what your chances would be of succeeding in college. . . .

Cl 11: That is, a speed test, you said. One where they clock you, like.

Co 12: Yeah.

Cl 12: I understand . . . that's always been. . . .

Co 13: That's always been a source of difficulty with you. . . .

Cl 13: You know, you get these in school, the I.Q. test, and . . . I had a test
for the Air Force and it was ninety questions and I had fifty minutes
to do it in, and of course, there was mathematics in it and I went right
through it and I did every one as they came, and, uh, the math you'd
think I could skip over and do them last and I did them and worked
them out and took my time and I got, I think, it was seventy out of
ninety done in fifty minutes.

Co 14: Apparently, the time there wasn't too much of a handicap.

Cl 14: Well, as far as getting them all done it was. They figured that was plenty
of time.

Co 15: Oh, I see. In other words, you should have been able to get through all
of them.

Cl 15: That's right.

In *Cl* 12, Richard tentatively begins to express a feeling of concern
about timed tests; the counselor goes along with this, dropping for the
moment the description of available tests.

To illustrate the practical value of client participation—in making a
good selection of tests—we include the next few minutes of the interview.

Co 16: Uh, huh, well, perhaps it would be, uh, be helpful if we gave you a
non-speed test, and this would tell you, uh, your college aptitude, when
you have all the time you want.

Cl 16: I think a speed test would be good, too, uh, I mean that would give you
a better idea of just, I mean, I can tell you that I'm slow but maybe this
test, uh, things would work out all right and I wouldn't be slow.

Co 17: First, we could, we could use both, and, uh, then we could see just what
the difference is. How much of a handicap you have because of speed.
This means more time, of course; one of them takes . . . the one that's
timed takes about an hour and the one that's untimed would take as
much time as you want but you could figure that if you work slowly, it
will take about three hours . . . How do you feel about it, do you want to
take both?

Since his reluctance to take a timed test has been accepted by the counselor in *Co* 16, Richard can go on in *Cl* 16 to suggest that both a speeded
and unspeeded test might be even better than one alone. Not only is this a
sound plan, but it is *Richard's*, with all the resulting advantages earlier
discussed: more motivation to take the tests, less defensiveness in discussing the results later, and so on.

Another example of flexibility occurs immediately afterwards; again the
client is more concerned with an associated feeling than with the problem
of test selection itself, and again the counselor follows him:

Cl 17: Oh, sure, yes, I'd like to very much. I often wondered um, what the
difference was between my father and I. Anything mental, uh, he can
do in a snap, whereas, things physical, he was never, you know, never
very good at, and it's just the opposite with me. A complete difference.
It's like night and day between my father and I. . . .

Co 18: Yeah.

Cl 18: I don't know. It must be the Irish in my mother. . . .

Co 19: Uh-huh.

Cl 19: But it's just like night and day between my dad and I. I mean, I was built for football, whereas, he wasn't and he, uh, had quite a bit of intelligence which he didn't want to use but then did use and, uh, he's quick at things like that.

Co 20: Mm-hm. Mm-hm.

Cl 20: You know, it's always seemed funny to me . . . as far as the difference between a man and his son could be so much.

Co 21: Mm-hm. Mm-hm.

Cl 21: Maybe it isn't, maybe it's just me, thinking it so much.

Co 22: Mm-hm. Mm-hm. (20 second pause). In other words, you expect that you would be more like him.

Cl 22: Well, you know, they always say you look like your father, you do that like your father and all.

Co 23: Mm-hm.

Cl 23: But, it's just like night and day. I don't even look like him.

Co 24: Mm-hm. Mm-hm, you just didn't take after his side of the family.

Cl 24: That's right.

Co 25: Mm-hm.

Cl 25: My sister, she did actually, 'cause she was very brilliant in school. She had to study though, to get it . . . I mean a lot of things seem easy to her.

Co 26: Uh-huh.

Cl 26: She won a scholarship and all . . . but there she's quick . . . in her mind.

Co 27: Mm-hm.

Cl 27: My brother, I think, is gonna be just like me.

Co 28: Mm-hm.

Cl 28: All sports and no study. I hope he's not gonna be . . . that's what it looks like now. . . .

Co 29: You sound like you wish that you could, you could have been a little bit different.

Cl 29: A little more like my father.

Co 30: Um. Hm. (20 second pause) Mm-hm. Sort of hoping that maybe these tests will show you as being a little bit more like him in ability than you, at the moment, think you are.

Cl 30: Maybe they will.

Co 31: Mm-hm. Mm-hm. (15 second pause) Mm-hm . . . Well, let's see, we've got a couple of academic aptitude tests now, uh, now another. . . .

In *Co* 30, the counselor seems to judge that the client has pursued this topic about as far as he can and returns then to testing. Other counselors might have been more aggressive in *Co* 31 and probed more or suggested interpretations of Richard's expressed feelings.

Miscellaneous

Several other points of technique need only brief mention:

1. The client's early statement of a need for tests should not be taken at *face value*. "I've always wanted to take a personality test" should not be followed by "All right, we'll give you one," but rather by an effort to

explore the meaning of this request. Is it simple curiosity, or has she been told she has "no personality" and expects the tests to contradict this, or is she anxious and perhaps depressed about herself as a person and really asking for help with this as directly as she can? The client often needs assistance in clarifying, for herself as well as for the counselor, what it is she wants and needs. For some, it is a matter of not really understanding what is troubling them and what needs to be done. Others sense the cause of the difficulty but cannot get themselves to reveal this to the counselor.

A general principle that is always in order, especially at the beginning of counseling, is to keep doors open for new hypotheses—as many as are at all reasonable—regarding the nature of the problem. At the same time, the principle of flexibility must be applied. When a client rejects the counselor's pet hypothesis, it may be a warning to drop it, at least for a while. This sometimes means that we go along with a client's request for a more superficial, informational service even when we are quite sure that this is not the "real problem." For that client at that point in time, this may be as much of a "real problem" as he can deal with.

2. *We all make mistakes.* In writing about these matters and discussing cases after the fact, it is possible to achieve greater approximation of perfection than in the midst of a counseling session itself. Even experienced and well-trained counselors look back at interviews and realize that they have missed an important client feeling or have subtly persuaded a client to take a test that really has no function save to satisfy the counselor's curiosity. Not infrequently, the counselor finds that he guessed wrong and that a test he thought would provide useful information makes no contribution.

3. *All existing sources of data* should be explored. A basic principle of information theory (see Chapter 2) is that we keep adding information only as long as something new is obtained. As Cronbach has explained (1955) additional achievement tests may add very little new information to what is already known from a record of grades and from previous achievement tests. Weitz and others (1955) have described a situation where college entrance tests already on file were ignored and additional tests were used to select students for special English classes. It was later found that the entrance exams in combination with certain grades were just as effective as the new tests for this purpose.

Counseling agencies frequently start from scratch with counselees, making no use of the accumulated information in school records and elsewhere. Counselors in all kinds of institutional settings sometimes move right into test planning after a particular need for information has been defined, without first attempting to explore with the client those of his previous experiences which might provide relevant information. For example, a question about chances of success in college can, for many colleges, be answered as well from a high school record as from new tests of scholastic aptitude. Likewise many clients can just as well describe their interests by recalling their reactions in a variety of situations as they can by taking most kinds of interest inventories available. With personality inventories, we frequently discover that people know about themselves just about what most paper-and-pencil inventories will reveal; using the interview rather than an inventory sometimes stimulates a self-descriptive effort, which may be more diagnostically valuable than formal measures. Also, self-description and recall of previous experiences have the inestimable value of making the client an active participant rather than a passive bystander in the appraisal process.

There is, however, one matter for concern in the use of previous information. Collection by the counselor of information from school records, employers, teachers, and others may encourage an attitude of dependence in the client. It is as if the counselor were saying (as some no doubt do), "I've looked through your records here, and I've sent away for your previous records, and so I know a great deal about you." To which the client might well respond, in attitude if not in so many words, "Fine, then you can now test me and tell me what you think I should do."

This difficulty may be avoided if the counselor shares with the client some of the decisions regarding use of record materials. The subject may be presented in such terms as: "Sometimes it's helpful to know how well you did in various school subjects, as a guide to your abilities and interests. Also, if you took any tests at————, we (or you) might ask that copies be sent here. How do you feel about doing that?" We have known occasional high school students and graduates to reject the idea, when they really have an opportunity to do so, on the grounds that they would "just as soon start with a clean slate," or they "don't feel my high school record is really a fair picture of what I could have done." In these instances, valuable discussion of the school situation may ensue. In some cases, genuine acceptance by the counselor leads the client to see that it is *his* information, to be used in making *his* decisions, and that he need not fear the counselor's reaction to the records and reports.

Perhaps the only thing the counselor who already has certain information about his counselee may do is to communicate his open-mindedness and intention to use information available only as the client is ready to accept it.

In whatever situation he finds himself, the counselor will find instances where he must choose between getting certain diagnostic information about a client and maintaining a relationship in which the client feels responsible and unthreatened. Giving in to the desire for more complete information about a school record may mean reducing the client's participation, confidence, or independence. Each counselor must find his own most effective range of behavior in such situations. The word *range* is used to suggest that for most counselors there will be some adaptation of procedure to the needs and characteristics of particular clients.

WHEN IS TESTING DONE?

Some counselors do all their testing of one client during a single period of time between two interviews. This is so routinized in some counseling centers that the staff refers to the second interview as the "close-out," with the assumption that a battery of tests is universally given between the first and second interviews. Others, as previously mentioned in this chapter, have a less rigid procedure, in which tests are used as deemed necessary: sometimes in a battery after the first interview, but at other times singly between interviews or during an interview, or whenever client and counselor decide that information is needed. In schools, testing is most often done *en masse,* sometimes as part of home-room or group guidance classes, but more often quite independent of any established counseling relationship. Some of the pertinent factors affecting these approaches have already been discussed—counseling school-of-thought, school or agency policy, nature of the clientele, and so forth.

The varieties of approaches seem to fall into the following major categories:

Uniform battery. All counselees take the same group of tests, which in agencies usually are comprehensive in nature, covering general intelligence, the major special aptitudes, interests, and personality. In school testing programs, a similar uniformity exists, but the tests ordinarily are taken over a period of years, perhaps general intelligence one year, interest another, and differential aptitudes another. Whether in schools or agencies, economy of staff time seems to be the major advantage of this approach. This method seemed to reach its peak in a few agencies during the period of overwhelming veteran caseloads after World War II. It is much less frequently heard of now, except in schools, because of many disadvantages—inappropriate and unnecessary tests being given to some, no client participation, and the almost inevitable assembly-line atmosphere.

Individualized Battery. Each client takes all *his* tests in a group but they are not necessarily the same as those taken by the others. This seems to be a frequent approach in agencies; "testing" is a separate phase (at least in time) of the counseling process, but it is tailored to the individual's needs, characteristics, and expressed goals.

Preliminary Screening Battery. This approach has been tried with both a uniform and an individualized battery of tests, usually apparently as a compromise between them. General tests, say intelligence and interest, are given first, to narrow down both the *level* and the *field* (Hahn and MacLean, 1955) of the client's possible courses of action. Then the counselor alone, or in co-operation with the client, selects a more individualized battery.

A theoretical rationale for a preliminary screening approach has been proposed, based on the concepts of decision theory (Cronbach, 1955). Applied particularly to group testing as practiced in schools, the suggestion is to arrange a program of "sequential testing." A short test, say of achievement or academic aptitude, is given to all. For some in the group, the necessary decision (choice of school, course of study or administrative assignment to sections) may be made on the basis of information from that test alone. Further tests continue to narrow down the decision for additional students until the added information for decision-making obtained from each new test is less than the cost of testing. Cronbach suggests another application—of value in individual as well as group arrangements: A relatively brief test of only moderate reliability is given, followed by longer, more reliable tests in those areas indicated as promising. This can even be done in the area of interests, a general inventory being used first to point up one or more broad areas for each student. Then each of the areas highlighted is further tested in greater detail than is possible with our present interest inventories, most of which are a compromise between the screening and detailed kinds of test. The two-phase approach to interest measurement is illustrated by the California Test Bureau's *Occupational Interest Inventory,* which samples six fields (such as Personal-Social and Mechanical) , and the six *Vocational Interest Analyses,* each of which provides a more detailed analysis of the individual's interests in that particular field.

A variant of this approach was proposed by North (1956), who suggested the development of short multifactor batteries for screening purposes, to be followed by selected long diagnostic tests in those areas highlighted in the battery.

Further support for this screening approach was given recently by West (1958) who objects to the tendency to assign the same tests to all clients rather than practice selectivity. West is especially concerned about lack of discrimination as to reading level and general level of mental ability and suggests the use of the *Kent E G Y* and the vocabulary section of the *Gates Reading Survey* to provide a brief (20-45 minutes) diagnosis of intelligence and reading level. Further tests can then be more specifically selected in terms of these variables. This approach may also provide valuable information so that appropriate occupational information may be used later in counseling.

Actually, for many counselors, interviews and records serve as informal screening devices to narrow down the choice of tests. *Types* of tests are suggested by reported interests, hobbies, and contemplated goals, and appropriate *levels* of tests are indicated by such data as previous educational attainments and verbal expression and understanding during the interview.

As-Needed. In the approach described by Super (1950), tests are more dynamically used and are more clearly interwoven with the ongoing counseling process than in the other approaches. There is no set point at which testing occurs; as a need for certain information or experience becomes manifest, a test or group of tests is used. The results are then discussed in relation to the topic that led to test planning. Further tests may then be planned, or not, depending on the needs defined in further interviewing. Many who have tried this method find that tests become less mechanized and less separated from the rest of counseling; they are really "tools," as almost all practitioners agree they should be. This approach may be less appealing to those who prefer to view appraisal as a process clearly isolated from the other elements of counseling and who like their testing to be done in neat packages rather than scattered unpredictably throughout the course of counseling.

Evaluation of the Four Approaches

Claimed differences among the approaches can be tested through carefully planned research studies, of which there seems at this date to be none bearing directly on the critical questions. As with many other important issues in our field, evaluation of the methods must therefore be based instead on logic, personal experiences, and the demands and limits of the local work situation. For us, the weight of logic is in favor of the As-Needed approach, in terms both of the likelihood that more appropriate tests will be used, and the likelihood that tests will fall into proper perspective—as reality testing devices (Bordin, 1955) which contribute to growth and development as well as to the decision-making process which is counseling as we view it.

GROUP TESTING PROGRAMS

At first glance, the principles and procedures thus far stated would not seem to be applicable to those situations in which tests are selected for groups rather than for individuals. In many colleges, for example, all entering freshmen take a battery of tests, such as academic aptitude and reading comprehension, although none may ever have expressed an interest in taking tests. Similarly, it is customary for entire classes in elementary or secondary schools to be administered the same tests of achievement, aptitude, and interest without any choice on the part of the students.

We may ask: First, is it absolutely necessary to give the same tests to entire groups in this way? Second, even in those situations where alternatives are not possible, can some elements of client participation be introduced? Our contention is that the answer to the first question can often be "No" and to the second, "Yes."

Is Uniform Testing Necessary?

There appear to be two reasons for the practice of giving all students the same tests: First, it makes possible the accumulation of local norms and local validity studies (Angell, 1959), as well as data for other research purposes. Second, it is more economical of staff time in the administration and scoring of tests. This is perhaps the more usual reason for the practice. However, a closer look at the conditions which usually prevail in group testing programs leads one to doubt that even these two purposes are well served. The fact is that unknown numbers of students take such tests with attitudes and a frame of mind hardly conducive to accurate measurement of ability, interest, and personality attributes. One who gains the confidence of high school and college students who have been through such mass testing programs will hear: "Oh, I didn't try very hard on that test— everybody knows that your score can't affect your standing in school." Or, "We all collaborated in Miss R's room; after all, nobody wants to look stupid." And, "Oh, that interest test? Everybody thought it was a big joke; no one took it seriously!" These students obviously had little appreciation of the possible value of these tests for later counseling. We may add to these cases those in which the student was overly anxious about the tests and did less well than otherwise he might. Adequate pretest preparation may reduce the level of anxiety by helping the individual (in groups or alone) to perceive the testing program more realistically.

For any serious use of the results of such mass testing, a counselor might well require a retest, since he could not be certain which scores were dependable. In this case mass testing is patently false economy; it is even dangerous, if undependable test data are ever used as a basis for important decisions, for development of local norms and local validity studies, or for other research purposes.

Hence, institutions using test results primarily for guidance purposes might well question their mass testing methods. In the long run, students might be served more adequately by individualized methods of test selection. The advantages of economy can be maintained by administering tests to groups; it is not necessary, however, for *all* students to take exactly the same tests. Careful scheduling makes it possible for individuals to take the tests they are ready for at the time they have reached the point of readiness. The result might be unsettling to the administrator or guidance worker who likes neatly packaged operations. Those who can live with the more dynamic approach, however, will probably find it superior in all the really important ways: improved morale, better motivation, and more learning from the test-taking process itself.

Incidentally, we are not excluding noncounseling testing programs, such as those used exclusively for curriculum evaluation or sectioning. Even in such instances, adequate preparation of the students is necessary, in order to maximize the reliability and validity of measurement.

Can They Be Improved?

Many institutions have been aware of the shortcomings of mass testing programs, and some have made efforts to improve the situation. Since the literature contains so few reports of any such efforts, we must deal essentially with impressions gained from personal contacts. Apparently, the most usual improvement attempted is the use of *group orientation meetings* prior to testing, in an effort to improve motivation and decrease undue anxiety. This method may be effective if given enough time and if the groups worked with are not so large that what ensues is not much more than lectures or pep talks.

One such program is reported by Malloy and Graham (1954). Groups of college students (restricted to about 20), previously screened as suitable for this approach, meet for about one hour prior to a uniform testing battery. The purposes of the tests are explained and questions are answered. The counselor tries to stimulate the development of some group structure; it is felt that the resulting identification with a group reduces tension during the testing itself. Although no research data are available, the writers also claim that this method of test structuring saves time. For those committed to the basic concept of spreading counseling services among a large caseload, this approach seems to offer at least some opportunity to reduce client passivity and to stimulate a feeling of involvement in the testing process.

An interesting technique is described by Slotkin (1954). A group of high school dropouts enrolled in required continuation courses was led to "standardize" a simple motor test. The interest which developed was then channeled into improving their understanding of tests in general. Unfortunately, no systematic or rigorous evaluation is reported, but it is claimed that there was ". . . greater interest engendered in the self-measurement process . . ." and ". . . greater comprehension of the meaning of particular test scores in the individual counseling that followed the self-measurement project" (p. 416).

What seems to be needed is the equivalent of group or multiple counseling, in which the individuals, though meeting in groups, can actually become active participants in a process which becomes meaningful to them. At this point, they may have some choice as to which test they will take (this is probably not as administratively impossible as it may seem), or they may all take the same battery. In either case, it seems likely that they will enter testing with some of the more positive attitudes and advantages which are claimed for client participation.

Broader Participation in Institutional Test Selection

When entire classes take the same tests, planning the testing program must necessarily affect others beside counselors and students. Teachers must often give up precious class time and sometimes are asked to aid in administration and scoring. The tests are sometimes intended for multiple use: curriculum evaluation, admission to certain programs and classes, and counseling. This necessarily affects curriculum specialists, administrators, department chairmen, and others. It seems obvious, then, that those affected should have opportunities for participating in appropriate ways in the process.

The reasons here are in general similar to those offered to support the idea of client participation. For one, more suitable tests would be chosen if all those who will later want something from the results play a role in the planning process. Second, teachers might be better motivated to administer the test properly if they had a feeling of identification with the program. Third, later application of the test results by teachers to improve instruction would be aided by the teachers' better comprehension of the tests and their purposes.

As with the question of *client* participation, here also we are dealing with hypotheses which seem to be logical and based on sound psychological knowledge. As before, careful research is needed to test the hypotheses.

The reader interested in much more extended discussion of this topic will find helpful material in Lindquist (1951), as well as in various textbooks on educational measurement (Greene, Jorgensen, and Gerberich, 1953, 1954) . General discussions of school testing programs and operations may also be found in two recent publications by Hill (1959) and Stoughton (1959). The former consists mainly of forms and procedures for evaluating a school's testing activities, but the latter contains many ideas and specific procedures for the use of tests in schools.

CHAPTER 4

Selecting the Test

We ADDRESS ourselves now to the question: *Which tests* will best suit a particular client or group? This question may be broken down into five component parts, which will serve as an outline for the chapter:

1. What purposes are to be served by tests for this client at this time?
2. What particular information, prediction, or description is needed in connection with the particular decision, plan, or action? Which of these can best be obtained through tests?
3. What information is already available? Of the remainder, which might best be obtained through tests?
4. What characteristics of the client define or limit the tests that might be used?
5. What are the relevant characteristics of tests that are to be matched with the needs as defined above?

PURPOSES OF TESTING AND OF TEST SELECTION

Having examined the purposes of testing in considerable detail in Chapter 2, we now go on to discuss their implications for the *content* of test selection. In that earlier chapter the counseling purposes of testing were organized into two broad categories—informational and noninformational—and then were listed as subdivisions of these categories. Each type of purpose may now be seen as a series of questions leading to the final question: Which test will serve this purpose best?

Informational Purposes

Precounseling Diagnostic Information

Is this person likely to benefit from my services?
What is the nature of the problem or need which has brought him here?

In what areas of his life is the problem or need?

How able is he to make use of a relatively cognitive, decision-oriented kind of service?

Are there any symptoms of disturbances or problems that would lead me to suggest referral elsewhere?

Information for the Counseling Process Itself

Within the range of services that I can provide, what are his particular needs?

How adequate is his knowledge of his abilities, interests, personality?

Is information his major need, or is it something like reassurance or resolution of a conflict?

Does he have a fairly realistic expectation of what tests can do?

Information Relating to the Client's Post-Counseling Decisions

Does he have any ideas as to what courses of action he might pursue?

Has he defined one or more such possible courses?

If so, how much does he know about the consequences of each?

How clearly does he see himself in relation to each of them?

What does he need with regard to each alternative: information about it, information about his relevant characteristics, or an opportunity to test his self-concept in relation to it?

What particular kind of information is needed—about aptitudes, achievements, interests, personality?

How much does he already know of what needs to be known?

Noninformational Purposes

Stimulation of Interest in Areas not Previously Considered

Are there areas, or courses of action, which the client has not considered and which seem to merit consideration as he approaches a decision or plan?

Are there abilities, interests, or other characteristics of himself that he seems not to recognize adequately?

Laying Groundwork for Later Counseling. Here there are really no particular goals of test selection; the results, usually of program testing, are presented in order to ascertain any immediate needs for counseling, and, if not, to indicate that "the door is open." The only implication for test selection is to select tests whose results are likely to be of interest to potential counselees.

Learning Experience in Decision-Making. The goal here is not so much the information which will come from the tests, but rather the contribution to the client's skill and confidence in making decisions. If the tests chosen turn out later to have been wise choices, the contribution toward self-confidence is obvious. Even if the choice should be a poor one, however, there can be value to the client in the experience, as he realizes that one can survive poor decisions and go on to benefit from them. As with the previous purpose, then, for this particular use of tests the tests selected are not nearly so important as the *manner* in which they are selected and the manner in which the counselor later helps his client to learn from the experience.

Research. Rarely do practioners use tests strictly for research purposes; when they do, the selection of particular tests should follow the procedures of good research design which usually include: definition of the problem and the purposes of the study, formulation of hypotheses, and selection or construction of appropriate tests. More often, however, the same tests used for counseling are also to be incorporated into a research project. Here one may run the risk of doing a disservice to one of the functions—research or service—through trying to perform both simultaneously. There is a temptation, on the one hand, to use a second-best test for a particular client or group, because one is interested in gathering research data about that test. On the other hand, a research project may be designed using a not-quite-appropriate test, just because one happens to use it frequently. A case can be made for either solution, with the rationale in the first instance that clients in general will be better served if more research is done, and in the second that the less-than-ideal piece of research which results is all that most of us can hope to do and is better than nothing. Sometimes a resolution may be, with the client's permission, to add the research-motivated test to batteries of which it would otherwise not be a part. Under these circumstances, fee-charging agencies should not charge for this test. The final resolution of these conflicts must, to some extent, remain the responsibility of the individual institution and counselor and will reflect their values and interest.

WHAT DO WE NEED TO KNOW?

Having defined the purposes of testing for a particular individual or group, we now go on to spell out the specific information or experience [1] that tests are to provide. It may be a matter of estimating the client's probability of succeeding in an occupation, in an educational program, or in a marriage with a particular person. Or it might be a question of the client's likely satisfaction with one or another of these courses of action.

[1] *Experience* is used here to indicate the noninformational purposes of tests. Included are experiences in decision-making and experiences of being stimulated to consider new areas or courses of action.

In the category of *precounseling diagnostic information,* it might be a need to appraise the client's degree of freedom from psychopathology or his likelihood of dropping out of school or of becoming delinquent. In the category of *information for the counseling process itself,* we may need to find out whether the individual has rather sharply focussed interests in one area of activities or conflicting interests in two or more areas, or whether, as he claims, he has "no idea at all of what I'm interested in."

In defining the particular need within one of our categories of purpose, there are two rather different "models" or approaches—the *statistical, actuarial,* or *mechanical approach* and the *clinical approach.* These will be explained in greater detail in Chapters 7 to 10; their implications for test selection can be treated briefly here. Models, though most practitioners do not follow them rigorously, are nevertheless valuable in aiding, even forcing, us to be conscious of the processes used in going from a test score to an interpretation, prediction, or piece of advice. Models are indispensable for careful research, providing, as they do, a proposed map or blueprint of the area to be studied.

Statistical Approach

Included here are such methods as norm comparisons, profile analysis, regression analysis, and discriminant analysis.[2] All have in common a more-or-less direct and more-or-less mechanical relationship between certain present characteristics of an individual and some criterion of success or satisfaction, usually in the future.

Thus we can estimate the probability of a student's getting a *B* in intermediate algebra if we have data for a comparable group showing the correlation between test scores and grades in that course. Or we can tell an individual what his chances are of *being* a chemist from knowledge of his *Strong Vocational Interest* profile. Or we might be able to tell what his chances are of being successfully married, or being an alcoholic, or benefiting from psychotherapy, if we have prediction or expectancy data for tests in relation to each of these contingencies. In each instance, we must have data available for *that* test, in relation to *that* school subject, occupation, or other condition, state, or "treatment," as these are all labelled in decision theory. None of this is to imply that *perfect* predictions are ever made, but simply to say that estimates or statements of *probability* are made within the limits of error (reliability) both of the test and of the criterion. It is also assumed that a suitable norm group is used, and that a relationship exists between predictor (test) and criterion (what is being predicted) .

Test selection using this model involves locating the test or tests which have been validated for the particular purpose we have in mind. Unfortunately, this is easier said than done. For most courses of action or

[2] These will be discussed in Chapter 8.

"treatments" (occupations, school subjects) the requisites for the statistical or mechanical method do not obtain. Either there are no normative or validity data for the particular "treatment" we have in mind, or there are no specific tests for that treatment, or if there are, they may have insufficient reliability, or perhaps the correlation between test and criterion is too small to be useful. For this reason, the clinical approach is the more usual one in counseling.

Clinical Approach

The process will be more extensively discussed in Chapter 9. In its most elaborate and rigorous form, the counselor begins by developing inductively a picture of the individual from the variety of data available. Inferences are first drawn from test scores and other data; they are then verified or contradicted by checking against additional facts; and then hypotheses are derived until a rather complete picture of the individual has been constructed. A deductive method is used for estimating how such a person would likely behave in a particular situation, whether school, occupation, or marriage. Finally, the counselor may make an over-all judgment as to the client's chances of being successful or happy in the situation.

This process is illustrated in the following test interpretation, which is presented here as the counselor might think it out loud:

Ted says he's unsure about engineering as a career but he seems vague in his reasons. As we were discussing it, interests seemed to be his main concern, but perhaps more important, though he is reluctant to admit it, is some concern about abilities. After discussing this for a while, we decided to use tests in both areas, since he seemed to block on any further discussion of his feelings and those of his family about this decision. College aptitude test scores are low average for freshmen at the college he's considering, which means they're even lower as compared with engineering freshmen there. This suggests (*inference*) that he would have a hard time in that program; incidentally, this is the same prediction I'd make from his high school record (*confirmation* or *verification*). Since he's well aware of the requirements for engineering college, why has he chosen this goal and why is he reluctant to discuss the ability area? Let's leave this for a moment and look at the interest profile. On the *Strong*, he has a much more pronounced cluster on Group IV (Technician) than on II (Physical Sciences), and his Occupational Level score is also more appropriate for the technician or even skilled-worker level. All this would imply that his expressed goal is at too theoretical a level and requires too much academic preparation. Why, then, did he choose it? Or did he? (Apparent *contradiction*, with just the suggestion of an hypothesis to explain it.)

What's the family constellation . . . father a draftsman . . . Ted said he was sorry he never finished college . . . mother was an elementary teacher before marriage . . . college graduate. I wonder if all these pieces fit together to form a picture of a boy whose own ambition and interests would lead him to a skilled mechanical or maybe a technician level—perhaps not unlike his father (*hypothesis*). Sounds like a socially aspiring family whose upward mobility requires college level goals for their children (*hypothesis*). Could it be that Ted's evasiveness when I asked him about his family's feelings about careers means that they're pressing him pretty hard to be an engineer? Might be even more specific than that—maybe father is projecting his own unfulfilled ambitions on Ted.

If this is true—and I'm not at all sure it is, but we can try to explore it when I see Ted again—Ted would receive considerable pressure at home not to give up his engineering goal; maybe I'd have to talk with his parents and try to help them to see the situation. Might even be worse than that: Ted's whole self-concept—the way he wants to live, kinds of friends, girl he'll marry—is based on a high professional occupational level. Is all this pressure so great that he'll just have to make a try at engineering? Maybe this would give him enough drive to study so that, especially at a less competitive college, he would make it.

This gives me some hypotheses to work on when I see Ted again. As we go over his test results—or maybe I can get him to talk about self-concept and family without bringing in the tests—I'll try to get him to explore some of these areas to see how accurate my "model" of him is. What would be his best choice? Well, we'll have to see first whether we've included all relevant factors; for one thing, I don't know how he really feels about all this—he was pretty evasive about it last time we talked. Then maybe I'll try to help him see the alternatives and the likely implications of each. After that, he'll have to decide which course of action is most likely to meet his (and his family's) needs. It might help to have his parents in for a talk.

Obviously a situation as complex as this doesn't lend itself to mechanical analysis and prediction, at least not at the current stage of development of the science and art of appraisal. The statistical or mechanical method might play a role *within* the clinical; if regression equations were available, we could estimate more precisely Ted's likelihood of success in College *A*, in Technical Institute *B*, or in Apprenticeship *C*. Such predictions would increase the counselor's confidence in his clinical analysis and would provide him with expectancy data which will probably be more acceptable to the client and his parents.

Implications for Test Selection

The two different methods do not necessarily lead to choice of different tests; the differences in some cases will be only in the process. In the statistical method, the counselor locates tests having such relationships with the "treatment" being considered that a direct statement of probability can be made. If it is a *precounseling diagnostic question,* for example, as to the client's likelihood of benefiting from counseling, the agency may have developed and validated a questionnaire including biographical and personality items which may be scored to yield a single number representing the probability of completing counseling successfully. Such an instrument might include questions about age, family composition, focal point of the problem, anxiety level, or dependence—whatever combination that agency has found, empirically, to predict success in counseling.

Not having such a locally validated instrument, the counselor would use a clinical method, perhaps in such a fashion as this:

Linda seems not to be entirely open with me; she says she's not sure about which career she wants, but I have the feeling that this isn't really the problem. She seems somewhat depressed, and she hasn't mentioned a thing about friends or dates. I wonder if the source of her difficulties is in the area of personal relations; there may be personality problems that she ought to be bringing to a different counselor. It might be helpful if she took the *MMPI* and maybe filled out our Activities Inventory. This could give me some clues as to the source of her anxiety and therefore some idea as to whether I'm the one to help her or whether I should make a referral.

In those instances where the same counselor handles both vocational and personal counseling, the foregoing analysis would be classified in our second category, as *information for the counseling process itself*. In that case, the counselor would be trying to determine which of his services is most likely to be helpful.

In the third category of uses of tests, *information relating to the client's post-counseling decisions,* we find most of the uses of tests, whether through the more direct statistical approach or the more indirect clinical approach. The case of Ted, cited earlier, illustrates test selection for this kind of purpose. As specifically as possible, counselor and client pose questions: (1) What are my chances of getting a passing average in College *A*? (2) Am I likely to be happier as a lawyer or as an accountant? (3) Is psychotherapy likely to help me with my marital problems? (4) Would it help my child to transfer him to a private school? (5) I'm thinking of quitting my job and changing to a similar job with another company; will this reduce the tension I feel in my work? (6) I've never done any organized thinking about my abilities; just what am I capable of doing? For some of these questions, such as the first, it may be possible to locate an expectancy table (see Chapter 7) which will provide a direct statement of probability of success in College *A*, given a score on Test *X*. In the case of questions such as the fourth, the data for a mechanical reply are not likely to be available, so that here it will be necessary to follow a more indirect (clinical) method. This might involve analyzing the question into its components, selecting those tests which are likely to give relevant information about the child, then developing one's picture of him, and finally concluding that this kind of child is likely to function in such-and-such a manner in a private school.

USING AVAILABLE DATA

Records and Reports

Having decided, one way or another, what information is wanted, should we use available data, including records of grades and previous tests, or is it better to give new tests? This question resolves itself largely to a matter of reliability and validity. To what extent can we rely upon a school or agency record as a dependable indication of abilities? Are grades in courses indicative of the student's capabilities, or even of his actual achievements? Schools differ vastly in their approach to grading, both with regard to standards and to the components of a teacher's grade: effort, co-operation, appearance, and the weight given to classroom versus tested achievements. Even *within* a school, there are often marked differences among teachers in the meaning of a grade. Is the record of extraclass activities accurate and complete, and can it be used as a basis for reaching conclusions about an individual's social relations and leadership behavior? Election to the Student Council in one school denotes recognition of outstanding scholarship, in another popularity, and in still another is a recognition of management ability.

How much confidence can we place in the recorded results of tests which have been administered and scored by a variety of teachers, guidance workers, and clerks? This question must of necessity be answered in relation to the particular institution and its characteristics. We have already commented (Chapter 1) on the amount of error in administration, scoring, and recording of test scores, particularly in schools. Also previously noted (Chapter 3) is the usual inadequate *preparation* for group testing, with resulting deficiencies in motivation, excesses of anxiety, and other undesirable effects.

All these problems are familiar to counselors in agencies and in schools and colleges that have made use of school records. The crux of the problem seems to be not knowing the significance and dependability of recorded information for that particular school. A counselor within an institution can eventually learn how to interpret Frank's 85 in English III with Miss Peterson and the significance of Marcia's selection as president of her class. He also has some basis for judging the reliability of administration and scoring of tests of various kinds in that school. His local experience may lead him to find increased value in all these sources of data, or, on the contrary, to conclude that certain of them are not usable.

A counselor outside of the particular institution where the record originates may also be able to learn some of these things, but with greater difficulty. College personnel workers often become familiar with some of their feeder high schools as they work with the graduates of those schools, correspond with their staffs, and use their records. By talking with the graduates of a particular school and comparing their college records with those from the high school, insights are gained that may be generalized to other graduates of that school. High school counselors gain similar insights about their feeder elementary schools.

Moreover, agency counselors can in the same way improve the informational value to them and their clients of data from local schools. All this requires effort; at best, extra-institutional counselors find that these data are of restricted and questionable value. Some decide that the results are not worth the amount of effort and therefore operate without any serious or systematic use of outside information.

The answer to our original question is now evident: it depends. Without personal knowledge of the institution from which the records are obtained, it is difficult to use the information. In such instances it is often better to use one's own tests, about whose administration, scoring, and recording more is known.

Checking Records for Dependability

Even in the absence of personal knowledge of the institution, certain checks may be made of the usability of the information. One such index is the apparent *completeness* of the transmitted data. Is the complete name of the test reported and its form? Is the date of administration included, as well as a notation of the norm group used? Absence of these may generally be taken as symptoms of carelessness, although their presence does not insure that the tests were properly administered and scored. A second index is *accuracy:* Are all test titles correctly given? Does the total of part scores agree with the total score? Was correct conversion made from raw score to converted scores, such as IQ, grade equivalent, and percentiles? Again, although complete accuracy is no guarantee that all is well, it is a symptom; if obvious errors appear on the records, we have reason to suspect the accuracy of administration and scoring.

Still another index is *consistency:* Are several measures of the quality (intelligence, achievement) given at different times? To the extent that they indicate a similar level of functioning, they are more usable. This is especially true, as with test scores in general, at the extremes; consistently low or consistently high scores are more likely to be significant than those in the middle of the range.

It may not be necessary to add that consistency is not invariably a virtue; people do change, and sensitive tests should reflect these changes. Discrepant scores, therefore, should not automatically be rejected as representing erroneous measurement or recording. Where consistency *is* appropriate, that is, where there is reason to think that the individual did not change over a period of time in a given characteristic, then consistency of scores can be taken as an index of the usability of the information.

Finally, the acceptability of the information from records may be checked with *the client himself.* What are his perceptions of his grades, test scores, and other recorded data? He may be able to confirm their accuracy by providing other data which support them, or simply by agreeing that they reflect his ability, interests, social relations, or whatever. He may, on the other hand, tell of inadequate motivation while taking the test, "co-operation" with other students, or excessive anxiety during the test.

Client Recall

Use of the client's own recollections and self-perceptions as a source of information not only may add valuable information relevant to the decision or problem, but also offers one more opportunity to make him an active participant in the process, at least to the extent of talking rather than listening or responding to test questions. As he remembers his experiences, the counselee has opportunities not only to add valuable data (some of them unavailable from any other source) but also to clarify his feelings about them. Also, as mentioned earlier, he may be able to confirm or question the accuracy of information in the record.

It is sometimes difficult for counselees to talk about their experiences. This may be an indication of dependence and passivity: They came to be asked, measured, and told. In other cases, reticence about past experiences may suggest an attempt to deny or reject them, as with students who know that their past records do not support a stated objective and are hoping that tests will somehow reveal a totally different picture of themselves. In still other instances, it may be simply a lack of awareness of the significance of past experiences in future planning; the impression is all too widespread that counseling, especially in educational and vocational areas, is based entirely upon tests.

Once the obstacles to client recall are reduced, valuable data, both diagnostic and predictive, may be forthcoming. The boy who is vacillating between mechanical work and engineering may derive much helpful information from a comparison of his experiences in shop courses and the more academic courses in high school. He may be able to decide, without any tests, which kinds of work he found more satisfying and in which he had greater feelings of success. The boy who wonders whether to enter his father's construction business or to try for architecture may have had some summer vacation contacts with the business, discussion of which might provide insights regarding his vocational self-concept. Taking plenty of time to talk about his experiences and his feelings about them may answer his own question: Do I want to make that my life's work? The skillful counselor helps his client by encouraging him to recall relevant experiences, by suggesting aspects which it may be useful to explore, and by keeping the focus on the *meaning* of these experiences in relation to the decisions and plans in question.

Counselor's Willingness

One factor of importance here is the counselor's willingness to let his clients reach decisions on the basis of recalled experiences. Some counselors feel an obligation to check always, through testing, the accuracy of the client's self-concept. This is the rigid approach to counseling which is so nicely satirized in Paul Meehl's story (1956: p. 263):

Once upon a time there was a young fellow who, as we say, was "vocationally maladjusted." He wasn't sure just what the trouble was, but he knew that he wasn't happy in his work. So, being a denizen of an urban, sophisticated, psychologically oriented culture, he concluded that what he needed was some professional guidance. He went to the counseling bureau of a large midwestern university (according to some versions of the tale, it was located on the banks of a great river), and there he was interviewed by a world-famous vocational psychologist. When the psychologist explained that it would first be necessary to take a 14-hour battery of tests, the young man hesitated a little; after all, he was still employed at his job and 14 hours seemed like quite a lot of time. "Oh, well," said the great psychologist reassuringly, "don't worry about *that*. If you're too busy, you can arrange to have my assistant take these tests *for* you. I don't care who takes them, just so long as they come out in quantitative form."

It is easy enough to fall into this kind of rut, because it offers the counselor a nice sense of security and a feeling that he is being thorough and objective. Further, there is the feeling that the counselor is doing something worthwhile, and that the client is getting his money's worth, only when something "new" is obtained through counseling. Yet frequently the client needs only an opportunity to reflect upon, and digest, old information, rather than to receive anything new. Finally, this approach —universal testing—may simply have been learned in graduate school, in field work, or on the job.

It is quite possible to be equally rigid at the other extreme. Here the counselor accepts a client's self-appraisal without question, refraining from suggesting tests because that would imply rejection of his client's self-concept. Counselors working in the area of educational and vocational planning in particular have an obligation to point out to an adolescent or adult the questionability or lack of validity of recalled experience, or the lack of relevance of that experience to the decision under consideration.

As in most things, balance seems to be the ideal. There are times when a client's recollections and self-appraisal based on those recollections are quite adequate as a basis for planning future activities. There are other times when one must reject, or at least question, the adequacy of an appraisal which has been made without test data.

Validity of Recalled Experiences

A factor which limits the value of client-recalled experiences (and which applies as well to similar information obtained from records and reports) is the questionable predictive validity of many kinds of experience data. It is well-established that high school grades are fairly good predictors of grades in many colleges. This is to say that high school grades have been validated with respect to the criterion, grades in college. What, however, can we say about the prediction of satisfaction as a machinist from expressed satisfaction in a high school shop course? What do we know about the predictive value of hobbies and leisure-time activities in relation to later occupations? Super (1957a) concludes that, with the exception of long-enduring interests (the boy who continues railroading as a hobby throughout the high school years), hobbies and other activities during adolescence cannot be relied upon as indications of vocational interests; instead they are usually variable ways of meeting needs at different ages.

Again, is leadership success in student government and other high school activities predictive of comparable success in college activities and of later success in business management or other occupational endeavors? Acceptable research evidence is scanty; some of the reports offer little support for the "obvious" relationships, whereas others, though promising, lack adequate statistical treatment (for examples, see Krumboltz on student leadership studies, 1957). One serious problem here, as with predictive studies in general, is that of the criterion: "Success" cannot be depended upon to mean quite the same thing in all settings, even within a single occupation. For example, Dr. Edward S. Jones, then at the University of Buffalo, reports in a personal communication that he followed-up graduates of the engineering school in three different companies. The criterion of success was "value to the company as indicated by speed of advancement in salary for five years." At Company A, engineers were used for experimental and developmental work; there college grades and aptitude test scores correlated well with the criterion of success. At Company B, engineers were used on a variety of tasks, but "politics and knowing the right people" were important for advancement. There the highest correlations were found with outside activities in college and a "worry index"—number of worries reported on a questionnaire when entering college. At Company C, engineers were used largely for maintenance and for supervision of semiskilled workers. There none of the grades, test scores, or other measures correlated significantly.

Add to the criterion problem the ambiguous meaning of many background data: school grades, elected offices, and so on. It is entirely understandable, then, that in one high school extraclass activities predict certain post-high-school criteria whereas in another they do not.

One implication of the foregoing discussion is the need for considerably more research of a substantial nature. A second implication is the likelihood that local validation studies will be needed in addition to those of more general applicability. Until we know the meaning of success in a particular situation, we cannot even try to validate certain data which may be available. The extent to which predictions may be made from such sources of data as records, reports, and client recall is limited until we know of the significance of the experiences in those particular situations.

Validity of Self-Estimates

Several recent research reports, with contradictory results, point up a topic of great interest in which further research is needed. How well can individuals predict their own success; in particular, how well can students predict their own grades? How well can counselees estimate their scores on tests? Answers to these questions would be useful in determining the value of the universal use of tests in counseling which we discussed earlier. Are students (or at least some of them) able to estimate their own abilities, interests, and achievements well enough that they don't need help from tests or counselors in this area?

Accuracy of self-estimates has itself been used as a criterion of the effectiveness of counseling, with the expectation that counselees' self-estimates will become more accurate as a result of counseling. Studies of this kind will be reported in Chapter 14; at present it will suffice to note that varying degrees of success in the self-estimation process have been reported. Some of the differences in results may be attributable to differences in the nature of the sample, in methods of data collection, and in the effectiveness of the counseling itself.

One study—perhaps the most optimistic in its results—will be summarized briefly as an example of this kind of research. This project focussed on the effectiveness of self-estimation itself rather than its use as a criterion for evaluating the effects of counseling. Young (1954) had each of 100 randomly selected college freshmen predict his own grades during a counseling interview, both before and after receiving reports of his test scores. The correlation between predicted and actual first semester grades was .68, exactly the same as that for the *counselor's* prediction and only one point lower than the students' predictive correlation *after* having a report of their test scores. Several features of the experimental design may have contributed to this unusual finding: First, the estimates were made during a counseling interview—a better controlled kind of situation for collection of data than the usual questionnaire. Second, the subjects had been shown a distribution of grades received by freshmen the preceding year—an experience likely to encourage reality orientation. Third, the estimates were made after six weeks of college classes, when students had some basis for judging their progress to date.

Further research in this area can make the self-estimate a valuable tool in counseling. For one, it gives an indication of the degree of development of the client's self-knowledge at the outset of counseling (Matteson, 1956); this would save time since counselor and client might then go on to fill the gaps in information (Gustad, 1951a). Next, the *accuracy* of the client's self-estimates may be a sign of personality integration; the unrealistic self-concept may signal defensiveness or poor reality orientation in general. Finally, since growth in realistic self-awareness is an important goal of counseling, it would be quite valuable as part of a total evaluation of counseling to have dependable instruments to measure self-concept.

SELECTING THE TEST: MATCHING CLIENT AND TEST CHARACTERISTICS

Having first defined the purposes of tests for a particular client or group, next the specific information or experience being sought, and finally having checked data already available, we now approach the actual choice of tests. Many counselors seem to draw upon a relatively small number of different tests in their work. This is especially true in schools and other institutions, largely because of the mass testing approach so much in vogue. There is a tendency, both for the individual counselor and for the staff as a whole, to use the tests they have come to know and to resist introducing different and new ones. This inertia to change seems to stem from several factors. First, one tends to learn about a limited number of tests from graduate courses, since instructors teach about those *they* know and like best. Second, experience in using a test improves one's skill with it and therefore its usefulness to clients. Third, it is difficult for most practitioners to keep up with the publication of new tests and validation data for them, let alone evaluate them enough to decide whether they are worth a try. Despite the number of resource materials, to be described later in this chapter, the average counselor simply does not have an adequate basis for judging new tests for five or more years after publication, which is the time usually needed before textbooks and other works provide fairly complete evaluations. Finally, to learn a test really well requires supervised experience with it, or at least the kind of help which comes from extensive discussions with other counselors. Too many practitioners are without ready access to either of these sources of help.

Possible Improvements

No easy solution of this problem exists. A number of steps can be taken, some of them by individuals, others by the graduate schools and by the profession in general through its associations. One is to make available as soon after publication as possible, thorough reports and critical evaluations of tests. The series of articles on The Use of Multi-Factor Tests in the 1956-1957 *Personnel and Guidance Journal,* also separately reprinted, is an outstanding and almost unique example.

Also of great value is competent professional supervision; this may be from a member of the staff, or from visiting consultants. As Mathewson pointed out several years ago, "The time is fast approaching, if it is not already here, when testing and measurement can no longer be put in the hands of persons with only a modicum of training in psychometrics, statistics, and measurement. Indeed, it now looks as if the growing significance of testing as well as the prospect of the emergence of more selective functions in American education might require the development of new measurement, not to say actuarial, functionaries in our pupil personnel work" (Mathewson, 1955, p. 221) . To do justice to their testing programs, schools and agencies need to have available, if only on a consulting basis, personnel who are thoroughly competent in the measurement area. The Veterans Administration has demonstrated the value, even to psychologists trained through the doctorate, of bringing in outside consultants, usually from university faculties.

Universities might do more with post-graduate institutes for counselors to bring them up-to-date in the testing area. Some of the short-term institutes which are open to all comers do not meet this need, because many of their students bring little or no previous knowledge, with the result that the work is done at an elementary level. The same result has been noted at some workshops sponsored by professional associations, State Departments of Education, and other groups. These too could make a contribution of the kind here envisioned if admission were restricted to those having necessary prerequisites.

Published Research

Published research on selection of tests by counselors is quite limited. A few reports have appeared of surveys of tests used in counseling agencies (Carpenter, Cottle, and Green, 1959; Darley and Marquis, 1946; Silvania, 1956) and colleges (Dragositz and McCambridge, 1952) . Failor and Mahler (1949) suggested a method for examining counselors' selection of tests, involving an inventory of the tests used in a sample of cases. They recommend that the resulting data be used as a basis for discussions of such questions as: What tests are used by the staff? Are they of enough variety to explore a wide number of vocational potentialities? Is there a tendency on the part of the counselors to concentrate on a particular test or to select tests in a rigid pattern without adequate regard to variations among clients?

The Factors to be Considered

It is not possible in a work of this kind to provide an encyclopedic discussion of the strong points, weak points, areas of special usefulness, and methods of use of particular tests. Such treatment is most nearly approached, at the level of the professional practitioner, in certain textbooks on tests and measurements (Cronbach, 1960; Super, 1949; Thorndike and Hagen, 1955) and in the valuable *Mental Measurements Yearbooks* (Buros, 1938, 1941, 1949, 1953, 1959). In addition, there have been occasional entire works devoted to a single test, notably the *Strong Vocational Interest Blank* (Darley and Hagenah, 1955, Strong, 1943, 1955) and the *MMPI* (Hathaway and Meehl, 1951; Welsh and Dahlstrom, 1956; Drake and Oetting, 1959). An annotated list of these and other resource materials is included in a later section of the chapter.

Lacking a single comprehensive encyclopedic resource covering the major published tests, one must perforce learn to use the variety of materials available. The remainder of this chapter is in part intended to provide assistance in this process. We begin with a list of those characteristics of tests which are to be matched with what is needed for a particular client. Some of these characteristics, such as validity and reliability of tests, receive only brief treatment here, since they are extensively discussed in textbooks on tests and measurements. Following this is an annotated bibliography of publications in which one may find information about these characteristics of particular tests.

Reliability

Other things being equal, we seek the most reliable test of the function to be appraised. Cronbach has already cautioned (1955), however, that there are situations where a test of less than optimal reliability may nonetheless be worth using because it adds new information. Another complication is the fact that reliability is not an all-or-none matter. A test may have evidence of internal reliability (split-half, odd-even) but not stability over time (test-retest); we could then be certain only of reliability of measurement of the characteristic at that point in time. Furthermore, reliability may vary with the age of the sample, their educational level, motivation, and so on. Finally, reliability statistics have to do with groups; much less is known about estimating the reliability of measurement of a particular individual. There are many warnings for the careful practitioner even with what on the surface seems to be a relatively obvious matter.

Validity

This is of course the central concern in test selection: Is this test capable of measuring the quality we are interested in, and do its scores correlate with the behaviors about which discussions and plans are to be formulated? It cannot too often be emphasized that the scores for a test are of value only to the extent that they have been demonstrated (logically or empirically) to bear a relationship to some extratest behavior, whether grades in school, supervisor's ratings on the job, compatibility in marriage, or whatever.

The validity may be of any of the four types commonly recognized (American Psychological Association, 1954):

Content. The test has been judged by competent persons to measure certain skills, knowledge, and understandings, usually those specifically labelled achievement and proficiency. We would seek evidence of this kind of validity to answer such questions as "what has he learned" and "what can he do?" If we wish to go beyond this point and estimate future success, satisfaction, and other behavior, it is necessary to have some logical or empirical support for this predictive inference (predictive validity). Content validity is also important in connection with the problem checklists, which usually have no more validity than this: "He checked five problems in what competent judges have deemed to be the area of personal relations." The question this would answer, then, is "What is he worried about (that he'll communicate to me via a checklist) ?"

Predictive. Some future behavior—success, satisfaction, adjustment— has been shown to be related to scores on tests given prior to the behavior. This is the kind of validity we seek most often in applications of tests in counseling, since we usually deal with future decisions and plans. Predictive validity data answer such questions as: "How likely am I to be a good typist?" or "What are my chances of making a passing average at the Technical Institute?" or "Do you think I'll have as much trouble in marriage as my mother did?" or "In what kind of work would I find the greatest satisfaction?" As we shall see in later chapters, only partial and qualified answers can be provided to these questions, in part because of the inadequacies of the tests themselves, but also because, even with tests of good quality, predictive validation studies are limited in number, scope, and adherence to rigorous research criteria.

Concurrent. Relationships are established with status or performance at the same time as testing rather than with future behavior. Appropriate questions are: "Are my interests closer to those of accountants or mathematics teachers?" and "How do my abilities compare with those of nurses —would I be out over my head in that field?" and "Am I neurotic?"

Construct. As contrasted with the other three categories, this one covers the psychological characteristics actually tapped by the test. Like content validity, it provides a basis for answering only descriptive questions: "How do I stand in reasoning ability?" or "What is my present level of anxiety?" Inferences to future situations, such as school, job, and marriage, go beyond the construct validity data and require either logical or empirical demonstration of a relationship between that characteristic and some other behavior of the individual. Thus we may justifiably say, "you are quite anxious at the present time," but we go beyond construct validity to suggest, "you probably would therefore do poorly in college next year." After all, it is just as conceivable that the anxiety level might stimulate extra efforts in studies and therefore even higher grades than would be predicted by the scholastic aptitude test scores. Which is more likely to be true can be ascertained by empirical studies yielding *predictive* validity data.

There is some difference of opinion as to the relative importance of construct and predictive validity. The position is held by some that construct validity is the fundamental kind; having it, all other types of validity must necessarily follow (Loevinger, 1957). This is also the position of those who insist that a theoretical rationale is indispensable for good tests (Flanagan, 1951; Travers, 1951). Others feel that the critical issue is the extent to which a test predicts behavior.

As with most such debates, a major obstacle is the insistence by either side that its favorite method is the *only one*. The theorist and fundamental researcher are interested in tests as instruments for testing hypotheses about human behavior in general; it is indeed indispensable for this application that tests have construct validity. For the practitioner with the usual empirical orientation, however, tests are useful to the extent that they improve the accuracy of future estimates; for this application, predictive validity is precisely what is needed. On the other hand, when using a test for self-concept development, where *description* of the person is desired, one may draw more on the construct validation for a test.

Norms

Ordinarily we seek the test for which are available normative data comparable to the individual's current characteristics (age, educational level, socioeconomic status) or to the characteristics of the group he is considering joining or competing with (dental students, carpenters). Sometimes it is helpful to have both kinds of norms: comparison with peers as well as with the future referent groups. A twelfth grade student may be above the average twelfth grader in clerical speed, but quite inferior to employed clerical workers.

It is most difficult really to evaluate the comparability of a set of norms. Consider the illustration just given; were the twelfth grade norms collected mostly at suburban high schools in middle-class communities, at a broad range central school, or at city schools in lower-class neighborhoods? The problem of drawing an adequate sample, and then of reporting adequately the nature of the sample, still plagues test developers.

Age

Usually the client's age as a factor is taken into consideration by using appropriate norms. There are, at the present time, however, at least two major problems in the use of norms. First, there is the problem of a young person who is considering a course of action for the future. This might be a junior or senior high school student who is considering a field of work that he might enter anywhere from one to fifteen or more years later. With some of the tests which might be most suitable for the occupation, such as the *Strong Vocational Interest Blank* or the *General Aptitude Test Battery,* norms are based on those already in the occupation. Here the question, usually unanswerable at present, is how much and what kind of change may we expect in this counselee between the time of counseling and the age of the norm group?

A different problem faces those who do counseling with older clients considering a change of occupation. What to do about the man in his forties or fifties who, for one or another reason, must change to an occupation that is, say, less demanding physically, or more challenging intellectually, or more mechanical in nature than his present occupation? Here it would sometimes be helpful to have information of the kind yielded by tests of general intelligence, special aptitudes, interests, or personality. Yet many of the tests one would normally use include norms only through adolescence, or, at most, through the early adult years. As before, the question is how much and what kind of change might have occurred in specific traits since this client was at the age of the norm group? And furthermore, is it better to compare him as he is now with the younger men with whom he will compete if he enters their occupation, or should his scores be adjusted for age before a comparison is made?

For both of these age problems, we need a good deal more longitudinal data than now available. We need many more studies, such as the Career Pattern Study (Super, 1957a), now some ten years under way, which follow up young adolescents until the time they are established vocationally. Then test scores of earlier testing may be compared with later test scores and with later criteria of success in the occupation. The manual for the *Differential Aptitude Tests* reports some follow-up data of this kind, but with limited samples.

At the other end, recent research suggests some modifications of earlier conceptions of the changes which accompany aging. It was thought, for example, that mental abilities generally decline with age, beginning as early as the twenties and thirties. More recently it has been felt (Bayley, 1957; Tyler, 1956) that previous results were due to the particular types of measures used, and to the fact that most of the studies were cross-sectional rather than longitudinal in method. Bayley's studies, for example, led her to hypothesize that the earlier research emphasized those particular abilities which happen to decline with age. Tyler discusses these and mentions in particular tests requiring adaptation to new situations, tests of processes which deteriorate through disuse, and highly speeded tests. Brown and Ghiselli (1949) add to this list tests of abstract and complex processes. Both Bayley and Tyler also emphasize the fact that the older subjects grew up in environments different from the environments of the younger subjects. In some recent longitudinal studies, people in their forties and fifties were found to continue to increase in certain measured mental abilities (Bayley, 1957).

For the counselor, the present situation leaves much to be desired. To a large extent he must resort to a good deal of guesswork with both kinds of age problem. Normally he will first seek tests having the most suitable, and most complete, norms for the particular client and his needs. To estimate the level of mental abilities of older adults, he will probably stress those abilities which are least affected by age. Where norms are available for different ages, he will see how his client compares with the different norm groups and modify his appraisal accordingly. He will exercise due caution in making interpretations in those cases where suitable norms and longitudinal data are not available.

Previous Experience

In selecting an achievement test for a particular individual, it is fairly obvious that the choice is based on previous learning experiences, formal and informal. A chemistry or physics achievement test, for example, will rarely be used with people who haven't had specific courses in these subjects (although there is an occasional individual who is self-taught and whose question is "how much *do* I know?").

The distinction is, however, less obvious with tests of aptitudes and interests. Quite clearly, it is inappropriate to give a college level numerical reasoning test to one who never got beyond the third grade in arithmetic. It may not be so obvious, however, that one with extremely narrow environmental background can do little with the questions on an interest inventory which deal with a variety of occupational activities. Recently, there has even been some evidence (Blade and Watson, 1955) that a spatial visualization test, which we would normally regard as relatively experience-free, is quite sensitive to specific related experiences *in college*. Groups of engineering freshmen in this study increased one standard deviation in scores on a space test after a year in college; the greatest increase was found in that subsample which had had the smallest amount of related experience (mechanical drawing, mechanical hobbies) prior to college. Mendicino, in a later study (1958), obtained contradictory results in a comparison of vocational and academic high school students; the vocational students showed no more gain from pre- to post-test than did the academic group. However, the vocational students' previous related experiences were apparently not controlled; it may be that they had already had enough such experiences to attain their maximal level on these tests.

As much as possible, then, is done to select tests which are appropriate to the individual's background; the effects of experience can also be considered later when the scores are being interpreted. What we do at that point is merely a special case of the general interpretive principle that a test score is the result of, among other things, specific learning opportunities and experiences. We say, then, "this is your score on such-and-such;

since you have had very little (or a great deal) of experience with things of this sort, the score probably is a minimal (or a maximal) estimate of your abilities." More of this in later chapters.

Reading Level

To the extent that a reading deficiency interferes with his performance on a test which is not intended in any way to measure reading abilities, to that extent a counselee is not being measured adequately. On tests of ability, the score represents his potentialities in that particular area (mechanical comprehension, spatial visualization) only partly; reading ability is also being measured. For some applications such contamination may be no real problem. For example, a college aptitude test consisting of reasoning items may also be tapping the ability to read the directions and the items themselves, and since grades in college courses also require this kind of reading ability, contamination may actually contribute to the efficiency of prediction. In other situations, however, it is desirable to measure reading ability separately from the other abilities, if only to enable examination of the contribution of each element to the final prediction.

With a number of formulas available for measuring reading ability and with the reading level of several tests already having been ascertained with the use of some of these formulas (Forbes and Cottle, 1953; Johnson and Bond, 1950; Pierce-Jones, 1954; Roeber, 1948; Stefflre, 1947), selection of the appropriate tests would seem to be a relatively simple matter of determining a client's reading level and assigning tests whose reading difficulty is within his range of capability. Unfortunately the measurement of reading difficulty of tests is far from the simple matter it might appear to be. The first complication is that different formulas yield different reading levels for a single test. Some formulas emphasize vocabulary level, others the use of personal pronouns, and still others the ability to interpret what has been read. There is no obviously best formula for most standard-ized tests. For some, such as interest inventories made up of short phrases and a relatively large per cent of difficult words, the formulas are either completely unsuitable or they provide unrealistic readability scores. A second complication arises from the fact that the readability of test direc-tions may be different from that of the items themselves or of the alterna-tive responses. Conclusive and universally accepted measurement of test reading levels has not yet been attained. However, we probably can make gross discriminations that are a good deal better than nothing, thereby at least avoiding grossly unsuitable tests.

Speededness

Reference has already been made to the decrease in performance on speeded tests which is associated with age. Other groups too suffer a handicap on tests in which speed is an important factor. Among these are the slow readers, the compulsively cautious persons who must check and recheck their responses, those handicapped sensorily (especially in vision) or in motor behavior (holding a pencil or turning a page), and the slow-to-warm-up. In all these instances power tests give a more adequate measure of level of capability, independent of speed. However, as Hanna (1952) pointed out, tests with time limits are usually favored since they may be more economically administered to groups. There are some instances where it is not desirable to eliminate the effects of speed. If, for example, speed is important in the clerical or assembly occupation being considered, then it may be entirely proper to use a speed test even with those so handicapped. This assumes that the handicapped person would be competing in a normal job situation rather than in a sheltered work-shop or other special environment.

Since high quality power tests are not available for all functions, we sometimes extemporize by giving a speeded test first with and then without time limits. This is easily done by noting the point reached by the subject at the end of the time limit and then permitting him to finish in his own time. The score without time limit cannot be interpreted in the usual fashion, since the norms are based on standard administration procedures. However, some value is often derived from this procedure in helping the client learn how much he is handicapped by speed requirements.

Paper and Pencil vs. Apparatus Tests

Assuming that both kinds of test give approximately similar predictions, apparatus tests are preferred for those who are uncomfortable with paper and pencil, perhaps because of experience. This happens especially in the area of mechanical and manual occupations, for which some apparatus tests of mechanical comprehension and spatial visualization are available. Unfortunately they are more expensive to administer, in terms both of initial cost and of the difficulty of giving them in groups.

One additional merit of apparatus tests is the greater opportunity to observe the subject's behavior in approaching the task, solving problems, and responding to frustration. In some cases the insights thus obtained are more valuable than the quantitative scores.

Individual vs. Group Tests

Any test may be administered individually, when it is important to observe behavior closely or when the individuals taking it do not function as well in group testing situations, because of tension or other factors. We are, however, now speaking particularly of those tests, such as the *Wechsler Intelligence* series and the various *Binet* tests, which routinely require individual administration. There is an erroneous assumption that the individual tests are for all purposes superior to group tests. The fact of the matter is that for most purposes group tests of mental abilities are better established as predictors of educational and occupational success than are individual tests. As to the "diagnostic" contributions of individual tests, in terms of such psychiatric categories as neuroses, psychoses, and character disorders, the research literature provides little foundation for this although clinicians continue to use them in this fashion. Finally, analysis of differential aptitudes and abilities is better accomplished through the multifactor group tests which have been developed for this purpose and whose part scores are reliable enough to permit profile examination.

One important use of individual tests remains—for those handicapped in some of the ways previously mentioned: reading ability, vision, motor skills, speededness. Even here, however, the individual tests are not always superior; approximately half of each *Wechsler* battery, for example, requires some amount of visual-motor co-ordination of a speeded nature.

The individual tests are indeed valuable, particularly in cases where careful observation of client responses is desired, and where it is helpful to be able to follow-up responses with requests for further clarification. For subjects handicapped in certain ways, they are often the best choice; for other cases, including many people with handicaps, group tests are as good or superior.

Amount of Time Needed

Test batteries often must have a time-limit, because of the counselor's heavy case load or because most counselees, individually or in groups, must restrict the amount of time taken from classes, jobs, and other demands. In fee-charging agencies where hourly rates prevail, clients sometimes restrict the amount of testing time because of costs. Actually the total amount of time spent taking tests must always be less than the total possible. Even if only one bit of information is sought, say speed in clerical tasks, there are several tests which might be used, partly to check on each other, partly to explore different facets of the question. Instead, we usually limit ourselves to one, perhaps to two tests, of a given function, though aware of the shortcomings involved.

Obviously a compromise must almost always be made between the amount of time that could be devoted to testing and the smallest amount that counselor or client would like to use. The end result in agencies is usually a battery including one or perhaps two tests of each function that is to be measured, such as interests or mechanical aptitudes. In school programs, an over-all plan is sometimes prepared for the several grades included within the school. Some tests, such as those of academic aptitude, may be repeated at intervals of two or more years; others, such as differential aptitudes, may be used only once; whereas achievement batteries may be given as often as annually. After a period of years, a considerable body of test data may thus be accumulated to provide not only the usual descriptive, predictive, and diagnostic data, but also a longitudinal and developmental picture of the individual.

Handicaps

Reference has already been made to handicaps under the headings of Age, Reading Level, and Individual vs. Group Tests. Numerous kinds of handicap affect test behavior: visual and auditory defects; abnormalities affecting control of hands, arms, and fingers, such as those caused by paralytic and spastic conditions; emotional disorders, such as excessive anxiety or impatience; and the effects of aging, including slowing-down and difficulty with new stimuli. Full treatment of this topic, including specific tests and techniques, would require a good deal more space than is here available. A handbook for testing those with handicaps of various sorts would be a real contribution at this time, both to the specialist in rehabilitation and to others who only occasionally test someone with a handicap serious enough to affect his test performance significantly. Valuable information may be found in such works as Lofquist (1957), Patterson (1958), and *A Manual of Norms for Tests Used in Counseling Blind Persons* (1958).

As has been previously mentioned, appropriate tests of good quality do not exist for many of the specialized uses occasioned by various handicaps. The skilled counselor and psychologist must therefore adapt available instruments by deviating from standard conditions of administration. The resulting scores are then interpreted as well as can be, but necessarily in less precise terms; predictions made from such data will have to be in terms of a broader range of possibilities than would otherwise be the case.

Despite the special problems of testing those with handicaps and the occasional need for different tools and techniques, the general principles and procedures of testing apply here just as they do otherwise. The purposes of testing are the same, although there often are additional specific ones, such as ascertaining work tolerances. The *process* aspects of test selection are essentially the same, although again with certain features found more often when testing the handicapped; for example, there may be a greater tendency for handicapped clients to be dependent. As to the tests themselves, many instruments in general use are appropriate, though sometimes with such modifications as reading the items aloud to the subject or writing his responses for him, instead of following standard conditions. Interpretation of results follows the same principles and procedures with the handicapped as it does with nonhandicapped counselees.

This is not to deny that some disabled people are beyond the present application of standardized testing; this is probably true, for example, of some active psychotics, the severe cerebral palsied, and those with marked deficiencies of attention and of motivation, whether as a result of mental retardation, senility, or some other specific condition. It is also true that testing handicapped clients is in general more difficult and demanding; this may be one of the reasons that some rehabilitation counselors do very little testing.

RESOURCE MATERIALS

Having determined what test characteristics are needed for a particular client (reading level, norms, validity for a particular purpose, and so on), the counselor needs to locate the particular tests which seem most closely to meet the needs. Lacking any single encyclopedic resource, he must refer to many. The following list includes published materials which are likely to be of greatest general assistance. Such lists go out of date rapidly, as new textbooks, monographs, handbooks, and other resources appear in print. There are also unpublished and locally published materials in some communities which may be of great value, such as information regarding the hiring standards of a particular plant or the entrance requirements of a community college or art school.

Our list begins with the more general works and moves toward the more specific. The questions which it is appropriate to bring to these materials are such as these: What abilities and interests are needed for success in a particular occupation? What is needed to succeed in college programs in forestry, and in the program at *X* University in particular? What interest test is most suitable for use at the tenth grade level? Is there a single nursing aptitude test of good quality that can be used with a high school senior? What tests are best to use for diagnosing reading disabilities?

General Treatment of Occupations, Educational and Training Curricula, and Other Criterion Variables (What Is to Be Predicted?)

DORCUS, R. M., and JONES, M. H., *Handbook of Employee Selection* (New York, McGraw-Hill Book Co., 1950).
Brief abstracts of research reports regarding tests used in employee selection. All abstracts pertinent to a given occupation may be found in an alphabetical index of occupational titles.

FRYER, D. H., and HENRY, E. R., eds., *Handbook of Applied Psychology* (New York, Rinehart and Co., 1950).
The two volumes contain a variety of articles; of particular relevance are those on Clerical Personnel, Mechanical Personnel, Retail Sales, and other occupational areas in Ch. V of Part I.

GHISELLI, E. E., *The Measurement of Occupational Aptitude* (Berkeley, University of California Press, 1955).
Review of the levels of validity of various types of test, for each of several categories of occupations. This is essentially a quantitive summary of ". . . all

investigations concerned with the validities of tests used in the selection and placement of workers. . . . The specific purpose of this monograph is to obtain a representative value of the validity of each type of test for each type of job." Appendix A contains a list of specific occupations, by *D.O.T.* classification, and the average coefficient of validity of various types of test, in relation both to training for the job and proficiency in it.

PATERSON, D. G., GERKEN, C. d'A., and HAHN, M. E., *Revised Minnesota Occupational Rating Scales* (Minneapolis, University of Minnesota Press, 1953).

In classified form are listed judgments by vocational specialists of the degree of each of the following kinds of ability needed for success in each of 432 occupations: Academic Ability, Mechanical Ability, Social Intelligence, Artistic Ability, Musical Talent, Clerical Ability, and Physical Agility.

ROE, A., *The Psychology of Occupations* (New York, John Wiley & Sons, Inc., 1956).

In five chapters are summarized some of the published research regarding individual differences as applied to occupations: Ch. 5, Physical Differences; Chs. 6 & 7, Psychological Differences; Ch. 8, Differences in Social Inheritance; Ch. 9, Differences in Education and other Biographical Factors.

Later, Chapters 13-20 summarize research on the characteristics of various occupational groups and of specific occupations.

STUIT, D. B., DICKSON, G. S., JORDAN, T. T., and SCHLOERB, L., *Predicting Success in Professional Schools* (Washington, D. C., American Council on Education, 1949).

Summaries of studies on prediction of success in professional education for engineering, law, medicine, music, agriculture, teaching, and nursing. Discussion of special problems of prediction in each field and implications for counseling.

SUPER, D. E., *The Psychology of Careers* (New York, Harper & Brothers, 1957).

The entire work contains a wealth of organized information about careers in general and their characteristics. Of special interest to the test user are three chapters which summarize the applicability of tests to various kinds of vocational areas: Ch. 14, "Aptitudes in Vocational Development," Ch. 15, "Interests and Vocational Development," and Ch. 16, "Personality and Vocational Development."

THORNDIKE, R. L., and HAGEN, E., *Ten Thousand Careers* (New York, John Wiley & Sons, Inc., 1956).

Follow-up study of 10,000 Air Force Aviation cadets reports their occupational status and success some 12 years later. A chapter on each occupational group summarizes their scores on Air Force tests, pointing out which discriminated best *among* the groups and which predicted success *within* each group.

United States Employment Service, *Estimates of Worker Trait Requirements for 4,000 Jobs* (Washington, D. C., U. S. Government Printing Office, 1956).

For each of 4,000 occupational titles are listed judgments made by occupational analysts as to the following requirements: Training Time, Aptitudes, Physical Capacities, Temperaments, Interests, and Working Conditions. There are also references to *GATB* test patterns in those occupations for which patterns have been established.

The judgments, it should be noted, are based on examination of occupational definitions rather than on direct observation of the job. Since the definitions are those of the *Dictionary of Occupational Titles,* the *Estimates* should be used in conjunction with the *D.O.T.*

WILLIAMSON, E. G., *How to Counsel Students* (New York, McGraw-Hill Book Co., 1939).
Most of the book is devoted to discussing 20 types of problems brought to counselors, such as Family Conflicts, Unwise Choice of Courses of Study and Curricula, Underachievement, Uncertain Occupational Choice, Problems of Self-Support in School and College, and Problems of Health and Physical Disabilities. The chapters on each of these problem areas follow the outline: Description, Incidence, Causes, Analyzing and Diagnosing, Counseling Techniques, Prevention, and Selected References. Relevant measuring devices are discussed under the heading Analyzing and Diagnosing. Though quite old, this is still the only work of its kind and is therefore included. For the beginning counselor, there are many helpful ideas.

A number of colleges are reporting to high schools certain facts about prediction of success in college, both from test scores and from high school achievement. One of the most elaborate has been produced by the Office of Testing and Guidance of the University System of Georgia. This document, which will be referred to in later chapters, contains percentile tables for each college in the system, as well as regression equations for estimating a student's probable grade at each college.

General Treatment of Various Tests

Textbooks

ANASTASI, A., *Psychological Testing* (New York, The Macmillan Co., 1954).

CRONBACH, L. J., *Essentials of Psychological Testing,* 2nd ed. (New York, Harper & Brothers, 1960).

SUPER, D. E., *Appraising Vocational Fitness* (New York, Harper & Brothers, 1949).

THORNDIKE, R. L., and HAGEN, E., *Measurement and Evaluation in Psychology and Education* (New York, John Wiley & Sons, Inc., 1955).

Such books contain discussions of types of tests and of specific tests, their reliability, validity, usefulness, and so on. Often there is critical commentary about particular tests.

Yearbooks

BUROS, O. K., ed., *The 1938 Mental Measurements Yearbook* (New Brunswick, N. J., Rutgers University Press, 1938).
———, *The Nineteen Forty Mental Measurements Yearbook* (New Brunswick, N. J., Rutgers University Press, 1941).
———, *The Third Mental Measurements Yearbook* (New Brunswick, N. J., Rutgers University Press, 1949).
———, *The Fourth Mental Measurements Yearbook* (Highland Park, N. J., Gryphon Press, 1953).
———, *The Fifth Mental Measurements Yearbook* (Highland Park, N. J., Gryphon Press, 1959).

One of the most valuable resources on educational and psychological tests, the yearbooks contain critical reviews and bibliographies of many tests. Since the volumes are not cumulative, it is often necessary to seek reviews of a single test in earlier volumes as well as in the most recent. This is not the resource in which one seeks detailed summaries of reliability, validity, and so on; the contribution of the Yearbooks has been, instead, in the critical discussions of selected aspects of the test. In many instances a single test receives multiple reviews in one volume of this series.

Journals

Journal of Consulting Psychology, "Psychological Test Reviews."
   Succinct critical reviews have been included in this department since April, 1956. Prior to that, shorter reviews were included in the section "New Books and Tests."
Journal of Counseling Psychology, "Test Reviews."
   A regular feature of each issue, this column contains descriptive as well as critical discussions, mostly of new tests. As a rule, all are written by the same reviewer.
Personnel and Guidance Journal, "Testing the Test."
   Initiated in November, 1959, and edited by David V. Tiedeman, this department seeks to supplement the *Mental Measurements Yearbooks* by reviewing tests not yet listed in the most recent Yearbook.
Personnel Psychology, "Validity Information Exchange."
   In each issue of this journal, beginning in 1954, appear brief outline reports of validity studies on various occupations.
Review of Educational Research.
   Each topic is reviewed once in three years on a regular cyclical basis. "Psychological Tests and Their Uses" is the most immediately relevant one and has been reviewed in February, 1959, February, 1956, and so on. It may also be useful to search the topic "Guidance and Counseling," the most recent review having been in April, 1960.
The Use of Multi-Factor Tests in Guidance (Washington, D. C., American Personnel and Guidance Association, undated).
   Reprints of the series of articles appearing in the *Personnel and Guidance Journal* from September, 1956, through September, 1957. Each of eight multifactor tests of mental abilities is first described by one of its authors and then reviewed critically by Donald E. Super. Included also are bibliographies for each battery up to 1957. A most valuable contribution to practitioners, this publication should be followed by others on different kinds of tests.

Individual Tests

Test Manuals

In recent years there has been considerable improvement in test manuals, both quantitative and qualitative. Two-page manuals are rarely seen any more, and some of the new manuals are so detailed and long that shorter, less technical versions are included for those who can't or won't use the complete manual. This presents something of a dilemma for the average test consumer, for whom the complete version is too technical, but for whom the briefer one lacks the data on which a critical analysis can be based. It may be that the practitioner, after detailed examination of a manual, will need to seek the help of a test specialist in making evaluations and choices of tests to include in his program.

Summaries of Research

Some test publishers bring together summaries of research on particular tests separate from the manual.

Test Bulletins and Other Publications

Several publishers issue free periodical publications, some of which include reports on some of their tests. The following list includes the major series of bulletins, usually available on request:

California Test Bureau, 5916 Hollywood Boulevard, Los Angeles 28, Calif.
Educational Bulletins
Summaries of Investigations

Educational Testing Service, 20 Nassau St., Princeton, N. J.
ETS Developments (Quarterly)
Evaluation and Advisory Service Series

Houghton Mifflin Co., 2 Park St., Boston 7, Mass.
Testing Today

The Psychological Corporation, 304 East 45th St., New York 17, N. Y.
Test Service Bulletins

World Book Co., Tarrytown, N. Y.
Test Service Bulletins
Test Service Notebooks

Books on Single Tests

Strong Vocational Interest Blank

DARLEY, J. G., and HAGENAH, T., *Vocational Interest Measurement: Theory and Practice* (Minneapolis, University of Minnesota Press, 1955).
LAYTON, W. L., *Counseling Use of the Strong Vocational Interest Blank* (Minneapolis, University of Minnesota Press, 1958).
STRONG, E. K., Jr., *Vocational Interests of Men and Women* (Stanford, Calif., Stanford University Press, 1943).
———, *Vocational Interests 18 Years After College* (Minneapolis, University of Minnesota Press, 1955).

Minnesota Multiphasic Personality Inventory

DRAKE, L. E., and OETTING, E. R., *An MMPI Codebook for Counselors* (Minneapolis, University of Minnesota Press, 1959).
HATHAWAY, S. R., and MEEHL, P.E., *An Atlas for the Clinical Use of the MMPI* (Minneapolis, University of Minnesota Press, 1951).
WELSH, G. S., and DAHLSTROM, W. G., *Basic Readings on the MMPI in Psychology and Medicine* (Minneapolis, University of Minnesota Press, 1956).

Journal Articles

Reports of research and practice with tests appear in a number of psychological, educational, and other journals. The up-to-date practitioner subscribes to some of these and arranges to scan at least some of the others. Those journals which are most likely to contain material of this sort are:

Educational and Psychological Measurement
Journal of Applied Psychology
Journal of Counseling Psychology
Personnel and Guidance Journal
Personnel Psychology

In the search for published material on a particular test, the following indexes are useful:

Education Index
Psychological Abstracts

By beginning with the latest number and working back, making use of the annual index for each volume (the *Education Index* also provides three-year indexes), it is possible to locate most of the published items about a particular test in a relatively short time.

Local Files

Counselors sometimes establish their own test reference files, including specimen sets of tests, normative data, and sometimes a collection of selected references—perhaps reprints of articles and summaries of other publications regarding the tests.

CHAPTER 5

Test Administration: Psychological and Mechanical Aspects

HAVING NOW reached the point of selecting the most suitable test for an individual counselee or for a group, class, or school, we approach the actual administration of the test. Despite the fact that tests are sometimes badly administered, we shall not be greatly concerned with the *mechanics* of giving tests in guidance work. This topic is well treated in a number of introductory textbooks in measurement, as well as in the better test manuals. There are matters which are more complex and which need more extended consideration. For example, how do *anxiety* and *tension* affect performance on a test of achievement or aptitude? Do they, as many test-takers will aver, reduce efficiency in taking a test, or do they have the opposite effect of increasing alertness and of bringing abilities up to a peak level of performance? Answers to these questions might make a considerable difference in the preparation we give to an individual or a class—whether we try to relax them or to increase their tension.

An additional matter is the problem of *faking* on personality and interest inventories. How frequent a problem is it, and how much *must* an individual distort his responses for the result to be different from a true picture? More information about faking and distortion would be especially important in testing groups, as in a school setting. Can we justify giving an interest or personality inventory to the whole ninth grade if it should turn out that, say 25 per cent of the group might, for one reason or another, so distort their responses as to give quite inaccurate pictures. Later we shall try to interpret some of the research in this area and suggest the implications for test administration.

Another matter of concern to test administrators is the effect of *coaching* and *practice*. With increased pressure from parents, especially in connection with college admissions, schools have instituted questionable practices such as setting up study groups for scholarship examinations. Sometimes students are encouraged to take the College Board examinations in the junior or even the sophomore year in high school. Although in some instances this is done for predictive purposes, in other instances it seems to be intended primarily for the practice value. Beyond the ethical question involved, is it worthwhile to give special practice and preparation for tests of this kind?

As a final illustration of the problems which might be included under the heading "psychology of test-taking," there is the question of *what a test score actually represents* in terms of the abilities used by the particular individual to solve the problems. For instance, one student may solve a mathematical problem correctly by remembering a similar problem he learned to solve in class. Another student may solve the same problem by recognizing the principles involved, and still another student, by a hazy, intuitive "feel" for the right answer. All receive the same score on the item and perhaps even the same total score on the test; yet the scores tell nothing about the *processes* by which they were obtained.

We shall, in the pages which follow, discuss problems of this sort; for some of the questions, there are currently available some fairly adequate answers from the research literature. In many cases, however, we can at present do little more than be increasingly aware of the problems, so that at least proper cautions may be taken in interpreting test results.

It is all too easy to regard the actual taking and scoring of tests as a simple and mechanical process which intervenes between what are regarded as more professional operations—the pretesting activities of analyzing the needs through interviews and study of records and the post-testing activities of interpreting test results to individuals, using test results to plan remedial work or to assign pupils to sections, and so on.

As we shall see, however, the taking of a test by an individual taps a myriad of attitudes, feelings, wishes, needs, abilities, interests, and, in fact, all the relevant experiences that he has ever had. Answering a single question on a test of mechanical aptitude, for example, can bring into play what Jack *knows* about various tools, how much he has been encouraged to help his father fix things around the house, what attitudes he has heard expressed by his family and friends about mechanical work and its "respectability," and even a host of specific skills in connection with reading, spelling, and mathematics.

In later chapters we shall discuss the impact of these factors on the *interpretation* of test results; the present purpose is to examine some of the ways in which these factors influence the actual *taking* of a test, which will, in turn, affect the interpretation of the scores.

The topics to be included in this chapter will be organized under three broad headings:

1. What are the effects of those things which have *preceded* the taking of this particular test—previous experience with tests, coaching and practice with that kind of material, and everything and anything that the individual has learned and experienced that has any relevance to what is being tested?

2. How does the individual *perceive* the test (e.g., as a threat or as a source of help), what *feelings* does he have about taking the test (e.g., anxiety and its effects), and how will these factors affect his approach toward the test (amount of effort, attempt to make a favorable impression, tendency to distort his answers)?

3. What happens during the actual taking of a test: What is the influence of distractions and what are the processes used by the individual in solving problems?

WHAT HAS PRECEDED THE TEST?

To some extent *everything* this individual has ever experienced could be considered here; after all, he brings to the taking of a test a variety of skills and knowledges, including reading, counting, analyzing, and "know-how" in taking a test. He brings also a variety of attitudes (aspirations, expectations of success or failure) and of interests, customary modes of behavior, and emotional characteristics. Many of these factors have already been discussed in connection with the purposes of testing and the selection of tests. Several topics, however, warrant consideration here.

Coaching and Practice

The more recent studies which bear specifically on this point (Dyer, 1953; French and Dear, 1959; Hay, 1950; Holloway, 1954; James, 1953; Lipton, 1956; Longstaff, 1954; Maxwell, 1954; Peel, 1952, 1953; Schlesser, 1950; Wiseman and Wrigley, 1953) show the noticeable but limited values of coaching and of other specific practice in preparation for taking tests. Research to date indicates that coaching and practice in taking tests may be effective in raising scores of individuals and groups who *have not had recent experience in taking tests of that general type, and who have not had recent experience with the subject matter of the particular test.*

Longstaff (1954) found, for example, that college students taking the *Minnesota Clerical Test* on three closely spaced occasions increased their mean scores (using norms for employed clerical workers) from below the 50th percentile on the first trial to the 72nd to 91st percentiles (for various subsamples) on the third trial. Schlesser (1950) reports that a group of students in a Navy Pre-Midshipman Refresher Program at Colgate University showed an average gain of 22 percentile points in score on the *American Council on Education Psychological Examination for College*

Freshmen between the beginning and end of the twelve-week course. He felt that the gains probably could be attributed to a combination of practice effects, regression to an earlier academic facility, maturation, and the specific effects of the training program.

Among English psychologists there has been considerable interest in the effects of coaching and practice, apparently because of the extensive use of tests in England as a basis for admission to "grammar" schools, which are the principal track to higher education. Among the more extensive studies is that of Wiseman and Wrigley (1953), who worked with 548 subjects in English schools. They set up three groups, one of which received six hours of coaching on verbal intelligence test items, one which received six hours of practice taking verbal intelligence tests, and, finally, a control group which received no special treatment. All subjects took an intelligence test before this period of training and then again three months later. In their second test, the coached group had a mean IQ gain of 6.5 points, the practice group a gain of 11 points, and the control group a gain of 4.5 points. Coaching seemed to have more pronounced effects at the lower end of the IQ range, whereas practice was more effective at the upper end of the range. Dyer (1953), however, reporting on a study in the United States with the *Scholastic Aptitude Test (SAT)* of the College Entrance Examination Board, concluded that coaching of able students in the senior year of a good secondary school is not likely to improve the *SAT-Verbal* score appreciably but could raise the *SAT-Mathematical* score if the students happened not to be enrolled in regular mathematics courses.

The most recent report, by French and Dear (1959), summarizes a series of studies carried out by the College Board with the *SAT* in a variety of secondary schools, both public and private. Several approaches were used in the studies, including group and individual coaching. They attempted to maximize the effects of coaching by using, in some of the studies, practice exercises and actual trial test items similar to those of the *SAT* itself. In almost every one of these studies the coached groups scored higher on the *SAT* after than before coaching, to an extent significantly different (statistically) from any increases attained by noncoached control groups. The differences, however, were relatively small, from a practical standpoint; at most, they were 20 points on the *Verbal* portion and 30 points on the *Mathematical* part. These amounts are both less than the standard error of measurement of the test (in which the mean is 500 and the standard deviation is 100). French and Dear conclude that ". . . an eager College Board candidate should not spend money on special coaching for the *SAT*. He would probably gain at least as much by some reviews of mathematics on his own and by the reading of a few good books" (p. 329). It should be noted, however, that their conclusion is based on *group* averages. What is not highlighted in these studies is the question of gains made by *individual* students. It may be that some students increased their scores by, say, 50 points; this could mean the difference between acceptance and rejection at a particular college. It would be valuable to separate out those who increased the most and to determine whether they might be identified in advance and advised as to the possible benefits to them of coaching and practice. The others might make better use of their time in other activities, such as cultural enrichment or scholastic acceleration. It would be interesting to know, for example, whether the greatest gains are made by those students who have not applied themselves in school and for whom intensive study groups might indeed be worthwhile.

Although we have not heard the last word on the subject of coaching, it would for the present seem justifiable to conclude that coaching will be of help to at least some individuals and is likely to be of greater help to persons who are "rusty" in the particular area being tested. Also, practice would seem to be especially helpful for those who have had limited recent experience in taking tests in general or in taking the particular kind of test which is in the offing.

For schools with fairly extensive testing programs in which students have had experience taking tests similar to those used for college entrance or for scholarship purposes, no special provisions for practice or coaching would appear to be necessary. With highly competitive examinations such as those used in connection with the National Merit Scholarship program, schools which have given their students good courses and adequate experience in taking tests probably need have little concern about the competition which their students will have from those in other schools. It is unfortunate that parental pressures, resulting from college-admissions anxiety, has led even schools with strong curricula and good teachers to institute special coaching classes, "scholarship clubs," and other such arrangements. For the schools which provide inadequate educational programs, coaching and test practice would seem to be short of an ideal correction of inadequacies. However, it must be admitted that for such schools coaching arrangements will probably help to raise the average scores of their students at least slightly.

For counselors who test individuals rather than groups, it may sometimes be desirable to give two different forms of the same test (say, Forms AA and BB of the *Minnesota Paper Form Board*), as a way of providing a warm-up experience for the "cold" client. This may be counter to the standard procedures for administering the particular test, in which case it introduces interpretive complications. Certainly with tests which have alternate forms, the manual should report the mean increase in score when both forms are administered with a short time interval. If a client has a much greater increase from first to second test than is true of people in general, we have reason to conclude that he was indeed in need of some warming-up.[1]

Another approach, particularly with tests which have time limits, is to note the item reached at the end of the time limit, and then to permit the examinee to finish the test without time limit. A great difference between the two scores—that with and that without time limit—may be an indication of "coldness" or "rustiness," especially on tests whose time limits are supposed to be generous enough that most people do not increase their scores appreciably with extra time. (As discussed later in this chapter, under the heading of "Speededness," such score differences may also result from other factors, such as overcautiousness).

Response Sets

This concept has received increased attention since Cronbach's review of the literature (1950). It is of interest as a general category into which can be fitted a number of more specific kinds of behavior and which therefore may offer new understandings of the psychology of test-taking. A response set is a tendency to take a given direction in answering test questions. There may be, for example, a set to answer "Yes" to questions of interest in various things or to answer "No" to any question regarding personal problems. There have been found sets to favor the first option or the last option in multiple choice items, or to avoid the extreme options in a personality inventory (Always, Never) in favor of middle or moderate options (Sometimes or Frequently). Another kind of response set is the tendency to guess freely or to hesitate to guess on a test of ability, achievement, or aptitude. Cronbach (1950) concluded that response sets are quite common and that they sometimes operate to reduce the validity of tests, since the individual is not necessarily answering the particular question but rather is responding to questions indiscriminately, as far as their content is concerned.

It is by no means clear at the present time just how prevalent are the various kinds of response sets, nor are their effects on test scores clearly established. Apparently they operate more often on tests with ambiguous instructions and on tests which are too difficult for the individual (Cronbach, 1950). In both of these cases the individual is projecting something irrelevant rather than responding to the question rationally. To a large extent, the prevention and control of irrelevant response sets is a problem

---

[1] Krumboltz and Christal (1960) found that the increase from test to retest over a period ranging from ten minutes to seven hours was about as great when they used two different forms of a test as when they retested with the identical forms. There was no practice effect when they used two different tests of the same ability.

for test constructors. We are concerned here primarily with the implications for test *users* of our current knowledge of response sets.

"Social Desirability" Set

One response set of near-universal occurrence is the tendency to give
"socially desirable" answers to certain questions on personality inventories, to picture oneself as well-adjusted, out-going, and mentally healthy.
The causes of this particular response set are somewhat more obvious
than are those of some others. Here it seems to be a matter of defending
oneself against an implied threat of criticism or of being discovered to be
"maladjusted." The extent to which this defensive response set is found in
middle-class groups has led test-makers to introduce devices of various
sorts to counteract it. For example, the *Minnesota Multiphasic Personality
Inventory (MMPI)* uses several validity scales, K, L, and F, to detect tendencies to deny pathology, to lie, or to give unusual responses which question the validity of scores on the various personality scales.

Edwards, in his *Personal Preference Schedule (EPPS)*, uses the forced-
choice approach, in which one must choose between two statements the
one which is more nearly true of him, the two options having been
matched for their social desirability. Despite the current controversy as to
the success of the matching process, this is a promising approach (Edwards, 1957). A recent variation is the *Adjective Checklist* in which the
respondent is asked to choose from each group of five adjectives the one
which is most descriptive of him and the one, least descriptive. All five
adjectives in each group had been placed together because they appeared
to be approximately equal in social desirability (Dunnette and Kirchner,
1960).

The counselor using personality inventories can approach this response
set from two angles. First, he may try to reduce the set in his clients by
establishing a relationship in which defensiveness will be reduced. Secondly, he may utilize inventories which provide either a *gauge* of this kind
of set (as in the *MMPI*) or a control over it (as in the *EPPS*). To know how
much a particular client has of the social desirability kind of set is in
itself information of some value since it tells us something about a dimension in which he differs from other people. A greater than average amount
of the need to give socially desirable answers may indicate insecurity, a
need to impress people favorably, or a need to conform to what one thinks
is expected of him.

Guessing

Another response set is readiness to guess the answer when the testee is
either uncertain or has no idea what the correct answer is. There is some
evidence that (1) the directions given to testees as to whether they should
guess make some difference in the amount of guessing that occurs; (2)

there are individual differences in readiness or willingness to guess, some people guessing under any circumstances, others being hesitant to guess under any circumstances; and (3) there may be a relationship between readiness to guess and certain personality characteristics. A good deal of the support for these generalizations comes from counseling practice, but there is also a small amount of research evidence for them.

The effects of giving different kinds of directions regarding guessing was studied by Swineford and Miller (1953). A vocabulary test containing regular items, exceptionally difficult items, and nonsense items was given to 801 subjects. The identical test was given to all subjects, except that the directions for some of them urged guessing, others discouraged guessing by emphasizing the penalty for wrong answers, and the remainder did not mention guessing. Only a slight difference was found between the do-guess group and the no-mention group in number of items tried (an index of guessing, since the groups were equated for ability), but there was noticeably less guessing on the part of the don't-guess group.

This same study offers evidence that some people will guess no matter what the directions. Several items were almost impossibly difficult and several were nonsense words, fabricated by the researchers. A subject's degree and selectivity of guessing could be gauged by the number of these difficult and nonsense items which he tried, as compared with the number of regular items that he tried. It was found that, even in the group explicitly instructed *not* to guess, the average subject tried 50 per cent of the difficult and nonsense words.

In counseling, one becomes aware, by talking to those who have taken tests, of some of the kinds of personal characteristics which appear to lead one person to guess more freely than another. Among these characteristics seem to be self-assurance, aggressiveness, motivation to do well, or in the case of random guessing throughout a test, lack of concern about doing well. Sherriffs and Boomer (1954) offer some support for one of these clinical hunches in a study of college students. They found that students low in self-esteem according to an *MMPI* scale tended to omit more items than did other students. They concluded that the usual right-minus-wrong (or a fraction of the wrongs, depending on the number of options in the item) correction for guessing penalizes those who are low in self-esteem.

Implications for Test Development. Among test developers, there continues to be a difference of opinion as to the desirability of encouraging guessing and of including some kind of correction-for-guessing formula in the scoring procedures (Cronbach, 1950; Doppelt, 1954; Stanley, 1954). Cronbach advises that subjects should be directed to answer *all* items, thus helping to overcome differences between the bolder and the more timid guessers. To do this would probably require the conditions of a power test, namely, enough time for everybody to try all items, or at least to try enough items that any further time allowance would not increase scores.

A rationale for a different approach is expressed in the manual for the *Davis Reading Test*. The authors of that test feel that it is undesirable to encourage examinees to try every item, first because such a practice is criticized by teachers as contrary to the principles of responsible scholarship, and secondly because it increases the proportion of the total variance of test scores which is attributable to chance. Their third reason highlights what is probably the most questionable assumption of correction-for-guessing from the point of view of counselors. This is to the effect that the formula compensates for any advantage which bold or sophisticated examinees have over cautious or naive ones. The reasoning seems quite valid with regard to responses that are "pure" guesses, since correction formulas assume that chance alone determines the number of such items that the person gets right, and the formula then deducts this same number of points from his score. However, there still remain the non-pure guesses, those on which the person *thinks* he knows the correct answer but is uncertain. On such items, the probability of getting the right answer is greater than chance, but bold and timid guessers are likely to differ in the percentage of such items which they will try. As a result, the timid ones are likely to get lower scores than their bolder fellows (assuming that both are equal in the particular ability), *whether or not* there is a correction procedure. With reference to this particular problem, Cronbach's position seems stronger, in that the timid ones would be compelled to try, even in those instances in which their self-confidence and boldness are not quite up to their ability. There is need here for research to ascertain the differential effects, if any, on the scores of more and less timid guessers, of different types of directions and different scoring methods.

Implications for Counselors. The practicing counselor must, of course, abide by standard directions for administration of a particular test. He advises his counselees to guess or not to guess in accordance with instructions in the manual (hopefully, all test manuals will before long at least be explicit as to which of these *is* the standard procedure). Similarly, tests must be scored in accordance with the procedures used in their standardization, using a correction formula whenever so directed in the manual. To deviate from either of these procedures may invalidate the test for that person or group and certainly makes it inappropriate to use the published norms. The counselor will be aware, however, of the possibility that the set to guess freely or not to guess freely may raise or lower an individual's score on a test. It is sometimes helpful to inspect answer sheets for omissions and errors, in order to get some idea as to the amount of guessing that has occurred. The results of this inspection may then be related to what one knows of the personality of the counselee. It is, of course, helpful in many such cases to discuss the matter with the client, both to try to ascertain what actually did happen and to help the individual to increase his self-awareness.

Speed

Not a great deal has been written about this kind of response set, so we must rely more on counseling experience than on research for our analysis.

One problem of speed is illustrated by the frequent experience reported by users of the *Differential Aptitude Tests* and mentioned also in the manual for this battery, namely, that the best students often do poorly on the Clerical Speed and Accuracy Test. The items for this part are easy, and a high score is largely a measure of speed. Bright youngsters (who usually do well on other parts of the *DAT*) sometimes are so set for accuracy that they cannot "let go" enough to get high scores on the Clerical test. It is often found that such subjects will get much higher scores on a second administration, after being urged to work quickly.

Less frequently found is the more deviant slowness of the person who is compulsively cautious, who double-checks and triple-checks where others would go on to the next item. Here again we see a response set which is reflective of a personality characteristic. Such clients may receive surprisingly low scores on time-limited ability tests, as contrasted, for example, with their grades in school. The latter may represent many extra hours of study and homework, in compensation for their compulsive slowness.

As mentioned in Chapter 4 and earlier in the present chapter, the counselor who is aware of the operation of this response set can at least ascertain its effects by doing one of two things. Either he may add an untimed test of the same ability (although these are all too rare), or he may deviate from the standard method of administration by permitting the counselee to have unlimited time to complete his test (after noting the number of items completed *during* the prescribed time limit). In either case, the difference between scores obtained with and without time limits may give an estimate of the handicap which this response set places upon the person. Mollenkopf (1950) has reported that added time to complete aptitude tests led to marked changes in the relative standing of some of the students in his study. There was very little, if any, benefit derived from added time, however, on such tests as Verbal Antonyms, where the item type is largely a matter of recognition. Mollenkopf concluded that additional time for slow test-takers is more likely to result in score increases when the type of item requires problem-solving.

For test administration in general, whether to individuals or groups, it is important that examinees are made aware of the importance of working quickly, on those tests in which speed is important. This can, however, be carried too far; Staudt (1948) found that under certain conditions pressure for speed increased the number of errors made on some tests.

Other Response Sets

Additional response sets have received some attention, but the work is too scattered to have much immediate value to test users. However, the occasional reports deserve some attention, if only to suggest possible interpretive clues. For instance, Asch (1958) studied a "negative response bias," a tendency to answer "disagree" to opinion items which were presented as a "Speed of Decision" test. Based on the premise that, in the American culture at least, people tend to agree rather than to disagree when in doubt (as an element of conformity or "other-directedness"), he hypothesized that those with a negative response bias of this sort are more maladjusted. He found some support for this hypothesis (by examining scores on the *MMPI, Rorschach,* and other tests) and concluded that negative response set is associated with a tendency to be neurotic and in particular to have obsessive-compulsive symptoms. Such results are far from conclusive and do not provide counselors with a specific tool or technique, but they are a source of inferences or hypotheses for the clinical process of interpretation which may be of great value in occasional cases.

Perhaps enough has been said about response sets, considering the speculative nature of much of our knowledge of this phenomenon at the present time. The practicing counselor can be alert to other and rarer response sets, such as Cronbach's (1950) case of the student who, from 90 items on the *Henmon-Nelson* (given with extended time limits), placed 30 of his marks on position "1" of the five response-choices for each item. Detection of such sets will require careful attention to each individual case, since they are not likely to be found unless one examines the answer sheet itself (see the discussion in Chapter 6 of the advantages of hand-scoring for this purpose).

PERCEPTIONS AND FEELINGS REGARDING A PARTICULAR TEST

Here we are dealing with the perceptions and feelings of an individual or group regarding a particular test and the particular counseling setting in which the testing is done. Excluded are the more "permanent" tendencies previously discussed as *response sets,* although it is obviously not possible to make a hard-and-fast distinction between the two categories. An individual, for example, who perceives a particular intelligence test as a threat to his self-concept may also bring to *all* tests a greater than average degree of defensiveness or timidity. These characteristics might then favor such response sets as lack of speededness and social desirability. The overlap notwithstanding, it is fruitful to examine separately the more particularized perceptions and feelings which people have in relation to specific tests.

To a large extent, the perceptions which a counseling client has of a particular test can be seen as a function of the *test selection process* discussed in earlier chapters. To the extent that selection of tests and preparation of the testees (in groups or individually) have been well done, we should expect that tests will be seen as important but not crucial, as helpful but not miracle-working, and as providing certain information that is relevant to some decision, plan, or other focal purpose.

In those cases in which the preliminaries have not been satisfactory, and to some extent even under the best of conditions, students or other testees approach tests with some negative perceptions (as a threat to self-concept or an obstacle to a desired course of action). These may lead to varying degrees of such cognitive and emotional results as faking, anxiety, and lack of effort, some of which we shall discuss in the following pages.

Faking and Distortion

It is now well-established (Furst and Fricke, 1956) that most interest and personality inventories, if not all, can be faked in a desired direction (see, for example, Cofer, Chance, and Judson, 1949; Cross, 1950; Garry, 1953; Gehman, 1957; Green, 1951; Kuder, 1950; Longstaff, 1948; Longstaff and Jurgensen, 1953; Mais, 1951; Wallace, 1950; Wesman, 1952). Not all tests are equally easy to fake on (forced-choice less so than free-choice, for example) and not all people can or do fake equally. The greatest amount of distortion can be expected in situations of an employment or admissions nature, where applicants try to present a picture of themselves which is as close as possible to their interpretations of the *desired* picture. Cross (1950), who asked high school and college students to fake their interests, concluded that ". . . when an applicant for a job has any idea of what job he is being considered for, his scores should be interpreted in the light of the knowledge that faking is possible *if he desires to fake*" (p. 277).

Some of the complexities of the faking phenomenon are suggested by Sheldon (1959) who points out, for example, that in many studies of faking, the results one gets depend in part on the sequence of instructions given the subjects—whether they are first given the inventory or questionnaire with instructions to fake or whether the first taking is with normal instructions. Furthermore, he highlights the importance of the *setting* in which the inventory is taken. The fact that it is possible to fake on an inventory does not necessarily imply that any particular individual or group of people *will* fake when taking it. Some support for this contention appears in the research of Mayo and Guttman (1959); Naval aviation recruits were given the *U.S. Navy Vocational Interest Inventory* and the *MMPI* under several conditions, some of which would be expected to produce more faking, others less. They were told, in one condition, that the information would be used in assigning them to jobs. In another condition they were told that there would be a lie score, while, in a third condition, some were *asked* to fake and were offered a prize for the most successful distortion. They found that none of the interest scores and none of the *MMPI* clinical scores was affected by these various instructions, although the F and L (validity) scores of the *MMPI* did seem to reflect faking tendencies appropriately. Here, then, is one setting in which one would certainly expect distortion to occur, and yet it was not evident.

Preventive Measures

In administering interest and personality inventories to counselees, one should in most cases be able to reduce faking or distortion to a minimum through proper preparation for testing, including client participation in test planning. A case can be made, and some have taken this position (Rothney, Danielson, and Heimann, 1959), for the point of view that when one has established such a relationship with his client that the latter is ready to be relatively open and frank in discussing his interests and personality, then it is not *necessary* to use standardized inventories; the skillful counselor can just *ask* his clients some of these questions. There is undoubtedly a good deal of merit in this position and in many cases there is indeed no need to use inventories. With proper rapport, one can ask a counselee to tell about his feelings or about his family relationships, or about his likes and dislikes, and thus obtain information that may be even more valuable than that obtained from structured inventories. To adopt this point of view completely, however, is to overlook some possible contributions of at least some of the standardized inventories. First, they sometimes help to *organize* the individual's various thoughts, opinions, and desires in a form which may help him to view himself more clearly. Second, they may help him to see how his responses compare with those of a *norm group*. Third, with some instruments, such as the *Strong Vocational Interest Blank (SVIB)*, information can be obtained from the scores which is simply *not available otherwise* (for example, that one's interests bear greater similarity to those of lawyers than to those of men-in-general).

With *group administration*, it is a good deal more difficult to overcome or reduce any tendencies to fake or distort responses. However, even with groups, one can try various methods of preparation for testing, such as group meetings or mimeographed explanations of the purposes of the tests. Even with these precautions, however, some in almost every group are likely to attempt distortion, consciously or otherwise. Counselors who work under these conditions (as in most school testing programs) must be cautious in accepting the resulting profiles as accurate reflections of interests, of typical behavior patterns, of feelings, or of whatever the inventory presumes to measure.

Distortion-Resistant Devices

Meanwhile, the counselor in any situation who has at least some "reluctant" or resistant clients will use his knowledge of tests to select those instruments which either (1) are resistant to distortion (as, for example, forced-choice inventories) or (2) have built-in "lie-detectors" such as the *L* scale of the *MMPI*. Some recent work suggests that it may be possible to develop measures of interests which are less susceptible to distortion than those currently in use. Dole (1958), for instance, describes the construction and standardization of the *Vocational Sentence Completion Blank*, a semiprojective device for tapping interests, and intended especially to give the subject more freedom of response than is usually the case with multiple-choice types of item. The manual is explicit in cautioning that the value of the *Blank* is diminished with resistant clients and ideally should be taken only with their willingness to do so. It would appear, however, that for some people such an instrument offers an opportunity to report their interests with less self-consciousness and less interference from unconscious tendencies to distort. This opportunity is similar to that offered by the projective devices in the personality area, such as the *Rorschach* and the *Thematic Apperception Test*. It is possible for an individual to be willing, even eager, to tell about himself, yet be unable to do so genuinely because with obvious items such as those on most interest and personality inventories, he can't help realizing what his parents or his teacher would want him to say, and these thoughts may get in the way of a genuine response. The *Forer Vocational Survey* uses a somewhat similar approach. Although published in 1949 and the object of several studies, this test does not seem to have received much use.

A few attempts have been made to use *pictures* in interest inventories. The *Geist Picture Interest Inventory* makes use of a forced-choice approach as does the *Kuder Preference Record*, but subjects are asked to make choices among drawings which depict various occupations and hobbies rather than among verbal descriptions of the activities. The *Vocational Apperception Test* is a projective device, in which examinees tell a story about each of the pictures and thus, presumably, project their attitudes, feelings, and interests about the occupations. A recent research report describes still another technique, this one not yet standardized (DeRath and Carp, 1959), which presents pictures of men in various occupations and requires the subject to select the one of each set that he prefers. In the case of all three of these graphic instruments, some research data are presented, but all are in an experimental stage, needing a good deal more research and tryout before being ready for routine use.

At this point it is appropriate to raise the question of whether there is something inherently wrong with this notion of measuring people against their will, or conspiring with them to outwit their conscious or unconscious tendencies to paint a distorted self-image when it is possible to do so, as it is with most inventories. There are many situations in which it would seem quite ethical and desirable to do this. In screening the student body of a school or college, for example, in an effort to locate those most in need of psychological help, it is sometimes those with the greatest need who are the most defensive and the most denying of their needs. In such cases the counselor is quite justified in using more subtle methods of screening. With *any* counselee, it seems justifiable to use such subtle or indirect instruments, certainly in those cases in which he understands and accepts the counselor's goals and purposes, and sometimes even when he doesn't. The counselor should be quite sure, however, that he is really operating in the client's interests and is not interfering with his freedom or invading his privacy beyond the bounds of ethical standards of practice.

For the most part, those doing counseling with relatively normal people about relatively normal problems will probably find it more valuable to devote their energies toward developing the kinds of relationships with clients that will maximize attitudes of candor and honesty on inventories. This approach would seem to be more fruitful than one which neglects the pretesting stage and forces the counselor to place more emphasis on distortion-resistant instruments and to question the interpretation of the results because of the possibilities of large-scale distortion.

There is a final consolation in the results of a study by Wallace (1950). College students were asked to make their answers on the *SVIB* simulate those of men in the occupations preferred by the students themselves. It was found that more successful distortion (comparisons between the "simulated" *SVIB* and that previously taken under normal conditions) was accomplished by students whose expressed and measured interests were similar than by those whose expressed and measured interests were discrepant. The "nondiscrepant" students also had had more opportunity to gain information about the occupation of their choice, and had less self-conflict about their vocational selection. Since all these characteristics of the "nondiscrepants" would be good supporting reasons for entering the particular occupation, it would appear that in these groups the largest amount of faking is done by those who are most appropriate for the occupation anyhow, so that nothing much is lost. It would be interesting to see whether this same phenomenon will be found with other samples.

Anxiety and Tension

Every user of tests can report, from his own observations and from testimonials of his subjects or counselees, that there is a considerable amount of anxiety and tension associated with taking tests. DeLong (1955) placed observers in elementary classrooms during the administration of tests to children who had previously been observed in the classroom. The observers reported many signs of disturbance during the tests, such as nail-biting, pencil-chewing, crying, talking to themselves, excitement, and noisiness. Yet observation reports of some of these test-disturbed children in their normal classroom settings contained very few instances of comparable disturbances. Though this was something of an exploratory rather than a controlled study, there is at least some support here for Lennon's contention (1954) that test-taking can be an upsetting experience for children and that it interferes with ideal teacher-pupil relationships.

It is not at all clear, however, what the *effects* of anxiety and tension are, and whether the effects are necessarily deleterious. Some people, after all, feel quite certain that a degree of tension increases their alertness and makes it possible for them to function at a higher level than when they are more relaxed. Before attempting to formulate conclusions or recommendations, we should examine some of the reported research.

Sears (1943) summarized the literature on this subject in 1943; most of the studies seem to have been done with *individual* tests of intelligence, and many are studies of emotional interferences with *learning* rather than with test-taking. His conclusions, nonetheless, have some relevance for our problem: ". . . good test performances are relatively frequent among the affectively abnormal—even in severe mental disorders, with the exception of organic brain disease" (p. 477). And later: "Within rather wide limits the essential factor determining whether the subject's motivational (affective and attitudinal) peculiarities will cause significant deviations of psychometric performance seems to be what the test situation means, consciously or unconsciously, in terms of this particular subject's individual patterning of complexes and desires" (p. 478). We shall return later to this latter point and will also add at that time Sears' suggestions for handling these "motivational" interferences in the testing situation. For now we are interested in his conclusion, based on an extensive review of the literature, that a wide variety of emotional disturbances, even neuroses and psychoses, do not have consistent or uniform effects upon test scores.

Sarason's Studies

A series of studies which bear directly upon the problem at hand is reported by Sarason and his associates (Gordon and Sarason, 1955; Mandler and Sarason, 1952; Sarason and Gordon, 1953; Sarason and Mandler, 1952; Sarason, Mandler, and Craighill, 1952). These research workers developed a test-anxiety questionnaire consisting of thirty-nine items (four of which are fillers that are not scored), including questions such as the following (Sarason and Mandler, 1952):

If you know that you are going to take a group intelligence test, how do you feel *beforehand?*

While taking a group intelligence test to what extent do you perspire?

In comparison to other students, how often do you (would you) think of ways of avoiding an individual intelligence test?

When taking a course exam, to what extent do you feel that your emotional reactions interfere with or lower your performance?

The split-half reliability of this instrument is reported as being .91 (Mandler and Sarason, 1952). The scoring key was empirically derived, being based on the median response to each item of a sample of college students (Sarason and Gordon, 1953). One indication of validity of the questionnaire is a correlation coefficient of .59 between scores on the questionnaire and independent ratings of the subject's perspiration, excessive movement, inappropriate laughter, and other signs of tension during the taking of individual tests.

Using this instrument, several studies were made to test hypotheses regarding effects of anxiety on test performance. Unfortunately, small numbers of subjects were used in some of the studies, with the result that differences between groups sometimes failed to meet the level needed for statistical significance. In one such study (Mandler and Sarason, 1952), it was found that subjects high in test anxiety (as measured by the questionnaire) got poorer speed scores on a block assembly test than did those with low anxiety scores, but the difference disappeared by the sixth trial. It was concluded that high anxiety interferes with test performance at first but that the interference diminishes with time. In the same experiment, some of the subjects were told that they had done very well, some that they had done poorly, and the remainder were given no appraisal (these "appraisals" were assigned to subjects at random and bore no relationship to their actual performance). The low anxiety students improved in score after receiving *either* a good or a bad progress report, whereas those high in anxiety score did less well after receiving either report. It may be that the progress report re-awakened in high anxiety students whatever blocking had been diminished through familiarity with the test situation.

In another investigation in this series (Sarason, Mandler, and Craighill, 1952), an attempt was made to explore the effects of *time pressure* and *ego-involvement* on the performance of high and low anxiety subjects. In the first instance half the subjects were told that they were expected to finish within time limits and the other half not. There was no significant difference between the high anxiety subjects given one instruction and those given the other. With low anxiety subjects, however, pressure for speed made a difference, leading to a higher mean score than without it. In the ego-involvement portion of this experiment, half the subjects were told that their scores would be studied individually, whereas the others were told that their scores would be used only for the development of group norms. Findings were in the direction hypothesized, but did not achieve statistical significance (again, with twenty-four subjects, significance of any kind is difficult to attain): The high anxiety group did somewhat better under non-ego-involving instructions, whereas the low anxiety group tended to do better under the other conditions.

Because of the small samples and nonsignificant findings, conclusions can be only tentative, but there does seem to be some evidence from this series of studies (not all the findings of which have been mentioned here) that test anxiety can be measured and that extreme amounts of it can interfere with test performance, at least in the subject's first efforts with a new test situation. It was also found (Sarason and Mandler, 1952) that social-class status was somewhat related to measured test anxiety, those below upper-middle-class status having higher test anxiety scores than those at or above this level. The interpretation suggested (and which was hypothesized in advance) is that at the higher social level there is not so much family pressure to achieve intellectually.

More recently Sarason and other associates have reported a group of studies on test anxiety in elementary school children (Sarason, Davidson, Lighthall, Waite, and Ruebush, 1960). It is not possible to do more than mention a few of the more pertinent highlights of their extensive theorizing and research. They found low but significant negative correlations between the *Test Anxiety Scale for Children (TASC)* and scores on intelligence and achievement tests. They also found that average *TASC* scores were higher among samples of children in England than in the United States. This difference had been predicted, on the grounds that in England tests are used as the primary basis for admittance to "grammar schools" and therefore are a greater source of anxiety to children.

Other Research

There is some evidence to suggest that anxiety operates differently with different kinds of tests. Pickrel (1958), for example, compared low anxiety and high anxiety subjects among Air Force recruits as to their scores on thirteen aptitude tests. He found that the low anxiety group had somewhat higher mean scores than the others on the tests. The differences between the groups were greater for tests involving complex tasks than for those involving simpler tasks. Sarason and others (1960), in their studies with elementary school children, concluded that the influence of anxiety varied according to the degree of threat which the child saw in a particular test. Anxiety seemed to play a greater role with verbal tests than nonverbal; this they interpreted to be a result of the fact that school children learn that teachers and parents place more weight on the verbal tests. They found also that anxiety played a greater part with tests of an unfamiliar sort. The interpretation here is that such tests are more threatening to anxious children. Some of these findings seem to confirm Sears' earlier suggestion (1943) that whether "motivational peculiarities" will affect test scores depends on the meaning to the subject of the particular test situation.

Negative results regarding the influences of emotional disturbances are reported in a study by Hanes and Halliday (1954). They tested several groups of prisoners; with some there was introduced a set of adverse and threatening conditions which seemed to function as a threat to self-concept. A few days later, another form of the same intelligence test *(Otis)* was given both groups but without the addition of the disturbing conditions. No differences were found for either group between first and second test, leading to the conclusion that this particular emotion-arousing set of stimuli did not interfere with test-taking efficiency. Of course, this sample is such an atypical one that one dare not generalize from it.

The question has been raised by several research workers as to whether test anxiety is really a separate entity or whether it is simply a manifestation of general anxiety. Martin and McGowan (1955) studied tension level by measuring palmar skin conductance. They concluded that Sarason's test anxiety questionnaire (slightly modified by them) may be measuring a general anxiety factor rather than one peculiar to test-taking. However, three other studies have found that correlations between measures of test anxiety and such measures of general anxiety as Taylor's *Manifest Anxiety Scale* are only moderate—in the .30s to the .60s (Gordon and Sarason, 1955; Sarason *et al*, 1960; Sinick, 1956b). It seems then that general anxiety level (if there *is* such a characteristic) cannot be an adequate index of an individual's anxiety in relation to tests.

Those studies which have been mentioned above and several additional ones (Branson, 1960; Kaye *et al*, 1953; Staudt, 1949; van Biljon, 1954; Welch and Rennie, 1952; Windle, 1955) offer a fair amount of evidence to support Sinick's conclusion that ". . . a high level of anxiety, whether existent or induced in Ss, generally brings about impaired performance, but occasionally causes improvement" (Sinick, 1956a: p. 317). One reason for the contradictory results, discussed elsewhere by Sinick is that people react differently to anxiety: ". . . some anxious subjects exhibit exceptional mental alertness, others seem to have their minds temporarily in deep freeze" (1953: p. 384). For some, anxiety causes difficulty in making decisions, whereas for others the same degree of anxiety may lead to unusually rapid decisions in order to escape from the uncomfortable situation.

In this regard, it is of some interest to look for a moment at a formulation of a theory of test anxiety which was made by Sarason and associates (1960) within the framework of psychoanalytic theory. They hypothesized for their series of studies that test anxiety among elementary school children is a reflection of relations between child and parents with regard to the child's abilities, his handling of hostility, and his feelings of guilt.

They concluded, from a variety of studies, that there is some confirmation of this theory.

Here we return to the formulation of Sears (1943), that one critical factor may be *what the test situation means to the particular individual.* For one anxious person, "failure" on a college aptitude test may represent relief from a threat of even greater failure if he *should* go to college. To another person the same amount of anxiety may lead to efforts to do well on the test because for him the greater threat is of *not* going to college. In addition to the specific situation and its meaning, we must also recognize the effects of *the individual's learned pattern of response to anxiety.* Some people tend always to respond to the discomfort of tensions and anxiety by going into action and trying to solve the frustrating, anxiety-inducing problem, thus removing the stimulus to anxiety. Others have a general tendency to run away from these threatening situations as another way of evading anxiety-provoking stimuli. Still others stay in the situation and attempt to deal with it, but are unable to function at their usual level of ability because of the effects of anxiety.

Implications for Test Users

What are the implications of all this research for the test user? Should he try to stir up moderate amounts of anxiety and tension in his subjects or try to relax them as much as possible? Should he offer reassurance and support or be more objective? The literature offers very little specific help with these questions. One study (Sinick, 1956a) of the relative effects of encouragement during testing versus nonencouragement yielded no significant differences, whether the subjects were low anxiety, middle anxiety, or high anxiety. The small samples in this study may offer a partial explanation of the failure to obtain statistically significant differences among groups. Perhaps equally important are the comments made earlier about the variety of behavioral results that occur in different people (even in the same person at different times) as a result of the same degree of anxiety. In order to know how to prepare a group for testing, it would be necessary to understand what meaning the test has for each person in the group, and to have some knowledge of each person's customary anxiety level in this kind of situation and his customary response to felt anxiety. This is obviously not a very practical approach.

Until a good deal more is known about this topic, counselors will probably be wise to seek to encourage only a moderate amount of tension, enough so that most subjects will be alert and ready to work. Those who bring more than what appears to be an optimal degree of tension may need help in relaxing somewhat before they are ready to perform optimally on tests. An interesting technique that was tried with achievement tests in an introductory psychology course (McKeachie, Pollie, and Speisman, 1955), was to give test-takers space on the answer sheet in which to write comments about test items. It was found that the permissive direction "Feel free to comment" led to higher test scores than did the conventional answer sheet. After a variety of experiments, the authors concluded that this modified answer sheet seemed to lead to a reduction of threat and a channeling of released anxiety.

One thing seems clear: Standardized conditions of test administration do not guarantee a uniform emotional response from all subjects. Some people will be quite upset by a test which others take in stride. The differences may be attributable to such variables as general anxiety level, ego strength, self-confidence, and the perceptions which the individual has of this particular test. He may perceive it as a threat, as a reassurance, or as just another piece of information to be added fairly objectively to what he already knows about himself.

We would hope that a considerable portion of the negative emotions related to test-taking (such as feelings of threat, tensions, worry and fear) will have been eliminated or considerably diminished by the application of good test selection procedures, as defined in Chapter 3. To the extent that each testee has developed some understanding and acceptance of the purposes of the tests and has identified with those purposes, to this extent we should expect reduction of negative feelings. Adequate preparation of counselees, whether through individual interviews or through small group sessions, should bring each one to a degree of readiness to approach tests with a desirable mixture of alertness, interest, and effort, but with a minimum of negative emotion.

In reviewing the test results of an individual, the counselor can make an effort to appraise the role which anxiety and tension may have played for that person. Perhaps some day there will be well-validated instruments to be administered along with other tests which will provide a systematic index of the degree of anxiety experienced by each person, along with some indication of corrections to be made in the scores because of the effects of emotional interference. For now, it would be desirable to experiment with such instruments as the *Taylor Manifest Anxiety Scale* and the test anxiety scales developed by Sarason and his associates, to see whether these can provide some gauge of the anxiety state of each person while taking the test. Appraising the *effects* of this level of anxiety must, for now at least, remain a matter for individual analysis, probably best explored during interviews before and after taking tests. The counselor might keep in mind some of the research findings now available and be especially alert to the influences of anxiety on tests of a complex nature, on tests of an unfamiliar nature, and on tests which are particularly threatening or important to the individual.

Effort and Motivation

Another result of the client's perception of tests is the degree of effort he expends. This aspect is related to the previous topic of anxiety, since we want our clients to be motivated to do well but not so much so as to be overly tense. We might suggest as an hypothesis (but without any research data currently available to test it) that clients who see the forthcoming test as potentially useful to them but not threatening are likely to exert optimal amounts of effort. *Lack of effort* may come from various sources: In some cases it may represent lack of interest in the test and lack of any expectation that it has something of value to offer. In other cases, lack of effort may represent just the opposite perception, that the tests are terribly important and even threatening. In such a case lack of effort may play a defensive role, permitting the individual to say afterward, "I didn't really try, because I wasn't interested in the results of this test, and they won't affect my plans in any way."

Gustad (1951a) has suggested the importance of ascertaining the client's relevant attitudes at the time of taking tests, and Flanagan (1955) has developed an "index of examinee motivation" for this purpose. Not much more has been heard of such instruments, but a contribution could be made, to group testing programs in particular, by a valid measure of degree of motivation to take a test.

One final point should be made here regarding the *degree* of effort. "Optimal" has been used as the adjective in this discussion rather than "maximal." It has often been assumed that an ability test should reflect the *highest* level of which the individual is capable. Thorndike and Hagen (1955) express the point of view that whereas personality measures should tell how a person behaves *typically,* on ability tests the person should be encouraged to try as hard as he can, so that we can have an estimate of what he *can* do rather than what he *does* do. Why is it not as important to know the individual's *typical* spatial ability level as to know his typical co-operativeness? Perhaps we would increase test validities somewhat if *usual* rather than *maximum* level of function was measured. After all, the criterion behavior we are interested in predicting—whether school grades, job satisfaction, or whatever—will be a function of his *usual* behavior as a student or as a worker. Perhaps it would be helpful to have a multiple report of an individual's ability in a given area: his *usual* level of functioning, his *maximal* level with great effort, and even his minimal level under stated conditions (lack of interest, fatigue) . This is an area worth some exploration with formal research studies, as well as through more informal observations in the testing and counseling process.

WHAT HAPPENS DURING THE TEST ITSELF?

It should not be necessary here to repeat the usual cautions regarding rigorous observance of standard testing conditions, such as time limits and standardized directions. The newer test manuals have in general been more adequate than many of the older ones by stating in detail the conditions of test administration. In particular, test administrators and proctors need specific guides as to how far to go in answering questions, both before and during the actual test. It simply is not adequate for a manual to advise giving "further explanation in individual cases as necessary to be sure that all students understand what they are to do." With such ambiguous instructions, we can expect considerable variation among examiners in the actual "explanation," some being more "helpful" than others.

This problem is less serious where trained counselors and psychometrists do the testing than it is in many institutional testing programs where it is common for classroom teachers (in schools) and clerks (in industry, the armed forces, and other places) to be the administrators. The responsibilities would seem to be twofold: for the test author and editor to give directions as explicitly and unambiguously as possible and for the responsible persons in school or agency to select test administrators carefully and provide them with suitable training and supervision. If these cautions are not observed, we must face a continuance of the present state of affairs, one result of which is that we are compelled to doubt the accuracy of test scores furnished by many schools and other institutions, because there is not enough assurance that minimum standards of test administration have been observed.

Having treated briefly this relatively simple and mechanical, though important, aspect of the test administration process, we now go on to consider several more complex aspects of the general question: What happens during the taking of a test that, as test interpreters, we need to be aware of?

Physical Conditions of Testing

It is generally advised that tests should be administered in well-lighted rooms, with suitable tables or other writing sufaces, and with a minimum of noise or other distractions. Attractive as is the logic of these *dicta,* there really is very little evidence that it makes any difference in the ultimate scores if the room is poorly lighted, if the seating is awkward, or if there is noise or other distraction. A very few studies bearing upon this point have been located and will be summarized in succeeding paragraphs.

A study by Henderson, Crews, and Barlow (1945) explored the effects of music as a source of distraction during the taking of a test (with implications also for the controversial question of whether listening to music interferes with studying). College freshmen women were administered the *Nelson-Denny Reading Test,* one group with popular music being played during the administration, a second group with classical music, and a third with no music. Since all had taken a different form of the same test some time previously, the effects of music as a distraction could be estimated from differences between the two sets of scores for the three groups. The only one of the three groups which showed any significant decrease was the popular music group, and they decreased only on the Paragraph Reading part of the test, and not on the Vocabulary part. There were no significant differences between those subjects who reported that they customarily studied with the radio on and those who didn't. The experimenters suggest that the results may be explained by two facts, first, that the popular music had a more distracting rhythm, and, second, that the Paragraph Reading part required more sustained concentration than the Vocabulary part and was therefore more sensitive to the effects of distraction. They concluded that the distractor effect of music depends both on the type of music and the complexity of the test materials.

Super and others (1947) introduced a series of distractions during the administration to graduate-student groups of the *Minnesota Clerical Test* and the *Otis Quick-Scoring Test of Mental Ability*. While the experimental group took its tests, conspirators played a trumpet in a nearby room, burst into the room to ask a question, and argued noisily just outside the door. The final touch was to have the timer go off five minutes prematurely, the experimenter then telling the annoyed subjects to continue for an additional five minutes. With all of this, there were no significant differences in test scores between this group and the control group, which had none of these distractions.

Another kind of distraction was used by Staudt (1948), who with one group sounded a buzzer every thirty seconds, announcing each time the number of problems that should have been accomplished (always a larger number than they were able to do). This group, when compared with a control group and with a third group which had no distractions but was urged to work accurately, had a somewhat larger number of errors on two tests, but they also had a larger number of *correct* items on two tests. Here again the distractions seemed to result in no net loss. The distraction in Staudt's study is different from the others mentioned, since it was relevant to the test and involved pressure to work faster on the test. For our present purposes, however, it is a distraction to the extent that it interrupted the subjects and apparently was a source of some annoyance.

The effect of noise on human functioning was recently studied in depth in a laboratory setting (Jerison, 1959). The effects were found to be complex in nature, sometimes impairing performance on certain tasks, sometimes not. They seemed in part to be a function of the nature of the task, and in part, of the sequence of activities and the particular points at which noise was introduced. Jerison suggests that noise has its effects by creating or increasing psychological *stress*, which in turn is the cause of changes in functioning.

Once again we find ourselves in the position of lacking sound research support for a common-sense principle. As is usual in such cases, most of us will continue to proceed on the basis of common sense, unless the weight of contrary evidence becomes so staggering as to be no longer resistable. It *does* make sense to be concerned about the illumination in a testing room, especially in the case of testees with defective vision. Likewise it makes sense to be concerned about distractions, especially in the case of those people who find it difficult to concentrate under such conditions. For the vast majority of test-takers, however, we can only hypothesize at this point that physical conditions of testing would have to be extremely bad (the lighting so poor, for example, that visibility is actually impaired) before scores are likely to be noticeably affected. It seems likely, from the limited evidence available, that these physical conditions are less important than the psychological conditions of testing, which have been discussed earlier under such topics as preparation for testing, feelings about tests, and attitudes toward tests. Although we have no specific research data to document these contentions, some indirect support comes from the classic studies of work efficiency at the Hawthorne plant of the Western Electric Company (Roethlisberger and Dickson, 1939), in which illumination and other physical conditions were found to be much less influential on production rates than were worker perceptions, attitudes, and feelings.

The Examiner and the Psychological Situation

In connection with the topic just discussed, a brief comment is in order regarding the lack of expressed concern in guidance testing with the possible effects of the examiner and of the psychological situation in which the test is taken. Clinical psychologists have become aware of the fact that a set of responses to an individually administered test of intelligence or to a projective test of personality can be adequately interpreted only in the light of the psychological setting in which the testing is done (White, 1952; Sarason, 1950). The setting includes the examiner and his behavior and how both are perceived by each testee—whether as a threatening or supporting or stimulating person, as someone to rebel against, someone to please, or someone who doesn't seem to care much one way or another.

Sacks (1952) studied the effects of the examiner's behavior on *Stanford-Binet* scores of nursery school children. An increase in score between *Form L* and *Form M* (with a ten-day interval) was greater for the group with whom she tried during the ten-day period to develop "good" relationships as an assistant teacher than for those with whom she tried to develop "poor" relationships in the same role. However, both groups' scores did increase, and a control group, with whom she had no contact during the ten-day period, showed no mean increase in score. She concluded that "heightened familiarity" with the examiner improved test scores and that a good relationship with the examiner produced greater improvement than a poor relationship. Sacks adds an implication for school psychologists, that it would be wise to know children in a school before testing them. The implication seems equally applicable to guidance counselors and to others who do testing in schools and elsewhere.

The book by Sarason and others (1960) which has already been cited offers some suggestions that are also pertinent here. As mentioned earlier, their theory is that test anxiety is a reflection of the child's relations with his parents. Therefore, they suggest, the child responds to someone administering a test to him with some of the same perceptions and emotions he has in relation to his parents when *they* talk with him about his abilities. Thus an examiner's efforts to be objective and to reject a child's attempts to be dependent may *arouse* anxiety in the child because it may be perceived as the kind of rejection and lack of emotional support which he has had from his parents.

This is a topic deserving of a great deal more consideration than it has received in the literature of counseling. Counselors, and others serving as examiners of individuals or groups, can gain at least some suggestions from the work mentioned above. They would do well to give some thought to the way they are perceived by their testees and the way the entire test situation is perceived and responded to.

Problem-Solving Processes

A test score in and of itself tells very little about the mental processes by which it was attained. Consider for example a spatial visualization item such as those used in the *Revised Minnesota Paper Form Board* test (see Figure 5.1). Two boys, Paul and Robert, both take this test and get identical scores—to make our point, let us even assume that they got exactly the same items right and wrong (and sat in different parts of the room!). It might be inferred that they have the same ability in spatial visualization of the kind tapped by this test. Yet if we could get them to think out loud as they take the test, we might find that they solve identical problems in different ways. For example, their thinking-out-loud in response to the item reproduced in Figure 5.1 might be as follows:

Paul: Not *A*, it doesn't look like the same pieces as the ones up there . . . not *B*, those pieces are different sizes . . . could be *C*, those pieces look like just the same shape and size . . . not *D*, they're different shapes . . . certainly not *E*, that has three pieces . . . it must be *C*.

Robert: Let's see, you'd call these four-sided figures oblongs, but not rectangles. *A* has two triangles, so it can't be right . . . *B* has a triangle and a five-sided figure, so that's out . . . *C* is made up of two four-sided pieces, and they're oblong but not rectangles . . . so that might be it . . . but let's check the others . . . *D* has two triangles, so that's out, and *E* has three parts, so that's impossible . . . it has to be *C*.

Both boys arrived at the correct answer, but through different methods; Paul has used a more nearly "pure" visualization method, apparently

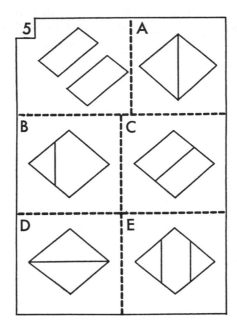

**Fig. 5.1. A Spatial Visualization Item from the Revised Minnesota
Paper Form Board**
(By permission of The Psychological Corporation.)

comparing shapes and sizes in a fairly direct visual manner. Robert has
used more verbalization, first identifying each of the disassembled parts
and categorizing it, then looking for parts which fit those labels; he may
do this mostly with *words* rather than by comparing images directly as
Paul seems to have done. Though their resulting scores may be the same,
these two boys may function quite differently in school courses or jobs
which include visualization activities. For example, Paul will probably
learn faster and more effectively through visual methods, whereas Robert
can be expected to learn better from verbal explanations, whether he
reads them or listens to them. Of course, in a specific situation involving
visualization problems, they may end up learning just as fast and may
function equally well, each using his own preferred approach. In that
case, the same prediction would be made for both from the same raw
score on the test. However, to the extent that they will function differently
in a particular situation, one learning faster than the other, one learning
more than the other, to that extent it would be a mistake to make the
same prediction just because they happened to have the same score on
the test. Yet, one has no alternative but to make the same interpretation

for both, since the scores do not reflect the mental processes which are used, but only the *products*.

There have been a few studies of this problem which lend support to the thesis that different problem-solving methods can lead to the same result on tests. Bloom and Broder (1950) had their subjects think out loud while solving problems and concluded that they varied so greatly in their attack on the problems that it was impossible to infer from the products what mental processes were used. Jones (1953) asked students in an educational psychology course to justify on a separate form their responses to fifteen multiple-choice items. He found there was considerable discrepancy between getting the item right and understanding why the right alternative was right. In fact, for three of the questions better reasons were given for wrong choices than for correct ones! Kropp (1953) studied the responses of high school juniors to a physical science reading comprehension test and concluded that (1) the fact that a student answered an item correctly could not be used as evidence of the fact that he used the same method of solution as did the "interpreter" when *he* solved the problem, and (2) a correct answer to an item was not sufficient evidence that the student could execute successfully the subsidiary behaviors in the "interpreter's" attainment of solution. These studies would indicate that the same score by two different people does not necessarily mean they possess the same amount of skill.

We are dealing here with a question of *construct validity:* the question of what human ability or other characteristic is being tapped by a particular test or test item. Unfortunately, we are currently unable to identify a specific mental process with a particular test and therefore have only very limited bases for describing a person's psychological life, or thinking activities, from knowledge of his test scores. Of course, a skillful counselor can sometimes make intelligent guesses, from examination of a person's responses to a group of items, or his scores on a group of tests, as to what went on in that person's thinking. This, however, is a "clinical" process and is severely limited by the personal skill of the test interpreter.

From the point of view of the counselor who uses tests primarily for predictive purposes, the problem posed here may be somewhat academic in nature. To the extent that a test correlates with a criterion of success, such as grades in school or ratings by supervisors on the job, to that extent the score obtained by an individual counselee may be sufficient information for the counselor's needs. He can, for instance, use an expectancy table to tell John Jones that he has eight chances in ten of getting a *B* average at *XYZ* college (or, more correctly, "that people with scores such as his have eight chances in ten"). It may be that, just as different people can get the same score on a given test through the use of different processes, so they may also be able to get the same grade in a course, or the same rating from a supervisor on the job, even though in the course or on the job they get their respective results by using different mental processes. What one student accomplishes in a drafting course through actual visualization, another may accomplish by means of verbal problem-solving, and still another by a more mathematical reasoning process.

It is likely, however, that we will in the long run have higher levels of predictive validity if tests are developed which have greater construct validity, in the sense that a test score can be interpreted as representing the product of a specific series of psychological operations. Furthermore, greater construct validity will give counselors the tools with which to do a better job of "descriptive interpretation" (see Chapter 7), that is, of understanding better how his counselee thinks and what kind of person he is. This understanding may be used without any predictive implications, simply to help the client know himself better. The understanding may also be used by counselor and client in the process of clinical prediction: the process by which the counselor develops a "model"·of this person, from which inferences may be drawn as to how he will behave in one situation or another in the future (see Chapter 9 for detailed discussion of this clinical process).

Tab Item

Ingenuity in the construction of test items may make contributions toward the improved construct validity of tests. One such method is the Tab Item, which was developed for the Air Force (Glaser, Damrin, and Gardner, 1954). The item type is illustrated in their report by an excerpt from a test of proficiency in diagnosing or trouble-shooting a defective television set. The subject is given a description of the symptom, in this case "the screen is dark, no picture appears." There follows a list of checks which might be made by the trouble-shooter: "Tuning: Tune in a station" or "Brightness and Contrast: Turn up brightness and contrast controls" or "Vertical Sweep: Connect headphones across vertical sweep coil"—in this particular item a total of eighteen different checks is available for the examinee's selection. Opposite each check is a tab which, when removed by the subject, informs him of the results he would have obtained if he actually had performed that procedure on the particular television set. For the first check quoted above, for example, the information revealed under the tab is "sound appears on all stations but no picture." Removal of the tab opposite the last check quoted above reveals the results of *that* test: "Loud, rough, roaring sound is heard."

As the authors suggest, the Tab Item can substitute for an actual work-sample test but without the necessity of expensive equipment and individual administration. It can be scored not only for the *number* of steps taken before the right answer is selected, but also, if desired, a record could be kept of the *sequence* of steps taken. In addition to the more obvious use of this kind of device for measuring job proficiency, this item type, or a modification of it, might contribute toward increased construct validity of aptitude and other tests by giving at least some information about the process by which an individual arrived at his answer to a question.

Self-Learning or Instructional Scoring Devices

Teachers sometimes go over classroom tests with their classes for the learning value of the experience. This seems to be a useful procedure, since students often are more ego-involved at such times than during normal class sessions, and learning therefore may be more effective. It has been speculated that it might be even more valuable to have an immediate report, to the person taking a test, of the correctness of each response as he makes it. This is in keeping with a principle derived from the psychology of learning, that the greater the proximity between a learner's response and the reward or other consequence of that response, the more effective will be the learning.

With this kind of rationale, devices have been developed which combine testing and instruction.[2] Usually the answer sheet is mounted on a punchboard, and the correctness of his answer is signalled to the testee in various ways, sometimes by the depth with which the pencil is permitted to enter the hole (Severin, 1955), sometimes by the color which appears under the hole punched (Jones and Sawyer, 1949). Favorable results have been reported with the use of these devices. Severin administered self-scoring achievement tests in academic subjects to college students and compared the results with those of other classes which took conventional tests. He concluded: "More learning occurs by taking a test with a self-scoring device than in the usual fashion. The range of errors is also much greater; since three times as many errors can be made, a greater discrimination in measurement might be assumed" (p. 330).

Useful especially with achievement tests, as reported above, self-scoring devices may also offer some promise if applied to tests of aptitude and to other kinds of tests. If nothing else, they may help discriminate between Student *A*, who knows, correctly, that the right answer is either option *a* or *d* but not *b* or *c* and chooses the wrong one of the first two, and Student *B*, who chooses the same wrong one, but in a blind guess. The first student, using a self-scoring device, will get the right answer on his second try, whereas the other student will have only one chance in three of guessing right on his second try. This, as Severin pointed out in the quotation above, should improve the discrimination of measurement, in addition to its value in helping testees to learn something about the material while taking a test. Of course, the latter value may also be a serious flaw in the

---

[2] These devices are related to the teaching machines in which there has been a recent increase of interest. Our focus here, however, is on the testing and appraisal aspect rather than the instructional.

process, since it is a threat to the confidentiality of test materials. Where this is a problem, or where one wishes to use the same test for the same person at a later date, as a measure of growth, then self-scoring devices may not be usable.

Other Learning During Test-Taking

As suggested in Chapter 3, a major argument in favor of client participation of some sort in planning a testing program is that it increases the likelihood that the client will learn something about himself while taking tests. Let us suppose that a client and counselor have decided to use a test of spatial visualization in order to provide some predictive information about the chances of success as a draftsman. The client with some understanding of the particular function which the test is to perform will, it is hoped, be more conscious of the ease or difficulty he has with this kind of material. His perceptions during the test should therefore give him some additional basis for deciding whether drafting is for him. Similarly, a client taking a personality inventory who has explored with his counselor the kinds of questions which the test is aimed at answering may actually clarify his self-concept as he thinks through his answers to each individual question. If this happens, the profile which emerges from the scoring of the test may be less valuable than the impressions and insights which the client gets while taking the test. When client and counselor confer together later, these impressions and insights may form the basis for a productive discussion of their implications for future plans and various courses of action.

Examiner's Observations During Test-Taking

In concluding this topic, only brief mention should be necessary of observations which may be made by examiners during the actual administration of tests to individuals or groups. Especially noteworthy are the following:

1. Symptoms of excessive tension and anxiety, such as perspiration, nail-biting, and trembling.
2. Symptoms of inadequate motivation or effort, such as day-dreaming and doodling.
3. Apparent fatigue, sleepiness, or illness.
4. Apparent efforts to copy from others.
5. Misunderstanding or difficulty in understanding directions.

Whenever possible, the teacher or other test administrator should make notes of his observations, at least of the unusual ones, so that the counselor, in reviewing the results later, will be aware of factors which may have influenced the results, and aware also of these additional facts about the counselee's behavior and personality.

CONCLUDING STATEMENT

As has been pointed out a number of times, the ills of test administration—inadequate motivation, exaggerated tensions, response sets which distort the client's image—are often the results of inadequate *preparation for taking tests*. A good program of test administration, then, begins long before the day on which tests are given; it begins with a study of the needs and readinesses of those individuals or groups who are to take the tests, it continues with selection of tests which are appropriate to those needs, and it includes as large a measure as possible of involvement and identification of examinees with the tests and with their anticipated contributions.

CHAPTER 6

Scoring the Test

In THIS CHAPTER, we shall consider several elements in test scoring, beginning first with the actual counting or other process which results in one or more raw scores. Next there will be some consideration of other kinds of information, both quantitative and qualitative, which one may extract from responses to a test. Finally there will be some attention to the use of norms and the conversion of raw scores to more meaningful scores, such as percentiles, IQ's, and grade equivalents.

SCORING METHODS

In most counseling agencies and clinics, the quantity of testing in any one day or week is not enough to warrant machine scoring methods, so that hand scoring is customary in these settings. In schools and other institutions, on the other hand, with *program* testing (entire classes or grades taking the same test), machine scoring is of increasing importance. The details of scoring tests with various kinds of machines are beyond the scope of the present work; those interested may obtain information from test publishers who provide scoring services, from manufacturers of the machines, from universities which have such equipment, and from state departments of education. Some of the approaches and possibilities are summarized in the *Proceedings of the 1953 Invitational Conference on Testing Problems* (1954).

Scoring Accuracy

Perhaps this is belaboring the obvious, but sometimes an idea as obvious as this is overlooked: If a counselor can't assume that the recorded score is completely accurate (within very narrow limits of scoring errors), the best tests in the world are absolutely no good to him and may even be dangerous. This principle is made vivid each time one has the experience of interpreting a set of scores to a counselee and then, because of what appears to be a contradiction or for some other reason, rescores the tests, only to find a serious scoring error. There follows a horrible sinking sensation, as one wonders how many other misinterpretations he has given other youngsters, without knowing it, and what the results have been. For some the result may be reduced confidence in the counselor, in tests, or in guidance in general. For others it may be confusion about their plans for the future or doubts about themselves. It is really not a sign of fastidiousness or compulsiveness to insist on two *independent* scorings of every test. There is enough inaccuracy in psychological and educational measurement that counselors can do nothing about; it is inexcusable to allow serious scoring errors to be added.

Machine Scoring

Scoring large numbers of answer sheets by machine provides rapid service with a minimum of manpower, but, as will be seen later in discussing hand scoring, one gives up opportunities for obtaining valuable qualitative information when mechanical scoring is done. It should also be noted that scoring machines are not infallible and, as with hand scoring, *two independent scorings of* each answer sheet may be necessary to assure accuracy.

Machine scoring may be arranged in several ways. One of the most popular, in terms of numbers of tests scored annually (though also probably the newest approach) is the package arrangement by which one contracts with a *test publisher* or *distributor* for use of his test booklets and answer sheets and for scoring and reporting of scores, sometimes on individual profile sheets, sometimes on group tabulation sheets. This arrangement is not entirely an unmixed blessing; the sheer convenience has all too often been the primary factor which sells the plan to schools, sometimes carrying far more weight than any considerations of reliability, validity, or norms. Also, the availability of multiple copies of profiles has led, in some schools, to promiscuous distribution of the profiles to students, parents, and others.

A second kind of arrangement is the *commercial test-scoring service* which is sometimes operated by a test publisher or distributor, sometimes by a company whose major function is scoring (Testscor, which specializes in the *Strong, Bernreuter,* and *MMPI*) and sometimes by a University Testing Bureau. Here the scoring is separate from the purchase of test materials; the cost per unit is usually inversely proportional to the number of answer sheets scored during a given period of time. This arrangement provides somewhat more flexibility, since under the package plan one cannot always have the materials when he wants them. A major disadvantage in using a test-scoring service is that the user must purchase and store his own test booklets and answer sheets all year, when he may use them only for a few days or weeks. It is wise to compare costs carefully, giving some thought also to the possibility of sharing the test materials with one or more other schools.

Sometimes *statistical services* may be arranged with the test-scoring service; these may include computation of local means, percentiles, correlations with local criteria, and other statistics. University Test Bureaus may be more likely to offer this service, since they tend to be somewhat more research-minded than other organizations. Making use of such services provides the local norms and other standardization data which can be far more valuable than those reported in test manuals. National data provide the foundation; they give a basis for deciding that a particular test has enough merit (in terms of various evidences of reliability and validity) and enough promise to be worth trying. The real value of many tests (particularly those of achievement, scholastic aptitude, and prognosis for school subjects) comes later, when local norms have been developed and when local validation studies have been completed. Then the counselor has substantial bases for making predictive statements for an individual or a group (Dyer, 1957). This point will be discussed in greater detail in later chapters.

Still another plan is to join a *testing program* such as those sometimes operated by universities, state departments of education, and other organizations, such as the Educational Records Bureau.[1] In these programs, one is in effect joining with a number of other schools in the purchase and scoring of tests and the pooling of information for the purpose of developing regional or other special norms. As usually operated, the central office maintains files of test materials, from which each member school selects those it wishes to use. After this point, the service operates much as do the package plans first mentioned, with testing dates being planned so as not to conflict with those of other schools. Some of these organizations publish bulletins and reports regarding test interpretation, and some sponsor conferences and workshops.

Some larger schools and school systems have rented or purchased their own test-scoring equipment. In some instances, several smaller systems share a machine among them, housing it in the most convenient location and arranging schedules where necessary to avoid conflicting dates. This is probably the least expensive of all the arrangements, provided the machine is kept busy enough of the time, but of course this provides only the minimum service of scoring.

Each school, agency, or other institution must decide which of these approaches best meets its needs. It is a mistake, however, to expect that any such arrangement can relieve the school of all responsibility for selecting

---

[1] An organization ". . . the main function of which is to assist its member institutions in the use of objective techniques in guidance" (Traxler, 1957, p. ix). Further details may be found in this reference.

tests suitable for its needs, characteristics, and goals. It is an even greater error to assume that using such a service, even the best of them, relieves the school of responsibility for having its own staff resources in the area of tests and measurement. Tests are never self-interpreting, even when they are almost self-scoring. Elaborate test profiles are of little value without competent local staff to interpret and apply them. Some of the services mentioned above are highly professional and will help schools to be aware of the facts just mentioned. Others, unfortunately, are highly commercial in nature and not motivated by professional and service criteria.

Hand Scoring

As with machine scoring, there must be assurance of *accuracy*. This can best be obtained by arranging for two independent scorings of every answer sheet or test booklet. Independence ideally involves two different scorers, the second going through all operations as did the first, rather than just *checking* the counting and addition of the first. Simply checking another's figures is not enough, as accountants can testify, since errors are easily repeated by suggestion when one sees the numbers which have already been written by the other person.

Some kinds of answer sheets are easier to use than others; one of the more convenient is the hole-punched stencil which fits over an IBM-type answer sheet, so that one can see instantly which correct answers have been marked by the subject. Scoring is then a matter of counting visible pencil marks. Perhaps even more convenient is the carbon-backed type of answer sheet, such as the Clapp-Young, in which carbon paper or carbon backing instantly records the subject's marks on a sheet which contains small boxes or circles, each one representing a correct response. Scoring here does not require a separate stencil; one simply counts the number of carbon pencil marks which are *inside* squares or circles, and this is the number of correct items. The California Test Bureau uses its own patented device, Scor-eez, which also makes use of carbon paper for automatic indication of right and wrong answers. The sheets on which the carbon marks appear are imprinted so as to show not only which items have been answered correctly, but also the type of material and the type of skill tapped by the item, so that a rapid visual examination may be made for diagnostic purposes. Finally, there is the pin-prick kind of answer sheet used with the *Kuder Preference Record,* which also permits counting scores without the use of stencils or other scoring devices.

All of these are easier to score than tests using the strip type of scoring device, in which there is a strip for each page of the test booklet, showing the correct word, letter, number, or whatever, for each item. One advantage of the strip device is that it permits the use of completion items, which require subjects to write something besides a vertical pencil line or an X. A disadvantage is the possibility of lower reliability of scoring, since the scorer must judge whether the letter written by the subject is an *a* or a *c,* or whether a word is spelled correctly. If nothing important is lost by being restricted to multiple-choice items, the stencil and the carbon types of scoring device are clearly superior in terms of convenience and accuracy of scoring.

The question of *who does the scoring* is not easily answered, except in general terms—that it should be someone who has the requisite abilities of perceiving, counting, adding, dividing, all with speed and accuracy, and who will approach the task with carefulness and a high regard for the importance of accuracy. Classroom teachers, psychologists, counselors, and psychometrists may or may not have this combination of qualities. Some of these people are too high in intelligence and some too low in patience to continue for long with the more-or-less routine task of scoring large numbers of tests. Some may simply lack the ability to perceive accurately under speed conditions.

Although this is speculation and needs empirical verification, the job would probably be done best by skilled clerks who have the requisite combination of specific abilities and who are neither too low nor too high in general intelligence. If this hypothesis is true, it is certainly unwise to ask teachers and other professional workers to do a job which most of them find unpleasant and burdensome.

Whoever does the scoring must be well-trained for the job and carefully supervised. There are possibilities of errors in all phases of test scoring, including the placement of the stencil on the answer sheet (being off by a quarter inch can give the impression of correct placement, since marks will appear under many of the windows), the actual counting, the recording of numbers, the division and subtraction involved in correction-for-guessing formulas, totalling of subpart scores, and conversion to percentiles and other equated scores.

Getting Additional Information from the Answer Sheet

Whether in school or agency, there are some techniques in the scoring process which can provide the counselor with useful information. The procedures which are here recommended include the following steps:

1. Indicating in some way which answers are right and which wrong. One simple technique is to put a red (or other distinctive) pencil mark on every wrong response. This is easily done with the stencil scoring device by making a red mark in every window that doesn't show a black pencil line; thus every item that has been answered incorrectly, or omitted, is noted on the answer sheet. With the various carbon-backed answer sheets, this step is unnecessary, since the subject's own pencil marks are already automatically recorded as right or wrong answers.

2. Recording on the answer sheet all numbers and computations involved in the scoring.

3. Recording on the answer sheet the equated score and the name of the norm group which was used.

If these steps are taken, the answer sheet (or test booklet if responses are written directly in the booklet) will contain a complete record of what happened. The values which may be derived from these steps include the following:

1. The red pencil marks quickly identify wrong answers. One use of the information is to make a *rapid check of the scorer's arithmetic* by counting wrongs (all items with red marks) and subtracting these from the total number of items. If desired, the original scoring may be checked by placing the stencil on the answer sheet and quickly looking for errors that were not marked in red.

2. Visual inspection of the red marks permits a *rapid survey of the distribution of errors.* They may be bunched toward (a) the end, indicating perhaps the effects of fatigue or, if the items are arranged in order of increasing difficulty, the fact that the subject reached his ceiling. They may be (b) bunched at the beginning, sometimes indicating the slow-to-warm-up person who didn't get the point at first. They may be (c) distributed throughout the test, in which case they may represent carelessness, guessing, or, in an omnibus test with different types of content, difficulty with certain types of material.

3. By going back to the test questions, one can *identify the kinds of material which the subject found most difficult.* On an omnibus test such as the *Otis* or the *Henmon-Nelson,* or any number of achievement tests, one can thus identify the sources of major difficulty, such as vocabulary, fractions, generalizations from given data, or whatever. This may suggest to the counselor certain hypotheses, which can be explored with the client, leading perhaps to recommendations for remedial work, or simply to increased awareness by the client of his strengths and weaknesses.

4. Still another value which may be obtained from the marking of errors is the opportunity to check with the counselee on *reasons for errors.* By repeating a missed item to the client and asking him to explain his choice of answer, we can sometimes identify sources of difficulty. Remedial work may be done right then and there (if it is an achievement kind of item) or referral made for remedial work. In the case of more basic aptitudes, this kind of diagnostic work will more likely be used for description of this person's psychological characteristics, with a view less toward remediation than toward seeking implications for career planning, choosing school subjects, or other decisions.

5. The suggested notation on the answer sheet of all computations in-

volved in the scoring might look like the following, on a test such as the *DAT Numerical Ability Test,* in which there is a correction for guessing:

$$27 - \frac{8}{4} = 25$$

This communicates to the counselor (who may not have scored the test himself) that there were 27 items right and 8 wrong, with an adjusted score of 25. He has an immediate *basis for checking all arithmetic,* and he can also check to be sure that the correction for guessing was made as directed in the manual for the test.

6. Inspection of the computation, such as that illustrated above, quickly reveals to the counselor something of the *test-taking approach of the person*—whether this is a person who guesses much or one who is cautious. The following computations, for example, based on a test which contains 60 items, all yield the same net score, but they represent differences in approach:

$$\text{Jack:} \quad 35 - \frac{0}{4} = 35$$

$$\text{Lucy:} \quad 37 - \frac{8}{4} = 35$$

$$\text{Victor:} \quad 40 - \frac{20}{4} = 35$$

Jack may be a slow but sure person who cannot or will not make even a slight guess, whereas Victor may be one who produces much greater quantity in a given period of time but at the cost of many errors. Lucy may be somewhere between these extremes. What the counselor does with the information is a question which need not be discussed further at this point, except to mention briefly that in one case we might try to help someone like Jack to be a little more daring, whereas under other circumstances we might help someone like this to select an occupation in which his kind of approach would be highly desirable. Similarly, Victor might, on the one hand, be encouraged to be more cautious, or, working from the assumption that he is not likely to change his approach very much, we might instead help him to plan a vocation in which this kind of approach is not detrimental and might even be a valued asset.

7. A notation of the converted score (IQ, percentile, grade equivalent) along with specification of the norm group used, as in the following example on the *Mechanical Reasoning Test* of the *DAT* battery:

$$35 = 15\text{th } \%\text{ile} - 12\text{th boys}$$

permits the counselor to be certain that suitable norms were used (12th grade boys) and to *check the conversion* rapidly by use of the table of norms in the manual. Having all the data right on the answer sheet is far more convenient than having to look for the raw score in one place (say the answer sheet), the percentile score in another (say the cumulative record card), and, to find out which norms were used, having to calculate the subject's age or grade at the time of the test, then check the table of norms for that age or grade level to see if suitable norms were used accurately.

CONVERTING THE SCORE

No attempt will be made here at systematic or thorough coverage of the various types of scores (percentile, IQ, grade equivalent, standard score, stanine). The subject is treated in detail in many basic texts in measurement and statistics and in a *Test Service Bulletin* of the Psychological Corporation (Seashore, 1955). The test interpreter should be aware of the statistical and other implications of each kind of score—which ones may be averaged, which ones actually represent a comparison with a group and which ones are just extrapolations. One particular problem, however, deserves extended treatment and will be discussed in the section which follows.

All Converted Scores Are Sample-Bound, Including the IQ

Whether one converts a raw score into an IQ, a percentile, a standard score, or a grade equivalent, he is in every case comparing one person's score with that of a particular group of people. There is a widespread misconception, even among those with some training in measurement, that some types of scores—particularly the IQ, but also the grade equivalent, especially as applied to reading tests—are more permanent, more dependable, more solid than other types of scores.

The origin of this fallacy is not entirely clear, but it is undoubtedly at least in part a reflection of the value placed on scholastic aptitude (often misnamed *intelligence,* which is really a broader concept) and on reading ability. These values long predate the Sputnik era, although emphasis on them has fluctuated over the years. The focus on scholastic aptitude in particular is quite understandably a matter of concern to parents, since the level of schooling their child attains plays a major part in influencing what he will do for a living, where he will live, who his friends will be, how he will spend his leisure time, whom his children will play with when young, and whom they will marry when they are grown. For each social-class level, educational attainment often represents the most important single means of climbing to the next level or even of holding on to one's status at his present level. We shall see later in some of the illustrative cases the role played by these sociopsychological factors in the process of test interpretation.

Since IQ is widely seen—by parents, students, teachers, and others—as the most important factor in setting the child's educational limits, it follows that much of a family's social-status anxiety is focused on his IQ. Perhaps this explains why it is so difficult to get people to understand that a child's IQ is just another kind of converted score, based on his responses to a group of items, and that the IQ represents a comparison of his number of correct responses on that test with those of a particular group of people of his age or grade level.[2] Otherwise responsible people, in schools and elsewhere, set up rigid IQ cut-off points—for special class placement, elimination from school, and other purposes—without specifying the particular test, grade level at which given, or circumstances under which given, as if the IQ is unchanging no matter what particular test is used or how nearly that particular testing session represents the usual or maximal level of functioning of the child. All too often one hears teachers and guidance counselors categorize an individual or a group by the IQ: "His IQ is 83," rather than "he got an IQ of 83 on the *XYZ* test in the sixth grade," or even better "his IQ has ranged from 76 on the *ABC* test in the second grade to 94 on the *JKL* test in the fourth grade to 83 on the *XYZ* in the sixth grade." Similarly, reading level is spoken of in these absolute terms, as if these tests also are free of the limitations of norms, validity, and reliability to which other tests are subject. With reading tests, one hears: "This boy reads at the third grade level; how can he possibly handle such-and-such material?," rather than, "on the Blank test of reading ability, he got a score which, based on national norms, converts to a 3.4 grade equivalent."

It is true enough that scholastic aptitude and reading ability are fundamental to progress in school and in some other life activities. It is also true that one's level of intelligence, as compared with his peers, is relatively constant throughout life. Neither of these truths, however, negates the fact that *tests* of scholastic aptitude, general intelligence, and reading, like all other tests, are samples of behavior in particular spheres, each of which yields a score which is given meaning by comparison with a norm group. The meaning of an IQ and a reading grade equivalent are no more universal than are percentiles, standard scores, or any other converted score.

LOCAL VS. PUBLISHED NORMS

Is it better to use the norms in the manual or to develop one's own? The answer depends on the test and on the use which is to be made of it. If we are dealing with an achievement or reading test which is to be used for placement of students in sections within a school, local norms will probably be more useful. If we wish to see how this school compares

[2] See in Chapter 12 the discussion of comparability of IQs among different intelligence tests.

with others in the state, region, or nation, then obviously we want state, regional, or national norms. If a youngster were considering becoming an auto mechanic, would it be more informative to compare his score on a mechanical aptitude test with the distribution of scores of a sample of auto mechanics (or mechanical trainees, or whatever) in the same city or town, or would it be more informative to compare his score with that of a national sample? Probably the former, for two reasons: First, the chances are that he will plan to work in that city or town, and he will be competing for a job and for promotions with the local mechanics. Secondly, "national" samples are rarely, if ever, really national in scope. Although some achievement and scholastic aptitude tests have been normed with samples intended to cover all parts of the country and to represent the various socioeconomic groupings, urban and rural populations, and so on, they are still quite the exception. For the most part, norms for tests are based on samples from only a few localities, and are further limited by the fact that they are obtained from those schools, colleges, counseling centers, employment agencies, or business establishments which have *consented to co-operate*. This is a further selective factor which limits the extent to which we can assume these norms to be representative of "schools in general" or "service stations in general." As a result, we simply cannot judge the applicability of a set of norms in relation to the appraisal of a particular client. If he should leave this area and move to another one which is 100 or 1000 miles distant, we usually have no way of knowing whether the published norm group is similar in distribution to the group *in the locality* in which he will be working.

What it comes down to is this: More times than not, a decision is to be made in relation to a particular high school, college, company, or other unit. What would therefore be *most* useful are norms for that *particular group*. In some instances, such norms are easily obtained; junior high schools should be able to obtain separate norms for each curriculum group in the senior high school (academic, business or commercial, vocational, agriculture) . Furthermore, junior high schools in a city which has specialized senior high schools (for skilled trades or for pre-engineering preparation) should be able without too much difficulty to obtain from each of these schools a set of norms for its entering class. Such norms would show their distribution of scores on whatever measures have been found to be relevant—scholastic aptitude tests, mathematics achievement tests, grades in particular subjects, or average grades in all subjects. This would permit counselors to report individual scores not in the usual general terms, but in a way that is much more meaningful to counselees: "Tommy, your score on Test *A* is better than four out of five sophomores at Technical High School, and on Test *B* you have a higher score than three out of five." Or: "Mrs. Williams, your daughter has scores on tests of clerical aptitude and scholastic aptitude which would make her an above average student in the commercial course of study in high school. However, in the academic or college prep curriculum she would be in the lowest fourth in scholastic aptitude and in her grades to date; she would still be above average in clerical aptitude but in a curriculum which doesn't make much use of that kind of ability."

College Norms

Similarly, local norms for particular colleges are far more useful than published norms which are based on samples of 5, 50, or even 500 colleges. What the student and his parents wish to know is not how the boy or girl will compare with college students *in general* in the United States. Nor do they wish to know how he compares with students in a total sam-

Table 6.1. Distribution of College Board Scholastic Aptitude Test Scores

	Men				Women			
	Verb.		*Math.*		*Verb.*		*Math.*	
	No.	%	No.	%	No.	%	No.	%
750-800	0	0	24	6	4	2	6	3
700-749	17	4	64	16	19	8	24	10
650-699	46	12	83	21	41	18	39	17
600-649	76	20	84	21	62	27	49	21
550-599	95	24	80	20	44	19	50	22
500-549	73	19	38	10	36	16	35	15
450-499	64	16	14	4	17	7	20	9
400-449	15	4	0	0	4	2	5	2
350-399	2	.5	0	0	0	0	0	0
300-349	0	0	1	.2	1	.4	0	0

SOURCE: *A profile of the freshman class, college of arts and science, the university of rochester,* 1959. Used by permission of the Director of Admissions, The University of Rochester.

Table 6.2. Scholastic Aptitude Test Median Scores

	Verbal	*Mathematical*
Liberal Arts and B.S. in Business Administration, Education, Industrial Management, Nursing (426 scores)	586	604
B.S. in Astrophysics, Biology, Chemistry, Geology, Optics, Physics (99 scores)	621	681
B.S. in Engineering (91 scores)	560.5	653
Total Class		
Men (388 scores)	573	632
Women (228 scores)	612	604
Men and Women together (616 scores)	586	622

SOURCE: *Ibid.*

ple which was drawn from a number of colleges of unknown or of mixed levels and types. It is much more valuable for them to know that Margaret would be in the top fifth (on a test or on high school average) at College *R,* in the middle fifth at College *S,* and in the lowest fifth at College *T.*

This kind of local norm has, in fact, been developed by some colleges, which transmit to high school counselors information about the test scores of their student body (see, for example, Table 6.1). If such information were available in a high school for all or most of the colleges its seniors apply to, a better job could be done of helping students to apply appropriately. There are objections to this by some college officials, and often for good reason: If a college is trying to raise the level of its student body, it may fear that distributing normative data based on its present students would result in discouraging better students from applying. On the other hand, some of the more selective colleges like to sprinkle their entering classes with some students who may not be outstanding academically but who have one or another desired characteristic: e.g., athletic skill, leadership ability in student activities and government, or artistic or musical accomplishment.

Some of the problems associated with the use of local norms for colleges apply also to local norms for particular high schools or for particular plants and offices. In part, these are problems associated with the actual collection of information within the school or company. A more serious obstacle, however, is communicating the resulting norms to school and agency counselors. There is required a high level of confidence in the professional qualifications and attitudes of these counselors—confidence that the information will be used judiciously and ethically—and this much confidence is not widespread, to say the least.

There is also a fundamental issue of public policy here: To what extent should a democracy put in the hands of counselors, or of anyone for that matter, such potentially powerful tools of manipulation? Will this deprive individuals and their families of freedom to try the "unadvisable" or the "unlikely?" Will it stereotype, to an undesirable extent, the populations from which colleges are filled and factories staffed? This certainly could happen, and we would be wise to weigh carefully the possible ill-effects resulting from this "efficiency" move. However, the fact is that local norms, for colleges certainly, are *already* in widespread use by high school and agency counselors; these norms, which are in the counselors' heads, are often of a vague and sometimes of an erroneous nature. As counselors talk with college representatives, as they visit college campuses, and as they talk with their own alumni who have gone to *X, Y,* and *Z* Colleges, they inevitably store up at least *impressions* of norms. They then use these impressions in informing their young clients that "X College never takes anyone with a College Board score under 550," or that "Y College uses its own battery of tests and requires a minimum score of such-and-so," or that "you'd never last a year at Z College, with your *SCAT* score." Perhaps it would be a *net* improvement over the present state of affairs, to collect and to make available to counselors the most accurate possible normative information.[3]

SPECIAL SCORES

Counselors sometimes develop for their own use special scores for standardized tests, scores over and above those provided in the manual. Most often these are used only by the particular counselor, school, or agency that developed them, with or without benefit of empirical verification of their value and significance. Occasionally these are reported in the literature. For example, Barnette (1955) reports the development of part-scores for the Vocabulary, Arithmetic, and Block-Counting items of the *Army General Classification Test.* He concludes that the part-scores have some diagnostic value despite their relatively high intercorrelations. Ebel (1954) experimented with rate scores on three college aptitude measures but found that they had little value in the prediction of academic success. Carrillo and Reichart (1952) offer a "caution factor" for use with the *ACE* examination, the factor being the ratio of the number of correct responses to the number of responses attempted. They report that use of this factor to adjust the usual Quantitative, Linguistic, and Total scores increased the test's validity for predicting grades of first-year engineering students. Fruchter (1950) offers some support for this approach from the results of his factor analysis study. He found that recording both rights and wrongs scores on four paper-and-pencil tests, with a sample of aviation students, produced in the resulting factor analysis a "carefulness" factor which would not have appeared if the usual right-minus-wrong scoring had been used.

Other counselors have no doubt developed special scoring methods of their own and have felt that these added usefulness to their tests. In the long run, such methods will be of greatest value, to their originators as well as to others, if they are supported by empirical research studies which are reported in the professional literature.

[3] At the time of writing, there are reports of a plan to publish norms on the tests of the College Entrance Examination Board, for some if not all the colleges which use those tests for admissions purposes. Some will remember that a number of years ago the publication of such norms for colleges using the *ACE Psychological Examination for College Freshmen* was discontinued because of objections from colleges (the list for 1934 is included in Strang, 1947). It is to be hoped that the advantages of such publication now will be found to outweigh any disadvantages, since such compilations could be extremely valuable, especially to counselors who lack the extensive personal experience necessary to collect their own "mental norms." A publication of this sort for the University System of Georgia is described in Chapter 13.

CONCLUSION

We have now considered some of the methods, some of the problems, and some of the issues related to the process by which a person's responses to a series of questions become translated into a score or set of scores. We turn now to the next stage of the process, that which we call *interpretation*, which deals with the derivation from a set of test scores of information and insights regarding a person.

CHAPTER 7

Foundations of Test Interpretation

ONCE WE HAVE in our hands a single score or a set of scores for an individual, what can be done with these scores to answer the kinds of questions with which we began: Should Joe enter a vocational, a general, or an academic high school program? Is Harriet likely to benefit from a second year in the fifth grade? Should remedial reading be recommended to Bill? Is commercial art an appropriate field of work for Martin? Then, for some counselors, there are questions outside the area of educational and vocational guidance. Should Frances be advised to undertake extensive psychotherapy? Is Bill Horgan wise in planning marriage at this time? Which youngsters in a neighborhood are most prone to delinquency?

All of these questions have some elements in common: From knowledge of a present characteristic or set of characteristics (whether intelligence, mechanical aptitude, or neurotic tendency), what statement can be made about the wisdom of a future decision or course of action? This is not to imply that in the counseling use of tests there is *always* specific reference to future action, plans, or decisions. Sometimes an interpretation is focussed on the present, as in that use of tests primarily for the purpose of self-concept development (see Chapter 2). In such uses and in others which will be discussed later in this chapter the focus may be on describing the person as he is now, or even as he was in the past, in an attempt to understand how he *got* to be whatever he is. In all of these, however, and in counseling in general, there is almost always an implicit *future* orientation. We try to help our clients, for example, to know themselves better, partly because we think that it is good for people to know themselves, but mainly in the hope that such self-knowledge will enable them to live more effective and more satisfying lives, to make wiser choices and more realistic plans.

Answers to the questions raised above involve a number of assumptions —about a present characteristic of the person, about the future event, and about the relationship between the two. It will be our task in this chapter to provide an overview of the major types of test interpretation and of the varieties of interpretive situations. In Chapters 8, 9, and 10, we will move on to more specific aspects of statistical and clinical methods of interpretation.

It may be tempting for the practicing counselor, whose interests, after all, are practical more than theoretical, to skip some of this material, leaving it for another day or for other readers. This would be unwise, for a number of reasons: First, some of the how-to-do-its will not make any particular sense without an understanding of their theoretical foundations. Secondly, to interpret tests without being aware of the theoretical foundations is to function as a technician rather than a professional worker. It means that one can do only as he is instructed rather than being equipped to select and adapt methods and materials as necessary for a particular person or group. It means also that one is unable to use new ideas and new findings as they appear in journals, in books, and in speeches at professional conferences, because he lacks a framework into which to fit them. Lacking the ability to read critically, to evaluate proposed new methods, and to integrate them with the old, the test user is at the mercy of every high-pressure test salesman and test author, for he has no choice but to believe them or not to believe them. Finally, to lack theoretical foundations is to function in a relatively superficial manner, with only limited understanding of *why* one does what he does.

For all these reasons, and others, it is worthwhile to struggle with the difficult ideas and theories. There is even the chance that, with some successful experiences in handling the more abstract, one may get to like it and seek more of the same. It is an expecially exciting experience (though one to be approached with caution) to gain a new insight into a counselee through applying a theory one has just read about. Likewise it can be rewarding to recognize in the discussion section of a research article an image of a client with whom one talked that very day and to see him more clearly than before, to have new understandings and therefore opportunities to try new techniques.

OVERVIEW OF THIS CHAPTER

Figure 7.1 presents diagrammatically the elements in the process of test interpretation, as we shall examine them. To the left is the test score itself; not a great deal need be said about it here since it has been discussed in considerable detail in Chapter 6. To the extreme right is the end result of the process of test interpretation. This might consist of a description of the way a person operates in certain situations or an estimate of his probable success or failure in a given endeavor. It might be a prediction of the degree of satisfaction he is likely to derive from a par-

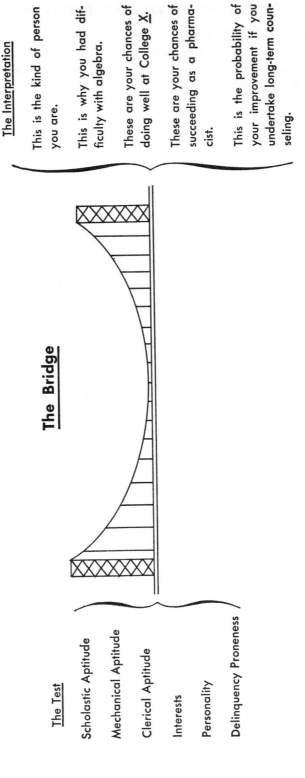

Fig. 7.1. Elements in the Process of Test Interpretation

ticular field of work or a course in school, or the expected outcomes for him of psychotherapy or of remedial reading, or whatever it is that he hopes to get from test scores. We shall need to pay a little more attention to *this* end than to the other, giving some consideration to the *criterion* problem and how it affects test interpretation. Finally our major emphasis will be on the "bridges" which connect the two parts. Our concern here will be both with the statistical or clinical structure of the bridge, as well as with the operations which the counselor engages in as he crosses the bridge. In succeeding chapters we shall give some attention to the clinical versus actuarial conflict in test interpretation, with the arguments regarding regression versus discriminant methods of bridging the gap between test scores and criteria and with a detailed consideration of the process by which a counselor derives meanings from numbers representing test scores.

Our approach is essentially eclectic; to each school of thought, to each theoretical point of view, and to each research finding is brought the question: "What does this have to contribute to the process of interpreting test data or to our understanding of this process?" As is usually the case, theories are rarely mutually exclusive; more often it is a matter not of which is "right" or even "best," but rather of what particular contribution each has to make, what kinds of insights each can facilitate, and what research approaches each might suggest.

We begin by summarizing the major types of interpretation and treatment of data, following this with illustrations of specific interpretive situations which may be found in practice.

DIMENSIONS OF INTERPRETATION

Perhaps we can best begin by outlining the kinds of interpretation that are made, to provide an overview of the structure. Figure 7.2 lists *four kinds of interpretation,* which we call Descriptive, Genetic, Predictive, and Evaluative; *two methods of combining data* to make interpretations —Mechanical and Nonmechanical; and *two sources of data* from which interpretations are made—Test Data and Nontest Data. Combining these three dimensions creates sixteen possible cells, each representing a type of interpretation made by treating in a particular way some data of a given type. Shortly we will have illustrations of each of these sixteen combinations. First, however, it is necessary to define each of the eight categories briefly before going on to the combinations.

Types of Interpretation

Each of the four types of interpretation is defined in terms of the kinds of questions that are brought to it.

1. **Descriptive.** What kind of person is this man, woman, boy, or girl?

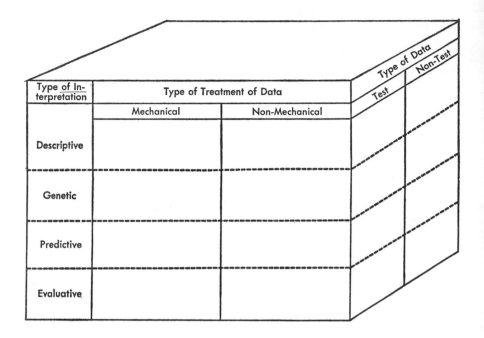

Fig. 7.2. Dimensions of Interpretation

How does he feel about getting close to people? How well does he handle numerical reasoning? How does his verbal intelligence compare with his nonverbal intelligence? What does he like to do?

2. **Genetic.** How did he get this way? Is his reading deficiency a result of emotional blockings, of inadequate development of basic skills, or of lack of interest? Does his expressed rejection of mechanical activities stem from parental pressures to avoid this area, from failure in the past when he tried to fix or make things, or is it a result of the fact that he likes many other things so much more?

3. **Predictive.** How is he likely to fare at college? How much satisfaction will he have in a vocational high school course? What degree of success will he have in typing as compared with selling?

4. **Evaluative.** What course *should* he take? Which college (if any) should he attend? Should he marry this particular girl? Should he become a salesman or an electrician?

In general, as one goes down the list from Descriptive to Evaluative, he is moving further from the data. The Descriptive kind of interpretation attempts no more than to tell what this person is like and how he functions right now. Genetic and Predictive interpretations leave the present, moving in two opposite directions. The first, Genetic, attempts to reach into the past in order to explain the development of the person as he is now. The second, Predictive, seeks to probe into the future, using facts about the person as he is now as a basis for inferring what he is likely to be. Finally, the Evaluative interpretation adds a value judgment to some other interpretation and is associated with advice-giving.

Some counselors—probably the least directive or leading—emphasize the first of these categories, leaving inferences to the client alone, or to a mutual client-counselor discussion. The Genetic kind of interpretation may be less used than the others, but it has an important place in the work of the counselor who is concerned with adjustment and with needed remedial work, since the genesis of a disorder has implications for its correction or remediation. Predictive interpretation is probably the most frequent, since counselors deal primarily with future plans, whether about school courses, occupations, or in some instances, plans regarding marriage or psychotherapy. Finally, Evaluative interpretation is an area of controversy and confusion among counselors: Should I give advice? Should I make a judgment as to which course of action is best for my client? These questions are beyond our scope here; they have to do with a counselor's point of view regarding counseling as a whole and include problems of a philosophical nature which are dealt with elsewhere. We can discuss Evaluative interpretations and consider the assumptions involved, but each counselor ultimately decides for himself whether he will *evaluate* or stop with *appraisal*.

Relationships of Interpretation to Test Validity

The four categories of interpretation have some relationship to the *types of test validity* delineated in Chapter 4: Construct, Concurrent, Content, and Predictive. The *Predictive* type of interpretation is directly linked with Predictive validity; predictions may be made which have been established as valid predictions from a given test. In a way Genetic interpretation may be seen as essentially the same process as Predictive, but in the reverse direction, in effect *post*diction; that is, from a present test score, we infer what happened *previously* in the individual's life. Postdictive validity can be established in much the same way as Predictive but perhaps more easily. Instead of having to wait for some period of time before validating a test, we can immediately seek biographical data about the members of the validation sample, with the goal of finding *past* behaviors which are correlated with present test scores. Some of the uses of this approach will be discussed presently.

Continuing the attempt to relate types of interpretation to types of test validity, we find that *Descriptive* interpretations draw more widely than the others—from Construct, Content, and Concurrent validities. To conclude from a set of test scores that Henry is better in verbal than in nonverbal reasoning, one may draw upon several kinds of validity of the tests: that there *are* such entities as verbal and nonverbal reasoning (Construct), that the items in the test have been found appropriate in terms of such characteristics as the vocabulary used (Content), and that this test correlates with outside and independent measures of these same qualities (Concurrent).

This analysis does not apply to our final type of interpretation—the Evaluative—which differs from the others not in terms of being based on different *sources* of test validity, but rather in terms of whether the counselor makes *recommendations*. The latter are based upon the probabilities which he has inferred through the use of one or another of the first three kinds of interpretation. As an illustration, suppose Susan asks about the advisability of electing Elementary Algebra in her ninth grade program. Suppose also that the counselor has found from an expectancy table that eight out of ten students with scores like Sue's on particular tests of intelligence and of Algebra Prognosis have been found to fail Algebra. He may stop with these facts (Predictive interpretation), or he may go on to give his personal advice (Evaluative). The latter, we are saying, is not based on any further data than the former. But suppose the counselor *does* base his recommendation on further data about Sue, say, that Sue is known not to have a very strong interest in academic matters and that she is not much of a scholar. What he has done is to bring in an additional source of *Predictive* interpretation, that is, the prediction of academic grades from interests, and he is still basing his recommendation on *Predictive* validity data.

This suggests a generalization which is of the most fundamental importance,[1] namely, *that any and every kind of test interpretation is based on at least the assumption, if not the fact, that there exists a relationship between a test score and the "thing" being interpreted—whether Descriptive, Genetic, Predictive, or Evaluative.* To say to Jim, "You are better in verbal than in nonverbal reasoning," is to assume that his scores on the tests which were used *do* represent verbal and nonverbal reasoning, respectively. This cannot be assumed from the *names* of the test, but there must be some kind of validation—be it construct, concurrent, or content—to support this interpretation. Similarly, in the case previously cited, simply to describe Susan's test scores, "You are below average in general intelligence and considerably below in algebra aptitude," is to assume that one test does indeed measure general intelligence (known perhaps from Construct or Concurrent validity) and the other algebra aptitude (known from Predictive validity). To go on then to say, "Since you are not much interested in academic subjects, I would certainly advise that you not take Algebra," is to give an Evaluative interpretation. What can

---

[1] The writer is greatly indebted to Dr. Benjamin Rosner, who has been a colleague both at the University of Buffalo and at Brooklyn College, for clarification of this point, as well as a number of others.

easily be overlooked is that there is an implicit Predictive interpretation which has intervened, namely, that Sue's limited academic interest will tend to reduce her Algebra grade even below what it would otherwise be. And *this* interpretation assumes that interest is predictive of grades (or at least that expressed or measured academic interest is predictive of grades in Algebra) ; here we are dealing with Predictive validity and must insist on some evidence for it.

Types of Treatment of Data

This brings us to the question: How *does* a counselor use validity data to make his interpretations? How does he bridge the gap (Fig. 7.1) between the test score on the left and the answer to the questions which have been asked on the right? Part of the answer to this question comes from a consideration of the second dimension of the chart depicted in Figure 7.2—the types of treatment of data. Later in the chapter and in Chapters 8 and 9, there will be a more extended treatment of the topic; our goal here is merely to introduce and to define the dimension.

Mechanical Treatment of Data [2]

This is the "cookbook" method (Meehl, 1956), introduced briefly in Chapter 3, about which there has been so much controversy. Although it is of very limited usefulness at the present time, because "recipes" are available for so very few of the interpretations we make in counseling, this method seems likely to be of increasing importance, perhaps someday becoming a primary method used by counselors for bridging the gap between a test score and a prediction or other interpretation.

Table 7.1 gives an illustration of the most usual kind of mechanical test interpretation device—*the expectancy table*. It is taken from a bulletin of Kent State University *(Guidance Before College,* February, 1956) and is typical of a kind of helpful data which colleges are beginning to supply to high school counselors. Suppose Mary Rinaldi has come to her twelfth grade counselor to talk about choice of college; her parents think Kent State is a good choice for her, and she asks what the counselor thinks. Using the data of Table 7.1 only, in a purely mechanical fashion, and knowing that Mary's score on the *Ohio State University Psychological Examination* was at the 65th percentile of high school senior norms, we can tell Mary that the chances are about 50-50 (actually 42 to 58) that she will have a *B-* or better average during the first four quarters at Kent State. This is a Predictive interpretation which was made in a Mechanical manner.

[2] The categories used here are Mechanical and Nonmechanical. Elsewhere in this chapter and in other chapters, other terms are used practically synonymously. Alternate terms for the Mechanical category are *Statistical* and *Actuarial;* for Nonmechanical, the alternate term is *Clinical.* The concepts seem to be closely related to what Williamson (1939) referred to as Experimental and Clinical methods.

READ GENERAL SCIENCE TEST

EXPECTANCY CHART

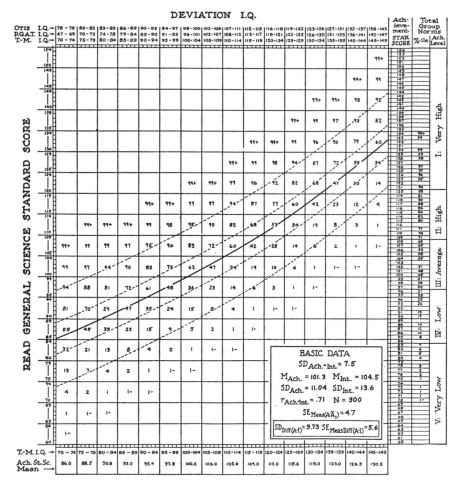

Fig. 7.3. Expectancy Chart: Read General Science Test and Three Intelligence Tests

(By permission of the World Book Company.)

148

Another kind of expectancy table is reproduced as Figure 7.3. Suppose John Winters, a junior high school student, is being seen by his coun-

Table 7.1. OSU Psychological Test Scores and College Marks

PERCENTILE SCORES ON OSUPT — FORM 23			PERCENTAGE MAKING THESE COLLEGE MARKS, FIRST 4 QUARTERS			
HS Senior Norms	College Fr. Norms	NUMBER OF STUDENTS	C—, D, F or below 2.0	C+ or 2.0 to 2.4	B— or 2.5 to 2.9	A, B+ or 3.0 & up
89 to 100	76 to 100	56	4	7	21	68
74 to 88	50 to 75	67	12	27	34	27
49 to 73	26 to 49	115	29	29	25	17
Below 49	0 to 25	160	51	36	11	2

This table is read as follows: Of the 160 students who as freshmen scored at or below the 25th percentile, 2 per cent made 3.0 or better; 11 per cent made 2.5 to 2.9; 36 per cent made 2.0 to 2.4; and 51 per cent made below 2.0.

SOURCE: *Guidance before college,* Bulletin of Kent State University, February, 1956, p. 4. By permission.

selor for a routine interview. We have John's standard score on the *Read General Science Test*—122, an obviously above average score—but wonder how to interpret it in the light of John's capabilities. We do know that his IQ as measured by the *Terman-McNemar (T-M)* test is 141. By referring to the chart, we see that, for his IQ level (next to last column on the right) John's *Read* score is slightly below expectancy, since only 30 out of 100 students in that IQ category get scores that low or lower on the *Read.* For John, then, the interpretation of his *General Science Achievement* is that it is slightly below what would be expected for the average student with an IQ at his level. For Carl Neumeyer, on the other hand, who also received a score of 122 on the *Read,* but whose *Terman-McNemar* IQ is 128, our interpretation is that he has done better than would be expected in General Science, since he has equalled or exceeded the scores of 82 out of 100 students at his IQ level. In both cases the chart has made the interpretation—essentially a Descriptive one—in a Mechanical manner.

An expectancy table which is used in industrial personnel work is shown in Table 7.2. This summarizes the experience of a large retail grocery organization in predicting ratings given trainees by members of the training staff (Low, Below Average, Above Average, and High). The predictor variable used in preparing this table was Part II of the *Store Personnel Test* (price computation and verbal reasoning items). A personnel technician in this organization can see in the table that applicants with error scores between 27 and 35 have only 26 chances in 100 of receiving an

Above Average or High rating. The employment manager of the company thus has an estimate of what he can expect if the minimum score for hiring

Table 7.2. Expectancy Table for the Store Personnel Test

Error Scores on Test	RATINGS RECEIVED BY TRAINEES Low (1-3)	Below Average (4-6)	Above Average (7-9)	High (10-12)	Totals
0- 8	—	—	2 (33%)	4 (67%)	6
9-17	4 (8%)	7 (13%)	27 (51%)	15 (28%)	53
18-26	6 (9%)	15 (22%)	30 (45%)	16 (24%)	67
27-35	4 (17%)	13 (57%)	5 (22%)	1 (4%)	23
36-44	2 (40%)	3 (60%)	—	—	5
45-53	1 (100%)	—	—	—	1

SOURCE: *Test Serv. Bull.* (Psychological Corporation), No. 37, p. 5. By permission.

is raised or lowered. (Naturally, other factors are also taken into consideration in setting minimum scores for hiring, principal among them being the supply of applicants in relation to the number needed by the company).

Another mechanical method is the *regression equation,* which is a relatively simple statistical procedure that is based on the correlation coefficient. Having found a correlation between predictor and criterion, the regression equation provides a rapid and mechanical method for estimating a person's standing on the criterion from his known score on the predictor. It appears that limited use is made of this method in schools, despite the fact that it is in just such institutions, where large numbers of students take the same tests and are graded on the same criteria, that it is most feasible and useful. One of the rare reports of the use of regression equations comes from Roslyn, New York, High School.[3] To help counselors and administrators make judgments in relation to such questions as underachievement and placement in curricula, first the correlation was computed between *Otis* IQ's and three-year average of students in the "Regents" (precollege) curriculum. The coefficient turned out to be .50, which is about par for a selected population of this kind. From the correlation data there was then computed the following regression equation:

$$\text{Academic Average} = .4 \; Otis \; \text{IQ} + 34$$

That is, if a student's IQ on the *Otis* is 110, his predicted academic average is 110 x .4, or 44, which, when added to 34, is 78. Furthermore, it can

[3] With thanks to William Rosengarten, Jr., Director of Special Services at Roslyn High School, who did the work reported here and who kindly gave permission for its release.

be said that, since the standard error of estimate is 7, the chances are 68 in 100 that this student's three-year grade average will be between 71 and 85, and 95 in 100 that his average will be between 64 and 92. These limits give a far from precise estimate and demonstrate the lack of precision associated with a correlation of .50. However, at least this procedure relieves the counselor from the necessity for *guessing* or using vague impressions as to the relation between IQ and grades. In effect, the method organizes and objectifies what is known about IQ's and grades at that school. The counselor may well add *a nonmechanical* prediction to the mechanical one. If he knows that a particular student with an IQ of 100 is highly motivated to do well in school, has good study habits, and receives encouragement and help at home, the counselor will estimate that his grades will be higher than those of the student who has a similar IQ but who lacks the other characteristics.

The school staff which was responsible for the statistical work just described went one step further and prepared a graph which provides a rapid reading of the mechanical prediction for a given student and makes unnecessary even the small amount of arithmetic required to use the regression equation (see Fig. 7.4).

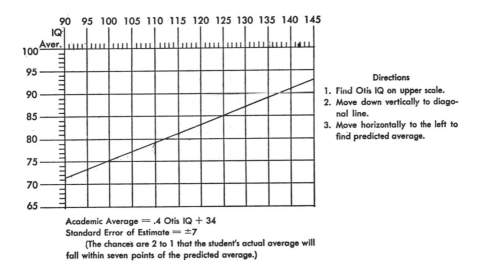

Directions

1. Find Otis IQ on upper scale.
2. Move down vertically to diagonal line.
3. Move horizontally to the left to find predicted average.

Academic Average = .4 Otis IQ + 34
Standard Error of Estimate = ±7
(The chances are 2 to 1 that the student's actual average will fall within seven points of the predicted average.)

Fig. 7.4. A Graph for Predicting the Three-Year Academic Average of Regents Students in Roslyn High School
(By permission of Roslyn, New York, High School.)

A graphic representation of an expectancy table is shown in Figure 7.5. This permits a high school or college counselor to estimate the Grade Point Average which a student may be expected to receive at Oregon

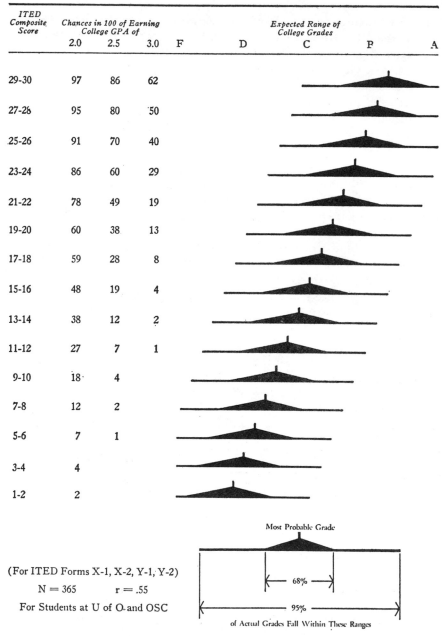

ITED Composite Score	Chances in 100 of Earning College GPA of			Expected Range of College Grades				
	2.0	2.5	3.0	F	D	C	B	A
29-30	97	86	62					
27-28	95	80	50					
25-26	91	70	40					
23-24	86	60	29					
21-22	78	49	19					
19-20	60	38	13					
17-18	59	28	8					
15-16	48	19	4					
13-14	38	12	2					
11-12	27	7	1					
9-10	18	4						
7-8	12	2						
5-6	7	1						
3-4	4							
1-2	2							

Most Probable Grade

(For ITED Forms X-1, X-2, Y-1, Y-2)

N = 365   r = .55

For Students at U of O. and OSC

68%

95%

of Actual Grades Fall Within These Ranges

Fig. 7.5 Expectancy Graph Showing Relationships Between Tenth Grade Composite Score on the Iowa Tests of Educational Development and Grade Point Average at Oregon State College and at the University of Oregon
(Carlson and Fullmer, 1959, p. 11. By permission of the University of Oregon.)

State College and at the University of Oregon, based on his composite score on the *Iowa Tests of Educational Development*. The tests had been taken in the tenth grade and the scores later collected from Oregon high schools by the University staff members who prepared the pamphlet from which this chart was taken. Similar graphs were prepared for the *Metropolitan Achievement Test* and the *Stanford Achievement Test,* both having been taken in the ninth grade, and for the *California Achievement Test* for both ninth and tenth grades. Another important feature of these graphs is the incorporation of the concept of standard error of prediction (to be discussed in Chapter 12). The graph in Figure 7.5 shows not only the best single estimate of GPA, but also the 68 per cent probability range (± one standard error) and the 95 per cent probability range (± two standard errors).

In a way, the simplest kind of Mechanical interpretation is reading a *table of norms*. To look up Nancy's raw score of 137 on the Numbers part of the *Minnesota Clerical Test* and to report that it is higher than that of 40 per cent of employed female clerical workers is to give meaning to the score in terms of Nancy's vocational planning, and this is a kind of interpretation of the score. Comparing two scores in an individual's profile is just one step removed from reading a table of norms. On the *DAT,* for example, Lawrence has a 90th percentile score on Verbal Reasoning, and 30th percentile on the Mechanical Reasoning Test. Since the two tests were normed on the same sample, the percentiles are directly comparable one with the other, and we may therefore conclude that Larry is better in Verbal Reasoning than in Mechanical Reasoning (as both are measured in this particular battery) —another Mechanical treatment of data yielding a Descriptive interpretation.[4]

Nonmechanical Treatment of Data

An illustration of Nonmechanical treatment of data was given in Chapter 3, where a counselor thought out loud his interpretation of Ted's scores on a battery of tests. As contrasted with the Mechanical approach, it tends to be more subjective, more vague, and sometimes intuitive. Furthermore, as Meehl has pointed out repeatedly (see especially 1954), in critical studies the Mechanical method has usually been found to be at least as efficient and in some instances superior to the other. Later, in Chapter 10, we shall discuss in detail the statistical-clinical controversy; our purpose at the moment is to define the dimensions just enough to provide a framework for the chapter as was depicted in Figure 7.1. Later we shall also describe in some detail the Nonmechanical (or clinical) process. For now suffice it to say that this process *must* be used extensively because the data needed for Mechanical interpretations (such as expectancy tables and

---

[4] The interpretation here assumes that the difference is statistically significant; this aspect is considered in Chapter 12.

equations) are rarely available to practitioners. Also, as another brief preview of a topic which is later to receive extended discussion, it may be said here that the Nonmechanical process, in part at least, has something in common with the Mechanical. As Horst has demonstrated (1956), the counselor as a clinical interpreter spends some of his time doing in his head what the table and the formula do mechanically. If, for instance, one didn't have an expectancy table relating *OSU* test scores to grades at Kent State University (Table 7.1), he might nevertheless be able to make some predictive interpretation if he had any knowledge of, or experience with, that particular school. Perhaps he has talked with an admissions officer of the college, or with some of his former counselees who went to Kent, or he may in some other way have obtained relevant information about grading practices there in relation to ability levels of students. He then uses his head as a crude table of norms or expectancy table.

The Nonmechanical process involves more than simply the aspect of it emphasized in Horst's analysis. As outlined by others (for example, Super, 1957b), it includes an inductive building-up of a "model" of the individual, from which deductions are later made as to his probable behavior in a given situation. Seen thus, it is quite different from the Mechanical process and will warrant more detailed study later.

Sources of Data

For the most part, we are dealing in this work with interpretation of data from *tests,* but counselors also make interpretations of data from a variety of sources other than tests. In an earlier illustration, a student's expressed lack of interest in academic subjects was used in predicting her probable success in Elementary Algebra. To the extent that there is substantial evidence of a relationship between that expressed interest and some criterion, it is a perfectly good source of data for making predictions. Similarly, broken homes have been found in many studies to contribute more than their share of juvenile delinquents. The fact of coming from a broken home, therefore, is a datum which may be used in the estimation of delinquency-proneness.

No matter what the source of data, the principle enunciated earlier is applicable: To be usable in the process of interpretation, there must be some evidence of relationship between the datum and whatever is being interpreted from it. In effect, nontest data must be validated in quite the same manner as test data.

ILLUSTRATIONS OF ALL POSSIBLE COMBINATIONS OF THE THREE DIMENSIONS

We now bring together the three dimensions: types of interpretation, types of treatment of data, and types of data. Figure 7.2 showed the interaction of the three dimensions. In the following pages each of the resulting sixteen cells is given with illustrations of the kinds of interpretive situations it includes. In many instances the illustration consists simply of a statement of the end-result of an interpretive process, as in the very first one listed. In other instances it has been necessary for purposes of clarity to describe the interpretive *process* which leads to statements about individuals or groups. All of this, it is hoped, provides a framework for what will follow it.

One final point: For purposes of definition, this discussion deals with interpretations made from one source of data at a time, combined in one way, leading to one type of interpretation. In actual practice, of course, there is rarely this degree of separateness, and the methods of several cells may be combined or done in rapid sequence to yield a single interpretive inference or hypothesis.

1. Descriptive - Mechanical - Test Data

Margaret is superior to 9 out of 10 girls her age in Clerical Speed and Accuracy on the *Differential Aptitude Tests.*

Bernard is better (stanine score 8) on the Assembly part than on the Memory part (stanine score 3) of the *Flanagan Aptitude Classification Test.*

Using a profile matching method in which *relative* scores on different parts of a battery are computed, the counselor found Tony's profile on the *Kuder* to be very similar to that of machinists but different from that of draftsmen.

2. Descriptive - Mechanical - Nontest Data

Laura has done better in her mathematics courses (average 82) than in her English courses (average 78) during her freshman and sophomore years in high school.

A review of teachers' ratings as recorded on the cumulative record card shows that Stephanie is above average in Responsibility and Accuracy but below average in Initiative.

Warner's Index of Status Characteristics (Warner and others, 1949), is a formula for estimating social-class status from such characteristics as occupation, source of income, and type of dwelling. The resulting estimate for Bill is in effect a Descriptive interpretation based on nontest data, and done in a purely Mechanical fashion.[5]

3. Descriptive - Nonmechanical - Test Data

Examining Harry's scores on the *Kuder* and *MMPI*, the counselor concludes that he seems to be oriented toward people, with a tendency to lead and dominate.

[5] This is one of several illustrations that are outside the usual scope of educational-vocational counseling. They are included because some counselors, in schools and colleges particularly, are also concerned about these and other problem areas, such as delinquency, alcoholism, personal-social development, and others.

From Albert's scores on a reading test and a personality inventory, it is judged that his slowness in reading is related to overcautiousness and lack of self-confidence.

From the fact that Barbara has a much higher score on several nonverbal than on verbal tests, it is judged that her IQ of 92 on the *Otis* is an underestimate of her general intelligence.

4. Descriptive - Nonmechanical - Nontest Data

From my observations of Mike around the school, I have the impression of a well-liked, socially skillful boy.

As he spoke of his school experiences in our interview, Bob revealed feelings of inadequacy regarding his ability to complete the college preparatory curriculum with a passing average.

Considering his father's semiskilled occupational level and the limited education of both parents, Eric expresses surprisingly high vocational aspirations in his expressed choice of "chemist" on our ninth grade questionnaire.

5. Genetic - Mechanical - Test Data [6]

Knowing Helen's scores on the various parts of a diagnostic arithmetic test and looking up that particular combination in a list of all possible combinations (this one is quite hypothetical!), the counselor finds that the most probable explanation is that she failed to acquire in the early grades an understanding of a particular number principle.

Given Joe's scores on the *Kuder* and on the *Primary Mental Abilities Test* and then looking up the resulting pattern in a special table, we interpret that he probably comes from a language-deprived home and, as a result, did not develop his potentialities in the verbal area.

6. Genetic - Mechanical - Nontest Data

Jill has been involved in two delinquent episodes in the past three months. We check on her grades for the previous year (several failures), her socioeconomic status (middle class, both parents college-educated), and reported parental goals for her (college education, professional occupation). We then consult a list of various combinations of these three variables and find that the most likely explanation of her delinquency is a combination of guilt feelings about school failure and hostility toward her parents because of their pressures.

John H. has started to drink heavily. Collecting data about his family background and present status, income, and social relationships and looking all these up in an appropriate table, the most probable hypothesis is that he feels failure in attaining the socioeconomic status which would be expected of him.

[6] To a greater extent than with any of the other types of interpretations, it has been necessary to *fabricate* illustrations of Genetic interpretations made in a Mechanical fashion. This combination is rarely found and perhaps will always be a rarity. Genetic interpretation, particularly in complex problems such as some of these used as illustrations here, are likely for some time to come to need a more Clinical approach.

7. Genetic - Nonmechanical - Test Data

Luis, aged 11, who recently arrived from Puerto Rico, receives an IQ of 76 on the *Henmon-Nelson* intelligence test, a reading score at the 2.5 grade level, and an IQ of 110 on a nonverbal performance test of intelligence. Our interpretation is that his verbal intelligence, in an English language situation, has not developed nearly to its level of potentiality because of his foreign language background.

Nancy's *Strong VIB* shows high scores in the Secretary-Stenographer and Office Worker scales, but her *Kuder* reveals very low scores in the Computational and Clerical areas. In interviews she rejects the *SVIB* scores but feels that the *Kuder* represents her interests correctly. Knowing that she comes from an upper-middle-class home (here we have brought in some nontest data), we guess that the self-concept which resulted largely from family expectations has led her to reject on the more obvious and therefore more distortable inventory (*Kuder*) the occupational activities associated with a low-level occupational group (office workers). On the *Strong*, which is a less obvious measure of interests, she is found to have much in common with office workers.

8. Genetic - Nonmechanical - Nontest Data

Mr. Stewart, age 36, tells his vocational counselor that he wonders whether he should change to a different occupation, since he finds engineering no longer satisfying. As he tells more about his daily activities, the counselor begins to hypothesize that Mr. Stewart's troubles stem from inadequate recreational and social life and that he is expecting his job to satisfy too many of his needs and interests.

Martin, a high school senior, insists that he wants to go to college and become a lawyer. The counselor knows that Martin has a barely passing average throughout high school. He also knows that Martin's father is an accountant who had to leave college after one year in order to help support his family. The interpretation begins to form: that Martin's unrealistic goals are related to his father's strivings and unfulfilled aspirations.

9. Predictive - Mechanical - Test Data

Emily's raw score on the *Orleans Algebra Prognosis Test* is 73. Using an expectancy table developed locally, her counselor tells her that of people with scores like hers, about 9 in 10 pass Elementary Algebra at that school.

The school principal asks the guidance director to identify for him those youngsters who are most likely to become delinquent, in order that a preventative program can be established. Administering the *K-D Proneness Scale* to all students in grades 7 to 9, the director selects out the highest scoring 5 per cent who, on the basis of validity data in the manual, have the greatest likelihood of becoming delinquent.

10. Predictive - Mechanical - Nontest Data

The guidance department is spearheading a drive to reduce the dropout rate at Van Buren Central School. Using information from the school records of dropouts over a five-year period, they found that several variables predicted early school leaving: failure in two or more subjects, having four or more siblings, coming from a broken home, and being a bus-rider (meaning that the family lives at least a certain distance from the school and is likely to own a farm). From these data, a formula was set up, in which each of the four variables is multiplied by a constant. The total weighted score for each student then in school was computed. The higher the score, the greater the likelihood of dropping out of school before graduation.

The *XYZ* Insurance Co. has found that annual sales by its agents are best predicted by certain biographical data: number of children, amount of life insurance carried by the agent, and number of social and fraternal organizations in which office is held. It has therefore constructed a brief questionnaire for applicants and is able to ascertain for each the probability that he will sell a specified minimum amount of insurance per year after the first year.

11. Predictive - Nonmechanical - Test Data

Each year in May, the staff of the Bradwin Elementary School goes over each pupil's scores on the *Lorge-Thorndike Intelligence Test* and the *Metropolitan Achievement Test* to decide whether the pupil should be promoted. In effect, they are estimating whether he is likely to gain more by going on to the next grade or by repeating his present grade.

Ronald Brown asks his counselor whether he is mistaken in aiming at a career in optometry. The counselor looks over the cumulative record and finds superior scholastic aptitude test scores, above average scores on science and math achievement tests, and high measured scientific, persuasive, and social-service interests. Based on his reading of the occupational literature and his knowledge of the occupation from other sources, the counselor tells Ronald that his chances of succeeding in optometry are very good.

12. Predictive - Nonmechanical - Nontest Data

The employment manager of an insurance office asks each applicant for a typist position to take a letter in shorthand and to transcribe it on the typewriter. Before deciding whether to hire the person, he also uses such information as school grades, letters of recommendation, and the results of a medical examination. When all these data are collected, he examines each application *in toto* and ranks it as to likelihood of success on the job.

Mrs. Axtell, the guidance consultant in Allen Elementary School, receives written referrals from classroom teachers for each pupil who is believed to need special help. From the information included—behavior in class, family composition, and attendance record—plus that available on the cumulative record card, Mrs. Axtell tries to decide whether to interview the child herself, to refer him to the school psychologist for psychodiagnostic testing, to schedule a case conference on the child at a future meeting of the pupil personnel staff, or simply to have a talk with the teacher, with the hope that this will suffice. Again this is in effect a matter of predicting the relative likelihood that each of the available courses of action will be effective.

13. Evaluative - Mechanical - Test Data [7]

At *ABC* college, several patterns of score on the *MMPI* have been found to be predictive of dropping out of college for personality reasons. A system was set up then to interview every student with any one of those patterns, based on the assumption that such students should be aided to improve their personal adjustment.

All ninth grade students whose scores on both scholastic aptitude and achievement tests are above a specified point are brought together for a series of group guidance sessions to help them plan their senior high school programs so as to utilize their superior abilities. The prediction here is that the group guidance sessions will improve students' planning. The value judgment is that this is worth the expenditure of student and staff time.

14. Evaluative - Mechanical - Nontest Data

Applicants for leadership grants (to encourage potential leaders to attend college) at the University of G——— supply information about their activities and offices held in high school. A specified number of points is assigned for each type of activity and each office held. Leadership grants are awarded to those with the highest total score (with financial need also taken into consideration, but separately).

At P. S. 17, a special remedial program at the third grade level is being instituted. Pupils who are nonreaders and whom teachers have rated as average or better in effort are automatically selected for it.

15. Evaluative - Nonmechanical - Test Data

On the basis of a battery of tests of aptitude and interest, a counselor at the State Rehabilitation Bureau approves an applicant's request for vocational training as being a realistic plan which is likely to lead to a higher level of functioning within the limits of the particular handicap.

Mark and his parents anxiously ask the counselor's advice regarding the boy's ability to handle a predental college course. The counselor, studying the test profile, says he is confident that Mark can make it and encourages the boy to try.

16. Evaluative - Nonmechanical - Nontest Data

Mr. Perkins, a history teacher at Jonesville Central School, is assigned to do college advising of seniors. Basing his judgment on his familiarity with colleges, he advises each student where to apply, using as criteria the student's grades,

[7] Not explicitly mentioned in each illustration, but assumed in all Evaluative interpretations, is that one particular course of action, an outcome, or a kind of personal trait is considered better than others. Each of these illustrations could be listed under one of the other three types of interpretation, were it not for the fact that a *value judgment* has been made and one alternative selected over others. There is here, in effect, a categorical choice rather than a statement of probabilities. With Descriptive, Genetic, and Predictive interpretations, alternatives are listed and the likelihood of each stated; with Evaluative interpretations, one of those alternatives is chosen and acted upon.

teacher's ratings and his own impressions of each student. He refuses to sign the application form whenever he feels that he cannot recommend a student to a particular college.

At Rentman Elementary School, the principal does all assignment of pupils to sections by examining each record card and talking with the pupil's present teacher whenever he has any doubts.

The sixteen groupings show the interactions of our three dimensions. There is nothing especially natural or inevitable about these dimensions. They are used here as a convenient way of organizing a large number of specific uses of tests. Some of the illustrations used above were taken directly from life, others are quite imaginary, sometimes because real life examples do not exist for those uses of tests. It seems clear that the Nonmechanical uses at present outnumber the Mechanical, at least in schools and agencies. However, with the demonstrated superiority of Mechanical over Nonmechanical methods of treating test scores for many kinds of predictions and other interpretations, the future may see a reversal of the ratio.

The illustrations show applications of these methods of interpretation in a variety of settings—in schools from the elementary to the graduate level, in business and industry, and in community agencies. The principles and basic problems are the same everywhere, but some of the specific instruments, techniques, operations, and problems differ.

It is hoped that the illustrations have shown at a concrete and applied level something of the nature of a variety of interpretations. As we go on now to more abstract and theoretical aspects of interpretation, the reader may find it useful from time to time to go back to the illustrations in order to help clarify the theories. At the same time, understanding of theory makes clearer what is happening in the applications.

CHAPTER 8

Statistical Bridges

W<small>E</small> MOVE on now to the middle portion of Figure 7.1—that which includes the *bridge* between test (as well as nontest) data on the one hand and interpretations on the other.

Essentially, in interpreting a test score we are seeking to find some meaning of that score *outside of* the test. We may ask, for example, what implication this score has for an individual's later success on the job or in a school subject or in a marriage (Predictive). Or, at a different level of interpretation (Descriptive), we wonder what may be concluded about this person's needs, feelings, or usual behavior, knowing his score on a particular test. The test score, after all, is not a *direct* measure of any of these things; it is a measure only of someone's responses to a set of stimuli at one particular time, in one particular place, under one particular set of circumstances. To say *anything* more about this person involves making *inferences* from the obtained score, inferences of this nature: The fact that he got fewer right answers on this test than did 80 per cent of his peers *means* that he thinks more slowly than most, or that he cannot handle problems of as great complexity as most, or whatever *generalization* we try to make. There must be some basis for such a *descriptive* generalization, as for any *prediction* that we might make about his behavior in the future. And the basis is to be found in the *demonstration of a relationship* between a score of that kind on this test and the psychological quality or future behavior that we seek to interpret from that score.

Lacking anything better, we must often be satisfied with a *logical* demonstration of such relations. For example, we observe draftsmen at work and agree that spatial visualizing is an important function. When Joe Doakes then asks for an appraisal of *his* likelihood of success as a draftsman, we give him a test which *looks like* it taps the same psychological function. If he does well, we conclude that doing well on the tested function means that he has the ability to do well on that function of the job which looks like the one measured by the test. This is obviously a very "iffy" kind of reasoning: *If* the test measures something reliably, *if* that something is very much the same as something done on the job, and *if* that something on the job makes a difference between success and failure, then our conclusions are all right. Even if we could assume all these "ifs," there remains the question: *How much* of this function as tested is needed for doing the job minimally well, average well, and very well?

Appalling as it may be, a great deal of present-day test interpretation is based on a foundation as uncertain as that described in the preceding paragraph. There are any number of test manuals which suggest interpretations for which there is little or no basis other than armchair speculation.

Statistical bridges are those methods of a quantified, empirical sort which tie together a test score or set of scores, on the one hand, with a human characteristic or set of behaviors on the other hand, as was depicted graphically in Figure 7.1. The statistical bridges vary in complexity and are described below in what is roughly an order of increasing complexity.

The statistical bridges are a direct source of the formulas, the expectancy tables, and the other techniques for making *Mechanical* interpretations. They also make some contributions to *Nonmechanical* interpretations, since the latter frequently are at least partly based on the interpreter's familiarity with such statistical data as test norms and validity coefficients of correlation. The difference between Mechanical and Nonmechanical methods, is that with the former there is *exclusive* use of tables, formulas, and the other devices which emanate from statistical bridges. Nonmechanical methods in addition make use of nonquantified information available to the counselor and also may make use of a model-building process described later under the heading "Clinical Bridges."

In describing statistical bridges the emphasis is on the concepts and the general procedures used, rather than on mathematical theories underlying them or on computational methods used to develop them. Most of all, we are concerned with the implications of these bridges for the counselor's interpretations of test data.

THE NORM BRIDGE

The simplest of all statistical bridges, the *norm* usually involves a direct comparison of the individual's raw score (or standard score or other converted score) with some table of norms. Here are a few examples of normative interpretations of test scores:

Joe's reading score on the *Co-operative English Test: Reading Comprehension* equals or exceeds that of 93 per cent of eleventh graders.

Harriet achieved a score on the Clerical scale of the *Kuder Preference Record* that is within the average range, to be exact, at the 63rd percentile.

Kenny's reading readiness score shows him to be at the level of the average child in the 6th month of the first grade.

Simple as these are, nonetheless, they involve assumptions that are not always obvious, the essence of which is that the norm group represents a meaningful basis for comparison. If Kenny's reading-readiness test score is to be used as a criterion for placing him in a particular section of the first grade, or if it is to be used by his teacher for grouping within the section, we must first assume that what is called "Reading" in the first grade of that school is related to what the particular test is measuring. We must then assume that the average child in the sixth month of the first grade at Kenny's school is equivalent in general ability, cultural background, and other relevant characteristics to the average child of that level in the norms for the test.[1]

Simple norm comparisons of this kind can be seen as the lowest order of score interpretation, involving probably the fewest assumptions and being the least removed, of all interpretations, from the test score itself. The greatest danger is that more will be assumed from a normative statement than is warranted. For instance, when one knows that Joe's reading score is at the 93rd percentile, it is tempting to conclude that therefore he is similar to people in verbal occupations or that he would probably be successful in such fields as writing or library work. These latter interpretations go well beyond the limits of what one may conclude from a table of norms. As we shall see later, there are special kinds of statistical bridges leading us to these more remote kinds of interpretation.

Another unwarranted assumption is that the higher the score in comparison with a norm group, the better. It is tempting, for example, to conclude that a person whose score on the *Bennett Mechanical Comprehension Test* is at the 90th percentile is a better bet for mechanical training than is one whose score is at the 80th percentile. (To help make this particular point, let us assume that the difference between the two scores is statistically significant.) This conclusion, however, cannot be justified unless more information is available than that contained in the table of norms. It may be, for example, that a certain amount of mechanical comprehension is needed for optimal learning of a skilled trade but that abil-

---

[1] For discussion of norms in relation to college aptitude, the reader is referred to the section "Predicting Success in College" in Chapter 13. There is also an example of "College Norms" in the section in Chapter 6 bearing that title.

ity beyond this point makes no difference. It is even possible to have too much of a particular ability for an occupation, since it may lead to boredom which then causes carelessness. Similarly, in the case of personality characteristics, the highest possible score on a scale called Social Adjustment does not necessarily represent the best chances for success in an occupation which stresses relations with people. Extremely high scores may suggest too much dependence on other people and too little ability to function independently. Congdon and Jervis (1958) have discussed this point with regard to interest inventories, and their study of interests of groups of college students majoring in four different areas proposes that an individual's score be expressed in terms of *deviation* from the average of a norm group, whether the deviation be above or below. They suggest that it may be possible to have *too much* measured interest of a given type, as well as too little.

Profile Analysis

A more complex form of norm comparison is encountered in the use of profiles. Here the individual's scores on two or more tests (or on subscores or parts of the same test) are compared with some norm group. Several examples follow:

Jerry's *Kuder* profile, as compared with the mean profile of physicians, as shown in the manual, is higher on Scientific, lower on Persuasive, and about the same on all other scales.

Harry's profile on the *Iowa Tests of Educational Development* shows him to be superior to our local norm group in Social Studies Background, Reading in Social Studies, and General Vocabulary; average in Correctness in Writing, Reading in Literature, and Uses of Sources of Information; and below average in Natural Science Background, Quantitative Thinking, and Reading in Natural Sciences.

On the *GATB,* John attained Patterns No. 15 and 17. (This is to say that his scores equalled or exceeded the minimum scores on the parts found to be critical for each of those patterns.)

Profile comparison data are available now for a number of tests. For example, the occupational profiles presented in the *Kuder* manual are just this. (We refer here to the *empirical* data which report mean scores on the various scales and not to the lists of occupations which are suggested for each of a number of combinations of interest scores—the latter lists are derived through armchair analysis and are indeed a kind of Profile bridge but of much more doubtful validity than the empirical ones). Group profiles are also to be found in the manuals for many tests which have part scores, including the *DAT,* the *Iowa Tests of Educational De-*

velopment, and, in fact, for most modern multiscore tests of aptitude and of achievement.

Profile Codes

For convenience, both in interpreting individual profiles and in summarizing group data for research purposes, systems of codes have been prepared for the *Strong VIB* (Crites, 1959) and for the *Kuder* (Callis, Engram, and McGowan, 1954; Frandsen, 1952; Wiener, 1951), all of which are similar to a coding scheme which earlier had been developed for the *MMPI* (Hathaway, 1947). Using the system proposed by Callis, and others, for the *Kuder,* for example, the code number 8'6-1'5 would be translated to mean "this client has a score at the 75th percentile or higher on the Social Service scale, between 65th and 74th on the Literary scale, at or below the 25th percentile on the Mechanical scale, and between the 26th and 35th percentiles on the Artistic scale." Then, if one has a card file, as these authors suggest, arranged in numerical order, he can quickly find that this client's profile is identical with the mean profile of Male Social Studies Teachers, as reported in the manual.

Statistical Methods for Profiles

Methods have been sought for handling several scores simultaneously in a mechanical or statistical fashion. Without such devices, we are often forced to use a profile essentially as a collection of individual scores rather than to make use of their characteristics *as a profile.* In Figure 8.1, for example, the *DAT* Profile of Robert Martin is depicted. At the simplest level, we can report each of his scores one at a time: "He is within the average band on Verbal Reasoning, Numerical Reasoning, and Abstract Reasoning, but below average on Space, and so forth." Would it add anything to know that there are 20 standard score points between his Verbal Reasoning and his Spelling score? Are there any meaningful behaviors associated with the large amount of scatter among the eight scores on his profile?

Several writers have considered the values which might derive from a statistical treatment of profiles and some have suggested specific procedures that can be used (Anderhalter, 1954; Block, Levine, and McNemar, 1951; duMas, 1949, 1953; Forehand and McQuitty, 1959; Jastak, 1949; Michael, 1959; Wittenborn, 1951). The mathematics of the statistical methods need not concern us here; they have to do sometimes with the *slope* of the line connecting any two scores on a profile, sometimes with the vertical *distances* between any two scores on a profile, sometimes with combinations of these and other measures. Whatever the method, the first opration is to find out whether there exists among a sample of people (in an occupation, college curriculum, or other group) some *cluster* of scores which characterizes that group. With a group of salesmen, for instance,

INDIVIDUAL
REPORT
FORM

DIFFERENTIAL APTITUDE TESTS

G. K. Bennett, H. G. Seashore, and A. G. Wesman

THE PSYCHOLOGICAL CORPORATION
New York 17, N. Y.

NAME	SEX	AGE YRS.	AGE MOS.	GRADE
Martin, Robert	M	17		12

PLACE OF TESTING	FORM	NORMS USED	DATE OF TESTING
	A	12th - boys	

	Verbal	Numerical	Abstract	Space	Mechanical	Clerical	Spelling	Sentences	VR+NA
Raw Score	25	24	28	28	25	69	93	63	
Percentile	35	50	30	20	05	85	95	90	

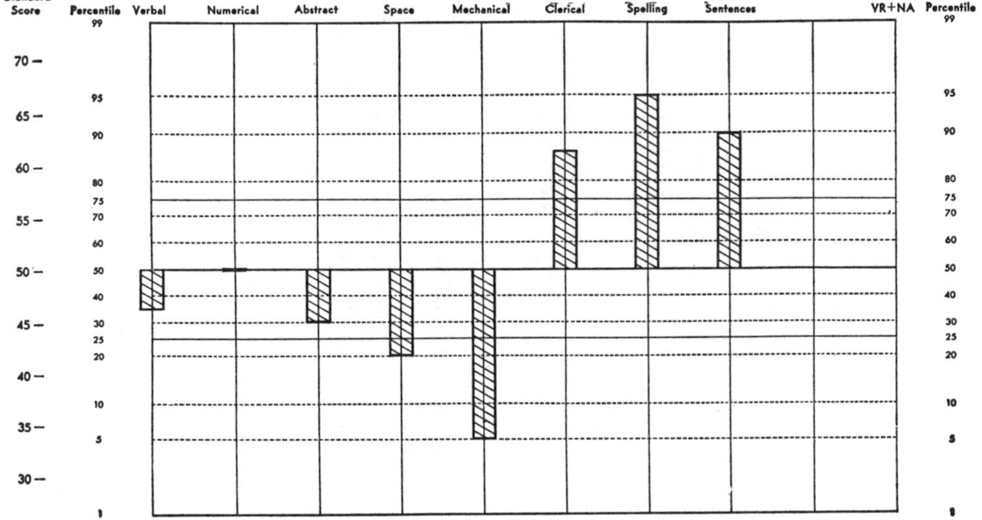

Fig. 8.1. Differential Aptitude Test Profile
(By permission of The Psychological Corporation.)

we might hypothesize a pattern on the *Guilford-Zimmerman Temperament Survey* consisting of high scores on Activity and Dominance scales. It might be that high score on neither one alone would be unique to this occupation but together they might distinguish salesmen from men in other occupations.

In fact, as has just been suggested, the situation is usually one of *comparing* two or more groups in order to find the profile which not only is characteristic of one group but which also distinguishes it from one or more other groups (this is discussed further during the treatment of Discriminant Bridges).

A few studies have been reported of efforts to test the value of some of these more elaborate statistical devices, with mixed results to date. Michael, in his review of these studies (1959) concludes that results have been disappointing, and that complex profile-analysis methods have added little to the information contributed by absolute scores on individual scales. He suggests that these results may be due to the fact that *differences* beween pairs of scores are less *reliable* than are the individual scores themselves. Further details of some of these studies will be reserved for later sections of this chapter, since each of them involved one of the more complex bridges, such as the discriminant and the regression, in addition to the table of norms. One that may be mentioned at this time (Wittenborn, 1951) concluded that a *difference* score (the difference between an individual's scores on two measures) added nothing to what could be predicted from each of the scores themselves. A number of studies will be reported in Chapter 13 on the possible interpretive significance of differences between the Quantitative and Linguistic scores on the *ACE Psychological Exam for College Freshman (ACE)*. Here too there have been mixed reports, some finding that the *difference* score adds information about the person which could not be obtained from knowledge of the two scores themselves and others achieving negative results with difference scores.

For the practicing counselor, statistical examination of profiles must be limited to what amounts to one-score-at-a-time treatment, since the data presently available for almost all tests do not provide for scoring of the *configuration* or shape of the profile in any statistical fashion.

Configural Scoring

Brief mention should be made of a technique similar to profile analysis, but applied now to the individual items of the test or inventory (Meehl, 1950). Of interest primarily to test developers, the approach has not yet reached the point of usefulness with any particular tests, and there is still some question as to its value. Essentially, it involves simultaneous scoring of the responses to two or more items on a test, so that the *pattern* of responses is emphasized. In the case of a personality inventory which provides for *Yes, No,* and *?* answers, this approach might show, for example, that a particular neurotic sample is characterized by a *combination* of a *Yes* answer to Item 17 and a *No* answer to Item 25, whereas a *Yes* answer to both or a *No* to both might be found to be typical of another diagnostic category or of none at all. This approach is an application of the basic Gestalt principle that the whole is greater than the sum of its parts, and that the *configuration* of the parts has meaning over and above the meaning of the individual parts. It is not clear at present how much this technique has to contribute toward increasing the validity of tests. At least one study found that configural scoring was less valid than the conventional technique based on scoring items one-at-a-time (Lubin, 1954). Horst (1954a), however, feels that configural scoring may become more useful with further statistical advances.

THE DISCRIMINANT BRIDGE [2]

Very closely related to the norm bridge, but somewhat more complex, is a kind of bridge which permits us simultaneously to compare an individual with two or more groups. This is extremely valuable, for this reason: To know that our client is similar to a particular group (say, of salesmen, or of neurotics, or of children who have learned to read in the first grade) is of limited value unless we know also that the profile which is characteristic of that group is *different from* profiles of other groups. For example, let us suppose that a study of a sample of engineering students has disclosed that their mean IQ on the *Otis* is 115. The fact that our client happens to get an *Otis* IQ of, say, 117 does indeed tell us that in this regard he is similar to the average engineering student in that sample. Suppose, however, we should discover that the student body as a whole, in the college from which we drew our sample of engineering students, has a mean *Otis* IQ of 115. Under these circumstances we are not able to tell our client anything about his suitability for engineering *as distinguished from* his suitability for any other college program. It is only when we find a test on which engineering students are significantly different from at least some other groups that we are able to give *differential* interpretations.

As another illustration, suppose that we have located a test which indicates that our client is more similar to the average engineering student than to the average college student in other departments (perhaps a test of proficiency in mathematics or the physical sciences). But our client must decide on the particular branch of engineering—electrical, civil, chemical, or mechanical—since the engineering school he is considering

[2] The label given this group of bridges derives from the Discriminant Function, which is one of the more important of the statistical methods for this kind of bridge. This category, however, is not limited to the Discriminant Function.

requires choosing a specialty at the time of admission. If we know nothing about any test differences among the specialties, we cannot provide any discriminating information for our client from tests. (Obviously there are other methods which can be used, such as helping him to learn something about the nature of the work in the various specialties, so that perhaps he can choose among them in terms of which seems most appealing). If, however, it has been found that mechanical engineering students as a group are superior to the others in spatial visualization ability, that the electrical engineers are superior in physics, and that each specialty differs from others in certain ways, we would have some basis for using test data to help our counselee to select his specialization area.

Perhaps the most widely known and used test having this bridge as its basic method is the *Strong Vocational Interest Blank.* A score of *A* on one of the occupational scales of the *SVIB* means that one is more similar in his inventory responses to the men in that occupational sample than he is to men-in-general. The scoring keys themselves were developed on a discriminant bridge basis. For any one occupation, only those items receive scoring credit (plus or minus) which have been found to discriminate the responses of men in that occupation from those of the men-in-general sample.

Statistically, the techniques used for this purpose include the discriminant function (see especially Tiedeman, 1954) and the various tests for the significance of differences between groups—critical ratio, chi-square, and analysis of variance. These methods generally involve administering tests to two or more different groups (from different occupations and college curricula) and then computing a score indicating the central tendency of each group on each test or subtest. Then these central tendency numbers are compared with each other to determine whether the differences between groups are significant. Following this, in some of the techniques, there is derived a formula into which can be placed the test scores of any one person and which yields a single number indicating the similarity of this person's scores to those of the reference groups.

An illustration of the use of the discriminant function to yield a formula is found in Stinson's study (1958) of engineering students in college. For five years he followed up a group of beginning engineering students who had taken the *ACE, Guilford-Zimmerman Aptitude Survey,* and the *Kuder.* After the five-year period, subjects were classified as either graduates from the engineering program, nonengineering graduates (those who had transferred to other programs and had graduated), or dropouts from college. The following formula was derived: [3]

$$V = 0.002092X_1 + 0.006168X_2 + 0.051452X_3 + 0.010834X_4$$

[3] The formula and other quotations from this article are reproduced with permission of the *Personnel and Guidance Journal.*

X_1 is raw score on *ACE*, X_2 is raw score on the Verbal Comprehension part of the *G-Z*, X_3 is raw score on the General Comprehension part of the *G-Z*, and X_4 is the Scientific Interest score on the *Kuder*.

The fact that these four scores are in the formula means that they are the ones which best discriminate among students in these three groups.

By substituting in this equation the mean raw scores of men in each of the three groups, Stinson obtained a *V* score for each group. These scores are as follows:

$$\text{Engineering Graduates } V \text{ score} = 2.048146$$
$$\text{Nonengineering Graduates } V \text{ score} = 1.673095$$
$$\text{Dropouts } V \text{ score} = 1.509139$$

He then took the midpoints between these scores as the "critical scores" to be used for individual cases. Thus, if one's *V* score is 1.860621 and above, he is considered to be most similar to the Engineering Graduate group. *V* scores between 1.591117 and 1.860621 are classified as Nonengineering Graduates, whereas scores of 1.591117 and below are closest to the Dropout group. Stinson makes it clear that other data than a student's *V* score should be taken into consideration, especially with borderline cases, but that the discriminant function helps to objectify and to integrate into a single number the predictions which come from the four most valid (for this sample) variables.

Tiedeman and his associates have described the method of discriminant analysis, which is essentially the kind of technique which has just been described, as applied by them to various problems (Tiedeman, 1954; Tiedeman, Bryan and Rulon, 1952; Tiedeman and Bryan, 1954). They arrive at a "centour" score for each individual which tells what percentage of successful or satisfied people in a group had combined scores on two or more tests which are further than his from the central tendency of the group. These workers feel that this is one of the more promising methods among those currently available for comparing an individual's scores with those of groups he is considering joining (such as a college curriculum or an occupation). Tiedeman points out, however, (1954) that at present the technique is impractical when several groups are to be compared on several test scores simultaneously, since volumes of tables would be necessary.

Evaluation of Discriminant Methods

Tyler has recently (1959) presented a theoretical analysis of the whole topic of individuality and of the psychology of individual prediction which has implications for the present discussion. Her conclusion is that noteworthy improvements in prediction of human behavior are less likely to come from our traditional measurement approach (which emphasizes *how much* of a trait one has) than from a "nominal" kind of measurement which seeks to characterize the individual's *customary pattern of choice* in life situations. Knowledge of the kinds of choices one has made in the past (as, for example, one's choices among items in an interest inventory) is then used to estimate how he will respond to particular school programs or occupations in the future. It is clear, however, that the prediction here is not in terms of success-failure but of choice-rejection of alternative courses of action in life situations.

As pointed out previously, others are less than enthusiastic about the discriminant approach in general (French, 1956). As French makes clear, the method of multiple discriminant analysis tells nothing about the individual's chances of being *successful,* or *satisfied, within* an occupation or school curriculum. A score or set of scores treated by the discriminant method tells only to what extent our client is *similar* to a particular group. The group may or may not have been selected so that there is some reason to consider them at least minimally successful, for instance, having been in the occupation for three years or having graduated from college. But no differentiation has been made *within* the group as to success or satisfaction. Therefore we cannot say whether our client is likely to be successful or happy *within* the particular group, only that he is *similar* to a given percentage of the people in that group in certain ways. It is tempting to assume, in the absence of contrary logic or evidence, that the *more* similar one is to people in a criterion group, the more likely he is to be successful or satisfied as a member of that group. Likewise, it is tempting to assume that the more one *exceeds* the mean of a group on some test score, the more likely he is to be a successful or satisfied member of that group. Neither of these assumptions has much merit, as was pointed out earlier in discussing the norm bridge. One can be too bright, for example, to be a longshoreman, in which case the *optimal* intelligence test score would be lower than the *maximal.* Similarly, an above-average Dominance score might be found to be typical of members of a particular occupation, say managers or salesmen. Beyond a certain point, however, additional dominance may be handicapping, perhaps because it might restrict too much the people being supervised or give prospective customers a feeling of being pushed too hard.

Furthermore, as French also points out, if the people who comprise the sample used in a discriminant type of study have some characteristic undesirable for successful functioning in that area, then we are likely to encourage more people with the same defect to enter that occupation. If, for example, present-day counselors are poor in mathematics, as compared with people in several other fields, the discriminant-analysis method would reflect this, so that the poorer one is in mathematics, the better his score would be for counseling as compared with other occupations he might be considering. Yet a different kind of approach might show that the *better* counselors are stronger in mathematics than the poorer counselors (the illustration used, it need not be added, is purely fictitious).

The method preferred by French, which takes into consideration differences *within* groups in quality of work done or satisfaction with a course or an occupation is that of *regression,* to which we now turn our attention. After the regression approach has been described, an attempt will be made to compare these approaches in terms of available research and to offer some synthesis and reconciliation.

THE REGRESSION BRIDGE

This has been for many years the mainstay of test interpretation. Here are to be found the thousands of correlation coefficients which have been computed to ascertain relationships between test scores and some criteria of success or satisfaction or whatever. Here also are the sources of the expectancy tables and regression equations of Chapter 7. In its elemental form, the procedure is, first, to select a sample within which there is variation on some meaningful criterion. For example, let us say that we wish to reduce the number of failures in a geometry course. Our sample might be all those taking the course this year. At the beginning of the year we administer to the group whatever tests we think might be predictive of grades in the course (which are to be the criterion of success in our study). If the students have already had one or more relevant tests, it may not be necessary to use new tests. Then the scores are filed away so that teachers cannot be influenced by them in making up their grades. At the end of the semester or year, grades are collected and a correlation coefficient is computed between each of the tests and the grades. To the extent that a correlation greater than zero is found, we will be in a position to attack the problem in one of two ways. Either we can *select* for the course only those who show promise over and above a certain point, or we can make predictive data available to the students during *counseling,* in the hope that they will make wiser judgments about taking the course as a result of the additional information.

French (1956) cites some data which highlight one of the major differences between this regression approach and the discriminant approach which was previously described. Four scores (Perceptual Speed, Mechanical Knowledge, Carelessness, and Speed of Judgment) were obtained from tests administered to vocational high school students who later became office workers, beauty operators, carpenters, and mechanics. The first two groups were girls and the second two were boys. Tables 8.1 and 8.2, taken from French's report, show, respectively, the correlation coefficients between test scores and grades in shop courses (regression approach) and the average scores of each group on each test factor (discriminant approach). Here is French's discussion of these data:

For the office worker group, Perceptual Speed and Speed of Judgment look good from the standpoint of the validity coefficients. Therefore, multiple regression would choose office workers who had high scores on these two aptitudes. Future office workers also have the highest mean score on these two factors. Therefore, multiple discriminant analysis would guide into office jobs girls who had high scores on Perceptual Speed and Speed of Judgment. Thus, here is a case where both multiple regression and multiple discriminant analysis would select the same people for the job.

For mechanics the validity coefficients recommend high mechanical knowledge, carefulness (that is, there is a negative validity for number of careless errors), and slowness of judgment (there is a negative validity for number of choices made). The means, on the other hand, show that the criterion group of mechanics had high mechanical knowledge, but they were the most careless of the four groups and were speedier of judgment than the carpenters. This is a situation where multiple regression would guide different boys into mechanics than would multiple discriminant analysis.

For beauticians and carpenters the two methods would also select somewhat different kinds of people.

Which method is the more suitable? Let me reply by asking a leading question. Do we want to encourage speedy, careless boys to go into mechanics just because mechanics are speedy and careless now, even though speed and carelessness correlate negatively with performance ratings? (pp. 41-42)

Table 8.1. Predictive Data from a Regression Approach: Correlation Coefficients Between Scores on Test Factors and Vocational Shop Grades in Four Occupational Areas

TEST FACTOR	Office Workers	Beauticians	Carpenters	Mechanics
Perceptual Speed	.46	*	*	*
Mechanical Knowledge	*	*	.39	.36
Carelessness	*	.33	*	—.27
Speed of Judgment	.31	.37	*	—.23

* Not statistically significant.
SOURCE: French, 1956: p. 48. By permission of the Educational Testing Service, Princeton, N. J.

Table 8.2. Predictive Data from a Discriminant Approach: Mean Scores on Test Factors for Students Who Later Entered Each of Four Occupations

TEST FACTOR	Office Workers	Beauticians	Carpenters	Mechanics
Perceptual Speed	58	52	47	47
Mechanical Knowledge	39	39	55	58
Carelessness	48	50	48	51
Speed of Judgment	53	51	48	49

SOURCE: French, 1956: p. 48. By permission of the Educational Testing Service, Princeton, N. J.

In his last paragraph, quoted above, French asks questions which affect not only our individual clients but also the community at large and society as a whole. Counselors would do well to ponder these questions as they make some of their test interpretations. Each time we interpret a score on the *SVIB* as encouragement for a counselee to enter a particular occupation, we are in effect assuming that the typical people now in this occupation are the kind who *should* be in it, both in terms of their own welfare and that of society.

Limitations of Present Regression Data

Although vast numbers of correlation coefficients have been computed between test scores and various criteria of success or satisfaction, they are of only limited use to the practicing counselor. There seem to be several reasons for this state of affairs:

1. First, most counselors have had acquaintance with, and have access to, only very small numbers of all the relevant correlational studies that might be applicable to their counselees. Even very well-trained counselors who struggle earnestly to keep up with current literature cannot hope to make much of a dent in the wall. There are available altogether too few well-organized and integrated reviews of the available knowledge in an area, such as predicting success in a particular school subject, or in an occupation. The better test manuals, textbooks, and some of the other resource materials listed at the end of Chapter 4 have a great deal to offer, but there remains a serious lack of *usable* conclusions for the practitioner.

2. Many of the reported studies are so seriously defective technically as to be of no use, or at best, very limited use. One of the major problems is that of the criterion, which all too often is an inadequate representation of those things which are valued by a school or an employer. Some other flaws in the studies are small size of sample, inadequate description of the sample, failure to use appropriate statistical techniques, and poor choice of tests (often resulting from insufficient study of previous research and insufficient thinking through of the problem). Some studies contain "contamination of the criterion," that is, judges, for example, teachers who assign grades or supervisors who rate workers, have been permitted to know the test scores and thus to be influenced by them in assigning grades or ratings. Unfortunately, much of the best quality research is to be found only in unpublished doctoral dissertations, which are quite useless to the practicing counselor until a textbook or article reports the work.

3. Many of the correlations reported in the literature are really too small to be of much real informational value to counselor and client. As Franzblau points out (1958), a coefficient of correlation must be at least .66 in order to yield a prediction, from one measure to another, which is 25 per cent better than a chance or random guess. The correlation must

be at least .86 to yield a prediction which is 50 per cent better than chance. Correlations of tests with external criteria rarely attain even the level of .66, and validity correlations of .86 are practically unheard of.[4] Ghiselli (1955), for example, has summarized hundreds of correlation coefficients reported in the literature during the period from 1919 to 1955, taken from studies using aptitude and personality tests in the selection and placement of workers. The *maximum* validity coefficient for tests of intelligence was .61, and the highest for all tests was .66, this with a test of mechanical comprehension. The *average* coefficients for all intelligence tests were .38 where the criteria had to do with success in training programs and .19 for those studies whose criteria had to do with success on the job. The *highest average* coefficient with a job proficiency criterion, strangely enough, was found with the use of "personal data" (the kind of biographical information often collected through a questionnaire) ; this was .41 and was quite a bit higher than most other averages.

In all fairness, and as a source of some consolation, it should be stated that the level of coefficients found in predicting school grades and other *educational criteria* is in all likelihood higher than those of Ghiselli's data, which have to do mostly with subcollege occupations and with specialized training rather than general education. However, even in predicting high school and college grades, which we do about as well as anything, the usual coefficients are found in the range .40 to .60. At best, then, we are dealing with quite unprecise predictions, in which statements of probable success or satisfaction must be stated in general and broad terms, with a wide range of error. Super includes a table (1949: p. 662) from which can be found, first, a person's most likely standing on a criterion, from knowledge of his score on a predictive test, and, second, the zone of approximation of the predicted score. When the correlation between test and criterion is .60, which is fairly high even for predicting school grades from scholastic aptitude tests, the zone of approximation (based on the standard error of estimate) is 8 standard score points. An illustration will convey something of the degree of crudeness of most predictions. If a student's score on a test is at the 79th percentile (standard score of 58) , and this test correlates .60 with some criterion, say school grades, then the table tells us that there are 68 chances in 100 that his grades will be between the 38th percentile (standard score 47) and the 90th percentile (standard

---

[4] This is an oversimplification of the problem. Cronbach and Gleser (1957) have discussed the problem in terms of decision theory. The "utility" of a test procedure is ascertained not by how much it improves decisions over *chance* but over the best available "strategy" without the test. In some situations a smaller validity coefficient may be more useful than the same size coefficient in another situation. Also they point out, in relation to the use of tests for selection purposes, that the "selection ratio" must be considered. Maximum utility value of a test "strategy" may be expected when the selection ratio is closest to 50 per cent, that is, when one is likely to be accepting, or hiring, or placing about half of the total number of applicants.

score 63). If we wanted to have 90 per cent accuracy in our predictions, rather than 68 per cent, we would have to extend the range of prediction down to the 21st percentile and up to the 96th percentile. And even at that, there is one chance in 20 that his grades will be below the 21st percentile and one chance in 20 that they will be above the 96th percentile.

McCabe gives a table (1956) showing the 68-chances-in-100 limits on the criterion variable that may be expected for each of fourteen validity coefficients from .30 to .95, and for each of thirteen different percentile or standard score levels on the predictor.

4. Unfortunately, few reports of correlations include expectancy tables, such as those in Figure 7.3 and Table 7.2. In this form, the known facts can be understood by both counselor and client, whereas the coefficient itself has for the latter no meaning and for the former only limited meaning in terms of the predictions that can be made. Test authors and publishers, as well as research workers, would render a great service by making expectancy tables a routine part of reports of correlation studies, at least in those instances where the correlations are high enough to be of any use.

Multiple Regression

As in our earlier discussion of the Discriminant bridge we found that several test scores and several criteria could be considered simultaneously, so it is with the Regression bridge. The basic method here is the *multiple correlation* coefficient; two or more tests used together often yield a higher correlation with a criterion of success than does either test alone. Thus it has been found that college grades may be predicted better by combining, say, scores on a scholastic aptitude test with those on an English test and perhaps adding high school average. The application of such findings to an individual client may be made, first, by substituting his scores in a *multiple regression* formula, in which each score is weighted according to what has been found to be the most efficient set of weights for purposes of prediction. The resulting equation will look very much like the one given earlier, from Stinson's study (1958), as an illustration of the discriminant function. For example, Garrett (1958) uses data from May, who studied the correlation between college grades and two predictor variables—general intelligence, as measured by a combination of group tests, and number of hours per week devoted to study. The multiple correlation turned out to be .83, showing unusually good predictability. Using statistical methods described in detail by Garrett (pp. 406-409), the multiple regression equation is:

$$X_1 = .57X_2 + 1.12X_3 - 66$$

X_1 is predicted honor points, X_2 is intelligence score, and X_3 is number of hours of study per week.

In the case of "William Brown," whose intelligence score is 120 and who studies 20 hours a week, the best estimate is that he will receive 25 honor points at the end of his first semester (each credit *A* receiving 3 honor points, each *B,* 2 honor points, each *C,* one honor point, and *D,* no honor points) .[5]

The second method is the *multiple expectancy table,* an example of which is shown in Table 8.3, taken from Lins' study at the University of Wisconsin (Lins, 1950). Here one enters the table with two different scores for each client: his *ACE* scores and his standing in his high school class (in terms of percentiles). At the convergence of the two scores one finds the probability of getting a particular grade average at that college. Here again, as with the multiple discriminant method, any attempt to set up tables for more than two variables simultaneously would require pages or volumes of tables.

Multiple Absolute vs. Multiple Differential Prediction

More complex than the multiple regression approach just described is the attempt to estimate from a set of test scores an individual's chances of success (or satisfaction, or any other criteria) in *two or more areas.* This, after all, was the hope of the multifactor tests, that a standard battery of aptitude tests could be used to make predictions about a variety of school subjects, occupations, or whatever. The alternative is the use of a different battery for each field being considered, say engineering, journalism, or drafting. Use of separate batteries of this kind is likely to yield the highest predictions, but the time involved to test each person is a serious drawback.

Horst has discussed the relative effectiveness of the two kinds of approach mentioned in the heading of this section (1954b, 1955). In the first of these, *multiple absolute,* a battery is developed with the goal of yielding the *highest possible correlations* with several criteria; in the second approach, the *multiple differential,* the purpose is to use a battery in such a way as to gain the *greatest possible differentiation* between or among criteria, that is, to yield the most clear-cut estimates of a person's *relative* chances in different fields. Applied to the problem of success in college, the first approach would give us the highest possible correlations between a group of test scores and grades in a *variety* of college majors, with the various tests being weighted differently as one predicts the client's chances in engineering and his chances in journalism. The resulting tables or multiple regression formulas would help a youngster who wonders whether to go into engineering, by giving the best possible estimate of his chances of doing well in that area. Similarly a youngster who is unsure of his ability to handle a journalism curriculum would receive the

[5] For further illustration of multiple regression equations as applied to college grades, see Table 13.4 in Chapter 13.

Table 8.3. Probability of Academic Success of New Male Freshmen Based Upon High-School Percentile Rank and Percentile Rank American Council Psychological Examination*

HIGH SCHOOL RANK PERCENTILE	GRADE LEVEL	AMERICAN COUNCIL PSYCHOLOGICAL PERCENTILE							
		0-24		*25-49*		*50-74*		*75-100*	
75-100	B C	14 49	63 (49)	19 56	75 (107)	32 51	83 (136)	45 45	90 (228)
	D Fail	33 4	37	20 5	25	15 2	17	9 1	10
50-74	B C	6 40	46 (85)	5 50	55 (83)	14 52	66 (91)	14 55	69 (65)
	D Fail	46 8	54	39 6	45	27 7	34	28 3	31
25-49	B C	1 28	29 (80)	0 33	33 (66)	8 40	48 (48)	0 64	64 (22)
	D Fail	55 16	71	41 26	67	44 8	52	18 18	36
0-24	B C	0 17	17 (60) †	6 24	30 (33)	0 47	47 (19)	18 24	42 (17)
	D Fail	50 33	83	40 30	70	32 21	53	35 23	58

* Probability of success is based upon experience with first semester freshmen 1948-49 who were graduates of Wisconsin High Schools. The interpretation might be as follows: It has been our experience that 83 per cent of the men ranking below the twenty-fifth percentile on the American Council Psychological Examination *(local norms) and in high-school class were not successful as first-semester freshmen.*

† The number in parentheses is the size of the sample. Numbers above the broken line are probabilities of receiving a C or B or better average. The sum of these two is the probability of success.

SOURCE: Lins, 1950: p. 389. By permission of *Educational and Psychological Measurement and the author.*

most dependable statement of his chances of receiving a given average grade in *that* area. If, however, we have a client who vacillates *between* engineering and journalism and is concerned not so much about his chances in either program but rather about which one he is likely to do better in, for this kind of problem, the multiple differential design is the one of choice. Here we may not predict grades in either field as well as with the multiple *absolute* method, but we will have a more useful answer to the particular question of *relative* chances.

The kinds of tests which are likely to yield the highest *absolute* predictions in any particular set of areas will probably not be the ones which yield the highest *differential* predictions (Michael, 1956). Super (1956) discussed factorial purity in this connection; the more pure a subtest is as a measure of a single mental ability, the more remote it is from the *combination* of factors which usually operate simultaneously in performing the operations required by a job or a school subject, and therefore the lower is the anticipated correlation with any *one* criterion. In addition to greater factorial purity, the better differential battery will include tests whose correlations with one criterion are very different from their correlations with others. Put another way (Wesman and Bennett, 1951):

> The tests which survive attempts to predict criterion differences directly are naturally enough those which correlate with those differences. . . . A scholastic aptitude test may be one of our best predictors of success in courses in a liberal arts college; but because that aptitude is very important to success in all courses taken by the freshmen, it will receive little or no weight in the prediction of *differences* in course grades. Success in each course may depend to a large extent on the aptitude measured by the test, while predictable differences in success may be the product of other characteristics or traits. Tests of these other characteristics or traits will receive greatest weight in the direct prediction of differences (pp. 266-267).

OVERVIEW AND RECONCILIATION OF STATISTICAL BRIDGES

At this writing, there is considerable disagreement among proponents of the different statistical approaches to bridging the gap between predictor (test) and criterion (school grades, job success). Critical experiments to determine the relative superiority of discriminant and regression methods have not been reported. The ideal studies are practically prohibitive; Wesman and Bennett (1951), for example, suggest that an experimental school be established in which approximately one thousand boys would spend a month in each of several training programs. It would be necessary to control properly the *sequence* of courses (they suggest rotating the order) and the important variable of effort, to insure that each boy is trying equally hard in each field. Pretests and post-tests would then be analyzed by various statistical methods to determine their relative efficacy.

A more modest comparison of discriminant and regression methods appears in a study by Dunn (1959). Using as subjects some 1,380 graduates of Brown University, she sought to ascertain whether the multiple discriminant or the multiple regression method could predict better the student's major subject in college (14 different subjects were involved). By use of the discriminant method, it was found that two discriminants accounted for most of the separation among groups of major students. For example, Discriminant 1 gave high positive weights to secondary school rank and to mathematics and science achievement test scores and highest negative weights to an English usage test score, to age, and to verbal aptitude test score. On this Discriminant, groups of students majoring in Chemistry, Mathematics, and Biology received the highest mean scores, and English and Modern Language majors had the lowest mean scores. As an example of the findings with the regression method, *grades* received by Chemistry majors were best predicted by verbal aptitude and reading ability test scores. That is to say, Chemistry majors as a group were differentiated from some other group by being lower on certain verbal abilities. Yet, *among* Chemistry majors, those with the higher verbal abilities tended to receive better grades. In general, the variables which were most predictive in the discriminant approach were quite different from those which were most predictive in the regression approach. Comparing the two approaches now as to their success in predicting, with a fresh sample, the subject in which students actually majored, the discriminant approach was found to be more effective.

As pointed out by Paul L. Dressel in his "Comment" appended to Dunn's article, the superiority of the discriminant method in this study may be attributed to the fact that the task is one which is inappropriate for the regression method. The latter has the function of estimating relative standing *within* a field, rather than comparing people in different fields. It is true, as Dunn points out, that use of regression data alone might lead a freshman or sophomore to choose a major subject in which he is likely to get the highest grade point average, but possibly only because he is in a department where the competition is not as great as in others. She mentions, for example, that a good mathematics student could expect to get a higher average in accounting than in a physics or applied mathematics program. It is also true that the regression method alone sometimes does not point out an ability which may be necessary to enter and stay in a major (say mathematics for Chemistry majors) but which does not correlate with grades in that major. As found in her study, Chemistry majors as a group are significantly superior to all other groups on Discriminant 1, which gives positive weights to mathematics and science achievement tests and to secondary school rank, but none of these was given high weights in the regression analysis, which instead emphasized verbal aptitude and reading ability. It would seem then that regression data alone might lead a student into a field in which he would lack certain abilities necessary for success, or they might lead him into a field in which he would make little use of some of his strongest abilities. However, the opposite is true also, namely, that discriminant data might lead someone into a field in which he lacks the abilities which make the difference between the better and the poorer students *within* that field.

An additional source of some comparative evaluation of Discriminant and Regression approaches is the recent report of Thorndike and Hagen (1959) of a follow-up study of 10,000 former Air Force trainees some twelve years after they had taken a battery of tests in service. Various criteria of civilian employment status and degree of success were obtained, and both methods—Discriminant and Regression—were used, the first to compare the scores of subgroups who had gone into different occupations and the latter to see how well success *within* each occupation would have been predicted by the tests. In general, they found only modest validities for both methods,[6] but the Discriminant approach was at a somewhat higher level of validity than the Regression. It would seem that, in line with Tyler's analysis (1959), we are presently able to predict occupational *status* or choice better than degree of *success* within that status.

It seems that whatever research is done will ultimately lead to the conclusion that each major statistical approach has its merits and its particular areas of usefulness. As shown in Figure 8.2, each method has a somewhat different contribution to offer the practicing counselor. If our counselee is trying to decide among the occupational areas listed in the left-hand column, the Normative bridge tells how his scores on a battery of tests compare with those of the people in each field. Next, the Discriminant method can tell which group he resembles most in his over-all makeup of abilities, interests, and other characteristics. This information gives him some basis for judging the appropriateness of each field for himself, assuming that similarity to people already in the field generally implies greater likelihood of success and/or satisfaction in this field than in others. Next, we would use data from Regression studies for some estimate of the extent to which our counselee is likely to experience success or satisfaction within each field (Multiple Absolute method)—certainly an important piece of information to have. Finally, especially when our counselee has found two or more of these fields in which he has pretty good expectancy of success, the Multiple Differential method can help answer the question: In which field am I likely to find the *greatest* success (or satisfaction)?

Some counselees will find the decision easy, because all approaches will point to the same field. For many, however, compromises will be necessary, as the advantages of each alternative are weighed. Two people may face a similar set of alternatives: They will find that they can both expect to do very well (in terms of grades or salary, or other criterion of this sort) in field *A*, but that in Field *B*, which both see as more interesting and

---

[6] These research workers used data from tests which had originally been chosen for the purpose of selecting aviation cadets. Higher validities might be expected with tests chosen with a variety of criterion occupations in mind.

TYPE OF STATISTICAL BRIDGE

Possible Answers for Counselee Considering These Three Occupations:	Norm or Profile	Discriminant	Regression	
			Absolute	Differential
	"How Do I Compare with the People in Each Field?"	"To Which Group Am I More Similar?"	"How Well Am I Likely to Do in Each Field?"	"What Are My Relative Chances of Success in These Fields?"
Engineering	Similar	Most	Moderately Well	Poorest
Selling	Somewhat Similar	Least	Moderately Well	In-Between
Drafting	Somewhat Similar	In-Between	Very Well	Best

Fig. 8.2. Contributions of Various Statistical Bridges

challenging, they stand lower in those characteristics which distinguish the better student or the better paid worker from the poorer student or the lower paid worker in that field. One man may choose Field *A* because to him the better grades or higher salary are more important. The other may settle for lower grades and lower salary in order to have what to him is the greater value of being with people with whom he shares certain interests and certain abilities. There are societal concerns here too: Do we as educators, as parents, and as citizens prefer that young people enter those fields which promise the best grades and the easiest "success," or that they seek those fields in which they may utilize their potentialities to the fullest measure, even though they may not be the *best* in the field, even though they may have to struggle much harder and perhaps for lesser financial rewards? These are not measurement questions, but they bear directly on what we do with tests.

For the counselor of today, much of what has been said here regarding statistical bridges offers hope for the future rather than immediately usable methods. Instead of the well-organized armamentarium of devices which would permit the series of statistical interpretations mentioned above, we have today a collection of odds and ends. It seems possible to say with some assurance only that, to date, the Discriminant framework seems more promising than the Regression. Apparently "success" in most occupations can be attained by such a variety of abilities, behaviors, and other characteristics that our Regression methods are of limited effectiveness. It will require a great deal of large-scale research of both a fundamental and applied nature to eliminate the tattered patchwork that is the current use of tests and substitute for it a solid structure of well-established statistical data and a collection of demonstrated techniques for use in individual counseling. While we await that utopian day, it is perhaps even more important now for the practitioner to understand the theoretical and technical matters which have been discussed, so that he can at least have some appreciation of the severe limitations of the imperfect data now available to him. Finally, the counselor who is aware of the topics which have been discussed here can make more effective use of what *is* now available.

CHAPTER 9

Clinical Bridges[1]

P OSTPONING for a brief while a critical comparison of Statistical and Clinical bridges, we must first examine the latter in some detail. In Chapter 3 we listened to a counselor thinking out loud about a set of test (and other) data; this was the clinical method, or at least one counselor's version of it. There have been several attempts in the counseling literature to describe this process and its characteristics. Most of the descriptions have in common an emphasis on the inductive-deductive process by which data are studied. Before going into this in detail, however, we should give brief attention to a minority point of view which sees the clinical process as essentially no different from the statistical. Later we shall attempt to synthesize the two points of view.

Horst (1956) seems to take the position that clinical test interpretation is nothing more or less than a mental, relatively unquantified equivalent of statistical interpretation. He points out that the counselor, in order to tell his client what the chances are of being successful in a particular activity, must must know certain things:

(1) He knows what kinds of things are to be done. (2) He knows what kinds of behaviors are regarded as desirable in what kinds of activities. That is, he knows what constitutes success in the various activities. (3) He has a way of indicating how desirable the various kinds of behaviors are even though these ways may be very crude. He has some way of making discriminations among behaviors. (4) The methods he has for discriminating among behaviors are reasonably consistent. He does not roll the dice or spin a roulette wheel in order to get numbers to characterize the performance of the client. (5) Whatever method the counselor

[1] The term *clinical* is not the happiest choice for this purpose since it also connotes what *clinical* psychologists do as contrasted with *counseling* and other psychologists. The adjective has, however, long been used in this connection (see, for example, Williamson, 1939: Ch. 4, "The Art of Diagnosing"), and no superior alternative has suggested itself.

uses, no matter how vague or crude, in evaluating behaviors in life activities, he does arrive at evaluations with which other persons including the client will tend to agree. (6) He has some system—certain items of information—in terms of which he describes people, no matter how simple or complex. (7) He has ways of indicating to what degree these various things about people can exist. These may be very crude or they may take on any degree of refinement which he chooses. They may be all or none, more or less, yes or no, maybe yes—maybe no. (8) He has ways of knowing to what degree each of these things about people are true about a particular client. (9) He is somewhat consistent in evaluating the client with respect to each of his descriptive categories. He does not describe the same behavior as withdrawn one minute and extroverted the next. (10) He has a system for discriminating the variables, or quantifying them, such that there can be at least some measure of agreement with other observers. (11) Finally, he has a method, or system of methods, whereby he can combine or synthesize information about people in such a way that the synthesized information will indicate to what extent the client will exhibit desirable behaviors in the various activities available to him (p. 167).

Horst explains each of these components in detail, and he makes clear the responsibilities of the counselor for being familiar with tests, with criteria, and with the psychology of individual differences. Also, he adds, the counselor has the responsibility for following up his clients as a way of checking his own validity as a predictor; that is, checking his statement of probabilities against what actually happened in the activity chosen by the client. He describes the bases of the counselor's skills in combining information about people with information about the activities in which the people are considering engaging (Horst's point 11 above). The counselor bases his predictions not only on his own experience with people and with their activities, but also on the experiences of other counselors and on the accumulated body of research.

Horst has quite properly emphasized the fact, which has been mentioned here more than once, that every test interpretation bears an assumption that there is evidence somewhere of a relationship between that test and whatever is being interpreted. The practicing counselor will benefit from occasional rereading of Horst's discussion, as a reminder of the responsibilities he undertakes if he is to help people to find out what is good for them and what is not. Whether he makes his predictions (or other interpretations) clinically or statistically, the basic assumption is the same, and as Horst points out, the crystal ball is not one of the acceptable bases for making predictions, even when the crystal ball is called ". . . something more respectable, such as insight, special skill, or even broad experience" (p. 168).

Studies of the Clinical Process

However, Horst has described only one aspect of the total process of clinical interpretation. That the process is more complex is attested to by the results of a study (Koester, 1954) in which ten trained and experienced counselors thought out loud (in the presence of a wire recorder) their analyses of the data from three different cases. Six categories were set up to represent what appeared to be the major steps in the "diagnostic" process (the term used by Koester to designate essentially what we are referring to as interpretation) : (1) Indeterminate response, including expression of uncertainty; (2) Interpretation of a datum in the case without reference to any other data in the case; (3) Comparison and evaluation of data, but without interpretation; (4) Hypothesis based on synthesis of data, in which an hypothesis is formulated to tie together several of the data; (5) Evaluation of an interpretation or hypothesis, by using a datum either to support or refute a previous interpretation or hypothesis, or by comparing two conflicting hypotheses and choosing one over the other on the basis of the evidence; and (6) Need for additional data.

The extent to which each counselor used each of these six types of response was ascertained by judges who read typescripts made from recordings. It was found that all counselors used all six categories of response, but to different degrees. For all counselors, however, the *smallest* percentage of responses was in category 1 above and the largest in category 4. Eight of the ten counselors were consistent in their patterns throughout the three cases. Qualitative examination of the typescript indicated that only two of the ten counselors did not use negative evidence as a way of testing the validity of hypotheses they had set up.

More recently, Parker (1958) reported a study using methods similar to those of Koester to test similar hypotheses regarding intracounselor consistency and intercounselor similarities in the diagnostic-appraisal process. He also tested several hypotheses regarding the extent to which certain characteristics of the counselor's diagnostic thinking were related to the accuracy of his predictions of what would happen in the next counseling interview. He had ten counselors read case materials and think out loud into a microphone. Then they listened to an interview and again spoke their diagnostic thinking into a microphone. Among his major findings were these: There was little or no evidence that any particular characteristic of a counselor's diagnostic thinking (frequent evaluation of hypotheses or number of hypotheses developed) is related to accuracy of prediction of what the client would say in the next interview. Second, there was no increase from the first to the third interviews in the "richness" and "diversity" of counselor hypotheses and conceptualization of the client. Little change in the "model" of the client was made as additional data were available. Both the researcher and Charles McArthur, author of the "Comment" which accompanies the article, suggest that counselors may be too hasty and premature in developing their hypotheses and in building their "model" of the client (more about this later) .[2] Also, there was not found to be a hierarchy of steps in the diagnostic process; instead counselors moved back and forth among the various operations—interpretation, synthesis, forming hypotheses, and evaluating hypotheses.

Finally, brief mention may be made of an earlier study in this area reported by McArthur (1954a) . Though of an exploratory nature and lacking the hypotheses and the quantifications of Koester's and Parker's work, McArthur's paper contains ideas which are now deemed to be some of the major principles of the clinical process of interpretation. A variety of visiting "scientists" (apparently mostly psychologists) were given selected pregraduation data about individual college graduates and then were asked to interpret the facts and to make predictions about the individual's later behavior. Since the subjects of all the cases had been out of college for ten years, criterion data were available. Less concerned about the accuracy of predictions than about the *processes* by which they were arrived at, McArthur and his associates concluded that equally successful predictions could come from a variety of psychological theories and tests. The critical element seemed to be that an individualized "model" or conceptualization of the subject was built up, and predictions were made from this model. It was not a matter of interpreting a test score or other datum to mean a given thing about the person and then to predict his later behavior from that interpretation. Rather here was a process, primarily inductive in nature, in which a *theory of the individual* was developed, from which inferences were then drawn as to how he would behave in such-and-such a situation.

The studies by Koester, Parker, Soskin, and McArthur are the only reported empirical research (and the first three the only quantitative ones) which actually describe the *process* of interpretation as done clinically. Other articles, to be reported later, are descriptions and discussions, no doubt in many instances based on counseling experience but nonetheless armchair in nature. It would be of some value to have replications of the procedures used by Koester, by Parker, by Soskin, and by McArthur, to see whether similar results would be obtained with different counselors, representing a variety of theoretical points-of-view in counseling, and in different settings (both Koester's and Parker's work were done at the University of Minnesota) . It would also be of interest to learn about differences

[2] A recent report by Soskin (1959) may offer further support for this conclusion. Psychiatrists and psychologists were first given biographical data about a theology student and then answered multiple-choice items involving predictions of the student's probable behavior in specified situations. The items were based on actual situations that the student *had* engaged in. Then the judges were given additional data; some were given the subject's Rorschach protocol. Others were permitted to observe the student in role-playing situations which they themselves were permitted to stage. Then both groups of judges answered the multiple-choice test items a second time. Neither group of judges showed any greater accuracy of prediction after the additional data than before.

between experienced and inexperienced counselors, between trained, partially trained, and untrained. (As we shall see in a while, there *have* been a few studies of the relative effectiveness of various kinds of test interpreters, but these tell very little about the interpretive *process* and so are not included at this point.) Lacking such research reports, we must perforce base a description of the clinical process of interpretation on the limited research and on the few published discussions of it, as well as on personal experience.

It may be mentioned at this point that three empirical studies which have been mentioned (Koester, 1954; Parker, 1958; Soskin, 1959) suggest that at least three samples of counselors were not making extensive application of what most writers agree are desirable principles of the clinical interpretive process. In all fairness to the counselors involved in the studies, it should be pointed out that each was limited to just one case and was able to study it only in a very second-hand way—by reading case materials, listening to a recorded interview, or at most, observing the person. Also, during the process of "thinking out loud" in two of the studies, important elements of their thinking may have been lost. It is certainly not justifiable to generalize from their diagnostic behavior in such circumstances to their normal behavior as counselors.

THE CLINICAL PROCESS

It is well to keep in mind the fact that we are dealing here only with the *bridges* between two points. The points themselves remain precisely the same as in the case of statistical bridges; at the one end are data about a person (obtained from tests, school records, interviews) and at the other end are the situations or activities which the person is considering entering or engaging in (a college curriculum, an occupation, a marriage, or psychotherapy). The basic model, for our present purpose, is the same: We stand on one side of a river with our client, trying to help him to explore some of the territory on the other side, so that he may better decide where among the various communities on that side he would like to live. The question at hand is: Which bridge would suit our needs best? To complicate the situation none of the bridges leads to the places being considered but only to points from which those places can be viewed, sometimes not very clearly. Furthermore, on the opposite bank one cannot travel very well between bridges, so that each time one has seen the view from the far end of a clinical or a statistical bridge, he must return to this side of the river. To get another view of the countryside, a different bridge must be crossed. Counselors can help their clients to locate the bridges, to make the trips across, and to try to make out the different views from the other side —of the job, the college, or whatever. Later, the client must make the trip to his destination alone, without the counselor as guide; only at that time will he, or we, truly know how he will fit into that community.

Since it is only the crossing which differentiates the two major methods, the interpreter needs the same minimum competencies regarding the two sides (see Fig. 7.1). On the one side, he must know his tests (and other sources of data) —their nature, characteristics, norms, and uses. Crossing to the other side, he must know a great deal about the territory there—the activities and the ways of living being considered. However, as we shall soon see, the clinical method requires even more of the counselor, in the way of these kinds of competencies, than does the statistical.

Steps in the Process

Coming now to the clinical process itself, and drawing heavily on descriptions by McArthur (1954a) and Super (1957b), as well as research reports previously summarized, it seems to involve a series of deductive and inductive reasoning activities, which increase in complexity as one proceeds. Some details of the process are depicted graphically in Figure 9.1.

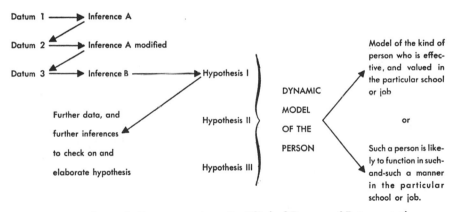

Fig. 9.1. Schematic Representation of a Clinical Process of Interpretation

The crux of the process is the building up of a model of the person, or as it has been called by others: a "hypothetical person" (Pepinsky and Pepinsky, 1954), a "clinical construct" (McArthur, 1954a), a "conception of a person" (Meehl, 1954), or a "picture of his client" (Super, 1957b). This model—as lifelike as we can make it—is then compared with the various situations or activities on the other side of the bridge, and judgments are formed as to how the two are likely to interact.

The model is built through a series of steps, beginning with *inductive inferences* from individual data, then comparing inferences with each other, retaining the compatible ones and rejecting or modifying others as contradictions appear, testing each inference against new data, and thus moving on to the next step of stating *hypotheses* which pull together several inferences into a broader pattern. The hypotheses are themselves tested for consistency with other hypotheses about the person and tested also against new data to see whether the hypotheses will accept them. At this point, there is one of the greatest challenges to the counselor's capacity for flexibility, for he must be able to give up or at least to modify an hypothesis in the face of contradictory data. This is, as emphasized by the Pepinskys (1954), one of the occasions in which the counselor functions both as counselor and as scientist. That is, while trying to be helpful to his client, he tries also to maintain the scientific attitude, which here is exemplified in a high degree of readiness to give up a belief or an hypothesis that does not hold up in the face of empirical data. There is at this point some *deductive* thinking: If this hypothesis is true, then it should follow that such-and-such would be found in further study of the case. Failing to find such-and-such, and finding instead its converse, we are forced to question the hypothesis as it now stands.

Also stressed by recent writers on the subject (McArthur, 1954a; Meehl, 1954; Shoben, 1956; Super, 1957b), is the great importance of building an *individual* model for each client and letting the model develop from the facts about him, rather than trying to force the facts to fit a preconception of the person—a stereotype based perhaps on an overly rigid theory or on a lack of awareness of the diversity and uniqueness of human personality.

Stern, Stein, and Bloom (1956) have contributed a thorough analysis of the *criterion* side of Figure 9.1. They propose a model-building process for the criterion which in some ways parallels the model-building process for the individual. Applied especially to the selection of students for admission to a college, they describe first the Analytic approach, which involves many hours of discussion with faculty members. Through the discussions and through intensive clinical study of selected students, they develop a model of the kind of student whose abilities, values, goals, and activities are most desired and most rewarded in that institution. With this kind of model available, the clinical interpreter can compare the model of an individual whom he is counseling with the model of the "ideal" student for a particular college or the "ideal" employee for a particular company.

These authors recognize the very time-consuming nature of the Analytic approach and suggest three other methods which have also yielded useful results. The Empirical approach is the familiar one of testing groups which have been previously identified as "good" and "poor" students, or employees, then looking for tests or test items which differentiate the two groups. The Synthetic approach involves first hypothesizing a personality variable which appears to be important in a particular school or job. Then an instrument is constructed to measure just that variable and is tried out with appropriate samples. Finally, the Configurational approach makes use of the discriminant function or of inverse factor analysis to seek configurations or patterns of traits which together lead toward success or failure in a particular school or company.

Stern, Stein, and Bloom are in all of this emphasizing the importance of knowing the specific situation about which interpretations are to be made. Clinical interpretation of tests should benefit greatly from more systematic study of the situations about which predictions and other interpretations are to be made. This is a point on which Horst was previously quoted, and it will be re-emphasized in Chapter 10.

The literature in guidance and counseling does not supply us with very many illustrations of this clinical process, but the few which are available may prove to be rewarding reading, particularly for the counselor who has lacked an opportunity to go over his cases in a laboratory or practicum setting. Actual case material and their interpretations may be found in the following sources: Bennett, Seashore, and Wesman, 1951; Bordin, 1955; Callis, Polmantier, and Roeber, 1955; Darley and Hagenah, 1955; Hahn and MacLean, 1955; Kirk, 1952; Rothney and Roens, 1949; Super, 1949. Also, the brief thinking-out-loud by a counselor, quoted in Chapter 3 of the present work, and the cases to be presented in Chapter 11 serve as further illustration of the process of interpretation.

For a more specific demonstration of some of the interpretive steps which have been discussed, the following tailor-made case is presented. It is fabricated, in that it is not based on a real-life case. On the other hand, very similar people with similar characteristics do exist and are familiar to many counselors. The "case summary" is given in brief excerpts. Between the excerpts are comments in brackets intended to indicate which steps and principles in the process of clinical interpretation are being illustrated.

THE CASE OF FRED

Fred, a high school sophomore in a community with a wide socioeconomic range, came to the counselor's office and, upon being invited to begin, stated that he was having difficulties with his school work and was in danger of failing some of his subjects. He asked for advice on raising his grades.

[What inferences or hypotheses can be made from the information so far? The number is so great that it would be uneconomical to spend time going through all the possibilities. A counselor who operates in a stereotyped fashion, perhaps because of an impossibly heavy case load, might at this point administer a reading comprehension test or a study habit inventory, or he might even start giving advice about studying more efficiently. In either case, he has in effect concluded that the problem in *this* case is one of defective reading or study habits, or at least he has decided, from the one fact given him, that one of these areas is the most likely to represent the cause of the problem. Whatever the inference, such an interpretation would represent a serious lack of individualization; instead, a pet theory is being applied to all.]

It was then learned that Fred was in the college preparatory curriculum.

[Here again is an opportunity to reach premature conclusions—for example, that Fred is in the wrong curriculum and should change, or that he should give up any plans to attend college. What inferences and hypotheses *can* validly be made at this point? Again the possibilities are so numerous that it would be unwise to go any further than the most tentative thought that our client may be in a program which is inappropriate for him.]

From his record card, it was found that, on a test of scholastic aptitude given in the eighth grade, the student had an IQ of 93.

[Now we really have the first basis for a specific *inference,* namely, that Fred may lack the degree of academic aptitude necessary for college and for a college preparatory course of study. We realize, however, that it would be foolhardy to reach a hard and fast conclusion from one datum.]

The counselor administered a different scholastic aptitude test and found that the IQ this time was 89. His judgment was that testing conditions were good, that the youngster was properly motivated, and that there was good reason to consider this an accurate reflection of Fred's present level of functioning.

[The inference from this datum is the same as before, and therefore the first one is supported.]

Looking at Fred's school record, it was discovered that the junior high school grades were not quite as bad as the current ones but nevertheless were below average as compared with his peers.

[Here is further confirmation of the *inference* that Fred's ability to do well in school is limited. The new information also suggests an *hypothesis*: that Fred has been approaching the limits of his capabilities with each succeeding year.]

It was also learned from the record that Fred did average work in elementary school.

[The *hypothesis* previously stated receives further support and is, therefore, retained. Now the temptation is great for the busy counselor to take action, say, to present Fred with the facts and expect to have him take the "reasonable" step, which might be to transfer to another course of study. The careful interpreter, however, knows that only one hypothesis is in and even that one is tentative.]

In the course of the interview, it was learned that Fred's father is an assembly worker in a local plant and completed two years of high school.

[A new *inference* is drawn, namely, that Fred selected the college preparatory curriculum through lack of parental guidance and that neither he nor his parents understood its purposes and the difficulties he was likely to encounter.]

A little later in the interview, Fred said that his mother was an elementary school teacher.

[The plot thickens. From his knowledge of occupational and social status and its effects on values, the counselor will *infer* that Fred's mother is likely to put great value on higher education and on the attainment of professional status. The *hypothesis* which now follows, from this *inference* and from the other data, is that Fred is in the college preparatory curriculum because of parental (at least *maternal*) pressure. There are now two contradictory hypotheses: one, that Fred's inappropriate placement in the academic curriculum is a result of *ignorance,* the other, that it is a result of parental *pressure.*]

Using a multifactor test battery, in order to help locate some noncollege occupational areas to suggest to Fred later, the counselor found that the boy was quite high on several nonverbal parts and consistently low on several verbal parts. He was especially low on a part which requires much reading.

[The situation is now becoming *more* complex rather than being solved. The counselor may now, from the *inference* of nonverbal ability being higher than verbal ability, *hypothesize* the possibility of a reading handicap or a more generalized verbal handicap. This could also explain Fred's relatively poor grades and his low scores on single-score tests of scholastic aptitude.]

Having by this time established a pretty good relationship with the boy, the counselor then asked Fred about his parents' feelings regarding his school work and his future plans. Fred opened up gradually and related that his mother has always been very ambitious for him and that she was critical of his poor school grades. His father, on the other hand, whom he feels more similar to in temperament, does not feel that college is especially important. Fred is quite confused between these two pressures.

[The counselor now feels ready for a *higher order hypothesis,* one which ties together several of the hypotheses already stated: Fred is capable of having done much better in school than his record would indicate, but has underachieved as a result of identification with his non-school-oriented father. In addition, the reading handicap may well be, as has frequently been found by counselors and psychologists, a way of fighting back against maternal pressure. This is no longer a "simple" problem of getting Fred and his mother to accept the idea of a transfer from one curriculum to another. Instead, having built up a picture— incomplete and sketchy as it is—of Fred and his family constellation, we now move in the other direction and try to *deduce* what might be the results of one or another course of action. What, for example, are the chances of Fred's recouping his previous losses and reaching the point of being able to do well enough in an academic program to get into a college? This will depend in large measure on his degree of motivation, which in turn will hinge on whatever resolution can be made of the parental differences regarding Fred's goals. Perhaps by talking with Fred we can get some clearer idea of his readiness to identify with his mother's goals (which may be more suitable than the father's, in terms of utilizing the boy's capacities), even though he does not identify strongly with her as a person.

It may be desirable to invite in one or both parents before we are ready to make a prognosis. After all, we know the situation only as Fred perceives it and is ready to report it. He may be misinterpreting the attitudes of one or both parents and may therefore be acting toward or against a straw man. It is quite certain that Fred's chances of succeeding in a college preparatory course at the present time are almost nil; this prediction can be made with confidence from available data, such as test scores, previous grades, and his expressed confusion regarding goals. If any of these can be changed—whether through remedial work, change of attitudes, or change of parental behavior—the prognosis might be quite different.

On the other hand, Fred may be a far happier and more effective adult if he becomes a skilled worker, or perhaps a technician. This would utilize the abilities which, at this point, are his strongest and would make unnecessary any major remedial work in reading and other academic areas. To explore this possibility, it might be helpful to use one or two interest inventories; even more important would be an extended discussion with Fred of his past experiences in various kinds of activities, and his feelings about the alternative vocational plans and the roles they imply.]

THE CLINICAL PROCESS: FINAL COMMENT

Before leaving the description of clinical test interpretation, a few further points should be made:

1. The logical analysis of the process, as reported above, may imply that the process as carried on by counselors is also that logical and neatly arranged. Actually there are probably wide differences among counselors in this regard (again we must depend largely upon speculation, because of the small number of research reports). However, it is not likely that many counselors follow very strictly the steps outlined in Figure 9.1: datum to inference, inference to additional data or further inference, inference to hypothesis, and so on. In actual practice, an hypothesis may come to the counselor's awareness in a fraction of a second, before he has *consciously* thought through the various data and their respective inferences upon which the hypothesis was based.

2. The total interpretation for any one case is rarely completed in a single period of time. More usually, it is a process which begins, consciously or otherwise, with the first contact either with the client directly or with any case materials—records, test data, or application form. Willy-nilly the counselor develops impressions and begins to conceptualize the client—to build his model—from the first moment on. Furthermore, the process continues throughout the duration of contacts with the case, both during and between interviews. As with all problem-solving—and test interpretations can be seen as problem-solving on the part of the counselor (Koester, 1954)—there is uneven progress, there are periods of stalemate, and there are periods of sudden insight.

Unfortunately, many counselors (especially in agencies) are unable to benefit from this "developmental" kind of interpretive thinking because their work is compressed into a short period of time and sometimes follows a stereotyped pattern: intake interview, tests, interpretive thinking, closing interview. In these arrangements, the full possibilities of interpretation may never be realized because of lack of calendar time, even when there is a generous amount of clock time. In schools and colleges, on the other hand, there is a greater potentiality for long-range developmental interpretation, since a "client" may be known to a single counselor, or at least to the guidance department, for a period of years. During this time, there are many opportunities for the counselor to continue collecting new data and to continue polishing and repolishing his "theory of the individual." Perhaps most valuable of all is the opportunity to see how predictions actually hold up as the student comes into interaction with various courses, teachers, and extraclass activities. This provides unequalled (though often untapped) opportunities to check oneself as an interpreter, to evaluate one's interpretive work, and to improve the quality of interpretations through this feedback.

3. Related to this developmental aspect of the clinical interpretive process is the *role of the client* in the process. Super (1957b) has pointed out, for example, that sharing tentative interpretations with the client provides a safeguard against serious errors in the process. The degree of participation permitted clients varies greatly among counselors; some counselors, at one extreme of this particular dimension, present the client with a finished product in the form of conclusions, recommendations, or statements of what they may expect if they choose this course of action or that. At the other extreme are counselors who do very little interpretive thinking themselves but who bring to the interview the individual test scores and then encourage the client to join them in a mutual process of educing implications from the scores.

Another facet of this problem is the effect on the process of appraisal of the personalities of both client and counselor. What information will be revealed by the client, whether through his responses in interviews or on tests, is itself a product of the kind and degree of relationships he has with the counselor. Similarly, the counselor's interpretations are a function of his own personality, insofar as it affects his understanding of a particular client. Gustad concludes from a review of work in this area: ". . . we should envision the evaluative process as one in which the client reveals or conceals, distorts or not whatever information he can; where the counselor perceives or neglects, ignores or distorts the information received; where the final product almost certainly contains significant traces of the counselor and, hopefully, fairly adequate descriptions of the client" (Gustad, 1957, p. 248).

We shall not pursue this point any further now, since it will be considered in the context of *reporting* test data in later chapters. For now, however, it may be said that, except for very few counselors, the client plays a part in the interpretive process, if only that of rejecting an interpretation.

CHAPTER 10

Evaluation of Statistical and Clinical Approaches

NOT VERY MANY STUDIES have been done of the efficacy or validity of clinical interpretations of tests. Counselors for years seem to have followed interpretive procedures learned in graduate school or, more often, developed by themselves on the job, without a great deal of effort to evaluate their work. During the 1940's and earlier 1950's, the counseling field, largely in response to the ideas of Carl Rogers and others, moved in the direction of placing more emphasis on the therapeutic than on the appraisal or diagnostic aspects of counseling. Renewed interest in appraisal was noted in the counseling literature of the mid-1950's, but now at a more advanced level. One of the most stimulating voices was that of Paul Meehl, at the University of Minnesota, whose book, *Clinical vs. Statistical Prediction* (1954), challenged many assumptions regarding the superiority of the clinical method of appraisal. Additional stimulation came from the Kelly and Fiske report (1951) of a large-scale attempt to predict success in clinical psychology training programs, in which report a few of our counseling instruments such as the *ACE* and the *SVIB*, used mechanically, outshone the far more expensive projective tests and clinical interviews in efficiency of prediction. In defense of the clinical approach there have been several articles in the journals and a number of speeches at professional conventions; they have, at least, begun the long process of finding out what the clinical method is good for and what its particular contributions may be, and how it may best be used.

FOR THE STATISTICAL APPROACH

To begin, Meehl's summary of the literature up to 1954, in his book, revealed that ". . . empirical evidence concerning the relative efficacy of the two methods of prediction is largely wanting" (p. 83). Counselors generally seemed to assume the superiority of the clinical method, whereas statisticians and many experimentalists assumed the opposite. Meehl disposed nicely of a number of philosophical arguments against his demand that the clinical method stand up *empirically*. His criterion for comparison of clinical and actuarial methods is simply this: Which one, in well-controlled studies, predicts more efficiently? This avoids some of the fruitless debates regarding the particular merits of each method and insists that whatever value a method has must be demonstrable in what decision theory refers to as the "pay-off." That is, the information yielded by any test interpretation must noticeably improve the accuracy of prediction, whether used for selection, diagnosis, or whatever. The clinical interpreter, Meehl insists, must state his interpretations in testable form: "If X enters this college he will probably achieve a barely passing average"; or "Y is likely to attain success in this occupation"; or "repeating the second grade should lead to improved reading and arithmetic attainment for Z." No one case can be a sufficient test of the interpreter's accuracy, any more than one case would be an adequate test of an actuarial prediction. When a number of cases are available, however, it becomes possible to compare the accuracy of clinical predictions with those which would come from chance alone, and to compare them with actuarial predictions.

With these stipulations, Meehl reviewed the available studies. A fairly typical research project was an early one by Sarbin (1943), who compared the prediction of grades in college by statistical and clinical methods. For the former, a clerk simply substituted each student's college aptitude test score and high school rank in a regression equation that had been developed from an earlier sample at the college. Clinical predictions were made by several counselors, most of whom had a doctorate. They were able to use, in addition to the college aptitude test score and high school rank, a variety of additional data including test scores, a biographical form filled out by the student, and an interview with the student. At the end of the first quarter in college, each student's honor-point ratio was ascertained, and correlations were computed between it and the two predictions—that from the clerk and that from the counselor. For the clerk, the correlations were .45 for men and .70 for women. For the counselors, the respective correlations were .35 and .69. The correlations for the statistical method were found not to be significantly different from those obtained by the clinical method. Sarbin also reports a number of other findings from his data, including the fact that his clinical predictors tended to overestimate grades, whereas the statistical predictions neither overestimated nor underestimated grades of the group as a whole.

Meehl (1954) analyzed a number of studies such as this one, including some which dealt with prediction of flying skill, of parole violation, and of the outcomes of psychotherapy. Each of the studies in some way offers a comparison of ratings made mechanically with those made by counselors, clinical psychologists, and others. Often there are aspects of the research design or of the statistics used in the particular study which preclude any hard-and-fast conclusions as to the superiority of one method over the other. One of the major problems is that some of the studies he examined were excluded from further consideration because the clinical and actuarial predictions were not made from exactly the same data. For example, he did not use most of the Kelly and Fiske material because the clinicians had available to them, at least for some parts of this study, information other than the tests—such as interviews and discussions with other clinicians. Meehl included in his final tabulation only those studies in which *sources* of information were the same for both actuarial and clinical predictions, so that the only variable would be the "method of combining data," or, as we have labelled it here, the bridge. This raises a serious question of methodology, which we shall pursue later.[1]

Using these ground-rules, Meehl reports that he found:

. . . from 16 to 20 studies involving a comparison of clinical and actuarial methods, *in all but one of which the predictions made actuarially were either approximately equal or superior to those made by a clinician.* . . . In about half of the studies, the two methods are equal; in the other half, the clinician is definitely inferior. No definitely interpretable, fully acceptable study puts him clearly ahead. In the theoretical section preceding, we found it hard to show rigorously why the clinician *ought* to do better than the actuary; it turns out to be even harder to document the common claim that he in fact does! (p. 119; italics in the original).

Since Meehl's 1954 appraisal of the literature, there have been reported several further documentations of the superiority of statistical-mechanical methods over clinical (Holtzman and Sells, 1954; Meehl, 1956; and Pierson, 1958). Meehl's 1956 report applied the same methods of comparison to the task of "personality description"—similar to our own Descriptive type of interpretation. He reported a doctoral dissertation done at Minnesota by Halbower in which there was developed a mechanical means for deriving from *MMPI* profiles a personality description of the person (the method is too complex to summarize here). Then a fresh batch of *MMPI* profiles was submitted both to the clerk and to several trained clinicians, including some with the Ph.D. and six years of experience. Not one of the clinical "personality descriptions" correlated as well as the mechanical "cook-book" approach with the criterion, which was a personality description made by therapists who had seen the subjects in therapy for at least ten hours and who also had available the case folder data.

[1] Even in some of the studies where clinicians had available to them *more* data than did the statistical clerk, the clinicians were inferior to the clerks in hit-rates.

FOR THE CLINICAL APPROACH

Support for the superiority of clinical methods of interpretation comes in two recent reports (Holt, 1958; Trankell, 1959). These studies contain some suggestions as to reasons for the findings of some of the other studies in the area. Holt criticized much of the earlier work on the grounds that, first, clinicians had not always used the techniques with which they were most skilled, and, second, that clinicians sometimes were making predictions about criterion situations that they were not well-enough acquainted with. He reports a study which was designed to test the validity of these ideas. Clinicians made predictions of the success of psychiatrists in training at the Menninger School of Psychiatry, in three different ways. First, they made "naïve clinical" predictions, with no prior study of the criterion. Second, they made predictions after having information which was based on an intensive study of the training program and the characteristics deemed necessary for success in it. For the third set of predictions they had, in addition to all the information about the criterion situation, a great deal of data about the individual, rather than just a test or two and an interview. This latter condition Holt refers to as a "sophisticated clinical" interpretation. Predictions made under the first and second conditions were not very successful, but the "sophisticated clinical" predictions were significantly better.

Holt's study points up some of the conditions which are necessary in order that clinical predictions may become more efficient than they have been found to be in much of the research. We shall return to this topic in a later section. However, his study does not offer an adequate set of data for comparing the *relative* merits of clinical and statistical methods. Very few details are given of the statistical approach as used in his study; for the most part, the tests used for statistical predictions seemed to be the ones which clinical interpreters had been using: *Wechsler-Bellevue* and *Rorschach*, plus the *Strong Vocational Interest Blank*. The failure of the *Strong* to predict the criterion in this study is indeed a point in favor of the clinical method. However, an adequate evaluation of mechanical methods would require a more thorough battery of tests than seems to have been tried here.

Trankell (1959) found that assessments by psychologists of candidates for airline co-pilot training (in Sweden) were more highly correlated with success than were test scores. In seeking to explain the superiority of clinical methods, he emphasizes the importance of the selection and training of the assessors, but unfortunately does not give very many details regarding methods of selection or training. His study also fails to be an adequate test of the relative superiority of clinical and mechanical methods. The clinical predictors had available to them several tests and other data (such as biographical information) which were *not* quantified and subjected to mechanical prediction methods. As with Holt's study, the major contribution seems to lie in the suggestions of conditions under which clinical interpretations are most effective.

An Evaluation

Additional discussions of the clinical-statistical controversy may be found in reports of symposia in the *Proceedings of the 1955 Invitational Conference on Testing Problems* (1956) and in the Fall, 1956, number of the *Journal of Counseling Psychology*. It seems to the author that at this point the weight of evidence is in favor of the accuracy of statistical or mechanical methods over clinical, *in those situations where both are used in their usual manner.* This is to say that regression equations, expectancy tables, discriminant functions, and other similar statistical techniques seem to do a better job of predicting success in schools and on jobs than do counselors with average or better training who have the usual amount of knowledge of the situations in which they work and about which they make predictions. It seems to be true that carefully selected and trained clinical predictors, who make an unusually extensive study of the criterion situation (as in the studies by Holt, 1958, and Stern, Stein, and Bloom, 1956) may do as well as, or sometimes better than, the clerk or machine. However, as Meehl has pointed out (1954), even if the clerk and the clinician do equally well in a given situation, the clinician's method is far more expensive. It makes sense in these situations to utilize the clerk for the predictive work and to save the more expensive and less available time of the clinician to do things that clerk and machine can *not* do as well. Suggestions along these lines will be offered in later paragraphs.

It would seem then that several kinds of action are implied. First, a large percentage of time and funds should be put into development of statistical interpretation formulas, tables, and other devices for as many as possible of the activities that our clients must choose among (school subjects, college curricula, and occupations). Second, we need to continue to study the advantages and disadvantages of each of the major approaches, in order to understand what the mechanical methods can do better and what the clinical methods can do better. Third, we need, as clinical interpreters, to find ways to do a better job of clinical interpretation in those situations where this approach is the superior one.

Succeeding paragraphs attempt to explore further some of these implications.

WHAT CAN EACH APPROACH DO BETTER?

Although a good deal more research is needed to answer this question at all adequately, some suggestions may be be made at this time.

1. For a large number of the *run-of-the-mill estimates* of how different kinds of people may be expected to function in various educational and occupational settings, mechanical methods seem to be the more promising. Mechanical methods in these applications seem to organize efficiently the relationships which exist between test and other data on the one hand and criteria of success on the other. The mechanical methods, when used well, provide information about which variables *are* related to the particular criterion (grades, supervisor's ratings) and which are not and should therefore be ignored in the appraisal of an individual. Mechanical methods also tell how each valid predictor should be weighted. There is some reason to think that counselors, when making clinical predictions, are more prone to be thrown off by irrelevant data about their clients and to give inappropriate weights to some data.

2. At the moment, *counselors have little choice but to use clinical methods for many situations;* the paraphernalia of actuarial interpretation —the tables, formulas, and machines—are with all too rare exceptions a vision of the future. The only alternative to clinical interpretation is not to use tests.

3. Even in the utopian era (some do not see it as such!) in which well-developed actuarial prediction tables and the other paraphernalia are available for large numbers of occupations, school courses, and for conditions such as juvenile delinquency and school dropout, *it is inevitable that for many of these situations there will not be tables or formulas.* Sometimes this will be true because the occupation or course is *new,* or has *recently changed* in some significant way. Sometimes there will be new criteria for old occupations or courses. In other instances, it may be that our client is considering a course of action which *happens so seldom* that statistical data cannot be accumulated in any numbers. For example, it might be that he is considering a rare occupation—one taken up by a very small number of people, such as city manager. Or perhaps he would like to institute a new kind of business enterprise, one that has never existed in just that form. In either case, the actuarial data are not available, and clinical predictions must be made.

4. Another instance in which actuarial methods are not likely to be of much help is that in which the *predictor is a rare occurrence.* Meehl offers this "special case" as an example:

If a sociologist were predicting whether Professor X would go to the movies on a certain night, he might have an equation involving age, academic specialty, and introversion score. The equation might yield a probability of .90 that Professor X goes to the movies tonight. But if the family doctor announced that Professor X had just broken his leg, no sensible sociologist would stick with the equation. Why didn't the factor of "broken leg" appear in the formula? Because broken legs are very rare, and in the sociologist's entire sample of 500 criterion cases plus 250 cross-validating cases, he did not come upon a single instance of it (Meehl, 1957: pp. 269-270) .

It is at times like this, says Meehl, that we should "use our heads instead of the formula."

In counseling we occasionally come upon an instance of a characteristic that is so critical (though rare) that we must permit it to override what would otherwise be the prediction. Take, for instance, the case of a college freshman who has high test scores but is somewhat lacking in self-confidence; the expectancy table might show that his chances of attaining a *B* average in college are 80 in 100. However, if he comes in the following week, quite distraught, and tells us that his father committed suicide and left little insurance, we would seriously reconsider our prediction, since we know these new data to be extremely important, even though we may know of no actuarial (or even clinical) data showing their relation to college grades. Similarly, we would generally be quite discouraging about any individual's plans for a career as a concert musician, knowing that even among those with high scores on appropriate tests and good grades in music courses, very few can expect success. But if Carol has studied for two years with Mrs. Winston, a music teacher whose judgment we know to be excellent, and is judged to have a rare talent, we might be inclined to change the prediction of success markedly, say from 1 in 1,000 to 1 in 10.

5. It also seems unlikely that actuarial tables will be of much use in some of the more *complex diagnostic interpretations,* as when we try to make sense of a set of apparently contradictory test scores, where we must take into account a whole host of factors—attitudes toward the tests, reading handicap, the effects of anxiety, the influence of home and family, and others. In these cases, there is a continuous process of interpretation, during which interview data lead to hunches which are tried out with tests, the results of which then lead to further hunches which are presented to the client in tentative form. Together counselor and client proceed through the learning process, as if groping their way through a maze. Probably the majority of Genetic interpretations would fall in this category. In trying to figure out how a person got to be the way he is, why he became a poor reader, or why he has unrealistic goals, we are far more likely to find our inferences and hypotheses in a clinical process of interpretation than by the use of mechanical interpretive devices.

We have dealt here with some of the *applied* considerations; the topic has been discussed at more theoretical levels (Humphreys, McArthur, Meehl, Sanford, and Zubin in *Proceedings of the 1955 Invitational Conference on Testing Problems,* 1956; McArthur, Meehl, and Tiedeman in the Fall 1956 issue of the *Journal of Counseling Psychology;* Meehl, 1954; Meehl, 1956; Meehl, 1957), and the interested reader is referred to these sources.

Finally, it should be noted that there are some who feel less sanguine about the long-range possibilities of actuarial bridges than has been the general tenor of our remarks. Super, for example, says:

Since in vocational counseling a great variety of data are evaluated, and since so many occupations are likely to be considered that regression data are not available, the first question (that of the relative validity of statistical vs. clinical prediction) is not of practical importance. The relative validity of regression and appraisal techniques needs to be considered in selection, but not in counseling programs (1957b: pp. 156-157).

McArthur (1956) seems to feel that the *Dynamic Model* (building up a picture of the individual in the clinical interpretation process) is inherently superior to the *Trait Model*. The latter is essentially the actuarial kind of bridge, predicting from a trait within the individual to a later behavior with which this trait has been found to be associated. In his view of the situation, it is not a matter of using the model-building approach only as a second-best method when actuarial tables are not available. Rather his judgment is that in the long run more accurate interpretations will be made from the Dynamic Model, because it provides a picture of the total functioning personality, from which many inferences may be drawn as to how this person will function in a variety of situations.

For now, this is as far as we can go with the debate on this one particular point. The weight of available empirical research evidence seems to be in favor of the efficiency of the actuarial method of handling test data, but there is a strong case for the value of clinical methods for at least some kinds of interpretation.

IMPROVING CLINICAL INTERPRETATIONS

No one is likely to deny that at present the actuarial method is of little practical use to counselors. Whether we use clinical interpretation as the method of choice or as a makeshift, we have a responsibility to use it as well as possible. Toward this end, the following suggestions are offered for *optimal effectiveness in using clinical interpretive methods:*

1. The counselor must *know his tests.* He must know them as a skilled cabinet-maker knows his tools—what each can actually do, what its special features are, and what it cannot do. He must know how dependable the scores are, what kinds of validity have thus far been demonstrated (even if not the specific validity he is looking for), and what the norms mean in terms of the people he deals with. These things are learned initially in courses in tests and measurement, but they change, and it is necessary to keep up with new developments as they are reported in journals, in books, and by test publishers in the form of revised manuals and other materials.

2. Since he uses test and other data to build a model of the person, it is

necessary that the counselor *know a great deal about people,* their personalities, their functioning, and how they differ from one another. This calls for a background in psychology, particularly in the areas of personality and individual differences, as well as in sociology and anthropology, to name only a few of the important related areas.

3. The clinical process, as described earlier in this chapter, involves careful reasoning, testing out of hypotheses against each other and against new data, and then deductive inferences as to how this person is likely to behave in such-and-such situations. Although we are sorely lacking any clear evidence as to the kinds of people who do this sort of thing best, there seem to be involved here at least two major skills. The first is *creative skill* in producing likely hypotheses—taking separate pieces and developing a structure to hold them together. Second, there is what might be characterized as *scientific rigor and cautiousness,* as seen in the willingness to modify or reject an hypothesis in the light of new data and the ability to stay with a set of data until quite certain that enough consideration has been given to various possible interpretations.

4. Moving on to the other side of the clinical bridge, the counselor must know quite a bit about the *situations about which he makes inferences.* If he is a junior high school counselor who helps ninth graders to select their high school curriculum, he really should know what is involved in the general course as contrasted with the commercial course and the vocational agriculture course and the other alternatives. This requires familiarity with many details: the specific subjects taken in each curriculum, something about the contents of each course, the kinds of youngsters in each curriculum, and the fields of work they are prepared for in each. Similarly, the vocational counselor in a high school or agency must know something about the actual activities in the particular occupation being considered, so that he may judge how this person as he sees him is likely to function. The educational counselor who works with high school seniors in choosing colleges must, if he lacks actuarial data, know something about each of the colleges being considered if he is to be of any help beyond the vague generalization: "Oh, you'll probably do about average in an average college, and not so well in a more competitive one."

How does the counselor know all these things? First, by using all the published resource materials he can find: college catalogs and directories, occupational monographs, briefs, and handbooks. Second, by keeping up with the professional literature which reports research pertinent to schools, colleges, and occupations. Any study of the predictive validity of tests for an occupation or a school course is potential grist for the counselor's mill. If he doesn't have any concrete evidence regarding what it takes to succeed at the *ABC* automobile assembly plant in his city, he can at least find out what the published research has shown to be the case at the *XYZ* assembly plant in another city. The list of resources at the end of Chapter

4 gives some idea of the materials which may be useful in this connection. Third, one can learn a great deal by visiting schools, colleges, plants, and business offices. Many high school counselors make it a rule to visit college campuses on a fairly regular basis, but it is probably not unfair to state that school and agency counselors for the most part have had personal contact with very few of the work situations which their counselees will enter. Yet it is difficult to conceive of meaningful clinical appraisals or predictions being made in the absence of detailed information about those situations. Finally, there are occasions when a professional counselor can receive help from specialists in occupational and educational information.

It is clear that the alternative to doing the research involved in the collection of actuarial data is itself no easier and no less demanding on the counselor.

5. The counselor needs to *study himself as an interpreter*, both to check on his hit-rate, as well as to find out something of his biases. An interesting approach toward the latter goal was reported by Barrett (1958). Although done in a situation where job candidates for industrial jobs were being appraised by a university testing bureau, the method itself could be used in counseling settings just as well. A factor analysis was done of the tests and other sources of data used in the appraisal program, including tests of intelligence and personality, projective tests, and interviews. Then the ratings of the "final rater" were correlated with these factor scores. It was found, for example, that ratings on Promotability were strongly affected by intelligence test scores. Another finding was that ratings in general were very much influenced by the judgments of an earlier interviewer and by the report of a clinician who used projective tests. A similar analysis might be made of the appraisal work of any counselor who will put his appraisal conclusions into some sort of systematic form, such as ratings.

Another approach to the evaluation of counselors' predictions is reported by Walker (1955). Data concerning sixty former high school students were given to twenty-five counselors five and six years after the students had left school. The counselors were asked to estimate the educational and occupational performance of these students after leaving school, and these estimates were compared with the students' actual later record. It was found that these counselors predicted success in school better than they did success on the job, and that their predictions for brighter students were more accurate than for duller students.

An interesting technique for improving the accuracy of prediction by a feedback method is described in a study by Thomas and Mayo (1957). The counselors in this study assisted Marine Corps recruits in deciding which one of eleven schools they would attend; each school trained men for a particular occupational specialty. These counselors made predictions, for each of 1315 recruit counselees, regarding the degree of success that the recruit was likely to attain in the school which he selected. Later, each counselor received a report regarding his counselees, showing the relation between his predictions and the actual grades received in school. He was also given the names of the counselees about whom his predictions were the most in error, with the suggestion that he study their records to try to locate the sources of error. Then predictions were made for the next 1647 recruits who were counseled. Major errors (those in which the prediction was more than one category removed from the actual grade attained) were reduced from 18.8 per cent of the total number of predictions to 10.5 per cent. Minor errors (one category off) were unchanged, and correct predictions rose from 31.9 per cent to 42.9 per cent. Another finding was that the counselors made fewer overestimates but more underestimates. This was attributed to the fact that among the first 1315 predictions there had been many errors due to overestimate.

Here again is a practical kind of research which can give counselors some idea of the accuracy of their test interpretations.[2] This kind of self-examination takes more than a little courage to undertake, but in the long run we should be able to expect improvements in test interpretation, both by the counselors who participate in the studies and by others who read published reports of their work. If it is even a small consolation, counselors who find that their predictions are not very accurate have lots of company, even among well-trained clinical psychologists who may spend a day giving projective and other tests and depth interviews, and who may then spend an equal amount of time studying their data before making interpretations.

WHAT OTHER THINGS CAN THE COUNSELOR DO?

Once the counselor accepts the fact that many of the kinds of predictions from tests he is called upon to make may some day be done better by the clerk than himself, he goes on to wonder what he *is* good for and what things he can do to be of service to his clients. There are a number of ideas that need consideration in this connection.

1. The counselor can put more time and effort into the *selection of tests*. By astute use of the interview, and by better acquaintance with tests

---

[2] A more theoretical kind of research is reported by Arnhoff (1954). Although it is not appropriate to report the study in detail here, one of his findings can be mentioned, in part because it is so striking, and also because a few others have reported similar findings. Arnhoff found that untrained college students were more reliable and less variable than clinicians in classifying schizophrenic test responses. The only generalization to be made at this point is that it cannot be assumed that professionally trained test interpreters are always superior to untrained people in their interpretations.

themselves, the counselor can make it more probable that for each client those tests will be used which can provide the best possible interpretive data.

2. The counselor can devote more of his time and energies to helping clients, primarily through the interview, *to deal with* interpretations of tests, and to *use* the information in planning and in making decisions. Meehl (1954) has made similar suggestions with regard to psychotherapy, and they are equally valid for counseling. The hours we can save by letting clerks or machines make some of our interpretations can be used to do more adequately the other things which are included in counseling—the things which *cannot* be done by a clerk or a machine. Horrocks and Nagy (1948) found, some years ago, that ability in diagnosis and ability in therapy are separate abilities, and that those who did well on one (in analyzing a case study) did not necessarily do well on the other. So there is hope even for those who have failed as diagnosticians. They may yet be worth their salt in other ways. In fact, tests at their best—and we are assuming that a good deal more research of the actuarial sort will help get the best out of tests—will surely fall short of perfect prediction. There will always be difficult decisions to make, as in those instances where two courses of action have equal promise, or where the criteria just are not very predictable. There will be lots of opportunity for counselors to exercise their professional skills in helping clients to wrestle with the information provided by tests.

3. In the appraisal process, counselors might well increase their emphasis on the use of *nontest methods of studying people*. Dailey (1958) , for example, has proposed a greater emphasis on the life history study, using the interview as the major tool. In a manner similar to that we earlier described as the clinical process of interpretation, Dailey suggests the organization of a "theory" of the individual (a "model," to use our earlier term) , from which are made inferences of his future behavior in given circumstances. The rationale is that *previous behavior in life situations* is the best possible source of predictions regarding *future behavior in life situations*. This seems to have some interesting similarities in its basic conception to Super's "thematic-extrapolative" method of studying career patterns (Super, 1957a) . There is also some similarity to Tyler's proposal (1959), which was cited earlier, that the individual's *pattern of choices* in the past is perhaps the key characteristic of him as a distinct personality and may be a better predictor of his future behavior than is a measure of his present characteristics. In any case, these would all support the use by counselors of a biographical-historical approach to the study of the individual. Of course, it is entirely conceivable that this approach too could be mechanized, with data collected through the use of standardized instruments and the pattern itself or the extrapolation (prediction) from the pattern arrived at by the use of formulas, tables, or by electronic com-

puting devices. Here again it will be a matter of setting up critical studies to determine the relative effectiveness of counselor and clerk.

The *interview,* although it may be inferior to tests as a source of predictive and other interpretations, could play an important role in providing in a brief period of time at least suggestions about a variety of hypotheses and of areas warranting further exploration. Cronbach (1955), for example, finds an important place for the interview in suggesting critical areas where further information should be gathered prior to any decision. Interviews used thus would be evaluated as contributors of suggestions rather than as precise measuring instruments.

It should not be necessary to belabor the point any further than to mention again that *whatever* kinds of data are used, the basic principle applies: There must eventually be produced acceptable evidence for the validity of predictions made from the data.

4. This brings us to another suggested activity for the counselor: *participation in, and at the very least support of, research.* The formulas and the tables used for actuarial interpretations are the product of research studies, many of them of a quite routine nature, in which relationships are sought between test scores and the criteria which are to be predicted or otherwise interpreted. Counselors are frequently in the best possible position to do these studies. For example, the counselor in a large high school has in his records test scores for all the graduates of his school. Over the years, he finds that quite a number have gone to each of three different colleges. Although he may have a pretty good "table-in-his-head" of the relation between test scores and later success in those colleges, he knows that his memory is far from perfect, and he may well be giving too much weight to his recollections of the graduates he knew the best, or to the ones whose later college records were especially noteworthy. Of one thing we can be quite certain: He is basing his "mental expectancy table" on those graduates who *happened* to report to him their later records at college. With the expenditure of not a great deal of time, this counselor could have a neat set of expectancy tables from which he could, in an instant, find for each student a statement of probabilities of getting certain grades at each college. He might find that this can be done without even the necessity of a follow-up of the graduates; many colleges are willing to furnish data regarding their students to interested high schools. All that might be necessary, then, is to send the college a list of one's graduates who attended there, asking that grade point averages, or whatever data are wanted, be inserted (for a summary of statistical techniques useful in such studies, see Seashore and Doppelt, 1949).

Those high schools which feed large numbers of dropouts or graduates to particular plants or offices can, with similar methods, establish expectancy tables for predicting job success from test scores. Not all companies will co-operate, and it may be necessary to solicit responses from the former students themselves. Here we run into problems of getting 100 per cent returns, and the problem also of the accuracy of some of the responses. However, the resulting data are almost certain to be far superior to the hit-and-miss impressions, of questionable reliability and validity, which are likely to be used instead.

The possibilities are endless: Elementary schools and junior high schools can develop expectancy tables or regression equations which will show the relationship between test scores or grades in that school and later success in a particular school curriculum (precollege, vocational). Similarly, one can study the predictability of success or adjustment in a particular section *within* a curriculum (accelerated, enriched, average, slow, or retarded). In fact, to use an illustration that has been repeated several times, a school can improve the placement of students into sections and into elective courses right in that school by developing expectancy tables for such criteria as grades in courses. In many instances, all the necessary data will be found in existing school records. At all levels, school counselors (and other counselors) could, through such research, save many of the hours that are now spent in trying to figure out the interpretations to be made of test scores and then trying to deal with the resistances of counselees to those interpretations. Both students and their parents (as well as classroom teachers, administrators, and other interested persons) are likely to be more accepting of empirical data than of what appears to be a counselor's subjective prediction. (An example of this kind of local validation work can be found in Fig. 7.4).

Finally, if past experience is any guide, counselors will more than once find that their armchair "guesstimates" have been quite inaccurate and that their advice and recommendations have not been in keeping with the facts.

All these suggested activities have thus far been put in terms of the *practical* values to be derived, and this after all is the primary concern of most counselors. However, the very same studies can also make more theoretical contributions as they accumulate among a number of schools and agencies. It then becomes possible for test authors and others to pull together the results of a number of studies and to reach *general* conclusions about the validities of a particular test or the validities of certain kinds of tests for certain kinds of criteria. Commenting on the general problem of the low level of success of all kinds of predictions—clinical and actuarial—Humphreys (1956) concludes:

... for the situation in which a clinician sees a person briefly and makes intuitive predictions of future status or behavior, I see little hope for the improvement of clinical predictions per se. There is a good deal of improvement possible on the other hand in predictions that we are calling actuarial. This improvement will not take place, however, without a good deal of research. We now have a situation in psychology in which we probably have more tests than there are psychologists doing related research. One of the several important characteristics of this situation is that it allows many degrees of freedom for the operation of chance. I would like to suggest to clinicians that they discard 75 per cent of their test repertoire, perhaps by lot, that they declare a moratorium on the development of additional tests by eager doctoral candidates looking madly for a dissertation topic, and that they concentrate on increasing the complexity of the nomological network, to borrow the term used by Cronbach and Meehl, concerning the tests remaining (p. 135).

A VIEW TO THE FUTURE

We have seen some of the things that are involved in translating a test score into information which will help an individual to grapple with the problems he brings to his counselor: the need to plan a career, to choose among school subjects, to remedy defects in order to be a more effective student or worker, or just to know himself better for the sheer satisfaction of that self-knowledge.

With the reawakening of interest in the appraisal process, now at a much more sophisticated level than before, we face some exciting developments as a number of theorists, researchers, and practitioners attack the problem. It seems likely that there will be considerable development in the next decade or two in both statistical and clinical approaches to test interpretation. The research and the theorizing, and the experience of counselors up to now, have provided valuable background for what is to follow.

CHAPTER 11

Interpreting Test Results:
Illustrative Cases

W E ARE READY now to return to tests at a somewhat more concrete level—where we left them at the end of Chapter 6. Having now built
up some foundations of theory and research, we become practitioners
again and see what applications may be made of the interpretive methods
discussed in the preceding chapters.

The plan is as follows: In this chapter there are several cases, drawn
from real life, but with names and other identifying information dis-
guised. Included for each one is a summary of background information,
the test results themselves, the counselor's interpretations of them, and
follow-up reports where available. In most instances, the test results are
shown on the profile form customarily used, to help recreate the situation
actually experienced by the counselor. In each case the test results are
grouped together so that the reader may conveniently study them and do
his own interpretive thinking before reading further.

The cases are not used for illustration alone; they also serve as vehicles
for explaining and demonstrating important techniques of interpretation.
For example, the case of Robert Martin includes detailed discussion of
the men's form of the *SVIB*, and the case of Kathy Musgrove provides an
opportunity for a similar discussion of the women's form. Within the case
discussions, especially in the earlier cases, there are frequent digressions
to consider principles and problems of interpretation of a particular kind
of test or in relation to a particular kind of situation. The case materials,
then, constitute an integral part of our descriptions and analyses of test
interpretation methods.

In the next two chapters there will be discussions of selected practical
topics regarding interpretation of test data. There is no attempt to bring
together all the information on which interpretations are based, since

that task is truly encyclopedic and worthy of a book itself. There are publications already in existence which include a great deal of material of this kind (see the list of resources appended to Chapter 4). Lacking a single compendium which conveniently brings together the vast amount of information on test validity for various criteria, practitioners will have to struggle with a variety of publications. These include textbooks on tests and measurements, books and pamphlets on the topics about which interpretations are made (occupations, school subjects, marriage, juvenile delinquency, mental retardation, and emotional illness), manuals, bulletins, research reports from test publishers, and relevant journal articles as they appear. To scan all this material is indeed a herculean task, which no counselor can hope to do in its entirety. By sharing the work, it may be possible for several counselors in a single school, college, or agency to develop fairly complete files which make readily available the major findings regarding the tests they use most frequently and the occupations, schools, and other life situations for which their counselees most often need test interpretations.

The following cases are limited to the kinds of educational and vocational counseling problems with which the author has had personal experience in community agencies and on a college campus. Hence they mostly involve adolescents and young adults. They are not intended to represent a cross-section of the kinds of counseling done with this age group or in this area of counseling; they are in fact a very definitely skewed sample. They were selected because they offered opportunities to illustrate principles and practices of test interpretation and because they are cases in which tests seemed to provide helpful information and insight. As a result they tend to include fairly large numbers of tests, and they tend also to be more complicated than usual in terms of the client's internal conflicts, difficulties in making decisions, and so forth. They are probably, as a group, more "difficult" than the majority of cases seen by counselors in schools, and even in many agencies.

Most of these cases have been used for several years in advanced measurement and counseling courses, and for many of the interpretive ideas the author is indebted to graduate students in those classes, who, unfortunately, cannot be credited individually for their contributions. For the interpretations themselves as reported here, however, the responsibility cannot be shared. It is important to underscore the fact that these cases represent primarily the interpretive thinking of one person, whose first-hand counseling experience has been limited to a community agency kind of setting. The author has been fortunate, however, in having had the opportunity for some ten years to participate vicariously, through contacts with graduate students, in counseling as carried on in schools, colleges, the Veterans Administration, vocational rehabilitation centers, and other agencies. Other counselors would undoubtedly have selected somewhat different tests, and the interpretations, especially of the clinical variety, would probably vary to some extent, but perhaps more in terms of emphasis rather than of serious disagreement on conclusions. This at least is the hope.

THE CASE OF ROBERT MARTIN

Contradictory Test Scores

Robert was seen by a counselor at a university counseling center to which he was referred by his high school guidance counselor for help in deciding on his vocational plans. Robert was 17 at the time and a senior in a suburban high school serving a middle- and upper-class community. He was of average height, somewhat slight in build, and had a poor complexion. He spoke seriously, in a controlled manner and with little spontaneity, without humor, often getting lost in details; his manner was in some ways more that of an adult than an adolescent. He expressed interest in mathematics and wondered what occupations related to math might be good choices for him. He said that engineering had been urged on him because "it pays more and is more secure." However, he reported, he hadn't had physics or chemistry and therefore would be handicapped in applying to engineering colleges. He was also considering "mathematician, accountant, and public relations work."

Robert's father was a real-estate broker and, according to the boy, would have liked him someday to go in the business.

The school record itself was not available, but Robert's recollection of his high school final examination grades was as follows:

9th Grade		10th Grade		11th Grade	
Latin	99	Latin	93	Latin	86
Elem. Alg.	84	Geom.	91	Int. Alg.	94
Gen. Sci.	81	Typing	"Passed"	English	86
English	88	English	82	World Hist.	81
Art	"Low"	History	79		

Summer School		12th Grade (1st semester)	
Health	92	Trig.	98
History I	84	Adv. Alg.	86

Unfortunately, the interview was not recorded, so we lack details regarding the reasons for selecting particular tests and the manner of test selection. A fairly comprehensive battery of tests was chosen. (This was an agency in which it was customary to do testing in this way, with the usual assumption that the second interview be spent in going over test results and discussing their implications for future planning. Further interviews were, of course, held as necessary in each case). The *DAT* was

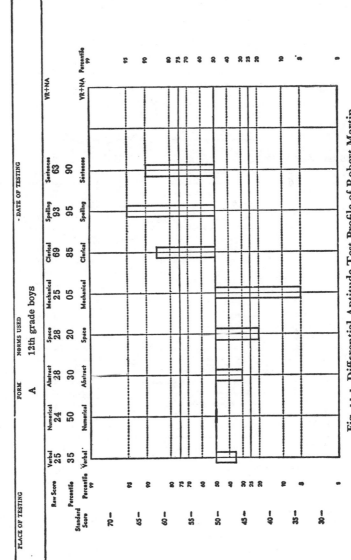

Fig. 11.1. Differential Aptitude Test Profile of Robert Martin
(By permission of The Psychological Corporation.)

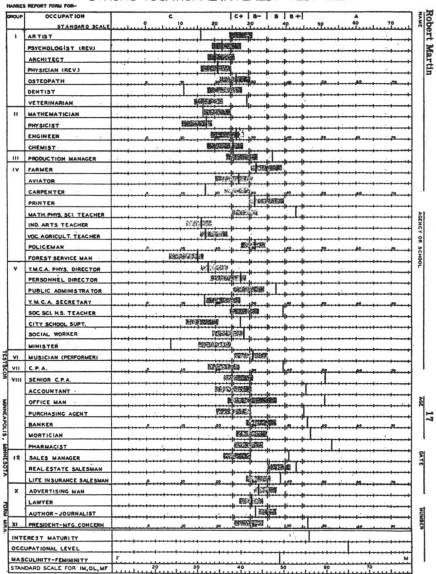

Fig. 11.2. Strong Vocational Interest Blank Profile of Robert Martin
(By permission of Testscor and Stanford University. Copyright 1938 by the Board of Trustees of the Leland Stanford Junior University.)

216

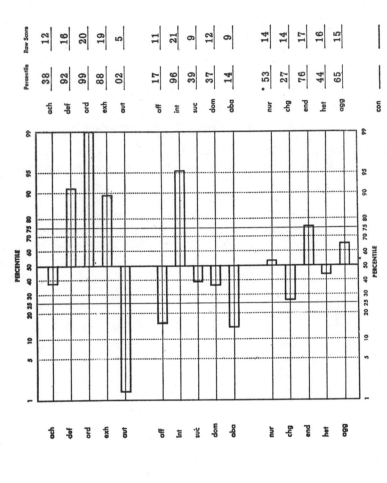

Fig. 11.3. Edwards Personal Preference Schedule Profile of Robert Martin
(By permission of The Psychological Corporation.)

used for information about aptitudes, especially in relation to college. The *Strong VIB* was used to help check the suitability of his interests in relation to the several college-level occupations he was considering. The *Edwards PPS* was apparently used as a general survey of personality rather than for any specific purpose. Finally, the *Cooperative Math. Achievement Test* was included for additional information in this area. which had been highlighted by Robert.

The results of the first three tests mentioned above are presented in profile form (Figs. 11.1, 11.2, and 11.3). The score on the fourth is as follows:

Cooperative General Achievement Test, Part III: Math
Raw Score: 32=80th percentile, 12th grade norms

[The reader may find it useful to study the data and formulate some of his own interpretations before going on to the next paragraphs].

Statistical Interpretations

1. At the simplest level are the percentile and other converted scores, using the most appropriate norms for each test. This step reveals extreme variation among the parts of the *DAT*, above average mathematical proficiency according to the *Cooperative* test, and a scattering of scores on the various scales of the *EPPS*. Statistical interpretation of the *SVIB* will be reserved for later, since the scores are really more complex than a simple norm comparison.

2. At the next level are profile comparisons. For the tests used here there are no known methods for doing this kind of comparison other than one-score-at-a-time. That is, there are no formulas or other methods for comparing Robert's profile on the *DAT* or the *EPPS* with that of any groups in terms of relative scores on parts, or slope between any two scores, or any of the other methods mentioned in previous chapters. We can, however, compare his *DAT* profile with that of a few pertinent groups (see *DAT Manual*, Table 21). We find, for example, that, as compared with a very small sample of college students majoring in science (which included mathematics), he is markedly below their means on all except Clerical, Spelling, and Sentences. The same holds true of his profile as compared with that of a group of Business Administration majors; however, since they are somewhat lower than the science majors on most parts, Robert's scores on the first five parts are not as inferior as before, and his scores on the last parts are even more superior than before.

We can go no further, in terms of prediction, or any other kind of interpretation, with these facts, since there is no mechanical way available for doing anything more with them.

3. At the discriminant level, we come to the *SVIB* scores. It is clear on inspection of the *Strong* profile that Robert's interests have been dis-

criminated fairly well by this instrument.[1] He has a primary pattern (majority of scores being A and $B+$) in Group VIII—the Business Detail group. Using Darley's criterion (a majority of scores to the left of the shaded area), there are no Reject[2] groups, but inspection of the profile shows that Groups I (Biological Science) and II (Physical Science) are very low, neither having a single score above $C+$. Group IX (Business Contact) qualifies as a Secondary group on the basis of a majority of its scores being $B+$ or B. None of the other groups is classified, indicating that they are composed mainly of scores which are below B and either within or to the right of the shaded areas.

Until one has seen a number of *Strong* profiles, it is helpful to check Darley and Hagenah's tables showing the frequency of occurrence of each type of pattern—primary, secondary, and reject—among their sample of college freshmen. Three of these tables are reproduced here.

Table 11.1. Frequency of Occurrence of Primary Interest Patterns on the Strong Vocational Interest Blank, Based on 1000 University Freshmen

Pattern	Number of Cases	Percentage of Sample
No primary	193	19.3
Single primary	410	41.0
Double primary	303	30.3
Triple primary	88	8.8
Quadruple primary	3	.3
Disagreement	3	.3
Total	1000	100.0

SOURCE: J. G. Darley and T. Hagenah, 1955. *Vocational Interest Measurement*. Minneapolis: University of Minnesota Press, p. 86. Copyright 1955 by The University of Minnesota. By permission.

Looking first at Table 11.1, we note that 41 per cent of that normative sample had a single primary group, so Robert's profile is not atypical from this point of view. The data of Table 11.2 show that his single

---

[1] Since a good portion of Darley and Hagenah's book (1955) is devoted to sample *SVIB* profiles and their interpretation, we will not attempt complete coverage of this topic but will, in our discussions here, apply many of the interpretive principles and techniques proposed by them and by Professor Strong himself (Strong, 1943). A recent briefer explication of the use of the *SVIB* (Layton, 1958) may also be helpful to those interested in this complex and fascinating instrument.

[2] The term *Reject* is an unfortunate choice for this purpose, since it implies a conscious rejection of occupational titles or of the activities which they represent. Actually, a low score on an occupational scale of the *Strong* reveals only that the individual's replies to 400 items are less similar to those of a sample of men in an occupation than they are to the replies made by a men-in-general group. *Reject*, then, should be read to mean "Different."

secondary group is also about par for the course, being found with 42.9 per cent of the college sample. His lack of even one reject group is atypical, but with two near-reject groups, Robert's profile is not very far

Table 11.2. Frequency of Occurrence of Secondary Interest Patterns on the Strong Vocational Interest Blank, Based on 1000 University Freshmen

Pattern	Number of Cases	Percentage of Sample
No secondary	260	26.0
Single secondary	429	42.9
Double secondary	234	23.4
Triple secondary	42	4.2
Quadruple secondary	2	.2
Quintuple secondary	1	.1
Disagreement	32	3.2
Total	1000	100.0

SOURCE: *Ibid.*, p. 87.

Table 11.3. Frequency of Occurrence of Reject Interest Patterns on the Strong Vocational Interest Blank, Based on 1000 University Freshmen

Pattern	Number of Cases	Percentage of Sample
No reject	64	6.4
Single reject	232	23.2
Double reject	399	39.9
Triple reject	251	25.1
Quadruple reject	47	4.7
Quintuple reject	2	.2
Disagreement	5	.5
Total	1000	100.0

SOURCE: *Ibid.*, p. 88.

from the average in terms of showing discrimination among groups.

The Interest Maturity *(IM)* and Masculinity-Femininity *(MF)* scores are close enough to the mid-point of 50 to require no special interpretations. The Occupational Level *(OL)* score is high, indicating that Robert has answered more like men in professional and high-level managerial occupations than like those in unskilled and semiskilled occupations (further interpretation of this score is of a clinical nature and will be offered later).

Little attention is paid to those groups which contain only single occupational scales—Group II (Production Manager), VI (Musician), VII (C.P.A.) , and XI (President of Mfg. Concern) except when one or another of these is especially relevant to the client's expressed interests, or when one is very high or very low.[3] In Martin's case the *B* on C.P.A. is worth noting because he mentioned accounting as an occupation being considered. Also, since some of his suggested occupations are in the field of business, the *A* on President of Mfg. Concern is also to be noted.

[*Individual* scales which are members of the multi-occupation groups are usually given less weight than is the *group* pattern in Darley's approach.[4] The rationale offered (Darley and Hagenah, 1955) is that it is usually more desirable for most clients to think in terms of *families* of occupations in order to avoid premature specificity. Also, the *title* of an occupation may have incorrect connotations to a person because of misinformation, bias, or other reasons. The danger of such misperception is reduced by the use of group titles, or of phrases descriptive of the kinds of work or other characteristics of people in that group, rather than the specific occupational title.

The individual scales may be used later, after some preliminary exploration, at the point where the client is ready to think of specific occupations. In some cases it may not be necessary to consider the individual scores at all during counseling, since often a specific choice within the field of work is postponed until general preparation for that field has been completed. Sometimes the individual scales are helpful as *examples* of the occupations to be found within a field. Finally, in rare cases, specific occupational letter scores may be used early in the counseling process. This might apply to those situations mentioned in Chapter 2 in which the counselee has a pretty definite idea of what he wants to do and seeks information of a specified nature to confirm his tentative choice.

In general, examination of a *Strong* profile is best done by moving from the more general to the more specific. First one scans the *entire* profile quickly in order to see whether it is characterized by many highs, many lows, or many moderate scores, or by a combination of these. Profiles in which there are few or no very high or very low scores have tended, in the author's experience, to be found with people who say, "I have no idea what I want to do," or, "I really don't have any strong likes or dis-

---

[3] In tabulating the frequency of group patterns for their norm groups, Darley and Hagenah (1955) absorbed these single-occupation groups into the larger groups with which they were most highly correlated; thus Production Manager was added to Group IV, C.P.A. was added to Group X, and President of Mfg. Concern was added to Group IX. The Musician key was dropped from the tabulations because its correlations with all other groups were too low.

[4] There are some differences of opinion about the merits of this approach, and the evidence to date is inconclusive.

likes; nothing especially appeals to me." Such cases may represent undeveloped or uncrystallized interests, in which case further exploration, tryout, or just a few years of developing may lead to a changed profile. In other cases, however, clients may have to resign themselves to the fact that they may never have a pronounced preference for any single occupation and may have to choose on the basis of other criteria.

At the next level of specificity, one examines the *group* clusters, having classified each one as Primary, Secondary, or Reject.[5] First, gross trends are sought—do the higher clusters tend to be among the first four groups (scientific and technical), in Groups V and IX (contact with people), or in Groups VII, VIII, IX, and XI (business)?

Then comes a study of the specific group scores and combinations of groups (for example, high I and X may suggest scientific writing) .

Finally, one looks at specific occupations, but within the framework of the previous analysis.]

Returning now to Robert Martin, it seems clear from the *Strong* profile that his interests are more similar to those of men in business areas than to others. The major similarity is to Group VIII—those who work in offices and whose functions are either record-keeping or management. There is a lesser similarity to Group IX men—those who sell. Accounting receives a little additional support from the Group VII score, whereas the management area is reinforced by the Group XI score. Robert is least similar to men in scientific occupations (Groups I and II) and bears little similarity to those in technical (Group IV) and social service (Group V) occupations. There is slight similarity to men in Group X (Verbal-Linguistic).

4. Using the regression kind of bridge, we would seek expectancy tables and formulas for estimating Robert's success in each of the areas being considered (plus any others which appear promising from the test data). Unfortunately, the manuals for the *DAT* and the *Cooperative Math Achievement Test,* the two most likely tests to provide predictions of success, provide neither formulas nor the needed expectancy tables. Therefore we will have to use less mechanical methods for this purpose, starting with the reported correlations between these test scores and various criteria of success. Starting with these data, we turn now to a clinical interpretation of Robert Martin's test scores.

Clinical Interpretations

The *DAT* profile presents a set of apparent contradictions. Since the two Language parts, Spelling and Sentences, are measures of school-

[5] It is important that every group be examined systematically and the numbers of *A*, *B+*, *B*, and left-of-shaded-area scores actually counted. Otherwise one runs the risk of overlooking groups that should be classified, because at first sight they don't happen to catch the eye. Also, an unsystematic examination sometimes leads to exaggerated weight being given to a group that has a single extremely high or extremely low score.

learned skills, we would normally expect them to at least approximate the level of Verbal and Numerical scores, which supposedly represent aptitudes for doing well in school. It is precisely in these cases with discrepancies between test scores which are normally at about the same level, that we may learn something useful about the person from an examination of the spread of scores. In Robert's case we would expect the average Verbal and Numerical scores to lead to no better than average grades in high school, but the Spelling and Sentences scores suggest a superior student. Robert's high school record in fact seems to lie somewhere between these two levels of expectation but is closer to the higher scores.[6] His over-all average in subjects for which grades are listed is about 88. To oversimplify the matter, we have a person who is either overachieving [7] or undertesting.

What do Robert's highest scores have in common? In general, they are previously learned material (Spelling and Sentences, also to some extent the *Cooperative Math Achievement Test*) of a relatively concrete nature. The Clerical test is not previously learned, but it is a simple task. Several of his lower scores, on the other hand, are on *new* kinds of problems, where a set of relationships must be figured out (Verbal, Abstract) through the use of inductive and deductive reasoning. His lowest scores, Space and Mechanical, raise serious doubts as to his suitability for engineering, in which he expressed some interest.

Now we can hypothesize that Robert does better with old-learned material than with new kinds of problems, that perhaps he is slow to warm up to a new kind of task, and that he works very hard in school to get the good grades he has received. These are all very tentative hypotheses, to be checked with other data as soon as possible. We might also speculate about a more remote hypothesis: Perhaps we are seeing the effects of excessive anxiety, since he seems to have done least well on the kinds of tests which some studies have found to be most sensitive to anxiety (see Chapter 5) .

Bringing in the personality test, we find significantly high needs (84th percentile or more, which is equivalent to one standard deviation above the mean) for Deference, Order, Exhibition, and Intraception. There are significantly low needs (16th percentile or below, equivalent to one standard deviation below the mean) for Autonomy and Abasement. On the borderline of significance is the low need for Affiliation. Deference and Autonomy can be seen together as lack of need for independence and a

---

[6] This interpretation is based upon knowledge of the particular high school which Robert attended and knowledge of the standards of grading which were customary there.

[7] Obviously this is logically impossible if taken to mean achieving beyond one's capabilities, since if one achieves at that level he must be capable of doing so. The term here is used in its ordinary connotation of achieving at a level higher than would be expected from our knowledge of the person's aptitude. Put somewhat differently, overachievement means a level of work beyond what the person might be expected to handle with reasonable effort and with freedom from excess tensions and other sources of interference.

willingness to do what others decide is worth doing. This combination could support our earlier hypothesis of a boy who works hard to do well in school on the tasks presented by teachers, such as spelling and grammar. Need for Order can also be incorporated into this developing picture of a person with compulsive characteristics—one who likes things in their place and who likes to know exactly what is expected of him. Finally, these characteristics would suggest a person who is rather anxious about school matters, including tests. The Exhibition, Intraception, and Abasement scores do not at this point seem to fit into this model, but, on the other hand, they do not necessarily contradict it. Perhaps as further data are collected and the model is further developed, these three scales will be more comprehensible.

The test data may also be related to three of Robert's statements on a questionnaire used by this agency. First, in response to the question, "What do you find especially difficult to do," he wrote "I find it hard to accomplish anything fast. I have to take my time." (Relate this to the hypothesis that he is slow to warm up to new tasks.) Then, asked to state the things he could do best, he wrote, "I am pretty good with figures and math." (Relate this to the Numerical score on the *DAT*, with which it is not congruent, and to the score on the *Cooperative Math Achievement Test,* with which it is more nearly in agreement). Finally, asked to list his extraschool activities and organizational memberships, he listed only membership in a church organization, no offices held, and no books read.

Add now his reported behavior in the first interview—controlled, serious, lacking spontaneity, and we seem to have a picture, though incomplete, of an inhibited person, one who focuses on details as a way of avoiding the anxieties of interpersonal relations, who is not an easily sociable person, and whose emotions, not given direct expression, reveal themselves in such behavior as blocking on new problem situations.

Second Interview

During the second interview, Robert's counselor reported the test results, throwing out as tentative interpretations some of those mentioned earlier: better on concrete than abstract problems, better with material he has had time to learn well than with new problems, and better with simple than with complex materials. Robert, as perhaps might have been anticipated, offered very little reaction to these suggestions, but he made clear his great surprise at the *DAT* results, particularly the Numerical part.

The counselor, too, at this point found it difficult to explain the *DAT* profile and suggested something that is occasionally helpful: going over some of the test items orally in an attempt to find out just what happened. This technique in effect provides some of the advantages of individually administered tests such as the *Stanford-Binet,* although, obviously, given orally it is no longer a standardized test, the standard conditions of administration having been abandoned. The purpose, however, was to understand the *causes* of the responses rather than to count the number of correct answers, and so the procedure is justifiable, so long as one is aware of its limitations and takes ordinary security precautions to protect the confidentiality of the test contents.

On the Numerical Ability test of the *DAT*, it was found that several errors were due to sheer carelessness and could have been avoided by reducing to simplest terms as called for in the directions for the test. The counselor then asked Robert orally to answer several easy items on the Verbal Reasoning part (having found from examination of the answer sheet that errors had been made throughout the test, on easy as well as difficult items). Asked in each case to tell why he selected that answer, Robert was quite vague, and it seemed clear that he was not approaching the items in a systematic manner but had instead used an intuitive method, almost guessing at some of the answers. The counselor then deviated even further from standard conditions of administration and asked Robert what the principle was for each item; he quickly got the idea and proceeded to answer correctly a number of items, including several difficult ones. The procedure here has much in common with "testing the limits" on the *Rorschach,* seeing whether, with increasingly greater suggestion, the subject can see things he could not see during the original "free association" responses. In this case it appeared that Robert's low score was in no sense a measure of his capabilities but instead a reflection of a disorganized and perhaps panic reaction to the test situation.

Robert gave very little reaction to interpretations of the other test results, relating very little to the counselor, participating almost not at all in the interpretation process, and asking only for conclusions and recommendations: "Does this mean I should go into Business Administration?" This continued for perhaps a half hour, and the counselor felt that little was being accomplished.

Robert's parents had come along and were now invited to join the client and counselor. The father turned out to be a rough-and-tumble, energetic extrovert, apparently disappointed that his son was not, like himself, a salesman by temperament. The mother had more depth and was more insightful. She confirmed the hypothesis about Robert's slowness with new learning situations; he had always been a plodder, she said, finally mastering each subject through dint of much effort.

Asked for implications of the tests regarding Robert's college planning, the counselor stated the *deductions* he made from the *picture* of the boy which had been developed from *hypotheses* based upon inferences: that Robert could be expected to have difficulty in college with each new subject, probably more so than in high school, because the material would be more difficult and the students more able as a group. It was suggested that he would need every minute he could get for his studies, and that therefore his chances would be improved by carrying as light an academic load as could be arranged, and by doing as little outside work as possible.

The College of Commerce seemed more suitable than the College of Liberal Arts (which they had been planning on), first because of Robert's measured interests, and second, because the student body was not as able academically in the former (normative information known by the counselor). All this was generally accepted by the parents and a tentative plan made to explore further the possibilities in accounting, real estate, and insurance before deciding on a specific major area within the College of Commerce.

Subsequent Developments

A year later, when Robert had completed one full semester in the University's College of Commerce, his mother called the counselor, quite frantic, reporting that Robert had "flunked completely." He had received three *F*'s, and his grades were not yet all in. They had had no idea that he was having trouble with his school work, and he had sought no help from his instructors, counselors, or anyone else, to the best of their knowledge. He had a part-time job and was working eighteen to twenty hours a week, apparently with his father's encouragement. Because of factors beyond his control, it was almost impossible for the counselor to see Robert or the parents at their convenience. Therefore he suggested that they talk ₍ₕₑ matter over with the Dean and then consider applying for either the two-year college or for the evening session, in both of which the competition and the pace would be less.

Discussion

In retrospect, it would appear that Robert was both an undertester and an overachiever. In high school, he was able to compensate by long hours of plodding for those factors which led him to do poorly on most of the aptitude tests. In college, perhaps because so much more was expected of him, in terms not only of quantity and quality of work but also in terms of working on his own, Robert "flunked completely." Which were the best predictors? His high school grades correlated best with the Spelling and Sentence scores, but both are poor predictors of college grades. Even the Verbal and Numerical scores, his lowest among the scholastic predictors, would have overestimated his achievement in college. Perhaps this is one of those cases in which the correlation coefficients between aptitude tests and school grades are reduced, because of personality factors which greatly influence the individual's functioning in particular situations.

The case of Robert Martin has illustrated a number of interpretive problems and principles, including the variety of interpretive bridges used with one case. It demonstrates also the need to favor the clinical bridge at the present time, especially for diagnostic work, and the various steps in the clinical process: inferences, hypotheses, an over-all picture of the individual, and finally deductions in relation to various situations and contingencies. Also illustrated is the use of the interview for checking hypotheses by collecting further data and by trying out hypotheses on the client and his family. A special technique used in this case involved extemporizing with tests and departing from standard conditions of administration when necessary for a specific purpose. Obviously more could have been done with the test data available and with further interviews. A different counselor might have used other tests, might have found additional interpretations, and might have been more effective in gaining acceptance from the counselee and his parents of the interpretations and their implications.

A counselor in Robert's school, knowing the teachers and the various subjects, would probably have found the school grades themselves a valuable source of information to contribute to the interpretive process. For example, the Latin grades decreased from 99 to 93 to 86, from the ninth to eleventh grades. Does this reflect the increased difficulty of the material, or increased rigorousness of grading? Perhaps it reflects differences in the *contents* of the courses—say a major emphasis on grammar in the first year (a relatively concrete subject matter which Robert could master through plodding) as contrasted with increased emphasis on reading and meaningful translation in the later years (a subject matter less compatible with Robert's abilities and study habits) .

A counselor with much knowledge of occupations might have devoted a larger portion of *his* appraisal time relating Robert's abilities and other characteristics to the demands of each of the occupations being considered. In any case, the interpretation reported here, long as it is, is only a portion of all the things that might be included in the appraisal of Robert Martin.

THE CASE OF RICHARD WILSON

Taking Stock Before Military Service

We met Richard in Chapter 3 (pp. 50-55), where excerpts from his first interview were used to illustrate principles of test selection.

The questions brought to tests were these:

What are his chances of succeeding in a college course?

What are the relative chances of success and satisfaction in the fields of merchandising, engineering, and teaching?

In particular, to what extent is Richard's slowness a handicapping factor in the area of academic aptitude?

For this latter purpose it was agreed to include both a speeded *(ACE)* and a nonspeeded *(OSU)* test of college aptitude.

Because Richard mentioned quite a variety of fields of work and because he felt quite unsure of himself, a rather comprehensive battery of tests was used. These included college aptitude (*ACE* and *OSU*) and differential aptitudes (*DAT*). Two measures of interests were used: *SVIB* and *California Occupational Interest Inventory*; these supplement each other, since the first is more for college level occupations and focusses on the characteristics of people in the occupation, and the latter covers a broader range and deals with the occupational activities themselves. Finally, there was a personality inventory (*Guilford-Zimmerman*), used partly because he expressed concern about this aspect of himself.

Here then are the results of this battery; the *ACE* and *OSU* scores are shown in Table 11.4. The others are presented in profile form (Figs. 11.4, 11.5, 11.6, and 11.7).

Table 11.4. Test Results of Richard Wilson

Name of Test		R.S.	Percentile	Norm Group
ACE Psych. Exam.	Q	35	24	College Freshmen
for College Freshmen	L	51	18	
	Total	86	18	
OSU Psychological	I	5	10	College Freshmen
Examination	II	10	04	
	III	20	12	
	Total	35	06	

Statistical Interpretations

1. At the first level are the *norm* comparisons of the various tests. It is quite clear that college aptitude scores are low for the samples of colleges used in the national norms. At first glance it appears that his slowness is not a particular handicap, since the *ACE* (speeded) scores are higher than the *OSU* (untimed). The differences between *ACE* and *OSU* scores are even greater than might appear, since at the extreme ends of the distribution, percentiles spread out much more than near the middle of the range, so that the difference between 18th and 6th percentiles is, in terms of ability differences, about as great as the difference between 50th and 75th percentiles. There is a complicating factor, however, which makes us much less certain about the difference; this comes from the fact that these are two different tests, standardized on different populations. Without having tables of comparable scores on the *ACE* and *OSU*, we cannot be sure that differences of the size mentioned here are really significant.[8] (Later, under clinical interpretation, we will offer additional hypotheses regarding these test scores).

[8] See the discussion in Chapter 12 of the variety of factors which might lead to differences in the scores made by a single person on two different tests which presumably measure the same thing.

DIFFERENTIAL APTITUDE TESTS

G. K. Bennett, H. G. Seashore, and A. G. Wesman

THE PSYCHOLOGICAL CORPORATION

New York 17, N. Y.

NAME   SEX   AGE   GRADE

Richard Wilson   M   YRS.   MOS.

PLACE OF TESTING   FORM   NORMS USED   DATE OF TESTING

A   12th -- Boys

	Verbal	Numerical	Abstract	Space	Mechanical	Clerical	Spelling	Sentences	VR+NA
Raw Score	24	6	35	38	46	54			
Percentile	35	05	60	25	45	40			

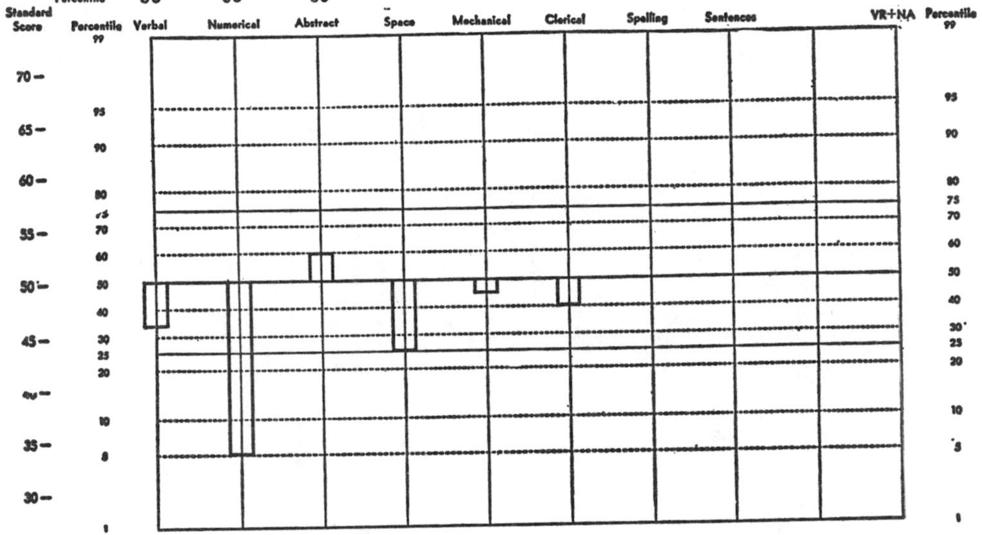

Fig. 11.4. Differential Aptitude Test Profile of Richard Wilson
(By permission of The Psychological Corporation.)

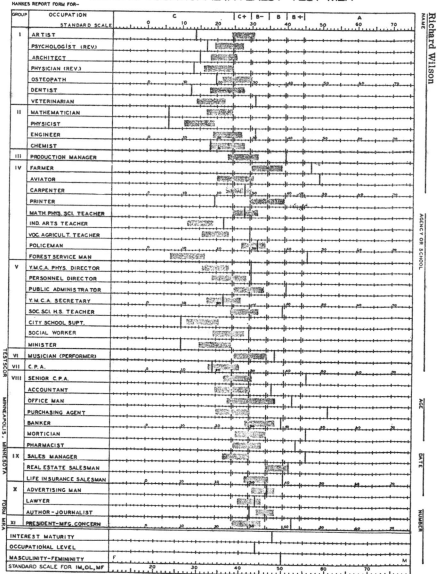

Fig. 11.5. Strong Vocational Interest Blank Profile of Richard Wilson
(By permission of Testscor and Stanford University. Copyright 1938 by the Board of Trustees of the Leland Stanford Junior University.)

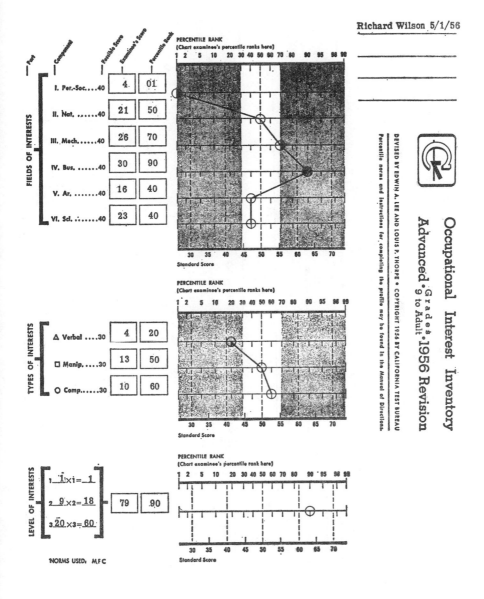

Fig. 11.6. Occupational Interest Inventory Profile of Richard Wilson
(By permission of the California Test Bureau.)

PROFILE CHART FOR THE GUILFORD-ZIMMERMAN TEMPERAMENT SURVEY
For high-school, college, and adult ages

Name: Wilson, Richard   Date: Comment:

C SCORE	G General Activity Energy	R Restraint Seriousness	A Ascendance Social Boldness (M / F)	S Social Interest Sociability	E Emotional Stability	O Objectivity	F Friendliness Agreeableness (M / F)	T Thoughtfulness Reflectiveness	P Personal Relations Cooperativeness	M Masculinity Femininity (M / F)	CENTILE RANK	NEAREST T SCORE
10	30 / 29 / 28	30 / 29 / 28 / 27	30 / 29 / 28 · 30 / 29 / 28 / 27	30	30 / 29	30 / 29	30 / 28 / 26 · 30 / 29 / 28	30 / 29 / 28	30 / 29	30 / 29 · 0 / 1	99	75
9	27 / 26	26 / 25	27 / 26 · 26 / 25 / 24	29	28 / 27	28 / 27	25 / 24 · 27 / 26	27 / 26	28 / 27	28 / 27 · 2 / 3		70
8	(25) / 24	24 / 23	25 / 24 · 23 / 22 / 21	28	26 / 25	26 / 25	23 / 22 / 21 · 25 / 24	25 / 24	26 / 25	26 / 25 · 4 / 5	95 / 90	65
7	23 / 22	22 / 21	(22) / 21 · 23 / 20 / 19	26 / 25	24 / 23	24 / 23	20 / 19 · 23 / 22 / 21	23 / 22	24 / (23)	24 · 6 / 7	80	60
6	21 / 20	20 / 19 / 18	20 / 19 / 18 · 18 / 17 / 16	24 / 23 / 22	22 / 21 / 20	22 / 21 / 20	18 / 17 / 16 · 20 / 19 / 18	21 / 20	22 / 21 / 20	23 / (22) · 8 / 9	70	55
5	19 / 18 / 17	17 / 16 / 15	17 / 16 / 15 · 15 / 14 / 13	21 / 20 / 19	19 / (18) / 17	19 / 18 / 17	15 / 14 / 13 · 17 / 16 / 15	19 / 18 / 17	19 / 18 / 17	21 / 20 · 10 / 11	60 / 50	50
4	16 / 15 / 14	14 / 13 / 12	14 / 13 / 12 · 12 / 11	18 / 17 / 16 / 15	16 / 15 / 14 / 13	16 / 15 / (14)	12 / 11 / 10 · 14 / 13 / 12	(16) / 15 / 14	16 / 15 / 14	19 / 18 · 12 / 13	40 / 30	45
3	13 / 12 / 11	11 / 10	11 / 10 · 10 / 9 / 8	14 / 13 / 12 / 11	12 / 11 / 10 / 9	13 / 12 / 11 / 10	(9) / 8 / 7 · 11 / 10 / 9	13 / 12 / 11	13 / 12	17 / 16 / 15 · 14 / 15	20	40
2	10 / 9 / 8	(9) / 8 / 7	9 / 8 / 7 · 7 / 6	10 / 9 / 8 / 7	8 / 7 / 6	9 / 8 / 7	6 / 5 · 8 / 7	10 / 9 / 8	11 / 10 / 9	14 / 13 / 12 · 16 / 17 / 18	10 / 5	35
1	7 / 6	6 / 5	6 / 5 · 5 / 4 / 3	6 / 5 / 4	5 / 4	6 / 5	4 / 3 · 6 / 5	7 / 6 / 5	8 / 7 / 6	11 / 10 / 9 · 19 / 20		30
0	5 / 3 / 2 / 1	4 / 3 / 2 / 1	4 / 3 / 2 / 1 · 2 / 1 / 0	3 / 2 / 1 / 0	9 / 2 / 1	4 / 3 / 2 / 1	2 / 1 / 0 · 4 / 3 / 2 / 1	4 / 3 / 2 / 1	5 / 3 / 2 / 1	8 / 5 / 2 · 21 / 23 / 25	1	25

Bottom labels (M / F):

	G	R	A	S	E	O	F	T	P	M
	Inactivity Slowness	Impulsiveness Rhathymia	Submissiveness	Shyness Seclusiveness	Emotional Instability Depression	Subjectivity Hypersensitiveness	Hostility Belligerence	Unreflectiveness	Criticalness Intolerance	Femininity Masculinity

Fig. 11.7. Guilford-Zimmerman Temperament Survey Profile of Richard Wilson
(By permission of the Sheridan Supply Company.)

2. Comparing Richard's profile on the *DAT* with those in the manual (Table 21) it is found that, with the exception of Abstract Reasoning he is below practically all the college student samples on all parts. As a whole, his scores seem to be closer to those of unskilled workers than any other group. Again, the Abstract Reasoning is the major exception, but Numerical Ability is well below the mean of *all* groups. All the remaining profile analyses will be made on a clinical basis, since no mechanical profile comparisons are available.

The *Occupational Interest Inventory* *(OII)* shows some spread of scores, from extremely low on Personal-Social to above average on Mechanical and very high on Business. Types of Interest are only moderately differentiated from each other, Verbal being low and Manipulative and Computational, average. Level of Interests is very high.

The *Guilford-Zimmerman Temperament Survey* shows a number of scores that deviate from the mean. High scores point toward Activity, Ascendance, and Sociability, whereas low scores are in the direction of Impulsiveness, Subjectivity, and Hostility.

3. Interpreted on a *discriminant* basis, the *Strong* shows a fair degree of discrimination of Richard's interests among the comparison groups. There are primary patterns in the two business groups, VIII (Business Detail) and IX (Business Contact), though the latter could almost as well be classified as a secondary pattern. The three *A* scores in Group IV (Technician) are noted, although the group as a whole cannot be classified as Primary or Secondary. Finally, there is a reject in Group I (Biological Science), and a near reject in Group II (Physical Science). As in the case of Robert Martin, this *Strong* profile shows greater similarity to interests of businessmen than to those of men in scientific occupations.

The nonoccupational scales are all rather close to the mid-point of 50, but the *OL*, which is at 46, is of some concern, since it may reflect a level of interests below that of some of the professional occupations being considered.

4. *Regression* formulas and expectancy tables not being available, we will have to do this kind of interpretation on a clinical basis.

Clinical Interpretations

Beginning with the two college aptitude tests, we seek possible explanations of the fact that Richard's scores are higher on the *ACE* than the *OSU*. Drawing from the factors which are listed and discussed in Chapter 12, we find several which might be applicable here. First, as has already been mentioned, the tests were normed on different populations, and the percentile scores may not be comparable. Second, the *ACE* is a speed test, the *OSU* a power test; this difference was the very reason for using both tests. The results would, if anything, show Richard to be better under the speeded conditions. Third, the tests differ somewhat in content: The *OSU* is almost entirely verbal and the *ACE* also includes numerical and abstract material. One must therefore consider the possibility that Richard is somewhat better with nonverbal than with verbal material.

With the two tests differing in so many ways, the score difference found between them cannot be interpreted without further data. Fortunately, it is possible to check at least one of the inferences, that dealing with the contents of the tests. If his *DAT* profile showed Abstract and Numerical to be superior to Verbal, this would support the inference that he is better with nonverbal than with verbal content. However, the *DAT* data offer no clear answer, since Abstract is higher than Verbal, but Numerical is lower. The matter remains unresolved, but, with *both ACE and OSU* as low as they are, the difference between them, if there actually is one, fades into relative insignificance.

The *DAT* profile reveals not a great deal of scatter among the part scores, except for Numerical Ability, which is considerably below average. All the other scores are within the average range, with Space being at the low end of this range. With Numerical Ability representing an important symptom of success with school subjects, the prognosis for college work from the *DAT* battery is no better than it was from the *ACE* and *OSU*. Trying to wrest some diagnostic hypotheses from the *DAT* profile, we might suggest that the higher Abstract score represents Richard's level of capability, whereas the Verbal and especially the Numerical scores signify underdevelopment of these more school-related abilities. Some support for this hypothesis comes from the interview excerpt (p. 55), especially Cl. 19 and Cl. 28, where Richard mentioned something he elaborated on in other portions of the interview (not reported in Chapter 3). His statement was to the effect that he had not applied himself to his studies but had put most of his time and energies into athletic activities.

The ability tests are quite consistent regarding Richard's *level*: It seems doubtful that he could handle the work required by most four-year colleges. He would probably have considerable difficulty even in most junior colleges, unless remedial work could change the level of some of the abilities measured here.

For some indication of *field*, we turn to the interest inventories (there has been some evidence that groups of college students in different fields of study differ more in interests than they do in abilities; see, for instance, Berdie, 1955). The *SVIB* and *OII* profiles both support the area of business. The *OII* "Type of Interest" scores also offer support for the hypothesis of greater nonverbal than verbal propensities. Also both interest inventories show a secondary mechanical leaning (*SVIB* Group IV and *OII* Mechanical scale). There seems, however, to be some difference between the two inventories in connection with the *level* of interests, the *OII* score being quite high and the *SVIB* somewhat below average. A suggested hypothesis based upon differences between the instruments is this: The *OII* is more obvious, in the sense that the Level score is based on the individual's choices among descriptions of occupations which are similar in field but at different levels. The status-conscious, aspiring person can easily discriminate the higher from lower-level occupations. On the *Strong*, however, the items which make up the *OL* scale require the respondent to indicate his liking for a variety of things, including occupational titles, hobbies, magazines, and types of people. It is therefore more a measure of one's liking things which are liked by people in higher-level as contrasted with people in lower-level occupations, and many of these differences are not obvious. On the basis of these facts, we hypothesize that Richard aspires to a high level of occupation but that his actual identification (in terms of the likes and dislikes measured by the *Strong*) is more nearly at an average level. The question still remains: What does this mean in terms of occupational choice? After all, the kinds of likes and dislikes measured by the *Strong OL* scale are largely *learned,* so that a boy who grows up in a lower-class family and has limited contacts with children whose parents are in higher-level occupations may have a low *OL* score on the *SVIB,* even though he is genuinely ambitious for a higher-level occupation and has the necessary abilities. Of course, we can deduce that such a person may find himself different from others in the higher-level occupation and therefore not in congenial company. Either he would have to be satisfied with this state of affairs or expect to change in some ways so that he can share more activities and conversational topics with his work associates.

Moving on to the *Guilford-Zimmerman* profile, we have a picture of a person who is outgoing (*S*), dominant (*A*), and spontaneous (*R*), but possibly in an immature way (the combination of *G* and *R*). There is also a tendency toward hostility (*F*). As suggested in the manual for this inventory, the combination of *G, R,* and *F* may be such as to get him into trouble, since it may mean that he tends to act out his hostilities.

Second Interview

The following is a copy of the counselor's notes on the second interview; it is reproduced here in its entirety (except for necessary changes to disguise the client's identity) because it adds to the appraisal picture by revealing the client's expressed feelings about some of the hypotheses:

Asked where he wanted to begin, he first said he had no particular ideas, but then went on to tell a little about his test experiences, said he saw a few weaknesses in himself—in English and Math. Found it a good selection of tests and he felt he learned quite a bit about himself while taking them.

After a few minutes, I suggested we might go over the tests. I interpreted college aptitude as pretty definitely low, with possibility of make-up work in Math and English bringing it up somewhat, but still marginal even for the two-year college. His reaction was that this was lower than he'd hoped, but about what he expected. Said it is a relief to know, that he learned something about himself—as to what he needs to study. He plans to take correspondence courses in the service —mainly in math. (He didn't express feelings to any extent, did much silent staring at *DAT* profile.)

After a long pause, he asked if this meant he should go into merchandising; I clarified concept of field and level; he then clarified that he meant the two-year college level. Again I said it seemed very marginal and we talked briefly about the procedures for entering the two-year college. Then I interpreted interest and personality inventories to help answer his question of merchandising as a career. Interests seem appropriate, and there were no problems here in interpretation or acceptance.

When I introduced *G-Z*, he had some reactions immediately, before I gave any interpretations. He had found it useful to take it and felt that it had helped him to understand himself better. The *G, R, A,* and *S* scores were all accepted and seemed to fit in with the merchandising interests, although I suggested that they pointed more to outside than inside work—perhaps selling. He said that outside buying was what he was thinking about. On the *F* score, he seemed to reject the interpretation and felt that his personal relations were not characterized by hostility or belligerence.

We concluded because of the time; earlier he had mentioned that this would have to be the last interview—he expected to be very busy the next weeks and wouldn't be able to get back in before leaving for the service. He said spontaneously that this had been helpful; I suggested that he had received confirmation of what he had been thinking. He said it had fulfilled his purposes, that he was less tense than when he started, that he had a pretty good idea of where he is heading, that he felt surer than before that he wants to try for the two-year college after getting out of service. I invited him to return at any time—before entering the service, while in, or afterwards. He seemed to have some real feeling on leaving—as if he had developed something of a relationship, though on the surface, one would have not thought so.

IMPRESSIONS: Perhaps he became as involved as he is capable of doing; seems flat affectively, inhibited, untalkative. However, at times, he opened up a little, though never expressing strong feelings directly. Seemed frank, though never got below a superficial level. Hard to judge how valid his final evaluation was; I did not feel that he had gotten as much out of this as he said he did, but maybe my own goals were too ambitious, or maybe there were things going on covertly that I wasn't aware of, in the way of his involvements.

Case closed for now.

Discussion

The test interpretations here seemed to help this client to know himself somewhat better, to confirm a tentative occupational choice, and to eliminate several other occupations which had been given slight consideration. He had already had some experience in a retail store, liked it, and had been encouraged by the officials of the chain to consider a career with them, leading ultimately to a management position. Although the tests could not definitely offer confirmation of his specific career plan, they indicated that the general area of work seemed about as appropriate for him as any. Opportunities in management in a retail business of this kind are available for those who don't have a college education, although some college is a help. Richard could probably handle selected courses on an evening session basis, even if he could not succeed in a full-time junior or four-year college program.

Finally, there is the possibility, as mentioned earlier, that lack of application in school has resulted in his test scores being something of an underestimate of his potentialities. If this is true, remedial work and other efforts to improve might make enough of a difference that he could be a marginally successful student in a college program.

In the preceding two cases, each type of interpretation—Statistical, Clinical, Discriminant, Regression, etc.—was discussed separately. Assuming that the didactic function of such separation has now been served, we will consider the test data of the remaining cases in a manner more nearly approximating that of the counselor on the job. Tests will be examined by *type*—aptitude, interest, personality. In the examination of each test or group of tests of a type, statistical and clinical interpretations will be combined.

THE CASE OF KATHY MUSGROVE

A Bright Girl

With the case of Kathy Musgrove, we have an opportunity to see the results of testing at two different stages: first as a high school senior and later as a college sophomore. The *Kuder* was used on both occasions, so we shall have an opportunity to study the changes occuring over a period of time. Finally, Kathy's case illustrates some interpretive aspects of the *Strong Vocational Interest Blank* for Women.

Phase I: High School Testing

When she came in early in her senior year in high school, at the age of 16, Kathy was reported by the counselor as being a ". . . large, not too attractive, older looking girl who related poorly. Her questions had to do with what college she should go to, since she was interested in journalism. The family had limited means for sending her to college, and preferred a Catholic college." Tests used at that time were the *Kuder Preference Record,* Form B, the *ACE Psych. Exam for College Freshman,* and the *Cooperative Reading Test.* The results are reported in Table 11.5 and Figure 11.8.

NAME _Musgrove_____ Kathy_____ AGE ____ SEX ____ GROUP _____ DATE OF TEST ____
Print   Last   First   Initial   M or F

PROFILE SHEET

• FOR WOMEN •

For Form BM of the
KUDER PREFERENCE RECORD

DIRECTIONS

Follow the directions below carefully. As soon as you have finished a step, place a check in the box at the right to show that you have completed it; then go on to the next one.

1. Fold the answer sheet on the dotted line so that the spaces for indicating scores are facing you. ☐

2. Find the total raw score for each of the nine areas by adding score *a*, which is found on one side of the answer sheet, and score *b*, on the other side. Enter these scores in the spaces marked *c* on the line labeled *Total Scores*. ☐

3. Check each total score again to be sure you have not made a mistake. ☐

4. Enter the nine total scores in the space provided at the top of the chart on this page. If you are a woman, use the chart at the right. If you are a man, use the chart on the other side of this sheet. ☐

5. Find the number in column 1 which is the same as the score you have entered at the top of the column. Draw a line through this number from one side of the column to the other. Do the same thing for each of the other columns. If your score is larger than any number in a column, draw your line across the top of the column; if your score is smaller than any number in a column, draw the line across the bottom of the column. ☐

6. With your pencil, blacken the entire space between the lines you have drawn in each column and the bottom of the chart. ☐

The result is your *"profile"* on this test. It should be remembered that the scores are not measures of ability, but that they represent the degree of your preference for activities in the various fields. Your adviser can tell you how to interpret the profile.

1 38	2 40	3 60	4 57	5 29	6 81	7 24	8 76	9 61
MECHANICAL	COMPUTATIONAL	SCIENTIFIC	PERSUASIVE	ARTISTIC	LITERARY	MUSICAL	SOCIAL SERVICE	CLERICAL

Fig. 11.8. Kuder Preference Record Profile of Kathy Musgrove: First Phase
(By permission of Dr. G. Frederick Kuder and Science Research Associates.)

238

Table 11.5. Test Results of Kathy Musgrove

NAME OF TEST		R.S.	Percentile	Norm Group
ACE Psych. Exam.	Q	*	86	College Freshmen
for College Freshmen	L	*	99	
	Total	*	99	
Coop. English: Reading	Voc.	*	96	College Freshmen
Comprehension	Speed	*	99	
	Level	*	96	
	Total	*	99	

* Raw scores were lost in the process of preparation of these case materials.

Brief Interpretation of the High School Testing

The ability tests leave little doubt of Kathy's capacity for success in any college, both in terms of general college aptitude and in terms of reading in particular. The *Kuder* shows scores above the 75th percentile on Computational and Literary scales and below the 25th percentile on Mechanical and Artistic. On the basis of this first set of test scores her college plans were supported, and journalism seemed not inappropriate in terms of abilities and interest.

Phase II: College Testing

Kathy returned to the same agency (but a different counselor, since the first was no longer on the staff). She was then a sophomore in a local Catholic college for girls, to which she commuted daily from her home. This counselor found her ". . . a tall, pretty, attractively dressed girl who expressed herself well and seemed to relate well to the counselor, but in a somewhat reserved way." (It is interesting to speculate as to whether these differences in perception reflect actual changes in Kathy over the two-and-a-half-year period, or whether they are due to differences in tastes or standards of the two counselors.) Returning to excerpts from the counselor's summary:

Kathy is an English major, has had mostly *A* grades, has decided she definitely doesn't want journalism or creative writing as a career, but is now thinking seriously of law. She wants security, she says, and an occupation that she could enjoy doing "in case I have to work for the rest of my life." She wonders how well qualified she is for law, and what schools might be suitable. We looked at the *Occupational Outlook Handbook* for further information about law but found little that she didn't already know. When we looked at the *Estimates of Worker Trait Requirements for 4000 Jobs,* she seemed delighted (and surprised) to learn that she was well above the minimum requirements for lawyer.

NAME ___Musgrove Kathy_____ AGE ____ SEX ____ GROUP _____, DATE OF TEST ____
    Print   Last   First   Initial   M or F

(Solid lines show later scores. Broken lines show earlier scores. Arrows show direction of change).

PROFILE SHEET

• FOR WOMEN •

For Form BM of the
KUDER PREFERENCE RECORD

DIRECTIONS

Follow the directions below carefully. As soon as you have finished a step, place a check in the box at the right to show that you have completed it; then go on to the next one.

1. Fold the answer sheet on the dotted line so that the spaces for indicating scores are facing you. ☐

2. Find the total raw score for each of the nine areas by adding score *a*, which is found on one side of the answer sheet, and score *b*, on the other side. Enter these scores in the spaces marked *c* on the line labeled *Total Scores*. ☐

3. Check each total score again to be sure you have not made a mistake. ☐

4. Enter the nine total scores in the space provided at the top of the chart on this page. If you are a woman, use the chart at the right. If you are a man, use the chart on the other side of this sheet. ☐

5. Find the number in column 1 which is the same as the score you have entered at the top of the column. Draw a line through this number from one side of the column to the other. Do the same thing for each of the other columns. If your score is larger than any number in a column, draw your line across the top of the column; if your score is smaller than any number in a column, draw the line across the bottom of the column. ☐

6. With your pencil, blacken the entire space between the lines you have drawn in each column and the bottom of the chart. ☐

The result is your *"profile"* on this test. It should be remembered that the scores are not measures of ability, but that they represent the degree of your preference for activities in the various fields. Your adviser can tell you how to interpret the profile.

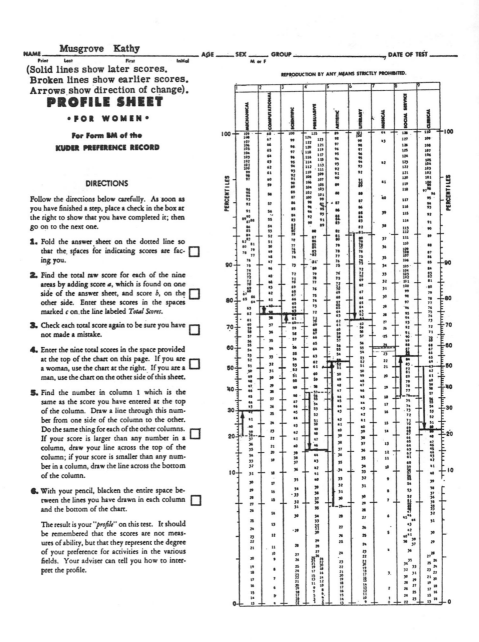

Fig. 11.9. Kuder Preference Record Profile of Kathy Musgrove: Changes from First to Second Testing
(By permission of Dr. G. Frederick Kuder and Science Research Associates.)

240

[For the benefit of the reader who may not have a copy of this resource, these minima are being in the upper 10 per cent of the general population in "General Intelligence" and "Verbal Ability", in the middle third in "Numerical and Clerical Abilities," and in the lowest 10 per cent in all other "Special Aptitudes." Temperamental traits deemed appropriate are those needed in situations involving "Dealing With People" and "Evaluation of Information Against Sensory or Judgmental Criteria." The Interests deemed appropriate are "Preference for Activities Involving Business Contacts with People" and "Situations Involving a Preference for Activities Resulting in Prestige or the Esteem of Others." Physical capacities needed are deemed "Light," and the only physical activities of importance are "Talking-Hearing."]

The counselor's notes continued: "With abilities for Law well-established, it was decided to use tests only in the areas of interests and personality."

Figures 11.9, 11.10 and 11.11 show Kathy's profiles on the *KPR, SVIB,*

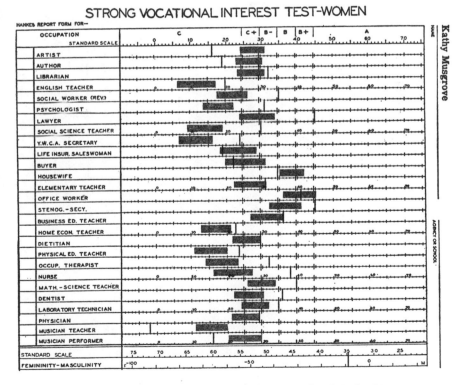

Fig. 11.10. Strong Vocational Interest Blank Profile of Kathy Musgrove
(By permission of Testscor and Stanford University. Copyright 1938 by the Board of Trustees of the Leland Stanford Junior University.)

Edwards Personal Preference Schedule

NAME Musgrove (LAST) Kathy (FIRST) SEX ______ NORMS USED College Women

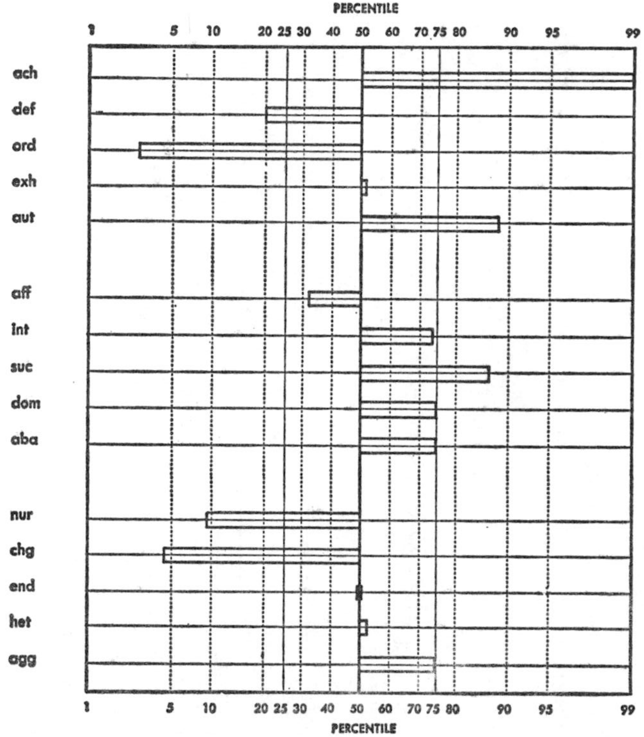

	Percentile	Raw Score
ach	99	24
def	21	9
ord	03	4
exh	52	14
aut	87	17
aff	32	15
int	73	20
suc	86	17
dom	74	17
aba	74	18
nur	09	10
chg	04	8
end	50	12
het	52	14
agg	74	13
con		

Fig. 11.11. Edwards Personal Preference Schedule Profile of Kathy Musgrove
(By permission of The Psychological Corporation.)

and *EPPS.* For ease of comparison, the earlier *Kuder* scores are noted on the new profile sheet.

Interest Measures

Five of the *KPR* scales have changed from one category to another, from significantly high (75th percentile) to the mid-range, from significantly low (25th percentile) to the mid-range, or from the mid-range to one of the areas of significant deviation. First, moving from significantly low to average are Mechanical and Artistic (obviously this method exaggerates some of the changes, as is seen, for example, in the case of Mechanical, which shifts from one category to another but with a percentile score change of only nine points) .[9] Looking at these two as a *craftsman* orientation, there seems to be an increase in this kind of interest. Next, the Persuasive score decrease, accompanied by the Social Service increase, would seem to indicate reduced interest in dominating and leading and increased interest in helping others. Literary goes from her highest score to high average, while Clerical drops from average to significantly low. During the next interview, in which these changes in the *Kuder* profile were interpreted, Kathy contributed to their interpretation by reporting that she was less concerned than formerly with such things as being elected to club offices (Persuasive) . She also said that she was less interested in routine activities and more interested in designing and other somewhat more creative enterprises (Clerical, Mechanical, and Artistic) .

Turning now to the *SVIB,* we find data leading to some interesting hypotheses. Since grouping has not been found to be as meaningful with the Women's form,[10] we devote our attention more to individual scores, with one exception: Approximately halfway down the list of occupations on the profile sheet are four occupations on which scores tend to intercorrelate and which have been called "noncareer" or "masculine association." These occupations as a group require shorter periods of education or training; they are, less often than most of the other occupations, entered into as lifetime careers, and they are more often seen as "fillers" between school leaving and marriage (or child-bearing) and as "something-to-fall-back-on-in-case." (For a discussion of a variety of women's career patterns, see Super, 1957a: pp. 77-78) . To have high scores on these four scales, then, is to have some *interests in common* with women for whom home-making and child-rearing are the major career. This is not to say that high scores on these scales necessarily imply interest in the *activities* of these occupations. Quite to the contrary, in counseling one finds numbers of girls and young women who have high scores on the Office Worker

[9] A table of significant differences for Form C of the *Kuder Preference Record* is reproduced in Chapter 12 as Table 12.2.

[10] As pointed out by Darley and Hagenah (1955) ". . . women's interests are generally less channelized or less professionally intense than are men's" (p. 70) .

and Stenographer-Secretary scales of the *Strong,* yet who have low scores on Computational and Clerical Scales of the *Kuder.* Although there is more than one possible interpretation of this combination of test scores, it is often found to reflect, on the one hand, a pattern of likes and dislikes similar to those of office workers, and on the other, a rejection of the *job activities* of these women. Such rejection of clerical activities on the *Kuder* may indicate, in some cases, genuine dislike for typing, filing, and other office functions. It may sometimes, however, mirror a *learned attitude* toward a kind of work that is regarded as low level by many middle-class and upper-class families.

In Kathy's case, we find something that is often a cause of internal conflict and anxiety among girls—tendencies toward both career and noncareer interests. Looking at the women's *SVIB* profile form, we see that those occupations listed first are of a career nature and tend to be verbal, social scientific, and management in nature. In Kathy's case, there is a high score on the Lawyer scale, and moderate scores on Librarian, Social Worker, and Psychologist. In the lower third of the profile form, among the technical and scientific career occupations, are a moderate cluster in Nurse, Math-Science Teacher, and Dentist. In the middle is a moderately high cluster on the four noncareer occupations: Housewife, Elementary Teacher, Office Worker, and Stenographer-Secretary. Finally, the *M-F* score shows a tendency toward interests more similar to those of men than of women, another symptom of a career orientation. Putting all this together, including the *Kuder* profile, we may hypothesize a combination of career and noncareer orientations, with possibly resultant feelings of conflict and anxiety, especially since this is a girl whose family does not seem to have encouraged her advanced education.

Personality Inventory

The *Edwards PPS* profile can be interpreted also to show a combination of tendencies which would support hypotheses already formulated. On the side of career orientation can be aligned the above average needs for Achievement and Autonomy, combined with a low average need for Deference; these could describe a person who wants to be looked up to as capable and who likes to work with some degree of independence. The above average Succorance score and the below average Nurturance score may be interpreted together as showing tendencies to be dependent on others emotionally, but not to want others to be emotionally dependent on her. This is as far as the counselor went in interpreting these scores prior to seeing Kathy for the next interview.

Second Interview

Since Kathy was so bright and seemed ready to play a rather active role in the counseling process, the test results and some of their interpretations were presented to her rather completely, and further interpretation was done co-operatively in the interview. The career versus noncareer issue received the lion's share of attention, at least partly because the counselor felt that it was likely to be important and therefore gave it emphasis. As the interview progressed it became evident that this did indeed represent one of Kathy's major needs for clarification. She had apparently done quite a bit of thinking about this aspect of her planning, and the counselor's interpretations and understanding, combined with the permissiveness of the situation, soon evoked her own statement of intention: to work for a few years, then marry, begin a family, and later, after ten years or so, to return to work. She did, however, express some concern about finding a husband; with the counselor's help, she soon developed a verbal blueprint for a husband (itself a kind of clinical prediction) : He would have to be accepting of her high level of abilities and interests and would therefore in all likelihood himself have to be functioning at a high level. Kathy added that he would also have to be brighter than she and taller (this would mean six feet or more) . Thus she made explicit a self-concept of a woman who combines a professional career—and some of the masculinity *this* implies—with a career as homemaker and mother—and the femininity which commonly goes with *this* role.

The test interpretations, although they added no truly new information, did serve to organize and clarify some of the major issues and areas of concern and thereby to help Kathy to know herself more completely. Not to be ignored is the strong possibility that Kathy received reassurance from the implications of the test interpretations, namely that this is a kind of problem which many other girls face, and that hers was not a unique or "abnormal" situation. Kathy also seemed to need, and to receive, some reassurance about her capabilities. Perhaps because of lack of parental encouragement or understanding of her high-level goals, she had found it difficult to accept herself as a person of really superior abilities.

Kathy left counseling with the stated intention of entering law school after three years of prelaw, perhaps also trying to get her B.A. in the three years by acceleration.

THE CASE OF HAROLD MANN

Underachiever?

Harold was a 17-year-old high school senior who had been referred by his high school guidance counselor. He knew that he would not graduate that year because of failures in several subjects, and he sought help in planning his further education. When discussing his activities, he told about liking to wash his father's car and take it to the service station for gas and servicing. He told also of a part-time job selling women's bags in a downtown store. Harold described with enthusiasm his great satisfaction in sizing up each customer when she walked in and trying to guess which models she would like well enough so that she might buy *two* handbags (prediction by the clinical method, based on nontest data!).

Harold appeared older than his age; his tenseness and restlessness, his deep voice, heavy build, careful grooming, and talkative, opinionated manner combined to give an over-all impression of an aggressive, outgoing man of action. One might expect him to ask for help in planning a career in the world of business—perhaps in selling or in small-business management—where his academic insufficiencies would not be a serious handicap. But Harold went on to tell, with equal aggressiveness and an air of self-assurance, of his occupational thoughts of the past: medicine, law, geology, forest ranger. He had dropped most of these, he said, for one reason or another, and now law was the major interest. Asked why he chose this, he mentioned, in this order: the prestige, the income, and the fact that you were helping people. Last, but by no means least, was the fact that his family and friends expected it of him.

Harold's father had a successful retail business of a semiprofessional nature (say, of the order of a pharmacy, in which both commodities and professional services are offered). They lived in a neighborhood consisting mainly of $15,000 to $35,000 homes (in terms of 1957 prices).

This, then, was the presenting problem: How can I attain my goal? How can I graduate from high school, go to college, and then law school? Harold was evasive when the counselor attempted to push beyond the presenting problem, and he avoided any topic which implied the possible inappropriateness of his stated goals or the existence of other problems. The counselor felt that it was futile to attempt at that point to get below the surface and that, if he was to help the boy at all, he would have to start with him on his own terms. Accordingly, tests were selected in two areas: differential aptitudes and interests (Harold rejected the suggestion of a personality measure on the grounds that he knew himself well enough). The profiles for the *DAT* and the *SVIB* are reproduced here as Figures 11.12 and 11.13, respectively.

Aptitude Tests

If approached "blind," with no other knowledge of the person, this *DAT* profile would be judged to be that of a boy who does his best thinking in the mechanical area, although not outstanding even here, and who would have a hard time in a college preparatory program. The likelihood of successful graduation from a college or a law school would receive, by either statistical or clinical methods, not a trace of confidence. Using the normative profiles in the *DAT* manual, for example, Harold's profile is seen to be, except for the Mechanical Reasoning score, below the averages

INDIVIDUAL REPORT FORM

DIFFERENTIAL APTITUDE TESTS

G. K. Bennett, H. G. Seashore, and A. G. Wesman

THE PSYCHOLOGICAL CORPORATION
New York 17, N. Y.

NAME: Harold Mann | SEX | AGE (YRS. MOS.) | GRADE

PLACE OF TESTING | FORM | NORMS USED: 12th - Boys | DATE OF TESTING

	Verbal	Numerical	Abstract	Space	Mechanical	Clerical	Spelling	Sentences	VR+NA
Raw Score	19	6	22	44	49	42	0	27	
Percentile	20	05	15	30	55	05	01	25	

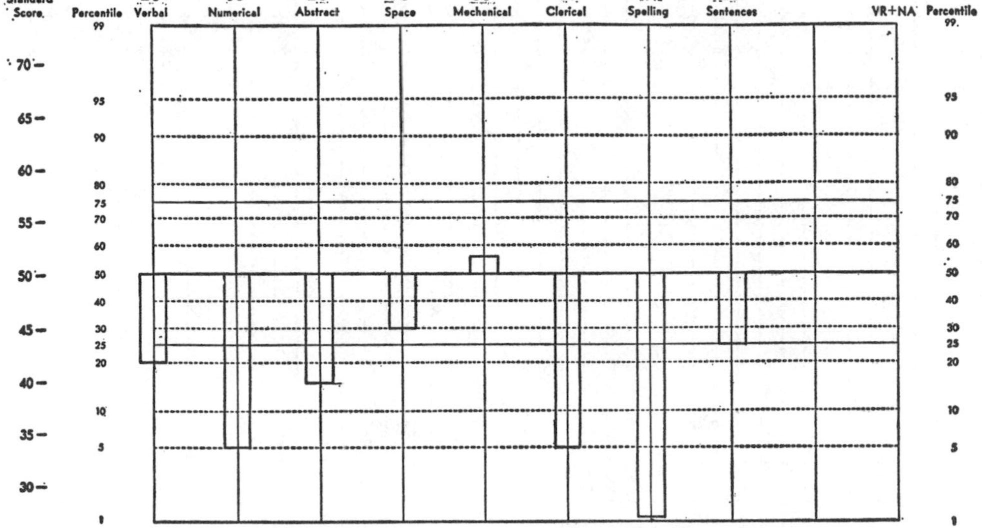

Fig. 11.12. Differential Aptitude Test Profile of Harold Mann
(By permission of The Psychological Corporation.)

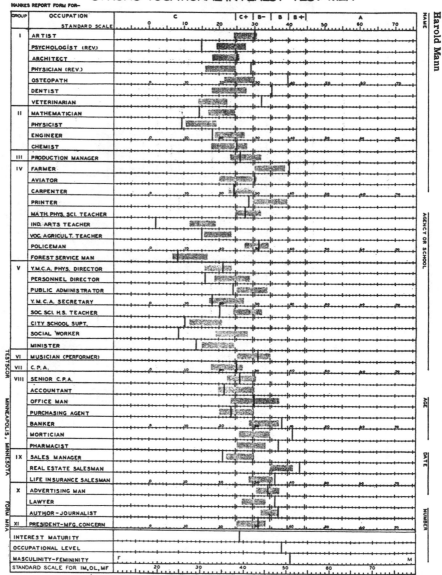

Fig. 11.13. Strong Vocational Interest Blank Profile of Harold Mann
(By permission of Testscor and Stanford University. Copyright 1938 by the Board of Trustees of the Leland Stanford Junior University.)

of all college and occupational samples, including the semiskilled and unskilled occupations.

These inferences received some confirmation later from test scores obtained from Harold's high school: In his sophomore year he had received an IQ of 86 on the *Otis Quick-Scoring Mental Ability Test*, and, a few months later, IQ's of 97 and 99, respectively, on the Language and Nonlanguage parts of the *California Test of Mental Maturity*. Considering that the *Otis* contains a combination of items similar to those included in the Verbal, Numerical, Abstract, and Space parts of the *DAT*, the average of these four parts might be compared with the *Otis* score as a *very* crude comparison. The average standard score of these four is approximately 40, which is one standard deviation below the mean. The *Otis* IQ of 86 therefore represents a rather close approximation of the *DAT* scores. (This kind of comparison ignores the fact that, even when standard scores are used, there is an assumption of equivalence of norm groups for the two tests being compared. See the discussion in Chapter 12 of this problem of equivalence of scores on different tests.) Compared in the same way, the *CTMM* scores are significantly higher than either *Otis* or *DAT*—a standard deviation higher. One possible explanatory factor might be sought in a tendency for the *CTMM* to yield higher IQ's than the *Otis* and some other intelligence tests of this kind. Unfortunately, the two studies reported are in disagreement, one (Los Angeles City School Districts, 1950) finding higher IQ's on the *CTMM*, the other (Mouly and Edgar, 1958) finding higher IQ's on the *Otis*. In any case, the highest estimate of mental ability is average. From his high school record (details not available, but reported in a phone conversation with the school counselor to be barely passing until the senior year, when he failed some subjects) and all available ability tests, college seems a remote possibility, and law school even more remote.

Interest Measures

The *Strong* profile shows only fair discrimination; there are no primary patterns, a clear secondary only in Group IX (Sales), and something short of a secondary in Group VIII (Business Detail). The group containing the Lawyer scale (X) consists of two *B*'s and a *B*—, a weak pattern indeed for serious consideration of the field. According to data reported by Darley and Hagenah (1955), and reproduced in Table 11.1, only 19 per cent of their sample of college freshmen had no primary groups, making this an atypical profile. Among the nonoccupational scales, Interest Maturity (Standard Score 40) suggests that Harold's pattern of likes and dislikes is more like those of 15-year-olds than of 25-year-olds.

[The psychological and predictive significance of the IM scale is not well understood. Strong (1943) felt that it represented level of general maturity and therefore could be used as an index of the probable stability of obtained scores; the higher the IM score, the more likely it is that the person is mature and that his interests are crystallized. Stordahl (1954), however, found that the degree of change among *SVIB* patterns of one group, from high school to college, were not related to their IM scores. Woolf and Woolf (1955) found one IM correlate that may prove to be valuable; in their study of college freshmen, lower IM scores were found more often in the cases of students whose Quantitative *(Q)* score on the *ACE Exam* was much higher than their Linguistic *(L)* score. It may be that this finding is related to an interpretation of increasing scores on the IM scale as representing lesser interest in things and greater interest in people. Perhaps those who are more interested in people are, as a result or as a cause, more able in verbal than in nonverbal reasoning. Darley and Hagenah's data (1955) would seem to support this interpretation; among their college freshmen, the highest mean IM score was found among those who had a primary pattern in the Social Service Group, whereas the lowest mean IM score was found among those with a primary pattern in the Physical Science group.]

In any case, Harold's *SVIB* profile must be interpreted with extra caution because of this low IM score. On the whole, we would see the profile as showing tendencies toward clusters in the Business areas, and quite clearly away from the Physical Science, Technical, and Social Service areas. This interpretation (essentially a statistical one) reinforces Harold's description of his bag-selling experiences but does not offer particular support for his expressed interest in Law as a career.

At this point in the appraisal process, a noncollege level of work in the business field, with emphasis on selling, seemed to offer the most suitable prospects for Harold. In addition, it would also be desirable that his occupation, or at least the specific job, make use of his mechanical comprehension, which was Harold's highest *DAT* score (and also an area of reported interest—working with the family car). As a matter of fact, a selling function in the family business seemed a good choice. The family business was thought of for one additional reason: With Harold's very poor school record and the unlikelihood of his being able to handle college work, his chances of getting a high-level job on a competitive basis seemed rather slim.

Subsequent Interviews

Harold was seen for three interviews after the tests were completed, with an additional interview occurring some months later. He was quite rejecting of the test data and especially of the *DAT* scores. (He rationalized and was quite evasive) when the implications of the test and nontest data were discussed, yet continued to return for further interviews. He said, for example, that his *DAT* scores would have been higher if he had worked harder in school. Asked to estimate how much higher they would have been, he was surprisingly modest, adding only an average of ten percentile points to each score. By the fourth interview, the counselor had moved quite a bit from his usual more permissive approach, since he saw the client getting nowhere, and he pressed much harder for a facing of reality. Finally, in the fourth interview Harold brought in the idea of taking a hotel management course or a general business administration course in college. He planned to arrange for tutoring or to attend a private college preparatory school in order to make up his deficiencies.

At no time was it expressed by Harold in so many words, but in effect he was during the process of counseling lowering his goals in the face of reality, as represented by the counselor and his tests, as much as he could. The fact is that there was no disputing the predictions emanating from the test data and from his school record. There was, however, a set of nontest data which led to a quite different prediction. These nontest data all have to do with his socioeconomic status; the prediction from *them* was that Harold *would* go to college. The implied "if-not" was indeed frightening enough to the boy to lead to all his rationalizations and evasions. Not to attend college and not to go into an upper-middle-class job might mean losing some of the things he valued—his family's approval, his friends, perhaps even the chance to marry one of the girls in his social circle. A whole way of life was threatened, and Harold found it difficult indeed to accept the counselor's version of reality.

The following fall, Harold called for another appointment. He was taking several very easy courses at his high school so that he could graduate in mid-year. His reason for coming was not made clear; he still insisted that he would make it and with a tone of bravado told the counselor he'd be back in four years, a college graduate.

Discussion

Two important interpretive principles stand out in the case of Harold Mann. First, there is the necessity of including significant nontest data in our predictive efforts. To do this in no way negates the validity of interpretations made from tests alone; rather it is a matter of reconciling contradictory predictions which stem from two different data. The final prediction one would make in such cases normally is a compromise between the two. In Harold's case, the best guess is that somehow he will get a high school diploma and that somehow, somewhere, he will get a year or two of college or some "respectable" post-high-school course, such as the hotel management course he suggested. He probably could not qualify for the semiprofessional education needed for his father's occupation; otherwise this would be our best guess for his future, with his later entry into the family business. He might enter the business, but as a salesman and manager rather than as a pharmacist.

A second principle to be noted is that our test (and other) data sometimes do not include important facts about abilities, interests, and personality traits. Harold, for example, had a "gift of gab"; his reported success in selling bags to women was entirely credible to the counselor in view of the way he handled himself in the interview. Yet, this fact would never be obtained from the *DAT* profile (nor from any other test commonly used in Guidance and Counseling). The clinical test interpreter, then, remembering that some highly significant human abilities are not measured at all by tests, must perforce seek evidence of these abilities elsewhere, especially in cases such as Harold's, in which a client with limited academic abilities tries desperately to find something positive on which to build. School, college, and other institutional counselors would seem to have an advantage here over counselors in separate agencies, in that they have access to many data outside of those usually available through tests and interviews. To name but a few, there are teachers' reports of classroom behavior, teachers' judgments of abilities and other characteristics, reports of extraclass activities, sociometric ratings by peers, and the counselor's own observations and his contacts with the student over a period of some years. Even when some of these data are not already recorded, institutional counselors frequently can arrange to get them. In the long run, then, they have the opportunity to collect a more extensive and a more developmental set of appraisal data than agency counselors who see their clients in a more limited way, both in terms of length of time and in terms of the variety of situations in which they see them.

THE CASE OF FRANK O'NEILL

Vocational Exploration in College

In this case, we have testing and counseling in two phases, the first prior to college entrance and the second three years later. The *Strong Vocational Interest Blank* was used on both occasions, so we have an opportunity to look for both consistency over the years and for reflection of any changes that might have occurred in the client. Finally, the case illustrates the use of local norms in the interpretive process.

First Phase

When first seen by the counselor, Frank was 24 years old. He was graduated from high school at the age of 18, having had a college entrance course, and then was employed for three years as a construction worker on dams and similar large projects requiring travel around the country. After this, he went into military service, where he spent two years. Upon discharge, he got a job in a woodworking mill but soon felt dissatisfied and began thinking about higher education. Now, at the age of 24, he was considering such fields as Engineering and the Physical Sciences. He struck the counselor as a rather poised, mature man; he played a fairly active role in the interview but related only at a superficial level, apparently not confiding to the counselor all that he was thinking about the matter being discussed.

A rather comprehensive battery of tests of abilities, interests, and personality was set up, since he was giving some consideration to a wide variety of occupations, though the major emphasis was on the Physical Science area. Also, he was quite concerned about his readiness to undertake college study. Since he had been out of school for six years and had had a barely passing high school record, an achievement battery was used. Since he was interested in attending one particular university, the ability tests included two which were normally used there for admission purposes: the *ACE* and the *Cooperative English Test*, Form PM, on both of which local norms were available.

The test results are reported in Table 11.6 and Figures 11.14, 11.15, and 11.16.

Table 11.6. Test Results of Frank O'Neill

NAME OF TEST		R.S.	Percentile	Norm Group
ACE Psych. Exam.	Q	47	65	Univ. of ————
for College Freshmen	L	80	75	Freshmen
	Total	127	80	
Coop. English, PM	Usage	97	35	Univ. of ————
	Spelling	12	15	Freshmen
	Vocabulary	61	85	
	Total	170	51	
Iowa H.S. Content	Engl. & Lit.	42	43	College Freshmen
	Math.	28	67	
	Science	55	93	
	History &			
	Soc. Stud.	17	01	
	Total	142	56	
Engrg. & Phys. Sci.	Math.	9	27	H.S. Grads. Enrolled
Apt. Test	Formulation	4	28	in Tech. Training
	Phys. Sci.			Programs at Penn.
	Comprehension	19	65	State
	Arith. Reason.	5	56	
	Verbal Comp.	27	79	
	Mech. Comp.	16	73	
	Total	80	37	Engrg. Freshmen,
				Penn. State
Rev. Minn. Paper				
Form Board Test		46	65	Engrg. Freshmen
Minn. Clerical Test	Numbers	44	01	Male Accountants
	Names	80	01	and Bookkeepers

NAME _____ O'Neill   Frank _____ AGE ____ SEX ____ GROUP _____ DATE OF TEST _____

Print   Last   First   Initial   M or F

PROFILE SHEET

• FOR MEN •

For Form BM of the

KUDER PREFERENCE RECORD

DIRECTIONS

Follow the directions below carefully. As soon as you have finished a step, place a check in the box at the right to show that you have completed it; then go on to the next one.

1. Fold the answer sheet on the dotted line so that the spaces for indicating scores are facing you. ☐

2. Find the total raw score for each of the nine areas by adding score *a*, which is found on one side of the answer sheet, and score *b*, on the other side. Enter these scores in the spaces marked *c* on the line labeled *Total Scores*. ☐

3. Check each total score again to be sure you have not made a mistake. ☐

4. Enter the nine total scores in the space provided at the top of the chart on this page. If you are a man, use the chart at the right, if you are a woman, use the chart on the other side of this sheet. ☐

5. Find the number in column 1 which is the same as the score you have entered at the top of the column. Draw a line through this number from one side of the column to the other. Do the same thing for each of the other columns. If your score is larger than any number in a column, draw your line across the top of the column; if your score is smaller than any number in a column, draw the line across the bottom of the column. ☐

6. With your pencil, blacken the entire space between the lines you have drawn in each column and the bottom of the chart. ☐

The result is your "*profile*" on this test. It should be remembered that the scores are not measures of ability, but that they represent the degree of your preference for activities in the various fields. Your adviser can tell you how to interpret the profile.

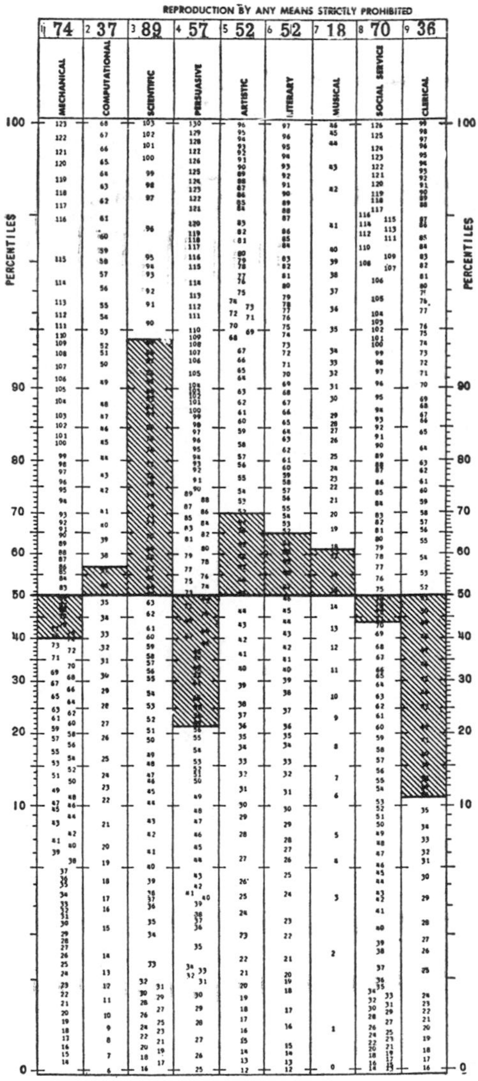

Fig. 11.14. Kuder Preference Record Profile of Frank O'Neill
(By permission of Dr. G. Frederick Kuder and Science Research Associates.)

254

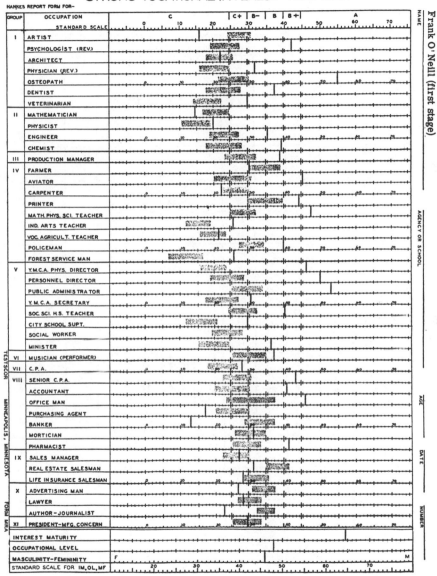

Fig. 11.15. Strong Vocational Interest Blank Profile of Frank O'Neill: First Stage
(By permission of Testscor and Stanford University. Copyright 1938 by the Board of Trustees of the Leland Stanford Junior University.)

255

Name __ O'Neill __ Frank __ __ Date __ Comment __
Last   First   Middle

C SCORE	G General Activity Energy	R Restraint Seriousness	A Ascendance Social Boldness		S Social Interest Sociability	E Emotional Stability	O Objectivity	F Friendliness Agreeableness		T Thoughtfulness Reflectiveness	P Personal Relations Cooperativeness	M Masculinity Femininity		CENTILE RANK	NEAREST T SCORE
			M	F				M	F			M	F		
10	30 29 28	30 29 28 27	30 29 28	30 29 28 27	30.	30 29	30 29	30 28 26	30 29 28	30 28	29	30 29	30 29	0 1	99	75
9	27 26	26 25	27 26	26 25 24	29	28 27	28 27	25 24	27 26	27	28	28 27	28 27	2 3		70
8	25 24	24 23	25 (24)	23 22 21	28 27	26 25	26 25	23 (22) 21	25 21	25	26 24	26 25	26 25	4 5	95 90	65
7	23 22	22 21	23 22 21	20 19	26 (25)	24 23	24 23	20 19	23 22 21	(23)	(24)	24	24	6 7	80	60
6	21 20	20 (19) 18	20 19 18	18 17 16	24 23 22	22 21 (20)	22 21 20	18 17 16	20 18	21 20	22 21 20	23 22	8 9	70	55
5	19 (18) 17	17 16 15	17 16 15	15 14 13	21 20 19	19 18 17	19 18 17	15 14 13	17 16 15	19 18 17	19 18 17	(21) 20	10 11	60 50	50
4	16 15 14	14 13 12	14 13 12	12 11	18 17 16 15	16 15 14 13	16 (15) 14	12 11 10	14 13 12	16 15 14	16 15 14	19 18	12 13	40 30	45
3	13 12 11	11 10	11 10	10 9 8	14 13 12 11	12 11 10 9	13 12 11 10	9 8 7	11 10 9	13 12 11	13 12	17 16 15	14 15	20	40
2	10 9 8	9 8 7	9 8 7	7 6	10 9 8 7	8 7 6	9 8 7	6 5	8 7	10 9 8	11 10 9	14 13 12	16 17 18	10 5	35
1	7 6	6 5	6 5	5 4 3	6 5 4	5 4	6 5	4 3	6 5	7 6 5	8 7 6	11 10 9	19 20		30
0	5 3 2 1	4 3 2	4 3 2 1	2 1 0	3 2 1 0	3 2 1	4 3 2 1	2 1 0	4 3 2 1	4 3 2 1	5 3	8 5 2	21 23 25	1	25
			M	F				M	F			M	F		

| | Inactivity Slowness | Impulsiveness Rhathymia | Submissiveness | Shyness Seclusiveness | Emotional Instability Depression | Subjectivity Hypersensitiveness | Hostility Belligerence | Unreflectiveness | Criticalness Intolerance | Femininity Masculinity | | |

Fig. 11.16. Guilford-Zimmerman Temperament Survey Profile of Frank O'Neill
(By permission of the Sheridan Supply Company.)

256

Aptitude and Achievement Tests

A first overview inspection of these results shows a wide range of scores, running from first percentile to 93rd percentile. With the *ACE* and the *Cooperative English* tests, it was possible to give specific *normative* interpretations, since these tests were given to all applicants at the university. Frank received above average scores on the *ACE,* whereas the *Cooperative* profile showed a strong foundation in Vocabulary, but weakness in the grammatical areas of Usage and Spelling.

Not available at that time, but issued later, was a set of *expectancy tables* for engineering students at that university. Although they were not used in the appraisal of Frank O'Neill, we will use them here, partly because they do aid in our consideration of the data, and partly because this gives us an opportunity, the first in this collection of cases, to demonstrate the use of the regression type of statistical bridge. Tables 11.7 and 11.8 are expectancy tables based on the experience of 113 engineering students at that university. It is clear that the *Cooperative* test discriminates better than the *ACE* for this sample (the *Q* score of the *ACE* was an even poorer predictor than the *ACE* total score) . As has often been found, frequently to the surprise of counselors, teachers, and students, verbal abilities frequently turn out to be better predictors of grades in engineering school than do nonverbal abilities.

Table 11.7. ACE Total Score and First-Year Grade-Point Average
of Engineering Students
(N = 113)

| ACE Total | Grade-Point Average | | | Combined Last 2 |
Score (Decile)	Below .75	.75 to .99	1.0 up	Cells (.75 up)
8-10	14%	45%	41%	86%
4-7	39	25	36	61
1-3	50	25	25	50

SOURCE: Memorandum from Dr. W. L. Barnette, Jr. By permission.

Table 11.8. Coop. English (PM) Total Score and First-Year Grade-Point
Average of Engineering Students
(N = 113)

| Coop. English | Grade-Point Average | | | Combined Last 2 |
Score (Decile)	Below .75	.75 to .99	1.0 and up	Cells (.75 up)
8-10	5%	21%	74%	95%
4-7	22	20	58	78
1-3	54	26	20	46

SOURCE: *Ibid.*

In Frank's case, we would read the table as stating that with *ACE* total scores such as his, the chances are 41 in 100 of having a grade point average of 1.0 (*C*) or higher in his freshman year, and 86 in 100 of attaining at least a .75 (*C*—) average. The *Cooperative* expectancy table gives 58 chances in 100 of having a 1.0 average, and 78 chances in 100 of having .75 or better, with scores such as Frank's.

These regression interpretations, then, used alone and without reference to any other data, indicate that Frank has about 4 chances in 5 of attaining a freshman G.P.A. high enough to keep him off academic probation (.75), and about a 50-50 chance of a solid *C* (1.0) average. Despite the fact that his scores on these two tests are 30 percentile points apart, the predictions yielded by them are almost identical. Inspection of the tables shows that this seeming anomaly results from the failure of the *ACE* to discriminate very well at the G.P.A. level of 1.0 and up. At this engineering school, to score high on the *Cooperative English* test provides much greater assurance of doing well academically than to score high on the *ACE* test.

Continuing our examination of the ability and aptitude tests and bringing in clinical methods, we find that the *Iowa High School Content* profile meshes with Frank's expressed interests—the scientific and mathematical parts being highest, English next, and History and Social Studies lowest. Since this is a fact-oriented test, we may conclude that Frank's *knowledge* of these various subjects is as indicated, but the *reasons* for the respective scores are not thereby revealed. His high science score might have resulted primarily from greater interest and effort in science courses in high school than in other subjects. The same set of scores might have resulted if he had done more reading in some fields than in others *since* high school graduation. Finally, an alternate interpretation (all these are of the Genetic variety) could be in terms of aptitude, that is, that he learned most effectively and retained most completely his learning in those subjects for which he had greatest aptitude. Whatever the Genetic interpretation, it is clear that at this moment Frank suffers serious deficiencies in some academic areas, most particularly in the Social Studies.

Analysis of the part scores on the *Cooperative English* test confirms the serious academic lacks. We might hypothesize that the higher Vocabulary score might have resulted from reading, whether in scientific or other fields, whereas the lower Spelling and Usage scores show lack of interest and effort in the specific English courses where these skills are normally developed.

Moving on to the remaining aptitude tests, we find on the *Engineering and Physical Science Aptitude Tests* (*EPSAT*) further evidence that his mathematical abilities are inferior to the others. In part this may result from the well-known fact that specialized skills such as those involved in solving algebraic equations (measured by Part I of the *EPSAT*) deteriorate rapidly with disuse—more so than skills which may be refreshed by newspaper and magazine reading (such as scientific and technical vocabulary, which is measured by Part V of this battery). Almost anyone who has learned the computation of square root and not used it for several years finds that he has forgotten how to do it; however, it is quickly relearned, thus revealing the presence of traces of the original learning.

Frank's *EPSAT* profile presents a difficult interpretive problem: To what extent should adjustments be made for the fact that he had been out of school for six years at the time of taking the test? How much better would he have done as a high school senior? How much better could he do after a refresher course in algebra? Unfortunately, these questions cannot be answered with any definiteness. In the absence of specific actuarial or clinical information [11] about the experience of similar students at that university, we can only speculate that Frank's chances are somewhat better than would normally be estimated from a profile such as his. There are other kinds of interpretations to be made of the same data; using our Evaluative type, for example, it can be recommended that Frank take refresher work in mathematics before attempting a college program in engineering. However, one would need a good deal more data before trying to answer the question: Which would be wiser, to aim toward engineering and the physical sciences after taking refresher work in mathematics or to assume that the profile as it stands is itself a reflection of too low a level of mathematical aptitude for these fields and that therefore it would be wiser to change to a goal requiring much less of this kind of aptitude? Essentially we are here applying Cronbach's (1957) two emphases, the "experimental" and the "correlational". With the former, we seek to find the treatment (a refresher course) which would most effectively help this person attain his goal. The correlational emphasis would instead suggest a change of goals, in the direction of utilizing his highest measured aptitudes (see Chapter 2 for a more extensive report of Cronbach's formulation).

Finally, the *Minnesota Paper Form Board (MPFB)* provides some support for the engineering goal, and the *Minnesota Clerical Test* offers no particular reason to consider the clerical area of work.

In summary, the results of the ability and aptitude tests show a mixed picture: College aptitude (for that particular school) is somewhat better than average but is reduced somewhat because of English deficiencies. The physical sciences seem to be the area of greatest promise, but present mathematical abilities are inadequate for programs such as engineering.

---

[11] It may well be that student counselors or administrative staff members in that particular engineering college have had enough experience with students like Frank that they *can* make clinical predictions of a more informed nature than could Frank's counselor.

Interest and Personality Measures

The *Kuder* contains only three scores which deviate significantly from the average band; above average is Scientific and below average are Persuasive and Clerical. Mechanical and Computational, one or both of which might be expected to be found high with engineers (see the Manual for the *Kuder*), are well within the average range. The *Kuder* profile seems to offer no contradiction to the previous interpretations derived from the aptitude and ability tests. Frank seems to like those things the most which he has learned the best. Naturally, the correlation here tells nothing about causation—whether the interests caused or resulted from the abilities, or whether both are the result of still other factors.

The *Strong* profile, however, introduces some complications. The strongest cluster—a Primary—is clearly in Group V, the Social Service group. Group VIII, Business Detail, is also a Primary. Neither of the scientific groups (I and II) qualifies even as a secondary cluster, though there are a few individual scores of *B* or higher. Group IV has a cluster of high scores but not quite enough of them to be classified. This seems to be the profile of one who works primarily with people rather than with scientific theories, computations, or laboratory apparatus.

How to resolve the apparent contradictory interpretations coming from the *Kuder* and the *Strong?* One line of speculation begins with the greater "fakability" of the *Kuder;* one who consciously sees himself as a scientist could be expected to check everything on the *Kuder* which sounds like a scientific activity—and this would yield a very high Scientific score, as in Frank's case. However, having the interests of scientists is more complex than this; they also have other likes and dislikes which differentiate them from men in general, and it is these which the *SVIB* measures (and also which some other scales of the *Kuder* may measure). Frank is not likely to know these other likes and dislikes, having lived in a nonscientific setting most of his life. Therefore, it would follow, his interest inventories show a stereotype of a scientist, or, put another way, his idealized self-image as a scientist.

Another line of speculation would begin with the assumption that Frank is genuinely interested in physical scientific subjects, perhaps finds them fun to read about, but is also quite interested in people and is not really attracted to the mathematical and the more routine aspects of a scientific career. Perhaps he doesn't *know* what a scientific occupation actually entails in terms of school subjects and in terms of job functions. The conclusion from this line of reasoning would be that he selected his tentative goals on the basis of incomplete, or inaccurate, information about what they actually entail.

At this point, it would appear, several hypotheses must be kept open for further consideration.

The *Guilford-Zimmerman Temperament Survey* results shed a little light on this question. Frank's responses here picture him as an outgoing person, dominating others, friendly, and co-operative. In general, people with such profiles would be expected more often to aim toward personal relations than scientific occupations. [A caution must be quickly added. Most occupations are in reality a cluster of occupations rather than a single homogeneous collection of functions and behaviors. Within any one occupation are a number of specialties which call for somewhat different personality constellations. For example, most physicians spend much of their time in direct contact with patients, but others work primarily in laboratories and spend only a fraction of their time in face-to-face meetings with patients (pathologists and physicians engaged in research). Other physicians are teachers (in medical schools) and still others administrators (of hospitals or medical schools). Analogies may be found in many occupations. This fact about occupations is often suggested as one important reason for the failure of personality inventories to predict success on the job. Especially in many higher-level occupations, it is possible for a variety of personalities to find, each one for himself, a niche in which he can function effectively and with satisfaction to himself. Nevertheless, it seems to be true, as witness the established validity of the *SVIB*, that there are more or less "typical" clusters of at least some kinds of personal characteristics in each occupation. See Super, 1957a, Ch. 16, for an extended discussion of personality and vocations.]

Returning to Frank O'Neill, and bringing together data from all the tests, it would seem to be desirable to seek out a vocational goal which has scientific *content* but which requires relatively limited mathematics, not much more than a bachelor's degree (because of limited academic aptitude), and which involves working with people. One such occupation is that of the secondary school teacher of science.

Second Interview

Although presented with these interpretations, O'Neill persisted in his earlier preference for a "scientific" goal in the narrower sense; engineering would have been first choice if not for his past difficulties with mathematics. He decided to postpone a specific vocational selection until he tried college mathematics courses. At this point his tentative choices were, in this order: physicist, engineer, and high school science teacher. The counselor felt that there were factors in Frank's thinking that needed exploration but which remained unexplained: Why did the client resist so strenuously the social service and other personal relations occupations pointed to by some of the test data? Why did he insist on trying engineering despite his mathematical weakness and lack of interest? Frank could not, or would not, dig into these motivational questions, and they remained unanswered.

Second Phase

Three years later, Frank made an appointment with the same counselor. He reported during the interview that he was now a junior, had just about a *C* (1.0) average, but that this was composed of quite a variety of grades: in English 2 *D*'s, in German 3 *B*'s, in History a *D*, in Chemistry a *D* and a *C*, in Biology an *F*, in Mathematics 2 *C*'s and an *F*, in Physics 2 *B*'s and a *C*, Geography *B*, and Psychology *C*. It was the two *F*'s he had just received that "shocked" him, and he was now "taking stock" before making further plans for the remainder of his college courses.

He wondered now whether the field of physics was a wise choice for him, since he knew that employment opportunities were limited unless one took graduate work, and his two failures left him with grave doubts as to his capabilities for undertaking graduate study. He was thinking now of high school teaching. Frank told of his rather extensive extra-curricular activities, including holding office and being an active committee worker in his dormitory and elsewhere on campus. Again the counselor's notes report the impression that O'Neill was "holding back," that he could not, or would not, confide in the counselor to the extent necessary really to get at some of the why's of the case. Accepting this rather superficial level of appraisal, the counselor engaged the client in a co-operative approach to test selection. They agreed to emphasize interests and personality, since two and a half years of college, and the first battery of tests, had provided considerable data regarding aptitude and abilities. A retest with the *SVIB* and the use of the *Edwards PPS* were planned, and, as a specific check on aptitude for graduate study, the *Terman Concept Mastery Test* was selected for its high-level and graduate-student norms. The results are shown in Figures 11.17 and 11.18.

The *Terman* results are as follows:

Raw Score: 70 = 32nd percentile for the norm group of Engineers and
            Scientists (of whom some had graduate work)
          = 08th percentile for the norm group of doctoral students.

The broad configurations of the *SVIB* profile are quite similar to those of the precollege one. Now the only primary cluster is in Group V; with the addition of the Social Worker key, which scores *A*, and an increased score on the Social Science High School Teacher scale, the group is somewhat stronger than before. Group VIII has changed from a Primary to an unclassified group as the result of decreases in three of the four scales which were previously *A* or *B+*. There are still no classifiable clusters in Groups I or II, though there have been some changes in both, the first gaining two *A* scores, and the second becoming slightly weaker than before. Group IV, the Technicians, has enough score increases to become

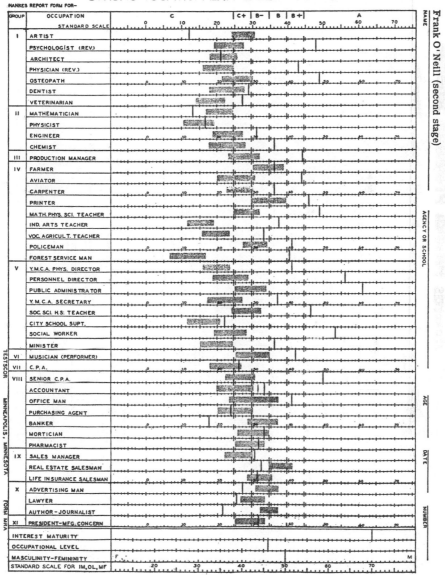

Fig. 11.17. Strong Vocational Interest Blank Profile of Frank O'Neill:
Second Stage
(By permission of Testscor and Stanford University. Copyright 1938 by the Board of
Trustees of the Leland Stanford Junior University.)

Edwards Personal Preference Schedule

NAME O'Neill   Frank   SEX M   NORMS USED College Men.
     LAST   FIRST

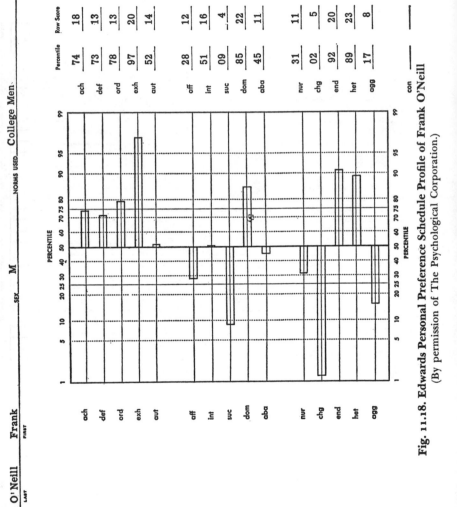

	Percentile	Raw Score
ach	74	18
def	73	13
ord	78	13
exh	97	20
aut	52	14
aff	28	12
int	51	16
suc	09	4
dom	85	22
aba	45	11
nur	31	11
chg	02	5
end	92	20
het	89	23
agg	17	8
con	—	—

Fig. 11.18. Edwards Personal Preference Schedule Profile of Frank O'Neill
(By permission of The Psychological Corporation.)

264

now a Primary group. A few decreases among the individual scales of Group VIII change this now from a secondary to an unclassified group. There seems then to have been primarily a sharpening of interests, with the major primary group becoming even stronger, and some of the weaker ones fading further into the background. Frank seems somewhat less a physical scientist and somewhat more a "helper" than before. Two kinds of teacher now get *A* scores: Math-Physical Science Teacher and Social Science Teacher.

The *EPPS* profile shows some of the outgoingness pictured three years before on the *Guilford-Zimmerman,* with Exhibition and Dominance both showing a need to be "visible." The high Endurance score was readily accepted by the client, who reported working well into the morning hours in order to keep up with both academic and extracurricular responsibilities. The low Succorance score can be interpreted as concurring with the counselor's impression of Frank as "holding back" in the interview; perhaps this means that the holding back is a way of avoiding emotional dependence on another person. The low score on Change was also quite acceptable to the client, who explained that in his precollege years he had satisfied his wanderlust and was now ready to stay put (this was discussed by the counselor and client also in relation to some kinds of technical jobs which would require frequent or occasional travel). Finally, the two remaining deviant scores—Heterosexual and Aggression—seemed to have no special significance in Frank's vocational appraisal. All in all, Frank again appears as a person whose satisfactions are obtained mostly from relationships with others, but relationships of a benign nature, in which he does not get very much emotional involvement (Succorance-Nurturance), and in which he does not fight for his ideas (Aggression).

Finally, the *Terman* score shows Frank O'Neill to be a borderline doctoral student and a barely average student in general among engineers and scientists. The prognosis from this score is not especially promising for graduate work.

Next Interview

Frank agreed that he likes working with people much more than working in laboratories. Most of all, he said, he likes science—but to *read* about, it developed, rather than to work with in a laboratory. Though Frank had mentioned teaching, even in his first series of counseling interviews three years before, he perceived as a new idea the counselor's suggestion that becoming a high school science teacher might afford him a combination of the things he *likes to do* and the things he *has done* successfully. At the end of the second interview of the second series, it was agreed that the client would seek out information about what he would need to take at the university in order to be certified to teach. He failed to appear for his next counseling appointment and for several appointments that were subsequently made, some at his request, others at the invitation of the counselor, and he was not seen or heard from again.

Conclusion

The case of Frank O'Neill illustrates a number of points, not the least of which is the frustration of the counselor when he must close a case with many key questions left unanswered. Frank was a late bloomer; a barely passing student in high school, he would have been given few chances indeed of getting through two and a half years in a competitive college program with a solid C average. Though he did finally bloom, Frank remained something less than a scholar, receiving much of his satisfaction from extracurricular activities. Finally, he persisted in working toward a goal which was rather clearly inappropriate, but he could not compromise until forced to do so by the irresistable reality of receiving failing grades in critical subjects. He might have avoided several failing and near-failing grades had he been more accepting of the interpretations made from his precollege tests.

Another counselor might have made better use of occupational information in the first phase of counseling to help Frank develop a more suitable vocational self-concept. Some counselors might have been able to "reach" Frank more adequately and to help him deal with the irrational drives which led him to continue butting up against a stone wall. This, however, is more a problem of counseling process than of test interpretation.

THE CASE OF RALPH SANTARO

Self-Confidence

Ralph Santaro was quite a different person from the others we have met, different in background and in the needs which he brought to counseling. The second and third interviews with Ralph were recorded on tape, and excerpts from them are used in Chapters 15 and 16, during the discussion of *reporting* of test results.

From the questionnaire filled out by clients at this agency, we find that Ralph is 28, married, and has an 18-month-old child. He owns a car but not a home. He began a "Business" course in high school but dropped out after completing the ninth grade. His grades, he says, were "average"; subjects liked best were Mathematics, Business, Arithmetic, and Book-keeping; those liked least were History and English. Asked, "What are your chief assets—the things you can do best?", he replied, "I like to sell." Asked next, "What things do you find particularly difficult or which give you a sense of failure?" he wrote, "Talking to a stranger or making conversation." His reported leisure-time activities were limited to watching TV and playing cards.

From the questionnaire and from information obtained during the course of the first interview, the story was pieced together. Ralph's father had died when the boy was 13, and an older brother assumed responsibility for supporting the family (which included also one sister younger than Ralph). From the time that Ralph left school until a few weeks before his first interview, he and his brother had operated a small fruit-and-vegetable store as partners. The brother, however, apparently was the "boss," frequently overruling Ralph's decisions. The two families—Ralph's and his brother's—lived in the same house, and the older brother paid the utility bills and in other ways played a protective role. Just a few weeks earlier the brother had taken a job with a large retailing chain, and they had then sold their business. Ralph was on his own for the first time and felt lost. He seemed quite insightful about the situation, telling about his lack of self-confidence due to the brother's overprotection. (Ralph didn't use these terms but expressed essentially these concepts in more concrete terms.)

Ralph also felt inadequate because of his limited education yet insisted that he would not become a laborer. He had thought about selling and mechanical work. The former was his major interest, yet he wondered whether he could sell, since "if a stranger hits me the wrong way, I can't talk." A few days previously he had gone down to a local department store to answer a help-wanted ad for door-to-door salesmen, but "I lost my nerve and didn't go in to apply." As to mechanical occupations, he had done very little specific thinking.

The counselor was careful to give Ralph every opportunity to deal with his feelings of frustration and lack of self-confidence, since Ralph was obviously quite anxious. After a half hour, however, Ralph seemed to have talked himself out, and the counselor summarized the situation as he saw it and then described briefly the services available. It was quickly decided between them that a battery of tests was an appropriate next step, since Ralph had some very real questions about his capabilities, interests, and personality. The battery was selected co-operatively and included mechanical and sales aptitude tests in addition to more general measures of mental ability, interests, and personality. Counselor and client also talked a little about the later applications of the test data. Ralph expressed his need for a feeling of security that would come from knowing in what occupations he would have a good chance of success. Asked what would be the case if tests did not give clear-cut answers of this sort, he said that he would then have to go out and build up his *own* self-confidence.

The counselor summed up his impressions of Ralph as follows:

This client presents first a vocational choice problem but soon expresses a concern about lack of self-confidence with regard to vocational success. At this point it does not seem clear as to his readiness and need for more extended counseling with regard to personality problems. His readiness to discuss the latter so soon may indicate that further exploration of this area, perhaps leading to referral, may soon be appropriate. On the other hand, it may be that a few sessions with me on this topic may suffice and a referral therefore be unnecessary.

Mr. Santaro's major problems seem to me to revolve around inadequate development of an adult self-concept. Dependence on an apparently overprotective older brother seems to have retarded the development of self-confidence in his own judgment and abilities. Vocationally, he is attracted to a type of work (selling) where his lack of self-confidence is a major handicap. His lack of formal education also contributes to this situation in two ways: first, it limits him somewhat occupationally, and second, it further aggravates his lack of self-confidence.

He seems to possess several assets, from the point of view of successful counseling and later adjustment. First, he expresses himself and communicates very well, considering his educational level. Secondly, he seems warm and outgoing, and he seems to be more capable socially and conversationally than his reported self-concept would indicate; in a word, he has the "gift of gab." Next, he seems relatively quite realistic and insightful in examining himself and his environment. He was able, for example, to discuss the relationship with his brother rather frankly, yet without rancor or apology. Finally, he seems to be ready for a good counseling relationship, in terms of degree of defensiveness and readiness to utilize reality data, such as those from tests.

The test results are reported in Table 11.9 and Figures 11.19 and 11.20.

Table 11.9. Test Results of Ralph Santaro

NAME OF TEST	R.S.	Percentile	Norm Group
Army General Classification Test	98	81	World War II Inductees
Bennett Mech. Comprehension Test, Form BB	26	30	Auto Mech. Applicants
Rev. Minn. Paper Form Board Test	41	60	Applicants for Apprenticeship
Bruce Test of Sales Aptitude	39	25	Salesmen
		54	Men in General

Test Interpretations

The *Army General Classification Test (AGCT)* was chosen as the general mental ability test in this case for two reasons. First, the items are of a somewhat more concrete nature than is true of most intelligence tests; for someone with limited formal education, such items would probably be more manageable and would provide a more accurate measure of general mental ability. Secondly, there are available for the *AGCT* extensive occu-

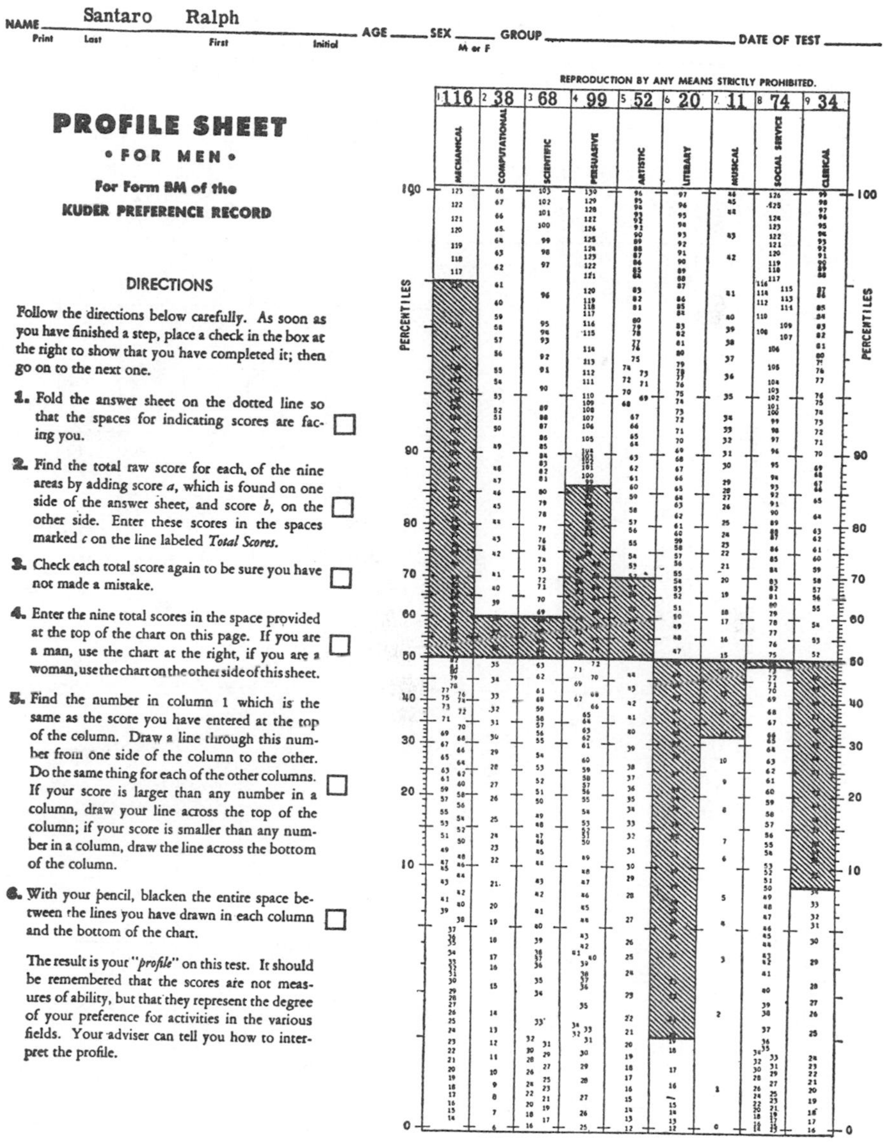

NAME ___Santaro___ ___Ralph___ _____ AGE _____ SEX _____ GROUP _____ DATE OF TEST _____
Print   Last   First   Initial   M or F

1 116	2 38	3 68	4 99	5 52	6 20	7 11	8 74	9 34

PROFILE SHEET
• FOR MEN •
For Form BM of the
KUDER PREFERENCE RECORD

DIRECTIONS

Follow the directions below carefully. As soon as you have finished a step, place a check in the box at the right to show that you have completed it; then go on to the next one.

1. Fold the answer sheet on the dotted line so that the spaces for indicating scores are facing you. ☐

2. Find the total raw score for each of the nine areas by adding score *a*, which is found on one side of the answer sheet, and score *b*, on the other side. Enter these scores in the spaces marked *c* on the line labeled *Total Scores*. ☐

3. Check each total score again to be sure you have not made a mistake. ☐

4. Enter the nine total scores in the space provided at the top of the chart on this page. If you are a man, use the chart at the right, if you are a woman, use the chart on the other side of this sheet. ☐

5. Find the number in column 1 which is the same as the score you have entered at the top of the column. Draw a line through this number from one side of the column to the other. Do the same thing for each of the other columns. If your score is larger than any number in a column, draw your line across the top of the column; if your score is smaller than any number in a column, draw the line across the bottom of the column. ☐

6. With your pencil, blacken the entire space between the lines you have drawn in each column and the bottom of the chart. ☐

The result is your *"profile"* on this test. It should be remembered that the scores are not measures of ability, but that they represent the degree of your preference for activities in the various fields. Your adviser can tell you how to interpret the profile.

Column headings (chart): MECHANICAL, COMPUTATIONAL, SCIENTIFIC, PERSUASIVE, ARTISTIC, LITERARY, MUSICAL, SOCIAL SERVICE, CLERICAL

PERCENTILES

Fig. 11.19. Kuder Preference Record Profile of Ralph Santaro
(By permission of Dr. G. Frederick Kuder and Science Research Associates.)

269

Name __Santaro__ __Ralph__
Last   First   Middle   Date   Comment

C SCORE	G General Activity Energy	R Restraint Seriousness	A Ascendance Social Boldness M F	S Social Interest Sociability	E Emotional Stability	O Objectivity	F Friendliness Agreeableness M F	T Thoughtfulness Reflectiveness	P Personal Relations Cooperativeness	M Masculinity Femininity M F	CENTILE RANK	NEAREST T SCORE
10	30 29 28	30 29 28 27	30 30 29 29 28 28 28 27	30	30 29	30 29	30 30 28 29 26 28	30 29 28	30	30 0 29 1	99	75
9	27 26	26 25	27 26 25 26 24	29	28 27	28 27	25 27 24 26	27 26	28 27	28 2 27 3		70
8	25 24	24 23	25 23 22 24 21	28 27	26 25	26 25	23 25 22 21 24	25 24	26 25	26 4 25 5	95 90	65
7	23 22	22 21	23 20 22 21 19	26 25	24 23	24 23	20 23 22 19 21	23 22	24 23	24 6 7	80	60
6	21 20	20 19 18	20 18 19 17 18 16	24 23 22	22 21 20	22 21 20	18 20 17 19 16 18	21 20	22 21 20	23 8 22 9	70 60	55
5	19 18 17	17 16 15	17 15 16 14 15 13	21 20 19	19 18 17	19 18 17	15 17 14 16 13 15	19 18 17	19 18 17	21 10 20 11	50 40	50
4	16 15 14	14 13 12	14 12 13 12 11	18 17 16 15	16 15 14 13	16 15 14	12 14 11 13 10 12	16 15 14	16 15 14	19 12 18 13	30	45
3	13 12 11	11 10	11 10 9 10 8	14 13 12 11	13 12 11 9	13 12 11 10	9 11 8 10 7 9	13 12 11	13 12	17 14 16 15 15	20	40
2	10 9 8	9 8 7	9 7 8 7 6	10 9 8 7	8 7 6	9 8 7	6 8 5 7	10 9 8	11 10 9	14 16 13 17 12 18	10 5	35
1	7 6	6 5	6 5 4 5 3	6 5 4	5 4	6 5	4 6 3 5	7 6 5	8 7 6	11 19 10 9 20		30
0	5 3 2 1	4 3 2 1	4 2 3 1 1 0	3 2 1 0	3 2 1	4 3 2 1	2 4 1 3 0 2 1	4 3 2 1	5 3 1	8 21 5 23 2 25	1	25
			M F				M F			M F		

Inactivity Slowness	Impulsiveness Rhathymia	Submissiveness	Shyness Seclusiveness	Emotional Instability Depression	Subjectivity Hypersensitiveness	Hostility Belligerence	Unreflectiveness	Criticalness Intolerance	Femininity Masculinity	

Fig. 11.20. Guilford-Zimmerman Temperament Survey Profile of Ralph Santaro
(By permission of Sheridan Supply Company.)

270

pational norms, making it more useful for one who is job- rather than school-oriented. Ralph's score is somewhat above average as compared with a men-in-general group. It seems likely that Ralph could have handled, and benefited from, a good deal more schooling than he received. The two mechanical aptitude tests show about average promise for this kind of work, as compared with people applying for mechanical jobs. On the sales aptitude test Ralph has a score which is average for men in general, but below average as compared with salesmen. Not as much weight can be given to low scores as to high scores on this test, since it appears to be essentially an achievement test, requiring the subject to select the best approach for each of a number of sales situations. In the case of a person without sales experience or with the limited kind of experience Ralph had, a high score could be interpreted as indication of a "feel" for selling, whereas a low score tells only that the individual has not developed these understandings. In some cases where the score is low, there may be potentialities which could be developed through training and experience. As with other tests of this kind, one would be more certain about interpretations of high scores obtained by an untrained and inexperienced person. In such cases, it is likely that the person does indeed have aptitude for that kind of work.

The interest inventory *(KPR)* highlights the Mechanical and Persuasive interests which Ralph spoke of in the first interview. There is also rejection of the Literary and Clerical areas. The low Literary score would seem to indicate that he is unlikely to endure extensive schooling and perhaps may explain Ralph's leaving school as early as he did. Even with the financial straits of the family, Ralph might have found some way of continuing his education if he had been more interested.

The *Guilford-Zimmerman Temperament* profile describes a socially inadequate person, characterized by inactivity, submissiveness, shyness, emotional instability, hypersensitiveness, and criticalness in personal relations. The femininity score might be further indication of lack of masculine assertiveness, or it might signify instead that Ralph has vocational and other interests which in our culture are more typical of women than of men (as with the *MF* scale of the *Strong*) .

All in all, these tests characterize Ralph Santaro as a person of above-average general intelligence, average to above-average mechanical aptitude, and about average sales know-how. As to interests, they would seem to be appropriate for either the mechanical or the sales fields. Measured personality, however, is patently inappropriate for selling. From these data, the mechanical area seems to be a better risk.

Second Interview

In the second interview, which will be reported in greater detail in Chapters 15 and 16, Ralph was quite accepting of the counselor's interpretation of the *G-Z* profile and told of his "bad personality." He described efforts to speak in public, in which he made "an ass out of" himself. It is important to note that though he feels socially inept, he is unwilling to *remain* this way. For reasons unknown, he wants to be socially aggressive and assertive and is attracted to selling occupations where these characteristics are usually necessary.

Ralph again offered explanations of his personality in terms of never having developed self-confidence because of overprotectiveness by his brother. During the years they were in business together, the older brother reinforced Ralph's inadequacies by "sheltering" him from "being hurt" in the "hard outside world." In effect, Ralph was, during this portion of the interview, giving both descriptive and genetic interpretations of the personality inventory results. The counselor added very little to the *content* of the appraisal process but instead acted primarily as a facilitator of the client's self-appraisal. The question might well be raised as to the necessity of using a personality inventory when the client is so ready to tell about himself directly. This is a moot question; with a person as anxious as Ralph, the inventory may have made a contribution in helping to organize his feelings and perceptions about himself in a systematic manner. On the other hand, skillful interviewing might have yielded similar outcomes without the use of a personality inventory.

In any case, the *G-Z* results and the ensuing discussion of them led the counselor to suggest referral to a personal counseling service to deal with some of these disturbing feelings. When they had reached a point at which Ralph seemed ready to have the counselor make a phone call to the other agency to get information about application procedures, the client suddenly asked about the sales aptitude test. In giving his interpretation, the counselor brought in the personality data, pointing out the close relationship between feeling confidently aggressive and selecting the "right" answers on the Sales Aptitude Test, which often were the most aggressive and most self-seeking alternatives. It was at this point that the counselor introduced the dichotomy which Cronbach (1957) has referred to as the "experimental" and "correlational" approaches. Here are the counselor's own words:

Co. 150: Now, you see, uh, we've got two ways of looking at this, personality, and also as it affects selling work. Um, on the one hand, we can say, well, this is the kind of person you are now, and let's see what field of work would seem to be most appropriate ... let's you and I try to find the most appropriate kind of thing. Well, that would immediately point away from anything having to do with selling or personal relations (CLIENT: "Mm-hm"). Um, on the other hand, we can take another point of view; we can say, um, this is the way you are now, but you're not satisfied (CLIENT: "No, I'm not") with the way you are now, and you'd like to change, and you'd like to become more confident and more outgoing, and more aggressive. And, uh, therefore, it would be a mistake to plan an occupation to fit your present personality, when you're hoping that you can change.

This seemed to make sense to Ralph, and it was the latter direction in which he wished to move, to try to change as a person so that he might be effective as a salesman. He planned to visit the personal counseling service in a few days; for now he wanted another appointment with this counselor in order to make immediate plans regarding employment. He said that he would also like to return after a few months to make more long-range plans. He was quite pleased to learn of the *AGCT* results and about the likelihood that he could get a high school equivalency certificate by taking the *General Educational Development* tests.

Third Interview

With this background information it is not difficult to understand the counselor's surprise at hearing, in the first minute of the third interview, that Ralph had applied for, and was expecting to get, a job as an inside salesman of large appliances, on a one-month trial basis. At the end of the month, the employer would decide whether to keep him on. Apparently Ralph had developed some confidence in his ability to make it, judging from the interview. The counselor tried to test out Ralph's reality orientation by getting him to tell what he knew of the job and of appliance sales. Apparently he had some substantial occupational information (his closest friend was in the business) and was not expecting miracles. Also, there would be some opportunity to satisfy some of his mechanical interests, in connection with technical aspects of his product.

Later in this interview information was disclosed which may shed light on Ralph's motivation for selling. His father had been, he reported, a successful small businessman, and Ralph identified strongly with the image of his father as a hard bargainer, but thoroughly honest. The client told of having turned down job opportunities of a "shady" sort, in connection with bookmaking and the numbers racket.

Discussion

In a way, Ralph Santaro may be seen as going through a somewhat belated adolescence. His first vocational choice—the junior role in the partnership with his brother—was apparently not really a choice in the true sense of the word. In some respects Ralph's position was similar to that of many young men who go into a family business in which a senior relative dominates the situation. Such young people may never go through a period of finding themselves and developing confidence in their own abilities to make their way in the world. Later, when for some reason they are thrown on their own, they may experience severe anxiety associated with being responsible for making their own choices. The anxiety can be as severe as a panic reaction, especially when, as in Ralph's case, the person has the additional responsibility of supporting a family.

This analysis, to the extent that it has validity in Ralph's case, can help to explain the apparent discrepancy between the Ralph depicted in the *Guilford-Zimmerman* profile (as well as his own self-portrait as painted during interviews) and the Ralph who applies for a job as a salesman. The first of these portraits may be markedly exaggerated by the anxiety of the panic state in which Ralph found himself. He may not have been nearly as shy and socially inept as he saw himself at that point. Certainly his behavior in the interview showed a great deal of verbal fluency and self-possession. A series of successful experiences, whether in selling or in club activities, might lead to the development of potentialities which were close to the surface and ready to unfold in the proper environment. If this hypothesis is correct, a retest with the *G-Z* after a period of time would give quite another picture.

Unfortunately the case of Ralph Santaro ends at this point, since Ralph's counselor found it necessary to cancel their next appointment, and letters offering substitute appointments were unanswered. No follow-up data are available, and so the various hypotheses must remain unchecked. It might be that Ralph Santaro was due for a major disappointment in the selling field. Perhaps he remained as the personality profile described him and therefore turned toward an occupation requiring little in the way of human relations skills. A more optimistic guess is that Ralph needed only these few interviews to help mobilize his inner resources. The test interpretations may have contributed by answering in the negative the question that was probably plaguing Ralph: "Am I good for nothing at all?"

ELEMENTARY SCHOOL CASES

All the case data and interpretive thinking for the following cases were supplied by Elaine Nitsberg, at the time a graduate student in guidance and counseling. These cases were prepared, along with several others, to meet the requirements for a graduate course in tests and measurement. For the most part, only minor editorial changes have been made, but some portions of the original document were omitted because they were not necessary for our purposes here. The author is indebted to Miss Nitsberg; it is difficult to find elementary school cases which illustrate guidance uses of tests.

These cases were chosen by Miss Nitsberg because they involve intelligence testing in relation to specific problems or decisions, and this was the focal point of her paper. They differ from the preceding cases not only in age level but also in the fact that they were studied by a classroom teacher in the setting of a school, rather than in a clinic setting. What brought these children to the attention of the person studying them were problems of teachers and of the school, and decisions which were to be made by the school rather than by the pupil. These, then, are not cases of individuals seeking counseling help for themselves, but rather of a school seeking to appraise pupils in order to use better its resources for their individual development.

In some of these cases, a more complete psychological study, including the use of individual intelligence tests, might have offered more information than that obtained from group tests. The circumstances in this particular school, as in very many elementary schools, simply do not permit any more elaborate work. In fact, it seems to the author that the use of tests shown in these cases is at a much more sophisticated level than would be found in most American elementary schools.

THE CASE OF THOMAS LOPEZ

How Capable?

Thomas is a bit taller than average and wears glasses; although he is a good student and admits liking school work, he is far from "all work and no play." He is active, has a good sense of humor, and is popular with his classmates; he seems to be a well-adjusted fifth grader.

His work is seldom neat, and he often neglects to do papers which he does not find interesting. Despite this, he has shown growth in reading, he shows insight into mathematical concepts, he has great interest in history, and he shows interest in and understanding of scientific principles. His written English is very poor, and his spelling is about third grade level. If he continues handing in untidy, poorly phrased papers with numerous misspelled words he is likely to obtain poor grades despite the fact that he has a good understanding of the subject matter.

Available Test Data

Tests already on record are listed in Table 11.10.

Table 11.10. Test Results of Thomas Lopez

NAME OF TEST	School Grade	Score
Local Reading Readiness Text	1st	80 Percentile
Pintner-Cunningham Primary	1st	107 IQ
Local Math. Achievement Test	1st	90 Percentile
Local Math. Achievement Test	3rd	80 Percentile
Otis Quick-Scoring Mental Ability	3rd	83 IQ
Metropolitan Primary Reading Test	3rd	2.5 Grade Equiv.
Local Math. Achievement Test	4th	40 Percentile
Local Math. Achievement Test	5th	80 Percentile

On the reading readiness test given in the first grade, there was every indication that he would have little difficulty in learning to read. Yet, the *Metropolitan Reading Test,* given in the middle of the third grade, showed one year retardation in reading. Upon entrance into the fifth grade, he was found to be one year retarded in reading. A number of factors may have been responsible. For one, Thomas was born in Puerto Rico, and English was his second language. There might have been lack of motivation at the beginning of reading instruction. The situation may have been aggravated by placement in a group of poor readers; even if he had greater potential, this placement might have discouraged his growth or at least failed to stimulate him and to provide the level and pace of which he may have been capable.

On the Arithmetic achievement tests, Thomas scored average to above average, all but one of the scores being at the 80th percentile or higher. The fourth grade score might have resulted from a temporary setback when multiplication was introduced, or there may have been some other specific cause, such as his physical or emotional condition at the time.

The two intelligence test scores are 24 points apart. Even though based on two different tests, a difference of this magnitude must be considered as representing a discrepancy. There are reasons to hypothesize that the higher score (IQ 107) is more nearly a correct indication of his level of intellectual development. In the fifth grade he has shown very good progress in mathematics, and he has done two years of reading advancement in the one grade. It may be that a visual defect was responsible for the lower score on the *Otis*. He started wearing glasses in the third grade but tends to forget to wear them unless reminded.

It is also noteworthy that the only low score in arithmetic was obtained seven months after the *Otis*. Although it may be only coincidence, the two scores may reflect problems of a motivational or other nature during that period.

Further Testing

In the fifth grade two questions arose: What level of work should be expected by the teacher, and should Thomas be placed in a different section? Regarding the first, his teacher had been giving him extra reading and spelling assignments but wondered whether he was being pushed beyond his capacity. As to the second, there were two choices: to place him in a class which was reading up to grade level or in a brighter class where the children were academically more apt.

To help answer these questions, and to supplement the information available from other tests, the *Primary Mental Abilities* test was selected. The particular choice was based on the fact that this test provides verbal and nonverbal IQ's, as well as separate scores for numerical and several other abilities. (Because of the low levels of reliability of factor scores on

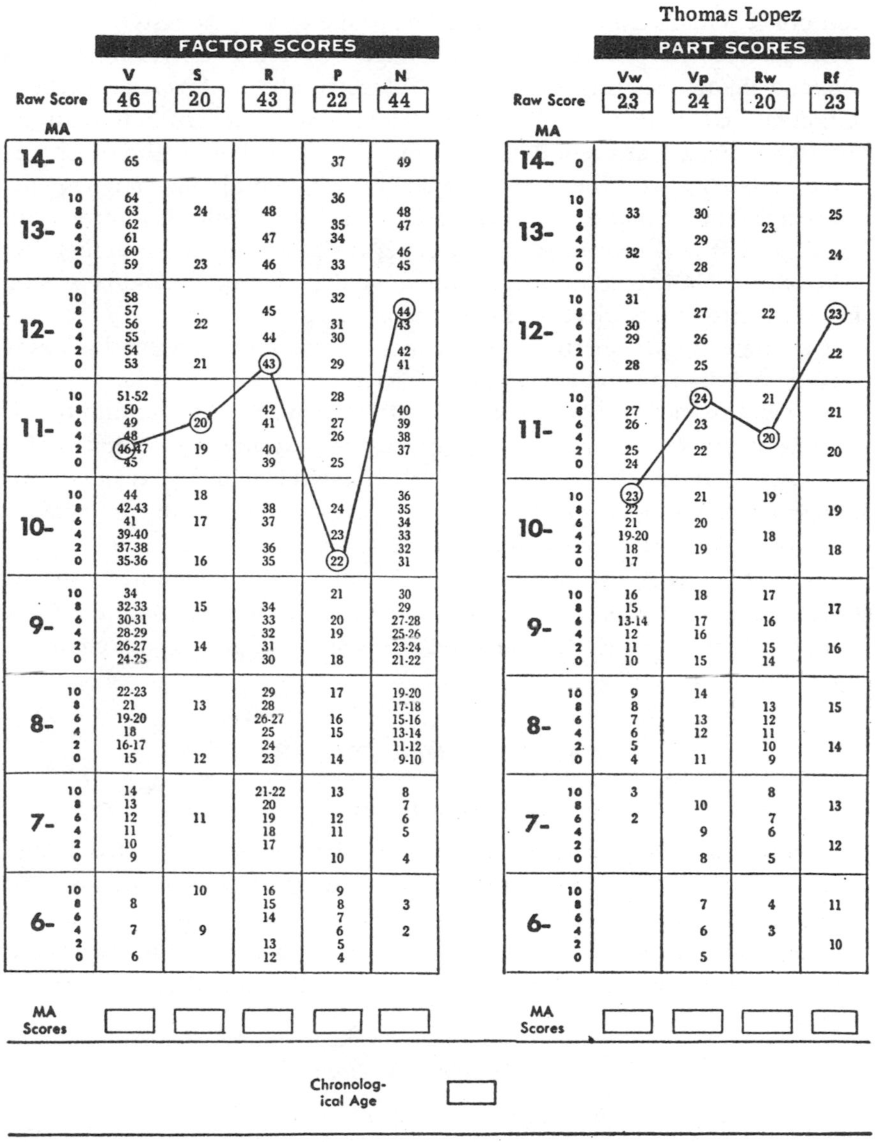

Thomas Lopez

FACTOR SCORES

Raw Score	V 46	S 20	R 43	P 22	N 44

MA		V	S	R	P	N
14-	0	65			37	49
13-	10 8	64 63	24	48	36	48
	6	62			35	47
	4	61		47	34	
	2	60				46
	0	59	23	46	33	45
12-	10 8	58 57		45	32	
	6	56	22		31	(44) (43)
	4	55		44	30	
	2	54				42
	0	53	21	(43)	29	41
11-	10	51-52				
	8	50		42	28	40
	6	49	(20)	41	27	39
	4	48			26	38
	2	(46-47)	19	40		37
	0	45		39	25	
10-	10	44				
	8	42-43	18	38	24	36
	6	41	17	37		35
	4	39-40			(23)	34
	2	37-38		36		33
	0	35-36	16	35	(22)	31
9-	10	34				
	8	32-33	15	34	21	30
	6	30-31		33	20	29
	4	28-29		32	19	27-28
	2	26-27	14	31		25-26
	0	24-25		30	18	23-24 21-22
8-	10	22-23		29	17	19-20
	8	21	13	28		17-18
	6	19-20		26-27	16	15-16
	4	18		25	15	13-14
	2	16-17		24		11-12
	0	15	12	23	14	9-10
7-	10	14		21-22	13	8
	8	13		20		7
	6	12	11	19	12	6
	4	11		18	11	5
	2	10		17		
	0	9			10	4
6-	10		10	16	9	
	8	8		15	8	3
	6			14	7	
	4	7	9		6	2
	2			13	5	
	0	6		12	4	

PART SCORES

Raw Score	Vw 23	Vp 24	Rw 20	Rf 23

MA		Vw	Vp	Rw	Rf
14-	0				
13-	10 8	33	30	23	25
	6 4		29		
	2	32			24
	0		28		
12-	10 8	31	27	22	(23)
	6	30	26		
	4	29			22
	0	28	25		
11-	10 8	27	(24)	21	21
	6	26	23	(20)	
	4	25			
	2		22		20
	0	24			
10-	10 8	(23) 22	21	19	19
	6	21	20	18	
	4	19-20			18
	2	18	19		
	0	17			
9-	10 8	16 15	18	17	17
	6	13-14	17	16	
	4	12	16		16
	2	11		15	
	0	10	15	14	
8-	10 8	9 8	14	13	15
	6	7	13	12	
	4	6	12	11	14
	2	5		10	
	0	4	11	9	
7-	10 8	3	10	8	13
	6	2	9	7	
	4			6	12
	2 0		8	5	
6-	10 8		7	4	11
	6 4		6	3	
	2 0		5		10

MA Scores ☐ ☐ ☐ ☐ ☐

Chronological Age ☐

Fig. 11.21. Primary Mental Abilities Profile of Thomas Lopez
(By permission of Science Research Associates.)

the short form of the *PMA,* it was not intended that a great deal of weight would be placed on these scores.) One further reason for additional testing was that all other tests had been given as part of a group testing program, so that one could not be certain as to the adequacy of testing administration nor Thomas's condition or behavior while taking the tests.

Thomas's *PMA* profile is shown in Figure 11.21. The reading IQ was 109, and the nonreading IQ was 113. These results confirm the teacher's judgment that the earlier IQ of 107 was a more accurate estimate than the *Otis* IQ of 83. From these data it seems likely that he has the ability to handle the extra work necessary to improve his spelling and language deficiencies and that placement in the brighter section would be appropriate.

The boy's superiority in mathematics is supported by his Number *(N)* score on the *PMA.* It seems reasonable to predict that mathematics will be one of his stronger subjects in later school years.

It is interesting to speculate on the possible relation between his lower Perception *(P)* score and his spelling deficiencies. This particular aptitude is supposed to measure ". . . the ability to recognize likenesses and differences between objects and symbols, quickly and accurately" *(Manual for Primary Mental Abilities,* 1948, p. 3). If this kind of ability is important in learning to spell, we may have here one specific factor to explain Thomas's relatively poor achievement in this area.

On the basis of this study, it was decided that Thomas would be placed in the brighter section. It was felt that not only could he handle the work there but that he would benefit from the more stimulating and challenging environment.

CASE OF ROBERT LING

Is He Gifted?

Robert is a short, well-groomed Chinese boy who was born in China and brought here shortly before entering the first grade. His speech is clear and his vocabulary well-developed. In the fifth grade he is seen as an excellent student, one with well-developed work habits, who is serious about his school work and who enjoys being one of the better students in his class.

Available Test Data

Tests already given are listed on Table 11.11.

Robert seems to have made good progress in reading; he read at grade level in the second grade, one year above grade level in the third grade, and, according to an oral reading test administered by his teacher, he was able to handle a seventh grade reader in the fifth grade. The slower progress in reading during the earlier grades may have resulted from his problems of adjustment to the new language and the whole new way of life. The later increases are felt to be at least partly a result of his variety of interests and his high level of motivation for learning.

Table 11.11. Test Results of Robert Ling

NAME OF TEST	School Grade	Score
Local Reading Readiness Test	1st	60 Percentile
Pintner-Cunningham Primary	1st	100 IQ
Local Math. Achievement Test	1st	90 Percentile
Local Reading Test	2nd	2.6 Grade Equiv.
Local Math. Achievement Test	3rd	90 Percentile
Otis Quick-Scoring, Alpha	3rd	109 IQ
Metropolitan Primary Reading Test:		
Word Meaning	3rd	4.7 Grade Equiv.
Reading	3rd	4.2 Grade Equiv.
Local Math. Achievement Test	4th	90 Percentile
Local Math. Achievement Test	5th	90 Percentile

Arithmetic achievement was consistently superior throughout the grades, seemingly reflecting a combination of aptitude and effort.

Two measures of intelligence—both nonverbal—show average to high-average mental ability. The nine point difference between the IQ obtained in first grade and that obtained in third grade may have no significance at all, especially since two different tests were used. However, the second was the higher one, which is in the direction in which reading scores moved. This may be further indication that the earlier measures (both of reading and intelligence) were not adequate representations of Robert's potentialities.

Further Testing

Normally in this school, in a case such as this, there would be no thought of retesting. The question was raised, however, whether Robert should be considered for a class for intellectually gifted (minimum IQ requirement 120). Because of his classroom performance, the trend toward higher reading status, the high mathematics scores, and all these in spite of any possible handicaps resulting from bilingualism and biculturism, it was felt that Robert might possibly have this high level of capability. Accordingly, the *Kuhlman-Anderson* was administered, with a resulting IQ of 112. This seems to confirm the earlier measures and indicates that Robert is functioning at high normal level. He will be placed in a bright sixth grade class but not in the class for gifted children. Although his school work is nearly up to the level of many of the children with IQ of 120, the competition of these brighter children is likely to have an adverse effect on Robert, especially since he is so serious about school.

FINAL COMMENT

The cases which have been presented, though hardly a comprehensive sample of the kinds of counseling situations in which tests are used, have nonetheless enabled us to observe the application of some of the principles discussed in earlier chapters. The methods used are basically the same, whether the problem is one of career planning, adjustment to college, decisions about marriage, or the prediction and prevention of juvenile delinquency. The actuarial tables and formulas for predicting success on the job, in college, or in marriage, are of the same form; only the contents differ. Likewise, the clinical process uses similar methods of inductive reasoning, model building, and deductive reasoning to lead to the conclusions, whether they be about school, job, or marriage.

Chapters 12 and 13 will focus on a number of topics associated with some special problems of test interpretation, most of which result from questions raised in the cases. Some of these topics, such as underachievement, apply primarily to one or another kind of interpretive situation. Others, such as interpretation of differences between scores, are more generally applicable to a variety of counseling situations.

CHAPTER 12

Interpreting Differences Between Test Scores

IN USING TESTS in connection with educational and vocational adjustment or planning, as with many other uses, counselors frequently make *comparisons* between an individual's scores on two different tests, or on two parts of a single test. The multifactor tests of mental abilities, in fact, had as one of their major *raisons d'être* the comparability of various parts one with another and thus were standardized and normed on the same samples of people. Many of the questions brought to guidance tests imply comparisons of two or more scores: In which school subjects does Frances have the greatest proficiency? In which subjects is she functioning below the level that might be expected of her? Which of Harry's aptitudes are his stronger and which his weaker? Are his interests greater in the mechanical area than in the clerical area? For which group of occupations does Martin have greater promise—selling, farming, or mechanical repair? Is Betty's social adjustment better than her family adjustment? Many such questions were raised in the cases included in Chapter 11: With Robert Martin, we wondered why his Spelling and Sentences scores on the *DAT* were so much higher than his scores on almost all the other parts. In the case of Frank O'Neill, there were a number of comparisons made between scores on tests of various aptitudes in an attempt to help Frank determine his chances of relative success in various fields.

A second group of applications of this kind of comparison between tests will be discussed in detail later in this chapter; these have to do with comparisons of two scores attained on tests *which presumably measure the same thing*. It is commonplace in many schools today, for example, to give intelligence (scholastic aptitude) tests at several points between kindergarten and twelfth grade. Comparisons are made to see whether there is consistency or whether there have been significant deviations. If the latter, further interpretive study is needed in order to find out the reasons: whether the person has actually changed in some way, whether one of the tests was administered or scored incorrectly, or whether the tests themselves are measuring somewhat different characteristics.

WHEN IS A DIFFERENCE REALLY A DIFFERENCE?

For now, we are concerned with only one element in all of these kinds of comparison: In consideration of the *errors of measurement* arising from the lack of precision of the tests used, how large a difference must there be between two scores before we will regard it as truly a difference? How far apart must Frances's scores on Spelling and Arithmetic tests be before we will say that she is better on one than on the other? How much higher must Harry's measured mechanical interest be than his clerical interest before we will say that he is more interested in one than in the other? How much difference must there be between a child's fifth grade IQ and his eighth grade IQ before we will say that there is a difference which requires further interpretive study?

Note that we are excluding from consideration all of the other elements implied in a comparison of scores on two tests. Most obvious is the *equivalence* of norms used in the two tests. If Frances took a Spelling test which was standardized on a national cross-section of American elementary schools and an Arithmetic test which was standardized in West Coast urban schools, a large difference between her two percentile or grade equivalent scores might mean only that the two norm groups are different in their average school achievement. Frances herself might actually be achieving about as well in one subject as the other. Similarly, there are other factors which might have caused differences between her two scores, such as differences in her *physical and emotional* condition on the two days the tests were administered, differences in her *motivation* on the two occasions, differences in *types of items* included in the test (essay versus multiple choice, for example), *scoring errors,* and others. These various elements are discussed later in this chapter, primarily with reference to "contradictory scores," scores on pairs of tests which presumably measure the same thing. Many of the factors to be examined at that time, such as differences in norm groups, are equally applicable to comparisons of scores on tests which do *not* presume to measure the same thing. For now we address ourselves to what must perforce be the first question in all the situations mentioned: Is there a difference, statistically speaking, large enough to be considered a significant difference and therefore to warrant further investigation into its meaning? The following section is intended to answer this question.

Standard Error of Measurement

Essentially the question here resolves itself to the *reliability* of measurement, which is usually represented by the coefficient of reliability, but which for our present purposes is better approached through the statistic of *standard error of measurement*. The concept, its mathematical origin, and its computation are included in most elementary statistics textbooks. The formula itself is simple (Thorndike and Hagen, 1955):

$$S_m = S_t \sqrt{1 - r_{11}}$$

where S_m is the standard error of measurement
S_t is the standard deviation of test scores
r_{11} is the reliability coefficient

The more reliable the test, the smaller the error of measurement.

The application of this concept is illustrated nicely by Thorndike and Hagen by use of one student's profile on the *Metropolitan Achievement Test* and *Otis* intelligence test. Figure 12.1 shows this profile as it is usually presented, with each score represented by a single point. One is tempted to characterize the Vocabulary score as being higher than Reading, and Reading in turn as higher than Arithmetic Fundamentals and Arithmetic Reasoning. However, this would assume that each score is absolutely precise and that there are no errors of measurement. Applying the standard error of measurement to this profile results in Figure 12.2, also reproduced from Thorndike and Hagen. Now each score is represented by a *line* instead of a point. The broader line extending above and below the actual score point (which now becomes the mid-point of a range of scores) shows the ranges plus and minus one standard error of measurement. The chances are 68 in 100 that this child's "true" score is within this range, or put another way, if it were possible to give this youngster the same test 100 times, it could be expected that 68 of those times the score would be within the range represented by the broad lines. We may appreciate the crudeness of this measurement by applying this degree of error to a bathroom scale. The per cent of variation represented by most of these broad bars would mean that if this third grader got on the scale once and had a weight reading of 60 pounds, we could expect that if he got on the scale 100 more times, 68 out of 100 of those times the weight would register between 54 and 66 pounds, and the remaining 32 times, it would be outside this range. We would probably not keep a bathroom scale of this sort for very long (without having it repaired). But our most reliable tests have only this degree of precision! To be right 68 out of 100 times, we would have to report this child's Arithmetic Reasoning score as between grade equivalent 3.2 and 3.6 (reading as best we can from this profile), but we would realize that there is practically one chance in three that the "true" score would be above or below this band.

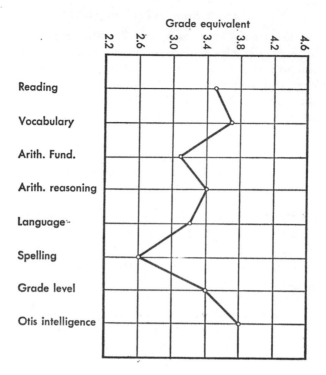

Fig. 12.1. Score Profile for Metropolitan Achievement Test Battery and Otis Intelligence Test
inted from R. L. Thorndike and E. Hagen, 1955. *Measurement and evaluation in psychology and education.* New York: Wiley. With permission.)

Studying the profile in Fig. 12.2 now in terms of the broader bars (± one standard error of measurement) and considering each score as a range rather than a point, we see that some of the "differences" have disappeared. Whereas the *mid-point* of Vocabulary is above the mid-point of Reading, the two bars overlap with the upper end of the Reading bar being above the lower end of the Vocabulary bar. The result is that we can no longer regard the Vocabulary score as being higher than Reading. The same thing occurs in comparisons of Arithmetic Reasoning and Language scores and in comparison of the *Otis* score with those on Reading, Vocabulary, and Arithmetic Reasoning. In these latter cases we might previously have said that this student was underachieving in these three parts of the *Metropolitan;* now there is no difference between intelligence and achievement in these areas (this assumes, of course, that the norms used for the *Otis* and the *Metropolitan* are equivalent or nearly so).

To be more conservative, we should extend our range to the points which include plus or minus *two* standard errors of estimate units; this would give us assurance that there are 95 chances in 100 that we have in-

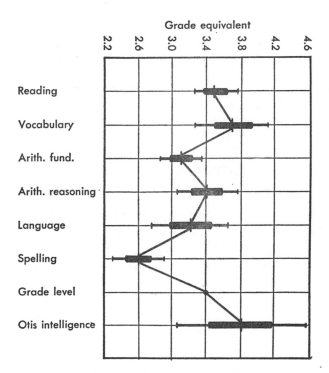

Grade equivalent

Fig. 12.2. Score Profile for Metropolitan Achievement Test Battery and Otis Intelligence Test, Showing Range of ± 1 S. E. of Measurement (Broad Bars) and ± 2 S. E. of Measurement (Narrow Bars)

(Reprinted from R. L. Thorndike and E. Hagen, 1955. *Measurement and evaluation in psychology and education*. New York: Wiley. With permission.)

cluded the "true" score. The narrower lines extending above and below the broader lines of Fig. 12.2 show *these* ranges. We would now be working more nearly at the level of accuracy of a good bathroom scale. However, we would have erased almost all the differences in this profile! Only those pairs of tests whose thinner lines do not overlap can be considered as being different. The only underachievement under these conditions would be in Spelling, and the Spelling score is the only one which can be considered to be different from any other score.

Although this concept has been understood for many years, and data regarding reliability reported in test manuals, the specific applications to particular tests have been used very little by counselors. Few seem to make the relatively simple translation from reliability coefficient or standard error of measurement to the "band of scores" used above. A promising sign, however, is the use of the band approach to score description in some recently published tests. Some manuals provide the test interpreter with a ready-made gadget for determining the range of scores included within a specified number of standard error of measurement units. In Figure 12.3

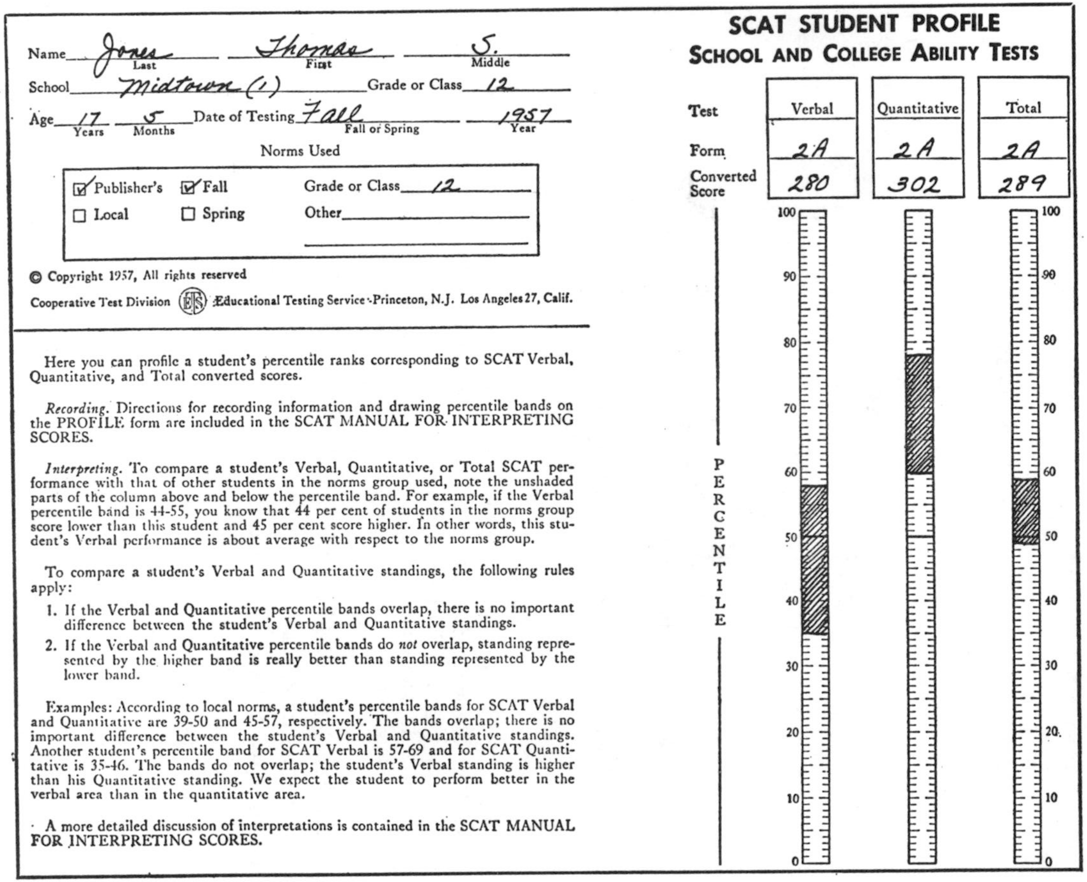

SCAT STUDENT PROFILE
SCHOOL AND COLLEGE ABILITY TESTS

Name Jones (Last) Thomas (First) S. (Middle)
School Midtown (1) Grade or Class 12
Age 17 (Years) 5 (Months) Date of Testing Fall (Fall or Spring) 1957 (Year)

Norms Used

☑ Publisher's ☑ Fall Grade or Class 12
☐ Local ☐ Spring Other

Cooperative Test Division ETS Educational Testing Service · Princeton, N.J. Los Angeles 27, Calif.

Here you can profile a student's percentile ranks corresponding to SCAT Verbal, Quantitative, and Total converted scores.

Recording. Directions for recording information and drawing percentile bands on the PROFILE form are included in the SCAT MANUAL FOR INTERPRETING SCORES.

Interpreting. To compare a student's Verbal, Quantitative, or Total SCAT performance with that of other students in the norms group used, note the unshaded parts of the column above and below the percentile band. For example, if the Verbal percentile band is 44-55, you know that 44 per cent of students in the norms group score lower than this student and 45 per cent score higher. In other words, this student's Verbal performance is about average with respect to the norms group.

To compare a student's Verbal and Quantitative standings, the following rules apply:

1. If the Verbal and Quantitative percentile bands overlap, there is no important difference between the student's Verbal and Quantitative standings.
2. If the Verbal and Quantitative percentile bands do *not* overlap, standing represented by the higher band is really better than standing represented by the lower band.

Examples: According to local norms, a student's percentile bands for SCAT Verbal and Quantitative are 39-50 and 45-57, respectively. The bands overlap; there is no important difference between the student's Verbal and Quantitative standings. Another student's percentile band for SCAT Verbal is 57-69 and for SCAT Quantitative is 35-46. The bands do not overlap; the student's Verbal standing is higher than his Quantitative standing. We expect the student to perform better in the verbal area than in the quantitative area.

A more detailed discussion of interpretations is contained in the SCAT MANUAL FOR INTERPRETING SCORES.

Test	Verbal	Quantitative	Total
Form	2A	2A	2A
Converted Score	280	302	289

Fig. 12.3. Specimen Profile for School and College Ability Tests
(*Manual for Interpreting Scores, S.C.A.T.*, p. 11, by permission of the Cooperative Test Division, Educational Testing Service.)

is reproduced an illustrative profile which appears in the Manual for the *Cooperative School and College Ability Test*. The band used there is read directly from the table of norms and requires no computation by the user. As described, the band includes one standard error of measurement.[1]

Tables applying this principle to a number of commonly used tests have been prepared by Dr. Frederick B. Davis, of Hunter College. Tables 12.1 and 12.2 are reproduced here as illustrations of his approach. Selecting the 85 per cent Confidence Interval, Davis has computed the number of points difference between each pair of scores that is the minimum at this level of confidence. Table 12.1 is read as follows: A difference between one's score on Verbal Reasoning and Numerical Ability (column 2) must be at least 7 standard score points before we can say that there are 85

Table 12.1. Significant Score Differences for Differential Aptitude Tests

Standard Errors of Measurement, 85 Per Cent Confidence Intervals for Single Standard Scores,* and Differences Between Pairs of Standard Scores* That Are Significant at the 15 Per Cent Level, or Better

Test	1	2	3	4	5a	5b	6	7	8	85 Per Cent Confidence Interval	Standard Error of Measurement
1. Verbal	7	7	7	7	8	9	7	7	7	9.1	3.2
2. Numerical		8	7	7	8	10	8	7	8	10.0	3.5
3. Abstract			7	7	8	9	7	7	7	9.1	3.2
4. Space				6	7	9	7	6	7	8.2	2.8
5a. Mechanical—Boys					8	10	8	7	8	11.1	3.9
5b. Mechanical—Girls						11	10	9	10	15.5	5.4
6. Clerical							8	7	8	10.4	3.6
7. Spelling								6	7	8.2	2.8
8. Sentences									8	10.0	3.5

* Standard scores are shown on the Individual Report Form of the Differential Aptitude Tests. The data on which this table is based are in Table 27 of the *Manual for the Differential Aptitude Tests*, p. 66. Except for the data pertaining to the Mechanical Reasoning Test, the data for boys and girls have been combined.

SOURCE: Dr. Frederick B. Davis, Hunter College, New York. Copyright, 1959, Frederick B. Davis. By permission.

[1] An earlier use of this same concept, though without the use of bands, is found in the *Differential Aptitude Tests*. The profile sheet for this battery is arranged in such a way that each inch of vertical distance represents ten units of standard score (see any of the *DAT* profiles used with the cases in Chapter 11 for illustration, although the reproductions here are reduced in size from the original 8½ x 11). The authors suggest in the Manual for the *DAT* that differences between two scores should be at least one inch to be certain that there is a real difference; this would result in very conservative estimates, since such differences are at the 1 per cent level of confidence.

Table 12.2. Significant Score Differences for Kuder Preference Record, Vocational

Vertical Distances on Profile Chart 7-299, Expressed in Sixteenths of an Inch, Corresponding to Standard Errors of Measurement and 85 Per Cent Confidence Intervals for Individual Interest Scores and to Differences Between Pairs of Interest Scores That Are Significant at the 15 Per Cent Level, or Better*

Test	0	1	2	3	4	5	6	7	8	9	85 Per Cent Confidence Interval	Standard Error of Measurement
					Differences							
0	13†	13‡	16	16	13	15	15	15	14	15	18	6
1		13	16	16	13	15	15	15	14	15	18	6
2			17	18	16	18	18	18	16	18	25	9
3				17	16	18	18	18	16	18	25	9
4					13	16	16	16	14	16	19	7
5						17	17	17	16	17	24	8
6							17	17	16	17	24	8
7								17	16	17	24	8
8									15	16	21	7
9										17	24	8

* Data in this table are based on reliability coefficients in a sample of 1,000 men reported in Table 5 of the *Examiner Manual*, Fifth Edition, (Chicago: Science Research Assoc., 1953) and are applicable *only* to Profile Chart 7-299.

† This entry indicates that a distance of 13/16, or more, of an inch between the points representing the outdoor interest scores of two individuals is significantly different from zero at the 15 per cent level, or better.

‡ This entry indicates that a distance of 13/16, or more, of an inch between the points representing the scores of one individual (or of two different individuals) on test O (outdoor interests) and test 1 (mechanical interests) is significantly different from zero at the 15 per cent level, or better.

SOURCE: *Ibid.*

chances in 100 that there is a "true" difference between the scores. Similarly, a girl's Mechanical Reasoning score must be at least 10 points from her Clerical score before the two may be considered different.

Table 12.2 gives similar information for the *Kuder Preference Record*. Here the differences are in terms of sixteenths of an *inch* of distance on the profile sheet; this was done because no standard score scale has been provided with the *Kuder*, as it was with the *DAT*. It is possible to use a ruler this way because the *Kuder* profile, although marked off in percentiles rather than standard scores, actually represents the spread of scores in standard score form, the percentile units being of different size at different points in the scale, as is proper.

Davis (1959) has discussed in detail the statistics of his approach. He points out that somewhat different formulas must be used for computing the standard error of measurement for each of several situations: for comparing an individual's score on one part of a test with his average on the total test, for comparing a person's score on a test with the average score obtained by a particular group, and for comparing the mean scores of two groups on a test.

It is to be hoped that soon it will be standard practice for publishers of multiscore tests to include not only technical information regarding reliability but also simple devices, preferably right on the profile sheet, which with little or no further computation will show the size of differences needed to be significant at stated levels of confidence. Until then, test interpreters can make use of the available materials such as Davis's tables. Counselors, especially those who use certain tests in quantity, can easily compute for themselves the number of points difference needed for statistical significance. This requires only information normally found in a test manual: the standard error of measurement or, in its absence, the standard deviation and reliability of each test. A simple graphical device can easily be made for application to profiles, perhaps a strip of cardboard which will show the ±1 and ±2 standard error of measurement limits for a test, or the spread necessary between any two scores for a given level of significance. This of course assumes that the standard error of measurement is the same throughout the range of scores on a test. To the extent that it is not, these methods are somewhat inaccurate.

CONTRADICTORY SCORES ON TWO OR MORE TESTS

In several of the cases in Chapter 11, it was found that two measures of the same interest or ability gave what seemed to be contradictory information about the individual. In each instance, an attempt was made to explain the discrepancy. Now we shall try to bring together in a single list a number of factors which may operate, singly or in combination, to produce such contradictions or discrepancies. We shall try to answer this question: What factors may explain differences between two test scores which are supposedly measuring the same thing? What might account for a difference of ten IQ points between a person's scores on two different intelligence tests? How can we reconcile the results of two interest inventories, one of which shows a high score on clerical interests, the other a low score? As applied to a group problem, what might have caused a class to score above average on one test of arithmetic and below average on another, when both tests presumably have been intended to get at the same ability? Such questions may be answered in terms of differences of three kinds: first, differences between *tests themselves;* second, differences in the *individual or the group* from one testing to the other; and third, differences in the conditions of *test administration* from one test to the other.

Differences Between the Tests Themselves

The fact that two tests carry the same designation—"intelligence" or "mechanical aptitude"—is obviously no assurance that they measure the same thing. It is not uncommon to find two such tests correlating with each other to the extent of .70 or less. Such tests, even when they do correlate highly enough to be considered in the same family, may nonetheless tap different aspects of a single quality, or they may have internal differences great enough to explain apparent discrepancies. Some of the ways in which the tests themselves may differ from each other are listed below.

Type of Test

We need not go into these in great detail, since they have been treated extensively in introductory measurement texts. Cronbach, 1960; Super, 1949; Thorndike and Hagen, 1955).

Individual versus Group Tests. For a particular person, there may be considerable spread between his scores on an individually administered and a group-administered test, as a result of this fact alone and apart from any other differences between the two tests involved. One youngster may concentrate and attend better in the individual situation and thereby get a higher score. Another may feel more self-conscious and become more tense in taking the test alone and therefore do less well than on a group test. Not a great deal is known about differences in scores arising from the individual versus group administration. As has already been pointed out (see Chapter 4), it is a mistake to assume that a more adequate measure is always obtained by an individual test. Until more facts are available, the effects of individual versus group administration for a particular individual remains a matter for clinical interpretation.

Power versus Speeded Tests. This question arose in the case of Richard Wilson. Some people seem to need more time than permitted even by generous time limits, in order to attain their maximal scores. This may be because they are slow readers, compulsive double- and triple-checkers, or because they become cripplingly anxious under speed conditions. Others may need the pressure of a time limit to exert maximum effort, and they may do poorly on power tests.

Worksample versus Abstract Test. The more closely the content of a test approximates the activity about which a prediction or other interpretation is to be made, the more nearly is it a *worksample* kind of test. Thus we may measure the mathematical aspects of aptitude for mechanical work by using a test such as the Shop Arithmetic part of the *SRA Mechanical Aptitude Test,* which requires reading of measurements on drawings of rulers and solution of practical shop problems, and is therefore something of a worksample test. We could, on the other hand, try to accomplish the same purpose with a general mathematics test, such as the mathematics section of one of the achievement batteries—*Iowa Tests of Educational Development* or the *Cooperative General Achievement Tests.* The fact that a particular boy did considerably better on one than the other may indicate that perhaps he found the worksample items more meaningful and understandable than the abstract problems of the other type of test.

Real worksample tests, such as the rarely used *Minnesota Mechanical Assembly Test,* are quite infrequent in guidance work, but there are situations, such as that in the illustration above, in which one test is more nearly a worksample than the other. In such instances, the worksample versus abstract qualities of the two tests may help explain differences between the scores attained by one individual.

Paper and Pencil versus Apparatus Tests. Like the preceding difference is the difference in the way in which responses are made, whether by marking with a pencil or by manipulating three-dimensional materials, such as pegs, blocks, or tweezers. As before, there are some people who find concrete materials more comfortable to work with and who may, therefore, get higher scores on, say, the *Minnesota Spatial Relations Test* (an actual form board) than the *Minnesota Paper Form Board,* which is a paper representation of a similar task. Therefore, when an individual has scored quite differently on two tests, one of which is paper-and-pencil and the other apparatus, interpretation of the difference in terms of this factor may be in order.

Type of Item

In addition to the type of test, explanation of discrepant scores may also be sought in differences in the types of item used in the tests, such as essay versus objectively scored, free-choice versus forced-choice, and so on.

Essay versus Objectively Scored. Except for some individually administered tests, such as the *Stanford-Binet* and the *Wechsler* scales, essay or open-end questions are rarely found in standardized tests. The convenience of scoring the multiple-choice item has contributed toward making it almost universal among standardized tests. There are some tests, however, such as the *Schorling-Clark-Potter Hundred-Problem Arithmetic Test,* in which the individual must write his own answers. Some people find such tests much more difficult than those in which all the possible responses to an item have been reduced to four or five from which they make their choice.

This factor also may be helpful in understanding the individual whose scores on standardized achievement tests are very different from those on teacher-made essay tests and on such essay items as those used in the New York State Regents tests. The nature of the task represented in essay tests seems to be somewhat different from that in objectively scored tests which purport to measure the same quality. This belief has led the Educational Testing Service to include an essay section in its *Sequential Tests of Educational Progress,* despite the added burden of scoring which results.

Free Choice versus Forced Choice. This dichotomy applies to measures of personality and interest. With statisticians and test-development theoreticians still debating the relative merits and effects of these two item types, we can only speculate as to whether the differences between an individual's scores on two inventories might have resulted from the difference in the types of items. For example, an individual might have an almost straight-line profile on the *Kuder Preference Record,* so that there seems to be no differentiation among his interests. Yet the same person might, on a free-choice interest inventory such as the *Cleeton Interest Inventory,* have very high scores on all or most of the parts, very low scores on all parts, or middle-range scores on all. The forced-choice nature of the *Kuder* results in a *relative* line-up of preferences, whereas the *Cleeton* shows *absolute* level of liking for the activities listed in each field.[2]

With personality inventories, the forced-choice approach has been used to reduce the effects of faking and of social desirability tendencies. Therefore if we find that a client has a "better-adjusted" profile on the *Bell Adjustment Inventory* than on the *Gordon Personal Profile,* we might hypothesize that it is because the latter is forced-choice and the former is not.

There are likely to be other effects of the forced-choice item type, some of them not as obvious as those already mentioned. The forced-choice test is often found to be more difficult and annoying to take, because of the necessity of making choices even when the person feels no preference for one of the alternative choices (as on the *Kuder* or the *Edwards Personal Preference Schedule).* This may in turn affect the person's responses so as to yield a profile different from what would result if he were permitted to answer each question individually "Yes" or "No," "Like" or "Dislike."

Here again, we find a scarcity of research, with the result that discrepant results on two interest inventories or two personality inventories, one of which is forced-choice and the other not, must be studied on an individual basis. In each case one applies clinical methods to ascertain the probable effects of the item type.

Characteristic Being Measured

We come now to the basic question of the particular validities of each test, that is, what specific characteristics each measures, what specific criteria each predicts. The *Ohio State University Psychological Examination (OSU)* and the *American Council on Education Psychological Examination for College Freshmen (ACE)* are intended to serve essentially the same function: to measure a cluster of mental abilities deemed important for success in college. Yet, the contents are different in several ways. The *OSU,* for example, contains mostly verbal materials, with a heavy emphasis on vocabulary and reading comprehension, whereas the *ACE* contains numerical and abstract reasoning material in addition to the verbal and has no reading comprehension part as such. For some subjects, then, a sig-

---

[2] In one of the few researches on this topic, Way (1953) found that a free-choice form of the *Kuder* led to much higher correlations (.37 to .92) among the scales than was the case with the standard forced-choice version. This led him to conclude that the differentiation among scales found with the *Kuder* may sometimes be attributed to the requirement that subjects make choices even when they have no feeling of preference among the options. He found also that the scales of his free-choice *Kuder* correlated only modestly (coefficients ranging from .09 to .57) with the same scales on the forced-choice *Kuder.* It seems to be true, then, that the type of item sometimes has a very marked influence on the results of testing.

nificant difference between scores on the two measures of academic aptitude may result from these differences of content. A clinical interpretation somtimes leads to fruitful hypotheses and conclusions; for example,
a lower *OSU* than *ACE* score may suggest a reading deficiency, which may
then be verified by administering a reading test, by checking school records for pertinent information, and by asking the client to tell what he
knows and thinks about his reading abilities.[3]

Some important differences in what is measured by tests are:

Old-Learned Material versus New Problems. We encountered this factor in the case of Robert Martin, where it apparently served to explain a
strange assortment of test scores and apparent contradictions between
scores on aptitude tests and high school grades. The plodder may do much
better on old-learned material than on new problems. The reverse may indicate either lack of exposure to the material (such as spelling) normally
learned in the past or lack of effort in the situations where the old material is normally learned.

General versus Specific Content. This applies particularly to achievement tests. The *Iowa High School Content Tests* represent one end of this
dimension, since they require recollection, or at least recognition, of
specific facts, such as dates of historical events, names of works of art and
their creators, and characters in novels. Sharply contrasting are the *General Educational Development Tests (GED)*, which have been widely used
as the basis for awarding high school equivalency certificates to those who
never graduated. This battery seeks to measure the *general* outcomes of
a high school education by emphasizing abilities required to read and
comprehend paragraphs in literature, the sciences, and social studies. The
Iowa Tests of Educational Development bring together in a single battery
both kinds of measure. A wide gap between an individual's scores on, say
"General Background in the Natural Sciences" and "Ability to Interpret
Reading Materials in the Natural Sciences," will in some cases be understood by considering whether specific or general content has been
measured.

Different Aspects of a Characteristic. Spatial ability is an example of a
mental ability which we often treat as a single entity, but which factor
analyses have shown to be a cluster of subabilities, each correlating with
the others, but not perfectly. Thus spatial ability may be broken down
into space perception, space relations, and spatial visualization, the first
of which has to do with recognizing the *shape* of figures, the second with
relationships between two or more figures, and the third having to do

---

[3] This is, of course, only *one* of the differences between the *OSU* and the *ACE* which
might have caused the discrepant scores. The fact that the *OSU* is a power test and
the *ACE* a highly speeded test is another. Still a third is the difference in norms
between the two (discussed later). Each factor receives at least momentary consideration in the clinical process of resolving contradictions in scores.

with mental *manipulation* of figures. Most space tests seem to involve a combination of two or all three of these subabilities, with the components being weighted differently on different tests. Another kind of breakdown can be made in terms of the number of *dimensions* involved; thus the *Minnesota Paper Form Board* involves two-dimensional figures, and the *DAT* Space test uses three-dimensional objects (which are, however, depicted in two dimensions).

Since abilities are known to be complex in every area (mechanical aptitude, clerical aptitude), it is not surprising to find that an individual gets quite different scores on two different tests bearing similar labels. Until a good deal more is known about the organization of mental abilities and about the specific validities of each test, we remain handicapped in attempting to reconcile discrepant scores on two or more such tests. Suppose Dick has a high score on the *MPFB* and a low score on the *DAT* Space test, and suppose Bill has the reverse profile. Assuming we have reason to believe that the differences are not due to differences in norms, motivation, or any factor other than the difference in the specific kinds of spatial ability measured by the two tests, what can we conclude? That Bill would do better as a draftsman or a sheet metal worker than would Dick, since both occupations involve working with representations of three-dimensional objects? Or that Dick would be more successful than Bill as a cutter in the garment industry, where two-dimensional spatial ability seems to be more important? Lacking anything better, the counselor does the best he can to tie the particular subability to what he knows about the specific requirements of each occupation.

The important point to be noted here is that different scores on different tests of presumably the same psychological characteristic may be found to differ because they actually tap relatively independent aspects or subdivisions of that characteristic.

Analogous conditions exist in the realms of interest and personality. Two interest inventories may have scales labelled identically, say "Mechanical Interest," yet the items which make up the two scales may be sampling different enough mechanical activities that a single person could score high on one Mechanical Interest scale and low on the other. Or, one interest inventory might ask the subject to indicate likes and dislikes for the *names* of occupations, whereas another sought to tap the same interests by soliciting reactions to *activities* included in the occupations. Here again a single counselee might have on two interest inventories apparently contradictory scores resulting from differences in the particular aspect of interests measured or the particular approach to interest measurement.

Perhaps the most important suggestion for the practicing counselor is that he know his tests as intimately and thoroughly as possible. This involves knowing the contents of the test from personal examination of them and knowing as much as possible about the specific validities of the test—what it measures and what it predicts. It seems clear that the known validities of *one* test of a given characteristic cannot be generalized to *another* test of the same characteristic without substantial evidence that the two are very highly correlated.

Level of Difficulty of the Test Contents

This factor may perhaps best be understood in relation to achievement tests. Suppose that Anne drops markedly in score on a reading test between the sixth and seventh grades. Different forms of the same test were used each time, the elementary form (intended for fourth to sixth grades) having been used in the sixth grade and the junior high form being used in the seventh grade. Having eliminated a number of other factors which might have caused Anne's drop in score (physical condition, motivation, anxiety), one would in such a case at least consider the possibility that the *difficulty level* of the two tests had something to do with the results. The elementary form of the test is made up of materials with which Anne had had almost three years of experience and on which she had attained enough success, at least with the easier items, to get a pretty good score on the test. The junior high form, however, might have as its *easiest* items material well above the lowest level tapped by the earlier test. Thus Anne had little opportunity to show what she *could* do, and, as a result, her score on the junior high form, although valid enough as a comparison with others at this level, does not tell the *whole* story about her reading.

This factor can also operate in relation to aptitude tests. An example is the *Bennett Mechanical Comprehension Test,* of which several forms are available, AA, BB, and CC, which are increasingly difficult. Each form is intended to discriminate best at one particular ability level. Even though we use the same norm group in each case, an individual might get lower percentile scores on the more difficult than on the easier forms. As in the case of Anne's reading test results, here also a youngster might do well compared to his peers with lower-level materials but not so well on more difficult material.

It is even conceivable that the reverse might happen, that a counselee might handle higher-level material (say, algebra and geometry) better than lower-level material in the same general academic area (say, arithmetic). Such a person would get a relatively higher score on a high school level mathematics test which contains a larger proportion of the more advanced mathematics than he would on a similarly titled test with a higher proportion of arithmetic. The writer has known at least one bright engineer who had had graduate work in mathematics but who had difficulty verifying his change at the store.

Norm Differences

In comparing two scores obtained from different tests, it is inevitable that the question of the equivalence of the norms on the two tests arises. This is an especially perplexing problem because it is usually impossible to check further on one's hypothesis without, in effect, collecting local norms. Suppose Gary's record shows a higher IQ on the *California Test of Mental Maturity* than on the *Otis Self-Administering Test of Mental Ability*. One of the more immediate hypotheses is that the *Otis* norm group was a brighter sample than that of the *CTMM* and that therefore a few points difference in favor of the *CTMM* is "normal." Counselors who use two different tests of a single type with their counselees soon develop their own impressions of whether there tends to be a difference between the two tests. One hears, for example: "IQ's on the *XYZ* test run about five points higher than on the *LMN* test, but *LMN* and *RST* tests run pretty much alike." These impressions are often quite vague and speculative, yet with relatively little research, counselors could have a much more dependable basis for equating scores on different tests. In schools where pupils have taken two or more different tests of the same type, the data may already be available for large numbers of cases. In other schools and in agencies, it would be necessary to set up a plan for giving two or more different tests to the same people so that this sort of data would be available.

This kind of research on *group intelligence tests* has been reported by several investigators; some details will be reported here, not only for the information which they furnish, but also to illustrate some of the methods used and some of the problems encountered.

Before proceeding to the studies, it should be noted that we are dealing here only with *normative* differences among tests. Even if two different intelligence tests were standardized on identical populations, it would not necessarily follow that a single individual would receive identical scores—IQ, percentile, or whatever—on the two. Besides the inevitable error of measurement, the tests might differ in content, one being more verbal than another, one requiring more reading than another, and one containing more numerical content than another. A youngster who is stronger in quantitative than in verbal reasoning would therefore be expected to do better on one than another test, even if the test norms were equated. Equating of norms therefore would make only a limited contribution, but an important one. At least one source of variation would be eliminated, and the counselor could concentrate on the others. If someone received an IQ of 120 on one test at the age of 10 and an IQ of 109 on another at the age of 13, and if we knew that most people score 5 to 10 points lower on the second than the first, we would not be likely to spend any great amount of time tracking down the reason for the discrepancy. Similarly, if someone had a 75th percentile score on a scholastic aptitude test and a 50th percentile score on an achievement battery, we would be in a better position to judge whether there was underachievement if we knew that the two tests were normed on comparable populations. It is entirely conceivable in this instance that the norms for the achievement battery came from samples of a more selected nature, or from more advanced school districts than the norms for the aptitude test; if so, the difference of 25 percentile points might turn out to be "normal."

Studies of IQ Comparability. The studies which have been made do little more than whet the appetite, since their findings are far from conclusive. This becomes immediately evident when it is discovered that in Los Angeles the *CTMM* was found to yield higher IQ's than the *Terman-McNemar* and the *Otis* (Los Angeles City School Districts, 1950), whereas in Milwaukee the reverse relationship was discovered (Mouly and Edgar, 1958).

Six fairly recent studies of this sort were found (Los Angeles City School Districts, 1950; Chicago Public Schools, undated; Lennon, undated; Mouly and Edgar, 1958; Justman and Wrightstone, 1953; Educational Records Bureau, 1955). The results of the first four of these studies may be compared with each other because all four had at least one test in common, and some of the studies had in common an additional test.[4] Table 12.3 is an attempt to compare selected results of these four studies. Since all four studies included one of the *Otis* tests, this was used as the anchor score; it should be noted, however, that two studies used the Beta level of the *Otis,* one used the Gamma, and the fourth used the older Higher Examination. Therefore, it was necessary to assume that IQ's on these three forms are themselves equivalent, thus introducing an additional possible source of variation among the studies. Some evidence for questioning this assumption comes in a study by Kazmier and Browne (1959), who reported that some of the "equivalent" forms of the *Wonderlic Personnel Test* are not truly equivalent to others.

For convenience of reading, only eleven score levels have been included in this table, beginning with IQ 85 and including multiples of 5 up to the highest, 135. Some of the studies reported equivalents for *Otis* scores below 85 and above 135, but not all did; in any case, for present purposes this range should suffice.

Next, since three of the studies also included the *California Test of Mental Maturity,* their respective results are listed in adjacent columns, for easy comparison. Similarly, three studies used the *Terman-McNemar Test of Mental Ability* and they are listed in the following three columns. The *Pintner General Ability Test* was used in two studies, and these re-

---

[4] The Educational Records Bureau report (1955) could not be used in this tabulation because differences (between *Otis Quick-Scoring* and *Terman Group Test* IQ's) were given by age levels rather than IQ levels.

Table 12.3. Summary of Comparable IQ's on Different Intelligence Tests as Reported in Four Studies

Otis	Calif. TMM (1)	Calif. TMM (4)	Calif. TMM (3)	Terman-McNemar (4)	Terman-McNemar (2)	Terman-McNemar (3)	Pintner (1)	Pintner (2)	Kuhlmann-Anderson (1)	Kuhlmann-Finch (3)	Lorge-Thorndike (1)	SRA-PMA (4)	SRA Non-Verbal (4)
135	139				142		145	139-40	135		137		
130	134		130*		138	140*	139	134	130	130*	132		
125	129		122*		133	133*	132	128	125	124*	127		
120	123	133	118*	123	127	127*	126	123	121	119*	121	117	141-42
115	118	126	110*	117	119	117*	119	117	116	111*	116	109	131
110	113	121	104*	111	113	111*	113	111	111	105*	111	102-03	125-26
105	108	116	99	105	108	107	106	106	106	101	106	96	117
100	102	109	93*	100	102	99*	100	99	101	95*	100	91	113
95	97	104	89*	95	96	94*	94	92	97	91*	95	84	105
90	92	98	84*	89	90	90*	87	85	92	86*	90	77	99
85	86		77		84	84	81	78	87	76	84		

* These values were interpolated from values reported in the study.

SOURCES: (1) Chicago Public Schools, undated. By permission of Dr. Max B. Engelhart.
(2) Lennon, undated. By permission of the World Book Co.
(3) Mouly and Edgar, 1958. By permission of The Personnel and Guidance Journal.
(4) Los Angeles City School Districts, 1950. By permission.

Table 12.4. Summary of Comparable Mean IQ's on Different Intelligence Tests as Reported in Three Studies

Study	Otis	CTMM	Terman-McNemar	Pintner	Kuhlmann-Finch	Kuhlmann-Anderson	Lorge-Thorndike	SRA PMA	SRA Non-Verbal
(1)	101.4	104.7	105.5	99.2*		103.9	102.3	96.4	118.2
(2)	103.7	114.2	112.7		106.7				
(3)	110.2	105.2							

* This figure is not really comparable with the others because in the sample of schools where it was obtained the mean Otis IQ was 99.2. In the Chicago study, only the Otis was used in all schools sampled; in addition, each school gave one of the other four tests.

SOURCES: (1) Chicago Public Schools, undated. By permission of Dr. Max D. Engelhart.
(2) Los Angeles City School Districts, 1950. By permission.
(3) Mouly and Edgar, 1958. By permission of The Personnel and Guidance Journal.

sults are shown next. Finally, each of five other tests was used in only one of the studies; these are reported in the last five columns.

The specific methods used varied somewhat from study to study. In some, all subjects took all of the tests being compared, in others each subject took two tests, one of which was identical for all subjects. The statistical method varied also from study to study; most used the equipercentile method, in which scores on two or more tests are considered equivalent when they are attained by the same percentage of subjects; the Chicago study used a regression equation method for estimating score on one test from that on another, based on the correlation between the two tests.[5] Finally, the samples differed in geographical location, in age level (seventh grade to twelfth grade), and in ability (the Mouly and Edgar sample in particular was above average in test scores). Some or all of the differences among studies might have affected their results.

Table 12.3 is read as follows: Moving across the line on which the *Otis* IQ is 110, we see that the Chicago study found that a *CTMM* IQ of 113 was comparable with an *Otis* of 110 for their subjects, whereas the Los Angeles study found that their *CTMM* equivalent was 121, and the Mouly and Edgar study had a *CTMM* equivalent of 104.

Examination of the table reveals a number of noteworthy points:

1. No pair of tests in any study yielded *exactly* equivalent IQ's at all points along the range, although some came very close. The *Kuhlmann-Anderson* IQ's, for example, are at most two points different from those on *Otis*.

2. The extent of similarity of IQ's among the pairs of tests varies quite a lot. Using *Otis* as the baseline, and dealing only with those values shown in the table, at one extreme are the *Terman-McNemar* (in the Los Angeles study), the *Kuhlman-Anderson,* and the *Lorge-Thorndike,* all of which have an average IQ deviation of one point from *Otis*.[6] At the other extreme is the *SRA Non-Verbal,* whose average deviation from *Otis* is 14 points. For all the values shown in this table, the average deviation from *Otis* IQ is 5 points.

3. In some instances, the very same pair of tests is found in different studies to have quite different relationships to each other. The largest variation is noted with *CTMM;* in Chicago it was found to yield scores on the average 3 points higher than *Otis,* in Los Angeles the average was 10 points higher than *Otis,* whereas the Mouly and Edgar data show *CTMM* scores to be about 5 points lower than *Otis,* on the average (all these computations are crude estimates based on the data selected out of

[5] Engelhart, who did statistical work and wrote the report of the Chicago study, has reported (1959) that the two methods produced very similar tables of comparable scores when applied to the same set of data.

[6] Justman and Wrightstone (1953), working with eighth grade pupils, found that the *Pintner* and *Henmon-Nelson* tests were also this close together.

these studies for inclusion in Table 12.3) . It should be noted that the Los Angeles study used the 1942 edition of the *CTMM* and Chicago used the 1950 edition; Mouly and Edgar do not specify which form was used. Normative differences between editions may explain some of the discrepancies.

The *Terman-McNemar* results show more consistency among the three studies reporting them, although even here one gets a somewhat different set of *Otis* IQ equivalents depending on which study is used. Lennon's data show *Terman-McNemar* to run about 4 points higher than *Otis,* Mouly and Edgar found a 3 point differential, and the Los Angeles data show only a one point difference. *Pintner* equivalents to *Otis* scores vary on the average by 3 points between the Chicago study and Lennon's study.

For the three studies which report mean scores obtained with the tests used, Table 12.4 summarizes their results. These data would for the most part lead to conclusions very similar to those derived from Table 12.3.

4. Relationships between two tests are not always the same throughout the range of IQ scores. The *Otis* and *Pintner,* for example, tend to be very close at the middle of the range, but they deviate more toward the extremes, *Pintner* being higher than *Otis* at the upper IQ end and lower than *Otis* at the lower end. This is probably based on the well-known fact that the *Otis* has a smaller standard deviation than most other tests of this kind and therefore yields fewer extreme scores. Justman and Wrightstone (1953) reported a similar relationship between *Pintner* and *Henmon-Nelson,* the latter tending to give higher scores below IQ's of 100 but lower scores with IQ's above 120.

5. From the Educational Records Bureau study (1955) mentioned earlier, there is evidence that relationships between IQ's on two different tests vary with the age level of the subjects. At ages 11 to 13, they found that *Terman Group Test* IQ's ran considerably higher than *Otis Quick-Scoring* IQ's. At age 14, the median IQ's on the two tests were only one point apart. Above this age, however, the tendency was for the *Otis* IQ's to be higher. Total figures for the sample of 163 high school pupils give no hint of these differences; of the total, 79 had higher IQ's on the *Otis,* 79 had higher IQ's on the *Terman,* and 5 had identical IQ's on the two tests. Furthermore, the median IQ's for the total group were only one point apart.

Conclusions Regarding Studies. It seems clear that a good deal more research is needed before we can have a table of IQ equivalents for the commonly used tests. At this point it is possible to state only very tentative conclusions, since contradictory or at least inconsistent results have appeared in different studies of the same pairs of tests. It is likely that some of the inconsistencies may be attributable to differences between studies in their methodology, in the specific form and level of the tests used, in age level of the samples, and intelligence level of the samples.

One other factor suggests itself. Since the tests also differ somewhat in content (some being more nonverbal than others, some having more mathematical content than others), it may be that in one school, neighborhood, or region, the children are relatively better developed in one type of ability than another, and that these differences may be reflected in disparate results. For example, it is conceivable that one school puts more emphasis on reading and vocabulary than others; children in the first school might therefore have higher IQ's on the test which requires much reading, whereas the children in another school, which does not emphasize reading so much, might have *their* higher IQ's on the test which requires less reading. Similarly, it is conceivable that children in lower-social-status neighborhoods might do better on tests whose contents are less academic and more practical but that middle-class children might show a reverse pattern. Thus it may be that attempts to equate different tests in terms solely of *normative* differences are complicated by *other* differences between the tests.

As it becomes more and more customary for new tests to be standardized on very large and very carefully selected samples, this problem of score equivalence will decrease in importance. For immediate purposes, counselors can make use of the few studies available for at least tentative data. In establishing new testing programs, it would seem wise to try to use tests which have different forms for different age levels, forms which have been demonstrated to yield very similar IQ's.

Physical Differences Between the Tests

The last of the factors within the tests themselves, this one includes such details as size of type, ease or difficulty of recording one's answers, and clarity of diagrams. Some counselees report more difficulty in using one kind of answer sheet than another. With the machine-scored type of answer sheet people sometimes have difficulty keeping their place, and occasionally someone skips or doubles up on an item, with the result that every response is one line off on the answer sheet; naturally, scores will be completely meaningless. As to size of type, visually handicapped subjects may do better on tests having larger and clearer printing.

Differences in the Individual or Group

The fact that a counselee received two "contradictory" scores on similar—or even identical—tests may indicate that the person himself, or at least his functioning, was different on the two occasions. This is a most perplexing group of factors because often a major purpose of counseling, as of school and college programs in general, is to effect changes in people. We certainly expect achievement test scores to increase from year to year, at least during those years in which that particular subject matter is being taught. We expect underdeveloped and disturbed youngsters to improve in measured intelligence after receiving remedial or therapeutic help. It is hoped by research workers (though not always found) that personality inventories will reflect reduced anxiety, increased self-confidence, and other sought-after results of counseling, of psychotherapy, of special attention by teachers, and of normal development through adolescence.

There are also changes of an undesirable nature; people deteriorate in many qualities through the normal and abnormal processes of aging. Anxiety increases for some people, and personality integration decreases for some, as the result of environmental and constitutional factors. Students in school sometimes experience a reduction of effort from one testing occasion to another and, as a result, do more poorly on ability tests even when the ability itself has not changed.

All of these changes, both the desired and the undesired, complicate the interpretive process in cases where the same characteristic measures differently at different times. The difficult distinction must be made between situations in which "contradictions" occur because of errors of measurement, differences in tests, or other extrinsic factors and those in which the person being tested *actually functioned differently* on the two occasions. These intrinsic changes, those within the individual or at least his behavior, can be broken down into several subdivisions:

Motivation

John's higher scholastic aptitude score in the eleventh grade than in earlier grades may have come about because he suddenly became aware of the importance of getting into a college and having high test scores. For Frank, the ninth grade may have been the turning point, when he recognized that school *was* important and that without a high school education, a number of desirable job opportunities would be closed to him. The resulting change in motivation could raise his test scores in two ways: directly, by leading him to try harder on tests, and indirectly, by changing his efforts in school, thereby improving some of the skills and knowledges measured by tests.

Motivational factors can play havoc with the results of interest and personality inventories. The writer has for years told with some relish of an experience he had along these lines. All applicants for the teacher-training program at a certain university took the *Minnesota Multiphasic Personality Inventory*. Those profiles which, in a general screening, contained one or more deviant scores were referred to the writer or another psychologist on the faculty for follow-up. In one case, the profile had several scores well above the T-score of 70 usually taken as the cutoff point for deviation on the *MMPI,* including some of the psychotic scales. The student was called in for an interview, and the *Rorschach* was administered. A week or so later, puzzled by the very marked contradictions between the *MMPI* on the one hand and the interview and *Rorschach* on the other (which seemed to show a normal amount of problems for a college junior but no serious neurosis or psychosis), we again called the young man in for an interview. This time, the *MMPI* booklet had been examined, and a number of questions selected which he had answered in the pathological direction. Several of these questions were asked orally, and in each case the response was in the opposite direction to those on the answer sheet. Finally, the student was faced with this fact and asked if he could explain it. With some embarrassment, he told the story: He had heard that the tests were not used at all in the selection of teacher trainees and were merely a formality. Since there was a baseball game in which he was to play later that day (he was a varsity athlete) and since he was anxious to leave as soon as possible, he just went down the answer sheet making marks with the electrographic pencil at random, completing the whole inventory in a few minutes. Were it not for this piece of detective work on the part of the interviewer, the student might have been rejected or perhaps admitted on probation, to be watched very carefully in class and in student teaching.

Group-testing programs are especially vulnerable to motivational problems of this sort, as has been discussed in some detail in Chapter 3. Group programs do not afford much opportunity to control and be aware of motivation of the subjects. As a result, the motivational factor must be given greater consideration in interpreting discrepant scores on group-administered tests (especially those of the program variety, where entire classes, grades, or schools take a test for which many of them may have little motivation) than on tests which have been selected on an individual basis.

Physical and Psychological Conditions

Not much is known about the effects on test scores of the various physical discomforts. Counselees are ready enough to claim a cold, or a fever, or a headache, or tension as causes of test scores lower than they think they should have received. It is conceivable that these conditions, when severe enough, might so reduce effectiveness of functioning as to affect test scores (see Chapter 5). In trying to explain a test score, therefore, that is noticeably lower than other scores attained by the person on the same or similar tests, it is sometimes fruitful at least to ask whether there was something unusual in his condition that day. It would, of course, be a great help if test proctors and administrators made note of such conditions observed during test administration, so that the interpreter might have some information in addition to the client's own recall of the situation.

Test-Wiseness

As summarized in Chapter 5, the research on coaching and practice effects seems to show that increases in score can be expected to result from practice, especially with subjects who have not had a great deal of experience with tests. Thus, if we find increased scores for such people, from an earlier to a later test, the factor may be found to be important. The same kind of phenomenon sometimes operates with students who are new to a school; here again higher scores on later tests may reflect an increased feeling of familiarity and ease in the school.

Changes with Time in the Characteristic Being Measured

Normal Growth and Development: Groups. There are, first of all, the normal changes in ability (and in attitudes, interests, and other personality attributes) associated with growth and development. As children and adolescents mature, they handle abstractions better, they generalize more from their own experiences, and they improve in a wide variety of specific skills—perceptual, spatial, quantitative, verbal. Later, in adulthood, some of these abilities begin to deteriorate, while others not only hold their own but even increase through the middle years (see Chapter 4). The use of appropriate age *norms* (and these are moderately available for some characteristics during the childhood and adolescent years but are much less available for adulthood) provides at least a basis for judging whether the amount of measured change is to be expected as a result of normal development in that society.

Normal Growth and Development: Individual. In addition to the *group* developmental trends, there are the "normal" *individual* developmental sequences. At one year level, especially during childhood and early adolescent years, an individual's scores, as compared with his age or grade groups, may be considerably higher or lower than in previous years. His IQ, for example—that unchanging measure—may suddenly drop ten points or go up as much. Assuming that other possible causes have been discounted—motivation, conditions of administration, differences in the contents of the two tests, and their norms—it may be hypothesized that this individual was for a year or so either in a spurt or a plateau in his own growth cycle and that therefore he compared differently with the peer group at that point than at other stages of his life.

Environmental Factors. The kinds of group trends and individual sequences of development discussed up to now have been *genetic and constitutional*, those which are an unfolding of human potentialities and probabilities. Over and above these kinds of development are those which are more nearly the results of *environmental and experiential* factors. Without implying that either heredity or environment operates apart from the other, it it nevertheless possible to examine separately the effects of each element. There have, for example, been some well-designed studies which show that when children move from educationally inferior to educationally superior communities and are tested before and after the move, they increase markedly more in measured intelligence and achievement than do their age-mates, who remained behind. This finding holds up when the subjects are Negroes who move from Southern to Northern states or whites who move from rural to urban areas. It follows that changes of this nature may be hypothesized in cases where a change of environment has occurred. Changes of this nature may occur even when the subjects do not move, but when their environment changes. This would occur, for example, if a school's curriculum, teaching staff, or administration were to change in significant ways; the average achievement level of the student body might show changes within a year or two. That such environmental-experiential changes can occur even in late adolescence and early adulthood has been demonstrated dramatically by Blade and Watson's study (1955) mentioned in earlier chapters. They found that even in the first year of engineering college an ability as "culture-free" as spatial visualization changed significantly for a whole group. The changes were most marked for those who had not had mechanical drawing, mechanical hobbies, or other mechanical experiences before college. A counselor seeing one of these students, then in his junior year, and noting a large increase in spatial visualization score, might well consider the hypothesis that particular experiences of that year were largely responsible.

Remedial work. A marked change in measured abilities may be noted following remedial work of some kind, whether in the area of reading, arithmetic, and other skills, in the form of improvement of study skills, or changes in attitude toward school. In all such cases, the person has changed largely in response to changes in his personal environment and experience. The implication for the test interpreter is alertness to the possibility that such environmental changes may have occurred during the period between two "contradictory" test scores.

Application to interests and personality. The operation of environmental factors has thus far been considered mostly in relation to abilities of various kinds. It may not be so obvious that they apply as well to changes in interests, attitudes, and personality characteristics of various kinds. The *Strong Vocational Interest Blank,* for example, has been found to show certain kinds of typical changes during the adolescent years; upon this finding, in fact, is based the Interest Maturity scale. It seems to be normal in our culture for boys to develop increasing interest in people and decreasing interest in mechanical and scientific activities as they move through adolescence. Aware of this, the counselor will not be surprised to note changes of this kind not only on the *Strong* but on the *Kuder* and other interest inventories.

The operation of *individual* developmental sequences may show itself, for example, in the early-maturing youngster whose interests change in a normal direction, but at the age of 12 or 13. Another example is the young man of 25, whose interests belatedly change in a direction that is usually found seven or eight years earlier and who comes to the counselor complaining that his mechanical-scientific job is no longer as interesting as it was, because there is not enough contact with people. In either case the discerning counselor can recognize and give assurance of the "normality" of the change reported.

The concept of vocational maturity is still so new that standardized instruments for its measurement are not yet available. Instruments of this kind were developed in connection with the twenty-year Career Pattern Study (Super, 1955a), and it may well be that when they have been validated in that study, they can be added to the armamentarium of the counselor for the appraisal of this important aspect of growth and development.

Then there are other, special, kinds of changes in interests, which occur outside of the "normal group" and "normal individual" developmental sequences. Some youngsters have a first experience with a scientific laboratory, or with a particular teacher, and suddenly express—orally or through inventories—strong interests in these areas. Roe has reported (1953) instances of eminent scientists whose first interest in scientific careers was said to have occurred during college in a particularly exciting course or as laboratory assistant to a stimulating professor.

In the case of Kathy Musgrove (Chapter 11), we saw changes in the *Kuder* over a three-year period which were interpreted by the counselor as representing more of a craftsman kind of orientation, greater impatience with details, and, in general, a broadening of interests.

Applied now to *personality inventories,* a variety of personal and environmental changes might show themselves in differences between two testings. People in general normally become more poised, more socially confident, and more outgoing as they move through later adolescence and adulthood, and such changes may be reflected on personality inventories. If home and family problems show a decrease from one testing to another, this may result from actual changes in parental and sibling behavior, or it may indicate a greater tolerance by the counselee. Finally, such changes may result from the development of outside interests on his part, so that he is less annoyed by the family idiosyncrasies, pressures, and demands. Neurotic and even psychotic patterns may increase or decrease as a result of less or more satisfying life experiences, as a result of increased or decreased sources of anxiety in the environment, or in response to psychotherapy and other forms of treatment. As in the case of interests and abilities, here too we can delineate the roles of normal group trends, of normal individual sequences, and of special individual factors.

Differences in Test Administration and Scoring

Last of the factors to be considered are those involved in the administration and scoring of tests. Although they should theoretically be among the least important of all the factors, unfortunately they must be considered all too often as primary hypotheses to explain contradictions in scores. Here as before, we operate with very little research evidence, but the observations of well-informed people (Durost, 1954) regarding frequencies of errors of scoring alone are enough to lead one almost always to consider such errors as possible explanations of discrepant scores. Until the administration and scoring of tests are far better controlled and more uniformly dependable than they are today, this attitude of skepticism on the part of interpreters of tests must continue. Since this subject has been discussed rather extensively in earlier chapters it is not necessary to expand any further on it at this point.

A counselor newly appointed to a school, college, or agency may find it valuable to check in some way on the dependability of test scores already on file, so that he has a basis for deciding whether to use these data in his own work with these counselees. It may be possible to make discreet inquiries among other staff members—teachers, administrators, or psychometrists—and perhaps among the counselees themselves as to the conditions under which administration and scoring were done. In addition, a random sample of answer sheets could be rescored to ascertain the amount of error which occurred in the scoring and recording processes. If this investigation reveals serious errors in administration, it might be wiser to discard the earlier results rather than make misinterpretations. If many scoring errors are found, all papers should be rescored. More specifically, errors of test administration and scoring may come from the following sources:

The Administrator

This may be a person of known carelessness or one who is known to be hostile regarding tests. He may be a person who for one or another reason does not motivate students properly, perhaps because of his own apathy, because of an overly mechanical approach to test administration, or perhaps because of his open ridicule of the tests. He may increase anxiety among testees by presenting tests in an overly threatening manner. On the other hand, perhaps through misguided sympathy, he may be too helpful to students in answering their questions and in extending time limits.

Physical Factors in Administration

It may be discovered that one set of tests was given under conditions of extreme discomfort or noise, or at a time of day, week, or year when students might be unusually fatigued, unusually uninterested (just before close of school for the year, or just before a big ball game), or for some other reason not able to function at their best. It may be discovered that tests were given in too large doses for the age group; if so, the results of the last hour or two of testing may be questioned. Although minor administrative lapses of this kind are not likely to cause much damage (see Chapter 5), knowledge of extremely poor conditions may justify disregarding those results or at least perceiving them as underestimates of abilities for most of the subjects.

Scoring

This topic ought not be belabored, but it warrants mention because, first, it is so *unnecessary* as a source of error. If we can assume nothing else about a test score, we should at least be able to assume that it represents near-perfection in accuracy of scoring and of transformation into percentiles, grade equivalents, or IQ's. If this assumption cannot be made and if large scoring errors occur with any degree of frequency, it is doubtful that the tests involved are useful, and they would better be discarded. Secondly, accurate scoring is so important because scoring errors can be large in size and yet impossible to track down logically. Other factors—motivation, norm differences between tests, difference in the contents of two tests, or the counselee's physical and psychological condition during testing— can at least be analyzed by the counselor by asking questions of the client, by using his own knowledge of the various tests, and by other techniques. But scoring errors have no logical relationship to other factors—a single scorer may be consistently too high, consistently too low, or just randomly too high or too low. There is usually no way to follow-up the hypothesis of scoring error except to rescore the test, and this may be impossible if answer sheets are not filed in some accessible place.

We cannot repeat too often that the school or agency that is unable to afford a near-foolproof scoring system simply cannot afford tests. If a high degree of scoring accuracy cannot be assumed by the test interpreter, those tests are at best worthless, at worst dangerous.

CHAPTER 13

A Potpourri of Interpretive
Problems

Eight INTERPRETIVE PROBLEMS have been selected for detailed examination. These eight were chosen for a variety of reasons: some because of the amount of research that has been done, some because they present perplexing problems to the interpreter, and still others because they have not been systematically discussed elsewhere in the present work. Those included here are:

Quantitative vs. Linguistic Abilities
Differential Prediction of School Grades
Intra-individual Scores—Scatter
Differential Predictability of Subgroups
Overachievement and Underachievement
Interests and Abilities
Interests and Achievement
Predicting Success in College

QUANTITATIVE VS. LINGUISTIC ABILITIES—INTERPRETED GENETICALLY, DESCRIPTIVELY, AND PREDICTIVELY

This topic might have been called Numerical versus Verbal Abilities or some other such title; the fact that it was not is testimony to the important role in American measurement played by the *ACE—The American Council on Education Psychological Examination for College Freshmen,* which has two parts: Quantitative *(Q)* and Linguistic *(L).* Though now discontinued by its publisher in favor of the *School and College Ability Tests (SCAT),* the *ACE* has been for many years a major instrument both of counselors and of research workers, as well as probably the most widely used device for selection of college students. Many users have been intrigued by the possible differential interpretations which might be made from differences between an individual's Q and L scores, each presumably representing one's ability to think, reason, and learn with that kind of material. Some have been particularly interested in the *predictions* that might be made from the Q and L scores separately and in combination. Others have focussed instead on *descriptive and genetic* interpretations of differences in Q and L scores for a given individual, particularly in terms of personality characteristics which might be associated with Q-L differences and which might have led to those differences. Although the *ACE* has been discontinued as an annually revised examination given to thousands of college applicants, this topic does not become academic in nature. For one thing, some in the field are certain to continue using the *ACE*, at least for individual counseling purposes; second, what has been learned regarding Q-L differences on the *ACE* may have implications for other tests which yield similar pairs of scores. What *has* been learned about Q and L scores?

1. A large number of studies, published and unpublished, seem clear on the subject of *academic prediction*. The L score is generally a better predictor of school and college grades than the Q score. Although there have been many exceptions, this trend has held up even in schools and curricula in which "common sense" would point toward the Q score as the better one, such as engineering schools or mathematics and physics courses. At present the best explanation of these findings is this: In schools and colleges the preferred mode of learning is almost universally the written or the spoken word. Even in subjects like mathematics and physics, students learn by *listening* to instructors and to other students in class, by *reading* and by *discussing* the material with others. In addition most instructors, consciously or unconsciously, judge a student's competence at least in part by the way in which the student *explains* what he knows, either orally or in written form; here again the student with greater verbal skills has an advantage.

2. Not nearly enough has been done to ascertain the extent to which relative Q-L scores are associated with *membership in certain groups*. One study of this kind was done by Di Vesta (1954) with Air Force officers. He found that Q-L differences were related to service occupations and to college majors; pilots tended to have higher Q scores and ground personnel had higher L scores. Arts and science college majors had higher L scores, and applied-science college majors (engineering and business) had higher Q scores. Although all these differences were statistically significant, they were nonetheless rather small in size. The largest difference, that between business administration majors and most of the other educational groups, may have quite another meaning: the mean Q score of former business students was not very different from the mean for most of the other groups, but

their mean L score was lower than most; what they may represent, then, is a less verbal, or a less scholastically successful, group than the others. Also, as Di Vesta points out, his data do not tell which come first, ". . . whether this pattern *(Q-L)* represents a predisposing factor or whether it emerges as a result of experience in certain areas" (p. 252) .

There is much too little research in this area to warrant any conclusions. Most studies deal with the relation between each test score and the criterion, rather than with the relation between intra-individual score differences (such as $Q-L$) and the criterion.

3. The relation between $Q-L$ patterns and various *personality and interest factors* seems to have received more attention than other aspects of this topic. Much of the interest in this area of research was stimulated by Ruth Munroe's study, reported in 1946, of Sarah Lawrence students. Those girls whose L scores were higher than their Q scores were found, on the Rorschach, to have a more "subjective" orientation toward reality (less use of form exclusively, greater use of human movement, and poorer form quality) . The higher Q girls were characterized as ". . . more bound to a rather literal construction of objective reality" (p. 315) .

Pemberton (1951) studied male executives with the *ACE* and several interest and personality inventories and reported results some of which agree with Munroe's. He found that "The higher L group was significantly more reflective and socially intraverted, with higher literary, esthetic, and theoretical interests. The higher Q group was more extraverted, socially conforming, interested in economic and practical affairs, and interested in persuasive occupations" (p. 162) . The Q group also were reported to have more "nervous tension" and lower masculinity of interests and attitudes than the higher L group.

The author's doctoral dissertation (Goldman, 1951) was an attempt to test the existence of similar relationships with a sample of high school students. However, the *DAT* was used rather than the *ACE,* and intra-individual scores were expressed as the difference between an individual's score on one test and his mean score on all the others. "High Verbal Reasoning," then, meant high on this part as compared to the subject's average score on the whole *DAT* battery (excluding Spelling and Sentences, which were not used) . As in Munroe's study, the *Rorschach* was used as the measure of personality structure. Very little support was found for Munroe's conclusions, but there was a tendency for higher Verbal subjects to be somewhat more "subjective." The only other cluster of relationships of any importance was found with the Clerical Speed and Accuracy test. However, since this test correlates low with all the others of the *DAT,* the findings may be a reflection of the lower academic aptitude of this group rather than of personality differences.

Two studies of relationships between $Q-L$ patterns and scores on the *Strong Vocational Interest Blank* (Gustad, 1951b; Woolf and Woolf,

1955) agreed at least that there are few, if any, *SVIB* occupational scales or group patterns associated with *Q-L* differences. Gustad found no such associations, whereas Woolf and Woolf found that the group made up of those with *Q* scores twenty or more points above their *L* scores had a lower mean Interest Maturity score and a lower score on Group V (Social Welfare) than the group whose *Q* and *L* scores did not differ by more than four percentile points. They also found that the higher *Q* group were poorer than the equal *Q-L* group on two linguistic tests: *Cooperative English* Form OM, and on both the Reading Speed and Comprehension parts of the *Cooperative Reading Test,* C-2. They interpret their findings in developmental terms, hypothesizing that there is a relationship between linguistic development and social development, and that those students whose *L* scores were markedly inferior to their *Q* scores were undeveloped in the linguistic area as a part of a broader underdevelopment as individuals. The fact that Gustad's study did not have similar results does not necessarily question the Woolf and Woolf findings. There were differences in sample (Gustad's were college juniors; the Woolfs used freshmen in a scientific-technical college) and in the design (Gustad divided all his subjects into three groups, dominantly *Q*, dominantly *L,* and nearly equivalent; the Woolfs used only two segments of their total population, those extremely *Q* dominant, and those nearly equivalent). The Woolf and Woolf study needs cross-validation, but with a similar design and sample, to see whether their results are merely peculiar to one sample.

Implications of the Research

There is not nearly enough published research to warrant any definitive conclusions about *Q-L* differences, and about related intra-individual differences in abilities in general. Meanwhile, counselors sometimes make interpretations of *Q-L* differences along some of the lines which have been discussed. Sometimes they make differential *predictions,* for instance, that one with higher *Q* than *L* would do better in technical-scientific-mechanical occupations, and one with *L* higher than *Q* would do better in linguistic-personal relations occupations. Some interpretations are in personality *descriptive* terms, for example, that those with *Q* higher than *L* are more rigid, objective, or constricted. Sometimes the interpretations are in developmental *(genetic)* terms, as, for instance, that those with *Q* higher than *L* are mentally underdeveloped, possibly as part of a general personal underdevelopment.

If nothing else, this situation demonstrates the inadequacies of our present understanding of human abilities and their development. The possible relationship between types of people in terms of personality constellation and types of people in terms of ability patterns, remains intriguing and is deserving of a good deal of research, whether carried on in the counseling room or in the laboratory. It may turn out that any such relationships are too minor to be of any value for individual appraisal and counseling. It is entirely conceivable that any given personality constellation can be associated with, and can function through, a variety of ability patterns. This would mean, for example, that one narrow, constricted, unimaginative person could have quantitative abilities superior to his own linguistic abilities and become the stereotype of a clerk, accountant, technician, or engineer. On the other hand, the same personality in another person might (whether for reasons primarily constitutional or primarily environmental) turn out to be stronger linguistically than quantitatively and be an unimaginative salesman, editor, or teacher. Conversely, an intellectually and emotionally expressive person could, on the one hand, be an imaginative engineer or, on the other, an imaginative editor.

The fact is that we have extremely limited notions of how abilities and aptitudes develop, whether they are the *results* of personality, whether the abilities are basic in the constitution and influence the development of personality, or whether the two interact in different ways in different people. At a much simpler level (simpler in terms of the conceptualization involved as well as in terms of the research implied) we know very little about the relationships, if any, between such differences as those between Q and L scores on the one hand, and success in school, success in occupations, or success in psychotherapy (regression bridges). Nor do we know much about the relationships between Q-L differences and the likelihood of *being* in one or another school program or occupational area (discriminant bridges).

DIFFERENTIAL PREDICTION OF SCHOOL GRADES

One particular facet of the topic just discussed deserves separate examination here. The *ACE* test, with Q and L scores, which the Thurstones developed was a forerunner of the multifactor tests which have blossomed forth in the past decade. The hope of authors of these tests has been, at least with regard to their use in schools, that having subscores on verbal, numerical, spatial, and other subdivisions of general mental ability, would permit better differential prediction for different school subjects.[1]

To see how this has actually worked, it will be profitable to examine some of the findings reported for the *Differential Aptitude Tests*. This particular battery was selected because it was extensively validated in school settings. The Manual reports large numbers of correlations with school

---

[1] A wealth of material on this subject is found in *The Use of Multifactor Tests in Guidance* (undated), which is a reprint of a series of articles which appeared in the *Personnel and Guidance Journal* from September, 1956, to September, 1957. Table 13.1 and Super's comments quoted in the following pages are also taken from that publication.

Table 13.1. Summary of Validity Coefficients Between Differential Aptitude Test Scores and Grades in Four Subject Matter Areas

SUBJECT	SEX	NO. OF R's		VR	NA	AR	SR	MR	CSA	Spell.	Sent.
English	Boys	43	Med.	0.49	0.48	0.32	0.26	0.21	0.22	0.44	0.50
			High	0.78	0.74	0.74	0.52	0.52	0.48	0.69	0.76
			Low	0.11	0.03	0.03	0.01	-0.12	-0.10	-0.13	0.02
	Girls	41	Med.	0.52	0.48	0.40	0.28	0.26	0.26	0.44	0.53
			High	0.78	0.71	0.66	0.63	0.54	0.51	0.69	0.77
			Low	0.22	0.23	0.09	-0.01	-0.23	0.03	0.12	0.22
Mathematics	Boys	36	Med.	0.33	0.47	0.32	0.26	0.19	0.16	0.28	0.32
			High	0.70	0.65	0.61	0.53	0.57	0.45	0.62	0.65
			Low	0.04	0.27	0.07	-0.09	-0.21	-0.10	-0.08	0.06
	Girls	26	Med.	0.45	0.52	0.38	0.37	0.26	0.22	0.30	0.40
			High	0.63	0.71	0.62	0.50	0.41	0.49	0.65	0.65
			Low	0.07	0.25	0.00	0.00	-0.29	0.06	0.11	0.06
Science	Boys	28	Med.	0.54	0.52	0.42	0.34	0.40	0.24	0.36	0.45
			High	0.80	0.74	0.67	0.50	0.58	0.46	0.70	0.78
			Low	0.10	0.10	-0.02	0.15	0.02	-0.14	-0.19	0.07
	Girls	25	Med.	0.55	0.50	0.45	0.39	0.37	0.27	0.36	0.52
			High	0.79	0.75	0.70	0.55	0.55	0.55	0.65	0.77
			Low	0.06	0.14	0.03	0.17	-0.12	-0.07	0.10	0.24
Social Studies	Boys	28	Med.	0.48	0.46	0.32	0.24	0.21	0.21	0.36	0.43
			High	0.72	0.76	0.74	0.55	0.47	0.47	0.68	0.73
			Low	-0.01	0.04	-0.12	-0.06	-0.15	-0.06	-0.08	0.20
	Girls	27	Med.	0.52	0.50	0.38	0.27	0.26	0.30	0.35	0.49
			High	0.79	0.74	0.62	0.55	0.49	0.54	0.67	0.83
			Low	0.27	0.25	0.17	0.06	-0.13	0.04	0.14	0.17

SOURCE: Bennett, Seashore, and Wesman, 1956: p. 85. By permission of *The Personnel and Guidance Journal*.

grades; these have been conveniently summarized in a single table by the authors of the *DAT* (Bennett, Seashore, and Wesman, 1956), which is reproduced here in Table 13.1.

The reader may find it interesting, and revealing, to inspect the table himself to see what he can get from it. For example, going down the columns, he finds that the highest median coefficient for boys with the Verbal Reasoning (VR) test is with science grades. However, this is also true with the Numerical Ability (NA) test, where again the highest median coefficient is with science grades. In fact, the same result is found with *all* the tests in this battery, save Spelling and Sentences, which have their highest correlations with English grades. One can also go across the rows, looking for that test which correlates highest for each subject. For English, with the boys it is the Sentences test (but the coefficient is only one point higher than that for the Verbal Reasoning test, and two points higher than for that for the Numerical Ability test). With girls, the highest median correlation with English grades is also found with the Sentences test; here again it is one point higher than the correlation with the VR test, and five points higher than that for Numerical Ability. With mathematics courses, differential prediction seems more successful, the NA test being the best median predictor for both boys and girls, noticeably better than most of the other tests.

Super, in his "Comments" on the article in which this table appeared, reports the results of his own examination of the data:

> . . . I took the median *r*'s in the table of validity coefficients in this article, and added additional columns from the manual so as to include commercial and shop subjects. Space prohibits including the material here, but the data justify a few generalizations. English is well predicted by verbal, numerical, abstract, spelling and sentence tests; so however, are *not only* social studies grades, but *also* grades in mathematics and science (in the last, spatial and mechanical tests help too). The tests look good for academic subjects, but not very *differentially* good: they seem to measure intelligence, and intelligence helps in all of these subjects. Now let us look at the business and shop subjects (in the Manual): number and language usage help in bookkeeping, but both also in typing; spatial predicts slightly for shop grades. Not much differential prediction here, either. The tests look like good academic ability tests with this type of analysis, not much else (Super, 1956: pp. 92-93).

It may be, as the *DAT* authors have pointed out in the manual, and as others have concurred, that the failure of differential prediction is a failure not as much of tests as of criteria. Perhaps science teachers are not different enough from English teachers in their specific bases for evaluating students; even some shop teachers may place more emphasis on student verbalizations than on actual proficiency with the tools and materials of that shop. There may be here a reflection of a general bias among teachers, which results in higher grades for the academically brighter youngster, the one who is strongest in the areas most valued by schools—essentially the verbal and numerical ones.

There is another facet of this problem, this one calling for a closer look at each of the school subjects.[2] Perhaps it is a mistake to lump together all English courses or all mathematics courses, or even all shop courses, as if to assume that because they are offered by the same department they are a homogeneous group. The demands and goals of a first-year language course may be so different from those of a third-year language course in the same school as to require quite different predictors of each. This very point was mentioned briefly in our case of Robert Martin. In a way, this is to say that the correlations between tests and school grades, if studied carefully for specific courses (and even for specific teachers), might tell as much about the demands and values of the course (and the teacher) as about the validity of the test.

Still another hypothesis worth exploring is this: Tests such as those in the Linguistic portion of the *ACE* and the Verbal Reasoning and Numerical Ability parts of the *DAT* are measuring the kinds of content which schools emphasize, more so than do the Q parts of the *ACE* and the Abstract, Space, Mechanical, and Clerical parts of the *DAT*. It would therefore follow that students in general have developed their potentialities in these emphasized areas to a greater extent than in the other areas. If this is so, the L tests and the VR and NA tests may be more valid measures —more valid, in the descriptive sense, as indicators of what students are actually capable of in those areas. In the other areas, such as Mechanical and Spatial, few students have had opportunities to develop their potentialities, and therefore the tests may be poorer indications of students' capabilities in those areas and in school subjects which tap those areas. There is some evidence to support this hypothesis in the oft-cited work of Blade and Watson (1955) who found that if a spatial test was taken at the end of the freshman year in engineering schools, it was a better predictor of grades in Engineering Drawing and Descriptive Geometry than if it was taken before the freshman year. They concluded that it might be advisable for engineering schools to postpone final selection of students until after the students have had a chance to take basic courses such as engineering drawing and descriptive geometry, ". . . so that ability in spatial visualization would be nearer its final plateau, and therefore a more effective predictor of success or failure in related studies" (p. 13).

Whatever the explanation, the fact seems to be that, with the *DAT*, in particular, and with other batteries which have also been used in school validity studies, differential prediction of grades from subscores has not been very effective. The best estimates of school grades for the most part

[2] For clarification of some of the ideas in this paragraph, the writer is greatly indebted to Dr. Martin Hamburger, of New York University, who expressed them in a lecture to the Guidance Institute at Rutgers University, July, 1959.

come from verbally loaded (and, at least in high school, numerically loaded) tests of the traditional academic aptitude type.

INTRA-INDIVIDUAL DIFFERENCES; SCATTER

Although there has been in *clinical* psychology considerable thinking, research, and writing about the significance and interpretation of the scatter or spread of an individual's scores around each other or around their mean (see, for example, Jastak, 1949), little has been done with this concept in counseling psychology. Yet, in terms of the demonstrated reliability and validity of the tests used, counseling psychologists have greater justification for doing studies of this kind. The questions to which investigations could address themselves are such as these: What significance can be attached to a very uneven profile on a multifactor test of mental abilities, as compared with a nearly straight-line profile? Similarly with interest inventories, what genetic or descriptive or predictive interpretations can be made of the fact that one person has about equal scores, say all about average, in a number of areas, whereas a second person has one or two extreme scores and all the others average, and a third person has almost no average scores but rather is characterized by extremes, both high and low?

In effect, we are returning to a topic in Chapter 8, which was there discussed in terms of profile scoring as a bridge between tests and criteria, and which we now approach again, this time asking what is known regarding interpretations to be made of given intra-individual spreads of scores. The earlier discussion of *Q-L* scores is a special case of this same general topic.

Actually we know very little about the meaning of scatter in the guidance and counseling use of tests. Few recent studies have appeared, and their results have enough contradictions to leave the question wide open. Tilton (1953), for example, found that, among achievement-test profiles of elementary school pupils, average children were likely to have the most even test profiles, and both above average and below average had more scatter among their scores. None of these group differences, however, was very great. Snodgrass (1954a, 1954b) followed up this problem, using the parts of a mental ability test, and found that much of the unevenness within profiles can be due to unreliability of measurement. However, the profiles of the bright pupils were found to be more reliable than those of either average or below average, and it was concluded that the profile unevenness of the brighter children was not attributable to unreliability of measurement. Somewhat different results, but with different tests (the *ACE* and a *Cooperative English* test) and a different sample, were obtained by Rausch (1948). He reported a general trend for the most variable subjects to have lower academic achievement, although variability was positively correlated with scores on the tests themselves, those scoring higher tending to have more variation.

Scatter on Interest Inventories

In the area of interest measurement, no studies of scatter were found, except the normative data provided by Darley and Hagenah (1955) regarding the frequency of occurrence of primary and secondary patterns on the *Strong*. Based on a small number of cases observed during counseling, the writer has hypothesized that, at least on the *SVIB* a profile with most of the scores down the middle—*C +*, *B −*, and *B −*, and very few *C* or *A* scores, is most likely to be found with the client who is most unable to make an occupational choice, who reports that nothing really appeals strongly to him. The *Strong* profile in effect may be saying the same thing, that there are no occupations (at least among those for which scoring scales are available) with whose members he has a marked identity of interests.

In such cases of middle-of-the-road profiles, lacking more precise bases for interpretation, clients have been told something like this:

Your interests are not very similar to those of people in any of the occupations or areas for which we have information. This might mean several things; it might be that you have a combination of likes and dislikes which is atypical as compared with any of *these* groups, but which might be similar to those of some occupations not represented here. Or your interests may be more suitable for a specialized job which involves a combination of occupations, and which is so rare as not to be considered an occupation unto itself, as, for example, a writer or editor in some scientific or technical field, whose interests are unlike those of either writers or scientists or technicians. Or, you might be one of those people, of whom there are quite a few, who just have no real differentiation of vocational interests and who may never find a job that gives them a great deal of satisfaction and who get their major satisfactions from other aspects of their lives —their families, travel, or recreational activities. For such people, choice of an occupation may be based mostly on factors other than their interests, such as the salary, working conditions, pensions, and so on. Sometimes the choice between fairly different jobs may be almost a matter of tossing a coin. Finally, there is the possibility (this especially for adolescents and young adults, and most especially when the IM score is low) that your interest pattern has not crystallized and may yet do so. In the latter case, it would probably be helpful to get acquainted with, and preferably to try out, a variety of activities, in the hope that latent interests might develop that way.

In individual cases, the counselor may have additional data which lead him to emphasize one or another of these alternative interpretations. For example, when there is evidence of immaturity—physical, emotional, or social—the last interpretation mentioned might be given greatest weight. If, on the other hand, there is no evidence of immaturity and the individual has explored many fields in school and on jobs, one of the earlier interpretations might thereby be given additional support.

DIFFERENTIAL PREDICTABILITY OF SUBGROUPS

A few studies have appeared which highlight the fact that not all members of a particular group are equally predictable and that by subdividing a group in certain ways we can sometimes raise the efficiency of prediction for at least some of its members.

One such study (Frederiksen and Melville, 1954) began with 154 engineering students who had taken the *SVIB* and the *Cooperative Reading Comprehension Test* and had completed one year in college. The Engineer Key of the *Strong*, to select one of those they used, correlated .10 with average grades in the freshman year. However, when the total group was divided into two parts, one whose Accountant score on the *Strong* was above average and the other whose Accountant score was below average, the correlations of the Engineer scale for the two subgroups were —.01 and .25, respectively. Their interpretation (and this is what they began with as a rationale for their study, so it isn't second-guessing) was that those higher on the Accountant scale are more compulsive and are therefore likely to study hard for *all* their courses, whereas those with the lower Accountant scores are less compulsive and are likely to work harder at those subjects they enjoy more. The latter group, the reasoning continues, are therefore more predictable because they permit their interests to affect the quality of their work more than do the compulsives. With similar logic, another test of the same hypothesis was made, using the difference between Vocabulary and Speed of Reading Scores on the *Cooperative Reading Comprehension Test* as an index of compulsiveness (those whose speed score was low in relation to their vocabulary score being considered the more compulsive). Again the hypothesis was confirmed, the college grades of the noncompulsives being more predictable from the *SVIB* than those of the compulsives. One need not accept Frederiksen and Melville's labelling of the trait they called "compulsiveness" to accept their conclusion that one can use such a method to improve the quality of predictions for some people. In the case of the reading scores, for example, it could just as well be concluded that those whose speed of reading was below their vocabulary level were simply inefficient readers, therefore more erratic students, and, as a result, less predictable. In fact the authors report that their two measures of "compulsiveness" correlated not at all with each other, which makes it somewhat difficult to regard them as measures of the same trait.

Ghiselli (1956) has furnished evidence of another sort on this topic. He found first that, for a sample of taxi drivers, there was practically a zero correlation between Occupational Level scores on an interest inventory (not the *Strong*) and a criterion of success on the job. A test of tapping and dotting yielded a low correlation (.26) with the criterion. Neither measure alone (interest level or tapping and dotting) was much of a predictor of the criterion. However, Ghiselli noticed that for those with low Occupational Level scores, there tended to be more agreement between their tapping and dotting scores and the criterion of job success. Therefore, a cross-validation (fresh) sample was selected and divided into three groups on the basis of their Occupational Level score. As hypothesized, the lowest third were the most predictable in terms of correlation between tapping and dotting score and the criterion (.66), whereas for the three thirds combined, the correlation was about as low as it had been for his original sample (.22).

Ghiselli suggests that, if one is using these tests for selecting taxi drivers, ". . . a first elimination of applicants can be made by dropping out those individuals for whom prediction of job success by means of the selection test is likely to be poor. Then a second elimination can be made on the basis of the selection test, picking those individuals whose scores are high" (p. 375). Ghiselli does not offer much in the way of speculation regarding the psychology of this situation except to suggest that the job of taxi driver is at the semiskilled level and would not provide sufficient challenge for those with higher ambitions. The latter people presumably are therefore less predictable on their jobs, because of motivational and other problems. Perhaps it can be hypothesized that men with higher-level interests who seek jobs as taxi drivers are not as well-integrated in total personality as are those who seek employment at a level more nearly their level of aspiration. The lower order of personal integration might itself make people less predictable, more erratic.

A third example of differential predictability is reported by McArthur (1954b) and McArthur and Stevens (1955) on the basis of still another kind of problem. In studies at Harvard of the predictive validity of the *SVIB*, it was found that Harvard College students as a group were not as predictable as were the Stanford University samples which Strong has worked with (predictable in terms of entering the occupation in which they obtained high scores on the *SVIB* while in college). Following up the proposition that the ". . . SVIB validly measured interests but that failure to predict what job a man would choose could be explained in terms of his making the choice on some basis other than interest" (p. 352), McArthur divided his sample into two groups—those who had gone to public high schools and those who had attended private prep schools. As hypothesized, the public school boys were about as predictable (from *SVIB* scores to later occupational status) as were Strong's Stanford samples. But the prep school graduates were much less predictable. McArthur's explanation is that the latter group are in many cases choosing their vocations in response not so much to their actual interests as in response to family expectations of what they will be, which are, in "the purest case," a choice among trustee, lawyer, or physician.

Implications of the Research

These three studies exemplify what may be an important technique in the future use of tests. For now, not a great deal can be offered the practicing counselor along these lines. Even these few studies cited, however, may offer the clinical interpreter some helpful insights. Certainly for counselors who have worked with individuals whose expressed vocational choice is quite different from their measured interests, the McArthur study should suggest that perhaps there are subcultural factors at work which will help explain the discrepancy and which should be understood in the total process of appraisal. Similarly, the Frederiksen and Melville work may offer some insights into the functioning of particular clients whose interests do not seem to be reflected in their achievements in different subjects.

For the research planner, there are numerous possibilities in this area for studies of both theoretical and applied emphases. Those interested will find some discussion of theoretical and statistical aspects of the problem in a paper by Saunders (1955) on the general topic of the "moderator variable."

OVERACHIEVEMENT AND UNDERACHIEVEMENT

Despite the twenty-year interval since their publication, not very much can be added to Williamson's two chapters on Underachievement and Overachievement in his 1939 *How to Counsel Students*. Not a great deal has been learned since then about diagnosis or specific treatment in these cases. Perhaps the major change is in treatment of those cases in which attitudes, emotional disturbances, and other such causal factors are important, for a good deal has been learned during the years about what is called "personal counseling," and "adjustment counseling." Changing of attitudes, changing of self-concept, and reorganizing of perceptions are known now to involve processes far more complex and less rational than were earlier recognized.

As to the appraisal process in these areas, there has been some recent research which confirms some of the earlier "clinical hunches." Hoyt and Norman (1954) have, for example, furnished evidence of the effects of maladjustment; they found that those college freshmen who were judged by their *MMPI* profiles to be maladjusted had among them higher incidence both of underachievement and of overachievement. As they predicted, the correlation between ability measures and grades was smaller for the maladjusted than for "normal" students. McQuary and Truax (1955) developed an achievement scale for the *MMPI* by locating twenty-four items which differentiated underachievers from overachievers.[3] Shaw and Grubb (1958) found that high school underachievers had higher scores on three different measures of hostility than did other students and concluded that hostility is a causal factor in underachievement. However, their data might just as well be interpreted the other way around, *viz.,* that underachievers become hostile as a *result* of their failure to achieve. Still another bit of evidence comes from a study by Drasgow and McKenzie (1958). Working from college transcripts, they separated from the others those which contained one *A* and one *F* and those with three or more *A*'s and three or more *D*'s. It was found that the members of both of these subgroups (the erratic achievers) had a far greater incidence of abnormal *MMPI* profiles than did the other students. A similar correlation was found between being a dropout from college and having an abnormal *MMPI* profile. All of these studies suggest that emotional factors influence the extent to which a person will achieve in accordance with his capabilities. Especially noteworthy is the fact that maladjustment can lead *either* to underachievement or to overachievement.

Several recent studies extend this idea and suggest further that *underachievement (and overachievement as well) is not a single syndrome* but results from *several different patterns.* Gebhart and Hoyt (1958), for instance, dug into some of the psychodynamics involved, again with emphasis on personality factors. They compared the *Edwards Personal Preference Schedule (EPPS)* of college freshmen whose first semester grades were lower than predicted by their test scores (underachievers) with those whose grades were higher than predicted (overachievers). They found that the overachievers were significantly higher on needs for Achievement, Order, and Intraception, and significantly lower on Nurturance, Affiliation, and Change. They speculate that there may be a *variety of personality patterns* associated with underachievement and overachievement. For overachievement, three patterns are hypothesized: *(a)* overachievement resulting from the drive to compete (high Achievement score); *(b)* overachievement resulting from the drive to organize and plan (the Order score); and *(c)* overachievement resulting from intellectual curiosity (as

[3] James D. McKenzie, Jr., University of Maryland, has kindly furnished a draft copy of his Ph.D. dissertation completed in 1960 at the University of Buffalo. He tried to develop *MMPI* scales for overachievers and for underachievers. Of seven such scales developed empirically for various ability groups, only one, for underachievement, held up in cross-validation. Even with this one, the discrimination between underachievers and normal achievers was too limited to be of practical use. He found also, like Hoyt and Norman, some evidence of greater anxiety among both the overachievers and the underachievers than among normal achievers. As McKenzie suggests, the kinds of items included in the *MMPI* may not be as sensitive as those on, say, the *Edwards PPS* to the personality factors which characterize overachievers and underachievers. This may be one reason that studies utilizing the *Edwards* have been more successful in discovering such personality factors, whereas the *MMPI* seems to give only a gross indication of "maladjustment" of underachievers or overachievers.

measured by the Intraception score). For underachievement, two patterns are suggested: *(a)* underachievement associated with the need for variety (Change score) in which cases academic studies may appear boring and routine and *(b)* underachievement associated with social motives (Affiliation and Nurturance) in which cases friendship may be placed above scholarship.

At least four other studies have used similar approaches (three of them, in fact, used the *EPPS*) and with results some of which are quite similar to those of Gebhart and Hoyt. Krug (1959) found that the *EPPS* scores of underachievers were higher than those of overachievers on Affiliation and Heterosexuality; this coincides very nicely with the *sociability* pattern reported by Gebhart and Hoyt. Krug also found that his overachievers were higher than underachievers on Achievement, Order, and Endurance. The first two confirm Gebhart and Hoyt's patterns, and the third introduces, as an additional pattern, the need to plod along until a job is finished. Krug made two further contributions: First, he found that the scales which differentiated underachievers from overachievers were, in that sample, statistically independent, thus lending further weight to the position that there are several separate *patterns* of achievement. Second, he studied separately an *aptitude* test (the College Board *SAT*) and *achievement* measures (several achievement tests plus high school standing). He found that the *EPPS* added something to predictions made from the aptitude test, but not to those from achievement tests. His conclusion adds an important dimension to this area: With achievement measures, the *EPPS* personality variables have already played their part, and their effects are already included in the achievement measure. The aptitude test is more nearly a measure of potentiality. Thus there is outlined very nicely the diagnostic process with overachievers or underachievers: when there is discrepancy between aptitude and achievement, we look for one of the patterns in the personality area.

Another study which used the *EPPS* was reported by Rodgers (1959); his subjects were freshmen in the Printing program of a technical college. Although he did not actually study underachievers and overachievers, he compared *EPPS* scores of students with higher grades and those with lower grades. He found a negative correlation between grades and the Affiliation score, thus confirming this sociability pattern as a factor contributing to low grades. He also found that the high achievers had a higher mean score on the Endurance scale than low achievers, confirming Krug's finding.

Diener (1960) also used the *EPPS*, as well as the *Kuder Preference Record*, and several additional sources of data. He found that only the Order score on the *Edwards* significantly distinguished overachieving from underachieving college freshmen. On the *Kuder*, only the Artistic scale was significantly related to achievement deviations (higher for underachievers). It was also found in this study that underachievers studied fewer hours per week and worked for pay more hours per week than did overachievers.

The final study of personality factors in relation to scholastic achievement to be discussed here is that of Middleton and Guthrie (1959). Using an inventory with categories, like those of the *EPPS,* based on Murray's analysis of needs, they did a factor analysis of the scores of fourteen higher achieving and fourteen lower achieving students. They tentatively identified five factors among the high achievers, which may be seen as patterns of achievement. They found that there were (1) those for whom achievement appears to mean power and approval, (2) those for whom it means prestige and influence, (3) those for whom it is an expression of resentment and independence, (4) those for whom it is an expression of dependence, and (5) those for whom it is a "hostile aggressive denial of tender socialized feelings." Among the low achievers there were four factors, which they characterized as: (1) preoccupation with pleasure, (2) extroversion in relationships, (3) need for disavowing social shortcomings, and (4) preoccupation with power and acceptance. This study differs from the others in several ways. Perhaps most important for our present purposes is that it made a somewhat finer breakdown of personality factors and sought to establish the *reasons,* in terms of personality dynamics, for some of the kinds of behavioral patterns. Whether this approach is more valuable for counselors is a moot question. On one hand, it may be sufficient to know that a student's grades are suffering from his overactive social life and that he can now be helped to learn a better balanced regimen. On the other hand, it may be necessary to identify the *reasons* for the overactivity (compensation for felt inadequacies or denial of hostile feelings) in order to attempt to remove the causes. Perhaps the answer will be different for different clients. Counselors will differ also as to the types of personality data which they seek for the purpose of getting clues and building hypotheses to understand overachieving and underachieving students.

Confirmation of the concept of multiple causality of underachievement comes also from very preliminary reports of a study of underachievers being conducted in New York City public schools, in conjunction with Columbia University's School of Engineering. Early impressions of some guidance workers associated with the project is that there are a variety of causes of underachievement and that individual cases frequently involve a complex of causes.

Finally, an important caution in all research and counseling regarding achievement is highlighted in a study by Krathwohl (1952). Through all the preceding discussion, underachievement and overachievement have been treated as if they are *general* characteristics of people. There has been an implication that one underachieves or overachieves, or achieves normally, about the same in all his school subjects. Krathwohl, however, found that achievement of a group of engineering college students varied among different subjects. For each student, there was computed an index of congruence between his score on an aptitude test for a particular college subject and his score on an achievement test, taken almost two years later, in that subject. A congruence score represented the degree of agreement between the aptitude and achievement scores. Correlations between congruence scores for the different subjects ran from .08 to .34, and only two of them were statistically significant (Mathematics with Chemistry being .34 and Mathematics with Physics being .18). Krathwohl concluded that overachievement and underachievement are *specific* to college courses. Of course, it is still possible that there were in his total sample a small number of students who were over-all overachievers and some who were over-all underachievers. These might be the kinds of students who were the subjects in some of the other studies which have been cited. Also, his sample consisted of technical students, who may differ from other students in achievement patterns.

Appraisal of Underachievement and Overachievement

The first step in detection of either of these deviations usually involves comparing an individual's scores on aptitude tests with a record of his grades in school. Both the objectivity and the precision of this first step would be improved by the use of local validation studies. This is simply a matter of computing correlations between a general or a specific aptitude test and grades in that school; from these data regression equations are produced which result in a predicted grade for each aptitude test score.[4] Even simpler, though less refined statistically, is the construction of expectancy tables directly from test scores and grades.[5] In either case there is a basis for judging whether an individual student is achieving more or less than is normal *in that setting* for one of his ability level. It is essential to consider both the predicted or expected "normal" grade, and the person's actual grade, as bands rather than points. Some "discrepancies" will disappear when the standard error is extended (both plus and minus) around both the predicted and actual grades.

Underachievement and overachievement may also be detected through test scores alone. Krathwohl, in a series of studies (1949a, 1949b, 1953) has demonstrated that differences between pairs of test scores for an individual can be used to predict later underachievement. In one study of English grades (1949a), a vocabulary test was used as a measure of aptitude and a test of mechanics of expression as a measure of achievement. The lower a student's mechanics score was in relation to his vocabulary score, the lower were the grades he was likely to receive in college English courses. In the other two studies (1949b, 1953), it was found that the

[4] An example is given in Figure 7.4.
[5] Expectancy tables are shown in Tables 7.1 and 7.2, and in Figure 7.3.

discrepancy between a student's score on a mathematics aptitude test and his score on a mathematics achievement test was predictive of later under-achievement in mathematics. Krathwohl labels the discrepancy lack of "industriousness"; this construct, however, as he points out in footnotes, is an arbitrary one on his part. The discrepancy between aptitude and achievement could just as well be labelled "maladjustment" or "under-development of skills." The fact is that his approach yields only an indi-cation of *degree* of underachievement, but no inkling of *causes.*

For appraisal of *causes,* one must collect additional data. Some of the research previously cited shows that personality inventories such as the *MMPI* and the *EPPS* may be helpful. This approach, however, gets at only a few facets of causation. Williamson's analysis of the problem (1939) is still quite helpful, since he points out a number of factors which may be important in different cases. Besides those which have been identified in the studies of maladjustment and of needs, one important causative factor is lack of identification with school and its middle-class values (this may be a problem for an entire school population or at least for those from the lower class). Also to be considered are deficiency in basic skills, such as reading or arithmetic, which may discourage even the student who wishes to do better work; here appraisal might be aided by the use of a battery of basic skills measures. Still another cause might be poor study habits; some of the special inventories may be helpful here.

For the most part, with both overachievement and underachievement, the appraisal procedures are primarily clinical in nature, although in-creasingly the data are becoming available for making more mechanical the first step, that of deciding that there *is* a deviation in achievement from what is normally expected (Descriptive interpretation). One extra precaution need be taken. Since verbal intelligence tests (such as *Otis* or *Henmon-Nelson*) correlate very highly with achievement tests (Coleman and Ward, 1956), the former may not tell much more about a person's potentialities than the latter. In many cases, a better measure of general ability would be a nonverbal (or at least *less* verbal) test, such as the *Lorge-Thorndike Non-Verbal, CTMM Non-Language,* and nonverbal portions of the multifactor tests of mental ability.

Further appraisal procedures (largely Genetic) begin with the percep-tions and opinions of the student himself and of others who are involved —teachers in particular. There follows an examination of existing test and other data, and the use of new tests as necessary to provide informa-tion about aptitudes, interests, personality adjustment, and personality needs. It may also be valuable to compare standardized achievement tests with teachers' grades, in cases where it is suspected that the student knows more, or less, than he gets credit for. As developed in the case of Robert Martin (Chapter 11), there may be *undertesting* involved as well as, or instead of, overachievement: The person's achievement may be a more accurate measure than his test scores of his comfortable level of capability. All of these procedures are obviously time-consuming and ordinarily will require a series of interviews, tests and other appraisal devices, and some time to think about the data. But, then, this is what we have learned to expect of the clinical process of interpretation as applied to almost any complex problem of appraisal. Counselors who don't have the time to do an adequate job may have to resort to more generalized approaches, such as giving reassurance or dispensing advice about study habits, and hope that they guess right once in a while.

INTERESTS AND ABILITIES

A chronic source of frustration is the failure of research reports to confirm what seems to be a perfectly logical expectation, that is, that interests and abilities will be closely related, and that most people will be *interested* in doing the things which they are most *capable* of doing. Counselors are tempted to see as vexing exceptions those cases in which interests and abilities point in different directions. Yet the fact seems to be, as concluded by Darley and Hagenah (1955) after a review of the literature, that ". . . there is a low relation between measured interests and measured ability or scholastic achievement" (p. 57). Their detailed consideration of theory and research on this problem is available for the interested reader and need not be repeated here. It does seem worthwhile, however, to consider briefly some of the major elements of the problem and to point up some implication for counselors.

First, let us exclude from this discussion *expressed* interests, to avoid additional complications. For example, expressed interests (what the person *says* he is interested in) can all too easily be influenced by misinformation as to what a particular occupation consists of. Also, an expression of interest in a particular occupation may be an echo of parental desires or a felt need for the prestige which the name of the occupation connotes to the person. These factors complicate the problem with regard to *measured* interests also, but to a lesser degree.

Secondly, we limit this discussion to abilities as measured by tests of aptitude and general mental ability, excluding *school grades, supervisors' ratings* and other such indices of *achievement*. With some of the latter, complications would be introduced: Teachers' grades and supervisors' ratings are both influenced by what are, for our present purposes, extraneous factors, such as manner of dress and grooming, co-operativeness, and pleasant personality. Furthermore, as Strong (1943) suggested, people sometimes work harder on the subjects in which they are weakest (and in which they may have little interest), sometimes because they feel challenged, sometimes because it is expected of them. As a result, the correlation between interests and achievement, and even between aptitudes and achievement, is attenuated.

Restricting our discussion then to interests as measured by inventories, and to aptitudes and general mental abilities as measured by tests, what are some of the factors which interfere with their complete agreement? First, drawing heavily on Darley and Hagenah, who in turn have built upon the thinking of Strong, Fryer, Carter, Bordin, Super, and others, what are the reasons for *expecting* agreement between measured interests and abilities? There are several theories regarding the development of interests, and they all seem to give abilities an important role in the process. In one theory, interests develop as a result of successful experiences; clearly, then, people should develop their strongest interests in the areas in which they have their best abilities. Another theory sees vocational interests developing as a way of life through which the individual satisfies his needs (for status, service to others, aggressiveness). However, the way of life is satisfactory only so long as the individual can attain at least minimal success, and this requires certain abilities. A third approach emphasizes self-concept, with the individual increasingly seeing himself as functioning most effectively, and with greatest satisfaction to himself, in a particular vocational role. Here too abilities are important, since they are a vital part of the self-concept, at least to the extent that the individual has realistic perceptions of his abilities.

In all theories, then, there appears to be an important association between abilities and interests, and we return therefore to the earlier question: *What are some of the factors which interfere with complete congruence between abilities and interests?*

1. One such factor is the influence upon measured interests of *family and social values*. For a long time, our cultural values have influenced young people to show interest in white-collar activities and in high-level activities, as a result of the prestige associated with both. Although these same cultural values may also influence the development of abilities (through greater emphasis in school and elsewhere), the latter appear to be less flexible and more limited by heredity and constitution.

2. *A single ability can find outlets in a variety of occupations.* Thus spatial visualization ability can be used in semiskilled or skilled mechanical jobs, but it can also be used in sculpture, dentistry, and engineering. On the *Strong VIB,* interests appropriate to mechanical occupations would appear in Group IV, those for sculpture and dentistry in Group I, and engineering in Group II. On the *Kuder,* we can expect a different pattern for each of these occupations among the ten scales, with some overlap perhaps in the Mechanical and Artistic areas. As a result spatial ability tests might show no clear-cut relation to measured interests.

3. *A single occupation offers possibilities for success to people with a variety of abilities.* A group of insurance salesmen may show equal degrees

of measured interests in selling in general and insurance selling in particular, but they may utilize quite different major abilities in attaining equal success. One may be especially able in *persuading* people, a second may be best in an analytical-mathematical process of determining the best insurance plan for a particular income, needs, and risks. A third may be best in developing friendly relationships with his clients, one in which there may be mutual liking and sharing of other experiences—such as bowling and fishing. These three men might not be equally successful in selling insurance to the same people, but in the long run they might earn equal amounts of money and receive equally satisfactory ratings from their superiors. They might have equally high measured interests in insurance selling, yet be different in measured abilities.

4. Even though interests may be a learned way of utilizing abilities, they also inevitably *reflect others of the individual's characteristics,* such as his level of energy-expenditure, sensitivity to his environment, his need to be recognized, or his need for closeness to or distance from people. Some of these, in individual cases, may lead to the development of vocational interests contradictory to those suitable to the person's abilities. The youngster who is very able mechanically may be so responsive to people and so in need of contact with people that he develops interests more like those of people in personal relations occupations such as selling or teaching. Thus the reflection of abilities in interests may be blocked by other characteristics of the individual.

5. It is well-established that *people are multipotential;* most have abilities which would be suitable for more than one kind of school program or occupation. As one of these abilities is favored by the individual and appropriate interests developed, the other abilities may fade into the background, or be utilized in leisure-time activities or in "do-it-yourself" projects at home. In any case, these other abilities may not correlate with the individual's job title or job functions, or, perhaps, with his measured interests.

6. Neither interests nor aptitudes nor abilities are measured reliably and validly enough that perfect correlation could be expected, even if it existed. Whatever association there *is* between these two classes of variables in people is attenuated somewhat in researches because of these *flaws in the tests and inventories.*

7. Finally, any relation that does exist between measured interests and abilities may be diminished by a particular factor common to the design of most studies: correlations are frequently between *absolute* level of interests and *absolute* level of abilities or aptitudes. That is, the customary correlation design tells whether those people in a group who have the higher mechanical interest scores also have the higher ability test scores in that group. It is possible, however, for an individual to be rather interested in mechanical activities and yet to have measured mechanical

aptitude which, though *his* highest aptitude, may still not be very high as compared with other people. In a correlational study, such a person might contribute to reducing the coefficient of correlation between interests and aptitudes.

There is in fact some evidence that this phenomenon does operate. Wesley, Corey, and Stewart (1950) designed a study in which college students took the *Kuder* and seven different tests of aptitude and achievement, each intended to measure an ability closely related to one of the *Kuder* scales. (Persuasive and Social Service scales of the *Kuder* were not used because of lack of adequate tests of ability in those areas). The customary zero-order coefficient of correlation was computed between each ability test and the corresponding *Kuder* scale. In addition, *intra-individual* correlations were computed; for this purpose a person's score on an ability test was expressed by the deviation of that score from *his* own mean score on all seven ability tests. Since the *Kuder* is a forced-choice inventory, its scores are already in intra-individual form and so could be used without further transformation. Coefficients of correlation were then computed between these own-mean ability scores and the *Kuder* scores. Table 13.2 is reproduced here as it appears in their report. In several of

Table 13.2. Correlations Between Interest and Ability Based on Deviations from Group and from Individual Means

Vocational Area	Group Means		Individual Means	
	N*	r	N*	r
Mechanical	131	.44	126	.50
Computational	115	.24	112	.47
Scientific	126	.33	126	.35
Artistic	131	.29	127	.31
Literary	125	.47	125	.68
Musical	122	.21	118	.23
Clerical	132	.07	125	.33
Mean		.30		.42

* The size of N in each case depended on the number of subjects for whom necessary data were available.

SOURCE: Wesley, Corey, and Stewart, 1950: p. 195. By permission of the American Psychological Association.

the areas, there was a noticeable increase in correlation by the intra-individual method. The mean coefficients of .30 and .42, respectively, differed significantly. As an additional test, each person's *Kuder* scores were ranked from one to seven, as were his ability test scores, and a rank-order correlation computed *for each individual*. The individual correlations ranged from —.57 to +1.00, with a mean of +.46; this value was also significantly higher than the value of .30 obtained from the traditional "group mean" correlations. These authors also report further work with the data in an effort to find out why some individuals have so much agreement between interests and the corresponding abilities and others so little. Measures of general mental ability *(Army Alpha)* and personality adjustment *(MMPI)* showed hardly any relationship with interest-ability congruency.

It would seem from the Wesley, and others, study that the deviations-from-individual-mean approach helps to increase agreements between interests and abilities. There is also a promising area for research here, particularly in further pursuit of possible factors associated with congruence and with discrepancy between an individual's interests and abilities. It might be hypothesized, for example, that correlations between a person's relative interests and his relative abilities will be highest in cases with the best level of personality integration. Another illustrative hypothesis is this: that the greatest congruence of interests and abilities will be found in those cases in which the ranking of the individual's abilities is in closest agreement with his family's value system. At least in the early stages of research in this area, it might be valuable to do case studies of congruent as compared with discrepant individuals; insights regarding the dynamics of interest-ability relationships might be obtained which would have immediate usefulness to counselors, as well as being valuable sources of hypotheses for research workers.

Implications for the Counselor's Use of Tests

One obvious implication is that lack of congruence between measured interests and aptitudes-abilities is to be expected in a fairly large number of cases and is not to be considered as prima facie evidence of the invalidity of one or both tests.

Second, it is wise to be sensitive to the possible presence of some of the factors emphasized by current theories as being sources of discrepancy between interests and abilities: family pressures, other needs of the individual which conflict with his interests, emotional disturbances, and lack of experience in utilizing certain abilities which the individual is relatively unaware of. Some of these the counselor may seek to correct, but with others it may be that the best that can be done is to help the individual be aware of the reasons for his leanings, without expecting that these will be modified to bring interests and abilities more nearly in line with each other.

Third, realization that there are multiple vocational outlets for any given ability and that there are multiple ways of functioning *within* any occupation, should reassure both counselor and client even when there is considerable discrepancy between interests and abilities. The boy with a high level of mathematical and scientific achievement but low interest in these areas and high interest in dealing with people has possibilities of interesting and remunerative jobs of an administrative, sales, or teaching nature in a scientific-technical setting. The man, like Ralph Santaro in Chapter 11, with better-than-average mechanical aptitudes but even stronger interests in sales can find, as Ralph did, an area of selling in which some mechanical competence could be of value. In some cases where there are serious contradictions and conflicts, the plan developed will be a *compromise* between occupational choices appropriate for the person's abilities and those appropriate for his interests. In many cases, however, it may be more of a *synthesis* (Super, 1957a) of various facets of an individual's total make-up. The difference between these terms— *compromise* and *synthesis*—is not as slight as it may seem; it may be of real help to a client to see that he is building a complex whole different from any of the parts alone, rather than having to give up one part for another.

INTERESTS AND ACHIEVEMENT

Much of the discussion in the preceding section is applicable here, but there are some additional points to be made. First, to define this particular topic: *achievement* as used here represents more specific learnings than *aptitudes* and *abilities*. It means especially those knowledges, skills, and understandings which result from particular courses in school and from training and apprenticeship programs in particular occupations (though these are usually labelled *proficiency*). These learnings are not readily acquired without specific school or out-of-school experiences with a particular subject-matter, as contrasted with the more basic aptitudes and mental abilities, which can be developed to their levels of potentiality through a variety of less specific life experiences.

One point to be made here is that, in counseling, the interest-achievement connection is a two-way track. That is, we use measured (and expressed) interests as one of the elements in helping an individual to decide in which direction to channel his future achievements. But we also can use past achievements (as evidenced in school grades, standardized tests, and the individual's own perception of what he has done well) as an index of interests. Those things which the individual has done best in the past are probably things in which he had greater interest than those things in which he did not do as well. This does not contradict comments made earlier regarding a tendency of many students to exert extra efforts even in courses they don't like, in order to keep up their grades. Strong (1943) hypothesized, and Frandsen (1947) has offered some supporting evidence, that interests will probably correlate better with achievement when achievement in an area is measured over a *long period of time,* say, the average of grades for a number of courses rather than for only one course.

There have been some efforts, of an inconclusive nature at present, to develop interest *tests* rather than *inventories,* in which an individual's achievements in an area can be used to tap his interests in that area. Super and Roper (1941) developed a technique in which an instructional film on nursing was shown to a group and the retention of details from the film, as measured by an achievement test immediately afterward, was used as an index of interest. Another approach is that of Greene's *Michigan Vocabulary Profile Test,* which measures familiarity with the meanings of a sample of technical words in each of eight areas, such as physical sciences, government, literature, sports. Again the assumption is that high school and college students have had opportunities to pick up this material in basic courses in the various subjects and through reading of newspapers, magazines, and books and that they will have learned and remembered the most words in the areas of greatest interest to them.

This is a knotty problem of cause-and-effect: Does interest lead to learning, or learning to interest? Also, there is an interaction here of interests and aptitudes, and of a number of extraneous factors in addition. Joe Jones's highest score on the *Michigan Vocabulary Profile* might have resulted from his *interest* in that area, and therefore from the greater time expenditure and other effects of motivation, but his score might just as well have resulted from his greater *aptitude* for this kind of subject matter than for others, or it might have resulted from the incidental fact that he happened to have one or two unusually effective teachers in that subject.

Fortunately, from a straight predictive point of view, it probably doesn't matter a great deal which of these is the cause of the present condition. Whether it was interest, aptitude, external factors, or a combination of these that was responsible, present level of achievement is an equally good basis for estimating further achievement. However, when we use clinical appraisal methods in an attempt to understand the person who is undecided or conflicted or underachieving, it is often desirable to separate out the effects of each factor as much as possible. In this way, the causes (genetic interpretation) of the present situation may better be ascertained and differential predictions may better be made: If such-and-such changes, this is likely to happen, and if such-and-such a contingency occurs, then another result is more likely to be the outcome. Sometimes this separating-out can be done by collecting various kinds of data—measured interests, expressed interests, aptitudes, achievement as measured by standardized tests and by school grades, and biographical data, whether from cumulative records or from the individual's own recollections—and manipulating all these in the usual clinical process. A knowledgeable school counselor may pick up clues in the names of instructors the student had for certain subjects (one known to be a stimulating and effective teacher, another dull and ineffective). An agency counselor might find hints in a questionnaire used with applicants, perhaps in a statement about leisure-time activities, or about parental ambitions. Then, using the interview to try out hypotheses, the counselor might gain further insights which lead to a dynamic description of the operation in that particular person of each of the elements: interests, aptitudes, stimulating teachers, and other factors.

Interests as Predictors of Status Rather than Success

The evidence has been marshalled elsewhere (Darley and Hagenah, 1955; Super, 1949; Strong, 1955), and the conclusion seems clear: Interest inventories are better established as predictors of the field the person will *enter* than of the degree of *success* he will enjoy within that field. This conclusion is particularly applicable to the *Strong VIB*, since so much of the research on which the conclusion is based was done with that instrument. An individual's *SVIB* profile at the age of about 17, and thereafter, is a pretty dependable index of *what* he will be doing ten and twenty years later. *How* he will do as compared with his peers in that field is not very predictable. The rationale seems to be this: People tend to enter occupations for which their interests are appropriate (at least for the higher-level occupations on which most of this research has been done), but once in the occupation, factors other than interests seem to be more important. However, at this writing the factors influencing success, especially in these higher-level occupations, have eluded scientific detection. One of the major obstacles in the way of further progress in this area of research is the near-impossibility of locating criteria of success in these occupations. Does one identify the most successful teacher, attorney, physician, business executive, or chemist by his income, by what his students, clients, patients, or customers say about the quality of his work, by judgments of his professional associates (few of whom can have actually observed him at work), or by any other of the presently available criteria? Hardly, each of these is much too sensitive to extraneous factors of geography, luck, slickness of manner, and others which may be quite irrelevant to the accomplishment of the basic functions and duties of the job.

For these reasons and others, we can say to clients, "Your interests are most similar to those of people in Field X; this doesn't mean that you are assured of *success* in this field, but people with interests like yours usually enter these occupations rather than others, and tend to stay in them rather than change to other occupations. We can infer, though this is not as well-established by research, that you would find your colleagues congenial company, since they would share your interests to such an extent, and we can infer that you would be satisfied in your work, since most people in the field are."

Although some would reject the use of interest inventories completely, because of these limitations on their use (Rothney, Danielson, and Heimann, 1959, question even the kind of limited interpretation made above), it seems that there is value to at least some counselees in knowing how their likes and dislikes, when organized systematically into scoring scales, compare with those of people in relevant fields of work. It is, of course, a responsibility of the counselor to see that proper interpretations are made and communicated to his clients and to do all in his power to insure that they do not come away with unfounded perceptions.

PREDICTING SUCCESS IN COLLEGE

The past record of tests in predicting success in college has been documented in detail (see, for example, Garrett, 1949; Travers, 1949), and the conclusion seems to be that of all predictors of college grades, the best single one is the high school average. Following this in usually decreasing order of effectiveness are: achievement tests of high school course contents, general college aptitude tests such as the *ACE* and the *Ohio State,* general scholastic aptitude tests such as *Otis* and *Henmon-Nelson,* and finally, the special aptitude tests, such as verbal and numerical parts of the multi-factor tests of mental abilities. It seems clear that the closer the contents of the predictor are to the contents of the criterion (college grades), the higher the correlation. There is some disagreement, however, as to the use of achievement measures versus aptitude measures for estimating the probabilities of success in college.[6] Some of the major issues and problems are the following:

1. A major point of disagreement has to do with the student who *underachieved* in high school for any of a number of reasons: inadequate motivation, lack of defined goals, emotional disturbance, bilingual home, and other family handicaps. The major producers of tests used for college admission and for scholarship awards seem now to lean toward the point of view expressed by two of the participants in the 1958 Invitational Conference and briefly summed up in these quotations:

> What the colleges require are students who have strong education foundations, not those possessing brilliant but undeveloped minds (Ebel, 1959: p. 91).
>
> The examination must make him [the applicant for admission or for a scholarship] feel that he has *earned* the right to go to college by his own efforts, not that he is entitled to college admission because of his innate abilities or aptitudes, regardless of what he has done in high school (Lindquist, 1959: p. 109).

The contrary point of view is taken by Wesman (1959), who emphasizes the "rescue" function of tests which show promise for more than the

---

[6] See, for example, a symposium on the subject in the *Proceedings of the 1958 Invitational Conference on Testing Problems* of the Educational Testing Service, listed in the bibliography under the names of individual participants: Ebel, 1959; Flanagan, 1959; Lindquist, 1959; and Wesman, 1959.

student has developed in high school. He cites data from a "large midwestern state university" in whose 1957 entering class were 188 students who were in the top 25 per cent on the *College Qualification Tests* but in the lowest quarter of their high school class. More than half of these attained an average of *C* or better during their first semester in college. An additional 314 freshmen in this same class were in the top quarter on the *College Qualification Test* but in the third fourth of the high school class; of this group three fourths earned a *C* average or better. If being in the upper half of the high school class had been a requirement for admission to college, here are some 300 students who would have been denied admission, who, it turns out, did succeed at least in attaining a *C* average. High school and college counselors can add many cases to these and can document them as to the factors which were responsible for greater effectiveness in college than in high school—the student who suddenly realizes how important college is as preparation for the goals he holds, the student who improves his study habits or who gets remedial work in reading or other areas.

It seems likely, however, that only a minority of students who did poorly in high school and have higher scores on aptitude tests will maintain a solid level of success in college (Wesman's data are for one semester only; some of these students might have regressed once they had overcome the hurdle of the first semester and thus earned the right to stay in college) . From the vantage point of a college admissions officer, the number of successes is seen as only one cell in the expectancy table: for almost every one of Wesman's subjects in the lowest fourth of his high school class who achieved a *C* average in the first semester in college, there is one person who failed to master even this minimum hurdle. From the point of view of the college, this may be too high a price to pay. From the point of view of many college instructors also, it is not especially appealing to know that of one identifiable segment of a class, half are almost sure to fail. The picture is even less attractive when we take note of the fact that often the poorer students enter the less competitive programs in college, in which success is not measured on precisely the same scale as in the others. Further, the *presence* in his class of many such students sometimes leads the conscientious instructor to exert extra efforts on their part— efforts which are not then available to other students. Finally, many teachers will tend to "mark by the curve," whether they believe in this approach or not, when they have large numbers of such students.

One's leanings regarding this issue probably will hinge largely on his identification and goals; for counselors whose major concern is with individual students and who feel their major goal is providing each one assistance in becoming whatever he is capable of and wishes to become, the "rescue" function will be important. Such counselors will find it useful to include in their test libraries, for at least special cases, tests of an aptitude rather than achievement nature (the older *ACE*, for example, rather than the newer *SCAT*). They do not need to give up one kind of test for another; for the fairly normally achieving student—the one who is functioning at about his level of capability—the achievement measure should do very nicely. For the others, counselors can add the information from the aptitude test, given either as part of the all-school program or on an individual basis. Upon verifying the hypothesis that aptitude is higher than achievement, they will use their armamentarium of tools and techniques to discover causes and to help the student, if he wishes, to plan necessary activities to close the gap. The counselor, however, must make the same judgment about his time expenditure as does the college; he will probably need to spend many more hours per counselee with the underachiever than with other students, and other services will necessarily suffer.

2. A second issue involved in the debate over the achievement versus the aptitude approach to college prediction has to do with the *possible influence which these tests have on high school curricula*. Critics, such as Wesman, of the achievement approach feel that it too readily becomes a goal of instruction, as happened in New York State with the Regents testing program.[7] Proponents of the achievement kind of test do not deny that many school administrators and teachers *are* unduly sensitive to such tests and tend to gear their course contents to what is expected on the tests. Nationwide, one of the major criteria for evaluating high school programs has become the scores attained by seniors on College Board examinations, National Merit Scholarship tests, and others of this nature. Not only are high school junior and senior courses being geared to these examinations, but in addition high schools have set up special "scholarship classes," "college clubs," and other cram groups.

Those who favor an achievement emphasis in the testing of college aptitude feel, however, that it is the responsibility of test-makers to do all in their power to reflect in test items the generally accepted goals of high school curricula. They feel that there is enough commonality among schools, in the way of knowledge and skills in applying that knowledge, to warrant measuring college aptitude through high school achievement. Some of them also feel that present tests of this sort are a long way from achieving these criteria.

3. A third argument against the achievement measure is that it *duplicates information* already available in the high school record. For some high schools this is undoubtedly true, but with the variety of schools in this country which prepare for colleges, differences in standards and in

[7] A statewide program of subject achievement tests which are used as part of the student's evaluation in the course and which are recorded separately on the student's record. "The Regents average" is used by many colleges for admission purposes and by various bodies for evaluation of instruction.

curricular content are so great that it is not possible to consider high
school grades an adequate indication of a graduate's attainments compared with those of others in the country. Some college admissions officers
use rank-in-class as an improvement over straight numerical average;
some go further and adjust the averages of students from different schools,
adding points to some and deducting from others in order to make them
comparable (although this is usually done *sub rosa* to avoid repercus-
sions). Many feel that the most defensible approach is to require the same
achievement tests of all applicants, thereby at least knowing what level
and type of achievement is represented by a given score.

Conclusion

This debate will undoubtedly continue, and we may see the pendulum
swing first in one and then the other direction. At this writing, the achievement emphasis seems to be in the ascendance. The abandonment by the
Cooperative Test Division of the Educational Testing Service of the *ACE*
and its replacement by the *School and College Aptitude Tests* is a major
example of this trend. Even the Psychological Corporation, whose policies
seem to represent an aptitude point of view, made their *College Qualification Test* heavily achievement in content. From the evidence currently
available, it would seem reasonable that, for high school students *as a total
group,* the newer tests should yield a somewhat higher level of predictive
validity in relation to later success in college.

Counselors, however, are concerned primarily with students as *individuals.* For those individuals who have worked at approximately their level
of capability, the achievement measure should be adequate (although it
may add little or nothing to the information already available from
standardized achievement tests used in the school). For those individuals
who have *not* worked up to capacity, it is often necessary to include a
college aptitude measure that is less dependent on specific learning in
high school courses. This is not to say that a test labelled "college aptitude" must always be used in such cases. A multifactor battery that was
given fairly recently and that has a high enough ceiling may provide
enough information for these purposes.

It may be well to note that a similar situation exists in connection with
appraisal of students who have achieved at a level *higher* than their
"normal" level of expectation. As in the case of Robert Martin (Chapter
11), such a student would be wise to plan his post-high school education
in the light of information from *both* achievement and aptitude kinds of
tests. He might, for example, set his sights at a level between the two
scores, reasoning that overachievement in college will probably be more
difficult to maintain than it was in high school. For such a student, the
achievement type of college aptitude test may provide an overestimate of
his chances in college.

The appraisal of individuals will therefore require a variety of types of college aptitude measures. In addition, counselors have a responsibility to pass along to all prospective college applicants the information that it is becoming increasingly necessary to develop their potentialities while in high school. With the trends in college admissions testing and the anticipated bulge in college applications, there will be fewer opportunities for "second chances" for those who have underachieved while in high school.

Specificity of College Predictions

It is not uncommon to hear it said that a particular student is "not college material." This could mean a number of things—that he is not deemed capable of *doing well* in an *average* college, that he is not capable even of *barely passing* in an *average* college, or that he is not capable of passing even in the *least selective* or *least competitive* colleges. Often the quotation above is an interpretation of our fourth type—Evaluative— and implies a value judgment on the part of the speaker, namely, that this student *should not* go to college.

As most counselors of high school seniors know, there are in this country close to two thousand institutions of higher education. Among them is an almost unbelievable *range,* not only of requirements for admission and retention, but also of other characteristics, such as specific goals of various curricula, criteria for grading, and the kind of student behavior that is valued. In such a situation, it is a rare student who can be characterized categorically as "college material" or "not college material." Instead, one must make a multiple statement about each student (with regard, for example, to his mental ability, achievements, social characteristics, and goals) in relation to each *kind* of college. In effect, this becomes a matter of using *local norms* with regard to *appropriate* variables.[8]

A penetrating analysis of this normative problem was made recently by Davis (1959), who reported some of his experiences in developing norms for sixteen colleges in a state system. The project included both the collection of local *norms* for each college on College Board *SAT* and high school average and also collection of data regarding the *validity* of each of these predictors at each college. Tables 13.3 and 13.4 illustrate some of the kinds of data included in the 1957 report of the Director of Testing and Guidance for the University System of Georgia.[9] The only change made in the original data is removal of identification of the particular colleges; the tables shown here are not direct reproductions of

---

[8] Slater (1957) has discussed the implications of this principle for research studies on prediction of college success. He pointed out that success in college can properly be evaluated only by relating each student's perceptions of the purposes and goals of college to the purposes and goals as perceived by that particular college.

[9] We are indebted to both Dr. Junius A. Davis, who was Director at that time, and to Dr. John R. Hills, the present Director, for their help in making the materials available and to the latter for granting permission to reproduce them here.

tables in the report but rather are excerpts. Table 13.3 is excerpted from one of the tables in the report and shows the proportions of male students

Table 13.3. Proportions of Students at Each of Eight Colleges with Various SAT-V Scores Who Make C or Better Their First Quarter

SAT-V Score	College A	College B	College C	College D	College E	College F	College G	College H
750	98	97	99	99	99	99	96	99
700	96	95	99	98	99	99	93	99
650	93	90	99	95	98	99	88	98
600	87	82	96	91	95	99	81	95
550	80	75	91	86	90	98	73	91
500	69	63	82	77	79	94	63	84
450	57	50	71	66	68	86	52	74
400	44	39	56	54	50	73	42	63
350	32	27	40	43	37	55	31	50
300	21	18	26	32	21	36	22	37
250	13	12	15	21	10	19	15	25

SOURCE: Regents, University System of Georgia, 1958. By permission.

Table 13.4. Regression Formulas for Predicting Grades in Eight Colleges from SAT-V and SAT-M Scores and High School Average

College	Formula	Sest.
A	$.042$ (SAT-V) $+ .028$ (SAT-M) $+ .669$ (HSA) $+ 25.833$	9.5
B	$.0059$ (SAT-V) $+ .0050$ (SAT-M) $+ .0734$ (HSA) $- 7.61$	1.39
C	$.036$ (SAT-V) $+ .024$ (SAT-M) $+ .457$ (HSA) $- 16.290$	7.1
D	$.035$ (SAT-V) $+ .008$ (SAT-M) $+ .542$ (HSA) $- 39.547$	7.5
E	$.0024$ (SAT-V) $+ .0027$ (SAT-M) $+ .0214$ (CR) * $- 2.21$	.53
F	$.047$ (SAT-V) $+ .014$ (SAT-M) $+ .049$ (HSA) $- 2.939$	5.8
G	$.021$ (SAT-V) $+ .033$ (SAT-M) $+ .342$ (HSA) $- 13.138$	7.3
H	$.0030$ (SAT-V) $+ .0024$ (SAT-M) $+ .0244$ (HSA) $- .62$	.67

* Converted Rank is used instead of High School Average.
NOTE: The formulas are not all directly comparable with each other, since these eight colleges use a variety of numbering systems for college grades and for high school averages.

SOURCE: *Ibid.*

with various *SAT-Verbal* scores who made *C* or better average in their first quarter in college. At College *A*, a student with *SAT-V* score of 500 has 69 chances in 100 of attaining an average of *C* or better. At College *F*, he would have 94 chances in 100 of attaining a *C* or better average.

Table 13.4 is excerpted from another table in the report and shows the regression formulas developed for these same colleges for predicting

**Table 13.5. Percentile Distributions of SAT Scores of Entering
Male Freshmen at Colleges D and E**

Score	SAT-M		SAT-V	
	College D	College E	College D	College E
640-659				
620-639				
600-619			99	99
580-599			98	97
560-579	99	99	95	96
540-559	97	98	91	95
520-539	97	96	88	92
500-519	96	95	85	86
480-499	95	92	82	80
460-479	92	89	75	74
440-459	86	86	68	69
420-439	80	80	62	62
400-419	76	69	52	51
380-399	70	60	41	43
360-379	63	50	32	36
340-359	55	40	25	30
320-339	44	31	19	23
300-319	32	21	11	16
280-299	23	13	7	8
260-279	15	8	2	3
240-259	8	3	1	
220-239	3			
200-219	1			
Mean	354	374.5	415	409.0
S. D.	82	87.6	84	87.6
Correlation with grades	.45	.53	.44	.58

Source: *Ibid.*

grades from scores on *SAT-Verbal* and *SAT-Mathematical* tests and high
school average. Unfortunately, it is difficult to make direct comparisons
between colleges because they used various different methods of calcu-
lating high school average and a variety of different numbering systems
for college grades. However, it can be seen, for instance, that the formula
for College *D* gives more than four times as much weight to *SAT-V* (.035)
as to *SAT-M* (.008), whereas at College *E*, *SAT-M* receives only slightly

more weight (.0027) than *SAT-V* (.0024) .[10] Yet the student bodies of these two colleges, as can be seen in Table 13.5, also excerpted from data in the report, are not very different in their distribution of *SAT-V* and *SAT-M* scores. As Davis points out (1959) , it is necessary to know not only the student's relative standing on tests and other measures, but also the relative importance of each measure as a predictor at each college. Being high on a test, as compared with students at a particular college, is in itself not enough information to conclude that the person has better than average chances of doing well there. For this purpose, it is necessary to have information of the nature included in Tables 13.3 and 13.4.

The discussion just preceding hearkens back to some of the bridges of Chapter 8. Data of the kind shown in Table 13.5 are of the Norm Bridge type (except for the correlation coefficients) , whereas data in the other two tables are of the Regression Bridge type.

Davis also points out a number of other subtleties in his data. For example, at three of the colleges there is almost identical correlation between *SAT-V* and grades, and at all three a score of 400 is exceeded by similar percentages of the freshman class. Yet, the chances of attaining satisfactory grades in the first quarter with an *SAT-V* score of 400 is quite different: In one college it is 80 in 100, in the second 73 in 100, and in the third 42 in 100. The difference is in attrition rates: The faculty at the third college had a higher cutoff point for failure.

Perhaps enough has been said to make the point; clearly one cannot characterize a student as "college material" without a good deal of further qualification. As if this were not enough, norms and correlations become outdated. As Davis points out, when a college sustains a 40 per cent increase in applications and the loss of a dormitory by fire, a score on the *SAT* which one year is at the 80th percentile for that college drops the following year to below the 50th percentile.

---

[10] Simplified regression equations and more convenient tables were used in the most recent publication of this same body, the Office of Testing and Guidance of the University System of Georgia (Hills, Franz, and Emory, 1959) . For example, a regression equation which in its original form read: ".024V + .019M + .628HSA + 38.788" was reduced to "V + M + 26HSA" with very little loss of predictive accuracy.

Another recent publication (Carlson and Fullmer, 1959) presents college predictive data of this kind in the form both of tables and graphs. One of these graphs is reproduced in Figure 7.5.

CHAPTER 14

Communicating Test Results:
Research Foundations

W E ARE NOW READY to rejoin the client. Since the end of Chapter 5 we have been operating pretty much alone—without the participation of the counselee, his parents, teachers or other persons for whom and about whom the tests are being used. During these intervening chapters, the counselor has been thinking about the test data, trying to make sense of them, and preparing to do something with his interpretations. True, the client has slipped in occasionally during this period to illustrate his role in the process of giving meaning to the scores and the other information. From time to time also, the counselor will have found it helpful to go over one or another inference or hypothesis with other people. This might be a classroom teacher who has seen the counselee function in a particular subject and who can help verify such an hypothesis as the one about Robert Martin (Chapter 11), that he is confused in his first contacts with new material but through much effort manages to learn it well. (As a matter of fact, in *that* case, it was the client's mother who verified the hypothesis). In a setting where there are medical personnel (a school, college, rehabilitation center, or hospital), the counselor will sometimes want to check the possibility that a learning disorder has a physical component or to seek advice as to whether the client's health would be endangered by the demands of a particular occupation. A clinical psychologist or psychiatrist might be consulted with regard to suspicions of serious personality disturbance.

Whatever other people may contribute toward interpretation of test data, the fact remains that this is an operation which is the *responsibility* of the counselor or counseling psychologist and is done mostly by him alone. In performing it, he draws upon his knowledge of people, of

343

groups, of occupations, of schools and colleges, of adjustment and maladjustments of various kinds, and, of course, of the tests he uses.

There are, however, large differences among counselors in the extent to which they invite clients to share with them in examining the raw test data and inferring therefrom predictions, conclusions, and recommendations. At one extreme there are probably some counselors who take little responsibility for interpreting tests beyond scoring them and converting the scores to percentiles or another form and then turning these over to their clients to interpret. This practice cannot be justified solely as a timesaver, but only if based on a purposeful, carefully thought-through plan of procedure in which the counselor emphasizes client participation for its learning values. However, test interpretation is more than a matter of their "meaning to the client." There is a body of knowledge regarding tests that forms a very major element of the process of interpretation; this knowledge, and the skills necessary for its application, are the counselor's important contribution, and interpretation without them is dangerously unprofessional.

Schools sometimes tend to neglect the counselor's responsibilities for test interpretation. It is not unheard of for students in high schools to take tests and inventories in home-rooms, to score them and prepare their own profiles, and then to be given only the most general interpretations in a group and frequently under the supervision of a teacher with little or no training in measurement. This sort of thing may sometimes be encouraged by using the package programs, in which answer sheets are shipped to the test publisher or distributor, who scores them and sends multiple copies of each pupil's profile back to the school. In some instances copies go to classroom teachers, presumably with the assumption that all teachers are qualified to interpret the results. Even more appalling, some schools turn over a copy of the profile to the student, asking that he take it to his parents for *their* interpretation.

In college counseling bureaus, in vocational guidance agencies, and in some other settings, it is more likely that the counselor has spent at least some minutes, perhaps an hour or more, studying an individual's test scores. Whichever the situation, and however detailed, complex, and deep-level are the interpretations, the counselor now is ready for the next phase in which he will try to communicate to someone (client, teacher, parent) the results themselves, or his interpretations thereof, or recommendations based on them. This is then a *process of communication* to which we now address ourselves. Though we examine the reporting process separately from the other aspects of testing—selection, administration, and interpretation—it is of course integral with all. As we selected our tests, administered them, and interpreted the results, we kept reminding ourselves of the purposes for which the tests were being used; these reach a focal point at the time that our findings are communicated to the people concerned.

For some counselors, this last step seems to be anticlimactic, a mere routine in which people are "told" what the counselor has spent minutes or hours finding out. These counselors have their greatest interest in the interpretive process itself—digging meaning out of the data. Some become extremely skilled in this process. However, there can be little doubt among those who have seen clients, and their parents, and their teachers, responding to these "objective" and "factual" reports that this final step is far from simple. In some ways it is more difficult than deriving the interpretations themselves, since the counselor is on the "firing line"—in a face-to-face situation where he has to think on his feet. He may indeed be well prepared to give his interpretations, but he must also be flexible in giving up hypotheses as they are disproved by new data appearing in the interview. He may expect to encounter any and all of the emotional responses of a person who is struggling with important personal matters —anxiety, defensiveness, under- or over-dependency. In addition to his skills as an interpreter, of which few of us have enough, the counselor must have the skills required in the face-to-face counseling situation; this is no small order.

In this chapter and the two which follow it, we will survey some of the variety of methods by which counselors communicate their findings to various people. Greatest stress is on the use of the interview for reporting to counselees and their parents. Brief treatment is given to other kinds of report, such as graphic devices, and written reports to other professional persons. As with the topic of Test Selection, we will deal both with theory and research, on the one hand, and with practice, on the other. First we must see how much direction can be obtained from published research on the value of test reporting in general and on the relative values of various methods of reporting.

RESEARCH ON TEST REPORTING

Although there are a number of relevant studies, most of them fail to isolate particular elements of the process, so that it is impossible to know which was responsible for the result. In one popular design, for instance, subjects who have received oral reports of their test results are later followed up to see how much increased knowledge they have about themselves. If they seem not to have learned what the tests show, one might conclude that the counselor failed to communicate. However, it might also be that the interpretations were too threatening for them to accept, or that the "facts" represented by the test scores and their interpretations were inaccurate, or that the whole process of test reporting was a waste of time because the subjects were not adequately motivated to learn these things about themselves.

If, on the other hand, subjects *do* show, after test reporting, self-perceptions similar to those which the counselor has tried to convey, this could be an indication of mere parroting, rather than of meaningful and persisting learning. Related to this is the evidence, from recent studies of *gullibility*, that people may accept uncritically a report about themselves, perhaps because it came from a psychologist or because it was based on a test or inventory. Forer (1949) demonstrated the gullibility effect with a group of students, who were given identical generalized personality sketches (drawn from dream books and astrological charts), which they were told were individual interpretations based on the instructor's scoring of an interest blank they had filled out. They all accepted the sketches as accurate descriptions of themselves (without realizing that everyone else in the class had exactly the same sketch). It may be that these subjects were not nearly so gullible, but were acting in accordance with a fairly widespread student code of behavior, which is to agree with the instructor when in doubt (and even sometimes when not!). However, Stagner (1958) had very similar results in using an adaptation of Forer's method with a group of personnel managers who were attending a conference. Fifty per cent of these subjects said that their "personal" interpretations were "amazingly accurate," 40 per cent rated them "rather good," and 10 per cent "about half and half." Nobody selected the categories "more wrong than right" or "almost entirely wrong." With another group, this time composed of industrial supervisors, 37 per cent chose "amazingly accurate" and 44 per cent "rather good." So this phenomenon does not appear to be peculiar to college students. In fact, Stagner found that a group of students with whom he tried his method were less accepting than the personnel men; 25 per cent of the students chose "amazingly accurate," and 37 per cent "rather good."

There are other methodological problems; most studies include only very short-term follow-ups. Even if counselees do seem to learn things about themselves, short-term follow-ups do not reveal how enduring the learning is or how effective it is in changing the individual's reality orientation and his plans (Hobbs and Seeman, 1955). To mention just one problem, few studies have included adequate provisions in their design or in statistical treatment of the data for controlling the variety of elements involved—the test interpretations themselves, interpretations of other data, the counselor himself and his competency, and other facets of the interview.[1]

For the reasons mentioned above, despite the fair *number* of studies now in the literature, few positive conclusions are available for the guidance of counselors. Let us see, however, what has been done.

[1] A much more extensive treatment of these and other problems in the evaluation of counseling is found in Chapter 12 of Tyler (1953).

Studies of the General Effectiveness of Test Reporting

With Self-Ratings as the Criterion

Several researchers have sought to measure the extent to which counseling (with tests as a major element) is followed by greater agreement between the individual's self-ratings and his scores on tests (Berdie, 1954; Froehlich, 1957; Johnson, 1953; Lallas, 1956; Robertson, 1958, 1959; Singer and Stefflre, 1954; Torrance, 1954; Wright, 1957). One additional study attempted to measure simply the extent to which clients *remembered* their test scores as told to them (Froehlich and Moser, 1954). In general, the results furnish little evidence for our more optimistic expectations of the influence of test information on self-concepts.

Among the more positive findings are those of Johnson (1953), who administered a self-rating form to one hundred clients before, immediately after, and one month after counseling. Client self-ratings of their aptitudes, interests, and personality traits were compared with the counselor's ratings, which were based largely on test results. There were significant increases in accuracy of self-ratings, and the subjects also showed gains in their ratings of certainty regarding their self-estimates. The largest gains in self-knowledge were for intelligence, followed by interests and then personality. In general, correlation between accuracy of self-estimates and the degree of certainty the person felt about those estimates was very low. This led to the conclusion that the client's expressed certainty about his abilities or other characteristics is no reason to assume that no tests are needed. One fact to be noted for later consideration is that the subjects of this study were voluntary self-referrals for counseling. It will later be suggested that one cause of the less positive results of some of the other studies may be their use of a "recruited" sample, one about whom it cannot be assumed that they are motivated for self-learning.

Berdie (1954) used a somewhat longer follow-up period (six months) with a group of college freshmen, and he also had a control group of students who had had no counseling during the period (students had been randomly assigned to experimental and control groups in advance). He computed correlations between the actual test scores and, first, self-ratings prior to any counseling, and, second, self-ratings at the end of one quarter in college. He found, first, that there were at best moderate correlations either time, indicating, if the tests are accepted as valid, rather limited self-knowledge on the part of students as to their standing compared with others. Secondly, he found essentially one characteristic, among those rated, on which the counseled (experimental) group improved significantly more than did the control group in agreeing with the test scores. This was in estimates of ranking of interests on the areas of the *Strong VIB,* where men in the experimental group showed an increase in agreement with the *SVIB* profile which was greater than that of men in the control group. For the characteristics measured by the *ACE* and the scales of the *MMPI* no significant improvement in self-knowledge was found for either experimental or control group. Berdie also used other criteria in addition to self-ratings, but these will be reported in a later section.

Three studies were done in connection with intensive orientation programs sponsored by colleges for prospective or accepted freshmen (Robertson, 1958, 1959; Torrance, 1954). Torrance asked entering freshmen to estimate their scores on tests of scholastic aptitude and achievement, first before a five-day orientation program, then at the end. They were also asked on both occasions to predict their grades. Few details are given of the study itself, since the article deals primarily with the implications of this self-evaluative approach for a faculty counseling program. It is not reported that control groups were used; without this, it is not possible to pinpoint the elements which were responsible for any results noted. Torrance concluded, however, that the self-evaluative set which was encouraged by the procedures had these results: more learning from the test experiences themselves, more learning from the orientation experiences, and more learning from later contacts with advisors and counselors. He reported that self-estimates bore little relationship to actual scores and grades. Students tended to overestimate their abilities at the preorientation point but they became more realistic on re-evaluation.

Contrasting with Torrance's result, Robertson (1958) found that a group of prefreshmen who had gone through a testing and counseling program tended on some tests to *underestimate* their scores, and on other tests there was no particular tendency one way or the other for the group as a whole. Of course, Robertson had his subjects do their ratings only *after* the counseling; without precounseling data it is not possible to judge whether this difference is a result of counseling, or of qualities peculiar to his population, or perhaps of the wording in his questionnaire. Robertson's conclusions seem overly sanguine regarding degree of correlation between student and counselor ratings of ability (both done after counseling). Although many of the relationships attained a level of statistical significance, they are not very impressive. For example, only 50 per cent of the subjects judged correctly in which fourth of the total distribution their test scores were. Student predictions of their grades correlated .43 with those of the counselor, a statistically significant level, but again rather modest in degree.

In a second study, Robertson used the pre- and post-counseling design, subjects being prospective freshmen. On various items, 43 to 80 per cent changed their self-estimates of ability and interests. This alone suggests some substantial impact of the program, and especially of the testing and counseling portions. Robertson went on to discover that 25 per cent changed their fields of study, but from the results of a follow-up done two years later, he concluded that the self-estimates did not have much stability. It would appear that, as Hobbs and Seeman (1955) said, changes in expressed self-concept may represent little depth and little permanence.

In one of the rare published studies using a group as young as high school age, Froehlich (1957) reports very limited effectiveness of individual counseling which included test reporting. Clients here rated themselves at the beginning and end of a summer school program, during which the experimental subjects received counseling by experienced counselors, each of whom used his own preferred methods. There was little change in accuracy of self-ratings for either experimental or control subjects.

Wright (1957) added a further dimension by comparing *group* reporting of test results with individual reporting, and both with a control group which received no report between pretest and post-test ratings. The group method utilized techniques similar to those used with individuals: There was a general discussion of tests and their uses and limitations and an explanation of the meaning of norms and percentiles; then each person received a slip of paper containing his own scores in quintiles. Finally, there was a discussion period during which questions could be asked and during which illustrative interpretations were given. Both counseled groups—individually and "multiply"—showed significant gains from pre-inventory to post-inventory in the accuracy of self-concept and other criteria. Both groups had significantly greater gains than the noncounseled control group, but there were no significant differences between individual and multiple counseling methods.

A comparison of individual and group methods of reporting was also made by Lallas (1956). In addition to the three groups which Wright had—individual counseling, group (or "multiple") counseling, and control—Lallas had a fourth group each of whose members received first a group interpretation of test results and then an individual interview. His eleventh grade subjects took the *Iowa Tests of Educational Development*; before and after taking this battery they estimated their rank in the various subtests and also their degree of confidence in their estimates. The greatest improvements in accuracy of self-estimates were found with individual counseling and group-plus-individual counseling. Somewhat less improvement was shown by those who had only group reporting, but all three experimental groups showed significantly greater improvement than the control group.

In another of the few studies done with high school students, Froehlich and Moser (1954) used no premeasure, so it is not possible to determine changes in self-estimate, nor did they use a control group. Instead, their design simply tested the extent to which ninth graders *remembered* their profiles on the *Differential Aptitude Tests* fifteen months after having received their scores and interpretations thereof both in groups and individually. Correlations between students' *actual* percentile ranks on the eight subtests and their *remembered* percentile ranks were between .41 and .57. In addition to this rather limited accuracy of recall, it was found that, first, the group as a whole remembered their scores as higher than they actually were. On closer examination, the phenomenon of regression toward the mean seemed to have been operating: The low scoring students remembered their scores as somewhat higher than they actually were, but also quite a few of the higher scoring students (though not as many as in the low group) remembered their scores as *lower* than they actually were. Some further details of this study will be reported in later sections.

Singer and Stefflre (1954) designed their study specifically to focus on *individual* discrepancies in self-estimates. They point out, quite correctly, that some of the research in this area deals only with *group* relationships. They give an example of a hypothetical situation in which every member of a counseled group has a greater discrepancy after counseling than before, between his self-estimates and actual test scores. Yet the correlation between self-estimates and test scores is *higher* after counseling than before. This would happen in a situation in which post-counseling self-estimates are all very distant from actual test scores, but all the *same* distance, whereas precounseling estimates were all closer to actual scores, but varying both in amount and direction, from a few points below to a few points above the test scores. Their own study therefore used *individual discrepancy* scores (the difference between self-estimated interests and scores on the *Occupational Interest Inventory*). However, they found almost no significant differences between mean discrepancy scores precounseling and those taken three months after counseling. Pushing their data further, they found a few more significant differences by comparing *standard deviations* of discrepancy scores obtained precounseling with those obtained post-counseling. Some of the standard deviations were significantly smaller after than before counseling, indicating a decrease in the number of subjects who had very large discrepancy scores. Even with these additional data, however, the results of this study do not show very impressive outcomes of counseling, since only five of a total possible twenty-four comparisons were statistically significant.

Finally, Froehlich (1954) sought to ascertain the effects on self-ratings of *taking* tests, without receiving any report of results. Using adult evening school students, he had his subjects rate themselves on seventeen abilities, interests, and personality traits, before and after taking an extensive battery of tests. Very few significant changes in self-ratings were found, and it was concluded that taking tests in and of itself does not influence self-description. To the extent that these results may be generalized to the other studies, they act as a control over this one element in the total process. Whatever improvement there is in accuracy of self-estimates, then, would not be attributed to the experience of *taking* tests, but to other elements, in particular to receiving a report of results.

An attempt will be made to summarize and evaluate the results of all this research after the next section, which adds several studies of a related nature.

With Other Criteria than Self-Ratings

In their review of studies of this nature, Hobbs and Seeman (1955) discussed the problem of lack of independence between the experimental variable (giving test reports during counseling interviews) and the criterion of success of this operation (the self-rating). Even if the client rates himself as the counselor would rate him, say, on intelligence, mechanical aptitude, or clerical interest, this may represent learning of only a superficial nature, a mere parroting, without any substantial or lasting change in the individual's self-concept or future behavior. They recommend the use of criteria which would require the subject to make more of an independent appraisal, such as asking him to predict his later grades. To some extent, this was done in the study by Berdie (1954), which has already been cited, and in a study by Young (1955).

Berdie, whose research emphasized self-ratings as the criterion, also included three other criteria, one of which required students to predict their average grades at the end of the first year. This is a somewhat more independent criterion than the usual self-description, but it is still a subjective report by the client which can easily mirror the content of the interview. There were on the whole very large increases in accuracy of predictions made at the end of the first quarter as compared with those made prior to college entrance. Perhaps the college experiences themselves and the receipt of first-quarter grades were a powerful force toward reality orientation. The men who received counseling increased significantly more than the control men in accuracy of predicting their own grades, an effect which presumably can be attributed to counseling, and the experimental group of women showed the same difference, but not to a statistically significant degree. The other two criteria were of a different order—comparison of the honor-point ratios of experimental and control groups at the end of two quarters and comparison of the percentages of students in each group who had dropped out of college by the end of two quarters. There were no significant differences between counseled and noncounseled groups in honor-point ratios, but there was a lower dropout percentage in the experimental than the control group, significant at the 5 per cent level. Although both of these have the merit of relative independence, that is, of avoiding mere parroting of counselor statements, they unfortunately do not serve very well to measure the effects of *test reporting*, since, in some cases, a lower honor-point ratio and dropping out of college might represent more realistic self-acceptance than continuing to "overachieve" and overaspire. In fact, if pushed a little deeper, even these criteria may turn out not to be entirely inde-pendent. A student who drops out of college may be doing precisely what his counselor told him was likely to happen.

The report by Young (1955) is one of the few which report details of the counseling procedures. He had a rather standardized 25-minute inter-view with each of 100 college freshmen in the course of which he made frequent use of statistical interpretations. Charts were employed to show the student how his test scores compared with those of freshmen in gen-eral at that college. Each individual's predicted grade-point average was explained (derived from a regression equation using high school rank and *ACE* score). Early in the interview and again after all the test inter-pretations had been reported, the student was asked to predict his first semester's grades. There was a control group of 100 students, matched one-for-one with the experimental group, who had not been called in for this counseling program (and had no counseling of any other kind that semester). The results of comparisons between experimental and control groups were essentially negative. There was no significant improvement in the accuracy of predicting one's own grades, and there was no differ-ence in the grade-point average between experimental and control groups. The counseled students, in answering specific evaluative questions asked by the counselor at the end of the interview, rated most helpful "know-ing" their test scores, next most helpful "seeing relation of individual grades to over-all achievement," and least helpful their own "guessing" of their test scores and their predicted grades. It is interesting that they were in effect rejecting what were probably the most active and self-involving parts of the interview and favoring the most passive parts.

Resistance to Change. Before evaluating the studies reported in this section and the one preceding it, one additional piece of research will help to highlight an important problem, that of resistance on the part of people to changing their self-concepts in the face of test reports. Hill (1954) administered the *Kuder Preference Record* to a group of college students, from whom he selected seventy-three who had very high and fifty-two who had very low scores on certain scales. Then he gave each of these subjects a series of home-made tests which they were to think meas-ured aptitude for the area in which the person had a high or a low score. Before taking the next test in his series, each subject received the results of the preceding one; his scores were always lower than what he had been told was the level necessary for success in that field. After completing all the discouraging "aptitude tests," subjects again took the *Kuder*. Com-parison of the two *Kuders* showed almost no significant changes in inter-est scores, with the exception of a very few special subgroups (for exam-ple, for those badly maladjusted according to their *MMPI* profiles who started with low interest in an area, measured interest in that area was reduced even further). It is interesting to compare one's reaction to the negative results of Hill's study with one's reactions to the essentially negative results of many of the other studies cited. Those of Hill are probably easier to understand and to fit into one's conception of counseling; one might say that these youngsters showed desirable resistance to false information, whereas the subjects of the other studies were often resisting *valid* and *genuine* information about themselves. Yet, from the point of view of the subjects, there may be no difference, since presumably they do not know in one case that the reports are fake and in the other case that they are genuine. In both approaches, then, a similar phenomenon seems to have been operating, namely, resistance to changing one's self-concept, attitudes, and aspirations.

Overview of Research on General Effectiveness of Test Reporting

As a group, these studies provide only limited evidence of the values derived by people from receiving reports of their test results. It is not clear why some studies had so much more favorable results than others, and one can only speculate as to reasons. As Roeber pointed out (1957), few research reports give enough details about *specific methods* used in communicating test information, so we cannot be sure what role this variable plays. A second factor is the nature of the *particular sample* used; those reported above included high school students, college students, and adults in different parts of the country. Some groups perhaps had had more experience with testing and counseling prior to the experiment than did others; if so, accuracy of self-knowledge before counseling could be affected, as could be the amount of improvement during the experiment.

There is some evidence that *short-term learning* from test reports is greater than long-term effects. It may be that this kind of learning is no more enduring than has been found to be the case with school subjects.

There is encouraging evidence from two of the studies (Lallas, 1956; Wright, 1957) that group reporting techniques may be as effective, or nearly as effective, as individual reports. In this connection it would be extremely helpful to have detailed reports of the group techniques used in these studies. As with individual counseling methods, it is not the approach in general that produced the effects but the particular application made by a person in a setting.

This raises the touchy but unavoidable question of individual differences among the counselors who did the test interpretations and reporting in these studies. Even when we are given information about their years of graduate training and of experience, we do not have enough information to judge the *quality* of their work. Even those who are quite effective in one setting, or with one kind of counselee or group, may not be so effective in other settings or with other counselees. This is a vexing problem that must await studies which are designed in such ways that the effectiveness of different counselors can be compared.

Still another factor which may be responsible for some of the different results obtained among these studies is that of *client motivation* to learn about self. Johnson's study (1953) used voluntary applicants for counseling; with such a group one may assume some degree of readiness for self-appraisal and self-learning. Several of the other studies, however, used samples of broader range populations, such as all students in a grade or all entering freshmen. In these latter cases a lesser degree of motivation for learning about abilities, interests, and other traits, may be assumed, and therefore less learning results. Froehlich's study (1957) offers a bit of evidence which does *not* support this reasoning. His high school student subjects were asked on a questionnaire whether they wanted an opportunity to talk with a counselor. Those who replied in the affirmative showed no more improvement in accuracy of self-ratings after test reporting than did subjects who answered this question in the negative.

Finally, in most of the studies the total testing and counseling process was begun and ended within a few days or a few weeks. The total *number of hours* actually spent by subjects in receiving information about themselves (whether in groups or individually) was very small—probably one to five hours. Perhaps it is unrealistic to expect a great deal of enduring learning to occur in such a short period of time. The time factor is particularly important with self-concept learning; this is not entirely a new subject of study for adolescents and adults. By the time they have reached high school, boys and girls have had many opportunities for reality-testing, and they may have reached a practical limit of their self-knowledge, or at least have reached a crystallization of self-concept that is likely to resist change. This "subject" is, after all, not quite as objective as history and mathematics, and learning here is likely to be much more complicated by emotional factors.

Studies of Relationship Between Clients' Characteristics and Learning from Test Reports

Just a few studies have been reported which provide insights into possible *client characteristics* favorable to the acceptance and incorporation of information about themselves given in test reports. Because of the complexity and other problems in doing such research well, very few except doctoral candidates seem to undertake them.[2] Conclusions must be quite tentative; the few studies located take somewhat different approaches, making it difficult to compare results of one with another. Replication of identical studies with different samples (high school, college,

[2] There may have been additional studies in this area which were done as doctoral dissertations but which, because they were unpublished, were less likely to turn up in the search of the literature than books and articles.

agency; rural, urban; different geographical areas) is almost unheard of, so that generalizations can rarely be made with assurance.

Most of the research to be reported aimed at discovering correlates of *learning* about self. However, first we should note Johnson's report (1953), from a study previously cited, that there was very little correlation between *self-knowledge* (about general intelligence, interests, and personality) and the personal characteristics which he examined, including intelligence level, educational attainment, and emotional stability. His conclusion was that counseling of this kind is useful for people of a variety of ages, levels, and other characteristics.

One of the more productive studies, in terms of meaningful results, is that of Kamm and Wrenn (1950). Unfortunately, details of the specific data on which the conclusions are based were not given, so it is not possible to judge their validity. The study used recorded interviews of an educational-vocational planning nature with self-referred college students. Just before and again a few days after the interview, each counselee completed a questionnaire regarding his future plans. One month, and later four months, after the recorded interview, the counselor again interviewed each client to get further evidence regarding the extent of client "acceptance of information." *Information* was defined to include advice, suggestion, emphasis, recommendation, interpretation, request, or explanation. The criterion of acceptance was a composite of decisions by judges who worked from "summaries" of "pre-interview and post-interview data." They judged that in 26 of the 40 cases the client "definitely" or "for the most part" accepted information presented in the interview. Even the brief report of this study in article form is too complex to summarize any further. The findings most pertinent to our present purpose are briefly these:

1. Client acceptance occurred most often in those situations in which both client and counselor were "completely relaxed"; in which there were "positive attitudes" expressed by the client; in which there appeared to be readiness on the part of clients to act regarding a felt need; in which information was directly related to the client's own immediate problem; and in which the information was not in opposition to client self-concept.

2. Acceptance of information was *not* found to be related to: academic aptitude, measured personality patterns, social status of the client's home, veteran status, or marital status.

Their conclusions seem to offer support for some of our earlier comments regarding possible reasons for the negative results of most studies. Emphasis in their findings is placed on attitudes and readinesses of clients to make use of the particular kind of information being given in the interview, which implies *motivation* for receiving the information. Also, they stress the importance of information being congruent with the individual's self-concept, which implies *lack of resistance*. With the additional fact that with only 26 of 40 *self-referred* clients was information judged to have been accepted, the generally negative findings of other studies with "recruited" clients seem not so surprising.

Froehlich and Moser (1954) included in their study, already described in detail, data showing the relations between *level of mental abilities* and accuracy of recall of scores on the *DAT*. Previously mentioned was their finding that not only did many lower-scoring students (about half of them) remember their scores as higher than they actually were, but also some of the higher-scoring students remembered *their* scores as *lower* than they were. (The authors point out the implication of this finding for counselors who are more reluctant to report low scores than high scores; both seem about equally hard to take!) However, there was a significant difference between the mean IQ of the subgroup whose members remembered correctly which of their scores was either first or second highest and the mean IQ of the subgroup whose members failed to report either their actual highest or second highest score as one of their two highest in the battery. The subgroup which remembered this fact had a mean IQ which was eleven points higher than the other subgroup.

Only brief mention is necessary at this point of the Tuma and Gustad (1957) study to which reference was made in Chapter 3. They found a little evidence that similarity between counselor and client in personality characteristics was associated with self-learning (as measured by self-ratings completed before and after counseling). As mentioned in the earlier chapter, however, the counselors in this study tended to be above average in "dominance," "social presence," and "social participation," the three variables on which counselor-client similarity was related to self-learning during counseling. As the authors point out, it may be that it was the fact that the *clients* were above average on these three characteristics that led to superior self-learning rather than the similarity between counselor and client. These findings then are equivocal. In the companion article (Gustad and Tuma, 1957) several additional findings are reported regarding client characteristics in relation to amount of learning about self. Only one such characteristic was found to be significantly correlated with the criterion of successful counseling, and that one was accuracy of self-estimates prior to counseling. In other words, those who knew themselves best before counseling (assuming of course that the test scores represent the truth about their abilities and interests) learned the most about themselves during counseling. Mental ability, as measured by the *ACE,* was not found to be related either to the amount of self-knowledge precounseling or to the amount learned during counseling. This latter finding is in concurrence with that of Kamm and Wrenn (1950) and in partial concurrence with the findings of Froehlich and Moser (1954).

Information pertinent to the present topic was also reported in the study by Froehlich (1957) mentioned earlier. His high school student subjects rated themselves before and after counseling on abilities, interests, and other characteristics. There was no relationship between the amount of improvement or deterioration in accuracy of self-ratings and any of the following characteristics: age, grade, score on *Primary Mental Abilities* tests, or scores on the *Youth Inventory*.

A study by Rogers (1954) will be described more fully in a later section. For now we are interested in his finding, contrary to most of the studies mentioned above, that those of his subjects who were above average on the *ACE* showed a mean increase in self-understanding scores after a test report interview, but those who were below average on the *ACE* did not as a group show a mean increase.

Implications of Research on Client Characteristics

One comment which preceded the review of studies in this particular subarea bears repetition: Very few conclusions can be stated with much assurance. Only a minority of the studies indicate that mental ability influences the amount of learning about self that goes on during short-term counseling. There is little evidence that any personality characteristics or other personal characteristics *in general* bear any marked relationship to learning during counseling. There is some evidence that the critical factors in the individual are those specifically related to his *felt need* for counseling *about that topic* and his *readiness to learn those things* during counseling. There is also confirmation of the logical expectation that people will accept more readily that information which is least in conflict with their self-concepts. The practical implications of these tentative research findings will be discussed later in this chapter.

Studies of Relationships Between Counseling Methods and Learning from Test Reports

Is there any evidence that the counselor's techniques make any difference in the efficacy of test reporting? It may be worth recalling briefly the analysis in Chapter 3 of arguments for and against client participation in selecting tests, since this appears to be a major point of difference among counselors with regard to test reporting as well. It was argued, on the one hand, that more client participation would be likely to decrease defensiveness, to increase motivation for taking tests, to decrease dependence on the counselor, to give experience in making decisions, to reveal more diagnostic information about the client, and to lead to the selection of more suitable tests. Against client participation were the arguments that the client lacks knowledge and competencies and also the objectivity to make such judgments, that excessive dependency and indecisiveness are problems for the psychotherapist rather than the counselor, and that, in any case, degree of client participation has no bearing on the effectiveness with which tests are used, that it is the *counselor's skill* in selecting and inter-preting tests that is the critical factor.

Theoretical Analysis

The theoretical positions regarding client participation in test inter-pretation are similar to those regarding test selection. The less "leading," more "client-directed" counselor is more likely to present his client with raw data, in the form of percentile or decile scores, profile charts, and to encourage the client to join him in the process by which interpretations —whether descriptive, genetic, predictive, or evaluative—are made. This counselor is also more likely to put stress on the client's *feelings* about his scores and their interpretations. The more "leading" and more "directing" counselor is more likely to present his clients with a finished job of in-terpretation, emphasizing the implications and predictions rather than the raw data from which they were derived.

Arguments for and against client participation in test interpretation seem to be as follows. *In favor* of client participation are these (Bixler and Bixler, 1946) :

1. The more the client participates in teasing meaning out of test scores, the more likely will he be to bring in new information about himself from other sources, and to produce new insights regarding the significance of all the data. This should then lead to *more valid interpretations* and there-fore to better decisions and plans.

2. The more he himself contributes to the conclusions reached from tests, the more *accepting* will the client be of those conclusions and of their implications regarding his future activities.

3. The more a client participates in the process of drawing inferences and hypotheses from his test scores, the more *involved* he will become. This in turn should lead to *greater effectiveness of learning* and *greater retention* of what is learned.

Arguments against client participation are rarely seen in print, perhaps because it has been so unrewarding, during the past ten or fifteen years, to express a "directive" point of view. It is, therefore, more necessary to base this list of arguments against client participation on speculation. (Another reason is the author's personal leaning in the opposite direction) .

1. Drawing implications and making predictions and other kinds of interpretation from test data requires the *knowledge, skills,* and degree of *objectivity* which counselors are a good deal more likely to possess than their clients.

2. It is the *responsibility* of the counselor, and an important element in his professional contribution to his clients, to do the thinking and research leading up to the finished interpretation. To ask clients to share this re-sponsibility is to slough off a part of the counselor's job.

3. Effective *learning* about oneself in counseling is a result not of the

amount of client participation in making the interpretation but of the counselor's skill in transmitting valid information.

As in Chapter 3, an attempted reconciliation and set of conclusions will be presented after the available research has been examined. The general picture regarding published research is very similar to that in the earlier chapter. Here, too, research evidence is sparse and inconclusive. Of the few studies reported, very little can be done to compare results since there are so many differences in research methods, instruments, and samples. Each study has asked somewhat different questions; without replications one must exercise great caution in generalizing from the answers. This is the best we have, however, and knowledge of these results may, if nothing else, caution against too ready assumptions regarding our pet theories and approaches.

Research Studies

Details of the Kamm and Wrenn study (1950) have already been reported in this chapter and their conclusions with regard to client characteristics stated. We need only add their findings regarding counselor variables in relation to their particular criterion, which was the degree of *acceptance* by the counselee of "information" (including advice and suggestions) given by the counselor. Their results are easily summarized: They found essentially no relationship between the counselor's approach and the client's acceptance of information. Also, no differences were found between "accepting" and "nonaccepting" counselees in *their* interview behavior, such as their use of various categories of client response (answering questions, asking questions, making statements regarding plans).

Nor were there differences between "accepting" and "nonaccepting" clients in the sequence of behavior during the course of the interview (for both groups, for example, there was a decrease in client statement of the problem and an increase in client statement of agreement, as the interviews progressed). Unfortunately, the design of their study permits only very limited conclusions, since one counselor did all the interviews and is reported to have used a similar approach with all subjects (little use of feeling-responses; less asking of questions and more giving of suggestions and directions as the interview progressed). What we can say, then, is that this approach is effective with some clients and not with others (in terms of their "acceptance" of the counselor's information and suggestions) and that what seemed to make the difference were the client's attitudes and his readiness to be helped. Whether other approaches would have a higher or lower success rate, in general, or whether they would have succeeded where this one failed cannot be known from this study.

Dressel and Matteson (1950) used seven different counselors and forty clients in an attempt to test hypotheses that clients who participated actively in test interpretation would gain more in self-understanding, would be more certain of their final vocational choice, and would be more satisfied with the experience than clients who participated less actively. Client participation was defined in a set of directions to the counselors, which included: waiting to discuss test scores until clients are emotionally ready to do so; giving test results via presentation of the profile; encouraging client expressions of feelings and thoughts regarding their tests; and not emphasizing test results too heavily. A rating scale covering these criteria was completed for each interview by four judges on the basis of transcriptions of the interview. Counselees completed a self-understanding inventory before and after counseling, and then again two months later. The two post-counseling questionnaires also included questions regarding satisfaction with counseling and degree of certainty as to vocational plans. Then rather complex statistical methods were used to discover the relationships, if any, between degree of participation in the interviews and the three criteria of counseling success: (1) self-learning, as measured by the increase, from the precounseling to the post-counseling inventory, in agreement between self-description and test scores; (2) satisfaction with counseling; and (3) degree of certainty of vocational goals. Their findings are moderately supportive of two of the hypotheses—gain in self-understanding and degree of vocational certainty. In both instances there was evidence that greater gains are made by counselees whose counselors elicited the greatest amount of client participation. The third hypothesis, regarding satisfaction with counseling, was not supported by the data.

A carefully executed and meticulously reported study by Rogers (1954) provides some modest support for the value of greater client participation. Working also with college students, he found that his two groups both showed significant increases in self-knowledge, but there were no *differences* between those who received their test interpretations by the "Test-Centered" method (client participation not encouraged and no effort made to draw in nontest evidence) and those counseled by the "Self-Evaluative" method (client participation encouraged throughout, and efforts made to bring in nontest data whenever appropriate). However, a difference *was* found when the actual amount of participation was brought into the picture. Each of the groups—the Test-Centered and the Self-Evaluative —was subdivided into two groups, those who *had* participated actively in the interview and those who hadn't. Of the four subgroups, the only one which showed a significant increase in self-knowledge was that made up of those who actually *did* participate in the participation-encouraged type of interview, the "Self-Evaluative." Finally, Rogers points out one aspect of his study that may be partly responsible for the something-less-than-overwhelming results of his study, namely, the fact that one counselor did all the interviews, with the result that he may not have differentiated enough the actual approaches and techniques used with the two groups.

Lane (1952) administered a single battery of tests to 111 high school juniors and seniors and then gave each of the subjects one of two types of test-interpretation interview. Half the subjects had "traditional" interviews, in which the counselor used "authoritative techniques," synthesized the data, and presented his opinions. The other subjects had "permissive" interviews, in which the counselor remained neutral and encouraged the client to synthesize the data. An important methodological check was to have judges rate recordings of a sample of the interviews as to technique used and as to over-all quality of counseling. This check indicated that the two types of interview did differ as to technique but were of approximately equal quality.

One week after the interview, and then again three weeks later, subjects filled out a questionnaire aimed at measuring memory of their test scores. Then groups counseled by the two methods were compared on this criterion, but no significant differences were found. However, as Lane points out in his discussion, his findings may be peculiar to the over-all program of which the interviews were a part. All subjects, for example, took the same battery of tests and all had one interview, which was limited to a class period. Lane concludes that, for this kind of situation (which may be typical of the way test reporting is done in many school and college programs) the techniques used may be of little import. He also adds a comment which is applicable to much of the research in this area, that the criterion of the counselor's effectiveness (memory for test information) is a very limited one and does not include such important outcomes as emotional acceptance of test information and integration of test information in the client's planning.

Finally, only brief additional mention is necessary of the Tuma and Gustad work (Tuma and Gustad, 1954; Gustad and Tuma, 1954). The design of this study promised to offer helpful information, since four different methods of test interpretation were to be assigned at random to both counselors and clients. However, the description of the four methods (Tuma and Gustad, 1954: p. 138) shows no difference in kind or degree of client participation in the interview, but only a difference in the extent to which the counselor was to relate his test report to the student's self-estimates. Nevertheless, it would be expected that those counselees whose counselors specifically related their test results to their own self-estimates would show more learning about themselves during the counseling process. The results of the study, however, show no differences among the four groups.

Implications of the Research

These studies provide at best moderate support for some of the claimed advantages of client participation. One of the major problems with these studies is the familiar dilemma: If one counselor tries to use two or more different methods of test reporting, he may be more effective with one than another, thereby influencing the results in an irrelevant way. On the other hand, if two or more different counselors are used, each to apply his own preferred methods, the results inevitably reflect any differences among them in over-all competence. Lane's (1952) precaution of having judges rate interviews as to quality may be a partial solution. Another approach, used in the Tuma and Gustad study (1957), involves assigning clients and counselors at random to different methods. However, this design necessitates finding a counseling center with a wide enough range of points of view among its staff; this problem is one of the major shortcomings, in retrospect, of the Tuma and Gustad study.

Another problem has been mentioned before: Few studies include any index of the client's degree of motivation for counseling; perhaps it is unrealistic to expect changes, of the kind envisaged in most of these studies, in subjects many of whom may come to counselors with only the slightest readiness for learning and for changing. Perhaps we should be satisfied with noticeable change in only a fraction of our counselees; this is especially pertinent in school and college counseling departments which see *all* students routinely.

Lastly, there remains one possible conclusion from all these studies, one which is painful but unavoidable at least as a possibility: It may be that we are as a profession not very effective in using our tools and techniques. Thus far we don't have much, except "belief" and our own and others' subjective impressions, to substantiate the validity of our services. It is small consolation that almost all of applied psychology shares with us this condition.

As in the discussion of Test Selection in Chapter 3, we must now turn to methods and techniques without a great deal of help from published research. As before, we will have to rely to a considerable extent on logic and personal experience for our ideas rather than on scientifically demonstrated facts. One generalization seems applicable here, as it was there: that it is quite likely that different counselors are achieving approximately equal success by the use of different methods. Probably the interaction is three-dimensional:

Counselor *A* is effective with Client Number 1 through the use of Method *X*, but he is effective with Client Number 2 only with Method *Y*, and he cannot effectively use Method *Z* with any of his clients. Counselor *B*, on the other hand, finds that Method *X* doesn't seem to work at all for him, and that Method *Z* is more effective than *Y* for most of *his* clients. Counselor *C*, finally, finds that he gets about equally good results with Methods *X*, *Y*, or *Z* with clients like Number 1, but he can't get anywhere, with any of the methods, with clients like Number 2.

The *dictum*, as before, is that each counselor must do research on himself, in an attempt to learn which combination of methods and clients is most effective for him. Even with a great deal more group research than has been done so far, this personal research will continue to be necessary.

This is not to reject the hope that research will some day point out that some procedures are better than others in general, and that some procedures work better with certain kinds of clients than with others, and even that certain kinds of counselors achieve greater success with one method than another, or with one client than another. But it would appear that, no matter how many general principles are delineated, it will remain necessary to calibrate each individual counselor, so to speak, to discover the optimal combination for *him* of technique, client, and types of outcome. This is not a matter which is peculiar to test interpretation and reporting, but applies to the counselor in all aspects of his work.

CHAPTER 15

Principles and Problems of Test Reporting

TEST REPORTING IS PART OF A COUNSELING PROCESS

This general principle would be too obvious to mention, were it not for the fact that it is so easily overlooked. Just as with Test Selection, there is often a tendency to see Reporting as something quite rational and objective, in contrast with those parts of counseling which deal with feelings, needs, and hopes. Reporting scores and their interpretations may indeed be rational and objective processes to the counselor, but they are unlikely to be so for the client. To the counselor, a score on a mechanical aptitude test is merely a description; to John Q. Client, the simple number or adjective may in fact represent a pat on the back that says: "Yes, you can accomplish what you hoped to in this area." It may represent a deeply-felt disappointment that he hears as: "You can't be what you want to be." It may be perceived as a threat: "You are fitted to do the kind of work for which your family and friends have only contempt." Because our tests seem to us so objective, rational, and factual, we as counselors need constantly to remind ourselves of the quite different perceptions of our counselees.[1]

To recognize these perceptions is to be more ready to handle the client responses which may result—defensiveness, rejection, argument, seeming inability to understand the points we make. Being so prepared, we may remember, for instance, to reflect or interpret the feeling being expressed

---

[1] To appreciate the client's perceptions in these situations, one need only recall a visit to a physician or dentist to receive *his* interpretation of a set of X-ray pictures. How great is the anxiety with which one awaits the "verdict"—must the tooth come out, *is* it an ulcer, *do* I have a cancer? And how grateful we are at such times to the sensitive physician or dentist who shows awareness of our feelings as he gives his report quickly, clearly, and adequately enough so that we can understand its implications, and yet unhurried enough that we feel free to ask our questions, no matter how naïve.

rather than to attempt to *persuade* the client that his rationalization is wrong or his rejection unfair. There is a tendency, as Bordin has pointed out, for counselors to assume that:

> ... they can be certain when a test score will be threatening or satisfying to a client. This erroneous belief is based on half truths, namely, that there are general social pressures toward higher achievements, so that any test result which seems to predict lower than average achievement is per se assumed to be a threatening test result. This fallacy springs from the common failure to allow for the variability hidden behind most of our generalizations about people. Despite the existence of an over-all pressure toward higher achievement, there are subgroups of persons who find value in one type of achievement and who may devalue others that are usually highly esteemed. When we get beyond the standards of a subgroup and come to the individual, we are now faced with a complexity of motivations that can discover almost any meaning in the results of a particular test. For example, a student who feels he is too effeminate and, in an attempt to deny this effeminacy, is planning to go into engineering, may be considerably threatened and disturbed by a test result that shows he has superior verbal and artistic ability. On the other hand, a student who feels under pressure from his parents to stay in school but wants to drop out may actually be motivated to treat a slightly below average college aptitude test score as though it were a sign of certain failure in college (Bordin, 1955: pp. 275-276) .

Basic Principles of Counseling

The basic principles of counseling as listed by Tyler (1953) will serve well: *understanding, acceptance, communication.* Being an effective test reporter requires *understanding* of the client, not only of his abilities, but also of his perceptions of his abilities—what it means to him to have low clerical aptitude or average college aptitude. In order to help Kathy to make use of our test interpretations regarding her career-marriage orientation (Chapter 11) , we need to understand how *she* feels about it and how she perceives the information we offer her—whether as reassurance, as a threat or as a new idea which arouses a little anxiety but also some interest.

Acceptance of the counselee's perceptions, feelings, and ideas also seems likely to improve the effectiveness of test reporting. What is being suggested is not a "front" or an "act" on the counselor's part, but genuine respect for the client's whole self as it exists, with all its irrationalities, contradictions, and blind spots. To *accept* his right to argue with the test implications or to aspire too high or too low, or to choose a type of school program or occupation that is inappropriate to his aptitudes, to accept these things is not the same as *approving* them or *agreeing* with them. It is, rather, first an expression of a humanistic regard for other people; second, an appreciation of some of the facts about human behavior; and third, a belief that we will in the long run be more helpful if we work *with* rather than *against* most counselees. To live by this point of view in no way prevents the counselor from disagreeing with a client's expressed goals. Nor does it prevent the counselor from pointing out the undesirable results which are likely to follow a particular course of action, or from questioning a client's reasons for reaching a particular conclusion.

Communication is a keystone of test reporting, as of all elements of counseling. Later we shall examine the more specific applications of principles of communication to the use of various types of scores, to graphic portrayals of test predictions, and to other elements in the process. For now, it should suffice to point out that one communicates several kinds of things during a test report: First, he communicates the "facts" themselves—the descriptions, genetic implications, predictive implications, and perhaps recommended actions. Second, he communicates his understanding of the client's feelings about, perceptions of, and reactions to these "facts." Third, he communicates a readiness to accept the client's view of all this.

We will now discuss a few specific counseling principles as they apply to test reporting:

Readiness of Client

This is a matter of good counseling practice rather than anything peculiar to Test Reporting and does not need extensive explication here. The fact that a counselee is seen *after* having completed one or more tests does not imply that a report of his results is automatically the first order of business of the interview. Yet this unfortunately is a routine procedure in some counseling offices, the second interview sometimes being referred to as the "close-out" (the term and its assumptions are persistent carry-overs from assembly-line procedures used in some centers during an earlier era in counseling). This approach serves to reinforce a frequent expectation of counselees: that they came to be tested and advised, rather than to engage actively in a learning and planning process.

The case of Bette Morgan (Callis, Polmantier, and Roeber, 1955) makes this point. The excerpt reproduced here is from the third interview, which follows the completion of a battery of tests. Bette is twenty-one years old and a junior in the College of Education:

Co 1: How are you this morning?
St 1: All right. (*long pause*)
Co 2: Well let's see, where did we (*pause*) get to?
St 2: Well, I think I've taken all the tests now. (*pause*)
Co 3: Yes. Would you repeat for me now the various questions you had as we ended last time?
St 3: Well, what I wanted to know is whether I'd be suited for a school teacher or not; and if not a teacher, what else? (*long pause*)
Co 4: What's been your thinking since our last talk (*pause*) in regard to that question?

St 4: I am a little undecided whether I'm going to come back to school next semester, *(pause)* so I'm just waiting to see what, how this,—I don't imagine this will have a whole lot of weight, because I know what I like.

Co 5: Mm-huh.

St 5: But I think it might tell me something that I want to know.

Co 6: Tell me a little bit about the question, coming back or not next semester. I think that is new as far as I'm concerned.

St 6: Mm-huh. Well, I thought I might take a commercial art course and really go on with it, I mean, if I like it. It's at least worth trying for, whether I succeed or not. If I enjoy doing it, I think it'll be worth it. *(long pause)*

Co 7: Yes. How about commercial art schools compared with art that you get here at the University?

St 7: Well, one of my majors has been art, and I've taken a few courses, but they haven't been commercial courses, been more fine art courses; and there's not many commercial courses offered here, and this correspondence course that I was thinking of is strictly commercial. It's commercial advertising.

Co 8: Where is this school? Where is it located?

St 8: (client states the name and location of a commercial art correspondence school). *(long pause)*

Co 9: And, then you would live at home? *(pause)*

St 9: That's the only hitch. *(laughs)*

Co 10: Mm-huh. *(long pause)* Well, is part of that the result of dissatisfaction with school here?

St 10: Well, I have been going with a fellow who is going to be stationed at Army Camp *A,* and he'll be coming home quite often.

Co 11: Mm-huh.

St 11: And I think that will probably help quite a bit, *(pause)* but I don't know whether it would be satisfactory or not.

Co 12: Now, what would be satisfactory?

St 12: Well, the fact that he'll be there on weekends.

Co 13: Mm-huh. *(long pause)* Well, what are your questions about it, whether it will be satisfactory?

St 13: Well, whether I could stand the family during the week, you know. *(pause)* Sounds terrible to say it this way, but— *(long pause)* (Callis, Polmantier, and Roeber, 1955: pp. 38, 45) .

The interview continues along this line. The editors inserted this comment after *Co* 2:

An opening response such as this gives the client wide latitude in choosing a topic to discuss. The counselor had expected to discuss rather fully the test results with the client in this interview. However, through a series of rather neutral counselor responses, the client was permitted to choose the topic for discussion; and she chose to ignore the test results. In fact, it was the counselor who introduced the rather meager discussion of the test data later in the interview (Third interview *Co* 47 ff.) The reader may question the advisability of having the client take a battery of tests and then not discuss them fully with the client. However, all of the test results were used. Although there was little "formal" discussion of the test results *per se,* the results were woven into the interpretations which the counselor made throughout the interviews. See especially *Co* 32 in the fourth interview in which the results of the *MMPI* were the basis for the interpretations made. Actually this is a more defensible procedure. Any interpretations which the counselor makes should be based on all data available, not just test data alone (Callis, Polmantier, and Roeber, 1955: p. 38) .

The converse is equally important; if the client is genuinely ready for a test report, this is the appropriate thing to do, even if it *is* the first topic in an interview. Sometimes the counselor suspects that the request for test results is but an avoidance of other, perhaps more sensitive topics. He may in some of these cases judge that more is to be gained by going along with the client, in the hope that there will be later opportunities to deal with the other material. In general, however, it seems to be easier to shift from a client-directed discussion of nontest topics early in the interview to a report of test results later, than to make the transition with the reverse sequence. A test-centered discussion tends to take the focus somewhat from the client and transfers it to the test data themselves, thus encouraging passivity. On the other hand, to start out with general leads such as, "What's on your mind," "How do you feel about such-and-such," and "Your opinion then is that so-and-so would be preferable," would seem to help set the stage for more client activity and involvement in later discussions of test results and their implications. This very point was the basis for one of Rogers' hypotheses (1954) , for which his data provided some support, as reported in the previous chapter.

An illustration of this kind of handling of a client request for test results is seen in the second interview with Ralph Santaro (see Chapter 11) , in which, with almost his first breath, he brings up the tests:

Co 1: How are you today?
Cl 1: *(lost)* —and you?
Co 2: Oh, fine.
Cl 2: That's good . . . How are my results?
Co 3: The tests, you mean? *(Cl:* Yeah) How did you feel about them when you were taking them?
Cl 3: All right . . . felt all right.
Co 4: Uh-huh . . . As you were taking them did you have any particular . . . did you get any ideas as to what kinds of things seemed to be easier for you and what kinds of things seemed to be tougher?
Cl 4: No, I didn't . . .
Co 5: You just went on through them?
Cl 5: Just went through them—that's all.
Co 6: Uh-huh. On the whole you felt pretty comfortable. You didn't feel that they were terribly difficult.
Cl 6: No, no—just on the one I had to figure out the circles, and chop them up. You get so many possible answers there that . . . screwed me up a little bit.
Co 7: Those, the spatial relations tests? *(Cl:* yeah) Uh-huh. Incidentally, we often make tape recordings of interviews, mainly to evaluate our own counseling. [*Long explanation of purpose of recording, requesting permission.*]

Cl 7: No, it's perfectly all right with me. Did you tape the last one?

Co 8: No, no, we don't tape them all. Uh, we'd have a whole room full of tapes before long, if we did. We do one every once in a while just as a way of looking at ourselves and seeing what kind of work we do, or to give us some material to use in teaching other people how to be counselors.

Cl 8: Mm-hm. It's very good. I mean, it seems a way of, uh, teaching other people about these things. Uh . . . I have no objections . . . (*Co:* Uh-huh) . . . I had quite a few disappointments this week. I have been out looking for jobs in my own field, and it seems to be kind of full.

Co 9: Uh-huh.

Cl 9: I went out even this week looking for produce jobs . . . .

Co 10: Uh-huh, there weren't many to be had, is that it?

Cl 10: No, no, I, uh, I've been to all the chains and everything—there's nothing there.

Co 11: Uh-huh. They're just not looking for produce clerks these days.

Cl 11: I don't know. Maybe I just don't fill their requirements . . . I don't know.

Co 12: Uh-huh. Did you get interviewed in these places?

Cl 12: Yeah, yeah, I left an application. Before they interviewed me, they told me there was nothing now, but if I would leave an application, and they would interview me, and then that would be it.

Co 13: Mm-hm . . . but you're not sure whether it's that they don't have jobs, or whether . . .

Cl 13: . . . being in the position I was in, in a store, uh, I don't know if it's just because they didn't want me, or if they were closed, or what.

Co 14: Uh-huh.

Cl 14: Because a lot of times, well, I hired a couple of people and if I didn't want 'em, I'd take their application and after they left, more or less file it in the garbage can, you know.

Co 15: Mm-hm, yeah.

Cl 15: So that it made me suspicious just wondering about that.

Co 16: Mm-hm, mm-hm. Yeah . . . so you're not sure whether or not they're telling the whole truth?

Cl 16: Mm-hm, it's a cruel world, I'm beginning to find out (*nervous laugh*).

As in the case of Bette Morgan, here also it was the *counselor* who reintroduced the subject of tests at the point that he felt it might provide relevant information. This happened about fifteen minutes later in this interview. Ralph had spoken of a number of things, most of which are sources of anxiety to him: his job-hunting frustrations, his wife's pregnancy, and his overweight. The counselor begins the new topic, after a fifteen second pause (*Cl* 56) which he took to mean that Ralph had pretty well gotten these other things off his chest:

Cl 54: Yeah, yeah, I think that's so. I don't want to start feeling sorry for myself, because I feel that that would be defeat there, the more you feel sorry for yourself, the worse it's going to get for you. (*Co:* Uh-huh) If you can sort of bolster up and face it, then you've got more of a chance, and like I say, my wife has been . . . consoling me you might say, in saying that, "There'll be something tomorrow, don't worry about it." (*Co:* mm-hm, mm-hm) "With the help of God you'll get something." . . . I think I'm more concerned than she is, actually.

Co 55: She's got more confidence in you than you have?

Cl 55: That's right, that's right. She sort of laughed yesterday, when I came home and told her that on account of my weight, why she says, "You've worked anywhere from 12 to 16 hours a day, why should that be any concern," she says, "I've *seen* you work," and things like that—sort of helps out the morale.

Co 56: Mm-hm, mm-hm . . . It helps to have *some*body who believes in you.

Cl 56: Yeah, yeah . . . even if they don't mean it *(nervous laugh)* *(Co:* uh-huh) but, I think she means it . . . *(Co:* uh-huh) *(15 second pause)*

Co 57: At this moment, you're not sure what *kind* of work is most appropriate for you to . . . .

Cl 57: No, I'm not. Actually I'm like a chicken with his head cut off, you might say *(Co:* mm-hm) . . . I'm grabbing for anything now.

Co 58: Uh-huh, uh-huh, rather than, rather than planning, and selecting, you're just kind of desperately grabbing for anything that could be a job.

Cl 58: Yeah, uh-huh.

Co 59: Well, maybe it would be a good time for us to take a look at some of these tests and see if they provide any kind of help in selection. *(Opens test folder)* Let's see, you had a general mental ability test, you had a personality test, you had two mechanical aptitude tests—one of them that spatial relations test that you mentioned, and the other one is more of, oh, a kind of mechanical problems test—there were gears that turned different ways, and there were tin cans over a stove . . . .

Cl 59: Yeah, yeah.

Co 60: And then there was a sales test, and then there was an interest test. So there were six different tests.

Cl 60: Yeah, that's right.

Flexibility

This principle of good counseling has application here as it did in relation to Test Selection (see Chapter 3). Despite the counselor's best intentions (or worst, depending on one's point of view!) a test report may not follow a neat and logical pattern. Clients insist on going off on tangents, sometimes to get away from unpleasant topics but sometimes for quite productive forays into important areas of their problems and plans.

Another excerpt from Ralph Santaro's second interview illustrates this principle of flexibility as well as that of dealing with what the client seems to be *ready* to talk about. It also points up the value of focussing on the client himself, both as a *source* of data and as the *user* of the information. Since *Cl* 60, about fifteen minutes have elapsed, during which the counselor has been doing most of the talking as he reported the *Kuder* profile and the mechanical aptitude test results:

Co 92: *(10 second pause)* Maybe we could also cut across now, and be looking at the personality test and I'll . . . .

Cl 92: I was just going to ask you about that.

Co 93: Uh-huh.

Cl 93: I, uh, I'm interested in that, uh, very much, to find out just what *(Co:* Mm-hm) type of personality I have.

Co 94: Mm-hm—you're *wondering* ....
Cl 94: Yeah.
Co 95: What kind of person you are.
Cl 95: Yeah, yeah.
Co 96: Mm-hm.
Cl 96: Care for a cigarette?
Co 97: No, thanks—you go right ahead.
(*10 second pause—client lights cigarette*)
Cl 97: This is, this is the one I was, I was wondering about mostly (*Co:* It was) what type of personality I would be put in the class of, uh, ... and you can usually help yourself by knowing what kind of a personality you are, *I* would think.
Co 98: Uh-huh, uh-huh. Well, I wonder—do you have some *feelings* right now as to ....
Cl 98: I think I have a very *bad* personality, actually, I have, uh, I have a little fear in me—I just can't explain it.
Co 99: Uh-huh, uh-huh, in bringing out certain things.
Cl 99: Mm-hm, which I believe would be a, uh, uh, better means of bettering my personality, if I could overcome these fears ....
Co 100: Mm-hm, hm-hm.
Cl 100: ... and, uh, there's a lot of things I'd like to talk about that I'm *afraid* to talk about, because possibly I don't know enough about 'em.
Co 101: Uh-huh.
Cl 101: ... and I, uh, it's a hard thing to explain.
Co 102: Uh-huh, uh-huh—it's a matter of your having some things that have been going inside you that you've never told anybody, that you wonder about, and worry about, and wish you could get rid of, get out into the open.
Cl 102: Yeah.
Co 103: Uh-huh, uh-huh ... the personality test results that we see here seem to show that.
Cl 103: Oh, yeah?
Co 104: Um, after all there's nothing on here except what you put into it—*you* answered the questions (*Cl:* That's right), as long as you answer the questions honestly (*Cl:* I did) ... they will tell some of the things ....
Cl 104: I would be only kidding myself if I didn't answer them right—I mean, if I came here to kid myself there's no sense in my coming (*Co:* Mm-hm) I came here to find out exactly, uh, exactly what's what.
Co 105: Mm-hm, mm-hm—well, these seem to indicate the fact that you're worried—that, uh, that you're not self-confident—uh, you seem to be, uh, shy—you seem to seek—or avoid, possible coming in contact with people because you're unsure of yourself, with people.
Cl 105: That's right, that's right.
Co 106: I think it indicates that you're not at all happy about this.
Cl 106: I'm not, actually I'm not—uh, I *would* like to be able to, uh, walk into a room that, uh, has people into it and really make conversation with them and, uh, become *part* of it, there's something else holding me back.
[Then, for five minutes or so, Ralph tells about difficulties he has had in getting up and speaking on the floor at meetings of a club he belongs to. He took a course in public speaking, but this didn't help because he was unable to overcome his tension and blocking. Then the counselor, to clarify further his appraisal

of the severity of the problem, asks about the duration of Ralph's emotional handicap.]

Co 115: ... it didn't meet your needs. Mm-hm ... This is something that has been of long standing—this lack of confidence in yourself (*Cl:* Yeah, yeah) this is not just something in the last few weeks, or a few months ....

Cl 115: No, no—it's the last ten years that I felt myself going down, being drawn into this little world of mine, you might say.

Co 116: Mm-hm, mm-hm—for about ten years, you've been becoming less and less social.

Cl 116: Yeah, yeah—I mean ever since I left school—and I didn't do much in school—I mean in activities—but, I used to get along, I mean, uh, I wasn't *too* afraid in school. I imagine I had the normal fears of school, but being in the classroom, if I forgot to do my homework, then I had a fear, but if I did my homework, then I was all right.

[Ralph makes it clear in the next few statements that the decrease in self-confidence began just about the time he left school, after the ninth grade. Now the counselor, continuing to explore the nature and severity of Ralph's problems, moves (*Co:* 122) in the direction of seeking reasons for this change for the worse.]

Co 121: Mm-hm, mm-hm, so somehow, somewhere around that time, you started losing ....

Cl 121: I started losing confidence in myself.

Co 122: ... losing confidence in yourself, uh-huh, and it's been continuing ever since. Mm-hm, and yet it's kind of hard for you to know what the causes were.

Cl 122: The causes I think, were, that my brother more or less took over the thinking part of it—uh, I relied more on his confidence than my own.

Co 123: Mm-hm.

Cl 123: Uh ... any problems—well, my brother took 'em ....

Co 124: Mm-hm, mm-hm.

Cl 124: ... and he solved them, and I was more or less a carefree person. I didn't have any problems that I had to solve and as the years went on, I just didn't have anything to worry about.

Co 125: Mm-hm.

Cl 125: There were times when we got into financial difficulties in the business, and uh, possibly, if I had had this confidence that I should have had ....

Co 126: Mm-hm.

Cl 126: I would have been able to solve them myself, but my brother used to solve them. I feel that although he did a good job in figuring out these things, that there was something left out for me, (*Co:* Mm-hm) I mean, I was under a protective shelter you might say, (*Co:* Mm-hm) and anything that would come, well, he would take care of it.

Co 127: So there was no necessity for you (*Cl:* That's right) to take over any of the responsibility, and you feel that this may be one of the reasons that (*10 second pause*) ....

Cl 127: Till like I told you before, now we're at the breaking point. I have to assume responsibilities that I never had to assume before.

Co 128: Mm-hm, mm-hm, responsibility for making your own job and ....

Cl 128: Decisions and everything, yeah.

Co 129: Mm-hm.

Cl 129: And I gotta face up to them, because, actually I got a family now to worry about, and, uh, I've got to do something about them ....

Co 130: Mm-hm.

Cl 130: I'll have to get hardened to this hard outside world here.

During most of this time, Ralph has been telling his own story, with a little help from the counselor, most of it in the way of nonleading statements of reflection and acceptance. Occasionally the counselor has encouraged his client to go in a particular direction: from *Co* 115 to *Co* 122, the counselor is looking for some indication of the *duration* of Ralph's personality handicaps, and then in *Co* 122 he shifts the emphasis slightly to an exploration of *causal factors*. Very little formal interpretation or other report is made from the *Guilford-Zimmerman* profile; in this instance it wasn't necessary, since Ralph could tell a good deal more than could the profile or the counselor. He was *ready* to talk about these things, and the counselor was *flexible* enough to shift from reporting scores to helping his client to talk.

PRINCIPLES MORE SPECIFIC TO TEST REPORTING

The Report Is Related to the Purposes of Testing

Here is another of those obvious principles that need occasional warming up, and again the problem is one of lack of individualization of test interpretations. It seems to be quite natural for one's manner of test reporting to fall into a pattern which varies little from one counselee to another. In some settings this might be quite appropriate, as, for example, when all members of a group—say ninth graders, or high school juniors, or college freshmen—are to be called for a brief interview after all have taken a battery of tests. The purpose may initially be the same for all—information about themselves to help them make plans for the future and to further the process of individual self-concept development. A counselor may find that for most of the group a fairly standard pattern works pretty well—say the use of charts and profiles, then asking the counselee to make certain inferences, and so on. Some individuals in the group may show particular needs which would then necessitate deviating from the pattern.

With a more individual use of tests, however, as with counselees seeking help with particular needs, the assumption of sameness of purpose is not nearly so tenable, although counselors sometimes act as if it were. At its best, testing for counseling purposes is a highly individualized matter, in terms both of the tests selected and of their interpretation. If, for instance, a purpose of testing with a particular counselee is *Precounseling Diagnostic Information* (see Chapter 3), appropriate tests will have been given, probably with emphasis in the area of personality. After his interpretive study, the counselor will have reached some tentative conclusions regarding the person's needs, degree of disturbance, and likelihood of benefitting from his particular brand of counseling. In the interview which follows, he may seek to test his tentative conclusions by trying them out on the client or by seeking further information. He will be ready, when this is appropriate, to discuss with his client the possibility of referral for other services. Returning again to Ralph Santaro, we have an illustration of this use of tests. A personality inventory (*Guilford-Zimmerman*) had been used, partly to explore the extent of Ralph's reported personality inadequacies. The extreme scores led the counselor to encourage Ralph in the second interview (see *Co* 92 to *Cl* 130 above) to discuss the duration and degree of his problems. In the next response, the counselor, having judged that this *is* a problem of long-standing and of a handicapping nature and that Ralph seems to want to do something about it, moves in the direction of referral:

Co 135: Mm-hm, mm-hm . . . well, we've been exploring a little bit some of these feelings you have; and I wonder whether you might feel it worth while to, uh, get another kind of counseling help, uh, something a little bit different from what we do here.

Cl 135: Uh-huh.

Co 136: Uh, something more in the nature of personal counseling, where you can, uh, discuss some of these things and try to work through them to the—to try to get some better understandings of yourself and why you feel as you do, uh, in the hope that this would help you to get more confidence in yourself and more insight into yourself. Uh, it's a kind of counseling that's available in different places in the city, and it's a kind of thing that usually lasts over a period of months rather than our kind of counseling service, which is more limited.

Cl 136: Mm-hm.

Co 137: We deal mostly with vocational matters themselves.

Cl 137: Mm-hm, uh, where would I go to get this kind of thing?

Co 138: Well, there are several kinds of places, uh, right in this building, here, there's a psychological clinic, where psychologists offer this kind of help, and, uh, you would, uh, first of all have an interview with somebody there—talk over the whole thing—they would give you, uh, some psychological tests, uh, and then, uh, if you and they both decided at that point that this was an appropriate place for them to be of help for you, uh, you would start a series of interviews—it might be once a week, or it might be twice a week, or it might be some other kind of arrangement, uh, and, uh, this could go on for, uh, as long a period of time you, uh, felt you were getting some good out of it. Uh, another kind of place where this sort of counseling is available is a social case work agency, and there are several in the city.

It turned out that Ralph did not follow through with the suggested referral. For this reason, the counselor was obliged to change his diagnostic thinking after the third interview and to feel now that perhaps the personality profile and Ralph's self-description were exaggerated due to the situational anxiety he was then experiencing.

If a major purpose of testing is to provide *Information for the Counseling Process Itself* (see Chapter 3), interpretation of the results will lead to appropriate action during the interview. With Kathy Musgrove, for instance (Chapter 11), the *SVIB* profile, along with other data in the case, led to the hypothesis that Kathy was having difficulty in reconciling career and marriage aspirations. Accordingly, this area was given emphasis by the counselor, and Kathy was encouraged to explore and develop her self-concept.

When the questions leading up to testing have to do with *alternative courses of action* and when tests are planned accordingly, the client has a right to expect that the test report will include reference to these questions, with some indication of the answers, if any, which come from tests. This doesn't mean that the counselor must feel obligated to give a definite answer, to say "Yes" to this school or "No" to that field of work. Nor does it mean that the completely undecided client must be presented with a specific goal and a specific plan leading up to that goal. It is unrealistic to expect such outcomes from testing. Furthermore, there is an overly narrow conception of test interpretation implied by such expectations. Instead, if test selection has been done well, definite answers of a final nature are not likely to be expected. Both client and counselor will have more modest expectations and will be ready to use test results and their interpretations as the beginning, rather than the end, of a process of discussion and exploration. Unfortunately, so many clients, especially those who go to the trouble and expense of obtaining counseling in a fee-charging agency, bring with them unrealistic expectations gleaned from magazine articles and other sources.

Similarly, with *other purposes of testing* the report of results should be related to the purposes. With dependent and indecisive clients, who have been helped to select tests as an experience in making decisions for themselves, the specific results may be less important than some recognition of their success in having made a decision, regardless of the merits of the decision itself. It is all too easy in such cases for the counselor to concentrate on the scores themselves and their implications and to neglect to follow-up the learning possibilities in the area of decision-making. Counselors sometimes find it difficult to take their eyes off the test scores and the occupational pamphlets and to see clients as human beings struggling with the responsibilities of independence and decision-making.

Before leaving this discussion of relationships between the purposes of testing and reporting of test results, one final point should be made. Despite the absence of research evidence, there seems to be some basis from the experiences and observations of at least one counselor to propose that the effectiveness of test reporting will be much influenced by all that has preceded it. This refers particularly to what occurred during the selection of tests, but also includes experiences during the actual test administration and all other contacts which the individual has with the total counseling process. If there is an overly casual atmosphere during the actual administration of tests, it seems less likely that counselees will come to the later reporting interview with a serious attitude. If there has been little preparation for testing, it seems likely that counselees will come to the later interview with slight understanding of the roles to be played by tests, by the counselor, and by themselves. Even if there was a preliminary interview or group session, preparation for testing may have been inadequate; if so, there is greater likelihood of a lack of readiness to make active and positive use of test results.

Even with the best conditions prior to test reporting, the task is not easy, requiring all the skill counselors can muster. And with all this, there will be many clients who cannot be reached, who persist in misinterpreting data, who are overly defensive, and whose counseling must be recorded as failures.

Relation of Test Reporting to Test Selection

More specifically, the *kind* of approach used in test selection should have its effects on the role played by counselees during the interpretative-reporting process. If tests were chosen by the counselor alone, even with explanations of their purposes, the client would be less likely to be ready to take an active part in the reporting process than he would if he had really exerted some efforts during the process of selection. Unfortunately there almost are no research data which test this hypothesis.[2] Until the necessary research is done, each counselor can try out various approaches to the selection process to see if any discernible differences are found. Our hypotheses are: First, there will be a correlation between client participation in test planning and client participation in the later stages of appraisal, interpretation, and planning. Second, the *nature* of the relationship which is developed during test selection (dependency, superficiality, overemphasis on fact, and neglect of feeling) will be reflected in the client's behavior in later interviews.

---

[2] Seeman (1949) found that clients of only one of his two counselors who used a client-participation approach to test selection expected to play an active role in the second interview. He concluded that counselors differ in the extent to which they facilitate client participation, even though they use similar techniques. This study was reviewed more extensively in Chapter 3.

CHAPTER 16

Methods and Materials of Test Reporting

IN THIS LAST CHAPTER, we move up to the level of actual techniques of reporting, having first built the foundation with a mixture of theory, research, and basic principles. There are undoubtedly many specific techniques developed by counselors on the job which have never been published and so are unknown outside of the local establishment where they are used. Those to be mentioned here then are only a very limited sample, based on a search of the professional literature and on the experiences of the writer and of other counselors with whom he has had contact.

We might well begin by reproducing in its entirety a list of suggestions prepared by the staff of the Tennessee State Testing and Guidance Program, which is administered by the University of Tennessee for the State Department of Education. This is school-oriented, but many of the suggestions are of general interest, and they may help make more concrete some of the points which have been discussed in more abstract terms.

Suggestions for Counseling with Students About the Results of Tests

1. Put students at ease.
2. Try to sense what the counselee is really seeking in being counseled. What did he hope to learn from the tests?
3. Relate the results to something the student has said, a question he has asked, or a choice that he has made.
4. Usually begin with interests or interest test results, high interests or scores first.
5. Help students see the relationship of measured interests to past training and experience in school subjects, hobbies or leisure-time activities, part-time work experience, family interests, and so forth.
6. Give time and opportunity for expressions of attitude about each test result.
7. Give information slowly, not all at once.

8. Give him an opportunity to indicate what the test results mean to him and to raise questions about them.
9. Show relationship of test results to failure or success in school subjects.
10. Help students face evidence of strengths and weaknesses in background and ability, and help them recognize that to do otherwise is unfair to themselves.
11. Discuss with students their comparative position in particular groups in terms of generalizations, such as upper third or lower fourth, rather than in terms of specific scores.
12. When dealing with intelligence, *high* scores might be interpreted as "can do the work assigned," "ought to have time for extra things"; as *average*, "can handle the work, but some things will be easy and some hard"; as *low*, "abstract work is difficult," "you find it hard to understand some things," "you will have to work hard to keep up."
13. Discuss test results with students without becoming involved in the I.Q. concept. If students ask for their "I.Q.'s," explain that it is not too meaningful and may change several points from one test to another. Reiterate, if necessary, the information as to relative standing.
14. When dealing with achievement results, emphasize the pattern of strengths and weaknesses interpreted in terms of his own level, rather than concentrating on the over-all level.
15. Suggest that tests may help the student understand the kinds of competition he may encounter.
16. Help students understand the meaning and importance of norm groups.
17. Discuss standardized tests in the language of students.
18. Give reasonable emphasis to any physical and environmental factors which may have influenced test scores.
19. Help students understand that test results are only one part of the evaluation of abilities and background.
20. Suggest that measures of special aptitude such as eye-hand co-ordination, spatial relations abilities, clerical aptitude, and others may fit into the total evaluation of abilities.
21. Indicate the importance of reading comprehension in certain areas of study and the part it may play in planning a study schedule. (Tennessee State Department of Education, 1956-1957: p. 15.)

DEGREE OF CLIENT PARTICIPATION IN TEST REPORTING AND INTERPRETATION

This is a topic which cuts across both the reporting and the interpretation processes, and about which not a great deal has been published since the classic article by Bixler and Bixler (1946), which has been drawn on heavily for the present discussion. The question is this: Should counselees be given only the *implications* and *conclusions* reached by counselors from tests (and other data, of course), or should they be given some of the "raw data," that is, the scores on particular tests? The following thumbnail sketches of three approaches highlight some of the major differences:

1. In this approach, the counselor reports individual scores in some meaningful form (percentile or quintile, grade equivalent, or other), shows profile sheets, and then encourages the client to join with him in

deriving interpretations. He aims at having the client take as much of the lead as he can in this process.

2. The counselor may report individual scores and perhaps show profiles, as in Method 1, but he also goes further, spelling out some of the implications, some of the predictions, and perhaps even makes recommendations. These latter, however, are explicitly related to the test data from which they stem.

3. The counselor gives conclusions, implications, predictions, and possibly recommendations, but without reference to the specific data from which they were made, giving no percentile or other scores on particular tests and showing no profiles.

In extremely oversimplified and condensed form, these three approaches may be illustrated by showing how their respective proponents would handle the same test report situation. These are contrived so as to make the desired distinctions and may actually resemble no counselor, living or dead:

Co A: Your preferences on this *Kuder* profile are above average in Mechanical and Artistic areas and below average in Computational and Clerical. Your score on the test of Mechanical Comprehension was in the top fifth (or "above average," depending on the counselor's preference for specificity) as compared with mechanical workers. On the spatial relations test your score was better than that of three out of four men on mechanical jobs. Finally, on the clerical aptitude test, your score on the Numbers part was in the lowest fifth as compared with clerical workers, and on the Names part it was in the lowest tenth. Now what does all this mean to you? (or: How do you feel about this?) .

Co B: From these tables (in the *Kuder* manual) , we see that your interests are quite similar to men in such-and-such mechanical occupations, whereas they are different from those of men in such-and-such clerical occupations. So we can say that your interests are most like those of mechanics, and you would probably enjoy that kind of work. As to your abilities, we also find that on the two tests which are closest to mechanical work, you had better than average scores, whereas the clerical aptitude scores were rather low. Adding mechanical aptitudes to mechanical interest, and adding also what you've told me about your hobbies and part-time jobs, the mechanical area would seem to be a better choice than clerical. How does this compare with your own picture of yourself?

Co C: In reviewing your scores on the various tests we gave you, and comparing them also with your experiences as you've told me about them, it seems to me that you would probably do the best and be the most interested in mechanical jobs rather than clerical jobs. Specifically I would suggest that you consider the occupations of *A, B,* and *C.*

Naturally, these are quite artificial, and counselors in real life rarely speak in so well-organized a manner.[1] Also, there are many intermediate approaches which combine some of the features of two or more of these. In particular, we should add the point made in connection with the Bette Morgan and Ralph Santaro cases, namely, that test reporting sometimes is not a separate and distinct element but rather is interwoven with appropriate interview topics. Some counselors, in fact, may almost never give test reports as such, but instead use the information derived from tests in planning and conducting interviews. But there does seem to be a real difference among counselors in this dimension, which has to do with *sharing* the appraisal process with clients, or at least with letting them in on it.

A Point of View

We take the position that Approach 3 is the least desirable and that Approaches 1 and 2 are preferable, with the assumption that the counselor in 1 will eventually bring into the discussion his own expert interpretation. In both 1 and 2, the client is at least *in on* the thinking which goes into the interpretive process, the difference between the two being the extent to which an effort is made to derive interpretations through the give-and-take of the interview. Counselor *A* feels that it is a more valuable learning experience for clients to play an active role in test interpretation. He may also feel that the *content* of the appraisal will be more valid if arrived at this way rather than by him alone. Counselor *B* probably feels less strongly about the learning values derived from having his clients work on the interpretation of scores. He may feel that his professional interpretation has greater value to the client, at least as a starting point in their discussion. On the other hand, he may use Method 2 primarily because he feels that Method 1 is too time-consuming. Counselor *C* is probably the person whom we discussed earlier, in Chapter 14, the one whose major concern is with the *appraisal process* and who is much less interested in counseling as a growth or adjustment process. The numbers of this type of counselor have probably been somewhat reduced as a result of developments in counseling theories during the 1940's and 1950's.[2]

---

[1] Those using Method 3 are perhaps most likely to give a prepared, well-organized talk. Bordin (1955) has pointed out the danger: ". . . . there is a danger that the counselor will approach his task in somewhat the same manner as the teacher approaches a formal lecture. He will have laid out a series of items which he is prepared to transmit to the client and will proceed to do this somewhat in lecture fashion" (p. 277).

[2] An interesting sign of this change is the kind of research reported earlier and more recently. In the 1920's and 1930's there were numerous studies comparing the later lives of counselees who heeded the advice of their counselors (usually regarding vocational choice) with those who did not. These were in effect validations of the counselor's *appraisal*, in other words of the *contents* of his interpretations. The more recent work on evaluation of test reporting, summarized earlier, in Chapter 14, has instead emphasized the different kinds of reports made by counselors and their differential effects on clients, all apart from the *merits* or validities of the interpretations themselves.

Much of the rationale for preferring a greater amount of client participation has already been discussed, both in the preceding chapter and in Chapter 3. Very briefly, it is likely that the client who participates in reaching the conclusions about himself from test and other data (1) is more accepting and less defensive about the interpretations, since they are in part *his;* (2) learns about himself more effectively and will remember better and longer what he has learned, because he was an active participant in the learning process; and (3) brings in more new relevant data about himself and family, his experiences, and so on, so that the interpretations finally arrived at are more valid than they would be otherwise.

Seeing the Source of a Score. One further specific argument in favor of greater participation by the client is that he will be less likely to view the tests as magical instruments which read his mind in some mystical way or find out things about him that he has never known about. This is especially true of the areas of interests and personality, but also applies to abilities and aptitudes. It is not uncommon to have counselees confide, after some of the initial barriers have been lowered, that they came with the hope of discovering their "hidden talents" or their "unknown interests" and to find out what they are "really like." Counselees sometimes come to an interview after they have taken one or more tests with expectations of "finally learning the truth." It seems preferable to communicate to clients the very unmystical and mundane sources of test interpretations. This can be done throughout the counseling process, but primarily at two points, first when tests are selected, and second, when their results are discussed.

The second interview with Ralph Santaro, from which we have seen a number of excerpts, contains a *Kuder* report and illustrates this point. In this instance, an unusual amount of detail about the inventory was given, partly because of Ralph's propensity to jump to conclusions, perhaps as a result of his anxiety and partly because of his limited previous experience with tests. With a more nearly "normal" client who has taken a number of tests in school and has received at least fairly adequate reports of his results, this much detail might be neither necessary nor desirable:

Co 63: Well, usually it, uh, seems to make sense to start with the most general kinds of tests first, and maybe that would mean interest test and the general mental ability test. So suppose we take a look at those two. The, uh, interest test you may remember, (*Cl:* Yeah) this is the sheet on which you punched your answers, and, uh, you remember that each time you had to choose the one out of three (*Cl:* Right) kinds of activities that you most prefer.

Cl 63: Uh-huh.

Co 64: And also, the one of the three that you least cared for, and when you punched those holes, that automatically put holes in certain circles (*Cl:* Uh-huh) and each set of circles here (*shows inside of Kuder answer sheet*) along a continuous line that represents one group of activities, and so when we get your score here, what we're really saying is, what kinds of activities in general, do you seem to prefer over other kinds of activities, when you have a choice.

Cl 64: Let me ask you a question here. If I don't hit the circles is that bad or what? I mean, like in a lot of these places, I didn't hit the circles.

Co 65: No, you see, you have to hit a circle somewhere. In different pages the circles are in different places.

Cl 65: Oh, yeah.

Co 66: See, in this first page, for example, these circles all represent mechanical (*Cl:* uh-huh) things, and any time you punched a hole opposite something mechanical, it came into one of these circles. Now, if instead it just happened that number, well, let's take number 2, which is computational —working with figures, numbers—you'll notice that here's a circle on the other side, where there isn't one here. So this means that this circle is probably opposite a question that has to do with using figures. And, if you had punched that, you would have gotten a circle on this page, but not on this one.

Cl 66: Oh, I see.

Co 67: And when we add up all of these circles and we simply get a score that tells us, uh, which ones you seem to prefer more of the time. Well, uh, it seems that the mechanical is, uh, by far, your first preference (*Cl:* Mechanical) and over, and over, and over, when you were given a choice between mechanical things and other things and it was mechanical more often than not. It's a very high score, which indicates it's a very strong preference with you.

Cl 67: Now, the next thing is how do I get into something mechanical, I mean, uh, actually.

Co 68: Of course, this represents only your preference and interest. (*Cl:* Mm-hm) It doesn't tell us as yet anything about abilities. (*Cl:* uh-huh) Uh, do you feel that this represents really your feelings about it?

Cl 68: Yeah, I really like to, uh, do a little mechanical work, but feeling I didn't have the schooling to go into mechanical work, uh, especially a, uh, car mechanic, let's say, or uh, an airplane mechanic or, a carpenter, or something, you know. (*Co:* Yeah) I never felt that I was qualified to do any of them jobs.

Co 69: Mm-hm, mm-hm—do you think that you'd like to do these kinds of jobs that you've mentioned?

Cl 69: Yeah, mm-hm.

Co 70: And have you looked into them—what they require in the way of schooling?

Cl 70: No, I haven't . . . I haven't checked into any of them yet.

Noting the kind of response given in *Cl* 67, one might well ask whether the counselor's detailed explanation was worth all the trouble. It is a moot question whether, with Ralph, it made much difference *how* the test interpretations were presented. The counselor went on, however, to engage Ralph in a discussion of his actual efforts to find out about mechanical jobs. This is an approach quite a bit like that of Counselor *A* in our earlier discussion, with the actual test results being given and then the client being encouraged to participate actively in a discussion of their meaning.

Many counselors have developed their own favorite techniques and "gimmicks" to facilitate client participation. A former colleague [3] developed a technique which involved asking clients to estimate what their interest inventory profile would look like, before he gave the report. This required that the counselee understand each category on the profile and sometimes necessitated some clarifying discussion before the estimate could be made. Thus, by the time the actual inventory results were reported, the counselee had been brought into at least some degree of active participation. Other counselors ask the client to summarize the thinking which led up to planning tests (see the excerpt from Bette Morgan's interview in Chapter 15).

SEPARATE VERSUS INTEGRATED REPORTS

Some find it convenient to take up one test at a time, covering all the tests and then going on from there. Others prefer to follow-up one particular question or hypothesis with a number of tests, thus building up to an answer or conclusion. For example, with a counselee who is considering both selling and teaching, one might have used a battery consisting mostly of interest and personality inventories. The counselor might go through each test, reporting the level of score on each scale, thus ending up with, say, twenty or thirty scores (many more if the *Strong* was used), each representing an aspect of the individual's interests, needs, or customary behavior. Then the counselor alone, or with his client, might use these twenty or more variables to reach hypotheses about the person and relate these to the fields of work being considered. An alternative approach would be to select from all the scores those relevant to selling and to build up the case for and against this field of work. Then, the counselor would go through a similar process with the scores relevant to teaching.

There does not seem to be an across-the-board superiority of one or the other of these approaches. The first is probably more time-consuming *during* the interview, but the second requires more preparation *before* the interview. In part, the choice is made on the basis of individual preference of each counselor. However, the particular purpose of testing may point toward one or the other in individual cases. For example, if a major purpose of testing in one case is self-concept development, the first approach would be more suitable, since it is in effect an *inventory* of the individual. If, on the other hand, a counselee has brought specific questions with regard to two alternative courses of action, a complete inventory may be quite unnecessary, and the counselor instead might select only the relevant scores and the relevant interpretations for reporting.

[3] Mr. Dominick J. Carminati, then of the U.S. Veterans Administration, now with the New York State Employment Service.

The "As-Needed" Approach

The foregoing discussion was based on the assumption that testing is done on the package plan—the "battery." If the "as-needed" method is used (see Chapter 3) there is often no choice to be made, since there may have been only one test taken between one interview and another. The as-needed approach also has other special implications for the reporting phase:

1. It is easier to relate the test report to its purposes, since a specific purpose in one interview leads to use of a particular test and then usually to discussion of the result of that test in the following interview.

2. There is less information for the counselee to absorb in any one interview when tests are spread over a series of interviews. It is true that reporting can be spaced over two or more interviews even with the battery approach. However, the longer the time interval between taking a test and receiving a report of its results, the greater are the difficulties in making use of a client's recollections of the test and of his test-taking experiences.

3. Client participation is probably easier to achieve in the as-needed method, since he is somewhat more likely to approach tests with understanding of the information to be sought from the results.

A possible disadvantage of the as-needed approach, however, is a fragmentation which may occur if the counselor does not take pains, from time to time during a series of interviews, to bring together relevant data from several tests and to relate them to each other. He may miss out on opportunities to use one test to confirm or question an hypothesis emanating from another, to compare implications from two different tests, and in other ways to add to the information derived from each test separately.

SEQUENCE OF REPORTING TESTS

Should interest scores be reported first or last? Should an individual's highest aptitude scores be reported first, and the lowest last (or perhaps never)? Here, too, the answers are for the most part determined by the personal style of each counselor, as well as by the particular needs of each client and the way the interview proceeds. A few comments, however, may be helpful. On the question of whether interest inventory results should precede those from aptitude and achievement tests, or *vice versa,* arguments can be made for both sides.

On the one hand, interests differentiate people in different fields of work better than do abilities (at least at the higher occupational levels). In addition, one is not likely to function with maximum effectiveness, certainly not with satisfaction, in a field not harmonious with his interests. Hence it would follow that interests should be examined first, as a way of narrowing down possible choices, and then information from aptitude and other kinds of ability tests could be related to these interests.

On the other hand, the individual or society, or both, may suffer if he does not utilize his best abilities. One can expect little success in a field for which he lacks the requisite abilities. Interests can be developed, it is argued further, through successful experiences, especially for those still in adolescence, certainly at junior high school age. In the individual case, there is a danger of premature crystallization of vocational plans if interest inventories are used too early in counseling (Di Michael, 1951). Di Michael also points out that interest scores are really complex data which are difficult to handle early in the counseling process. Better, he suggests, to build up a foundation first, through interviews, and then to report interest scores only when there is enough understanding by the client to permit using them properly.

Segel and others (1958) have gone further and proposed that testing in the secondary school proceed in two stages: In the first, abilities are measured and curriculum choices based on these; later, measures of interests and personality are brought in for purposes of checking and further planning.

It is unlikely that counselors will give up the time-tested practice of using *both* interest and ability data in helping adolescents and adults to make decisions and plans. Which comes first probably makes little difference in a particular interview or series of interviews, so long as the counselor is alert to the possibility of overlooking *any* relevant data. In some cases, interests may be deemed less important, for one or another reason; in others they may be emphasized as the major focal point. In the first category might be cases in which an impoverished environment has provided limited opportunities to develop latent interests or cases in which there are several equally strong interests. In neither of these situations are developed interests a very good basis for initial narrowing down of choice. In the second category are those cases in which abilities are all high enough for almost any field (as, for example, Kathy Musgrove in Chapter 11). In such cases one looks to interests for help in narrowing down the range of possible choices.

It may also be wise, at least in some cases, to offer counselees an opportunity to help decide the sequence of tests to be reported. For one, this may help to structure test reporting as a process in which the client is expected to participate actively. Secondly, it may be that a counselee is really concerned about one particular area—say college aptitude or personality—and he may be so preoccupied with that one area that he will not learn much from discussions of tests in other areas.

As to the other issue, whether to report high scores first or low scores, again there seem to be some general principles but again there is the need for adaptation to individual cases. As a general rule, it makes good sense to emphasize the positive, to help people build on their assets rather than to bemoan their liabilities. In individual cases, however, there are times when it is most salutary for an individual to face an inadequacy squarely, to struggle with it, and finally to make peace with it. To be explicit and direct with counselees regarding faults they have refused to face requires more courage on the counselor's part than to avoid the subject. To collaborate with the client's weakness by joining him in evading the low scores may be not only an indication of inadequacy on the part of the counselor, but, even worse, it may do the client a serious disservice.

The amenities of everyday social relations call for "looking for the silver lining" and "accentuating the positive," but counseling requires a somewhat different kind of relationship. Sometimes the greatest contribution one can make to an individual counselee is to be quite honest with him about his shortcomings. Actually, as students of counseling have long known, this kind of honesty really implies more *acceptance* of the individual than does the opposite approach. To avoid mentioning "negative" things, to be constantly reassuring about any faults or lacks of the counselee is in many cases to be seen as *rejection* of these negative aspects. In effect, it is saying to the client: "There are some things about you that are so horrible and so fearful that I'll pretend I don't know about them, and you would be wise to do the same and deny to yourself that they exist." If one accepts people, he accepts them as they are, the good with the bad, the strong with the weak. This kind of acceptance is one of the major contributions which counselors have to offer their clients, since it helps them to face themselves more openly and to build their lives on a more complete and more accurate understanding of themselves. It is commonly agreed that such openness and self-awareness are important foundation stones for a healthy and productive personality.[4]

TYPES OF SCORES FOR REPORTING

Assuming that one is to use Methods 1 or 2 in reporting the results of tests, the question arises as to the kinds of scores which are reported to counselees. Are standard scores preferable to percentiles, should IQ's be reported, should actual numbers be used (78th percentile, 10.6 grade equivalent) or more general descriptive terms (above average, superior)? To some extent, the answers depend on the age of the counselee, his level of comprehension and of intelligence, and his sophistication regarding testing "lingo." This is, after all, a problem of communication, so that we must take into consideration the understandings of the person to whom

[4] This is also related to one of the elements which Hahn (1955) listed as making up the unique pattern of function of the counseling psychologist. Hahn characterized this element as " . . . the casting of a psychological balance sheet to aid our *clients* to contribute to, and to take most from, living in our society" (p. 282; italics in the original) .

we are trying to communicate certain information. The elementary school child may not be able to handle any more complex a concept than "You're better in arithmetic than in reading," or "Your spelling is not up to what you are capable of doing." The young adolescent may find meaning in such statements as: "You are better than three out of four youngsters your age in your vocabulary." To older adolescents, college students and adults, there may be value in explaining the operation of an expectancy table or a multiple discriminant statement: "People with your abilities on these tests succeed in this field of work 70 times in 100," or "Your pattern of likes and dislikes is most similar to that of people in field X." With these general comments, a few specific points may be made:

1. Although *standard scores* are preferred by statisticians, they are not as meaningful to counselees as the more frequently used *percentiles*. Even counselors who have a good grasp of standard scores probably find themselves doing some quick mental translation into percentiles: "Let's see, his standard score on that test was 61, which means it's just about one standard deviation above the mean, which puts him at the . . . let's see, 50 plus one half of 68 . . . would put him at the 84th percentile." The major disadvantage of percentiles—the fact that they are not of equal size throughout the distribution—can be overcome to some extent by having handy a chart which shows that percentiles are more crowded together at the center than at the extremes of a distribution. The profile sheets for a number of tests do just this; included are many of the multifactor tests, such as the *Differential Aptitude Tests, Holzinger-Crowder Uni-Factor Tests,* and *Multiple Aptitude Tests,* and others, such as the *Iowa Tests of Educational Development, Kuder Preference Record, Occupational Interest Inventory, Guilford-Zimmerman Temperament Survey, Edwards Personal Preference Schedule,* and many others. Some of these are reproduced in connection with cases in Chapter 11. Attention to *distances* between two scores on such profile sheets rather than to the *number* of percentile points of difference between the scores will help counselors to avoid the errors of underemphasizing large differences and overemphasizing small differences.

An interesting modification of standard scores has been suggested by Seigle (1953). Beginning with the premises that standard scores are superior statistically but are difficult for the layman to understand, Seigle proposes the *W*-score, which is a standard score scale in which the mean is 85 and the standard deviation is 5. With this arrangement, the range of plus and minus three standard deviations, which includes over 99 per cent of the cases in a normal distribution, will lie between 70 and 100. The main advantage of this plan would also seem to be its main disadvantage. The *W*-scores will probably be seen by students, parents, and others, as comparable to the numbers used in teachers' grades. The result may be that they perceive a *W*-score of 85 on an aptitude test as above average (which it would be as a teacher's grade in many schools) rather than as a just-average score. They may see a score of 99 as near-perfection (which it usually represents on a teacher-made test) when it means only that the person got a higher score than most people who took the test but tells nothing about the percentage of items correct.

Durost (1959) describes the use of *stanine* scores in a school system in Florida. Stanine scores are a standard score arranged in nine categories (the term was derived from the two words *stan*dard and *nine*), with a mean of five and a standard deviation of two. Durost reports that stanine scores were easy to compute by a counting technique and were easy to explain to parents and pupils. With only nine categories, they are not too fine a score and are therefore more stable than many other kinds of scores. Finally, they lend themselves to easy statistical analysis, since, like all standard scores, they may be averaged and in other ways used directly in computation. As described by Durost, the stanine score may provide a means for retaining the advantages of standard scores without the major disadvantage of other kinds of standard score, that is, the difficulty of communicating their meanings.

Hart (1957) also found the stanine method useful, in a New Hampshire high school. The purpose there was to combine a variety of scores and teachers' judgments into a single number in order to place students into homogeneous sections for tenth grade English. She reports that the method was so successful in yielding a predictor of high reliability (the total composite stanine score) that it was later used for estimating success in algebra, French, Latin, and science.

2. It is probably wise to report scores in terms of gross categories such as *fourths, fifths,* or *tenths,* rather than in terms of hundredths, the latter being, of course, the unit of percentiles. A spurious sense of precision is communicated when a score is reported as "36th percentile" or "better than 35 out of 100 boys your age." Such statements imply that we know that he is neither at the 35th nor the 37th percentile but exactly at the 36th. It would be more in keeping with the errors of measurement of most tests to report such a score as "low average" [5] or "better than one out of three." In fact, to be really scrupulous, one should add and subtract at least two units of the standard error of measurement, thus getting the range within which we can be 95 per cent certain that the person's "true score" lies. With many tests we usually regard as "average" all scores between the 25th and 75th percentiles. For personality and interest inventories, where reliability is lower, even broader limits for the "average range" are in order.

3. It is important that the client understand as well as possible the *nature of the norm* group with which comparisons are made. With the

[5] Berg (1956) suggests that it may be more desirable to use descriptive terms of this kind and to omit all references to numbers.

multiscore batteries of aptitude or achievement tests, this is not quite so serious a problem, since at least all part scores are compared with the same norm group. (Even here, however, there are problems; to tell a student that he is superior in mathematics according to his score on the *ITED* may be confusing if he is in a school where mathematics is taught unusually well and where he is just slightly above average as compared to his mates. Local norms would, of course, take care of this situation.) The problem is more complex when two different tests are used and different norms. He may be average on one test whose norms are "easy," and below average on another test with "tougher" norms, and actually be about equally good in the two aptitudes or abilities. He may seem to be much lower in engineering aptitude than in general scholastic aptitude, but only because the engineering test was normed on engineering college freshmen and the scholastic aptitude test on high school seniors or on general college freshmen. These distinctions are often difficult even for beginning counselors to make, so the task of communicating them to counselees is not an easy one.

4. Is it wise to *show the counselee his profile?* Again the answer depends in part on the individual's level of intelligence and maturity, but there are several reasons for a counselor's reluctance to let his clients have access to the actual profile. If the entire profile is shown, one has to be ready to explain any and all parts of it. With the *Strong VIB,* for example, clients are apt to be concerned about the three nonoccupational scales (Interest Maturity, Occupational Level, and Masculinity-Femininity) and often ask for interpretations of these scores. The counselor may be reluctant to get involved with interpretations of such scores, perhaps because of the difficulty of explaining them, perhaps because in most cases the information derived is too little to warrant the time and trouble. Yet one cannot brush aside a counselee's request for an explanation without running the risk of implying that something is being concealed.

Secondly, the profile probably shows raw scores and percentile scores in specific number form, with all the disadvantages thereunto pertaining (see point 2 above). Third, some tests do not lend themselves at all to client examination of the profile because of the risks of misinterpretation. For example, one is not likely to show an *MMPI* profile to his counselee, for fear that the latter will become unduly anxious about the psychiatric labels attached to the scales. Fourth, there is the danger of misinterpretation of percentile differences, as discussed in point 1 above. A score at the 55th percentile may erroneously be seen as "above average," and a difference between two of the individual's scores (say 10 points in the middle of the distribution) may be exaggerated.

With all these disadvantages, why consider showing counselees their profiles? First, as Bordin has pointed out (1955) ". . . proponents of this procedure maintain that this is the most effective way of stimulating the client to react freely to test results in terms of their meaning for him. In effect, the profile operates like a projective test" (p. 278). Secondly, there is the well-founded belief that a graphic report improves the process of communication. Done well, a profile should aid in the process of learning, in terms of perceiving, understanding, and retaining. Perhaps we need to develop special profile forms for use in reporting scores, forms which would show the relative position of an individual on one or more measures, without all the disadvantages listed above. This might be done by omitting all numbers referring to raw scores, percentiles, or grade equivalents, and showing only a cruder division, say, into fifths. Also desirable would be the depiction of scores as *ranges,* so that a score would be represented by a band rather than a point. Figure 16.1 shows how such a form might look (this is very much like the form used with the *Sequential Tests of Educational Progress*). Until standard forms of this sort are available for the tests they use, counselors could easily make their own for "showing" purposes, retaining the more detailed profile for themselves, if they wish. Actually the form here recommended would probably serve *all* the counselor's purposes better than the usual detailed profile sheet and would serve as a constant reminder of the crudity of our measurement.

It should be noted that the profile format suggested above does nothing about differences between norm groups on different tests. Unless there is substantial basis for concluding that the norms for two different tests are

	Test 1: Mech. Apt.		Test 2: Cler. Apt.		Test 3: Engrg. Apt.	
Superior						
Above Average						
Average						
Below Average						
Inferior						

Fig. 16.1. Suggested Form for Profile to be Used in Reporting to Counselees, Parents, Teachers, and Others

very similar both in central tendency and dispersion, it is probably wiser not to place the scores on a single profile sheet.

GOING BACK TO THE TEST ITEMS

In the case of Robert Martin (Chapter 11), the counselor found it helpful to ask orally, during the interview, some of the questions which Robert had missed on the *DAT*. This technique permitted the counselor to develop an hypothesis which could explain the marked discrepancies among Robert's test scores and between his test scores and school grades. This same technique, used in that case primarily to sharpen the *interpretation* of the data, is valuable occasionally in the reporting process. Counselees sometimes reject a score on an interest inventory or on a personality inventory with the objection that it is not an accurate reflection of them: "But I'm not interested in that," or "That's what the *test* may say, but I don't like to work with my hands," or "Sure, I like to listen to music, but it certainly isn't my main interest in life," or "But I'm not that kind of person at all." In such cases, it is sometimes helpful to point out that "after all, nothing can get on a profile that you didn't put there," and then to go further and show how the score is derived. On the *Kuder,* for example, one might explain just how the two pinpricks in each triad lead directly to points of score on particular scales. By putting the answer sheet back in the booklet, one can locate items of the kind which led to the rejected score, and can show the person just how he himself caused his Mechanical or Musical score to be so high. In somewhat similar fashion, a counselee's objections to interpretations of reported scores on tests of aptitude and achievement can sometimes be handled by going over selected items, showing him just how he attained his low score (or his high score).

Two cautions are in order: First, the contents of tests must be safeguarded in terms of confidentiality. If one is too free with right answers to questions, as he goes over items with a client, the scores of that counselee (and of his friends) may be raised on a later administration of the same test. Some counselors may indeed judge that, with certain counselees, perhaps with their whole case loads, it is unwise ever to go over test items. Used with discretion, however, this technique is occasionally useful.

A second possible danger in using this technique is that one may overlook *other meanings* of the client's protestations regarding a test score. A counselee's inability to accept an aptitude test score may be indicative of an unrealistic self-concept stemming from overly high parental ambitions. With such a person, one should not be surprised to find that the act of pointing out some of his errors on the test does not lead to immediate acceptance of the test's implications. Instead, it is more likely that he will rationalize or otherwise defend himself against the attack on his self-concept. Likewise, the youngster with a very high musical preference score on an inventory, who denies any interest in a musical career, may be reflecting parental or peer disdain for occupations in the field of music. Going over some of the inventory items may help persuade him that he really is interested in musical activities, but still we should not be surprised if he again becomes defensive and refuses to see the (counselor's) logic of the situation.

In the kinds of cases just referred to, a more suitable counseling approach is likely to be one which attempts to deal with the counselee's unrealistic self-concept, its origins, and the needs it serves. This is not to deny that even in such cases it may be helpful to go over selected test items with the client, at appropriate points, as part of the process of improving his reality orientation. Furthermore, one cannot always know in advance that going over test items will be futile; it is sometimes necessary to try this before realizing that there are irrational factors underlying the unrealistic self-concept and that it is not just a matter of the client's not *knowing* his abilities or his interests.

RELATING TEST REPORTS TO OTHER DATA

Although this point has been implied repeatedly throughout many of the chapters, perhaps it is worth mentioning separately here, particularly as it applies to reporting of test results. Tests are just one set of tools used in educational and vocational planning to sample client behavior. Nontest data (which include biographical information, records of school grades, anecdotal reports, rating scales, information and opinions given by the person who made the referral, and information of various kinds obtained in interviews) are used earlier in the counseling process in considering the needs for tests and deciding which tests, if any, to use. Later in the process, nontest data are combined with test data in making interpretations of the results. This can be done even with statistical interpretations, as was suggested in Chapter 7. It is fairly common practice, for example, for colleges to combine high school average and scores from college aptitude tests in a formula of some sort, or in an expectancy table, in order to arrive at a multiple prediction. Insurance companies long ago found that certain biographical data, such as number of children and amount of life insurance carried, are predictive of success for insurance salesmen.

As used in test selection and interpretation, nontest data help the counselor in analyzing an individual's needs, in choosing tests which are most likely to meet those needs, and in getting meaning from test results. As applied now to test *reporting*, nontest data again help to verify interpretations ("Does this agree with your experience with mathematics in school?" or "As you think of your likes and dislikes for school subjects, how do they compare with this profile?"). They serve a further purpose, however, that of helping the client to understand his test results and to appreciate their implications for his plans, decisions, and adjustments. Thus, as a counselee ponders the question, "How do your school experiences compare with this test profile?" he has an opportunity not only to contribute to the testing of hypotheses regarding his abilities, but he may also be increasing his understanding of how his abilities have affected his school grades in the past and how they may affect his grades and his job functioning in the future. In fact, often a major contribution of tests is not so much the new information they provide the client as the insights which they help him to gain regarding his functioning in various situations. In receiving results of interest and personality inventories, in particular, the counselee often finds that there are no "unknown interests" or "real self" revealed, but that, with the help of a skillful counselor, he emerges with a clearer, more self-assured picture of himself and therefore with a better foundation for planning his future.

Some counselors, as a matter of fact, prefer to withhold test information until there has first been a discussion of the client's own remembered experiences (Di Michael, 1951). Later, test data are brought in to confirm a point, to clear up confusion, and in other ways to play a role subsidiary in importance to that of the nontest data.

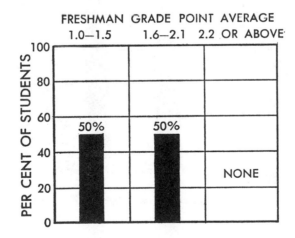

Fig. 16.2. Graph I
This graph shows how former students of this school who had scores on the Terman-McNemar Test similar to yours did in their first year at the state university. Half of them had a grade point average between 1 - 1.5 (C to C+) and half of them had a grade point average between 1.6 - 2.1 (B— to B). None of them obtained higher than a B average. An undergraduate average of B or higher is necessary to be admitted to graduate work.
(McCabe, 1957, p. 450. By permission of the *Personnel and Guidance Journal.*)

GRAPHIC AIDS IN REPORTING SCORES TO COUNSELEES

There are probably any number of homemade devices in use around the country, although very few have been described in the literature. Mc-Cabe (1957) shows one such graphic aid, which is reproduced in Figures 16.2 and 16.3. The data from which these charts were made were found in the files of a high school in California to which the state university had sent reports of the freshman grades of their graduates. The appropriate one of the two graphs, in mimeographed form, is given to each student who is planning to attend the state university. Graph I (Fig. 16.2) is given to those whose *Terman-McNemar* IQ is between 100 and 120; it tells the student that, with *T-M* scores such as his, there are 50 chances in 100 of attaining a freshman GPA of 1.0 to 1.5, 50 chances of attaining a GPA of 1.6 to 2.1, and zero chances of having a GPA larger than 2.1. Graph II (Fig. 16.3) gives similar information for those whose *Terman-McNemar* IQ was in the range of 121-140; here there is a further break-

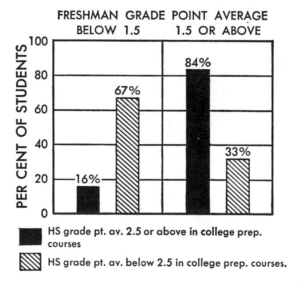

Fig. 16.3. Graph II

This graph shows how former students of this school who had scores on the Terman-McNemar Test similar to yours did in their first year at the state university. Notice that 84 per cent of those who had a high school grade point average of 2.5 or better (B+) obained a grade point average at the university of 1.5 or better (C+), 67 per cent of those who had a high school grade point average below 2.5 (B+) obtained a grade point average at the university below 1.5 (C+).

(McCabe, 1957, p. 450. By permission of the *Personnel and Guidance Journal*.)

down according to high school average—in effect, this is an expectancy table combining test and nontest data. (For those with IQ 100 to 120, high school average was not found to be related to college GPA and so was not used on the graph.)

Another kind of graphic aid is used in the "Student Report" form published by the Educational Testing Service for use with the *Sequential Tests of Educational Progress (STEP)* and reproduced here as Figure 16.4. This furnishes a *descriptive* interpretation, in terms simply of comparisons with a norm group, whereas the McCabe form previously described and illustrated is *predictive* in nature. The *STEP* report form (on a page not shown here) also explains how to compare any two scores of the individual, using the concept of the *band* of scores rather than the single point.

Devices such as those mentioned above can readily be made locally; in some instances they might be prepared for projection on a screen and used in connection with group guidance sessions. Busy counselors in schools might well find that the time needed to prepare charts, graphs, and tables would result in less time needed for reporting scores to individual students. Therefore more time would be available to help these individuals to digest the information and do something with it. It should be stressed, however, that "gadgets" of this kind are never a substitute for counseling, but only an *aid;* if anything, it might well be that they would increase the demand for individual counseling, as has been found to be the case with group guidance activities in general.

REPORTS TO TEACHERS

Counselors in *schools* have a splendid opportunity to enlarge the scope of effectiveness of tests by communicating some of their findings to teachers and administrators. Whereas counselors in agencies ordinarily can work only with the client, and perhaps his parents, and must do all their test reporting in a short period of time—perhaps one to five hours of individual interviews—those in schools can extend the values of tests into every classroom and into supervisory and administrative offices. Yet informal observations in a number of schools show scanty evidence of this kind of activity. Of late, however, some of the large-scale testing programs have encouraged teacher and administrator reporting by providing forms for that purpose and, in some instances, statistical summaries of test results for entire classes and grades. As was pointed out in an earlier section, however, communication is often inadequate, in that translation is not made into a language understandable to people with little or no training in measurement.

Several evaluative and descriptive studies have been reported and will be summarized in the next few paragraphs. The first to be mentioned is

_____'s standing on each of the tests taken is indicated by the shaded area.
(name)

Ability, as measured by each test, is compared with that of a sample of students in grade_____in the
(grade)

_____.
(national or local group)

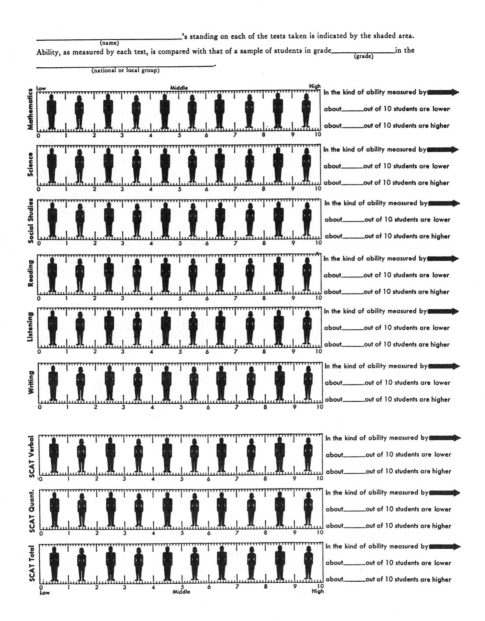

(To find out how to compare a student's own performance on any two tests taken, turn to page 4.)

STEP
Mathematics . . . measures your ability to understand numbers and ways of working with them (for example, addition and division), such symbols as $+$, $\sqrt{}$, and $<$, relationships between objects in space, how two changing things can depend on each other (for example, distance and speed), how to draw conclusions from facts, and how to make estimations and predictions when you do not have all the information. Mathematics teachers call these concepts *number and operation, symbolism, measurement and geometry, function and relation, deduction and inference,* and *probability and statistics.*

STEP
Science . . . measures your ability to recognize and state problems relating to science, to select ways of getting information about the problems, to understand and judge the information you get, to predict what the solutions to these problems may be, and to work with symbols and numbers used in science problems. Some of the questions are about biology materials; some are about chemistry, physics, meteorology, astronomy, and geology. All of the questions present science in practical situations (for example, in the home, on the farm, and at work).

STEP
Social Studies . . . measures your ability to understand the kinds of social studies materials which a citizen in a democracy should be able to deal with. These include maps, graphs, cartoons, editorials, debates, and historical documents. There are questions about history, geography, economics, government, and sociology.

STEP
Reading . . . measures your ability to read materials and then answer questions about what you have read. These questions ask you to remember specific things the author said, to understand what he meant and why he might have said what he did, and to criticize his ideas. The reading materials include directions, announcements, newspaper and magazine articles, letters, stories, poetry, and plays.

STEP
Listening . . . measures your ability to listen to materials and then answer questions about what you have heard. The Listening test is very much like the Reading test except, of course, you *hear* instead of *see* the things you are asked to remember, understand, or criticize.

STEP
Writing . . . measures your ability to criticize materials written by other students in terms of the ways they are organized or written. The questions ask you to pick out errors or weaknesses in the writing and choose revisions which best correct the errors or weaknesses. The materials were written by students in schools and colleges in various parts of the United States; they include letters, answers to test questions, school newspaper articles, announcements, essays, outlines, directions, and stories.

SCAT
Verbal . . . measures your ability to understand sentences and give the meanings of words. This ability is most important in such school courses as English, foreign languages, and social studies (history, civics, etc.).

SCAT
Quantitative . . . measures your ability to perform operations with numbers and to solve mathematics problems stated in words. This ability is most important in such school courses as mathematics and science.

SCAT
Total . . . combines your scores on SCAT Verbal and SCAT Quantitative to provide the *single* best measure of your general capacity to do the work of the next higher level of schooling.

Fig. 16.4. Inside Pages of Student Report Form for STEP and SCAT
(By permission of the Cooperative Test Division, Educational Testing Service.)

more a report of action than of research but is one of the very few reported at the college level. Smith (1954) selected six English instructors, three of whom had favorable and three unfavorable attitudes toward the value of receiving personal information about their classes. An interview was held with each, in which tables and graphs were used to describe their classes in terms of high school average, test scores, and family characteristics. Smith reports that all reacted positively to the interviews and later said they had made use of the information for instructional purposes. An important by-product was improved relations between these instructors and the counseling office.

Evidence of the values of reports to teachers is offered in a study by Spivak (1957). He sent two seventh grade teachers summaries of the frequency of problems checked by their pupils on the *SRA Youth Inventory*. Two other classes were reserved as controls, and no reports were sent to those teachers. In midyear, the *Youth Inventory* was again administered to all four classes and comparisons made of October and January problems. Although the two control groups showed a small decrease in mean number of problems, it was not statistically significant. The experimental classes showed a larger, and a statistically significant, decrease in mean number of problems. Spivak points out some technical problems in the design of the study which limit the confidence that can be placed in the results (for example, the experimental classes by chance turned out to have a much larger mean number of problems than the control classes, on the October test). It would be extremely valuable to replicate this study in other schools. If similar results are obtained, here is a technique which requires very little time of the counselor and teacher and yet seems to improve the teacher's effectiveness in reducing problems among students.

Additional support for the value of the report-to-teachers comes from Baker and Doyle (1959). Using both tests and other sources of data, such as sociometrics and autobiographies, they tried to help teachers increase their effectiveness in assigning grades relative to each child's capacity. They reasoned that the more effective the teacher was, the more independent his grades should be of measured intelligence; this would indicate that teachers were making a discrimination between general mental ability and specific subject-matter achievement. Therefore the correlations between intelligence test score and grades should decrease. Using pupils in sixth to eighth grades whose teachers had received the in-service training with emphasis on tests, they found some evidence that this did happen. For one thing, there were a larger number of unsatisfactory grades reported for these children than had been the case three years earlier; this was interpreted as showing greater confidence on the part of teachers in their appraisal ability. Second, correlations between intelligence test scores and grades in reading and spelling declined (from .45 to .25 with reading, from .38 to .19 with spelling) from those of three years earlier. However, correlations with grades in language and arithmetic remained the same. As its authors point out, the design of this study does not permit identification of the specific factors leading to these changes. One bit of evidence offered, however, is that some years previously they had tried to communicate the "relative grading" point of view to teachers, but at that time no changes in grading practices resulted. This time the emphasis was placed on tests and on other data regarding pupils, so they feel that it is this element which was responsible for the success obtained.

Diffenbaugh (1950) used a somewhat different approach in a consolidated school, where the ninth grade dropout rate was very high among pupils who had just entered from elementary schools in 24 surrounding school districts. Counselors saw each new student in the first few weeks of the school year and prepared a "thumbnail sketch" of each to pass on to teachers. The sketches included both test data (Mental Age, Algebra Prognostic score) and nontest data (residence, weak and strong subjects, pertinent family information, health and other special needs or problems). Whereas dropouts had "amounted to as much as 35 per cent," they were 7 per cent during this experimental year. It is also reported that teachers frequently requested the sketches and commented on them. The study as reported is, like much of action research, lacking in the controls and statistical niceties which would permit a firmer conclusion as to the effectiveness of the technique. Replication in the same school and in other schools would help establish the reliability of the findings. Some provisions for control groups would lend assurance that it is the techniques under study and not some other factor that is responsible for the change. Finally, it would be important to test the effects of the technique for a second and perhaps third year in order to be assured that it isn't just the novelty that is arousing teacher interest and producing these results.

Still another kind of report is described by Bowman (1952). This consists of a chart which, by a single entry for each student (by number), shows simultaneously his standing on an intelligence test, on an achievement test, and in grades. This is done by using one dimension for the intelligence test, the other for the achievement test, and a code number to designate school grades. It is possible to examine a chart of this sort for a class or a grade and, in a few minutes, to select out those who seem to need special help, those whose grades are lower than their test scores or the bright high achievers who are too old for grade level.

The Great Neck, New York, Public Schools have prepared, through their Central Testing Office, a mimeographed "Portfolio—How Teachers Use Test Results." Included in the Portfolio are summaries of important facts for teachers to know about each of the tests used, suggestions for using test results, and other useful information. Although this kind of

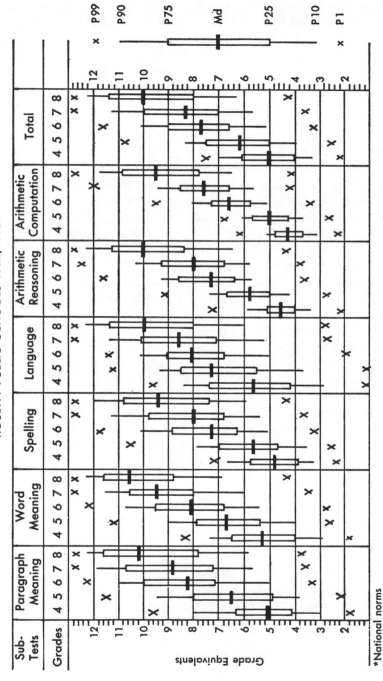

Fig. 16.5. Local Norms for the Stanford Achievement Tests
(By permission of William Rosengarten, Jr., and Roslyn, New York, High School.)

material is not an actual *report* of test results, it can be a helpful part of the total process of communicating test information.

To give one final illustration of methods of reporting to teachers and other school staff members, Figure 16.5 reproduces a chart prepared by William Rosengarten, Jr., of the Roslyn, New York, public schools. It is accompanied by a three-page memo, which explains the chart and its applications and implications. A covering memorandum to principals and guidance counselors adds, "I shall be happy to accept invitations to speak to faculty meetings and other groups on how to interpret the results."

As with almost any mechanical device of this sort, there are dangers of improper use. Counselors may feel that their responsibilities are ended when they have turned their reports over to teachers. They may not follow through with the informal teacher conferences which are necessary to clarify points and to be sure that teachers are not misusing the data. On the other hand, counselors may emphasize reports to teachers at the expense of working directly with students.

These dangers seem relatively small compared to the value to classroom teachers of having information regarding needs and characteristics of their pupils. In addition, information of the kind provided by Bowman's charts could be invaluable to supervisors, administrators, and curriculum co-ordinators in all aspects of planning and operating the school program. Such charts contain answers to questions such as these: To what extent are our students achieving up to capacity? Who are the under-achievers, and in what grades is this problem most serious? Are the brighter youngsters utilizing their abilities? Is our curriculum organized to meet the actual capabilities and past achievements of our student body?

The charts alone and any accompanying statistics—means, standard deviations—do not themselves provide answers. This fact is evidenced by the bewilderment with which school superintendents sometimes ask for explanations of simple mean scores of a grade on an achievement test. Yet such data for groups should be approached in the same way we approach a set of test data regarding an individual—as a problem of test *interpretation*. Many of the principles and methods of clinical interpretation apply here: drawing inferences which lead to hypotheses, these in turn being compared with new data and with other hypotheses, until a "theory" is developed to describe or explain the group. As with clinical interpretation in individual cases, it is necessary to seek out nontest data, in this case consisting perhaps of teachers' judgments regarding their classes, parental reactions obtained formally or informally, and opinions of the students themselves as reported in interviews, group discussions, questionnaires, and in other ways. In Rosengarten's chart, for example (Fig. 16.5), it is clear that these pupils are performing at a level higher than that of the national norm group. This is merely a fact; its meaning and the conclusions based on it require further data and some thinking: What kind of population is represented by the published norms? To what extent are these results reflecting strengths in the curriculum and in teaching, and to what extent are they reflecting superior (innate or developed) academic aptitude of the pupils who attend these schools? Would these pupils do equally well on a different battery, one which emphasizes somewhat different competencies? As further data are sought to answer some of these questions, hypotheses emerge and are tested, and ultimately conclusions and recommendations are in order.

This is the appraisal process, and it requires the skills and understandings of one who is well versed in measurement and who has also some understanding of curriculum and of educational psychology. Rarely is this combination found in one person, so that the problems of interpretation often require the combined efforts of measurement, curriculum, and other personnel. It may also be helpful to bring in consultants from outside the school who can bring to bear specialized competencies in measurement, as well as a fresh view of the situation. Even the larger systems which have their own research and evaluation bureaus may find it helpful to bring in outsiders for consultation.

REPORTS TO OTHER PROFESSIONAL WORKERS

School and college counselors rarely make formal reports of test results for the use of other counselors, psychiatrists, or social workers. Usually, the scores themselves are recorded on cumulative record cards or in folders and these are consulted by others who may need the information. On transfer to another school, or upon graduation from elementary, junior high, or senior high school, the entire record, or excerpts from it, may be sent to the new school. Although test scores may be included, these are not test reports in the sense in which we are using the term here. Counselors in agencies are occasionally asked to write separate reports, based on tests and other data, which are intended as appraisals of individuals. Sometimes these requests come from the school or college which the counselee attends and which often does not offer as extensive a testing program as does the agency. Sometimes the counselee is under treatment by a psychiatrist, who seeks advice from the counselor as to appropriate educational and vocational goals. Still other times, the request comes from a community agency which is providing family counseling, or rehabilitation training, during the course of which questions arise regarding the individual's educational and vocational capabilities. Counselors and counseling psychologists on the staffs of hospitals and of multifunction agencies may be asked to write appraisal reports for the use of other specialists or as part of a broader study by a team of which the counselor is a member.

Occasionally the client himself asks that a report be sent to his employer or to some other person.

A related but somewhat different kind of reporting is done when testing and appraisal are done by one person and counseling by another. Some of the state rehabilitation offices operate in this manner, as do some college and community agencies which offer vocational counseling services. (We exclude from this discussion those agencies—governmental and other—in which a clerical or subprofessional worker administers and scores tests, records the scores, and perhaps reports observations of the client's behavior during testing, but does not interpret or appraise.)

A number of problems arise in connection with these various kinds of reports. Should the test scores themselves be reported, or only the interpretations? How detailed should the report be? Is it ever justifiable to withhold certain information? One generalization is that obviously the answers to these questions depends upon the recipient of the report: his qualifications, his purposes, and his reputation. Beyond this generalization, each question needs some discussion.

What Should Be Reported—Scores or Interpretations?

This is a question largely of communication; one communicates information which is expected to be comprehendible and usable. Test scores themselves, whether in the form of percentiles, age or grade equivalents, or standard scores, are meaningful only to those who have had some training in tests and measurements and in statistics, as well as related background in psychology, particularly in the area of individual differences and in some or all of the following: psychology of personality, educational psychology, and psychology of careers. In brief, these are the competencies expected of readers of this book. Lacking these qualifications, the recipient of a report cannot be expected to make constructive and valid use of test scores. Instead, it may be necessary to go one or more steps away from the raw data in the report. If the person for whom the report is written has some related professional training, say in psychology, social work, or psychiatry, we may be able to start at a point only one step beyond the scores themselves and *describe* the person in terms of achievement, aptitudes, interest, and personality, and then go on to state the implications of these characteristics. If we cannot assume that the recipient understands these descriptive data, then the first of the two steps above must be omitted, and the report will include only the *implications* of the data for whatever actions or decisions the recipient has in mind. For instance, if the report is to be sent to an employer who is thinking of transferring our client to a different job and if he has no relevant professional qualifications, it may be proper to tell the employer only what kinds of work are most (or least) suitable for the client on the basis of our appraisal. Such a report would not indicate the test scores themselves and might not tell very much about the characteristics of the individual which led to the counselor's conclusions.[6]

It is clearly the responsibility of the person writing the report to find out exactly what information the recipient needs, what he plans to do with it, and what qualifications he has. This is obviously somewhat time-consuming, requiring at the least a telephone call, and possibly some correspondence. However, to do anything less is to run the risk of doing harm to a client, by having data misinterpreted or by placing confidential material in the hands of one who may not respect the confidence. What is needed is, first, a general policy for the school, agency, or other institution in which the counselor works, as to what kinds of information will be released, to whom, and with what provisions (such as the written consent of the counselee or his parent). Second, a judgment must be made for each individual case, which involves the application of the general policy. Counselors should not have to operate entirely "by ear"; there should be an explicit statement of policy regarding such matters. If a telephone call requesting information about a person comes to a school or agency office, from another agency or school, from an employer, from a psychiatrist, or anyone else, the proper procedures should be clearly understood by all concerned. Lack of such explicit policy is all too frequent, particularly in schools. As a result too much confidential information is probably released indiscriminately.

True, the ethical situation is somewhat different in schools and in agencies. In the former, test-taking is not a voluntary activity of students, and so the results belong to the school, to be used at their discretion. In agencies to which people go voluntarily for help, it is usually understood that the information is confidential to the client and to the staff of the agency and is released to anyone else only with the client's written consent.

Should Selected Information Be Withheld?

The question raised here is different from that discussed in the preceding section, in that we are now concerned with the advisability of reporting "good" things and withholding "bad" things. Ralph Santaro, for example, told his counselor in the third interview that he had named the latter as a reference in applying for a job as a salesman. If the employer telephoned or wrote with a request for information, what should the counselor report—that Ralph lacks self-confidence, that his measured sales aptitude is below average as compared with employed salesmen, and that his mechanical aptitudes are higher than those for sales? Or should he omit all these facts and report only that Ralph is above average in

---

[6] It is assumed here that the individual who took the tests is the client. In those instances in which the client is the present or prospective employer, the situation is reversed, and only limited information may be given to the testee.

intelligence, that he speaks easily and expresses himself well, and that he is eager to succeed on the job? Suppose a prospective employer calls the school from which the applicant recently graduated, asking for an appraisal. Should *all* relevant information from the record be reported, or should emphasis be given to those data which are favorable to the individual?

Our own practice has been to inform counselees, when they ask if we will send a report or act as a reference to an employer, that we will do so upon the client's written request, but that we must report all the facts that appear to be relevant—both favorable and unfavorable. In effect, we refuse to act as an endorser or recommender, but rather as an objective professional consultant. The counselee decides whether he wishes a report sent under these conditions. This arrangement permits the counselor to maintain his professional integrity and to respect the confidentiality of case materials. Of course, it is only natural that counselors will exert somewhat greater effort to find favorable things to report about clients than unfavorable. This is not the same, however, as consciously omitting unfavorable information which is clearly pertinent to the questions asked by the person getting the report. To seek out the favorable is a very human kind of behavior; consciously to omit the unfavorable is to play the role of attorney, friend, or public relations man, none of which is an appropriate role for counselors.

This problem is usually of lesser concern when reports are to professional workers, such as psychotherapists, social workers, and personnel workers in schools. Although there are exceptions, it should generally be correct to assume that these people practice within a code of ethics and are concerned primarily with service to clients. Having obtained the client's permission to send a report, all relevant information may then be included—unfavorable as well as favorable.

A related problem is that of the school counselor who reports test results or their interpretations to classroom teachers, but who knows that certain teachers may misuse the information or violate the confidence. An equally ticklish situation arises when such a teacher approaches the counselor asking for information about a particular pupil's test results. The idealistic answer, of course, is that teachers are trained professional people and that one may therefore assume that they are both willing and able to treat confidential information with discretion and good judgment. Realistically, however, there are few school systems in which it can be assumed that *all* teachers have both requisites: professional competence and professional attitudes. The dilemma is not easily resolved. At the very least, however, counselors should, in conjunction with responsible administrators, evolve a policy to guide their day-by-day actions. The specific policy will depend on the caliber of the faculty, as well as on the personal predilections of the school's administrative and guidance staff.

Some will lean in the direction of a liberal policy, perhaps with the hope that even the less professional teachers will be stimulated to function at a higher level by the information given them. Others will tend to withhold information from *all* teachers because of the danger of abuse by some. Some will work entirely or primarily on an individual basis with teachers, revealing to each whatever they feel that person is capable of handling; the great danger here is that some teachers may find that they have been denied information which is freely shared with others.

Specific Contents and Format of Report

This is largely an individual matter, but just a few general points can be made (Di Michael, 1948; Hammond and Allen, 1953). First, the report should be aimed as directly as possible to the particular questions asked; this is a rather obvious matter of economy of time and of adequate communication. To be avoided is the stereotyped quality which so often characterizes reports of psychologists in schools and elsewhere. If a specific question is asked, say, about a youngster's potentialities for learning something-or-other or about his suitability for a special class, it can often be answered without relating all the tedious details about his "fund of information," "social comprehension," "attention span," "responsiveness to stimuli from his environment," which are soon recognized as a score-by-score run-down of the intelligence and personality tests used or rigid adherence to an outline learned in a graduate course.

It is usually helpful to have a terse summary-and-conclusion paragraph at the end, for the convenience of the reader. This is especially desirable with long reports. A summary also forces the report writer to organize his thoughts, to select the most important points, and perhaps also to relate them to the specific purposes of the report.

Finally, brief mention may be made of a rather specialized kind of report which seems to be a novel and worthwhile idea. This is a report to colleges by a high school, which describes the students of that high school, and particularly its senior class.[7] This is now the reverse of a growing practice among colleges, of feeding-back information to high schools, in order that students may choose more wisely (see Tables 6.1, 7.1, 13.3, 13.4, and 13.5 for illustrations). This high school's guidance staff felt that colleges could choose more wisely among applicants if they had more information about the school. The three-page printed report therefore includes information about the distribution of IQ's and of College Board test scores in the school, as well as explanations of the school's grading system and special curricular arrangements.

[7] The author is indebted to Arthur E. Pankow, College Consultant at Amherst Central High School, Snyder, New York, for supplying a copy of the report.

REPORTING TO PARENTS

Those who work with children and adolescents are well aware of the fact that often it is the parents rather than the children who are most in need of the information provided by tests. Try as we may to help youngsters to develop self-sufficiency and independence in making their adjustments and plans, experience teaches us that their conflicts and their unrealistic plans are often reflections of parental attitudes. In many of these cases little change can be hoped for without parental involvement in counseling. Managing an interview in which both parent and child are present and maintaining a fairly objective position with regard to both calls for all the art and science we can command, but it can be an instructive and productive experience. One of the best ways to understand the irrational goals and emotional behavior of a youngster whose problems stem in part from the home, is to observe the parent-child relationship as it is actually lived in the counseling office. It is a difficult situation to handle but well worth the effort, in terms both of the additional insights it may provide, as well as its contribution toward problem-solving.

One of the errors frequently made by counselors who invite parents in for interviews is to assume that the parent, unlike his child, is quite reasonable and objective about the matter, and that all that one need do is present the facts. Actually, parents bring to interviews many of the same kinds of unreasonable aspirations, blind spots, and defense mechanisms as their children. To be effective with parents, then, one should be ready to give enough time, perhaps to have more than one interview, and to deal with the feelings and attitudes involved.

Another error is to fall into the trap of taking sides, either with child or parent. There may indeed be extreme cases in which one is justified in doing this, but more often it is a mistake, because the counselor finds it increasingly difficult in such situations to remain objective. As a result, there may be *three* unreasonable and emotion-driven people in the room instead of two. It is a ticklish business, trying to avoid identification with one or the other protagonist when there is conflict between parent and child, especially since the counselor finds himself sometimes in agreement with one, sometimes with the other, sometimes with neither. It is possible, however, to play this role, stating explicitly if necessary, the "ground rules" by which we operate.

As to the specific techniques of reporting tests to parents, little need be added to the principles previously defined. One tries to understand the purposes of the parent in seeking information about his child. One tries to communicate in language and in concepts which are comprehendible and meaningful. One uses the interview both to test the validity of interpretations further (thus continuing the appraisal process) and to help the parent to understand and accept them.[8]

An interesting specific technique for reporting test data to parents was described by Hoover and Micka (1956). In a farm-area high school, juniors and their parents take the *Kuder Preference Record* at the same time, the students answering in the usual manner, but the parents answering as they think their sons and daughters would. A composite graph is prepared, using different colors to show the three profiles: students' preferences, mother's scores, and father's scores. Later the counselors have joint interviews with parents and child, at which time there is an attempt to reconcile differences, if any, and to plan for the future. The study lacks controls, so it is not possible to conclude that the changes observed are the result of this particular technique rather than of anything else. However, the authors report several facts which they feel can be viewed as indicators of the success of this particular method: First, before the project began, 10 per cent of the graduates sought further training, but for the period of 4 to 7 years afterward the rate was 35 per cent (without controls, there is no way to know that this would not have happened anyhow, perhaps as a result of changing economic and social conditions, or of improved guidance services in general). Second, they report improved school-community relations, including active support of the guidance program and of other activities of the school. Third, almost 100 per cent attendance is reported at the meetings during which the interest inventory is administered, and it is felt that parent-child relationships are improved as these matters are considered and discussed by both together.

A small group conference technique for reporting to both students and their parents is reported by Bidwell and Temple (1957). Each group consists of about six to eight students of a similar level of ability and achievement, and their parents. The counselors explain test results both in terms of national norms (using percentiles) and local norms (using stanines). They report favorable response from parents during the five years that the program was then in operation.

From informal observations, it appears that there is an increasing tendency to invite parents to share test interpretations. Some schools schedule evening hours specifically for this purpose. Others use both group and individual sessions with parents on a routine basis, in some instances making this a requirement before a student's program of studies is approved. Counselors in schools and in agencies which deal with adolescents might well consider the possible values of increased work with the parents of their clients.

---

[8] A number of helpful specific suggestions for reporting to parents are contained in a recent *Test Service Bulletin* (Ricks, 1959).

Bibliography

American Educational Research Association, 1955. *Technical recommendations for achievement tests*. Washington: National Education Association.

American Psychological Association, American Educational Research Association, & National Council on Measurements Used in Education, Joint Committee, 1954. Technical recommendations for psychological tests and diagnostic techniques. Supplement to *Psychol. Bull.*, 51, No. 2.

American Psychological Association, Committee on Ethical Standards for Psychology, 1953. *Ethical standards of psychologists*. Washington: American Psychological Association.

American Psychological Association, Committee on Ethical Standards of Psychologists, 1958. Standards of ethical behavior for psychologists. *Amer. Psychologist*, 13, 266-271.

ANASTASI, A., 1954. *Psychological testing*. New York: Macmillan.

ANDERHALTER, O. F., 1954. An application of profile similarity techniques to Rorschach data on 2161 Marine Corps officer candidates. *Proceedings 1953 invitational conference on testing problems*. Princeton, N.J.: Educational Testing Service, pp. 47-53.

ANGELL, M. A., 1959. Multiple differential prediction: significance for college academic counseling. *Personnel guid. J.*, 37, 418-423.

ARNHOFF, F. N., 1954. Some factors influencing the unreliability of clinical judgments. *Dissertation Abstr.*, 14, 867-868. (Abstract).

ASCH, M. J., 1958. Negative response bias and personality adjustment. *J. counsel. Psychol.*, 5, 206-210.

BAKER, R. L., & DOYLE, R. P., 1959. Teacher knowledge of pupil data and marking practices at the elementary school level. *Personnel guid. J.*, 37, 644-647.

BARNETTE, W. L., JR., 1955. Diagnostic features of the *AGCT*. *J. soc. Psychol.*, 42, 241-247.

BARRETT, R. S., 1958. The process of predicting job performance. *Personnel Psychol.*, 11, 39-55.

BAYLEY, N., 1957. A new look at the curve of intelligence. *Proceedings 1956 invitational conference on testing problems*. Princeton, N. J.: Educational Testing Service, pp. 11-25.

BEILIN, H., 1956. The utilization of high level talent in lower socioeconomic groups. *Personnel guid. J.*, 35, 175-178.

BENNETT, G. K., SEASHORE, H. G., & WESMAN, A. G., 1951. *Counseling from profiles*. New York: Psychological Corporation.

BENNETT, G. K., SEASHORE, H. G., & WESMAN, A. G., 1956. The Differential Aptitude Tests: an overview. *Personnel guid. J.*, 35, 81-91.

BERDIE, R. F., 1954. Changes in self-ratings as a method of evaluating counseling. *J. counsel. Psychol.*, 1, 49-54.

BERDIE, R. F., 1955. Aptitude, achievement, interest and personality tests: a longitudinal comparison. *J. appl. Psychol.*, 39, 103-114.

BERG, I. A., 1956. Test score interpretation and client confusions. *Personnel guid. J.*, 34, 576-578.

BIDWELL, M. B., & TEMPLE, E. S., 1957. Small group counseling conferences at the senior high school level. *Test Serv. Bull.* (World Book Company), No. 87.

BIXLER, R. H., & BIXLER, V. H., 1946. Test interpretation in vocational counseling. *Educ. psychol. Measmt.*, 6, 145-155.

BLADE, M. F., & WATSON, W. S., 1955. Increase in spatial visualization test scores during engineering study. *Psychol. Monogr.*, 69, No. 12 (Whole No. 397).

BLOCK, J., LEVINE, L., & McNEMAR, Q., 1951. Testing for the existence of psychometric patterns. *J. abnorm. soc. Psychol.*, 46, 356-359.

BLOOM, B. S., & BRODER, L. J., 1950. Problem-solving processes of college students. *Suppl. educ. Monogr.*, No. 73.

BORDIN, E. S., 1946. Diagnosis in counseling and psychotherapy. *Educ. psychol. Measmt.*, 6, 169-184.

BORDIN, E. S., 1955. *Psychological counseling.* New York: Appleton-Century-Crofts.

BORDIN, E. S., & BIXLER, R. H., 1946. Test selection: a process of counseling. *Educ. psychol. Measmt.*, 6, 361-373.

BOWMAN, H. A., 1952. Techniques for graphical representation of pupil personnel data to indicate individual deviates and to provide a basis for more adequate guidance. *Educ. psychol. Measmt.*, 12, 490-502.

BRANSON, B. D., 1960. Anxiety, discrimination, and self-ideal discrepancy. *Personnel guid. J.*, 38, 373-377.

BROSS, I. D., 1953. *Design for decision.* New York: Macmillan.

BROWN, C. W., & GHISELLI, E. E., 1949. Age of semiskilled workers in relation to abilities and interests. *Personnel Psychol.*, 2, 497-511.

BUCKTON, L., & DOPPELT, J. E., 1950. The use of selection tests at Brooklyn College. *Occupations*, 28, 357-360.

BUROS, O. K., (Ed.), 1938. *The 1938 mental measurements yearbook.* New Brunswick, N. J.: Rutgers University Press.

BUROS, O. K. (Ed.), 1941. *The nineteen forty mental measurements yearbook.* New Brunswick, N. J.: Rutgers University Press.

BUROS, O. K. (Ed.), 1949. *The third mental measurements yearbook.* New Brunswick, N. J.: Rutgers University Press.

BUROS, O. K. (Ed.), 1953. *The fourth mental measurements yearbook.* Highland Park, N. J.: Gryphon Press.

BUROS, O. K. (Ed.), 1959. *The fifth mental measurements yearbook.* Highland Park, N. J.: Gryphon Press.

CALLIS, R., ENGRAM, W. C., & McGOWAN, J. F., 1954. Coding the Kuder Preference Record—Vocational. *J. appl. Psychol.*, 38, 359-363.

CALLIS, R., POLMANTIER, P. C., & ROEBER, E. C., 1955. *A casebook of counseling.* New York: Appleton-Century-Crofts.

CARLSON, J. S., & FULLMER, D. W., 1959. *College norms.* Eugene, Ore.: Counseling Center, University of Oregon.

CARPENTER, S. J., COTTLE, W. C., & GREEN, G. W., 1959. Test usage in state vocational rehabilitation. *Personnel guid. J.*, 38, 128-133.

CARRILLO, L. W., JR., & REICHART, R. R., 1952. The use of a "caution factor" to increase the predictive value of the A.C.E. examination for students of engineering. *J. educ. Res.*, 45, 361-368.

Chicago Public Schools, Bureau of Child Guidance, undated. *Equivalence of intelligence quotients of five group intelligence tests.* Chicago: Author.

COFER, C. N., CHANCE, J., & JUDSON, A. J., 1949. A study of malingering on the Minnesota Multiphasic Personality Inventory. *J. Psychol.,* 27, 491-499.

COLEMAN, W., & WARD, A. W., 1956. Further evidence of the jangle fallacy. *Educ. psychol. Measmt.,* 16, 524-526.

CONGDON, R. G., & JERVIS, F. M., 1958. A different approach to interest profiles. *J. counsel. Psychol.,* 5, 50-55.

CRITES, J. O., 1959. A coding system for total profile analysis of the Strong Vocational Interest Blank. *J. appl. Psychol.,* 43, 176-179.

CRONBACH, L. J., 1950. Further evidence on response sets and test design. *Educ. psychol. Measmt.,* 10, 3-31.

CRONBACH, L. J., 1955. New light on test strategy from decision theory. *Proceedings 1954 invitational conference on testing problems.* Princeton, N. J.: Educational Testing Service, pp. 30-36.

CRONBACH, L. J., 1957. The two disciplines of scientific psychology. *Amer. Psychologist,* 12, 671-684.

CRONBACH, L. J., 1960. *Essentials of psychological testing.* (2nd ed.) New York: Harper.

CRONBACH, L. J., & GLESER, G. C., 1957. *Psychological tests and personnel decisions.* Urbana: University of Illinois Press.

CROSS, O. H., 1950. A study of faking on the Kuder Preference Record. *Educ. psychol. Measmt.,* 10, 271-277.

DAILEY, C. A., 1958. The life history approach to assessment. *Personnel guid. J.,* 36, 456-460.

DARLEY, J. G., & HAGENAH, T., 1955. *Vocational interest measurement.* Minneapolis: University of Minnesota Press.

DARLEY, J. G., & MARQUIS, D. G., 1946. Veterans guidance centers: a survey of their problems and activities. *J. clin. Psychol.,* 2, 109-116.

DAVIS, F. B., 1959. Interpretation of differences among averages and individual test scores. *J. educ. Psychol.,* 50, 162-170.

DAVIS, J. A., 1959. Non-apparent limitations of normative data. *Personnel guid. J.* 37, 656-659.

DELONG, A. R., 1955. Emotional effects of elementary school testing. *Understanding the Child,* 24, 103-107.

DERATH, G., & CARP, F. M., 1959. The Picture-Choice Test as an indirect measure of attitudes. *J. appl. Psychol.,* 43, 12-15.

DIENER, C. L., 1960. Similarities and differences between over-achieving and under-achieving students. *Personnel guid. J.,* 38, 396-400.

DIFFENBAUGH, D. J., 1950. Thumb-nail sketches help teachers. *Occupations,* 28, 230-232.

DIMICHAEL, S. G., 1948. Characteristics of a desirable psychological report to the vocational counselor. *J. consult. Psychol.,* 12, 432-437.

DIMICHAEL, S. G., 1951. Interest-inventory results during the counseling interview. *Occupations,* 30, 93-97.

DINGILIAN, D. H., 1956. How basic organization influences testing. *Proceedings 1955 invitational conference on testing problems.* Princeton, N. J.: Educational Testing Service, pp. 66-77.

DIVESTA, F. J., 1954. Subscore patterns on ACE Psychological Examination related to educational and occupational differences. *J. appl. Psychol.*, 38, 248-252.

DOLE, A. A., 1958. The Vocational Sentence Completion Blank in counseling. *J. counsel. Psychol.*, 5, 200-205.

DOPPELT, J. E., 1954. The correction for guessing. *Test Serv. Bull.* (Psychological Corporation), No. 46, 1-4.

DORCUS, R. M., & JONES, M. H., 1950. *Handbook of employee selection.* New York: McGraw-Hill.

DRAGOSITZ, A., & McCAMBRIDGE, B., 1952. Types of tests and their uses in college testing programs. *Amer. Psychologist*, 7, 299-300 (Abstract).

DRAKE, L. E., & OETTING, E. R., 1959. *An MMPI codebook for counselors.* Minneapolis: University of Minnesota Press.

DRASGOW, J., & McKENZIE, J., 1958. College transcripts, graduation, and the MMPI. *J. counsel. Psychol.*, 5, 196-199.

DRESSEL, P. L., & MATTESON, R. W., 1950. The effect of client participation in test interpretation. *Educ. psychol. Measmt.*, 10, 693-706.

DUMAS, F. M., 1949. The coefficient of profile similarity. *J. clin. Psychol.*, 5, 123-131.

DUMAS, F. M., 1953. Quick methods for the analysis of the shape, elevation, and scatter of profiles. *J. clin. Psychol.*, 9, 345-348.

DUNN, F. E., 1959. Two methods for predicting the selection of a college major. *J. counsel. Psychol.*, 6, 15-26.

DUNNETTE, M. D., & KIRCHNER, W. K., 1960. Psychological test differences between industrial salesmen and retail salesmen. *J. appl. Psychol.*, 44, 121-125.

DUROST, W. N., 1954. Present progress and needed improvements in school evaluation programs. *Educ. psychol. Measmt.*, 14, 247-254.

DUROST, W. N., 1959. The use of local stanines in reporting test results in a large cosmopolitan school system. *Sixteenth Yearbook of the National Council on Measurements Used in Education*, pp. 140-147.

DYER, H. S., 1953. Does coaching help? *Coll. Bd. Rev.*, No. 19, 331-335.

DYER, H. S., 1957. The need for do-it-yourself prediction research in high school guidance. *Personnel guid. J.*, 36, 162-167.

EBEL, R. L., 1954. The characteristics and usefulness of rate scores on college aptitude tests. *Educ. psychol. Measmt.*, 14, 20-28.

EBEL, R. L., 1959. What kinds of tests for college admission and scholarship programs? *Proceedings 1958 invitational conference on testing problems.* Princeton, N. J.: Educational Testing Service, pp. 88-97.

Educational Records Bureau, 1955. Comparison between Terman IQ's and Otis IQ's for a group of independent-school boys. *Educ. Rec. Bull.*, No. 66, 78-79.

EDWARDS, A. L., 1957. *The social desirability variable in personality assessment and research.* New York: Dryden.

ENGELHART, M. D., 1959. Obtaining comparable scores on two or more tests. *Educ. psychol. Measmt.*, 19, 55-64.

FAILOR, C. W., & MAHLER, C. A., 1949. Examining counselors' selection of tests. *Occupations*, 28, 164-167.

FLANAGAN, J. C., 1951. The use of comprehensive rationales in test development. *Educ. psychol. Measmt.*, 11, 151-155.

FLANAGAN, J. C., 1955. The development of an index of examinee motivation. *Educ. psychol. Measmt.*, 15, 144-151.

FLANAGAN, J. C., 1959. Criteria for selecting tests for college admissions and scholarship programs. *Proceedings 1958 invitational conference on testing problems.* Princeton, N. J.: Educational Testing Service, pp. 98-103.

FLANAGAN, J. C., & DAILEY, J. T., 1959. Prospectus for the Talent Search. *Personnel guid. J.*, 37, 387-389.

FORBES, F. W., & COTTLE, W. C., 1953. A new method for determining readability of standardized tests. *J. appl. Psychol.*, 37, 185-190.

FOREHAND, G. A., JR., & McQUITTY, L. L., 1959. Configurations of factor standings as predictors of educational achievement. *Educ. psychol. Measmt.*, 19, 31-43.

FORER, B. R., 1949. The fallacy of personal validation: a classroom demonstration of gullibility. *J. abnorm. soc. Psychol.*, 44, 118-123.

FORGY, E. W., & BLACK, J. D., 1954. A follow-up after three years of clients counseled by two methods. *J. counsel. Psychol.*, 1, 1-7.

FRANDSEN, A., 1947. Interests and general educational development. *J. appl. Psychol.*, 31, 57-66.

FRANDSEN, A., 1952. A note on Wiener's coding of Kuder Preference Record profiles. *Educ. psychol. Measmt.*, 12, 137-139.

FRANDSEN, A., & SESSIONS, A. D., 1953. Interests and school achievement. *Educ. psychol. Measmt.*, 13, 94-101.

FRANZBLAU, A. N., 1958. *A primer of statistics for non-statisticians.* New York: Harcourt, Brace.

FREDERIKSEN, N., & MELVILLE, S. D., 1954. Differential predictability in the use of test scores. *Educ. psychol. Measmt.*, 14, 647-656.

FRENCH, J. W., 1956. The logic of and assumptions underlying differential testing. *Proceedings 1955 invitational conference on testing problems.* Princeton, N. J.: Educational Testing Service, pp. 40-48.

FRENCH, J. W., & DEAR, R. E., 1959. Effect of coaching on an aptitude test. *Educ. psychol. Measmt.*, 19, 319-330.

FROEHLICH, C. P., 1954. Does test taking change self ratings? *Calif. J. educ. Res.*, 5, 166-169; 175.

FROEHLICH, C. P., 1957. A criterion for counseling. *Psychol. Monogr.*, 71, No. 15 (Whole No. 444).

FROEHLICH, C. P., & MOSER, W. E., 1954. Do counselees remember test scores? *J. counsel. Psychol.*, 1, 149-152.

FRUCHTER, B., 1950. Error scores as a measure of carefulness. *J. educ. Psychol.*, 41, 279-291.

FRYER, D. H., & HENRY, E. R. (Eds.), 1950. *Handbook of applied psychology.* New York: Rinehart. 2 vols.

FURST, E. J., & FRICKE, B. G., 1956. Development and applications of structured tests of personality. *Rev. educ. Res.*, 26, 26-55.

GARRETT, H. F., 1949. A review and interpretation of investigations of factors related to scholastic success in colleges of arts and science and teachers colleges. *J. exp. Educ.*, 18, 91-138.

GARRETT, H. E., 1958. *Statistics in psychology and education.* (5th ed.) New York: Longmans, Green.

GARRY, R., 1953. Individual differences in ability to fake vocational interests. *J. appl. Psychol.*, 37, 33-37.

GEBHART, G. G., & HOYT, D. P., 1958. Personality needs of under- and overachieving freshmen. *J. appl. Psychol.*, 42, 125-128.

GEHMAN, W. S., 1957. A study of ability to fake scores on the Strong Vocational Interest Blank for Men. *Educ. psychol. Measmt.*, 17, 65-70.

GHISELLI, E. E., 1955. The measurement of occupational aptitude. *Univer. Calif. publ. Psychol.*, 8, 101-216.

GHISELLI, E. E., 1956. Differentiation of individuals in terms of their predictability. *J. appl. Psychol.*, 40, 374-377.

GLASER, R., DAMRIN, D. E., & GARDNER, F. M., 1954. The Tab Item: a technique for the measurement of proficiency in diagnostic problem solving tasks. *Educ. psychol. Measmt.*, 14, 283-293.

GOLDMAN, L., 1951. Relationship between aptitude scores and certain Rorschach indices. *Microfilm Abstr.*, 11 (2), 421-423. (Abstract).

GOLDMAN, L., 1954. Counseling: content and process. *Personnel guid. J.*, 33, 82-85.

GORDON, E. M., & SARASON, S. B., 1955. The relationship between "test anxiety" and "other anxieties." *J. Pers.*, 23, 317-323.

GRANT, C. W., 1954. How students perceive the counselor's role. *Personnel guid. J.*, 32, 386-388.

GREEN, R. F., 1951. Does a selection situation induce testees to bias their answers on interest and temperament tests? *Educ. psychol. Measmt.*, 11, 503-515.

GREENE, E. B., 1952. *Measurements of human behavior.* (Rev. ed.). New York: Odyssey.

GREENE, H. A., JORGENSEN, A. N., & GERBERICH, J. R., 1953. *Measurement and evaluation in the elementary school.* (2nd ed.). New York: Longmans, Green.

GREENE, H. A., JORGENSEN, A. N., & GERBERICH, J. R., 1954. *Measurement and evaluation in the secondary school.* (2nd ed.). New York: Longmans, Green.

GUSTAD, J. W., 1951a. Test information and learning in the counseling process. *Educ. psychol. Measmt.*, 11, 788-795.

GUSTAD, J. W., 1951b. Vocational interests and Q-L scores on the A.C.E. *J. appl. Psychol.*, 35, 164-168.

GUSTAD, J. W., 1957. The evaluation interview in vocational counseling. *Personnel guid. J.*, 36, 242-250.

GUSTAD, J. W., & TUMA, A. H., 1957. The effects of different methods of test introduction and interpretation on client learning in counseling. *J. counsel. Psychol.*, 4, 313-317.

HAHN, M. E., 1955. Counseling psychology. *Amer. Psychologist*, 10, 279-282.

HAHN, M. E., & McLEAN, M. S., 1955. *Counseling psychology.* New York: McGraw-Hill.

HAMMOND, K. R., & ALLEN, J. M., JR., 1953. *Writing clinical reports.* Englewood Cliffs, N. J.: Prentice-Hall.

HANES, B., & HALLIDAY, R. W., 1954. Unfavorable conditions in intelligence testing. *J. genet. Psychol.*, 85, 151-154.

HANNA, J. V., 1950. The test-obsessed client. *Occupations*, 28, 244-246.

HANNA, J. V., 1952. Use of speed tests in guidance. *Occupations*, 30, 329-331.

HART, I., 1957. Using stanines to obtain composite scores based on test data and teachers' ranks. *Test Serv. Bull.* (World Book Company), No. 86.

HATHAWAY, S. R., 1947. A coding system for MMPI profile classification. *J. consult. Psychol.*, 11, 334-337.

HATHAWAY, S. R., & MEEHL, P. E., 1951. *An atlas for the clinical use of the MMPI.* Minneapolis: University of Minnesota Press.

HAY, E. N., 1950. A warm-up test. *Personnel Psychol.*, 3, 221-223.

HENDERSON, M. T., CREWS, A., & BARLOW, J., 1945. A study of the effect of music distraction on reading efficiency. *J. appl. Psychol.*, 29, 313-317.

HILL, G. E., 1959. *Evaluating the school's testing program.* Pupil Services Series, No. 2. Athens, Ohio: Center for Educational Service, College of Education, Ohio University.

HILL, J. M., 1954. The effects of artificially measured low aptitude test scores on change in vocational interest. *Dissertation Abstr.*, 14, 781. (Abstract).

HILLS, J. R., FRANZ, G., & EMORY, L. B., 1959. Counselor's guide to Georgia colleges. Atlanta: Office of Testing and Guidance, Regents, University System of Georgia, 244 Washington Street, S. W., Atlanta 3, Georgia.

HOBBS, N., & SEEMAN, J., 1955. Counseling. *Annu. Rev. Psychol.*, 6, 379-404.

HOLLOWAY, H. D., 1954. Effects of training on the SRA Primary Mental Abilities (Primary) and the WISC. *Child. Develop.*, 25, 253-263.

HOLT, R. R., 1958. Clinical *and* statistical prediction: a reformulation and some new data. *J. abnorm. soc. Psychol.*, 56, 1-12.

HOLTZMAN, W. H., & SELLS, S. B., 1954. Prediction of flying success by clinical analysis of test protocols. *J. abnorm. soc. Psychol.*, 49, 485-490.

HOOVER, K. H., & MICKA, H. K., 1956. Student-parent interest comparisons in counseling high school students. *Personnel guid. J.*, 34, 292-294.

HORROCKS, J. E., & NAGY, G., 1948. The relationship between the ability to make a diagnosis and to select appropriate remedial procedures. *J. gen. Psychol.*, 38, 139-146.

HORST, P., 1954a. Pattern analysis and configural scoring. *J. clin. Psychol.*, 10, 1-11.

HORST, P., 1954b. A technique for the development of a differential prediction battery. *Psychol. Monogr.*, 68, No. 9. (Whole No. 380).

HORST, P., 1955. A technique for the development of a multiple absolute prediction battery. *Psychol. Monogr.*, 69, No. 5. (Whole No. 390).

HORST, P., 1956. Educational and vocational counseling from the actuarial point of view. *Personnel guid. J.*, 35, 164-170.

HOYT, D. P., & NORMAN, W. T., 1954. Adjustment and academic predictability. *J. counsel. Psychol.*, 1, 96-99.

HUMPHREYS, L. G., 1956. Clinical versus actuarial prediction. *Proceedings 1955 invitational conference on testing problems.* Princeton, N. J.: Educational Testing Service, pp. 129-135.

JAMES, W. S., 1953. Symposium on the effects of coaching and practice in intelligence tests. II Coaching for all recommended. *Brit. J. Psychol.*, 23, 155-162.

JASTAK, J., 1949. Problems of psychometric scatter analysis. *Psychol. Bull.*, 46, 177-197.

JERISON, H. J., 1959. Effects of noise on human performance. *J. appl. Psychol.*, 43, 96-101.

JERSILD, A. T., 1957. *The psychology of adolescence.* New York: Macmillan.

JOHNSON, D. G., 1953. Effect of vocational counseling on self-knowledge. *Educ. psychol. Measmt.*, 13, 330-338.

JOHNSON, R. H., & BOND, G. L., 1950. Reading ease of commonly used tests. *J. appl. Psychol.*, 34, 319-324.

JONES, H. L., & SAWYER, M. O., 1949. A new evaluation instrument. *J. educ. Res.*, 42, 381-385.

JONES, S., 1953. Process testing—an attempt to analyze reasons for students' responses to test questions. *J. educ. Res.*, 46, 525-534.

JUSTMAN, J., & WRIGHTSTONE, J. W., 1953. A comparison of pupil functioning on the Pintner Intermediate Test and the Henmon-Nelson Test of Mental Ability. *Educ. psychol. Measmt.*, 13, 102-109.

KAMM, R. B., & WRENN, C. G., 1950. Client acceptance of self-information in counseling. *Educ. psychol. Measmt.*, 10, 32-42.

KAYE, D., KIRSCHNER, P., & MANDLER, G., 1953. The effect of test anxiety on memory span in a group test situation. *J. consult. Psychol.*, 17, 265-266.

KAZMIER, L. J., & BROWNE, C. G., 1959. Comparability of Wonderlic Test forms in industrial testing. *J. appl. Psychol.*, 43, 129-132.

KELLY, E. L., & FISKE, D. W., 1951. *The prediction of performance in clinical psychology*. Ann Arbor: University of Michigan Press.

KIRK, B. A., 1952. Individualizing of test interpretation. *Occupations*, 30, 500-505.

KITSON, H. D., 1942. Creating vocational interests. *Occupations*, 20, 567-571.

KOESTER, G. A., 1954. A study of the diagnostic process. *Educ. psychol. Measmt.*, 14, 473-486.

KRATHWOHL, W. C., 1949a. An index of industriousness for English. *J. educ. Psychol.*, 40, 469-481.

KRATHWOHL, W. C., 1949b. The persistence in college of industrious and indolent work habits. *J. educ. Res.*, 42, 365-370.

KRATHWOHL, W. C., 1952. Specificity of over- and under-achievement in college courses. *J. appl. Psychol.*, 36, 103-106.

KRATHWOHL, W. C., 1953. Relative contributions of aptitude and work habits to achievement in college mathematics. *J. educ. Psychol.*, 44, 140-148.

KROPP, R. P., 1953. An evaluation of two methods of test interpretation and the related analysis of oral problem-solving processes. *Dissertation Abstr.*, 13, 1090. (Abstract).

KRUG, R. E., 1959. Over- and underachievement and the Edwards Personal Preference Schedule. *J. appl. Psychol.*, 43, 133-136.

KRUMBOLTZ, J. D., 1957. The relation of extracurricular participation to leadership criteria. *Personnel guid. J.*, 35, 307-314.

KRUMBOLTZ, J. D., & CHRISTAL, R. E., 1960. Short-term practice effects in tests of spatial aptitude. *Personnel guid. J.*, 38, 385-391.

KUDER, G. F., 1950. Identifying the faker. *Personnel Psychol.*, 3, 155-167.

LALLAS, J. E., 1956. A comparison of three methods of interpretation of the results of achievement tests to pupils. *Dissertation Abstr.*, 16, 1842. (Abstract).

LANE, D., 1952. A comparison of two techniques of interpreting test results to clients in vocational counseling. *Dissertation Abstr.*, 12, 591-592. (Abstract).

LAYTON, W. L., 1958. *Counseling use of the Strong Vocational Interest Blank.* Minneapolis: University of Minnesota Press.

LENNON, R. T., 1954. Testing: bond or barrier between pupil and teacher? *Education*, 75, 38-42.

LENNON, R. T., undated. A comparison of results of three intelligence tests. *Test Serv. Notebook* (World Book Company), No. 11.

LINDQUIST, E. F. (Ed.), 1951. *Educational measurement.* Washington: American Council on Education.

LINDQUIST, E. F., 1959. The nature of the problem of improving scholarship and college entrance examinations. *Proceedings 1958 invitational conference on testing problems.* Princeton, N. J.: Educational Testing Service, pp. 104-113.

LINS, L. J., 1950. Probability approach to forecasting university success with measured grades as the criterion. *Educ. psychol. Measmt.*, 10, 386-391.

LIPTON, R. L., 1956. A study of the effect of exercise in a simple mechanical activity on mechanical aptitude as is measured by the subtests of the MacQuarrie Test for Mechanical Ability. *Psychol. Newsltr, NYU*, 7, 39-42.

LOEVINGER, J., 1957. The nature of validity. Paper read at Amer. Psychol. Ass., New York, September, 1957.

LOFQUIST, L. H., 1957. *Vocational counseling with the physically handicapped.* New York: Appleton-Century-Crofts.

LONGSTAFF, H. P., 1948. Fakability of the Strong Interest Blank and the Kuder Preference Record. *J. appl. Psychol.*, 32, 360-369.

LONGSTAFF, H. P., 1954. Practice effects on the Minnesota Vocational Test for Clerical Workers. *J. appl. Psychol.*, 38, 18-20.

LONGSTAFF, H. P., & JURGENSEN, C. E., 1953. Fakability of the Jurgensen Classification Inventory. *J. appl. Psychol.*, 37, 86-89.

Los Angeles City School Districts, Curriculum Division, 1950. *A comparative study of the data for five different intelligence tests administered to 284 twelfth-grade students at South Gate High School.* Los Angeles: Los Angeles City Schools.

LUBIN, A., 1954. A methodological study of configural scoring. *USA Personnel Res. Br. Note*, No. 42.

McARTHUR, C., 1954a. Analyzing the clinical process. *J. counsel. Psychol.*, 1, 203-208.

McARTHUR, C., 1954b. Long-term validity of the Strong Interest Test in two subcultures. *J. appl. Psychol.*, 38, 346-353.

McARTHUR, C., 1956. Clinical versus actuarial prediction. *Proceedings 1955 invitational conference on testing problems.* Princeton, N. J.: Educational Testing Service, pp. 99-106.

McARTHUR, C., & STEVENS, L. B., 1955. The validation of expressed interests as compared with inventoried interests: a fourteen-year follow-up. *J. appl. Psychol.*, 39, 184-189.

McCABE, G. E., 1956. How substantial is a substantial validity coefficient? *Personnel guid. J.*, 34, 340-344.

McCABE, G. E., 1957. Test interpretation in the high school guidance program. *Personnel guid. J.*, 35, 449-451.

McKEACHIE, W. J., POLLIE, D., & SPEISMAN, J., 1955. Relieving anxiety in classroom examinations. *J. abnorm. soc. Psychol.*, 50, 93-98.

McQUARY, J. P., & TRUAX, W. E., JR., 1955. An under-achievement scale. *J. educ. Res.*, 48, 393-399.

MAIS, R. D., 1951. Fakability of the Classification Inventory scored for self-confidence. *J. appl. Psychol.*, 35, 172-174.

MALLOY, J. P., & GRAHAM, L. F., 1954. Group orientation in guidance services. *Personnel guid. J.*, 33, 97-98.

MANDLER, G., & SARASON, S. B., 1952. A study of anxiety and learning. *J. abnorm. soc. Psychol.*, 47, 166-173.

A manual of norms for tests used in counseling blind persons, 1958. Research Series No. 6. New York: American Foundation for the Blind.

MARTIN, B., & McGOWAN, B., 1955. Some evidence on the validity of the Sarason Test Anxiety Scale. *J. consult. Psychol.*, 19, 468.

MATHEWSON, R. H., 1955. *Guidance policy and practice.* (2nd ed.) New York: Harper.

MATTESON, R. W., 1956. Self-estimates of college freshmen. *Personnel guid. J.*, 34, 280-284.

MAXWELL, J., 1954. Educational psychology. *Annu. Rev. Psychol.*, 5, 357-376.

MAYO, G. D., & GUTTMAN, I., 1959. Faking in a vocational classification situation. *J. appl. Psychol.*, 43, 117-121.

MEEHL, P. E., 1950. Configural scoring. *J. consult. Psychol.*, 14, 165-171.

MEEHL, P. E., 1954. *Clinical vs. statistical prediction.* Minneapolis: University of Minnesota Press.

MEEHL, P. E., 1956. Wanted—a good cookbook. *Amer. Psychologist*, 11, 263-272.

MEEHL, P. E., 1957. When shall we use our heads instead of the formula? *J. counsel. Psychol.*, 4, 268-273.

MENDICINO, L., 1958. Mechanical reasoning and space perception: native capacity or experience. *Personnel guid. J.*, 36, 335-338.

MICHAEL, W. B., 1956. Development of statistical methods especially useful in test construction and evaluation. *Rev. educ. Res.*, 26, 89-109.

MICHAEL, W. B., 1959. Development of statistical methods especially useful in test construction and evaluation. *Rev. educ. Res.*, 29, 106-129.

MIDDLETON, G., JR., & GUTHRIE, G. M., 1959. Personality syndromes and academic achievement. *J. educ. Psychol.*, 50, 66-69.

MOLLENKOPF, W .G., 1950. Slow—but how sure? *Coll. Bd. Rev.*, No. 11, 147-151.

MOULY, G. J., & EDGAR, SR. M., 1958. Equivalence of IQ's for four group intelligence tests. *Personnel guid. J.*, 36, 623-626.

MUNROE, R. L., 1946. Rorschach findings on college students showing different constellations of subscores on the A.C.E. *J. consult. Psychol.*, 10, 301-316.

NETTLER, G., 1959. Test burning in Texas. *Amer. Psychologist*, 14, 682-683.

NORTH, R. D., 1956. The use of multi-factor aptitude tests in school counseling. *Proceedings 1955 invitational conference on testing problems.* Princeton, N. J.: Educational Testing Service, pp. 11-15.

PARKER, C. A., 1958. As a clinician thinks . . . *J. counsel. Psychol.*, 5, 253-261.

PATERSON, D. G., GERKEN, C. d'A., & HAHN, M. E., 1953. *Revised Minnesota occupational rating scales.* Minneapolis: University of Minnesota Press.

PATTERSON, C. H., 1958. *Counseling the emotionally disturbed.* New York: Harper.

PEEL, E. A., 1952. Practice effects between three consecutive tests of intelligence. *Brit. J. educ. Psychol.*, 22, 196-199.

PEEL, E. A., 1953. Footnote on "Practice effects between three consecutive tests of intelligence." *Brit. J. educ. Psychol.,* 23, 126.

PEMBERTON, C. L., 1951. Personality inventory data related to ACE subscores. *J. consult. Psychol.,* 15, 160-162.

PEPINSKY, H. B., 1948. The selection and use of diagnostic categories in clinical counseling. *Appl. Psychol. Monogr.,* No. 15.

PEPINSKY, H. B., & PEPINSKY, P. N., 1954. *Counseling: theory and practice.* New York: Ronald.

PICKREL, E. W., 1958. The relation of manifest anxiety scores to test performance. *J. counsel. Psychol.,* 5, 290-294.

PIERCE-JONES, J., 1954. The readability of certain standard tests. *Calif. J. educ. Res.,* 5, 80-82.

PIERSON, L. R., 1958. High school teacher prediction of college success. *Personnel guid. J.,* 37, 142-145.

Proceedings 1953 invitational conference on testing problems. Princeton, N. J.: Educational Testing Service.

Proceedings 1955 invitational conference on testing problems. Princeton, N. J.: Educational Testing Service.

RAUSCH, O. P., 1948. The effects of individual variability on achievement. *J. educ. Psychol.,* 39, 469-478.

Regents, University System of Georgia, Office of Testing and Guidance, 1958. *Distribution of 1957 entering freshmen on pre-admissions indices, University System of Georgia.* Research Bulletin 2-58. Atlanta, Ga.: Author, 244 Washington Street, S. W.

RICKS, J. H., JR., 1959. On telling parents about test results. *Test Serv. Bull.* (Psychological Corporation), No. 54.

ROBERTSON, M. H., 1958. A comparison of counselor and student reports of counseling interviews. *J. counsel. Psychol.,* 5, 276-280.

ROBERTSON, M. H., 1959. Results of a pre-college testing and counseling program. *Personnel guid. J.,* 37, 451-454.

ROBINSON, F. P., 1950. *Principles and procedures in student counseling.* New York: Harper.

RODGERS, F. P., 1959. A psychometric study of certain interest and personality variables associated with academic achievement in a college level printing curriculum. Unpublished doctoral dissertation, Univer. of Buffalo.

ROE, A., 1953. *The making of a scientist.* New York: Dodd, Mead.

ROE, A., 1956. *The psychology of occupations.* New York: Wiley.

ROEBER, E. C., 1948. A comparison of seven interest inventories with respect to word usage. *J. educ. Res.,* 42, 8-17.

ROEBER, E. C., 1957. Vocational guidance. *Rev. educ. Res.,* 27, 210-218.

ROETHLISBERGER, F. J., & DICKSON, W. J., 1940. *Management and the worker.* Cambridge: Harvard University Press.

ROGERS, C. R., 1942. *Counseling and psychotherapy.* Boston: Houghton-Mifflin.

ROGERS, L. B., 1954. A comparison of two kinds of test interpretation interview. *J. counsel. Psychol.,* 1, 224-231.

ROTHNEY, J. W. M., DANIELSON, P. J., & HEIMANN, R. A., 1959. *Measurement for guidance.* New York: Harper.

ROTHNEY, J. W. M., & ROENS, B. A., 1949. Counseling the individual student. New York: Sloane.

SACKS, E. L., 1952. Intelligence scores as a function of experimentally established social relationships between child and examiner. J. abnorm. soc. Psychol., 47, 354-358.

SARASON, S. B., 1950. The test-situation and the problem of prediction. J. clin. Psychol., 6, 387-392.

SARASON, S. B., DAVIDSON, K. S., LIGHTHALL, F. F., WAITE, R. R., & RUEBUSH, B. K., 1960. Anxiety in elementary school children. New York: Wiley.

SARASON, S. B., & GORDON, E. M., 1953. The test anxiety questionnaire: scoring norms. J. abnorm. soc. Psychol., 48, 447-448.

SARASON, S. B., & MANDLER, G., 1952. Some correlates of test anxiety. J. abnorm. soc. Psychol., 47, 810-817.

SARASON, S. B., MANDLER, G., & CRAIGHILL, P. G., 1952. The effect of differential instructions on anxiety and learning. J. abnorm. soc. Psychol., 47, 561-565.

SARBIN, T. R., 1942. A contribution to the study of actuarial and individual methods of prediction. Amer. J. Sociol. 48, 593-602.

SAUNDERS, D. R., 1955. The "moderator variable" as a useful tool in prediction. Proceedings 1954 invitational conference on testing problems. Princeton, N. J.: Educational Testing Service, pp. 54-58.

SCHLESSER, G. E., 1950. Gains in scholastic aptitude under highly motivated conditions. J. educ. Psychol., 41, 237-242.

SEARS, R., 1943. Motivational factors in aptitude testing. Amer. J. Orthopsychiat., 13, 468-492.

SEASHORE, H. G., 1951. Human resources and the aptitude inventory. Test Serv. Bull. (Psychological Corporation), No. 41.

SEASHORE, H. G., 1955. Methods of expressing test scores. Test. Serv. Bull. (Psychological Corporation), No. 48.

SEASHORE, H. G., & DOPPELT, J. E., 1949. How effective are your tests? Test Serv. Bull. (Psychological Corporation), No. 37.

SEEMAN, J., 1948. A study of client self-selection of tests in vocational counseling. Educ. psychol. Measmt., 8, 327-346.

SEEMAN, J., 1949. An investigation of client reactions to vocational counseling. J. consult. Psychol., 13, 95-104.

SEGEL, D., WELLMAN, F. E., & HAMILTON, A. T., 1958. An approach to individual analysis in educational and vocational guidance. U. S. Department of Health, Education, and Welfare Bull. 1959, No. 1.

SEIGLE, W. F., 1953. The teacher reports test scores to parents. J. educ. Res., 46, 543-549.

SEVERIN, D. G., 1955. Appraisal of special tests and procedures used with self-scoring instructional testing devices. Ohio State Univer. Abstr. of doctoral Dissertations, No. 66, pp. 323-330.

SHAW, M. C., & GRUBB, J., 1958. Hostility and able high school underachievers. J. counsel. Psychol., 5, 263-266.

SHELDON, M. S., 1959. Conditions affecting the fakability of teacher-selection inventories. Educ. psychol. Measmt., 19, 207-219.

SHERRIFFS, A. C., & BOOMER, D. S., 1954. Who is penalized by the penalty for guessing? J. educ. Psychol., 45, 81-90.

SHOBEN, E. J., JR., 1956. Counseling. *Annu. Rev. Psychol.,* 7, 147-172.

SILVANIA, K. C., 1956. Test usage in counseling centers. *Personnel guid. J.,* 34, 559-564.

SINGER, S. L., & STEFFLRE, B., 1954. Analysis of the self-estimate in the evaluation of counseling. *J. counsel. Psychol.,* 1, 252-255.

SINICK, D., 1953. Anxiety in the testing situation. *Personnel guid. J.,* 31, 384-387.

SINICK, D., 1956a. Encouragement, anxiety, and test performance. *J. appl. Psychol.,* 40, 315-318.

SINICK, D., 1956b. Two anxiety scales correlated and examined for sex differences. *J. clin. Psychol.,* 12, 394-395.

SLATER, M., 1957. Perception: a context for the consideration of persistence and attrition among college men. *Personnel guid. J.,* 35, 435-440.

SLOTKIN, H., 1954. A technique for self-measurement. *Personnel guid. J.,* 32, 415-416.

SMITH, R. E., 1954. Presenting the psychological dimensions of classes to instructors. *J. educ. Res.,* 48, 149-151.

SNODGRASS, F. T., 1954a. The relation between profile unreliability and acceleration in school. *Bull. maritime Psychol. Ass.,* (Spring), 14-16.

SNODGRASS, F. T., 1954b. Unreliability of group test profiles. *J. educ. Psychol.,* 45, 129-142.

SONNE, T. R., & GOLDMAN, L., 1957. Preferences of authoritarian and equalitarian personalities for client-centered and eclectic counseling. *J. counsel. Psychol.,* 4, 129-135.

SOSKIN, W. F., 1959. Influence of four types of data on diagnostic conceptualization in psychological testing. *J. abnorm. soc. Psychol.,* 58, 69-78.

SPIVAK, M. L., 1957. It pays to tell the teachers. *Personnel guid. J.,* 35, 452-453.

STAGNER, R., 1958. The gullibility of personnel managers. *Personnel Psychol.,* 11, 347-352.

STANLEY, J. C., 1954. "Psychological" correction for chance. *J. exp. Educ.,* 22, 297-298.

STAUDT, V. M., 1948. The relationship of testing conditions and intellectual level to errors and correct responses in several types of tasks among college women. *J. Psychol.,* 26, 125-140.

STAUDT, V. M., 1949. The relationship of certain personality traits to errors and correct responses in several types of tasks among college women under varying test conditions. *J. Psychol.,* 27, 465-478.

STEFFLRE, B., 1947. The reading difficulty of interest inventories. *Occupations,* 26, 95-96.

STERN, G. G., STEIN, M. I., & BLOOM, B. S., 1956. *Methods in personality assessment.* Glencoe, Ill.: Free Press.

STINSON, P. J., 1958. A method for counseling engineering students. *Personnel guid. J.,* 37, 294-295.

STORDAHL, K. E., 1954. Permanence of interests and interest maturity. *J. appl. Psychol.,* 38, 339-340.

STOUGHTON, R. W., 1959. *The testing service.* Hartford, Conn.: Bureau of Pupil Personnel and Special Educational Services, State Department of Education.

STRANG, R., 1947. *Educational guidance.* New York: Macmillan.

STRANGE, F. B., 1953. Student self-selection of group tests. *Personnel guid. J.*, 32, 30-33.

STRONG, E. K. JR., 1943. *Vocational interests of men and women.* Stanford: Stanford University Press.

STRONG, E. K., JR., 1955. *Vocational interests 18 years after college.* Minneapolis: University of Minnesota Press.

STUIT, D. B., DICKSON, G. S., JORDAN, T. T., & SCHLOERB, L., 1949. *Predicting success in professional schools.* Washington: American Council on Education.

SUPER, D. E., 1949. *Appraising vocational fitness.* New York: Harper.

SUPER, D. E., 1950. Testing and using test results in counseling. *Occupations*, 29, 95-97.

SUPER, D. E., 1954. Guidance: manpower utilization or human development? *Personnel guid. J.*, 33, 8-14.

SUPER, D. E., 1955a. Dimensions and measurement of vocational maturity. *Teach. Coll. Rec.*, 57, 151-163.

SUPER, D. E., 1955b. Personality integration through vocational counseling. *J. counsel. Psychol.*, 2, 217-226.

SUPER, D. E., 1956. The use of multifactor test batteries in guidance. *Personnel guid. J.*, 35, 9-15.

SUPER, D. E., 1957a. *The psychology of careers.* New York: Harper.

SUPER, D. E., 1957b. The preliminary appraisal in vocational counseling. *Personnel guid. J.*, 36, 154-161.

SUPER, D. E., BRAASCH, W. F., JR., & SHAY, J. B., 1947. The effect of distractions on test results. *J. educ. Psychol.*, 38, 373-377.

SUPER, D. E., & ROPER, S., 1941. An objective technique for testing vocational interests. *J. appl. Psychol.*, 25, 487-498.

SWINEFORD, F., & MILLER, P. M., 1953. Effects of directions regarding guessing on item statistics of a multiple-choice vocabulary test. *J. educ. Psychol.*, 44, 129-139.

Tennessee State Testing and Guidance Program, 1956-1957. The place of standardized testing in a guidance program. *Tennessee State Testing and Guidance Program Annual Report, 1956-57.* Nashville: Tennessee State Department of Education.

THOMAS, D. S., & MAYO, G. D., 1957. A procedure of applying knowledge of results to the predictions of vocational counselors. *Educ. psychol. Measmt.*, 17, 416-422.

THORNDIKE, R. L., & HAGEN, E., 1955. *Measurement and evaluation in psychology and education.* New York: Wiley.

THORNDIKE, R. L., & HAGEN, E., 1959. *Ten thousand careers.* New York: Wiley.

TIEDEMAN, D. V., 1954. A model for the profile problem. *Proceedings 1953 invitational conference on testing problems,* pp. 54-75.

TIEDEMAN, D. V., & BRYAN, J. G., 1954. Prediction of college field of concentration. *Harvard educ. Rev.*, 24, 122-139.

TIEDEMAN, D. V., BRYAN, J. G., & RULON, P. J., 1952. Application of the multiple discriminant function to data from Airman Classification Battery. *USAF Hum. Resour. Res. Cent., Res. Bull.*, No. 52-37.

TILTON, J. W., 1953. Factors related to ability-profile unevenness. *Educ. psychol. Measmt.*, 13, 467-473.

TORRANCE, E. P., 1954. Some practical uses of a knowledge of self-concepts in counseling and guidance. *Educ. psychol. Measmt.*, 14, 120-127.

TRANKELL, A., 1959. The psychologist as an instrument of prediction. *J. appl. Psychol.*, 43, 170-175.

TRAVERS, R. M. W., 1949. The prediction of achievement. *Sch. & Soc.*, 70, 293-294.

TRAVERS, R. M. W., 1951. Rational hypotheses in the construction of tests. *Educ. psychol. Measmt.*, 11, 128-137.

TRAXLER, A. E., 1957. *Techniques of guidance.* (2nd ed.) New York: Harper.

TRAXLER, A. E., 1959. Testing for guidance and evaluation. *Sixteenth Yearbook of the National Council on Measurements Used in Education,* pp. 1-6.

TUMA, A. H., & GUSTAD, J. W., 1957. The effects of client and counselor personality characteristics on client learning in counseling. *J. counsel. Psychol.*, 4, 136-141.

TYLER, L. E., 1953. *The work of the counselor.* New York: Appleton-Century-Crofts.

TYLER, L. E., 1956. *The psychology of human differences.* (2nd ed.) New York: Appleton-Century-Crofts.

TYLER, L. E., 1959. Toward a workable psychology of individuality. *Amer. Psychologist,* 14, 75-81.

United States Employment Service, 1956. *Estimates of worker trait requirements for 4,000 jobs.* Washington: U. S. Government Printing Office.

The use of multifactor tests in guidance, undated. Washington: American Personnel and Guidance Association.

VANBILJON, I. J., 1954. The influence of emotional tension and lability upon the performance of certain aptitude tests. *J. soc. Res., Pretoria,* 5, 51-59.

WALKER, J. L., 1955. Counselors' judgments in the prediction of the occupational and educational performance of former high school students. *J. educ. Res.,* 49, 81-91.

WALLACE, W. L., 1950. The relationship of certain variables to discrepancy between expressed and inventoried vocational interest. *Amer. Psychologist,* 5, 354. (Abstract).

WARNER, W. L., MEEKER, M., & EELLS, K., 1949. *Social class in America.* Chicago: Science Research Associates.

WAY, H. H., 1953. The relationship between forced choice scores and differentiated response scores on the Kuder Preference Record—Vocational. *Dissertation Abstr.,* 13, 1097-1098. (Abstract).

WEITZ, H., COLVER, R. M., & SOUTHERN, J. A., 1955. Evaluating a measurement project. *Personnel guid. J.,* 33, 400-403.

WELCH, L., & RENNIE, T. A. C., 1952. The influence of psychopathological emotions on psychological test performance. In Hoch, P. H., & Zubin, J. (Eds.), *Relation of psychological tests to psychiatry.* New York: Grune and Stratton, pp. 271-289.

WELSH, G. S., & DAHLSTROM, W. G. (Eds.), 1956. *Basic readings on the MMPI in psychology and medicine.* Minneapolis: University of Minnesota Press.

WESLEY, S. M., COREY, D. Q., & STEWART, B. M., 1950. The intra-individual relationship between interest and ability. *J. appl. Psychol.,* 34, 193-197.

WESMAN, A. G., 1952. Faking personality test scores in a simulated employment situation. *J. appl. Psychol.,* 36, 112-113.

WESMAN, A. G., 1959. What kinds of tests for college admission and scholarship programs? *Proceedings 1958 invitational conference on testing problems.* Princeton, N. J.: Educational Testing Service, pp. 114-120.

WESMAN, A. G., & BENNETT, G. K., 1951. Problems of differential prediction. *Educ. psychol. Measmt.*, 11, 265-272.

WEST, D. N., 1958. Reducing chance in test selection. *Personnel guid. J.*, 36, 420-421.

WHITE, R. W., 1952. What is tested by psychological tests? In Hoch, P. H., & Zubin, J. (Eds.), *Relation of psychological tests to psychiatry.* New York: Grune and Stratton, pp. 3-14.

WIENER, D. N., 1951. Empirical occupational groupings of Kuder Preference Record profiles. *Educ. psychol. Measmt.*, 11, 273-279.

WILLIAMSON, E. G., 1939. *How to counsel students.* New York: McGraw-Hill.

WINDLE, C., 1955. Further studies of test-retest effect on personality questionnaires. *Educ. psychol. Measmt.*, 15, 246-253.

WISEMAN, S., & WRIGLEY, J., 1953. The comparative effects of coaching and practice on the results of verbal intelligence tests. *Brit. J. Psychol.* 44, 83-94.

WITTENBORN, J. R., 1951. An evaluation of the use of difference scores in prediction. *J. clin. Psychol.*, 7, 108-111.

WOLFLE, D., 1958. Guidance and educational strategy. *Personnel guid. J.*, 37, 17-25.

WOOLF, M. D., & WOOLF, J. A., 1955. Is interest maturity related to linguistic development? *J. appl. Psychol.*, 39, 413-415.

WRENN, C. G., 1952. The ethics of counseling. *Educ. psychol. Measmt.*, 12, 161-177.

WRIGHT, E. W., 1957. A comparison of individual and multiple counseling in the dissemination and interpretation of test data. *Summary of the Dissertation, University of California, Graduate Division, Northern Section.*

YOUNG, F. C., 1954. College freshmen judge their own scholastic promise. *Personnel guid. J.*, 32, 399-403.

YOUNG, F. C., 1955. Evaluation of a college counseling program. *Personnel guid. J.*, 33, 282-286.

Appendix
List of Test Publishers

Abbreviation	*Address*
ACE	Veterans' Testing Service, American Council on Education, 6018 Ingleside Avenue, Chicago 37, Ill.
AGS	American Guidance Service, Inc., 720 Washington Avenue S.E., Minneapolis, Minn.
Bruce	Martin M. Bruce, 71 Hanson Lane, New Rochelle, N. Y.
Calif.	California Test Bureau, 5916 Hollywood Boulevard, Los Angeles 28, Calif.
CEEB	College Entrance Examination Board, c/o Educational Testing Service, 20 Nassau Street, Princeton, N. J.
CPP	Consulting Psychologists Press, Inc., 270 Town and Country Village, Palo Alto, Calif.
ETB	Educational Test Bureau, 720 Washington Avenue, S.E., Minneapolis, Minn.
ETS	Cooperative Test Division, Educational Testing Service, 20 Nassau Street, Princeton, N. J.
Hawaii	University of Hawaii Bookstore, Honolulu 14, Hawaii
HM	Houghton Mifflin Company, 432 Park Avenue South, New York 16, N. Y.
Iowa	Bureau of Educational Research and Service, State University of Iowa, Iowa City, Iowa
Kansas	Bureau of Educational Measurements, Kansas State Teachers College of Emporia, Emporia, Kan.
McKnight	McKnight & McKnight Publishing Company, Bloomington, Ill.
Ohio	Ohio College Association, Ohio State University, Columbus, Ohio
PP	Personnel Press, Inc., 188 Nassau Street, Princeton, N. J.
Psych. Corp.	The Psychological Corporation, 304 East 45th Street, New York 17, N. Y.
PTS	Psychological Test Specialists, Box 1441, Missoula, Mont.
SRA	Science Research Associates, Inc., 57 West Grand Avenue, Chicago 10, Ill.
Sheridan	Sheridan Supply Company, Box 837, Beverly Hills, Calif.
Stoelting	C. H. Stoelting Company, 424 North Homan Avenue, Chicago 24, Ill.
TC	Bureau of Publications, Teachers College, Columbia University, New York 27, N. Y.
USES	United States Employment Service, Washington 25, D.C.
Wonderlic	Wonderlic Personnel Test Company, Box 7, Northfield, Ill.
World	World Book Company, Tarrytown, N. Y.
WPS	Western Psychological Services, 10655 Santa Monica Boulevard, Los Angeles 25, Calif.

Index of Names

Index of Subjects*